/s/

PEARL WEDDING

This is the story of Colin Whimboyne, of his parents, his brothers and his friends. It covers half a century in a man's life and gives the reader vivid impressions of public figures between the wars, of the great historical events of the period and of the changing values since the beginning of this century. Throughout it is distinguished by the vivid characters that illuminate the scene. For instance, we meet such singular personalities as Colin's wife, Elizabeth, a vibrant, dominating, yet somehow vapourish figure, flitting through the pages like a restless ghost disturbing the lives of the family; Violet, purposefully handling her husband and her lover; and young Norman, brought up by Elizabeth and eventually battened on by her; there is, too, Yvette, an extraneous item so far as Elizabeth is concerned, but a prime essential in Norman's life.

This book possesses many other dynamic characters; and they and their share in Colin's story give immense colour, warmth and vitality to a captivating, nostalgic and altogether monumental family saga.

STEPHEN McKENNA

PEARL WEDDING

HUTCHINSON & CO. (Publishers) LTD
London   New York   Melbourne   Sydney   Cape Town

First published 1951

*Printed in Great Britain
by The Anchor Press, Ltd.,
Tiptree, Essex*

TO
FLAVIA

LEIT-MOTIV

PEARL WEDDING

"WHIMBOYNE—GERROLD.—*On December* 2, 1918, *at the Register-Office, Kensington,* COLIN WHIMBOYNE *to* ELIZABETH GERROLD. *Present address: Ridgeway House, Marlborough, Wilts.*"

Leit-Motiv

OPENING CHORUS

RANDOM READERS. "A 'Pearl Wedding' is a new one on me. A 'diamond' or a 'ruby' one knows. And, of course, the 'silver' and 'golden'. Nineteen-eighteen? Ah! A pearl wedding must be the thirtieth anniversary. 'Colin Whimboyne'? That's not the dramatist-fellow, is it? Never knew he had a wife! Truth to tell, I didn't know he was still alive. It's a good many years since he produced anything. Not likely to be two Colins with a surname like Whimboyne, though. And Gerrold is an odd name too, spelt like that. Well, as I don't enjoy the *entrée* to Ridgeway House, Marlborough, Wilts, I shall not send a telegram of congratulation."

*   *   *   *   *

SELECTED READERS.

BARBARA GERROLD. Have you seen this, Martin? Your mother and Colin are celebrating their pearl wedding.

MARTIN GERROLD. It was only the other day that they had a silver wedding. These anniversaries are becoming a habit, which should not be encouraged.

BARBARA GERROLD. You'll have to send a telegram. After all, she has been *terribly* generous to us.

MARTIN GERROLD. Oh, she has all the virtues except that of being even faintly interesting. How Colin, who is by way of being intelligent, has stayed the course for thirty years entirely defeats me. All right! Here's a nice half-crown for a nice telegram. Thank goodness we aren't being roped in for a party!

*   *   *   *   *

HUMFREY GERROLD. Once again the invaluable Dr. Brewer, of *Phrase and Fable* fame, has saved the situation. A pearl wedding, my dear Monica, is celebrated after thirty years of marriage.

MONICA GERROLD. And every one is expected to weigh in with a

9

present of pearls. Can you get a few on your way to the Temple?

HUMFREY GERROLD. They'll have to be artificial. Anything more artificial than my sainted mother's second marriage would be impossible to imagine.

MONICA GERROLD. I suppose they were in love at some time.

HUMFREY GERROLD. You have no conceivable grounds for a statement of that kind! When my father was killed in '16, Colin as an old family-friend leapt into the breach with offers of help and, as my mother was rather more than usually helpless at the time, he decided that the most helpful thing he could do was to marry her. I was still in the nursery, of course, but I've been told since that Colin's friends were rather disappointed. He had waked a few years before to find himself famous and was making a pot of money with his plays.

MONICA GERROLD. I've always understood that Colin married on the rebound. The love of his life was Lady Isabel Pryde. And he was the love of hers, but I suppose she thought the chance of being Duchess of Abbotsbury was too good to miss. Well, what are we going to do about it? A telegram of congratulations and good wishes? She never forgets *our* wedding-day.

HUMFREY GERROLD. I leave it to you! Good-bye! I've a case in the Court of Appeal.

*   *   *   *   *

THE DUKE OF ABBOTSBURY. Wasn't Colin Whimboyne a friend of yours at one time, Isabel?

THE DUCHESS OF ABBOTSBURY. I saw a certain amount of him before I married. Not since. Why do you ask?

THE DUKE OF ABBOTSBURY. He's celebrating his pearl wedding. Didn't know there was such a thing! We ought to have celebrated ours some months ago, my dear! Elizabeth Gerrold?

THE DUCHESS OF ABBOTSBURY. She was a Cheshunt, if that means anything to you. I remember the name because Colin used to talk about her. I knew her first husband before she did. Colin? It must have been in the middle of the 1914 war, when I was working in London for our prisoners-of-war. He was the literary lion of the moment and one ran into him at all the parties.

THE DUKE OF ABBOTSBURY. I had an idea that your reading in those days was confined to 'Jorrocks' and the 'Irish R.M.' What you and Whimboyne found to talk about . . .

THE DUCHESS OF ABBOTSBURY. Love, my dear, love! Love in a cottage, love in a castle, love in a shooting-box and a studio, love in the Shires and in the civil service! You never met him when he was private secretary to Claude Axminster? And did no one ever tell you about us? I fondly imagined we were one of the major scandals of London.

THE DUKE OF ABBOTSBURY. So *many* people were in love with you, my dear, and you were in love with so many people! Or *thought* you were. Was this any more serious than the rest? After thirty years I shan't be jealous. Nor, I should think, would Mrs. Whimboyne.

THE DUCHESS OF ABBOTSBURY. After thirty years I find it impossible to say! We both *thought* we were quite desperately in love. He was very good-looking and *very* attractive, but I could never be sure that he was capable of a grand passion. I was apparently attractive enough to make him very unhappy. I honestly don't know! There were so many complications. Perhaps we should never have fallen in love if we hadn't felt in our bones that nothing would ever come of it. You may call it romance or being in love with love. Perhaps something *would* have come of it if people had left us alone.

THE DUKE OF ABBOTSBURY. Meaning that your father shewed him the door?

THE DUCHESS OF ABBOTSBURY. Oh, far from it! My brother Lascombe had known him at Oxford and he seemed to think that on the strength of one or two successful plays, which was all that Colin had written then, he could relieve the family of all responsibility for me. No, I was wondering what might have happened if other people had left us alone. We were both in the limelight, you see, and neither of us made any secret of our feelings. I suppose the sheer improbability of the whole thing added to the general interest. Colin often said that he would like to write a play about us. Two people without one interest in common! Horses and hunting on one side, books and the theatre on the other; and a good or bad fairy coming to our christening with this singularly inappropriate present! Love! And nothing else! We were told that was all that mattered, we were told that it mattered less than almost anything, we were told it wasn't true love if we couldn't blend ourselves and our lives into one. I don't know! The pace was too hot to last and our nerves began to suffer. With me it took the form of wondering whether Colin could ever bring himself to say: 'The world-and-my-career-with-it well lost for love!,' which was absurd and unfair. If we *had* married, we should have depended on his career for our daily bread. Then, fortunately for every one, you came along. Fortunately, too, Mrs. Whimboyne's first husband had been killed in Flanders. . . . At least, when I say 'for every one', I haven't met him since I became engaged to you.

THE DUKE OF ABBOTSBURY. It must have been 'fortunately' for them too if they've stuck together in sickness and health, weal and woe, for thirty years.

THE DUCHESS OF ABBOTSBURY. I've no idea whether they have. Colin's name was coupled with Violet Oakhirst's at one time, but I never heard whether there was anything in it. Well, after all this time I don't feel inspired to send a telegram of congratulation.

*   *   *   *   *

VIOLET OAKHIRST. Have you seen this about the Whimboynes' pearl wedding, Nigel?

NIGEL OAKHIRST. Is that thirty years? I should have thought they had been married longer than that.

VIOLET OAKHIRST. No doubt it seems longer to poor Colin.

NIGEL OAKHIRST. The world, knowing less than we do, would hardly call him 'poor'. He has succeeded in two careers, which I should never have prophesied for him when we were at school together. I suppose he'll get a K.C.B. before he retires from the civil service. He had a longer run than most men as a playwright, never achieving an absolutely first-rate line.

VIOLET OAKHIRST. You don't think he would have been first-rate if Elizabeth hadn't kept him back?

NIGEL OAKHIRST. I don't admit that she did. He'd had his first successes before he really knew her or Isabel Pryde or you, who I suppose have been the three greatest feminine influences in his life. He might have written better plays if he had married you; he would have given up writing altogether if he'd married Isabel. Conceivably Elizabeth would have held him back if he had given her the chance, but in all their boasted thirty years of connubial bliss they only saw each other at week-ends till this last war. Perhaps it would have been better if they'd never married at all; but, when they discovered their incompatibility, the sensible thing was to avoid getting in each other's way. Elizabeth's only interest was her children: she cared nothing for public affairs, or London society, or Colin's literary life. Any more, my dear, that you in your heart of hearts cared for politics!

VIOLET OAKHIRST. But I made myself care about them, Nigel, because they were your *career*. I never once failed you as a political hostess.

NIGEL OAKHIRST. Whereas the world might fairly say that I'd failed you as a political careerist and everything else! When our friends talk about us, do you suppose they say that perhaps it would have been better if *we* had never married, better if you had divorced me when you had the opportunity, better if you had married Colin? Looking back, I can see now that I hadn't the makings, whatever they may be, of your first-rate politician. The cabinet, yes, a secretaryship of state, yes; but Downing Street and the mantle of Gladstone, no! I feel the same about old Colin in both his careers. He would never have been a Morant or a Chalmers or a John Anderson, even if he had wished or tried; he would never have been a Shaw or a Pinero in the theatre. All the same, the world would say he had had a very happy life.

VIOLET OAKHIRST. I wonder! As a matter of form, I suppose we shall have to send our congratulations.

NIGEL OAKHIRST. Oh, yes! We've known each other for close on fifty years now and there aren't so many of the old brigade left. I'm not sure, as a matter of form, that we oughtn't to give a party for them. We might ask Clement Phayre and his wife. He's one of the few survivors.

* * * * *

MARGERY PHAYRE. Are you doing anything on the ninth, Clement? The Oakhirsts want us to dine. Violet is trying to get the Colin Whimboynes.

CLEMENT PHAYRE. Is there to be any one else? A rally of the 'old-school ties' is no use to me. Nigel lost his very moderate news-value years ago; and Colin's only good for a couple of paragraphs when he has a new play.

MARGERY PHAYRE. Can you make anything out of a pearl wedding? He and Elizabeth are advertising theirs. I should think you could pad out a column with a general review of his work.

CLEMENT PHAYRE. That's an idea! As it happens, I was talking to our O.C. Graveyard only last week about bringing Colin's obituary up to date. With a very few alterations . . . Turn up *Who's Who* to see how old he is. I should think he'll be retiring soon. No reason why he shouldn't be made to employ his well-earned leisure on a volume of reminiscences. A man is not on oath in a gossip-writer's column. Let's see! '*If a woman is as old as she looks and a man as old as he feels, the ever-young Colin Whimboynes may have some difficulty in convincing their numberless friends that to-day is the thirtieth anniversary of their wedding. As one who had known "Collie" in his top-hat and Eton-collar days at Westminster, I was amongst the first this morning to present myself at the famous* atelier.' Give me the blasted address, Margery. '*Both of us found it hard to believe that blank years had passed . . .*'—I shall want his civil-service record—'*since Colin Whimboyne entered the Lord Keeper's Department.*' And a list of the Lord Keepers he served under, with their dates. '*And it was blank years, we found, since watchers of theatrical skies . . .*'—Give me his first big success . . . —'*discovered that a new planet had swum into their ken. At different times Colin Whimboyne has been compared with Oscar Wilde and Henry Arthur Jones, with the early Somerset Maugham and the later Freddie Lonsdale, with A. A. Milne and Alfred Sutro. My own opinion . . .*' I shall want a few minutes to think what my own opinion is. The usual question about having a new play on the stocks . . . No, the last time I mentioned him (though nobody's likely to remember) I made rather a point of saying that he'd finished with plays. No reason he shouldn't write something else, though. '*Discussing his plans for the future, Colin Whimboyne reminded me that he would very soon be retiring from the public service. "I hope," I said, "that means you'll have more time for writing. Another play . . ." "No more curtain-calls for me," he answered.*' Can you imagine Colin using a phrase like that, Margery? It's what the public would expect him to say, though. ' "*I shall devote my leisure to writing my memoirs. In the last thirty years I've met every one—as the saying goes—who is any one?".* Then I shall want a spate of big names, with a few anecdotes that I can make up. At the end I shall suggest calling it a 'success-story'. Success in two careers. I shall make him come over all modest, of course: "Call no man successful till he's been dead a century". I shall say I can call him happy without waiting till he's dead. He'll agree, *"gratefully, almost humbly, with a sudden softening"* and all that. Then I'll make him say *"with a queer glad air of discovery"* that perhaps this is the only success worth having. Yes, by Jove, that ought to fill the column. A good idea of yours, Margery! Well, about this party that the Oakhirsts are throwing: ring Violet up and say we'll come. And ring up old Colin if he's in London. Don't tell him that I've warmed up his obituary in honour of his pearl wedding, but offer him our congratulations. It's an ill wind that blows nobody good: I was well and truly stuck over my precious column for to-day. God, who would be a gossip-writer, if he could break stones by the roadside?

SOLO RECITATIVE

SOLOIST: COLIN WHIMBOYNE.

I suppose even gossip-writers have their place in Nature's scheme. Eliminate them; and, as in most crusades against seemingly useless pests, you would upset the intricate balance by which every species checks or helps, however remotely, the development of every other species.

Eliminate a single one, as it might be Mr. Clement Townley Phayre, and you would end the infinitesimally small influence that he has exerted shamefully long over the more debased readers of the *Evening Chronicle*. Does he in fact hinder or help the development of any one but the readers of newspapers produced —in the classic phrase—by office-boys for office-boys? My press-cutting agency has to-day sent me a long and purely fictitious interview which he purports to have had with me; and after a brief explosion of homicidal fury I have been trying to get the two of us into perspective by considering what difference (if any) it would have made to any one if "The Piccadilly Johnny" had been drowned at birth and if I had never been embarrassed with news-value.

To the victim of his interview it would make the difference that this seedy, needy scavenger would not have given me a certain idea which, if I follow it, may determine the course of my life and work for most of my few remaining years on earth. Evidently there are still pearls to be found on the unlikeliest of dunghills! I am not going to write those memoirs—of *"a distinguished public servant and a yet more distinguished man of letters"*— which he has invented as my great future preoccupation; but I feel a passing interest in his superficial chatter about success and happiness. Are they the same thing? In some ways I have been more than ordinarily successful; at times I daresay I have been happier than the average. In the two spheres that have brought me this distinction I imagine most civil servants and many writers would envy me. Clement Phayre, who has failed in both, predicts that my autobiography will reveal a *"first-class success-story"*.

Is this the whole truth? What does he know about it, any way? I am now the far side of sixty; and, looking back with the eyes of a professional psychologist, I believe I can assess quite

16

objectively whatever happiness or success I have enjoyed. I am sure, though, that no one else, be he close friend or intelligent onlooker, can. Making every allowance for the sentimentality released by this announcement of my pearl wedding, I feel that Mr. Clement Phayre and his readers can have no picture that I at least should recognize of what my real life has been. I had none myself until a few hours ago, when I turned from the impertinent reference to *"the devoted partner of my triumphs"* and my *"brilliant son"* to think critically of the road—sometimes stony and sometimes flower-strewn—that I have so literally been taking in my stride till I find myself nearing the end of it. For the moment I can think of nothing else. My life: what do I make of it now that I can see almost the whole of it dispassionately and in proportion? What sort of autobiography should I write if I could set down the truth, the whole truth and nothing but the truth?

Though Clem Phayre has probably forgotten the occurrence, he once shewed me the obituary that he had written in my honour for the *Evening Chronicle*. Since his interview repeats the very words of the obituary, I know what one newspaper will say of me if I die to-night; and, while the facts and dates are more accurate than I should have expected, I find the general verdict so wrong and so wrongheaded that I do not recognize myself. This inspires me to wonder whether any one else would recognize me if I had written the obituary or if I were now to write my own story.

I have no intention of undertaking either task; but I do not see why the public should not be encouraged to accept Clem Phayre's hint that I am engaged on my reminiscences. When I leave the Lord Keeper's Department in a very few months now, I shall have more time on my hands than ever in my life before; and I shall no longer have my old excuse for living by myself "within ten minutes of Whitehall". My friends will want to know what I am doing with my leisure. Am I, they will ask, working on another play?

For some reason, it would hurt my pride to admit that, as a dramatist, I am written out or that, as a professional psychologist, I have survived impotently into an age when I no longer have any idea how young people think or even talk. My stepsons and their wives explain me tolerantly as "pre-war"; but in all the not infrequent family-crises of the last few years I have felt that I was "pre-the-1914-war". I do not understand the language or the

B

ideals or the philosophy or the standards of my son's generation. I shall therefore not attempt another comedy of contemporary manners.

The more finally that I am dated, though, the greater the historic interest of the memoirs that I may pretend to be compiling. When my first play was produced, I had to win my foothold against Shaw and Granville Barker, Pinero and Galsworthy, Barrie and Maugham. I was private secretary to the now almost legendary Axminster when he condescended to become Lord Keeper in Campbell-Bannerman's administration. From these beginnings, as Clem Phayre makes me say in that apocryphal interview, I have known *"everybody who was anybody"* for the best part of forty years. I have, as the interview elegantly insists, "the goods", if I choose to deliver them. I shall not; but, if it is believed that I am preparing a gallery of celebrities in undress, I shall have an unassailable reason for continuing to live in the old Grosvenor Road workshop.

No publisher, in these days of paper-famine, is likely to offer me a contract for an unwritten book; and I am therefore not obliged to warn him that I shall never write the book that is being so officiously fathered on me. Why should I? How could I? What scrap of literary confession or political eavesdropping could I profitably spread before the circulating libraries? The political giants of my youth and middle age have long since been decently interred, in official two-volume biographies; and, even if I had a taste for anecdotage, I doubt whether many readers in 1948 are much interested in the great parliamentary figures of an age that ended in 1938, still less of one that ended in 1918. I could perhaps write with some knowledge of the changing social scene from the last years of Queen Victoria and of the nineteenth century; but the men and women whose names would look most alluring in my index were men and women that I had met as friends, I entered their houses as a guest and, as I should have thought it insufferably vulgar to earn a guinea by describing a house-party at Milden or Saxby or Ashworth, so now I should think it equally vulgar to publish an account of people or places that I knew on the privileged footing of private friendship.

Of the literary giants, too, I have almost nothing to say that has not been said already; and, if any one wishes to know how this or that play of mine came to be written, I am not certain that I could tell him, but I am quite certain that I should not try.

Successful I have been by the standard of long runs and box-office receipts; but no serious critic of the English theatre would say that I had contributed anything but so many thousand nights of innocent diversion to so many hundreds of thousands of play-goers. Somerset Maugham, in writing of his own literary work and life, begins most properly by focusing himself, without tiresome posturings of mock-modesty, as a person of some consequence. It is my considered judgement, delivered also without false modesty, that in any long perspective of literature I am a person of no consequence at all. By now, I have a good deal of work-shop experience; my technique is neat and my invention fertile; though I have made money, I have never written for money; my artistic honour is unsullied; but no one will ever mention me in the same breath as Wycherley or Congreve, Goldsmith or Sheridan, Wilde or Synge. If I thought it worth while to write a single page about my literary work, I should invite attention to it as an interesting combination of high ambition, extreme conscientiousness, hard work and good luck. I succeeded in doing well something that was perhaps not worth doing at all, but something that the public wanted done. By pure chance I wrote the kind of play that Willie Maugham had been writing infinitely better in the days of *Jack Straw* and *Lady Frederick* and that he had decided to write no more. Fortunately for me, the London playgoers who wanted more did not get quite what they wanted from St. John Hankin or R. C. Carton. They were to get it in a slightly different and far wittier form later from Freddie Lonsdale, better still and with the stamp of genius on it from Noel Coward. In the language of advertising, I was for some profitable years a useful substitute which was swiftly refused when the genuine article came on the market again.

In addition to commercial success, I have had great pleasure from writing my plays. Is pleasure the same as happiness?

Is happiness dependent on success? Have I had a happy life?

In the interview that he invented for me, Clem Phayre used the terms as though they were interchangeable. "A successful career in two distinct fields . . .", he kept saying. "A happy life . . ." Has it been? The test, I suppose, is that a man should say there is nothing he would change if he had his time over again. There are many things that I would change. At the end of a successful life, I presume that a man should be able to say complacently that "everything has gone according to plan". In my own life I can think of hardly anything that has gone according to plan. Has my life, then, been a failure?

Had I at any time a plan of any kind? In one thing, yes: I always wanted to be a writer. I wanted to be a writer before I was able—in the school-room sense—to write at all. Naturally, I could read before I learnt to write; and it was in the nursery at Ridgeway House, long before I was promoted to the school-room, that some stranger, addressing me as a "studious little man", asked what I meant to be when I grew up and I replied without hesitation (though with a faint lisp that I afterwards outgrew) that I wanted to be a "w'iter".

Success or failure? Who can say? Happiness or unhappiness? Who can care? What interests me is the difference between the obituary that Clement Phayre wrote for the *Evening Chronicle* and the obituary that I should write myself. It is as great a difference, I believe, as I presented in my own person when I attended a *levée* at Buckingham Palace one morning and submitted myself, stripped equally of clothes and importance, for medical examination at a recruiting-office in the afternoon.

It is this stark Colin Whimboyne, whom no one has seen for more than a moment at a time, that I want to examine against the background of Colin Whimboyne, the well-known playwright, in the *levée*-dress that he wore as a distinguished civil servant to be invested with his C.B.

PART ONE

I

THE time and place of my birth, though they are two of the
very few facts on which my autobiography and Mr. Clement
Phayre's obituary-notice would be in complete agreement, are
only of importance now in that, having been born at Ridgeway
House in 1888, I was old enough by the middle nineties to understand a little of the grown-up conversation that I heard when my
governess, Miss Flora Parsons, brought me down to lunch with
the family on Sundays. The iniquities of Gladstone's last administration were my weekly intellectual fare long after "that Grand
Old Mischief-maker" had been laid to rest; and, as they were
made the excuse for the revolution that was threatening the
Whimboyne fortunes at this time, I feel that, though the house
was the only home that I had ever known, I had hardly become
acquainted with more than the nursery-wing before the grown-
ups were warning me that it would soon be my home no longer.

With a deeper understanding of my father, I can now see that,
whatever the government in power, he would sooner or later
have ruined himself by always living a thousand or two beyond
his means; but, rather than reduce the style that he conceived to
be required of his position, he contrived that by selling and
mortgaging he should make Ridgeway House last his time. At
his death there would be little or nothing on which any one could
maintain a position; but by then there would probably be no
position for any one to maintain. He counted on living till
seventy and laid down port to be finished in the perfection of
maturity on his seventieth birthday. He also arranged for an
annuity to be paid to my mother, who—being five years younger
—could be expected to live five years longer. What more could
any man do except, perhaps, make the notorious socialism of Sir
William Harcourt a plausible and dignified screen for his own
practical incompetence?

" 'We're all socialists now'," he would quote with little gasps
of rage that I can still hear. "*Are* we?"

In a scheme of life that may now seem rather excessively ruled

21

by tradition my brothers and I went through this first initiation-rite in the hushed and gloomy dining-room on the Sunday after we became seven years of age. In the September following our eighth birthdays John and Charles, Harry and I were sent to Westcliffe House, Broadstairs, where we remained until we had exhausted the precarious possibilities of scholarship-hunting. Then at thirteen or fourteen, with or without a benefaction, we proceeded to Westminster, where—traditionally—every male Whimboyne had been educated since the first of a line that now rivalled the record of Phillimores, Waterfields and Madans had his name painted "Up School" against the date 1752.

By 1895 John and Charles were already there; and Henry, who had won an exhibition at the last "Challenge", was on his way there. At the first Sunday-luncheon that I can remember, the new vicar—an old Carthusian—wondered aloud how long it would be before Westminster followed Christ's Hospital and the rest into the country; and since that day I have sometimes wondered to myself whether the announcement that his old school was migrating from London would have convinced my father that one essential piece of traditionalism had broken in his hands or that he might usefully consider the wisdom of adapting himself to new conditions. I am inclined to doubt it. Had the scale of fees gone up or the standard of education down, there would have been grave shakings of head as the heavy cut-glass decanters circulated in their gleaming coasters; but it was the business of any school chosen for his sons to turn out scholars and gentlemen, he thanked God that in spite of Radical confiscation he could still afford to educate them as he himself had been educated and, though he knew of other establishments, West-minster was for him the only school in England, as Wiltshire was the only county, Brown's the only hotel, the *Morning Post* the only paper and the Army and Navy the only stores.

In the matter of adjusting himself to new conditions, why!, this was what he had been doing ever since he could remember or at least ever since the rascal Harcourt introduced his death-duties.

"You must adjust or perish!," he declared to the sombrely nodding Major Plimsoll and Canon Drake, without, however, revealing how he had ever adjusted himself to any change in the tradition that he had inherited and crystallized. "By the time these boys are ready to be launched . . ."

Traditionally, after five or six years at Westminster, young male Whimboynes went to Oxford or Cambridge, with or without a close scholarship to Christ Church or Trinity; and four years later again they were set—in the traditional phrase—to seek their fortunes, in circumstances that I now see seldom entailed much seeking and never resulted in a fortune. The hardiest article in my father's social faith, now defying Harcourt and later circumventing even Lloyd George, was an unbounded belief in the efficacy of "a word to the right man", resulting in suitable appointments with appropriate salaries. The eldest Whimboyne son, destined to inherit Ridgeway House, was traditionally not put into a profession, but was attached instead to some one's staff while he waited for his father to die or was sent to read in friendly chambers so that he might have a smattering of the law that he would afterwards dispense as a magistrate. The second son, as often as not, would find himself pushed into a family living; the third might hope to pick up a sinecure under government; and, if there were more than three sons, the youngest would have a word spoken for him to the right man in the City.

A "Radical rag" might fulminate against jobbery by parasites; but my father did not allow his house to be contaminated by Radical papers and, if mannerless phrases of this kind were quoted by apoplectic neighbours, he shewed himself to be more puzzled by their ignorance than resentful of their vulgarity.

"If any one wants to draw indictments against entire classes," he asserted at this memorable first luncheon, "the true 'parasites' in this country are the industrialists who have been infecting it since Arkwright and Stephenson. The landed gentry . . ."

To what followed I did not listen attentively, as I was troubled to hear my adored Stephenson, of "The Rocket", dismissed as a germ of social poison by my father, whom I had been brought up to regard as infallible. Very soon, however, I was to find that his speech was a stock piece which he repeated on three Sundays out of four; and, as my faith in his infallibility waned, I came to see him chiefly as an ineffectual, but adamantine, figure who refused politely and without ever raising his voice to compromise with the Industrial Revolution and all its evil consequences of swollen cities, franchise-extensions and general selling of the eighteenth century for thirty pieces of silver. Ineffectual in his hankerings for a vanished civilization, he was adamantine in his determination to preserve the best of an idealized, Roger-de-Coverley atmosphere in one small and steadily dwindling estate on the Marlborough Downs. He read the lessons and listened critically to Canon Drake's sermons from his corner of our box-pew; on his way to the lych-gate he enquired searchingly of the bobbing figures on either side why their husbands had not been in church; and at luncheon he worked methodically through the vicar's report on the moral and spiritual health of his flock for the past week. To his friends in other villages he was always "your excellent squire"; to his enemies he was "your local little tin god". There is no reference to him and hardly a mention of Ridgeway House in Phayre's obituary; and yet the man and the place have left their mark on the whole of my later life.

Ineffectual and adamantine? After fifty years I am inclined rather to call him effete and inflexible, from lack of joints or stiffness in such as he possessed. He very effectually achieved his unavowed aim of living and dying as an English country gentleman of the old school; and, if he consumed his sons' patrimony in the process, he gave them the best start in life that circumstances and his own mental limitations permitted. If—perhaps through no fault of his—he lacked the vital energy to repair or renew his failing fortunes, he was shrewd enough to see that his children would be unable to exist without working; and, if his vision was bounded by influence and good marriages, the explanation is that by 1895 he could not assimilate the idea of his sons' going on the Stock Exchange or taking up a government grant of land in Canada.

"Adjust or perish!," I have quoted him as saying; and that Ridgeway House might not perish before him I know now that he had begun to adjust himself some years before I was old enough to understand the grown-up conversation that followed its unchanging course when my mother had shepherded the other ladies to the saloon. Quite regularly in those years my father, it seemed, was selling a wood here and a farm there. If he did not live too long, he might perhaps at least die in the place where he had been born. After that?

I believe I am still nearly word-perfect in the speech that he invariably delivered at this point: After that? The deluge, he supposed! If he were not the last Whimboyne to own this house, he would be the last to reside here unless John married an heiress or discovered a gold-mine. All the boys, in fact, must now fend for themselves: no more loafing as honorary *attachés* at agreeable embassies or serving on some good-natured Viceroy's staff. He would, of course, speak a word to the right person when he knew where his sons' bent lay; but for the first time in the history of the family all four of them must support themselves by their own efforts.

"These death-duties . . . ," my father would end. "It's a matter of elementary mathematics! If these robbers take one slice and then another and then another . . ."

I fear that, after the first time, I did not concern myself with these attacks on "that rascal Harcourt": I was more interested to speculate about the immediate and personal implications of his rascality. I suppose I had come by now to understand that even fathers did not live for ever; but, almost immortal though my own seemed to me, this house was still more nearly immortal. It was the house that had sheltered generation after generation of Whimboynes; and, though I knew that younger sons quitted it in the course of nature, it seemed against the very order of nature that my brother John should not be acclaimed our father's heir and associate-ruler when he came of age and that he should not in the fullness of time succeed to the hereditary place on the local bench and on the hunt committee and to the half-hereditary privilege, which we shared with the Plimsolls, of representing this division of the county in Parliament.

I have little doubt that I am telescoping several of these Sunday luncheons into one; but it seemed at the time, when it was being hammered into me week after week, and it still seems, after half a century, that I had been promoted to a place in the candle-lit dining-room, with its lines of stately Chippendale chairs under the lines of massively framed and smoke-begrimed family portraits, just in time to be told that it was all to disappear next day. At the impressionable age of seven the lost child thinks himself lost for ever; and I was not yet able to share my easy-going elder brothers' Micawberesque conviction that something was sure to turn up. Hitherto I had not felt any strong affection for the mellow Georgian house that I had always taken as much for granted as the beechwoods that sheltered and separated it from the bleak Wiltshire Downs with their ancient trackways and barrows, their dolmens and hill-top earthworks; but I know that my love for it was born at the moment when I dimly apprehended that it was under sentence.

I sought the reassurance of Miss Parsons, who had remained behind as surety for my good behaviour, but was silenced by a quelling: "Hush, Colin dear! And don't fidget with the nut-crackers!" Major Plimsoll, our member, was talking about "entails"; and I heard my father explaining that Ridgeway was not entailed.

"It's left in trust to my widow for her life-time," he continued. "The wine stands, Colin! After that, if any of these boys have made enough money to buy it at auction . . . I shall give them the best start I can."

I have an impression that from this moment the conversation revolved exclusively about the quarters in which influence could be used and the influential friends on whom my father could count. I was thought young enough, I suppose, to be ignored; and I presume that my brothers were away at school. Certainly their futures and mine were discussed and arranged without reference to us. If in any way, therefore, my life has gone accord-ing to plan, as the obituary would have its readers believe, it has not, fundamentally, been according to any plan of mine.

"John will go from Oxford into the army," my father declared, "and it will be his *career*. If in his spare time he marries a rich wife . . . Charles, from his reports, has a rather unusual head for figures: his destiny lies in the City and I have good reason to think I can arrange the right kind of opening for him there. Henry would like nothing better than to succeed his uncle as rector of Aldington, but the hunting parson will be an extinct species by the time he's ready to be ordained and in any event I no longer have the presentation to the living. Henry will have all the hunting and shooting he wants if I can get him appointed agent to some one like Claude Axminster or Burncote. There has been no time to think about Colin yet, but a nomination to some post in the civil service . . . Thank Heaven, there are still a few that are *not* filled by this pernicious competitive-examination! But we must see first how he does at school. Yes, he will follow his brothers to Westminster. After that, if he can get a scholarship or exhibition to the House or Trinity . . . After that . . . It's only right that their tastes should be consulted."

How far my brothers' tastes were consulted I cannot say; but, to judge by results, I should think that each of them submitted without protest as I was myself to submit when my turn came. John, having no suggestions of his own to offer, received a commission in the Wiltshire Regiment and made the army his career until he was invalided out in 1915. Though he married twice, neither wife was a rich wife; and, far from buying Ridgeway House in when it came under the hammer, he was glad to supplement an insufficient pension by becoming resident-secretary to a golf-club. Charles secured his promised opening with a firm of export-merchants and was himself promptly exported to Valparaiso, where he died without ever returning to England. Henry became agent to Lord Drury until the Fremantle estates were turned into a limited-liability company; but he too failed to marry an heiress and indeed died insolvent. I, still stubbornly set at twenty-two on becoming a writer, was without difficulty persuaded that I should have all the time I needed for writing in the civil service and that, if I put myself under the protection of my father's friend Lord Axminster (a right man, though a Liberal in politics), I should find that it was still possible to secure myself a snug niche in Whitehall without the indignity of competing with board-school boys for the favours of the civil-service commissioners.

All this, however, lay half a generation ahead of the Sunday when I was first allowed to lunch downstairs, the day when for the first time I began to see Ridgeway House and my father in perspective, though not yet in focus. That was to come much later, if indeed it came at all.

II

THE "happy" life that I am popularly supposed to have led is a conception to which I have not—until the last few days—given sixty minutes' thought in sixty years.

For more than forty of them I have been too busy observing, analysing and classifying other people to have much time for studying myself; and, though I have written many plays with so-called happy endings, I have not until now tried to define happiness, which I am inclined to fancy is linked with its opposite like light with darkness. If I applied the rather crude test: "Is there much that you would change, if you had your time over again?," I might reply: "Everything!," unless indeed I replied: "Nothing!" It is obviously not a matter for tinkering. As a tea-planter in Assam or a veterinary surgeon in Dumfriesshire, I might have known a different and a greater happiness; but, unless I change the whole pattern of my life, I do not feel that the substitution of one thread for another—Winchester for Westminster or Cambridge for Oxford—is worth considering.

Certainly, for the readers of Mr. Clement Phayre's column of gossip, there is little that I should wish to change in the biography that I revise annually for *Who's Who*; but, until I was securely launched on the civil service and my father could wash his hands of me, it might be said with some justice that my life was not my own. Should I wish then, to alter anything in the years when I was *in statu pupillari*? I must again answer "Everything!," unless I answer "Nothing!" I was happy enough, that is to say, within a certain framework; but I am not prepared to declare off-hand that in 1948 I would choose that framework again for my wiser, better and happier life, were it beginning again in 1948. Public schools, for example, have been so much criticized since my boyhood that I pondered for years on the best education that I could give my own son. In the end I decided that, whereas members of a certain class had once gone to public schools as a matter of course and whereas some of us might see a time when as a matter of course the same class shunned public schools, that time was not come yet. In the years between the wars it was still expected that a boy like Norman should go to a public school; and to a public school accordingly he went. How very much stronger were the arguments for conformity in 1900 when I drifted in my brothers' wake to Westminster with an exhibition which was followed two years later by a scholarship!

My father's decision, then, is certainly not one that I would have changed at the time; nor, as affecting the last year of Queen Victoria's reign, would I in retrospect change it now. Accepting the classical framework, I find no fault with the education that I received; I was successful in work, at games and in the position that I attained as head of my house, a school monitor and *princeps oppidanorum*; I made two or three of my best friendships in these years; and, if I was ever unhappy, it was with the unhappiness of boredom. Like Max Beerbohm at Charterhouse, I never completely assimilated the public-school convention. Many of our cherished customs, much of our esoteric language and most of our fierce, petty loyalties seemed then, as they seem now, rather infantile.

So much admitted, I should have been no happier anywhere else in this period of history. Between us, my three brothers and I spanned about fifteen years, the last of Rutherford's reign and the first of Gow's. For my brothers' friends as for mine our father, sporting a faded pink tie and quoting his own Latin epigrams, kept open house; and, though I failed to overlap either at school or at the university some of the most distinguished scholars and athletes in this astonishingly rich period, I knew almost all of them as guests at Ridgeway House and I came to know the rest by sight as they returned and returned again to the school with fresh and fresher laurels to ask for additional half-holidays in celebration of their latest triumph.

Has any school of the same size a record to match ours in those fifteen dazzling years? Have we ourselves another noon-tide splendour to equal this one? Leaving out the pure academics, who may have conquered no further worlds after their double firsts and their university prizes and their All Souls' fellowships, I could compile from memory as fast as my pen would travel a list containing one Master of the Rolls in Wilfred Greene, one Chief Justice of India in Maurice Gwyer, a President of Magdalen and a Principal of Brazenose in Tizard and Stallybrass, two Fellows of the Royal Society in Tizard—again—and E. D. Adrian, one of the most brilliant writers in A. A. Milne, an outstanding conductor in Adrian Boult and an editor of *The Times* in Robin Barrington-Ward. This, or part of it, was the company that I was privileged to join in 1900; and, if I were going to a public school again, I could hardly ask for a better.

From the bow-fronted work-room window of my house in Grosvenor Road I can see the Houses of Parliament, where Nigel Oakhirst and I exercised our cherished privilege of entering in scholars' caps and gowns to hear the debates; I can see the Abbey roof on which Clayton Mandeville and I walked as founder-members of the illicit and short-lived Climbers Club. Every stone of the precincts enshrines a memory for me; but I believe it was the London outside these precincts—the theatres that I visited on wet half-holidays and the houses where, as a weekly boarder, I stayed at week-ends—that possibly made my later life different from what it might have been if I had gone elsewhere. Among my first acquaintances—not yet a friend—was Austin Gerrold; and obviously, if I had not dined with him a dozen years later at his house in Montpelier Square, I should not have been adopted into the family by his wife; and, if I had not met Elizabeth at this time, I could not have married her after Austin was killed in 1916. It was under the living pyramid of my first "pancake greaze" that I met and mauled the Honourable Anthony Pryde; and both of us recalled the encounter half-way through the 1914 war when he invited me to dine with his sister Isabel and himself. The Cheshunts, as a family or a social phenomenon, I did not come to know well until I was an undergraduate and they were established in the full magnificence of Coverley Court; but Philip and Maurice were friends of Vaughan Drake, our vicar's son, and I was taken by him once or twice to lunch in Saint John's Wood with "Old Alec" and his homely "Martha".

Doubtless, if it was preordained that we were all to play a part in one another's lives, we should have met, in Destiny's good time, wherever we had been at school; and perhaps my father's choice of Westminster only resulted in my coming under the influence of half-a-dozen friends somewhat earlier than if I had gone to Eton or Oundle. In contributing, however, to happiness or success, how great has that influence been?

"*The captain of the Hampshire grenadiers*" may not have "*been useless to the historian of the Roman empire*", but did the insignificant author of *Summer Lightning* owe anything to the Westminster exhibitioner or king's scholar? When this first play of mine was produced at the Welbeck Theatre before the 1914 war, Austin Gerrold's telegram of good wishes on my first night ended with the warning that, as he had set my youthful feet on the playwright's path, he expected a half-share of the profits. When the play was withdrawn after one of the shortest runs in the history of the London stage, I invited him to dine with me on my losses; and I seized the opportunity to point out that I had decided to be a dramatist many terms before he and I formed the habit of going to *matinées* whenever the weather released us from the purgatory of compulsory cricket. Far from encouraging me to write, I reminded him, he was then solely concerned to act and to make his friends act with him. I might occasionally be allowed to compose a duologue (which he carved up to give himself an ampler part); but this was only a sop to secure my support for the Christmas pantomime which he organized in our dormitory or for the dramatic society which he failed to impose on a wholly uninterested school or for the touring company which he aspired to inflict on the country houses of his acquaintances during the summer holidays. That shared passion for the theatre which I have mentioned really began and ended with our half-holiday ventures in gallery or pit; after that, we separated mentally, Austin giving imitations of George Alexander or Charles Wyndham on our way back to school and I wasting an hour of evening preparation on rewriting with topical embellishments the comedy that we had just witnessed.

The lure of the footlights weakened for Austin when he joined the Oxford University Dramatic Society and was told that despite his partiality for the music of his own voice, despite even his clearly chiselled Sherlock-Holmes profile, he lacked the makings of even a bad actor; but in his schooldays no house-party that he attended was secure from the menace of private theatricals. He came to Ridgeway House at least once; and with us, as with every one he visited, his plan of campaign was to unearth a deserving charity, collect a company, choose a play and round up the neighbourhood on behalf of a cricket pavilion or a cottage hospital. In this sparsely populated part of Wiltshire, his chief difficulty was to persuade even half-a-dozen self-conscious and unenthusiastic men and maidens to form his company; and, being throughout his short life the most outspoken of all my friends, he did not conceal his disappointment.

"Shakespeare's country!," he would groan. "No wonder Ben Jonson was 'rare'!"

We, on the other hand, though often startled and occasionally shocked, were never disappointed with Austin. He was too forthright, too dynamic, too full of new ideas and passions for that. The only child of well-to-do parents, indulged at home and untamed at school, he had been allowed to say whatever came into his head; and, since he was equally devoid of reverence and malice, his criticism of life was generally diverting and occasionally stimulating. If he did not set me on the road to becoming a playwright, Austin Gerrold flung open more intellectual doors for me than any six other men of all my acquaintances: and, looking back over more than forty years, I see him as really the first man who led me outside Ridgeway House, outside the Whimboynes and—most of all—outside myself, bidding me look down on them as they slept and as my awakened spirit accompanied him to the Downs that overhung our "mortuary".

That, he insisted, "with all respect to the Squire", was the proper word: my father and his fox-hunting, port-drinking

cronies were dead, but not yet buried, temporarily stretched on
their slabs for the interested public to view. The odour of
dissolution surrounded them; and my brothers were already
exhibiting the inertia and rigidity of death. What a cemetery this
part of the country must be if it could not produce even six
intelligent and presentable men and girls to play in my *Man
Overboard*! Where did they hide themselves between the closing
point-to-point of the spring and the opening meet of the autumn?

"Sleep-walkers!," he shouted to the placid landscape.

Had I ever asked my father and the other "old buffers" in their
low-crowned black hats and their tailed tweed coats and their
canvas gaiters what they imagined they were *doing* with their
lives? Farming at a loss, pursuing vermin on horseback, dis-
pensing justice that a stipendiary could handle in half the time
with twice the knowledge and planning, plotting, scheming and
contriving that their eldest sons should perpetuate this living
death for another generation! Good heavens, this was the
Richard-Jefferies country: did none of them ever want to write a
book? A day's ride would take them to Lawrence's birthplace:
did none of them ever want to paint a picture? Had we no friends
under ninety? Was this an Eveless Eden?

" 'Don't know, I'm sure, where you'll find the gals,
Gerrold!,' " Austin continued in exquisite mimicry of my father.
" 'Not many young people at this end of the county. No. Never
heard of any that could *act*. The wine stands, Colin.' "

I have sometimes thought that Austin could have supported
himself on the variety stage by quick-change impersonations. As
he talked of the "old buffers", I could feel them materializing
round me in their faded pink or rusty black or pepper-and-salt.
At the moment, however, I was pondering his phrase about an
Eveless Eden.

"I suppose, if we had any sisters . . . ," I remember beginning.

And then his phrase and any discussion to which it gave rise
were forgotten till the night, fully ten years later, when we dined
together at the Garrick for the last time before he went to his
death in Flanders. By then he was a married man—I still thought,
a happily married man—with two young boys, a charming house
where he entertained delightfully and the promise of a distinguished career in the civil service. By then I had made something of a name, thanks to *The Stormy Petrel* and *Objection
Overruled*, with more money that I had ever expected to handle in

a lifetime. I must also have made a different kind of name as— what he called—an eligible bachelor, for I recollect that Austin with his customary directness asked whether I had a wife in mind, whether I was ever likely to have one, whether I had ever fallen in love and, if so, whether the experience had enriched my knowledge of women and of life. Then, without waiting for an answer, he reminded me of our walk and talk together as school- boys over the Downs to Barbury Castle and his comment on the oddly celibate life that we lived at Ridgeway House.

"I suppose, if we'd had sisters . . . ," he murmured in words which I now recognized as my own. "My people did at least try to import some suitable female society for me, but then I was always susceptible to women, interested in them, romantic about them. I could never feel that your brothers and you *were*. All of you worshipped your mother and judged every other woman by her, ultimately picking on the girls who promised to become most like her. *Or* being picked on *by* them. Well, I suppose you'll do the same! Whatever happens, I wish you luck, Colin, but I must say I'm appalled to think sometimes how little you and I knew about women in the days when I was blindly idealizing them and you were blandly ignoring them as frills and fripperies on the pattern of your serious, your oh-so-serious, existence! Well, I hope you won't have to pay a heavy price for your superiority and indifference!"

I remember protesting that I had never felt superior and that, if my youthful approach to life and work now seemed a trifle solemn, Austin himself was chiefly responsible.

"That afternoon on the Downs," I told him, "you gave me my greatest shake-up. If ever I saw a light or heard a call, that was the time it came to me. A most illuminating—and offensive! —phrase about the mortuary in which we were all stretched on our slabs. Even my brothers, you said, were beginning to stiffen. I decided then and there that you should never say that of *me*. I would live all out, like you, putting every ounce of myself into everything I did."

"And that you've done, more than your three brothers put together. To be offensive again, whenever I've been with any of them, I've felt I was carrying a corpse about with me. I'm sure they're most worthy members of society; but there's no energy, no joy of life, no adventurousness about them. I used to think of Ridgeway House as a upas-tree, drugging you all to your long

C

last sleep; but *you've* escaped its influence, Colin. Perhaps all families stagnating in the backwaters of the world tend to lose their vital energy till something comes along to stir them. The pinch of poverty . . ."

We talked for a while of Ridgeway House as Austin first remembered it and as it was now. My father was still some months short of the seventy years that he had allowed himself; but, if he caught a chill on his birthday, I felt sure that he would do nothing to throw it off. The wine that he had laid down would last his time; but he was laying down none for our mother, who would not be entertaining when he was gone, nor for John, who had married (or been married by) a girl as ill-endowed as himself. It was to be hoped that the roof and the drains would also last his time.

"*You* look like being the rich member of the family," Austin observed, when I had done. "If the place *is* put up for sale . . ."

"I shan't bid for it on the strength of two successful plays and one failure. It will cost a small fortune just to put into repair. When you come to installing electric light and building additional bathrooms . . . Besides, I don't want a country house while I'm a bachelor with a seven-day-a-week job in London. If I married, still more if I chucked the civil service . . ."

"In your place, I shouldn't do *that*," Austin broke in with a gravity that seemed faintly incongruous with the lighthearted spirit in which he had defied his own departmental heads, taken a commission and telephoned to me an hour or so before to say that he had told Elizabeth she must consult me if she needed money or advice. "The play-going public is a fickle fairy, Colin, but the Treasury is a most dependable paymaster. Stick to your job, however many successes you have. I was only thinking that you're fond of Ridgeway House, your brothers are out of the running and you could have great fun modernizing it. Till you find a wife, I presume you could always let it."

"I'm not so sure. You yourself called it a ' dead-and-alive neighbourhood. Incidentally, if the hypothetical wife didn't take kindly to it . . ."

"If the hypothetical wife is some one who won't live anywhere outside the Shires . . . As you can't do your present job from Melton Mowbray, you would have to keep on your London quarters and visit her at week-ends. Which might not be at all a

bad arrangement. I'm sure most husbands and wives see altogether too much of one another. . . . However, I don't want to
arrange your married life for you. I was trying to put myself in
your shoes and wondering how I should feel if I allowed a place
I loved to pass into the hands of strangers. Have you in fact ever
considered the idea?"

I said that I had not; and, though I fancy it is widely believed
that I was my father's only surviving son and succeeded automatically to Ridgeway House on his death, the true account—for
whatever it may be worth—is that my two eldest brothers were
both living when our widowed mother found that she could not
afford to keep the place in commission, that we held a family-
council to decide what should be done, that the others waived
their seniority and that I was told I was welcome to anything I
had the money to buy, with their blessing, if I thought it would
amuse me.

I did not think it would amuse me; but I thought it might be
a sanity-saving distraction. When the family-council met, Austin
was no longer alive to be told whether I yet had a wife in mind,
or whether—as certain newspapers had alleged—Lady Isabel
Pryde and I were engaged to be married. As all newspapers had
been proclaiming for the past week, she was engaged—more
suitably in every way but one—to the Duke of Abbotsbury. Since
I had no other hypothetical wife in view, it was no longer worth
considering whether she would care to have Ridgeway House as
her home. I did not myself care at this time whether it was
destroyed by a Zeppelin or turned into an orphanage; but of a
sudden I remembered Austin's saying that I should have great
fun over making the house habitable. I was not indeed looking
for fun; but I sorely needed something that would keep me from
thinking.

I have allowed my pen to run away with me. An hour ago,
when I took it up, I was trying only to clear my head over the
popular conception of happiness and success, of lives in which
one would change nothing if one had one's time over again and
of lives that had triumphantly proceeded according to plan. I
must have been successful to have amassed money enough to buy
Ridgeway before I was thirty, but I never planned to buy it. I
never planned to amass money; but the influence and example of
Austin inspired me to live, in a favourite phrase of his, as though
every hour were my last and I fancy that in a world only half

awake or even half-alive the very few who live fully will to some
extent be successful. My life might indeed have been wholly
different if I had gone to another school, it might have been
happier or more successful if I had never gone to a public school;
but, such as it has been, I owe much to Austin and to the accident
of my meeting him at a hero-worshipping and malleable age.

For the rest and but for him, I must confess again that my
sturdiest recollection of six years in most distinguished company
at a most famous school is one of persistent mild boredom which
lifted only when I went to Oxford in 1906.

III

WHEN writing of Austin Gerrold in his school-days, I had
almost forgotten—and I have always been too ready to forget—
his talent as a caricaturist.

Though defamatory drawing—in a short life clamorous for
self-expression—was his sole contribution to creative art, I fancy
that he was a little ashamed of his facility. Untaught and too
impatient ever to take lessons, he knew that his success in catching likenesses and his unerring eye for absurdity were not enough
to hide faulty draughtsmanship; and, after spending two hours
on a composition, he would chuckle over it for two minutes and
then tear it in small pieces. Though I was suffered to keep one of
his most ambitious efforts, he stipulated that it should remain
under lock and key. And so it has remained, from the day when
he gave it me after my coming-of-age until now, when I have
been ransacking a box of private photographs.

It is entitled *Sauve Qui Peut* and represents my lean and tall
father, with his melancholy brown eyes and his greying thatch of
black hair, as Napoleon at Waterloo. The conventional half-
furled map in the right hand reveals, in place of the usual battle-
plan, the south elevation of Ridgeway House; and in honour of
my birthday the order—"Every man for himself"—is addressed
to me, though my brothers with the same eyes and hair, the same
spare frames and clean-shaven, flat-cheeked faces, are identifiable
in the middle distance. Camp-followers and civilians, in the
confusion of imminent defeat, mingle freely with the scattering
military; John and Henry are escaping with *vivandières* who bear

an unmistakable resemblance to the lately chosen chocolate-box beauty Blanche and the Spanish gypsy Constance, while I—a diminutive drummer-boy—am being helped off the field by the excessively whiskered Lord Axminster. From the conversational balloons issuing from the mouths of Napoleon's marshals (or, alternatively, my father's Wiltshire neighbours) the emperor and his map will stand their ground till a merciful shot shall bring the empire itself to an end. An *aide-de-camp*, opening an anachronistic bottle of Gould Campbell '72, hopes anxiously that it will not be corked, since it is the last in the imperial cellar. On the sky line the familiar outline of Wellington's hat, surmounting the unexpected features of Lloyd George, is suggested rather than drawn; and instead of a marshal's baton the duke carries a scroll marked *PEOPLE'S BUDGET*.

I can well understand Austin's unwillingness that my father should see himself as his youngest son's least reverent friend saw him; but I think discretion would have been satisfied if he had pledged me only to keep this best of all his cartoons hidden during my father's lifetime. With trifling changes it could be made to fit the circumstances of a thousand families like the Whimboynes and a hundred houses like Ridgeway. The "little Welsh attorney" was completing in 1909 the ruin begun by "that rascal Harcourt" fifteen years earlier; the necessitous landed gentry must look after themselves as best they could; before the bonds of discipline were finally relaxed, the emperor had provided for his children according to his powers; he could now only wait for the sun to set on his empire, himself and his last bottle of Gould Campbell 1872.

I never heard whether Austin meant to lay most emphasis on the doomed Napoleon or his doomed army or the doomed house depicted on his map; but I, so long habituated to hearing that the whole of our social order was doomed, find the chief interest of the picture in the artist's suggestion of our possible escapes. We are all, to be sure, still on the battlefield; but my brothers and I look as though we knew whither we were fleeing, for us at least there must be a friendly cottager who will give us food and shelter and the diminutive drummer-boy has the broad-backed protection of Axminster. This interests me to-day, as it interested me forty years ago, for the answer it furnishes to the otherwise perplexing question how cheerfulness kept breaking through our father's efforts to make philosophers of us. My three years at

Oxford from 1906 to 1909, roughly the first three years of the last Liberal government in English history, were probably the three unhappiest years in "the Squire's" life; he took heart for a time from 1910 when first the Land Budget and then the Lords and finally Ulster held out the precarious promise of a reprieve; and, when war broke out in 1914, he descried a mist-ringed hope for the landed gentry of England (though he, by his time-table, would not live to see it); but in general, throughout my undergraduate days, he was like Austin's figure of Napoleon, stoically waiting for the sun to set on the stricken field of Waterloo. For me, on the other hand, the years from 1906 to 1909 were without exception or qualification the happiest of my life. As Austin may or may not have divined, we knew—my brothers and I—that we were predestined to escape unharmed from the battle-field.

Consciously or subconsciously, we had always taken it for granted. Not, I suppose, until I made play-writing my vocation did I include either of my parents in my case-book of psychological studies: natural affection, so called, and inculcated reverence, which made me believe as blindly in my white-haired, weather-beaten mother as in my still handsome and incurably sad father, were succeeded in our early manhood by impatience and fault-finding, which gave place—in the pathetic, bewildered creatures' last years of helplessness—to compassion, but, until we were all established in careers and homes of our own, we never doubted our father's ability to extricate us from a crisis, even so comprehensive a crisis as the collapse of the English landed gentry. When Vaughan Drake or Clement Phayre or Nigel Oakhirst asked me what I was going to do when I came down from Oxford, I replied by rote that I was going into the civil service; when, possibly reflecting on my undistinguished academic record, they hinted that I was scarcely good enough for any but the least coveted branches, I quoted as a matter of course my father's phrase that there were, thank God, still a few positions that a gentleman could fill without submitting to competitive examination; and with unshakable faith in that word spoken in the right quarter, a faith already justified with my three brothers and to be justified for me while I was still a freshman, I went on to explain that my father's old friend Lord Axminster had said that he would keep an eye on me. Of Axminster I shall have more to say later; but his importance in my life from 1906 to 1909 was that his vague influence and vaguer promise to use it in my behalf rendered my time at Oxford more carefree than any that I have known before or since. The drummer-boy of Austin's picture seems to be enjoying every moment of his poor father's Waterloo.

In one hand he carries a portfolio entitled *PLAYS*. I do not remember that I made at this time any public confession of my ambition to be a writer, but a one-eyed man must have seen that I was thinking of little else. All my spare time, with much that I ought not to have spared, and all the money that I could afford, with much that I could not, were devoted to something that I loosely called "The Theatre" as a convenient name to cover play-buying and play-reading, play-reading clubs and the play-acting of the Oxford University Dramatic Society, anonymous play-writing and amateur play-producing, most important of all the methodical analysis of plays and the psychological study of characters and situations that promised to supply the raw material of plays. All this I owe, through my father, to Axminster.

The series of little note-books that I have been filling throughout my working life were begun in my first term when our vicar, Canon Drake, suggested that I should find it interesting to keep a diary and I quickly decided for myself that it would be far more interesting to sketch the new friends, with the old friends in new dress, who wandered through the pages of my daily life. And so it proved. Even forty years later there seems a rather creditable amount of shrewdness and discernment in my youthful observation, though there is even more shortsightedness of which at the time I was wholly unconscious. In three years, for example, no woman's name appears in these note-books! Did I imagine that plays could be produced without leading ladies? Did I think that the celibate conditions of which Austin had complained at Ridgeway House would be continued throughout my life? Perhaps my brothers and I developed late; possibly we knew that we were ignorant and were ashamed of our ignorance. I can only record that on the evidence of my note-books I was not interested in this side of play-writing or of life.

In term-time this was natural enough: there was an iron curtain in those days between the men's and women's colleges, "North Oxford" with its sprinkling of dons' wives and daughters was a place of penance to be visited ceremoniously when we set out in blue suits and bowler hats to call on our tutors after a gargantuan Sunday-luncheon and, for the rest, our adventures into female society were limited to a few best-behaviour parties

in Eights' Week and one or two Commemoration balls when the
unvarying and unflattering formula of invitation was: "If you'll
see me though with my people, I'll see you through with yours."
For me at least this celibate habit was natural enough in my
vacations as well, since houses were few and distances long in our
part of Wiltshire. When I stayed with friends up and down the
country, I was indeed dimly conscious of sisters generally too
young for me to notice or too old to notice me; but my note-
book addiction was already so strong that I could not spare time
for these shadowy figures in the background until I had finished
my rough sketches of the "fellows" that I had known at school,
the "men" that I was meeting at Oxford, in their appropriate
setting of houses and parents and neighbours. Why sisters and
sisters' friends of my own age should have formed no part of this
setting I cannot imagine unless, having none of my own, I
decided—as Austin was to hint many years later—that they did
not matter.

And yet it was during this time that I met two of the three
women who have mattered most to me in my whole life; but the
meetings made so little impression on me at the time that I should
not believe they had taken place if I had not this old box of faded
snapshots and smudged programmes to convince me. Isabel
Pryde and I apparently took part in the same lawn-tennis tourna-
ment ten years before our disastrous encounter in London; and I
was grouped with Elizabeth Cheshunt in some week-end party at
least five years before she married Austin. I do not know that I
was shy or ill at ease with girls (though Isabel was to ask me later
whether I had ever met a woman before her); I remember
telling myself at some time that I should have to study "this love
business" (which I think I called "the Life Force") in my self-
planned training as a playwright; but at the moment I was more
interested in my new friends, still more in those whom I have
called my old friends in a new dress, most of all in the hitherto
unregarded structure of society.

My note-books, which had begun with sketches of isolated
individuals, soon became filled with elaborate backgrounds
against which the individual was projected as the creature of
environment; and the phrase that I have just used—or, at least,
the idea underlying it—I owe to my indolently good-natured
eldest brother, who took me for an improving walk on the
Downs a few days before I went up for matriculation, as—six

years earlier—he had taken me for a chastening walk a week or so before I was admitted an exhibitioner of Westminster. John's advice on both occasions was primarily that I should comport myself with humility: the shining light of a preparatory school became an obscure fag at a public one; however glorious the figure that I had cut in the previous July, I should by the second week of October be only an indistinguishable item in a rabble of wholly uninteresting freshmen. My Westminster friends would invite me to breakfast; and, if I were lucky, I might be asked to join one of their messes in Hall, but I should be taken on my merits and I might discover that merits at Oxford were not quite the same as at school.

"Men tended rather to despise one for *not* getting into the Seventh and *not* rising even to house-colours," he continued. "At Oxford they some of them shewed social qualities—I really can't say what they were—that made great successes of them. Curious . . . I found the same thing when I joined my regiment."

I was reminded of this conversation a few weeks later as I watched the wilting of sundry school-heroes and the burgeoning of others, pre-eminently of two brothers who had been hardly more than acquaintances of mine at Westminster. Though I was to become their brother-in-law, I had not only scorned Philip and Maurice for their lack of conventional achievement, but I had also damned them, when Vaughan Drake took me to their house, for a flashy, man-about-town bearing that I thought unsuitable in schoolboys. At the House, their wide-spread popularity persuaded me that, unless all the rest of our undergraduate world was wrong, I must have been prejudiced. Beyond question the Cheshunts had arrived. Was Oxford in 1906, so many stages nearer than the public schools to the Edwardian social scene, more susceptible to the lure of the long purse and the open hand? These red-and-black barbers' blocks may have been envied or admired at Westminster for their Savile-Row clothes, their Jackson-of-Piccadilly food-supply and the signed photographs of musical-comedy favourites which they kept pinned to the inside of their locker-doors; but they were regarded by masters and boys as two of Nature's bounders. At Oxford, though the fastidious might dismiss them as vulgarians, they were accepted as authentic members of a rich sporting set that took as its motto: "On the Turf and under it all men are equal."

I meditated long and deeply on them as they progressed from

tentative whip-cracking and subdued view-holloas in my quadrangle through conscientiously intemperate attendances at
Corinthian dining-clubs to the final glory of the Bullingdon with
its blue-and-white ties and grey bowlers. Brooding over that
phrase about old friends in a new dress, I accepted an invitation
to spend a week-end with the family in Hampshire in the hope of
determining whether they or I had changed, whether they were
still as richly common as I had once thought them, whether I had
become more tolerant or whether Oxford had brought out
qualities which I was slow in recognizing.

Even forty years later I should have difficulty in answering my
own questions; and I suppose I am lingering over my first visit
to Coverley Court for the light it may possibly throw on my
literary development. Evidently before I even sketched my first
scenario, I was preoccupied with the niceties of English caste; and,
if all my many plays have followed a single track, it is because
the comedy of modern manners viewed under one aspect has
interested me to the end as it interested me from the beginning. I
may admire the whimsicality of Barrie, the moral earnestness of
Galsworthy or the sociological passion of Shaw; but I know
better than to imitate them even if I could. It was the workings of
caste that engrossed me when I stayed with the Cheshunts in
Hampshire. There, as at Oxford, these hard-living young men
and their dashing sisters were successfully asserting themselves
as they had not asserted themselves in Saint John's Wood.
Noticeably more opulent, with the enhanced confidence in
themselves that prosperity brings to those who measure their
fellows by a champagne or Rolls-Royce or grouse-moor standard,
father and sons, daughters and friends might have applied to
themselves a later phrase and said that to their ambitions the sky
was the limit.

Were the Cheshunts and their like, I asked myself in my
current note-book, taking the place of the Whimboynes and
theirs? By diligence and sheer ability old Alec had risen from a
clerkship in a firm of old-fashioned stockbrokers to the senior
partnership in a firm that paid its overhead expenses from broker-
age and made its profits as an issue-house. The profits must have
been enormous. When I returned to the shabby and neglected
Ridgeway House, still puzzled by the new dress that Philip and
Maurice now wore, I could only say that Coverley Court was the
richest house of my acquaintance. There were horses for any one

with habit or breeches, cars for those with driving-licences and chauffeurs for those without; the game-keepers and gardeners, the men-servants and maid-servants were in scale; and at different dates I met at Coverley my first hard-court, my first swimming-pool and my first landing-strip. It was already being hinted that Mr. Alexander Cheshunt, justice of the peace and a deputy lieutenant, hoped for a peerage when the next Conservative government was reminded of his lavish year as high sheriff; and, though he died unhonoured, perhaps unwept and certainly unsung, the appropriate works of reference shewed that he had at least collected several members of the more indigent nobility for his numerous sons and daughters.

Inexhaustible material here for the student of modern manners! And yet, when all this has been said, I feel that I am little nearer to defining the impact of the Cheshunts on the society of their day. They founded no line; they left no mark that I can see on the political or economic or cultural history of their time. Nevertheless, before their garish pleasure-domes collapsed in two world-wars, they seemed to have England at their feet. If they disappeared as suddenly as they had appeared, is the explanation that, unlike the patricians whom they copied and the middle class which they derided and the manual workers whom they ignored, they had no roots anywhere? I am still as much perplexed by this family into which I was afterwards to marry as when I first left Coverley Court, a little dazed by the noise, a trifle liverish from too much good living and faintly abashed by my obvious deficiency in vital energy. I felt no great desire to go back; and, but for the evidence of one faded photograph, I should not know that I had now met Elizabeth Cheshunt or that Austin Gerrold was already attracted to her by her unlikeness to her assertive sisters and brothers.

This visit, however, belongs to my second year at Oxford, when—as I have always and perhaps uncharitably assumed—the Cheshunts decided that a man who stayed regularly with the Axminsters was worth cultivating; and this brings me back to Austin's *Sauve Qui Peut*. In this overthrow of squirearchy by Lloyd George I at least am less interested in the mob of fleeing squirearchs than in the chosen few with a talent for self-preservation. If the young Whimboynes had not yet made fortunes or married heiresses, John was living on his pay in a line regiment and had become engaged to a lady with expectations (which were never realized), Henry was training to be a land-agent and Charles had begun to learn Spanish and merchant banking, whatever that might be. As for myself, the civil service and the consolidated fund were to be saddled with me. Starting as a supernumerary private secretary to Lord Axminster, I was to be added later to the strength of the Lord Keeper's Department; and thereafter nothing less than embezzlement or the betrayal of state secrets could endanger my salary and its periodical increases or my pension on retirement or my chances of a C.B. and, later, of a K.C.B. If I wanted to write, said the genial Axminster, I should have plenty of time. That was settled, then; and neither the Squire nor I need worry.

I do not know that either of us had ever worried, I about the omniscience of my father or my father about the omnipotence of Lord Axminster. As I watched the establishment of my three elder brothers, I came to feel that his most careless word would be more binding than another man's bond and that, whatever happened to the Liberal government and the Lord Keeper, nothing could ever upset the plans that I was making for life. In retrospect, I hope my manner was not offensively smug, but my attitude to the world and its problems was undoubtedly complacent.

What my scheme of life was planned to be at twenty I am not sure that I could state precisely now, though I remember certain things that it was expressly not to include. I would not resign myself, like my still respected father, to a conception of the world as a colossal shipwreck in which the far-sighted few had supplied themselves with life-belts to prolong their agonies till they reached a desert island; I would not allow myself, like my placid brothers, to drift into a good berth or to be prodded into a good marriage. I would live, I said, like my keen, acquisitive friend Austin, as though every moment were my last and best, I would drop down in harness, honourably worn out; and, whether or no my name were ever known outside my own street or village, the wine-cup that fell from my nerveless fingers should be drained empty.

I was resolved, though, that my name should be known: in general, it was to be known as that of a twentieth-century blend of Congreve, Sheridan and Wilde, but in seasons of political excitement I saw the Lord Keeper's supernumerary private secretary becoming a power behind the throne and in times of private ferment I combined both parts, leaving the Cabinet Room to take a curtain-call and returning to steer ministers through yet another crisis. My day-dreams were never disturbed by the knowledge that the Liberal government—Lord Axminster with it—could not last for ever; even in 1909, when I came down, I would not let myself be persuaded that the so-called German Peril was a dislocation to be regarded seriously; and, when I thought aloud of some abandoned Suffolk wind-mill or reconditioned Martello tower, as a retreat where the rising young author could work undisturbed, I ignored the warning voices of sceptics who wondered how my wife would like a home of that kind. The answer was too easy! I should never have a wife. Against women and marriage I had no sort of prejudice; but I took little interest in the first and had no time for the second. My art was to be my mistress and wife.

It is faintly consoling that, though I occasionally thought in those terms, I never spoke in this strain; and, if any of my friends had troubled to describe me at this time, I think they would have said that I was sociable by fits and starts, but that I seemed to spend my days buying books and my nights poring over them till I drifted into another world and age. Presumably it was a literary world, as I had already begun to write, though nothing in these years was published or produced. This, they might have added truthfully, did not seem to distress me: I always had the air of being satisfied with my lot, perhaps even with myself.

And why not? To count my blessings, as I certainly did not count them at the time, and to put them in an order that I should not at the time have followed, I was enjoying at twenty the almost perfect bodily health that I have known all my life; my mental health was mercifully free from morbid fears and unwholesome attractions; the social position of the Whimboynes, though I gave it little thought at the time, was good enough to dispense me from trying to improve it and secure enough to keep me from ever wondering whether perhaps I was not being taken at my own proper valuation. I received, as might have been expected of my father, an ample allowance; and when his careful time-table brought this to an end, I should by the efforts of Lord Axminster be supported by the British tax-payer until the day of my death. A young man so endowed, taking with both hands and so far requiring to give nothing in return, would have been hard to please if he did not feel that the foundations of a happy life had been finally laid.

Perhaps this is why these years seemed then, and seem still, a golden age. Nineteen-hundred-and-six to nineteen-hundred-and-nine: the heyday of the Edwardian Era! True, there was a Radical government in power, but the House of Lords was effectively curbing its worst excesses. The country was abnormally prosperous; London, when I went up for the Oxford-and-Cambridge match, was feverishly gay. Even in 1909, though Haldane was equipping his reorganized army with an expeditionary force and McKenna was insisting on more Dreadnoughts, no one believed that the exuberant Kaiser's periodical sabre-rattling would ever lead to a European war. For youth, the England of these years was the Land of Promise; these years were the Years of Opportunity.

And for me the promise and the opportunity were possibly greater than for most.

"I never expected you to get a first", my cherubic little tutor told me when I dined with him after the results of the final schools had been published. "I shouldn't have been disappointed if you'd taken a third. You're a dark horse, Whimboyne, and you'll win races when you've found your distance. A first isn't everything." Since Reginald Chalmers had taken three, I found this comforting. "You've made a host of friends in all parts of the college," he continued, "you're good-looking and you have backers in high places. You're going to make a mark of some kind, but what it will be I can't tell you. . . . Your friend Gerrold will make a mark too, if he's not in too much of a hurry. He has got his first all right. And he'll pass high into the home civil. I'm sorry he's not having a shot at a fellowship, but he says he wants to be *established* as soon as possible. You know he's engaged to be married? I don't think there's any secret about it. Rather on the young side, I should have thought, but I'm one of Nature's bachelors . . ."

I said that I was another; and the conversation turned to an account of Oxford in the days when the undergraduate Marquis of Axminster drank claret at breakfast and kept his private barge on the Isis and was sent down—at the instance of Chalmers himself—for fighting a duel.

IV

THE friends who on Clement Phayre's prompting assume that
I shall devote the leisure of retirement to writing my memoirs
begin always with a general reference to the literary and political
celebrities—from Pinero to John Drinkwater, from Asquith to
Ramsay MacDonald—with whom I am known to have been
associated and then go on to cite the late Marquis of Axminster
as a man about whom a whole book could be written.

They have apparently forgotten, if indeed they ever knew,
that whole books have in fact been written about him, that whole
chapters about him have been interpolated into books written
about other people and that there are allusions to him in almost
every book concerned with the social, sporting and political life
of Edwardian England. I gravely doubt whether I could add
much to the exploits and sayings that have been attributed to
him; I am quite sure that I have no wish to swell the spate of
irrelevant anecdotes that continues to grow even twenty years
after his death. I owe to him an introduction to certain houses
that I probably should not have entered otherwise; thanks to
him, for some years I lived on the fringe of a world that has now
disappeared for ever and that the Axminsters by sheer force of
personality kept alive from the Regency; I saw him as often in
his old-fashioned night-shirt as in his Garter robes or even in his
famous strapped trousers and blue frock-coat; and yet the one
thing that I care to say about him at this moment is that he was
the only man I ever heard describe himself as a Whig.

Others must have heard it too, but I do not recall that any one
has seized this as the master-key to a complex character and
career. Axminster has been variously described as the most
representative Englishman of his day, as the last of the Mohocks,
as a rebel and a reactionary, as a promiscuous lover and a concentrated hater, as a law unto himself and as a man born out of his
time; but, if he had described himself, I believe he would have
said that he was a Whig, adding "like my father and grandfather
before me".

The addition is all-important. Other men might be called
Whigs by their admirers or detractors; but the Whigs were
dropping out of political history before Gladstone became prime
minister for the first time and Whig principles, Whig houses and

great Whig families had lost their place in current jargon before I was born. Axminster, like his father and grandfather before him, gloried in the name and outdid Conservatives, Tories, Reactionaries and Last-Ditchers in regarding his own political faith as inspired and immutable. Hence the contempts and hatreds that made up much of his bellicose life! Tories like Harry Chaplin he could understand, even bring himself to respect if they remained Tories and did not whitewash themselves into Conservatives, like old Bob Salisbury, or—still worse—into Tory-Democrats, like that slippery Jew Disraeli; he tolerated Liberals as young Whigs born the wrong side of the blanket and, if a Radical were uncompromising enough, he admired him for the highly characteristic reason that, if he had been compelled to fight for what came to him at birth and what he would hand on to his son Honiton at death, he would himself have been a Radical. It was for the Whig who had struck his colours, like Lansdowne, or who called himself a Liberal-Unionist, like the Duke of Devonshire, that he reserved his hottest scorn and loathing. Once a Whig, a man must always remain a Whig; if the Whigs embraced electoral reform or free-trade or home-rule (which he continued to call "repeal"), no single Whig was at liberty to go against the party; and I have always presumed it was because his father had been a home-ruler, his grandfather a free-trader and both of them reformers that in 1905 the reigning Axminster could indicate to Campbell-Bannerman, without waiting to be asked, what office he was willing to accept.

It was generally believed that C.-B. made him Lord Keeper to inspire confidence in the hearts of timid voters who might have hesitated to support the new administration if Radicals like Lloyd George had not been balanced in the Cabinet by a few figureheads of substance and tradition. Axminster, with his fabulous wealth and his string of titles, could be trusted to see that no policy of general confiscation was followed and that no attack was launched on the hereditary principle His popularity caused King Edward to say that, if the monarchy were elective, "Claude the First" would be at least his immediate successor. And his modesty in taking an office without powers or duties fostered the belief that this champion of privilege and patronage was disinterested. To me—and doubtless to others—he declared that he could not be bothered with departmental routine, but that he did not mind attending an occasional Cabinet to hear

what was going on. It would, by the way, be my first task to tell
him what was likely to be going on, to look through those
ridiculous telegrams that the Foreign Office sent him every night
and to take charge of the infernal little key that he was always
mislaying. For the rest, I was to accompany him like his own
shadow; and he hoped that I was a good traveller, as he had to
get through a devil of a lot of travelling.

Since he had houses (always in full commission) in four
counties, with a flat in Paris, a villa at Cannes and a palace in
Rome, this did not surprise me; but after a year I decided that "a
lot of travelling" was a serious understatement. I very often
spent four consecutive nights in the same place, since very many
of the principal race-meetings occupied four days; but I seldom
passed a whole week anywhere, even in London, even when
parliament was sitting. I should like to think that I earned my
salary; but, if Axminster had demanded a premium, no sum
could have paid for the experience gained in the twelve months
after I came down from Oxford. Though my duties were exacting
and various, my hours undefined, I contrived to fill a number of
my little note-books; and, whereas my early sketches of types and
backgrounds came to be modified and elaborated with time, the
observations and discoveries in this crowded year were of a kind
that needed little later touching-up. No critic of my plays has
ever said that I have made a duke or dustman speak out of
character; and, because I had never met either a dustman or a
duke when I became Axminster's travelling secretary in the last
months of Edward the Seventh's reign, I made it my business to
study the speech and clothes and whole outward man of every
one I met. In my travels with this huge, untiring playboy I
became acquainted with many kinds of women and men, from
princesses of the Blood Royal to programme-sellers and from
broken-down tipsters to stewards of the Jockey Club. Ever since,
I have lifted them from my note-books as I needed them; and, if I
know at all how a Commodore of the Royal Yacht Squadron or a
government-office messenger should appear on the stage, I owe
most of my knowledge to the year in which the Lord Keeper ran a
race with the demon of his own restlessness and I panted after him
from Newmarket to the House of Lords, from Cowes to Argyle-
shire, from Covent Garden to Longchamps and from the Lord
Keeper's Department in Queen Anne's Gate to the Old Bailey. If
the murderer whom we saw being tried had been executed in

public, I doubt not that Axminster, like his grandfather before him, would have attended the hanging.

At the end of a year, startlingly mindful of his responsibility for my future, the Lord Keeper established me in London and appointed a new supernumerary private secretary to open his cabinet-boxes and skim his *Most Secret* papers for him. I was now, in my patron's view, fitted for a place on the very small regular strength of his department; and he would not feel that he had fulfilled his promise to "little Johnny Whimboyne" unless he had me settled before he was himself transferred. Yet more startlingly mindful of my own ambitions, Axminster recalled that I had once talked of wanting to write. He did not himself know much about writing and would not sign his own cheques if he could find some one to forge his signature, but he presumed that I had not had much time for writing in the last twelve months. Well, here was my chance.

So it came about that the moment the second general election of 1910 was over I became a first-division clerk in the Department of the Lord Keeper, with my name and salary published in *Whitaker's Almanack* and a room in Queen Anne's Gate overlooking Birdcage Walk; I also became a member of the Garrick Club and tenant of half the house which I still occupy in Grosvenor Road.

"It now rests with you," said my father in the course of a dinner at Brown's Hotel, when he was paying one of his rare visits to London for the ostensible purpose of seeing that I was fitly equipped for the battle of life and with a mournful air of discharging himself from his final trust.

Unlike Lord Axminster, he saw nothing freakish in a young man's aspiring to write plays, but he hardly troubled to hide his conviction that I should never make a success of it, still less earn enough money to bid for Ridgeway House when it came under the hammer. This phrase faltered to his lips more and more often as he drew nearer and nearer to the end of the span that he had rather arbitrarily, though—as it proved—quite accurately, allotted himself; and by the time his youngest son was set to seek his fortune he had decided that the three eldest would not find theirs. John was now married, to the pretty and penniless daughter of a neighbouring squire; but Blanche's shadowy expectations had already been shattered by her godfather's inconsiderate whim of taking a second wife; Henry too was married, but the expectations of Constance were only that some man somewhere would be found to support her alluring person; Charles, working in Valparaiso and living at Viña del Mar, could as yet hardly pay for his polo-ponies. Ridgeway House seemed so irretrievably doomed that, when my father examined the appointments of my new home, he wondered aloud whether he could not spare me certain odd unwanted pieces of family furniture.

Since the house in Grosvenor Road had been adequately equipped a year or two earlier by Nigel Oakhirst, with whom I was to share it until he married into a nearby house in Barton Street, I was more grateful to my father for his offer of servants. Young Alfred Winter, the second footman, was engaged to Margaret, our still-room maid; and they wanted to go out into service together. They would look after me well, my father assured me; and he would be glad to feel that he had got them a good place before the final break-up. I should say here that they came for a month on trial and have remained with me for all but forty years, returning to Wiltshire when I moved out of London in the 1939 war and coming back to Grosvenor Road in 1945 when the house was recommissioned.

"It ought to help you in your writing," said my father, "if you leave all your domestic affairs in the hands of people you can trust. When do you begin?".

I explained—with an odd premonition that this might be my last, as it was my first, opportunity of speaking intimately with my father—that I had begun at Oxford, perhaps even at school, to study the technique of the art that I aspired to practise. Doubtless I should make my first practical attempt when I had found something worth saying. I did not tell my faintly dazed and visibly ageing parent that my brain was already seething with plots and situations, characters and curtains, for the sufficient reason that I knew it to be seething. My year of peripatetic service to Axminster had given me more experience than I had yet found time to assimilate; I regarded myself as a finished man of the world, perhaps as a man of many worlds; but I needed time for all the glittering pieces in my kaleidoscope to settle. That time, I thought, might well be provided in the year of mourning after Edward the Seventh's death.

Possibly it was; but in looking back on my first twelve months in London I now feel that I was chiefly engaged in making a niche for myself among old family-friends of the Whimboynes, among new friends at my new club, even among new colleagues in Whitehall. During my travels with "the Flying Dutchman", as Austin was quick to christen the Lord Keeper, I had lost touch with my Oxford contemporaries and I returned to find that, though they had generally remained in one place, life had stood less still with them than with me. Before I had found anything worth saying or had learnt how to say it, here was Nigel Oakhirst, with whom I had listened to debates as a Westminster scholar, already called to the bar and opening the north-eastern circuit, already prospective Liberal candidate for a constituency in County Durham and a member of the Reform Club, already engaged to Miss Violet Pelman. Here were the Cheshunt brothers, already members of the Stock Exchange, already reputed to be minting money, Philip already married to the Marquis of Dromore's daughter Mary Tavish and Maurice to Earl Gullane's sister Jane Culme. Here was Clement Phayre, of Westminster and Balliol, a free-lance in Fleet Street, but already with the promise of a contract from the Amalgamated Press. Here was another school-friend, Clayton Mandeville, "the Laughing Cavalier", already a leader-writer on the *Sunday Post*, already married to Kitty Cheshunt (and surprisingly soon to be divorced by her). And here was the keen-faced, dynamic Austin, already married to another of them, already a father, already a coming man in the Home Office, the writer of signed reviews in three papers and a host whose invitations to dine in Montpelier Square were already valued.

When he heard that I was established in London, Austin announced that he would give a party to celebrate my escape from the clutches of the Flying Dutchman. He mentioned that Elizabeth wanted to ask the girl who was to marry my stable-companion and that, if it would amuse me, he would try to get hold of the celebrated Lady Isabel Pryde, whose brother Lascombe I doubtless remembered at school and Oxford. In the event, though Lady Isabel accepted, she was prevented from coming by an accident in the hunting-field. Violet Pelman, however, was there, pensively beautiful as a Mona Lisa to whom the Sphynx had whispered her secret a moment before; and I have more than once reminded myself that, but for Isabel's broken collar-bone, I should have met for the first time on the same evening at the same dinner-table the three women who have played the greatest part in my life.

Strictly speaking, I know that this was not my first meeting with Elizabeth, but I remembered nothing of her at Coverley Court and during this dinner I caught myself thinking once or twice that there was, comparatively, nothing to remember. She was pretty and her sisters were handsome; she was pale and they were high-coloured; her eyes were blue-grey, her hair flaxen, theirs were brown and black; she was soft in voice, when she spoke at all, and demure in manner, they were strident and bold from sheer excess of animal spirits and complete absence of inhibitions. It was, I reflected, easy to see why she had been overlooked in her parents' house; it was no less easy to foresee that she would be overshadowed in her own house if this party was a fair sample of the social life that Austin had decreed they should lead. I sat on Elizabeth's left; and some question about Axminster set me talking on that inexhaustible subject, without comment from her, till I felt that I had said enough and perhaps more than enough. Before I could open a fresh theme, the conversation had become general; and against the impetuous flow of Austin, the quiet assurance of Violet Pelman, the dogmatism of Nigel Oakhirst and the sledge-hammer attack of Clayton Mandeville I felt that the whispers of my mouselike hostess would pass unheeded and probably unheard.

Clearly, too, this party was a perfect sample of Austin's Montpelier-Square manner. The food, the wine and the service were above criticism; the guests had been carefully chosen; and the conversation was as good as I could have wished to hear anywhere. Still living his life to the full and being barred as a civil servant from talking partisan politics, my host seemed to have staged a gladiatorial show for his own entertainment between his brother-in-law and Nigel. When we turned from politics to literature, a second contest seemed to have been staged between Kitty Mandeville and Violet Pelman. And so throughout this very pleasant evening. Over our port Austin confided that it was his ambition to collect the best talkers in London round the dining-table in Montpelier Square; and, as we had a last drink after the others had left, he invited me to come again one night in the following week.

"If that means I've passed muster as a good talker," I said, "I shall be honoured."

"It will only be a small party," he answered, "but I've had no chance of getting you to myself to-night. Come to think of it, you know, we've hardly met since our last term at Oxford."

"Since which time," I reminded him, "you've managed, as usual, to cram in as much as any three ordinary men."

"Well, I still can't stand people who are only half alive," he laughed. "That's the one thing," he continued with his old out-spokenness, "that reconciles me to my in-laws. They're vulgar, cheap, useless, anything you like to call them, but they have genuine *joie-de-vivre*. Even that ghastly megaphone Kitty . . ."

A little embarrassed, I said that I had always liked her husband.

"He won't be her husband long," Austin predicted.

"But it's only about a year . . . Why did he marry her?," I asked.

"Because he didn't know our father-in-law as well then as he knows him now. Old Cheshunt has a set speech, you know: 'I don't make settlements. I expect any man who marries a daughter of mine to be in a position to support her.' Where money's con-cerned . . . I should think old Alec spends thirty thousand a year on being ostentatious at Coverley, but he wouldn't help to save an Old Master from going to America, he wouldn't endow a bed at a hospital, he wouldn't give his cherished daughters a hundred a year pin-money. And why? So that, when he dies, his precious estate shall touch the million-mark. My amiable brothers-in-law are just the same."

I said that, as Austin had married into the family, I did not feel it was for me to criticize them.

"I was attracted to Rella because she seemed so *different* . . . ," he began.

"Rella?," I repeated.

"Sorry! A pet name: Cinderella. In that *milieu* it was so refreshing to meet a girl who wasn't an Amazon! I suppose I'm swimming against the stream, but I still like a woman to be womanly. Keen on her house, interested in her children. If you take Violet Pelman . . . By the way, you had a great success with her."

I said, in all sincerity, that I thought Miss Pelman one of the best-read, most intelligent and sympathetic girls that I had ever met.

"Nigel's a lucky fellow," I added.

"I should never say that of any man till he's been married ten years," Austin rejoined cynically. "I asked Violet how she'd got on with you and she said that, if she'd met you first, she would never have become engaged to Nigel. There's a feather in your cap, my lad! I don't think Nigel liked it particularly. He could never take a joke. Well, we shall see you next week? Violet's coming. Have you any objection to podgy and uninteresting babies? Elizabeth is sure to drag you up to see ours."

V

On the fly-leaf of my battered and bulging first news-cutting album there is pasted a half-obliterated telegram with the cryptic message *"WELL SWUM VIOLET."* I cannot now read the name of the office at which it was handed in thirty-six years ago; but I fancy it was at some mining-village in her husband's constituency. By 1912 Nigel had been married a year and a member of parliament for two. He had moved into the Barton Street house which Violet and he have occupied, off and on, ever since; and I remember that I, in sole possession of the place in Grosvenor Road, was wondering how long I could afford to live there and pay the Winters' wages if, as by now seemed but too likely, I discovered that Nature had after all never intended me to be a playwright. It was not that I had nothing to say: between 1910 and 1912 I completed four three-act comedies and sketched the outlines of another two. My trouble, in what Violet and I have always called our darkest hour before the dawn, seemed to be that I did not know how to say it.

I owe the application of the phrase to her, as I owe to her the plural of the possessive pronoun with its suggestion that we were working in partnership and that, if I wrote the plays, she supplied the faith that they would be produced when "our" day broke. At our second meeting in Montpelier Square, Elizabeth once again gave me a cue for talking about myself by asking whether I was still composing "things" like the one that I had written for Austin (on some forgotten occasion) to inflict on a house-party at Coverley Court. I said that, like Mr. Gibbon, I was "scribbling, scribbling" all the time, but that as yet I had achieved nothing worth the cost of typing. Though at this date I could never be sure that Elizabeth, always silent after her one question, was even listening to the answer, I held forth for a time about stage-craft;

and, when I felt that I had talked enough, I was a little disconcerted to find that Violet, on my other side, now wished to
take me, point by point, through a dissertation in which she
challenged most of my premises and disagreed with all my
conclusions.

"I've had a passion for the theatre," she explained, "ever since
my first Punch-and-Judy show. And, being quite incapable of
writing a line myself, I'm fascinated by the way other people
write. After meeting quite a fair number of authors, I feel that
with all of them, though they might not care to say so . . ."

As she paused, I asked her to say whatever it was for them.

"That there's *something*," she answered, slowly, "certainly
with plays, something beyond their *control*. . . . Well, it *happens*
to them, without any kind of warning. . . . Or else it *doesn't*! If you
think of Browning, Swinburne, Stevenson, Henry James! It's
like swimming! One day you're still sinking like a stone, the next
you've discovered the knack and you never lose it as long as you
live. It will suddenly happen to *you* . . ."

"Or not, as the case may be," I put in.

How long could I afford to allow myself? How much pride
should I have left if I confessed myself unfit to write and com-
posed myself for the living death of a superfluous civil servant
in an office that should have been abolished seventy years ago?
My father was not alone in thinking that I should never make
money by my pen: before leaving Grosvenor Road, Nigel was
giving me the names of barristers and members of parliament
who would be glad to share the house with me and, when I
arrived for dinner that night, Austin had murmured that, if I
wanted to sublet, he could find me a tenant there and then. Young
Bracton, who had married Elizabeth's eldest sister Phyllis,
needed to live conveniently near the House of Lords; and
"Cupid", as the Viscount Scaling was known to his intimates,
would have to settle within easy reach of the Foreign Office when
he married the next sister, May. Naturally, if I had a wife in view
for myself, I should not want to turn out; but for a bachelor the
place was a white elephant. Forthright as ever, Austin declared
that he had never seen me as a successful dramatist.

Had any one? Would any one?

The quiet voice of Violet Pelman seemed to be asking
whether she might see something that I had written.

"If I think it shews promise . . .", she continued, "And I

believe I *shall*. . . . Hearing you with Elizabeth, I have more faith in you than you have in yourself! . . . I could try it on my father. . . . Or W. L. Courtney . . . Or William Archer . . . They're always dining with us."

She spoke with a tranquil sincerity that made me feel she would never praise from politeness and with an air of authority which suggested that in literary discussions at "the Master's" house she was accepted by Archer and Courtney as an equal. So indeed it proved when I dined in Russell Square a few nights later to meet Walter Raleigh and Clutton-Brock; so it proved again when at last I plucked up courage to send Violet the script of *Summer Lightning*. She begged me to put it on one side for future rewriting: the theme was amusing, but it was not yet "good theatre". I had learnt the motions of swimming, she continued, but I had not yet put them into practice.

In the next two years a very similar criticism was levelled against *The Stormy Petrel*, *Objection Overruled* and *Old Father Hubbard*, though she found an improved technique in the first two and said of the third that I could almost certainly find a manager to accept it, though he would quite certainly lose money over it.

"I believe you could get any of them accepted," she went so far as to say. "And perhaps they would be carried off by sheer acting. That's not at all what we want, though, Colin. We want these plays to stand by themselves, not to depend on Irene Vanbrugh or Gerald du Maurier. We want them to read as well as they act, to read and act as well in a hundred years' time as now. That's why we must keep them in a drawer till we've found what's lacking. It's something so small . . ."

"Merely the spark of life, the touch of magic, the *practice* of swimming . . . ," I broke out with the petulance of one who hopes for praise and receives truth instead.

"I wonder whether you would pick it up if some one pushed you in and you found you must swim or drown. I'm going back, my dear, on all I've said, but I do sometimes ask myself why any one should be expected to know how plays should be written— with a company, to help or hinder, for an unpredictable audience, to help or hinder, too,—till he's had one *produced*. I don't know what to say, Colin! You would learn a lot by seeing *Summer Lightning* put on, but you would be terribly disappointed when it was taken off at the end of a week. Well, perhaps it won't be!

When you come to rewrite it, you may find that you've mysteriously learnt how to swim."

This conversation must have taken place late in 1910, as Violet was not yet married to Nigel and I can still see her pale face and slight figure against the dark background of books which her father—the last of the dilettantes, in her own phrase—had collected in the house that was so excusably mistaken for an overflow from the nearby British Museum. At one time, I fancy, Mark Pelman had been an official of the printed-books department; but, inheriting a little money and marrying more, he had devoted most of his life and all of his widowerhood to collecting and, when the house would hold no more china or glass, no more pictures or books, he began to collect people. Knowledge, of course, he was always collecting; and without premeditation he had collected a number of separate and distinct reputations which led almost automatically to his catholic collection of artists, authors, antiquaries and connoisseurs who came to him as the final court of appeal in erudition and taste. Tall, thin and erect, with silver hair and a Vandyke beard, a dandy on lines of his own, he impressed me, when I first saw him in his claret-coloured velvet smoking-suit, as the most distinguished-looking man that I had ever met and as the most fastidious speaker that I had ever heard. I readily understood his daughter's casual remark that she had met quite a number of authors; I myself seemed to meet one or two of the most famous whenever I went to Russell Square and, if they did not go to be helped out of a difficulty, they commonly awaited the Master's *Nihil Obstat* before venturing into print.

Inevitably I tried to sketch Mark Pelman for my note-books, but he proved too delicate and elusive for me. So, I imagine, did Violet, as I essayed nothing more subtle at this time than a catalogue of physical characteristics. "*Her father's fine head and clean-cut features,*" I recorded, "*but brown hair and very deep, very deep-set brown eyes. My first two epithets would be 'quiet' and 'grave': she speaks (and perhaps thinks) in undertones, hardly ever laughs and seldom smiles. An endless range of twinkles are the outward signs of her most discriminating sense of humour.*"

It is a measure of Violet's discernment that the conversation which I quoted a moment since took place when I had finally decided a couple of years later that I must try my luck with what I had written or else give up trying to write. Hence her question whether any one could know how to write a play till he had seen one of his own produced. In rewriting *Summer Lightning* I evidently did not learn how to swim: though it was accepted by the fourth manager to whom I offered it and cut about till I hardly recognized it for my own, it was taken off as soon as another play could be put into rehearsal and Violet's telegram—*"WELL SWUM"*—was despatched when I told her that I had that day signed my first contract. When it was too late to save myself from this first rash plunge, I did indeed discover that the producer, the actors, the audience and the critics had combined to give me something that I can only call the sense of the theatre; and to my other manuscripts I could now impart the spark of life as quickly as I could rewrite them. Despite the alarming failure of *Summer Lightning* in 1912, the *Stormy Petrel* was accepted in the following year; and thereafter, instead of my waiting on managers, it was the managers who waited on me.

Looking back on our long literary partnership, I feel it is a measure of Violet's literary integrity that she never pretended in early days to think I was in the first class of writers or ever should be. As a friend, she hoped and believed I should be successful; she respected my industry and admired my technical adroitness; but she never encouraged me to think that I was more than a public entertainer.

"Why should you want to be?," she asked one summer's day in 1914. Her father had died a few months before; and I was in Barton Street helping her to arrange the books which she had chosen from his library. "What was good enough for Shakespeare should be good enough for you; and I'm sure he never looked beyond the play that would *go*. I don't want the stage to become a platform. A flawless entertainment like the best plays of Somerset Maugham, say . . ."

"And yet," I reminded her, "what was good enough for him when he had about four plays running in London simultaneously isn't good enough for him now. Luckily for me!"

"Why luckily for you?"

"Because the Maugham of *Lady Frederick* and *Mrs. Dot* evidently supplied a demand that has remained unsatisfied since he developed a new manner. There's a fortune waiting for the man who can step into the shoes of Maugham the First; and the compliment that I value most is that a play of mine is even faintly reminiscent of, let us say, *Jack Straw*."

As I paused, Violet murmured that, if I was two years her senior, I must be twenty-six. I had made a name for myself; but was I happy, should I be content to go on as I was doing, had I no ambition higher than to fill the shoes that Somerset Maugham had discovered unworthy of his mountaineering powers?

"Nigel won't be happy," she added with a pensive glance towards the Victoria Tower, "till he's on the woolsack. If then! He always wants to run before he has learnt to walk. To take silk before he's been called, to get into the Cabinet before he's got into the House. Whether ambition makes for happiness . . . But you've no ambition, Colin, except to take your creative impulse for its daily air and exercise? You've no desire to fall in love, to marry and have children, to get a handle to your name, to make a splash like Elizabeth Gerrold's *rather* deplorable father?"

I said that, though I could now support a wife, I did not want to marry for marrying's sake; and for all their good breeding and —occasionally—their good looks, I had never felt tempted to fall in love with the generally tongue-tied and vacant *débutantes* that I used to meet in my short-lived dancing days.

"For which I'm selfishly thankful," said Violet. "Your friendship has always meant a lot to me, Colin, more than ever since father died. If you had a wife, I don't think she would let us be the friends we are."

"And yet you have a husband who doesn't seem to mind . . ."

"Oh, he's grateful to you, my dear, for keeping me amused. Nigel is essentially a realist. His career being all that counts with him, he wants a wife who will entertain for him and look decorative on his platform, but he does not want to lose his head about her, he doesn't want to complicate his life with children till he's in sight of a peerage. If he thought about it, he would want me to be happy and, as he's no good on books and plays, he's thankful that I have a friend who will take me to first nights while he's reading briefs or stewing in the House. It's a perfect arrangement for all parties!" she continued with a touch of unwonted irony that reminded me rather uncomfortably of Austin's warning that no man should be called happy till he had been successfully married for ten years. Was Violet disappointed in Nigel? "So long as it doesn't bore *you* . . . ," she ended with a shrug.

I told her, as she should have known without being told, that anything I had done in the last four years I owed entirely to her.

"That's nonsense," she broke in, "but we've had great fun

working together. Well, let me say: so long as I don't get in your
way . . . No, let me finish, Colin! You say you've never been in
love and I want to say this before you are. I'm terribly fond of
you and always shall be, but _your_ happiness would always come
first with me. If you ever meet somebody you want to marry, you
mustn't think of our friendship. Even if she insists on your
dropping me, which she probably will . . . I don't know why I'm
talking like this! It's highly immodest for a respectable married
woman to be telling a respectable unmarried man that she's
terribly fond of him, but for all your cleverness you're extraordinarily blind sometimes, my dear, and I wanted you to know,
in case I died tonight, what a difference your friendship has made
to my life. Is it only four years since we met at the Gerrolds'?"

Having no vision of the four years that lay ahead of us in
1914, I said that publicly and privately we had compressed about
forty years into the last four. After this unexpected lapse into an
intimacy that we had not achieved before and perhaps did not
desire now, I think we were both glad to seek refuge in an impersonal review of the changes that had overtaken our little world
since we all embarked on the adventure of life in London.

"The Lloyd-George budget and the constitutional crisis,"
I enumerated. "The change of kings, the general elections and
the parliament-bill, Irish home-rule and Welsh disestablishment,
the Suffragettes and the Marconi scandal."

"Which nearly involved _you_ in another kind of scandal!"

"You mean, over Axminster? I hoped that had been hushed
up, but you know the sort of man he is! Or perhaps you don't!
We were at a City dinner, where some little dago from the
Bolivian Legation so far forgot himself under the influence of
wine as to become offensive about English hypocrisy. The
Marconi business had shewn that our public men were just like
all the rest. Lloyd George, Rufus Isaacs, Elibank . . . I suddenly
found Axminster leaning over my chair and asking me whether
I would act for him. Then he threw a glass of wine into the dago's
face, informed him that Elibank was a Scot, Lloyd George a
Welshman and Isaacs a Jew, scattered some uncomplimentary
remarks about Bolivia (which he seemed to think was in the
Balkans) and returned to his seat. The dago was too much scared
to bother about his diplomatic status; and the evening ended
quite pleasantly when he had apologized and been taken home.
That's as near as I have ever come to ordering pistols for two and

coffee for one. People sometimes complain that there are no excitements in the civil service: I have rather too many. Should I be a great fool if I chucked everything for writing?"

"Austin was saying the other night that you wouldn't be allowed to go," Violet answered. "You would be a permanent under-secretary and a K.C.B. before you knew where you were. I always thought the Lord Keeper's Department was a sinecure."

It was so much a sinecure, I explained, that with never enough work to occupy me in Queen Anne's Gate I had been lent far and wide, now as secretary to a royal commission, now in a team to set the new health-insurance act working, now on a task that I was not at liberty to discuss, but which was in fact the preparation of the "war-book" for the Committee of Imperial Defence. It was useful and interesting experience, I added; but I should like more time for my own work.

"It's a pity that the gifts of the gods sometimes come in such a rush!", said Violet. "Nigel has a whole-time job at the bar, but he got into the House at a moment that was bristling with opportunities for a good platform-speaker. And he has done so well for the party that he'll be given office any day now. I hope he won't kill himself. If the next four years are going to be as busy for all of us as the last . . . Austin, by the way, is rather unhappy in mind about things abroad. This Servian business . . . And now a very good chance of civil war in Ireland. I don't want to ask any questions that I shouldn't, Colin . . ."

I assured her that, if she did, I should be unable to answer them. There had been an almost annual crisis abroad, I said, ever since the unhappy, peace-loving Liberal government came into power: over Algeciras, over Bosnia, over Agadir, over the two Balkan wars and now over Serajevo. The present trouble was rather less our concern than any of the others; but, once a fire started, no one could tell how far it would spread.

"Austin said that there would be war this summer," Violet informed me, "and that we should be dragged in. He says that Lord Fisher foretold the day and the hour before he left the Admiralty. Nigel wouldn't hear of it! Scaremongering! I just wondered what you thought."

"At the moment, I'm thinking, a little selfishly, that, if we go to war this summer, it's a cheerful prospect for *Man Overboard*, which I hoped to finish rewriting in time to have it produced in September. Of course, if there's a war . . ."

"Oh, if there's a *war* . . . ," Violet sighed.

And then we both of us indulged in a number of prophecies which seem almost worth recalling for their fantastic falsity. I said that, if there were a war, the theatre would slump as never before: in fact, it boomed as never before. I said further that, if *Man Overboard* were produced, I should not be there to see, as every one must agree that my obvious duty was to take a commission; in fact, every one with any control over my destiny agreed that my obvious duty was to become secretary of the War Stores Purchasing Commission and to retain that office until I was lent to the Ministry of Munitions on its formation. Though I had not myself worn uniform since my cadet-corps days at school, I mentioned to Violet that Austin had joined the Inns of Court when Haldane launched his Territorial Army and I added that, since the Home Office would certainly not spare him, I thought his gesture in setting an example rather public-spirited: in fact, he defied his superiors, went out with one of the earliest drafts and begged me to believe that he was studying his own inclinations, no more and no less.

"Nigel joined at the same time," Violet told me. "If there's a war, *he'll* go, unless, of course, M.P.s are told to stay put."

In fact, M.P.s were left answerable to their own consciences. Many went and some did not return; but in the shuffling of offices after the resignation of Morley and Burns an under-secretaryship was offered to Nigel and he decided that he would be more usefully employed in Whitehall than in Flanders. Turning to friends of her own sex, Violet predicted that women without husbands in England would go as nurses and that the others would stay at home: in fact, she herself—to take one instance— closed the Barton Street house, sent Nigel to live at one of his clubs and spent the best part of four years abroad, first driving an ambulance and then nursing, while Elizabeth—to take another—remained in Montpelier Square to look after her boys and to be at hand if Austin returned home on leave or wounded.

Finally, *Man Overboard*—a youthful, high-spirited piece wholly out of tune with the grave mood to be expected of a European war—had not only a greater success than *Objection Overruled*, but has also been for five-and-thirty years the most successful play that I have written.

It was, moreover, the only play in which I had to do without Violet's help. The rewriting took me longer than I had expected when we talked of it that summer afternoon in 1914; and, before it was ready for her criticisms, war had broken out and we were separated. She has told me since that it contains nothing that she would have wished to change: by now the knack of swimming had come to me and I could not forget it if I tried.

"*If the war ever ends,*" she wrote from Salonica two or three years later, "*I hope you will let me continue to watch you at work, though I don't suppose you need any suggestions from me now. The technique of writing is still my abiding passion, but you've shot ahead so far and so fast that I'm afraid my ideas would seem rather crude to you and very presumptuous to your wife. Are you married yet, by the way? I saw in some paper that you were engaged (or soon would be); but I felt sure that you would have let me know so that I could be the very first to wish you all happiness.*"

In my reply I said that to the best of my knowledge and belief I was still single, though a number of so-called Society papers had been busily marrying me off. As *prima facie* evidence that I was an eligible bachelor, I continued rather ponderously, I supposed that I ought not to mind, though I felt a little sorry for any girl who was married off—with as little foundation in fact— to me. If the paper that Violet had seen was coupling my name with Lady Isabel Pryde's, I could assure her that we never had been engaged and now presumably never should be, as she was marrying the Duke of Abbotsbury in a few weeks' time.

Certainly, I said, Violet would be told before any one if I contemplated changing my condition; but marriage, from all I could hear of it, demanded more time than I could spare. I was already leading a pretty full double-life in Grosvenor Road and the Ministry of Munitions; and this would become a treble-life in the near future, if I became a landed proprietor. Then, thankfully dropping my stilted jocularity, I explained that I was playing with the idea of buying Ridgeway House in the hope of making my mother's last days there rather more comfortable.

Since Violet—in a postscript—had asked for news of common friends, I told her—also in a postscript—that Elizabeth Gerrold had been left completely shattered and helpless by Austin's death. I was doing my best, I said, to straighten her affairs for her; but, as she was quite unfit to look after herself, I really hoped—for her sake and the boys'—that after a decent interval she would marry again.

I suppose that in these few indifferent words about Isabel Pryde I had written nothing but the truth, but it was not the whole truth. I am interested to note that more than thirty years later I shrink, as much as I shrank then, from exposing my wounds; and yet, if I do not tell the entire truth, I feel that a cardinal decision which shaped the whole of my later life and appeared inevitable at the time will seem as trivial as the marriage-proposal of the young man in *Punch* who, after two dances, could think of nothing else to say.

VI

INNUMERABLE books have been written to trace the influence that moulded one man or another into a poet or a novelist; but I cannot recall many that have treated of the poet's or novelist's vocation as an influence in remoulding the man. Do dramatists, for example, tend to regard themselves as actors and life as a play with the curtain falling at one dramatic moment on one scene and set of costumes, to rise again on a different scene after so many hours have elapsed?

Looking back on my own life, I am certainly conscious of a literary temptation to have more clear-cut divisions in time and place, less gradual merging of one phase into another, than the facts—on further examination—really warrant. It would, for instance, be so easy to ring one curtain down on my father's death and to ring another up on my own marriage; but it would be misleading. Though the theatre demands intervals, life in general and my own life in particular appear to stream steadily on with very few complete breaks such as a long illness or many years' absence abroad might provide and with still fewer completely new starts.

I used to think that for men and women of my age an act or even an entire play ended on the Fourth of August, 1914; and perhaps I should have been right to think so if I had returned in 1918 to Grosvenor Road or Queen Anne's Gate or Ridgeway House, after soldiering in France or the Middle East, to find the explanatory note: *"Four years have elapsed"*; but in fact there was no such abrupt change of scene or action. At the beginning of the war I was a youngish civil servant, more often on loan to other departments than at work in my own; and, financially at least,

E

I was a successful playwright. At the end I was still a civil servant, with a C.B. to put after my name and a D.D.G. before it, I was now almost permanently on loan and I was a more successful playwright than ever, with one production following another and with money pouring in from England and America more quickly than I could spend or even invest it. As I observed, however, to Clayton Mandeville when we met—for the first time in four and a quarter years—on Armistice Day: "Everything's very much the same as before with me, only perhaps rather more so." Recalling our last meeting, as we waited to hear whether Germany would send a reply to our ultimatum, Clayton—a Laughing Cavalier who had lost his smile—commented that of all who had met in Grosvenor Road that night I was probably the only one who could say this of myself.

"And how many of them are still alive . . . ," he added. "We must meet again, Colin, and have 'a nicht wi' Burns'!"

As he hurried off, I tried to remember who had been with us on that last night of peace. My brother John, summoned to the War Office on business that he would not divulge, had telegraphed to beg beds for his wife and himself; my brother Henry, accompanied by Constance, arrived with the same request, but without telegraphing. I believe that this was the first time that I ever saw him in his yeomanry uniform; and his attitude to the changing company of men and women who drifted in for news or drinks and sandwiches was that we civilians had now best leave things to the soldiers. I fancy it was the last time till 1918 that I saw Clayton in a tweed suit, as he was already transforming himself from a leader-writer into a war-correspondent. Austin and Nigel dashed in and out several times, leaving their wives as security that they would come back for a buffet-supper. And there were many others who perhaps said nothing memorable and have therefore faded from my recollection. At eleven o'clock we should know the worst; and, as we listened to Big Ben sounding the quarters, I felt that we had gathered to see a slow curtain descending on an act that contained all our youth and hope.

My impression then and now is that those who talked most did not necessarily say most that was worth hearing. Nigel, for instance, was bursting with rumours of ministerial resignations that had been tendered and withdrawn every few hours. Austin rehearsed in full the speech that he would deliver if war broke out and his superiors tried to keep him shut up in the Home Office.

My sister-in-law Blanche maintained a dreary tirade against "the politicians" who had brought us to this pass. Whatever I thought then, I am disposed to think now that the most eloquent of my visitors were those who remained dumb and dazed at the horror and wickedness of war between nominally civilized Great Powers in the year of human redemption one thousand nine hundred and fourteen. It is the memory of these shocked and bewildered faces that makes me see this vague gathering in Grosvenor Road as the *ensemble* before the final curtain.

And, if we had one feeling in common, I should say it was that this was not the moment for keeping up pretences. Violet, I remember, in refreshing contrast to those who assured me that they had always regarded this war as inevitable, confessed that until now she had never believed in the German Peril, but that her father had prophesied a clash from the day of the Anglo-French convention and had insisted that she should train as a nurse and learn to drive a car. She added that, as a tribute to his memory, she was offering the government a fully equipped motor-ambulance. A little later, Clayton suggested a new point of view by asserting that most of us (if we could stop humbugging ourselves) had contributed to make war inevitable by requiring a solvent which would end various things that we could not end for ourselves.

"For years," he reminded me, "I've been saying every Sunday in my rag that we were heading for civil war. The Lords and the People, Capital and Labour, now the North and the South in Ireland. The old respect for law and order has gone. I don't believe that anything less than a war in which we're fighting for our lives will bring the factions to their senses."

"It's a big price to pay. . . ," I began.

"Perhaps. If we're *honest* with ourselves, though, war is not an unmixed evil for the individual. I don't think I *could* have stood my present job much longer, Colin, but Fleet Street may seem quite charming after a few months as 'Our Special Correspondent'. I'm always surprised that a restless and adventurous old bird like Austin has stood his present life so long: this is an opportunity he wouldn't miss even if it cost him his job and his pension. Incidentally, it's an opportunity of another kind for Nigel: he's pretty sure to pick up something in the great reshuffle."

I looked across the room at Elizabeth, whose flaxen hair was lank and whose pale face seemed puffy and stained from weeping.

"She doesn't look as though she thought this was any kind of opportunity for her," I observed.

"Oh, she would back down on Belgium and leave France in the lurch if she could keep us out of war. She would offer the fleet to Tirpitz if she thought *that* would make Austin stay safely in England. Poor Rella! She *needs* some one to lean against . . ."

"Well, with two small boys and a house . . . It'll mean a big drop in their income if Austin gives up his literary work. And, by Jove, if anything happened to him . . ."

Clayton assured me that Austin was as likely to survive as any one else, but that he and Elizabeth both needed a change.

"Once again, a war ending what you can't end for yourselves," he concluded. "I don't think Elizabeth would at all mind being a grass-widow for a few months. The children are her real interest; and I should think she finds Austin a bit too uxorious at times. And he'll just love holding the thin red line for a few months. I always said he wasn't cut out for a civil servant."

As Clayton kept speaking of a few months, I asked those nearest to me how long they thought a European war could be carried on under modern conditions. Philip Cheshunt replied without hesitation that everything would be over by Christmas; Lady Mary corroborated that it was a question whether the Russians could get to Berlin before the Germans got to Paris.

"Otherwise," Maurice predicted with an air of giving me the Stock-Exchange view, "the whole world will be broke. I mean to say, international trade and credit . . ."

"Whatever happens," Lady Jane contributed, "it'll be a good few years before we get back to our present standards. Taxation."

It was the cumulative effect of many speeches like this that wakened the latent playwright in me and turned my book-lined work-room into a stage on which we awaited a catastrophe that revealed itself little by little as a doom not to be escaped. Even with the inside information that trickled through to the Lord Keeper's Department from the morrow of the Serajevo assassinations, I had continued until the bank-holiday week-end to believe—as indeed I had told Violet several weeks ago—that the latest crisis would blow over like the rest; I was stunned by the appearance of my brothers in uniform and by their insistence that war was a certainty. Throughout the long evening one person after another was saying that war would mean the end of this or that; I lacked the imagination, or perhaps the will, to picture what would happen when the war itself ended; the latent play-wright, now in complete control of me, only repeated that the comedy was finished.

That Clayton's few months would produce a new play or that one act of it would be the biggest of my life so far never entered my head as we all divested ourselves of the costumes that we had assumed for the piece now ending. Henceforth, I told myself, we should most of us be in uniform: Philip and Maurice, their brothers-in-law Bracton and Scaling. We should all of us be more or less bereft of individuality, all without exception smartly obeying words of command. Phyllis Bracton and May Scaling were at this moment consulting Violet about ambulance-driving. Clayton was explaining that, as a war-correspondent, he would be in some kind of non-combatant khaki: when Elizabeth had pulled herself together, I presumed she would appear with red crosses on a white apron and cap; and Violet I should probably next see in a forage-cap, tunic and breeches. It was to be a very complete dispersal; and among the many wagers that were offered and taken that night no one thought to bet that I, already armed with a letter of introduction from my brother John to his colonel, should never leave London—except for a mission to Washington —till the war was over.

"Don't get up to mischief, Colin," Violet adjured me at parting, "when I'm not here to keep an eye on you."

"I shan't be here myself for more than a day or two," I answered, wondering whether I could find any one to take the house in my absence.

How would the next act have developed, would there ever have been a next act, if Violet too had remained in London till the war was over, a stone's throw away in Barton Street?

"Write to me when you can," she begged. "It's all going to be very strange for all of us."

I promised that I would; and, if I was slow to begin fulfilling my promise, the explanation is that I was slow in apprehending how little change the war would make in my daily life and how little I should find to say. The first of many mild surprises came in an uncompromising refusal—from Axminster himself—to let me apply for a commission. He might change his mind later, I told Violet, but for the present I was destined to fight my war on the home front.

And that front, I wrote a few weeks later, was utterly different from anything that I had expected. London was fuller than I ever remembered it at this time of the year; and, when leave began, there was more going on than in the height of a peace-time season. Every restaurant, theatre and music-hall was filled to capacity; the demand for light entertainment exceeded the supply; *Objection Overruled* had been revived and was playing to crowded houses; *The Stormy Petrel* was still a steady draw; and, if we could overcome certain difficulties in casting *Man Overboard*, I might live to see three plays of mine running in London at the same time.

In fact this happened—for a very few weeks—in 1916; but, when writing to Violet in the summer of my *annus mirabilis*, I had graver matters to discuss than the doubtful pleasure of being lionized, which she assumed—from the frequent appearance of my name in the press—to be my present fate. It was at the beginning of July, in the first days of the Somme battle, that Elizabeth telephoned to say Austin had been reported *"missing"*; this was followed in due course by the now sadly familiar announcement: *"Previously reported missing, now believed killed"*. I had kept in regular touch with Elizabeth ever since Austin went out, dining with her or having her to dine with me about once a week, helping her to the best of my ability in the hundred-and-one business matters that now devolved on her shoulders, pooling the letters that each of us had received from the Front and essaying a weekly appreciation of the war. I feel, looking back over thirty years, that I ought at this time to have come to know Elizabeth very much better: almost always we dined alone, always we seemed to talk with perfect frankness and, though she was inclined to be monosyllabic, I never thought her uncommunicative, still less secretive, when I asked her about her brothers or herself or the house in Hampshire, now a military hospital. In fact, when the blow fell, I knew little more of her than at the first meeting, which I never remember and sometimes deny, at Coverley Court.

"She would be an easier person to help," I wrote to Violet, *"if I had a better mental picture of her background. What other friends has she, for instance? How does she get on with her parents and brothers and sisters? Is she, as I sometimes suspect, self-isolated and am I an officious intruder? If so, has she aid outside herself that she can summon (by which I mean religion)? At the moment, she's completely bludgeoned; and the poor best that I can do is to tell her again and again that 'missing' men do sometimes turn up."*

How far I convinced or even encouraged her I cannot say. After the second announcement she continued to repeat by rote that perhaps Austin was a prisoner whose name had not yet come through, perhaps he was wounded and had lost his identity-disc, perhaps his memory had temporarily left him. I do not even know how far she wished to be encouraged. Very conscious that I was making no progress, I once told her that, if she ever needed money or advice, she must come to me; she replied that in due course her solicitors would no doubt explain her position to her and she would then know whether she could keep on the house in Montpelier Square and what she could afford for feeding, clothing and educating Martin and Humfrey. No one, she hinted, could help, though—as an afterthought—she would like to feel that she could always consult me.

Rightly or wrongly, I decided that she wanted to be left alone with her children till she had in some measure recovered from the loss of Austin and the overthrow of whatever plans they had made for themselves and the boys. I was not sorry to accept my dismissal, since at this time I had no vitality to spare for pumping consolation into some one who occasionally gave me the impression of not wanting to be consoled. By 1916 the Ministry of Munitions had been safely brought to birth; and I was not so nearly working round the clock as in 1915. On the other hand, *Man Overboard* was going into rehearsal for early production; and, as I had not taken a day's holiday since 1913, I applied for a fortnight's leave. Some part of it I had intended to spend at Ridgeway House; but my father, who had timed himself to die in 1917, was already making his final preparations and I was warned that I might upset him if I appeared before the death-bed summons. I therefore spent my leave in London and took the most satisfying, if negative, holiday of my life by not going to an office at 10.0, not talking departmental business throughout luncheon on six days a week, not dining at 9.0 without time for a bath, not returning to my office after dinner and not taking papers home with me.

"*I am looking forward to the change,*" I wrote to Violet, who was now nursing in a hospital on the Normandy coast. "*When we said good-bye in* 1914, *I felt that one act was ending and that the next might open in Belgium or Egypt or India; I feel now that I'm living in an* entr'acte *that has already continued for two years and may easily continue for another two. 'Living', I say; and then, my dear, I ask myself whether it is living. If my war is to be an indefinitely long* entr'acte *and nothing dramatic is going to happen when the curtain goes up on the next act* (Scene: the same *which of course will be Grosvenor Road.* Time: the morning after peace has been declared, *whenever that may be*), *I really must make use of this interval by going out for a cigarette, calling on So-and-So in her box, strolling into the* foyer *on the look-out for friends on leave. There are several good plays (in addition to my own!) running in London at the moment, but I've not had time to see the inside of a theatre for twelve months. Here's my opportunity. The friends on leave are legion—I'm dining with one and going to a show this evening: did you ever meet him, Tony Lascombe, son and heir of Wansborough (perhaps even more notably brother to Lady Isabel Pryde)? At Westminster and again at the House I always suspected that he despised me as over-studious and insufficiently sporting, but now he has discovered that apparently there's money in play-writing, and would like to become part-lessee of a theatre. The unhappy Prydes are all so desperately poor that money tends to play too big a part in their thoughts . . ."*

And yet from the very little that I knew of Wansborough, he differed in degree, but not at all in kind, from my own queer father. Layton was four to six times the size of Ridgeway House and he was the sixth earl: his standards were more exalted and his difficulties greater, but he displayed rather less flexibility in any effort to adjust or perish. Unlike Ridgeway House, Layton was entailed and had long since been loaded with all the mortgages that it could bear; but, so far as I ever heard, the shadow of insolvency perturbed the Prydes no more than the Whimboynes. They hunted with the Quorn, they shot and fished, they raced and occasionally ran their own horses, they relaxed at Monte Carlo while their house in Hill Street was being got ready for the season's entertaining and they entertained, regardless of cost, till it was time to go north for the Twelfth. While we were still at Oxford, it was accepted that Lascombe would have to marry an heiress; but, like my brother John, he married a pauper. Of the girls it was said that they would have to marry rich husbands; but all three were still unmarried when I first met them and by now it was beginning to be said that the men who married them would have to be brave as well as rich.

When he invited me to dine, Lascombe mentioned that his sister Isabel was a great admirer of my plays and would be "no end thrilled" to meet me. From the little that I had heard of her from Austin I thought it unlikely that she knew even the name of anything I had written or would be thrilled by anything in a theatre, unless it were a wild and dangerous adventure such as throwing lighted matches about the auditorium to see whether the resultant fire was really as alarming as most people made out; and, as I drove to Hill Street, I wondered whether Lady Isabel would at all live up to the reputation—for exploring to find anything that would really frighten her?—that had gathered about her ever since she came out.

When I passed through Leicestershire with my Flying Dutchman, every other conversation began with the question: "Have you heard Isabel Pryde's latest?"; and I remembered that, when Austin invited me to meet her at dinner, she was incapacitated at the last moment with a broken collar-bone. Lord Milner's famous advice that the Lords should throw out the land-budget and damn the consequences had inspired her, I was told, to murmur:

"Surely that's what consequences are for."

If she had a fear, I felt it might have been of the camera. For all her fame or notoriety I do not think I had ever seen a photograph of her; and, despite our single, forgotten meeting, I did not know whether she was tall or short, thin or fat, dark or fair when I was shewn into a shadowy drawing-room and a rather languid, husky voice murmured:

"Tony will be down in a minute. I'm his sister Isabel. You were a friend of his at Oxford, weren't you?"

The voice proceeded from an armchair; its owner was reading in a circle of light thrown by a table-lamp which illuminated her paper, but left herself in shade.

"We had rooms on the same staircase," I answered, "but I hardly knew him till we'd both come down and he invited me to dine with him on Bank-guard."

"That was before you were rich and famous? He wouldn't bother about you till then."

I said that this seemed hardly fair on Lascombe, to whom a writer—as such—would be as uninteresting as an astronomer; of the fame and riches attributed to me, I added, it was for others to speak.

"And they've *spoken*! 'I say, Bel! The feller who wrote that thing *Objection Overruled*: I find I know him. Point of fact, bumped into him to-day in Pall Mall. He's packin' up a *parcel* over these plays of his! Couldn't help thinkin' that if I got a theatre and he wrote me a play . . . Man to cultivate, me dear!' So . . . you have come to be cultivated! Tell me some time how you like it! I've seen so many unfortunates being put through the mill, but they were mostly inarticulate. It's your *trade*, of course, to express yourself. I've heard of you from the Axminsters, but I've not seen any of your plays: Tony was lying politely when he said I admired them." Putting her paper down on the table beside the chair, she pulled the shade of the lamp so that it shone for a moment on my face: "You're not at all what I expected from Austin Gerrold's account."

"And whether you're what I expected," I said, "I can't tell in this light."

"The switches are by the door, if you're curious. Well, whether you are or not, here's Tony, who will save you the trouble of answering. If you'll turn on the lights, Tony, you'll see that Mr. Whimboyne is here and that you're late, as usual. I think a word of insincere regret is indicated. And then you might introduce us."

As Lascombe explained that he had been dressed and down-stairs for ten minutes, but that, when they saw me getting out of my taxi in a white tie, Isabel had hunted him upstairs to put on a tail-coat, I wondered whether she had planned an undeniably effective scene by seating herself in a twilit room, making me first acquainted with her through that husky, intoxicating and ever-unforgettable voice, stealing a short march by looking at me before I could see her and then abruptly having every light in the room turned on her. I remember thinking that I might use the device in some future play.

Gladys Cooper I mentally cast for the part: Isabel Pryde's hair and eyes were astonishingly like Gladys Cooper's.

Definitely, I then decided, this scene had not been staged; and I doubted whether any one so supremely sure of herself would waste a moment on contriving effects. It was a failure in me always to be thinking of lines and situations. Perhaps writing plays tended to turn a man into a playwright even when he was off duty. Perhaps? I did not know.

I doubt if I know even now.

VII

IF for the last thirty years I have shrunk from speaking, and have
tried to avoid even thinking, of Isabel Pryde (or, more properly,
the Duchess of Abbotsbury), I might defend or explain myself
by saying that I have only been obeying—as best I could—the
last injunction that she ever gave me: "The *one* thing you can do is
to forget my existence."

This, to be sure, was not the same as forgetting her; but to
think about her, I soon discovered, was not going to bring her
back and to talk about her, even to myself in the long silence of
a sleepless night, would not stanch the wound that she had dealt
to my spirit. "*Why* . . . ?" I used to begin, only to check myself
with the sorry decision that we could do no good to ourselves
or to each other by holding solitary *post-mortem* examinations of
a dead love that we had so often and so unprofitably dissected
together. Many weeks before she consented to marry Abbotsbury,
Isabel had made up her mind that, if I were the last man living,
she was not going to marry me; some months before that, she had
persuaded herself that for all our maddening need of each other
we should not be happy together as man and wife; and, as our
frayed nerves snapped and joined and snapped again under an
utterly intolerable strain of excitement and frustration, she sometimes shook my own conviction that we should be very much
unhappier apart. It is not perverted vanity, but ingenuous shame,
that makes me feel I must have hurt poor Isabel as deeply as she
hurt me; and, when at the end I collected myself to wish her all
happiness and she exclaimed that she had long since given up
expecting happiness for either of us, I decided that our precarious
makeshift contentment—the best that either of us could now hope
to achieve—would have but a short life if we met to compare
wounds and their treatment. And so we have never exchanged
a word or a letter since the evening when I left the Hill Street
house for the last time, carrying to the post the announcement
of her engagement and proceeding thence to a first-night supper
and dance on the stage which should have convinced the most
sceptical that I had no wounds to treat.

As explanation or defence to myself I might argue that it is
always idle to brood over anything that cannot be changed; but
I fancy that my strongest reason for refusing to dwell on this

cardinal chapter of my life is that all those years ago I understood it no more than a dumb animal and that I understand it little better now. What madness possessed us that we should hurt each other, night and day, when each would have endured death by slow torture to keep any one else from hurting the other? To fall in love, for the first time and almost at first sight, is no doubt a sufficient explanation of everything for those who believe that falling in love is enough to change any man beyond recognition; but, for me, it poses three unanswerable questions for every one that it answers. On her own admission, this was the first time that Isabel had been in love; and she made the discovery at some moment in that first evening when, apparently, we were both inspired to talk so brilliantly that we missed the entire first act of the *revue* to which Lascombe was taking us. I have been told that Lady Wansborough afterwards drawled some comment on my having "struck fire from the flint"; Wansborough, I believe, was good enough to say that "Bel might go farther and fare worse". In all the changing of places at the theatre, I was always left next to Isabel, feasting on her soft hair and dark eyes, her eager red lips and gleaming neck, her slender arms and white shoulders. I understand that Lascombe's verdict was: "Looks like bein' a walk-over for Whimboyne."

What the *revue* was I doubt whether either of us could say, as I cannot think that we saw the stage or the auditorium; if we talked, I have wholly forgotten what we said until I jerked myself awake and erect for *God Save The King* and heard a voice—still husky, but no longer languid—murmuring:

"And what *now*, Colin?"

I felt for my cigarette-case and then put it back in my pocket because my hand was trembling.

"Will you and your brother come to my place for a drink?," I asked, as the box emptied.

"I've ordered a table at Ciro's," Lascombe, overhearing, intervened. "The others will be waiting for us there."

Isabel's hand touched mine, as though to say: "Leave this to me!"

"Then obviously you must go and look after them," she decreed. "I don't feel much like dancing to-night."

To me, when we were alone, she suggested—with a glance of loathing at the jostling crowd on the pavement—that we should walk till we found a taxi; and, while I was trying to remember the number in Hill Street, she enquired where I lived and, repeating "Grosvenor Road", advised me to keep the taxi while we had supper. She had been too busy "cultivating" me at dinner to eat much and now felt famished. Presumably I had food of some kind; if not, we might try to get a lobster at Scott's.

"Have it here!", I said, pointing to the doorway of the Carlton Grill-Room. "If you don't mind supping unchaperoned . . ."

"If I minded, should I be coming to your rooms, flat, studio or whatever it is, alone and defenceless? What I *do* mind, always and everywhere, is eating in a restaurant where you have to shout. You're not afraid of being compromised, are you? Or of compromising me? If you're afraid of your servants, the sooner they get accustomed to me the better. If I cultivate you seriously, they'll be seeing quite a lot of me. Grosvenor Road . . . That's the continuation of the Embankment, isn't it? I want to see your house, Colin. If it's as different from the studio I imagine as you are from Lord Axminster's secretary and Austin Gerrold's odd friend who wrote plays . . . Do you like being cultivated by me? That's really a point that we ought to clear up here and now!"

"If I knew what the process would entail . . . ," I began.

"I'm only interested in what it has entailed already. Do you like being in love with me? Most men find it a transfiguring experience, for a time, but Austin used to say that for a writer you were curiously uninterested in women. Perhaps you haven't yet discovered . . . I can assure you from a wide study of the symptoms . . . Here's a taxi! You haven't answered my question, you know. Do you *like* . . . ?"

As I opened the door for her, I asked whether my "yes" or "no" would make any difference to the address I was waiting to give: was it to be Hill Street or Grosvenor Road or Ciro's or the Berkeley?

"Does it matter?," she returned. "You really *must* give me some supper, even if we never meet again afterwards. Perhaps it would be better if we didn't! I can't say yet: it's the first time this has happened to me."

"The first time," I repeated, as I sat down beside her.

In the half-light of the dimmed street-lamp I felt a movement that I could not see. Isabel was straining against me, her lips on mine, her arms round my shoulders. I could feel the wild beating of her heart; my own missed a beat, as though her soft, hungry mouth were drawing the very life out of me; the scent of her skin and hair made me giddy; and, as I clasped her to me, her rigid body suddenly relaxed as though she had fainted.

With one cell of my brain, I remember thinking that I had a dozen times written the stage-direction: *They Kiss.* "They" had never kissed like this in any play of mine.

The inanimate body came slowly to life again. Isabel passed her hand over her eyes and mechanically straightened the Chinese shawl that had slipped from her shoulders.

"If you can't finish your sentences for yourself," she told me, "I must finish them for you. The first time . . . It's the first time *I've* been in love . . ."

"And you find it a 'transfiguring experience'?"

"It reminds me of the first time I tasted champagne, the first time I made a *coup* at Monte Carlo, the first time I drove a car at seventy miles an hour. It certainly goes to your head! You wonder what's going to happen next."

As we drove in silence across Parliament Square, I wondered too.

"Why did you say," I asked, "that perhaps it would be better if we didn't meet again?" As she shook her head limply, I continued: "This is Grosvenor Road; and the next corner-house is where I live. It's too big, of course; but I love the view up and down the river, I've lived so much of my life in the shadow of the Abbey and the Houses of Parliament and Whitehall. The rooms are not bad for entertaining; and I have space for my books. Well, I'll tell the man to wait and, if I may leave you for five minutes, I'll see what food I can find. My servants will have gone to bed, I'm afraid."

I am so much habituated to a place that has now been my principal home for two-thirds of my life that I can hardly imagine how it would impress any one who saw it for the first time. My work-room with its vast writing-table and model theatre, its breast-high cream bookcases round all four walls and its deep chairs on either side of the fireplace has changed little in character during the last thirty years: I have weeded out certain books to make space for certain others, there are more signed photographs of theatrical luminaries on the top of the cases and in 1916 there were but three or four of the framed play-bills announcing a "comedy", a "romantic comedy", an "extravaganza" or an "entertainment" by Colin Whimboyne. According to her moods,

Isabel loved and hated the place, at one moment returning in the hope of recapturing the magic of her first night there and at another crying out that she could not enter a room that would haunt her with memories on her death-bed. I am inclined to think that she loved and hated it at different times for the same reason: that it was mine, but I feel sure that the first time she visited it— at midnight, five hours after we had met for the first time—she did not see it at all.

And, when I arrived in the work-room with a tray, to find her turning the pages of my latest press-cutting book, I saw only a lovely sphinx with a tongue of fire and—now—with a brain of ice.

"This is a charming place of yours, Colin," she informed me without looking up. "I said what I did, by the way, because I felt it would be a tragedy if anything were allowed to spoil the evening."

"Is there any reason why anything should?", I asked. "You and I, who had never met till to-night . . ."

"It would be a comedy, bordering on farce," she laughed, "if you and I, *you* and *I*, dear heart, Mr. Colin Whimboyne, the well-known dramatist, and Lady Isabel Pryde, who is well-known enough to dispense with a label, you and I without one idea or taste in common . . ."

"I was working on the assumption that we had *one* thing in common, I should have thought the only thing that matters. . . . I hope there's something here that you can eat."

Isabel looked critically at the *chaudfroid* of chicken, the salad and the prawn-savoury that had been prepared for me by Mrs. Winter before I received Lascombe's short-notice invitation. She then inspected the bottle of champagne that I had opened with an intuitive conviction that neither iced water nor neat brandy could make us either less or more exalted than we already were.

"Well-known dramatists do themselves well," she observed.

"My excellent father, now dying beyond his means, taught us all to put up uncomplainingly with the best till we could find something better. Another idea in common, possibly? And yet another, surely, in our attitude to tragedy and comedy? Tragedy is the havoc that underlings allow the stars to make of their lives. You, Isabel, have never allowed anybody or anything to influence *your* life. Comedy . . ."

"Has anybody or anything ever influenced *yours*, Colin? Don't say: 'Not until to-night'! Nothing has happened to-night that we can't dismiss as a dream. A *vivid* dream, if you like, but if we decide while there's still time . . ."

She seemed to be pleading with me, hands clasped and outstretched, as a suppliant; and I, remembering how I had thought she was swooning in my arms, felt that she was throwing herself on my mercy.

"Nothing's going to 'happen'," I assured her. "You're as safe here as in your own house. If you imagine, though, that I shall ever say: 'That was a curious dream!' and then forget all about it . . . To our next meeting!"

I raised my glass; but Isabel, sinking into a chair, sat staring at me, then at the wine-cooler and then at the table that I had put between us.

"We have *taste* in common," she conceded, "if not *tastes*. Is your excellent father responsible for the house or is it a reflection of you? A reflection? The successful author in his private shrine? A pity, that! If I told you that I wanted to change everything, that I couldn't live with Crown Derby or Chippendale . . ."

"I should find it hard to believe, as you can apparently live with it in your father's house. Any way, when two reasonable, civilized creatures . . ."

"Discover that they're two unreasonable, savage egoists?"

"I don't recognize either of us by that description. Won't you drink my toast?"

Isabel glanced slowly round the room, as though to persuade me how justly my play-bills and press-cuttings merited her mocking title of a shrine.

"If our next meeting is to be like this one . . . ," she then answered. "With you talking like one of your plays and me talking like myself. 'I don't recognize either of us by that description'. Well, to our next meeting! After all, it doesn't matter our being egoists, Colin, so long as we never take each other seriously. You haven't yet given me your definition of comedy, but I think one form of it is the contrast between your life as you know it to be and your life as other people imagine it. Yes, we can go on meeting so long as we can go on laughing. You can be in love with me as long as you like provided you never ask me to marry you. That would knock the bottom out of the comedy! I must go soon, but I want to be shewn your house so that I can tell Tony about it. He was so right! He said you were a man to cultivate, one of the Wiltshire Whimboynes, y'know, in the stud-book all right. Poor Tony thinks that sort of thing matters! He said I should like you: no airs about the feller! Well, now, I believe there's a lot of comedy in store for both of us if we think what people are saying about us, what they've begun to say already at Ciro's. The *amazement!* Isabel Pryde and Colin Whimboyne! The *relief* of every one who wants to see me properly established, the horror of every one who knows I should ruin you in a month, the hints and whisperings about an engagement, the astonishment when we say we're not engaged and never shall be! All the time, by contrast, our life as we know it to be . . . You can see why you must never propose to me. It would spoil everything. Besides, I couldn't bear to hurt you. . . . Now, is that your dining-room in there?"

After more than thirty years I believe I have summarized with fair accuracy a conversation that was as remarkable for its brevity as for its pregnancy. Isabel, by the chiming of Big Ben, was in my house for less than half-an-hour; we were less than an hour together from the moment when we left the theatre to the moment when I watched her letting herself into her father's house. As we got into the taxi, she casually suggested lunching with me "to see what we think of each other by daylight"; as the taxi entered Hill Street, she warned me that, if I wanted to kiss her good-night, I had better not wait too long; and, as she felt for her latchkey, she turned to say:

"If you telephone to cancel the luncheon, I shall understand. Didn't Oscar Wilde complain that women spoilt every romance by trying to make it go on for ever? I shan't do that, but I think it more than likely that *you* may. Oh dear, I should be so much happier if I thought you knew the meaning of *romance!*"

"Oscar Wilde also said that to love oneself was the beginning of a life-long romance. Since you've decided that we're both incorrigible egoists . . ."

"It may be the beginning of a life-long tragedy if two people love themselves when they imagine they're loving each other."

I doubt whether either of us at the time understood the implication of these words; but I feel now that the whole of our brief, torturing time together was foretold in this tentatively epigrammatic line which might have meant much and might have meant nothing. I have called the time brief, though it ran from the autumn of 1916—when I was eight-and-twenty—until the

F

autumn of 1918—when Isabel was twenty-six (a most significant difference in age!) and I have called it a torturing time, though I think we were both happy enough for the first three months, meeting every day and telephoning every night, exploring each other's personality and all the while being simply, blindly, mentally, nervously and physically in love. The difference in age— a trifling matter of four years—I began to notice only when Isabel began to harp on our opposed egoisms. I did not, and still do not, believe that we were exceptionally egoistic, but I think that she lagged fully four years behind me in outgrowing an innocent youthful liking for lime-light. As it seems to me now, we were both immature, we had both become celebrities of a kind, we were not going to let our newly achieved individualities be swamped by anybody or anything and we were slow to discover —she four years after me—how little we really cared about being clean-cut, dominating personalities.

"Lady Isabel Pryde, who is well-known enough to dispense with a label."

She had made herself well-known in an age when, artists and actresses apart, a woman generally remained unknown until she was married. Miss Margot Tennant, to be sure, was the heroine of a thousand stories, before she became Mrs. Asquith; and at this moment there was a quip going the rounds that a Canadian officer had come to London for the whole of his first leave with the resolution to see Saint Paul's Cathedral and Lady Diana Manners. These ladies, however, were exceptional; and, whether or no the triumph was worth achieving, I can see now that in 1916 it was a triumph for any girl to be so well-known that she could dispense with a label.

The triumph, I think, had gone to Isabel's head. From the first night, when she challenged me to say what I should do if she declared that she could not live in Grosvenor Road, with Chippendale and Crown Derby, I feel that she was tormented by the fear that in marrying me she would become merely the wife of that well-known author Mr. Colin Whimboyne, unless I became merely the husband of Lady Isabel Pryde. She could never persuade herself that I was by now bored with photographs and anecdotes of myself in the cheap press; and at the time she could never imagine herself indifferent to the gossip-writer's chronicling of her exploits. There were other, deeper differences; but I am convinced that this one was present from the first.

Still in a mood of banter and using the stilted idiom of comedy-dialogue, I asked her at our second meeting whether she was any less misogamous than she had been the night before.

"If that means: am I less unwilling to marry you?," she replied, "the answer is in the negative."

"Now, I wonder *why*! There would be so many good reasons if we hadn't seemed to agree last night . . . Surely, when people are in love, they want to marry . . ."

"Or to sleep together?," Isabel interrupted with a harsh directness that rather disconcerted me. "If that's what you want, why not ask?"

"I want you to marry me. I want you to say I may go to your father . . ."

"It's more likely he'll come to you. Financially as well as socially you have now been passed as satisfactory."

The bitter weariness of her tone made me wonder how often the lovely and accomplished Lady Isabel Pryde had heard that she would have to marry a millionaire.

"That would make it all the easier," I said. "You receive very few presents if you elope."

"But why marry when you can get all you want without it?," Isabel enquired dispassionately. "It's different for women, who generally want a home. If I were a man with money and a career . . ."

Comedy, romance, tragedy, the women that men married and the men who were married by women without knowing it; I was transported from Grosvenor Road to the Garrick Club, from a September afternoon in 1916 to the February night in 1915 when Austin Gerrold dined with me for the last time before he went out to Flanders and we talked till the early hours of love and passion, but chiefly of our own perilous and alarming ignorance. Our sisterless state, the monastic smell of Ridgeway House, the tendency of the young Whimboynes to measure all women by the standard of their own mother: his phrases tumbled back into some sort of order in my recollection as though he were miraculously alive and in my work-room, sardonically asking whether my Victorian mother and Isabel Pryde had much in common.

I remained so long silent that Isabel asked a little contemptuously whether I had been shocked by hearing a woman speak naturally.

"For some unknown reason I was thinking of our friend Austin," I replied. "It's easy to see why he and you became friends: you have the same way of dashing through life at top-speed, living all out for every moment of the day, doing whatever you've a mind to, saying whatever comes into your head . . ."

"In your calm, deliberate fashion you've probably just caught up with what I said last night: Austin could never understand how you presumed to write about women when you weren't interested in them. I admit I've not seen any of your plays . . ."

"Would *you* say, after last night, that I wasn't interested in women? Or at least in one woman?"

"I thought, in spite of Austin, that you were a flesh-and-blood man. I don't think you were awake before. You certainly weren't aroused. I wondered at the time whether you'd ever met a woman before. *Passion* . . ."

I asked whether Isabel would think it presumptuous for a physician to treat a woman when he was not in love with her. I should have said that he could diagnose and prescribe better if he regarded her dispassionately as a name in his case-book. So, I submitted, with a novelist or playwright.

"I'm so much interested in women," I continued, "that four-fifths of the sketches in my note-books are of them."

"And have your studies led you anywhere?"

"I believe that, though we may not yet be able to live with members of your sex, most men quite certainly can't live without them."

"Have you had time to include me in your collection?"

"Time, perhaps; inclination, no."

I looked out towards the Embankment, where I had walked for an hour to clear my head and cool my blood after taking Isabel home. She was right, so far as she had gone, in saying that I had never been awake before; but she could not know the power of the forces that she had aroused. If we continued to kiss as we had kissed the night before, if she again melted in my arms with the same abandonment of surrender, I could not answer for my self-control. Should I telephone to cancel the invitation? I decided that it would surely be safe to meet in broad daylight under the eyes of my butler.

"Let me know when you begin," said Isabel, "I can help you a lot."

In the last thirty years there has been abundant time for me to complete a dozen sketches, all different; but there has until now been less inclination than at this second meeting when Isabel lay curled provocatively in a chair opposite mine, her white arms and shoulders gleaming through the black lace of her sleeves, her red lips parted and inviting. When one is in love with a woman, one does not wish to analyse her; and, when one is out of love with her, perhaps—as she was herself to suggest—one had best try to forget her.

And yet I am not sure! If I had been able to see her then as I am beginning to see her now, I might have found a means of reconciling our egoisms, as she was so fond of saying, or maybe I might have recognized that they were irreconcilable. Those everlasting references to people who were worth cultivating! I thought the jest a thin one, perpetrated at Lascombe's expense, and threadbare at the second repetition; but I believe now it was the cry of one who could feel iron lodged in her soul and knew that she had herself planted it there. Brought up in a wanton luxury that the Wansboroughs could not afford, Isabel knew that to maintain it she must marry a rich husband; she despised in advance the vulgarians who would gladly buy her for the reflected glory of a courtesy-title and she despised the vulgarian in herself who might consent to be so bought. To foreswear the life of luxury was beyond her powers and opposed to all that she thought due to herself; in her rare day-dreams she saw herself married for love to a rich man who was not a vulgarian—the Duke of Abbotsbury, for example, if any sane woman could imagine herself being in love with a man so irredeemably dull and worthy, or myself, for another example, if she thought I was capable of being in love with any one—and in her more frequent moments of cynicism she planned her life in neat compartments which were to give her the ecstasy of fulfilled passion with one man and the solid security of a wealthy marriage with another.

Had I put Isabel into my current note-book at the time, I fancy that this is the sketch I should have made; and doubtless I should have been wise to decline this second meeting. Wise, but hardly human! There was I in love, for the first time and at first sight; and for all my ignorance of women in love I knew that Isabel was somewhat more recklessly in love with me. Physically I could do with her what I liked; and in my innocence I imagined that a girl whose body could be mine for the asking would yield in something that—to me—seemed infinitely smaller. I wanted to be her husband, not her lover; I wanted her for our lifetime, not until she married either into the Blood Royal or into the aristocracy of commerce; I wanted her body, though I shrank from admitting it, but I wanted her independently of her body.

It would have been wise and perhaps not inhuman to refuse a third meeting: I could feel that this second had not been a success and perhaps I ought to have seen that self-control was already being mistaken for indifference. Alone at last, when Winter had brought the coffee and liqueurs into my work-room, she observed enigmatically:

"We are not drinking, then, to the next round?"

"If we either of us think of this as a prize-fight . . . ," I began.

"More fight than prizes! O God, what fools we are! Both of us fighting to get our own way! Both of us knowing that, while we go on fighting, there'll be no prize for either! Perhaps, in our hearts, both of us suspecting that we shall neither of us *get* our own way! Is it worth going on, do you think? Will the pleasure of being together outweigh the exasperation of being at cross-purposes? I've always understood that being in love is a nerve-racking business at the best of times: excitement and frustration, jealousy and suspicion. . . . Even when you're out for the same things, which—unhappily—we are not . . ."

As she paused in apparent utter despair, I implored Isabel to say what she wanted, of me and of life. So far she had expressed a perfunctory wish to see where I lived, a second wish that I should see her by daylight and, unintelligible and negative, a wish that I should not "spoil things" by proposing to her.

"You're not engaged already, are you?", I asked, with a feeling that my heart had suddenly stopped beating.

"You would soon get over it if I were, wouldn't you?," she asked in her turn.

"People get over it if they lose both arms and legs. They're not quite the same afterwards as before, of course."

"And you mean it *would* make that difference? If you never saw me again? I feel it would to *me*—that's why I'm here now, against my better judgement—but I can't help wondering whether it isn't just because we're in love . . . Or think we are . . . A little mad, not ourselves . . . People most certainly get over being in love. I have no doubt that I shall, unless I'm different from every one else. You? The trouble is, I don't know whether you *are* in love with me, Colin. As I understand it, I mean . . ."

I said that I thought she should have been convinced when I kissed her the night before.

"But *to-day*!" she cried. "I wonder whether you're capable of it!"

With a dreadful foretaste of all that was to follow, as Isabel began to lose her temper, I began to lose mine.

"It's a little perplexing," I said, "when I hold you in my arms one moment and you tell me the next not to 'spoil things'. I don't yet know whether some other man . . ."

"If I ever thought of being engaged to another man, do you suppose I should have let you kiss me? No other man ever has. If you took me now, I shouldn't become engaged to another man till we'd said good-bye for ever. It looks as though, when I'm in love, I'm in love! You? I feel that, if you were in love, you couldn't sit calmly there, smoking and arguing . . ."

"I'm trying to keep my head! I don't know what might happen if I lost it! That makes me a little afraid . . ."

Isabel looked at me with the expression of puzzled incredulity that she always assumed when any one admitted that he was afraid of anything.

"If I'm not afraid . . . ," she began impatiently. "Of you . . . Of my reputation . . . Of the consequences . . . I'm not even afraid of losing a romance, because in my heart of hearts I never really expected it. Or happiness? I wonder whether there *is* such a thing! *Afraid?*"

"I'm afraid of losing *you*, Isabel! Afraid of spoiling *everything*! Sooner than risk that, I would never see you again."

A short silence followed; and I felt that each of us was trying to assess the other's endurance.

"Well, you obviously don't want that," she then said. "No more do I! It's a pity we want different things! I must go now, Colin, and I must leave you to decide whether we're to meet again. Kiss me good-bye, if it *is* to be good-bye! Frankly, *I* would rather not see you again than watch the two of us getting on each other's nerves."

As I took her in my arms, all resistance seemed to die out of her. With new confidence in my power over her, I whispered that we did indeed not want different things. I loved her, I wanted her to be my wife. We should never, in her shocking phrase, get on each other's nerves.

Then I set her free; and we spent the next two years proving that she had been right and I wrong.

VIII

BEAUTY in ruin has an honoured place in the affections of the English, who would resist the rebuilding of Fountains or Tintern Abbey almost as bitterly as the destruction of Durham Cathedral or York Minster. By the sight of beauty becoming a ruin they are less attracted; and appeals are launched every other week for vast sums to save this or that threatened church. I have myself never perfectly grasped the logic of repairing the roof of Ripon and refusing to put a new roof on Jedburgh; but I share the common distaste for watching decay at work and I carry my own distaste to its highest point where human beauty is falling into ruin. The inevitable fading of Helen's loveliness—till a younger generation could ask whether this truly was the face that had burnt the topless towers of Ilium—is to me only one degree less painful than the decline, sudden or lingering, in the loveliness of her first passionate days and nights with Menelaus.

After all these years I still believe that there was a certain wild and perhaps sinister beauty in the love that flamed for a few months between Isabel Pryde and me; there may be some beauty, though I have failed to find it, in the charred ruins on which we gazed when the fire had burnt itself out; but I am very sure there was no beauty to watch as love blackened and died. I have no wish even now to think of 1917 or the first three quarters of 1918; it is hard to believe that I ever cared to think even of the last quarter of 1916, my *annus mirabilis*.

Nevertheless, the three months that ended at Christmas seemed at the time the happiest of my life; and the stimulus supplied by the daily presence of this young and lovely creature, so radiant with vitality, so fearless and unashamed, inspired me to write my two best, if not my two most successful, comedies and to sketch the *scenario* of another. I wrote like a man drugged, for Isabel, who was always less interested in the plays than in the playwright, gave me no encouragement to neglect her for my work; and I doubt whether I should have dragged her to my first nights if she had not seen in them an incomparable opportunity for playing the queer, bitter comedy of her own that she had foreshadowed the evening that we met.

Shall I say that she was taking her revenge on the people who were always talking about her by giving them something to talk about? And what more appetizing to talk than the hint that Lady Isabel Pryde, so long and so hopelessly loved, by so many more eligible suitors, was now hopelessly in love with the unlikeliest man in all London?

How unlikely I was she left others to say; and they said it. How impossible I was for her to contemplate as a husband she told me as often as she told me how impossible she would be as my wife. It was, of course, wonderful to be in love, wonderful to know it and to confess it proudly, wonderful to meet every day and to let the cold-blooded world see what love was; but did I, as a dedicated student of men and women, believe that the fever would last? Could I picture what our life together would be when we were once more sane? Did I imagine that by sharing a house and having children, by cleaving to each other and becoming one flesh, we should cease in five or fifty years to be the unchanged, unchanging, unchangeable Isabel Pryde and Colin Whimboyne that we were now? Was I deceived by the world's nonsense-talk of compromise, of adjustment, of give-and-take? Did I not see that I as Lady Isabel's husband, or she, as the wife of that so distinguished author, that so highly respected civil servant, Colin Whimboyne, should cease to exist as personalities or even persons?

"What will remain? Nothing!," she would say, again and again.

"Except our love," I always reminded her.

"And when that ends . . ."

"Why should it ever end? I'm not thinking of passion only . . ."

Perhaps, Isabel warned me more than once, it would be a good thing if I did. She might, of course, be wrong; our love might be more than a hunger that we could satisfy at will until it ceased to torment or even to interest us (after which we could part); but at times she wondered whether it was even as much as that. I might think I wanted her; but it was a queer kind of want if I could always keep primly at a distance, like a well-conducted servant-girl dreaming of the day when she could have marriage-lines to sew inside her scrupulous stays.

"The scruple is not confined to servant-girls," I was on one occasion stung into saying. "Since you like plain speaking, I was not invited to your house by Lascombe as the eventual seducer of his sister. I think people cheapen, perhaps spoil, marriage if they can't wait. As a substitute for marriage . . ."

"Or as something not evenly remotely connected with marriage? Call it romance, call it passion . . . I suppose I shall marry some day, but I doubt whether it'll be passionate and it certainly won't be romantic. For you either, my poor Colin! We shall have had our romance. This is a thing we can neither of us hope to repeat. Or perhaps *you* can," she continued with the first flare of temper that I had seen. "Perhaps it's all you *can* do, as a bloodless butterfly, flitting from one pierrot passion to another . . . I'm evidently made differently: to marry a man who's not interested in women except as studies for his plays . . . Well, we're at least providing London with a great deal of free, innocent amusement!"

At the end of three months I was to discover that, if not amused, a far wider area than London was interested, puzzled and occasionally scandalized. How the news reached Ridgeway House I have no idea; but, when I went there for Christmas, my father—now very near the end of his appointed span—asked me on the first night whether "these papers" (which he had long given up reading) were right in saying that I was more or less (whatever that might mean) engaged to a daughter of his old friend Toby Wansborough. I said that I hoped it might prove an instance of what the papers themselves called intelligent anticipation. How far, he then asked, had things gone? Had I spoken to the girl or to her parents? To be blunt, our names were apparently being coupled rather freely.

"That's inevitable," I replied, "seeing the amount we've been about together."

"You don't want to get the gal talked about."

"People are going to talk about Isabel whatever happens. She's used to it, perhaps she rather likes it. I *don't*. I want to announce our engagement, to have an engagement that I *can* announce; but it's no good hurrying her. In time and with patience . . . She's as much in love with me as I am with her, she would be the first to tell you so, but at present she sees chiefly the incredible comicality of our being in love at all. *She* and *I*!"

"And how much longer," my father enquired with sudden tartness, "are you going to grin sheepishly while she enjoys the funny side of adding a Whimboyne scalp to her collection? In your place I should make up my mind to the one thing or the other. Propose to her! Marry her, if she says 'yes'. Bite on the bullet if it's 'no'. But there's been enough, more than enough, of this playing about. As this is probably the last piece of advice I shall give . . ."

I told my father that I would follow it, though with the mental reservation that it would not be for his reasons. I did not consider—what man in his dealings with women ever does?—that Isabel was making a fool of me; and if others—my father included—thought that she was, I did not care. Only Isabel and I could know what we meant to each other; and the more the people that smiled at us the more the people that envied us. Was it, however, conceivable that I was making a fool of myself? Since the night of our first meeting, I had known that I had the whip-hand: why not use it? I might say that no man living could coerce Isabel; but, if I issued an ultimatum, she would coerce herself.

" 'Yes' or 'no'," I murmured. "And, if it's 'no', if she even asks for time, I must make my bow. We can't go on like this. It will very soon send us both off our heads."

On my return to London, I prepared my ultimatum and delivered it the next time that Isabel dined with me in Grosvenor Road. Would she marry me, I asked, or must we harden our hearts to saying good-bye? The present uncertainty was getting on my nerves.

I know now that I ought to have said that it had already got on my nerves. That whip-hand, which I prided myself on possessing, was powerful enough to startle Isabel, who asked in the accents of uttermost defeat: "D'you mean that, if I won't promise to marry you, I shall never see you again?"; but I threw away my victory when—for the first time in her life, I should think—she began to cry. It was also the last moment of anything that either of us could call our happiness. I insisted on an answer then and there; Isabel warned me that, if I could not wait a night, the answer must be "no". I said "good-bye"; and, when she telephoned in the morning, begging me not to spoil both our lives, I lacked the strength to hold out against her. Thereafter she knew that my whip-hand was an old glove stuffed with sawdust.

And thereafter, for a year and three-quarters, we watched our love falling into ruins. Trials of strength, promises and retractations, bargains, quarrels, reconciliations, a great and general tarnishing of all that once seemed beautiful: I do not want to think of it now. Let my final word be that I certainly do not wish to blame Isabel. Perhaps, if I had become her lover, she would have ceased to wonder—in that disastrous old phrase—whether I, more fiercely tempted than all the saints in the calendar, was capable of passion; perhaps she would have married me; or perhaps she would have ordered me away the moment she was sated. Perhaps, if I had turned a deaf ear to the telephone that fatal morning, she would have accepted me on my own terms.

If I have not succeeded in forgetting her, I am not forced to think about her now except for certain effects of our ill-starred love. For two years I was entirely enslaved to her; and in looking back I sometimes feel that those two years were passed in a trance. I kept no diary; but my old engagement-books for this period have survived to remind me that I was cramming three lives—official, literary and social—into one, lunching and dining out daily whenever Isabel had arranged that we should be invited together, attending polyglot conferences on munitions-supply and looking in at the rehearsal of a new play. And but for the little books I should deny that I had done any of these things. Was there really such a woman as Mrs. Ajax L. Templett? Did I know her? We seem to have exchanged hospitality; and I apparently spent a week-end in her house near Beaconsfield.

It would appear that I went to America in the spring of 1917 and held forth interminably on machine-tools and high-precision instruments; it would appear that my visit coincided with the production of my latest play in New York and that I was lionized by a number of hospitable ladies whose very names I have forgotten. On my return I was given a C.B.; and after leaving Buckingham Palace I must have roused for a moment to reflect on the contrast between the scene there and the next. In response to an outcry against the fit young men who were sheltering as "indispensables" beneath government umbrellas, I was on my way to a medical examination and, though I knew in advance that the ministry would not release me, I recollect wondering whether any one could in fact stop me if I copied Austin Gerrold and signed on for the army without waiting to be released.

"It would be an easy way out of everything," I exclaimed in a rare interval of lucidity, taking it for granted that I should also copy Austin by getting myself killed.

It seems, from the published histories, that my period of private trance covered certain pregnant chapters in the war abroad and at home. The Asquith coalition was replaced by the Lloyd-George coalition; the United States came in and Russia went out; for a moment, while Isabel and I were tormenting each other, an order of the day announced that our armies were fighting with their backs to the wall; then, as we parted to torment ourselves, the enemy began to collapse; and, when I roused finally, the war was over. Nevertheless, it was not the maroons on Armistice Day that waked me, but a tear-sodden letter from Isabel to say that she had promised to marry the Duke of Abbotsbury.

While I was still in my trance, I must have been told that my father was dying, but I am almost sure that I did not see him till he was dead. I know that he was buried in the family vault at Ridgeway and I suppose I attended the funeral. Doubtless I received many letters of sympathy; and I should like to think that I really answered all that I ticked in red ink, but I suspect some of my replies were not posted and I recall that, when I met Elizabeth Gerrold in the street for the first time in many months, she asked whether I had ever had her note of condolence.

"Austin used to speak so warmly about the old days when he stayed with you," she went on.

"In one sense of the word," I said, "he spoke very warmly indeed about the house, which he called a mortuary, and the inmates, whom he likened to corpses on slabs. You can hear him saying it! 'The sickly reek of the Morgue!' I don't know whether it's a pleasure or a pain, Elizabeth, for you to talk about him: to me, his vitality was so enormous that even death could not extinguish it. Whenever I come to Montpelier Square . . .

"Which hasn't been for a long time now, Colin. Are you doing anything to-night, or will you dine with me—just the two of us—and talk about old times?"

I said that I should be delighted. Now that I was out of my trance, I remembered that I had not seen Elizabeth for more than two years. At our last meeting, to be sure, she had given me the impression of wanting only to be left alone till the earth had ceased to quake beneath her feet; but I had promised Austin that I would look after her while he was abroad and my conscience smote me that after some years of air-raids, some months of epidemics, I had not until this moment known or even cared whether she was alive or dead. Had she not, on the last occasion, talked of seeing Austin's solicitors and finding out whether she

could afford to go on living in Montpelier Square? Had I not said
that I would advise her about the boys' education when she knew
how much she could spend on it?

"You stuck it out in spite of the Zeppelins and Gothas?,"
I asked in the hope of learning whether she was still at the same
address.

"My sister Kitty offered to share the house," she answered,
"while she was working at the Admiralty. I couldn't desert her.
Will eight o'clock be all right for you? I've had to have the house
repainted outside, but otherwise I don't think you'll find much
change."

There was certainly no change in the welcome accorded me
that evening by Austin's admirable butler, Cruikshank, nor in the
excellence of the food and wine provided by Elizabeth. There
was no change, either, in her conversational technique, which
was to ask me a question—"Haven't you been in America since
last I saw you?"—and then leave me to conduct a monologue,
though on this occasion she was obliged to think of a second
question—"Is your mother at Ridgeway House now?"—when
we adjourned to Austin's book-room for coffee.

From time to time I varied my monologues by putting a
question to Elizabeth about her brothers, her children, her
activities during the war and her plans for the future; but I
evoked no monologue in return and any addition to my scant
knowledge of her affairs was made more by inference on my side
than by expansiveness on hers. The Cheshunts, I gathered, were
drawing in their horns somewhat: the loan of Coverley Court as
a military hospital provided one excuse, an income tax of six
shillings in the pound another; but a considerable fortune in
Russian securities had been sunk without trace and, whatever
Elizabeth's income, she was living on Austin's pension and on
the interest of such investments as he had left her.

Once satisfied that these were adequate, I allowed my conscience to stand easy. Without help or guidance from me, Elizabeth seemed to have established herself upon an impregnable
basis. The house, though small, was perfectly appointed; the
staff, represented by Cruikshank and his wife, kept everything
polished and shining; the mistress of the house, I was ready to be
told, knew all that needed to be known about domestic science;
and, for me, the result was a dinner of all my favourite dishes
accompanied by the burgundy and port that had always been the

cream of Austin's cellar. As I came to the end of my cigar, which was obviously from his choicest cabinet, I felt that Elizabeth had, a little surprisingly—bloomed out into a better hostess than any one would have thought possible in the days when the over-shadowing Austin kept the reins and keys of everything in his own hands.

Did I let her replenish my brandy-glass once too often? Though the dinner had been dull under any conversational aspect, it had been pleasantly restful by contrast with my last dinner in Isabel's company, when the nerves of us both were snapping. I enjoyed and partook liberally of everything that was offered me; and it was only when a mood of something like cheerfulness was followed abruptly by one of maudlin self-pity that I began to wonder whether the complete breakdown that I had been expecting for weeks was going to overtake me that night.

We were talking, I remember, of my mother; and I told Elizabeth that my brothers and I were worried about her. By my father's will, drawn under the shadow of "that rascal Harcourt's" death-duties, she was to live for the five years that he was allowing her at Ridgeway House on an annuity that should have satisfied all her wants in the middle nineties. Twenty years of neglect, however, had brought the house into a state in which she must repair it or leave it; and war-time taxation had cut her annuity in two. How was she to be made happy or even comfortable for the last months of her life?

"She's too old to uproot," I continued. "My brothers aren't in a position to help. At one time Austin suggested that I should buy the place. He said I should find it amusing to modernize the house."

"I should have thought you had enough on your hands already," said Elizabeth, "without amusements of that kind."

"If it kept me so busy that I couldn't lie awake at night . . . ," I began unguardedly, thinking aloud. "But it's my mother I have to consider, not myself."

"Poor Colin!," Elizabeth murmured, standing up to find an ashtray and then sitting down on the sofa beside me and giving my hand a little pat of sympathy.

It was the tone that I had heard, the gesture that I had seen, a dozen times when one of her boys had hurt himself; and, because I was more like an hysterical child than a self-controlled grown man, it was the one approach that I could not stand without disgracing myself. Blindly, convulsively I turned to Elizabeth and laid my bursting head on her breast. I could feel her shaken by my own dry sobs; and, as she held me in her arms, rocking and crooning, I was too weak to tear myself away and tell her that it was not my mother for whom I was breaking my heart, but Isabel Pryde.

As I became gradually calmer, I tried to apologize. Elizabeth whispered that I must not try to talk yet; and then, like a mother distracting a frightened child, she herself talked at greater length than I had ever heard before. "Poor Colin!" changed to "Dear Colin!" When we met in the street that afternoon, I was looking miserably ill. Hence her invitation! Probably there was nothing that she or any one could do, but at least she knew the devastating sense of loneliness when one had lost somebody that one loved. From Austin she knew how dearly I had loved my father.

In fact this was not true; but in the bliss of relaxation from the racking of the last two years I could not rouse myself to correct her. I had always respected my father, at times I had feared him and at times I had shunned him as he seemed so perversely to withdraw from life before life was ended; but I did not now regret him, I was not missing him and I did not doubt that, when I was myself again, I should be able to contrive something for my mother's comfort. What good, though, should I do by trying to explain all this to Elizabeth? I was beginning to know peace for the first time since I said good-bye to Isabel: why disturb it?

With luck, I told myself, I might be able to sleep when I got home; perhaps I might reach my bedroom without averting my gaze from the thronging ghosts of Isabel that haunted every corner. Already, still with my head pillowed on Elizabeth's soft breast, I was so drowsy that I could hardly speak; but I remember thinking with agreeably candid self-reproach that I had never done her justice. Until this night, I had seen her as a pretty, placid, well-dressed shadow of Austin, only materializing to a flesh-and-blood woman as the mother of Austin's children. She was so little of a conversationalist, so much less of an intellectual, that I had sometimes wondered whether her brilliant, restless and eruptive husband was not occasionally bored by her; but I decided now that a good wife and a devoted mother were perhaps of more lasting value for him than a professional wit and that a well-arranged dinner in a well-run house was more important than dinner-table pyrotechnics.

However that might be, Austin had quite obviously been in love with her; remembering how often I had wondered why, once again I felt that I had not done Elizabeth justice. When I was feeling that I should never have eyes for another woman, I became conscious that she was not unattractive. Perhaps any woman who had played the mother to me at that moment would have seemed attractive; but I doubted whether any woman could have given me the same sense of healing and hope. I felt that I could lie for ever like this, with her arms securely holding me, her steady heart-beats calming me, her tranquil murmur coaxing me back to sanity; and yet I was sure that she knew best when, the clock striking eleven, she whispered that I must go to bed and leave orders that I was not to be called in the morning.

"I'll give you another cigar," she added, as she took her arms away from me. "Austin always used to say that you must never relight a cigar that has gone out."

"I wanted to talk about him," I told her, "and I've only talked about myself. You must forgive me, Elizabeth! What with the Ministry and my family affairs and various other things, I've felt for some time that I was heading for a crash."

"And your plays! How many . . . ?"

"I couldn't carry on without *that* part of my work. In every sense. *You* know how civil servants are paid; and, though I've not written for money, I've got used to always having plenty. But I don't think I could have stood the war, I couldn't have stood life in a government office or life at all, for the matter of that, if I hadn't created a world of my own into which I could retreat. The sense of *making* something, however ill-favoured . . . But I suppose it was a greater strain than I imagined. Am I forgiven for making an exhibition of myself?"

As she proffered Austin's old mahogany cigar-box, Elizabeth answered that there was nothing to forgive.

"I only wish I could help," she added. "If talking to me makes it easier, I hope you'll dine again. I *couldn't* talk to any one after Austin was killed. And, until Kitty came to share the house, I was absolutely alone after the children had been put to bed. If I'd had a dog, even . . ."

"I wish you had let me know, Elizabeth. I promised Austin . . ."

"Well, you can look after me *now*! Or at least as soon as I've finished looking after you. Promise me you'll go straight to bed . . ."

"Will you promise to dine one night soon and tell me all about yourself and the children? To-morrow? That's excellent! And now, my dear, good-night and more thanks than I can possibly express."

I leant down to kiss her good-bye; but the movement seemed to take her by surprise and she turned to the bell, saying that she would ring for Cruikshank to get my coat.

"Would you like a taxi?," she asked.

"I'm more likely to sleep if I have a walk first," I answered.

In fact I walked only half-way through Montpelier Square and then sat down on a doorstep till a startled and suspicious constable gave me the support of his arm to the nearest cab-rank. I have written figuratively of the fever that had been wasting me for two years; and, now that it was passed, I felt so weak in body and tired in brain that my legs gave way under me and I had to hand the taxi-driver a visiting-card for my address. I believe he helped me into my house, where I collapsed in the hall; and, when I had dragged myself to bed, I was far beyond wondering whether I should be pursued thither by the fiery, passionate ghost of the newly wed Duchess of Abbotsbury.

For this, I supposed, I had Elizabeth to thank; and once again I reproached myself for having misjudged her. Isabel, who found her dull and stupid, would have asked whether she was still as completely colourless as when she married. This evening I had not found her colourless. A little unready in speech, she had revealed a rare sympathy and an intuitive maternal understanding. I looked forward to seeing her at dinner the next evening. If any fools still classified women as natural wives or mothers or mistresses, Elizabeth must—as I had always suspected—be seen as a natural mother; and I wondered again why Austin, who needed mothering less than any man, had chosen her for his wife.

"If *he* had paired with Isabel," I mused sleepily, "leaving *me* . . . No one would ever use of him that accursed phrase about not being interested in women. Whether Elizabeth's interested in men, except maternally . . ."

I was puzzled and perhaps faintly disappointed by her sudden primness in drawing back when her utterly exhausted and deeply grateful patient sought to shew by a most passionless kiss on the forehead how much he felt he owed her at that moment. For heaven-knew-how-long I had been lying with my head on her breast; she had clasped me to herself; and her lips had brushed my ear as she whispered: "Poor Colin . . . Dear Colin." To be sure we never yet had kissed; but, as two men will often shake hands when they find that they have passed through a similar ordeal, I wanted to shew Elizabeth that I understood her desolation of spirit when she lost Austin. In some way, too, not easy to define, I wanted her to know that she had given me hope—shall I say, the hope that the endless night of the last few weeks would in truth end some day?—and I wanted to give her a similar hope.

I could look after her when she had finished looking after me: had that been her phrase? Though she would never know it, I believe that the bitterest drop in my cup had been the thought that no woman would ever need me to look after her: I had wanted Isabel, as a companion, a wife and an inspiration; but I had also wanted her unselfishly, as some one to protect.

IX

WORDS, originally intended to express (or, possibly, to conceal) thoughts, often come to acquire the hypnotic force of a spell, weakening resistance and paralysing individual initiative. I feel that, in the months immediately before and after Armistice Day, "reconstruction"—one of the hardest-worked shibboleths in the vocabulary of journalists and politicians—became also one of the most potent. Instead of buying a new suit, Philip Cheshunt told me that Lady Mary and he had "carried out a survey" of his "wardrobe with a view to reconstruction". Had my father survived into 1919, I feel sure he would have told our Wiltshire neighbours that we must "reconstruct or perish".

And did reconstruction mean picking up the threads of the life interrupted in 1914 or planning a wholly new one? Should I, for example, after the excitement and importance of my time at the Ministry of Munitions, when the heavy industries hinted at directorships and even the Treasury trembled at my nod, go tamely back to the leisured obscurity of the Lord Keeper's Department? Should I retire from the civil service altogether, to give myself more time for writing? Should I abandon the profitable vein of a public entertainer and try to create a masterpiece or two that would outlive me? I was now thirty. Did I mean to remain a dining-out, week-ending London bachelor, occupying a house too big for me and waking up one day to find myself called a crusty old bachelor—or worse—the club bore? Should I put Ridgeway into repair and settle there, as a small country-gentleman with literary foibles, when the place had served my mother's turn?

All these points, with many others, were included in the monologue that I delivered when Elizabeth came to dine with me and played her conversational part by asking why I did not go abroad for the winter, to the West Indies or Honolulu.

"I should have to apply for sick-leave," I told her, "and no doctor would certify that I couldn't stand any number of English winters. For that reason I've sometimes wondered whether it wouldn't be more comfortable if I were my own master. This country, from November to March . . ." I shivered. "I don't know that I should care much about travelling alone, but the feeling of *freedom* . . ."

Elizabeth touched the old-fashioned gold locket in which she carried miniatures of her two boys.

"A bachelor . . . ," she began.

We digressed to exchange news of her brothers and mine. By now Philip had two sons, Alexander and Hilary; and Lady Jane had presented Maurice with two daughters, Aileen and Frances, and a son, Angus. My own relations had been less assiduous in repairing the wastage of the war: both John and Henry were still childless and Charles had broken his neck at polo two years earlier in Valparaiso. If the name of Whimboyne was to continue, it looked as though I must bestir myself.

Did I care whether it survived or not? I could feel a wave of the old hopelessness beating against me.

"I think that women too should take stock," I made haste to tell Elizabeth. "What's *your* plan of life, now the war's over? For yourself, for your children? Will you stay in this country? Are you going to marry again? Have you chosen careers for Martin and Humfrey?" The wave was receding; and I hurried on before it could turn. "Here," I expounded, "is an opportunity for shewing whether we have it in us to do better than our elders did for us. It's now or never, though."

"When you marry and have children, your life's settled for you," said Elizabeth.

For a few minutes we talked of the plans that she had made when she married Austin. They both wanted a family of Victorian dimensions, Elizabeth (though delicacy prevented her admitting it in so many words) because children and childbirth, childish ailments and the upbringing, education, clothing and feeding of children were obviously the great and perhaps the sole interest in life for her, Austin (if his loudly proclaimed prenuptial theories had stood the test of marriage) because it was race-suicide unless every married couple more than reproduced its own two selves. The advent of their children was to be prudently spaced to safeguard Elizabeth's health and to ensure that Austin's income would increase proportionately with their growing family. They both held that the children should be left to discover their vocations; and the overriding consideration by which every step and act had to be tested was that the young Gerrolds, boys and girls, should have at least as good a start in life as their parents.

"Martin and Humfrey were put down for Austin's old house at Westminster," Elizabeth told me, "the day they were born. If either had been a girl, it would have been Wycombe Abbey."

"And, after that, Oxford?," I asked. "Or are they to decide?"

"Well, as Martin's only six and Humfrey three, we needn't make up our minds yet. And perhaps, when the time arrives, we shall find that our minds have been made up for us. It's very sordid, Colin, but everything nowadays seems to turn on what one can *afford*. I'm wondering whether I ought to break the lease in Montpelier Square when Kitty goes."

Since Elizabeth had not consulted me about her affairs when Austin was killed, I suggested that her solicitors (in whom she apparently had complete confidence) were the best people to advise her; but she answered, a little gloomily, that no two people ever gave the same advice. The City, according to her father, was looking forward to a gigantic boom in which every one would have money to burn; but Bedford Row, as exemplified by Austin's cautious and old-fashioned executors, made her head ache with unintelligible talk about "paper prosperity" and "the printing-press" (whatever that might mean!). Surely, if the Germans paid for their war, the income-tax could be reduced at once.

"And then we *might* be able to make both ends meet," she added. "At present the price of everything is just ruinous. No, my dear, it's quite useless for you to explain about 'inflation'! Either a pound's worth twenty shillings or it isn't. And I wish to goodness the government would go back to sovereigns instead of these wretched Bradburys."

Disclaiming all comprehension of economics, I said that in time of inflation land had the merit of not running away and, if the rent of her own house seemed reasonable, I recommended her to extend the lease and to sublet, if she found London too expensive. These, however, were only parts—perhaps small parts— of my far bigger question: were we going to patch and mend the old life of 1914 or were we going to reconstruct our lives as a whole?

"*You* may call it a small part, Colin," Elizabeth sighed. "If you were a woman who had *not* been trained to business and was responsible for two small sons . . ."

Remembering how she had comforted me the night before, I told her that, if I could help her in any way, she had only to command me. We were sitting in my work-room, she in the winged armchair that for two years had been consecrated to Isabel and I opposite her on the other side of the big open fire. Though her stolid presence was more than a match for any ghost that might dispute her right to be there, I seemed for a moment to look through her to a figure normally flashing and electric, but now cold, dark and dead, the figure of Isabel Pryde crumpled and weeping. If I could help Elizabeth, I might feel somewhat less unwanted and useless.

"I've not been trained to business either," I said. "With a certain horse-sense, though, and the help of an agent, a solicitor and an accountant . . . Remember, my dear, that I was to look after you when you'd finished looking after me. If you *care* to tell me about your position . . ."

"What is there to tell? If the executors say I can't afford this or that, we must go without it. No, it's the idea of those two boys growing up without a father. If anything happened to *me* . . . A helpless pair of homeless little orphans!"

As her voice quavered and died, I ostentatiously took a writing-block and pencil.

"I don't know whether you've made a will," I began. "You must be entirely unsentimental, Elizabeth, about the *facts* of life, which include death, and, as no one knows when his life will be required of him, it's your *duty* to appoint a guardian for your sons. Everything in black and white! If any money you're leaving them is to remain in trust till they're, say, twenty-five . . . By the way, you must remember that marriage invalidates a will. If you marry again . . ."

The threat of a lacrimose scene had passed; and Elizabeth was watching with childlike interest the swift movement of my pencil, only breaking silence to say: "Are you drawing up my will for me?" and "If I'm to say all this to the solicitor, you must write the letter for me. I'm no good at that sort of thing." The question of a possible remarriage, however, roused her to ask who in the world would think of marrying a middle-aged widow with a ready-made family.

"If you call yourself middle-aged . . . ," I expostulated.

"I'm twenty-eight," she returned.

"Then I, at thirty, must be more than middle-aged! I'm not trying to flatter you, Elizabeth, but you don't look a day older than when you married."

"So you think there's still hope for me?," Elizabeth asked, smiling. "Don't forget that ready-made family."

I replied that, when a man was in love, he was in love—at one remove—with his wife's children and parents and friends.

"Her cats and dogs . . . ," I continued. "Oh, sorry! I'd forgotten you told me last night that you hadn't a dog! You see what I mean?"

"I don't quite . . . If you were in love with me, you would take Martin and Humfrey as *part* of me? And I should take this place and your admirable butler—Winter, is his name?—as part of you?"

"If we can't do that as a matter of course, we're not in love."

"I see what you mean. Is this a proposal, Colin?"

I wondered whether it was. Thirty years later I am still wondering. Nothing certainly had been farther from my thoughts when I asked Elizabeth to dine with me; or, perhaps I should say, from my conscious thoughts; or at least from the half of my brain that housed my conscious thoughts. I am not so sure about the other half, the mysterious half that normally did most of my creative work for me by accepting an idea at night and returning it to me, as a plot or scene or character, in the morning, a silent and observant half that had taken no part this evening in our rambling conversation and yet had given us the key and had again and again recalled us to it with the clear, directing note of a tuning-fork. Assuredly I had never intended to ask Elizabeth or any other woman to marry what Isabel had left of me; and yet I knew in some part of my brain that I could not face perhaps another forty years of life alone. It was the eternal mother in Elizabeth that had appealed to me the night before; and yet in my everlastingly excited, everlastingly unsatisfied state almost any woman would have attracted me. Even at one remove I could never be in love with most of Elizabeth's assertive relations and I should not have recognized Martin or Humfrey if I had met them in the street without her; and yet, when I saw her pathetic inability to cope with the responsibilities that Austin had always shouldered, I wanted to shoulder them for her. Never, indeed, should I say of her, as I have lately written of Isabel, that she had inspired one or two of my best plays; but I must have had a strong, hardly suspected strain of domesticity in my nature and I feel that, whether we were in Grosvenor Road or Montpelier Square, the second half of my brain was whispering insistently to me: "A home, a wife, children."

Aloud I said:

"It is not good for man to live alone, Elizabeth, or for woman either. *Will* you . . . ?"

"Oh, my dear, you must give me a *little* time . . . ," she began and then held up her hand as Big Ben chimed the four quarters before the hour.

I looked at my watch and nodded. Eleven o'clock? Then all this had happened in less than three hours. Eleven o'clock . . . If I remembered aright, it used to take upwards of a minute for Big Ben to strike ten; and my parsimonious housemaster maintained that this was time enough for us seniors to get up to our dormitories and on the last stroke would turn off our study lights at his private switch-board. Elizabeth had asked for a little time; and a little time she should have. When the last reverberation had died away, I decided that she had now had time enough. I must insist on an unequivocal "Yes" or "No".

"Will you marry me, Elizabeth?," I demanded. The grating harshness of my tone made me wonder even at the time why she did not stalk out of the room; it was, however, no longer a man of polite breeding, no longer a courteous host, who had set himself to browbeat her, but the escaped victim of a torture-chamber who would kill himself to avoid recapture. A little time? Isabel, when cornered, would ask for a little time. Not willingly nor with open eyes would I stretch myself on that rack again. "I am neither mad nor drunk . . . ," I continued with a queer, cold rage.

"But do you *imagine* . . . ?" she gasped.

I suppose she wanted to say: "Do you imagine you're in love with me?"; and, if she had finished her question, I could have answered truthfully and brutally that I neither knew nor cared. It was not a question of imagination, but of true, brutal instincts, checked—if she liked—by feminine intuition. We had known each other for some years, I told her; she must have some idea of my circumstances and prospects. The sixty-odd seconds that I had given her should have been enough to enable her at least to say whether she would refuse to marry me, if I were the last man in the world, whether she knew in her bones that I should or should not make a good husband and father, whether she was set unshakably against a second marriage.

"Austin always said that, if anything happened to him, I *ought* to marry again," she faltered.

"*He* knew that you would always need some one to look after you," I said.

"But *you*, Colin . . . I never dreamt that *you* . . ."

"I shouldn't have asked you if I hadn't meant it. And, if you can't say 'yes' here and now, I don't want you to say it at all. Tell me that you'll marry me the moment I can get a licence . . ."

I stopped in mid-sentence, with a disabling sense that, if I wrote a scene like this for a play, my luckless actors would be hooted off the stage. Did Mr. Whimboyne, the critics would ask next day, really believe that this was the way any man wooed any woman? Well, it was not a way that many playwrights would dare to attempt; but, then, the play-going public had but a limited credulity. Art, evidently, was afraid to catch up with nature. Here was a conventional young woman, no shrew, being tamed by a conventional young man, no shadow of a Petruchio, who (a neurologist might say) was snatching some transient strength from the uninhibited state of his nerves, which at this moment were a hair's-breadth removed from breakdown. I did not care whether Elizabeth accepted me or not; but I cared with almost homicidal passion whether she kept me waiting for her answer.

And it was the wooing that Elizabeth welcomed. Did she, with her queer blend of obstinacy and helplessness, want to have her mind made up for her? Was she afflicted by a literary and rather morbid desire to be dominated, like the heroine of novelettes, by some ruthless male? Had she shut her eyes, since the night before, to my neurotic excitability and was she saying that, when I was normal again, I certainly could give her just the support that she needed? Was she thinking that any one who needed a woman in his life as desperately as I seemed to need her in mine would be an easy husband for her to dominate?

I cannot answer my own questions; but, however extravagant the scene might have appeared on the stage, I must record that my unorthodox wooing overpowered her. I seem to hear myself barking at her: "Yes or no, Elizabeth! And *now*!"; I seem to hear a small, frightened voice saying: "If you *won't* wait . . . Oh, Colin! . . . I suppose it's 'yes'. I do hope we're not both being quite mad!"

Mad or sane, we then became fantastically prosaic; and to this day I never see a copy of *Whitaker's Almanack* without remembering how it helped to shape our destinies that night. I read aloud all the available information about special licences; I calculated times and proclaimed the hour and place at which we were to be married. I drafted the announcement for *The Times* and explained that I should dispatch it on our way from the register-office to the station, but that we could neither of us possibly want to publish our engagement and expose ourselves to interviews and con-gratulations and enquiries about presents. Ostensibly I con-sulted her about our honeymoon; but in the winter of 1918 there was no question of our being able to go abroad and, among south-coast watering-places, we must take what we were offered.

"Axminster used to say," I recalled, "that, if ever I married, he would lend me any of his castles, seats, villas and so on that he didn't happen to be using at the moment. I've not seen him, though, since Honiton, his only son, was killed and I'm told he's still badly broken up. Any way, even if I pledged him to secrecy, the news would get about; and I feel I just couldn't *stand* the fuss and general inanity that people keep on tap for a wedding. I shall apply for leave from the Ministry without saying what it's for. I shan't tell even my mother till it's an accomplished fact. After all, it's nobody else's *business*. I suppose I must let my solicitors into the secret. Yours too, if you'll tell me who they are . . ."

"On account of the will?," Elizabeth asked, wrinkling her forehead. "You said that marriage upset a will or something . . ."

"On account of the settlements," I told her. "I presume there was a settlement when you and Austin married? Otherwise . . ."

"I don't think I ever heard of one. Daddy gave me an allowance. And Austin . . . *Austin* made a will, of course. I remember he signed it in the vestry. And *he* said something about marriage upsetting wills. It can't upset *his* will if I marry you, can it?," she asked in sudden dismay; and, when I had reassured her: "Then I don't see why you're bothering about a settlement! Apparently I got on quite well without one before. But, Colin, you were saying something about a guardian for Martin and Humfrey. If I marry you, do you automatically . . . ?"

With what patience I could muster I told Elizabeth the elements of English law as it affected marriage-settlements and married women's property, wills and intestate estates, trustees and guardians, wards of court and wards in chancery. There was much that I did not tell her, knowing that my stock of patience had run low and fearing that I might say too much if I said anything about her hardly credible ignorance of matters that concerned vitally her daily bread and the clothes on her children's backs. It was incomprehensible to me that her father and brothers should not have taught her the rudiments of affairs, that Austin —apparently—should have given her no guidance and that his solicitors should content themselves—in her own phrase—with saying what she could or could not afford; but still more incomprehensible was her obvious indifference, at least until an unworthy suspicion inspired her to look at me as though I wanted to marry her for her money.

"It's always rather invidious," I said, "for a man and woman, or even for their parents, to argue and bargain about how much each is going to bring into settlement. If the solicitors on both sides . . ."

"But if I didn't have a settlement before," Elizabeth interrupted, "why should I need one now? Anything that came to me from Austin was for me and the boys . . ."

"Which I'm not trying to disturb. And, so long as I'm alive and married to you, I'm responsible for you and any children we may have. But if I die . . . It's for your own protection; but, if you don't want it, I certainly shan't force it on you. Let's talk of something else!"

I fancy I have remarked of Elizabeth's conversational technique that, though she came to a dinner-party primed with two questions that should unloose a monologue from each of her neighbours, I could never be sure from her later contributions—

"Oh, yes?" . . . "*How* right you are!" . . . "I *do* so agree!"—
whether she thought over, or even listened to, what was being
said. On this strange evening when we became engaged I decided
that such sentences as happened to interest her effected a lodge-
ment in her mind and that she would bring them out, unassimilated
and indeed hardly tasted, when a moment of silence offered her
the opportunity. Petulantly urged by me to talk of something
else, she now begged for an explanation of things that I had
almost forgotten saying. A guardian for Martin and Humfrey:
should I, in marrying her, automatically become their guardian?
Ought she to appoint a guardian to look after them if she died
before they grew up? What would my position then be as their
stepfather? As with the settlement, she was inclined to say that
the boys had got on very well without a legal guardian so far
and she saw no purpose in making any change. I said that this
was for her to decide; and, remembering my stand-and-deliver
proposal of marriage, I wondered whether poor Elizabeth felt
that she must entrench herself against me if she was to retain any
independence. Rather than have her affairs discussed by me with
her solicitors, she would forgo the protection of a marriage-
settlement; and she would dispense with any advice that I might
give her about her sons rather than invest me with a legal right
to interest myself in them.

Or so I rather impatiently fancied; but already she was reminding me of something that I had said about the lease of her
house. Should she give notice to terminate it, should she transfer
it, were we going to live here? Everything had happened, was
continuing to happen, so quickly that she must be forgiven for
feeling a little confused.

"We can't live in more than one house at a time," she continued with a glance at the framed playbills that now surmounted
the bookcases on three sides of my work-room. I chose to think
she was saying to herself that this was my home, as Montpelier
Square was hers, and that we could not both of us retain our
homes. Who was to give way? "It *must* be London, I suppose,
whatever happens?"

As long, I told her, as I remained a civil servant; and, though
we had touched briefly on this subject at dinner when we were
discussing whether we ought to reconstruct our lives, we must
discuss it seriously now that our lives were being reconstructed
more completely than either of us could have thought possible

a few hours earlier. Rather to my surprise, Elizabeth quoted almost the last piece of advice that Austin had given me, when he contrasted the fickleness of the playgoing public with the dependability of an official paymaster. She hoped that my success in the theatre would continue; but, since I was giving her the right to an opinion on any course that affected us both, she trusted that no man who was making himself responsible for a wife and family would do anything so irresponsible as to throw away a certain income for an uncertain one. Perhaps she had been unduly scared by her father's tales of the fortunes that had lately been lost between night and morning, but it seemed so necessary to provide for every imaginable future that she had really been shocked to hear me talking, lightly, of making an offer for Ridgeway House.

"I don't blame people who refuse to start a family," she added, "until they feel they can see a *bit* of light ahead."

"Incidentally," I reminded her, "Ridgeway too was an idea of Austin's. But, whereas *he* talked lightly of it as a distraction, I look on it as a promising investment. Owing to the state of the house, the valuation will be absurdly low; for a few hundreds I can make it habitable for my mother, who can't have many years to live; afterwards, for a few thousands, I could so modernize it that, if we didn't want to live there ourselves, we could let it at a handsome profit. There's a general dearth of houses and a special dearth of moderate-sized houses. If I let *this* place to a member of parliament, say, or another civil servant, I could do a pretty piece of profiteering. So could you with yours. Would it be a wrench for you to give it up? It has been your home ever since you married Austin, it's the only home that Martin and Humfrey have known . . ."

"But *you* wouldn't want to leave here and go there!," said Elizabeth.

Forty-eight hours earlier I should have said that I would rather sleep on the Embankment than continue to live in a haunted house; but the sense of Isabel's presence had weakened and would doubtless in time pass completely away. I was attached to my home in Grosvenor Road as I could never be to a home that had been designed for my wife by her first husband; and there was ample room for the two boys with all the additional servants and governesses that a ready-made family entailed, all the nurseries and nurses that would be required by a family still to make. I hoped that Elizabeth would decide against Montpelier Square on her own account; but I did not want to see her again digging trenches to safeguard the individuality that I was apparently always threatening.

"I shall leave you to choose," I answered. "Whichever you think will be better for you and the boys . . ."

"This is much nearer your work, of course . . . ," she began.

"If we're profiteering," I interrupted, "we ought to consider what will pay best. I believe Austin's lease and mine were very similar: twenty-one years with power to break on six months' notice after seven or fourteen. We've both had nearly seven; and, if we're going to break, we must give notice next March to terminate at Michaelmas. Your neighbourhood being more fashionable, you can profiteer to greater advantage; but I don't think either of us will have any difficulty in finding a tenant. If you think it's a gamble that you would rather not take, you can fire in your notice, assign the last few months of your lease . . ."

I stopped on discovering that I was talking as though Elizabeth had already decided in favour of Grosvenor Road. In fact she had; and I felt it was only a formality that she should ask to be shewn over the house before making up her mind.

"If I *can* turn an honest penny for the boys by subletting . . . ," she murmured. "It will pay me back for all that ruinous painting I had to do. . . . How much do you think I ought to get, Colin?"

"I've no idea how rents run in that neighbourhood; but, if you're willing to let furnished, with immediate possession, to some one who's just desperate about getting a roof over his head . . ."

"My sister Kitty is. I promised her the first refusal if I found I couldn't afford to go on living there."

"That's rather unfortunate in one way! You can hardly squeeze your own sister as you might squeeze a total stranger. However . . . If you ask your solicitors to suggest a figure . . . Don't tell them *why* you're giving up the house. We shall have time enough for all that when we come back from our honeymoon."

This is perhaps the place to record that everything was arranged several days before we started on our honeymoon; but, though the house went to Kitty Mandeville, I was never told the terms proposed or accepted. The preliminaries were indeed completed by telephone that evening, as a culminating incongruity in the most incongruous betrothal that I could imagine. I still see myself ordering a taxi and, while we wait for it, helping Elizabeth into her cloak and putting on my own greatcoat. I remember my impulse to laugh hysterically when I remind her that we have not yet sealed our bond with a kiss. And I think I shall always recall the queer expression in her eyes, though I can still find no word to describe it, as she exclaims:

"Just a moment! The taxi's not here yet, is it? I've just thought that, if I may use your telephone, I shall catch Kitty before she goes to bed."

X

THOUGH I have never thought about it from that day to this, I believe that my insistence on marrying first and announcing our marriage afterwards was attributable to a superstitious fear that, if I proclaimed my intention to do anything at this season, an angry Heaven would have hastened to teach me the unwisdom of boasting. The parting gift of the newly wed Duchess of Abbotsbury was an acid capable of eating all my confidence in myself; and for the first time in my life I added "D.V." to the invitations that I issued and accepted, I refused to say that Ridgeway House was mine until the conveyance had been signed and the purchase-money paid in full, I fenced with any questions about my next play and, when our secret engagement became public property, I tried to propitiate Nemesis with the words: "Unless Elizabeth thinks better of it . . ."

When my nerves became steadier, I could see that she was unlikely to think better of it. The secrecy of our engagement was violated the morning after we became engaged, when Elizabeth— in the presence of "Aunt Kitty"—explained to Martin and Humfrey that they were soon to "have a new daddy"; at luncheon that day Kitty broke the news in strict confidence to Clement Phayre, who honoured me with three paragraphs in his column of gossip; and that evening in Saint James' Park poor old Axminster stopped to offer his congratulations and to ask whether we should care to make use of Bowbury Castle for our honeymoon. By the time that all the available Cheshunts and Whimboynes had telegraphed their good wishes, we were too publicly committed for either of us to leave the other stranded at the registrar's door. Still intermittently uncertain of myself, I postponed buying the ring until the last possible moment; but in writing to accept Axminster's offer I could declare with an assumption of jocularity that only sudden death or serious illness would now turn us from our purpose.

And, as we drove to Paddington, man and wife for almost a quarter of an hour, I felt that we had only short-headed Nemesis and that another day or two of nerve-racking would have produced just that illness at which I professed to mock. I am not concerned to make excuses for myself; and in long dispassionate retrospect I greatly doubt whether our marriage would have turned out differently if we had lingered longer over a different kind of engagement, but I cannot deny that, if possibly Elizabeth had thought better of her promise, I had given her ample justification. And, had I thought better of my proposal, it is but fair to say that she exasperated me as much as I exasperated her and with less excuse. It was my fault that our time for preparation was so short; it was hers that she wasted so much of it on irrelevancies.

I can see now that to her they were not irrelevant; but there were moments in every day of our engagement when I longed to snap at her: "If you can't help, don't hinder!" or even "*You* mind *your* business; and *I'll* mind *mine*!" Whose business was the purchase of Ridgeway House? It was the place where I had been brought up, the place where my now old and ailing mother was ending her days in discomfort that I should not have tolerated for myself; regarded simply as an investment, I believed that it was more than sound, but, if it had been the maddest sort of gamble, the money was mine, I had earned it by the ink of my pen and, though it seemed to be a strange thing to be saying thirty years later, I had at this time more than I could spend. If Elizabeth had agreed to my proposal for a marriage-settlement, she might have been entitled to an opinion; but our unending arguments carried her no farther than the statement that, if I was working in London, I could not need a house in the country and, if I really meant to make myself responsible for a wife and a ready-made family, I had better put my savings into war-loan or whatever it was that the government was always urging us to buy.

This source of wrangling was stopped only on the afternoon before our wedding-day, when I told her that the title-deeds were

now lodged with my bank; and I tried to soften her disappointment by suggesting that a country house might have its uses for
Martin and Humfrey in the school-holidays.

"If I thought you had *them* in mind . . . ," Elizabeth began, to
continue rather less ungraciously: "I'm sorry, Colin, but I sometimes feel you don't understand. . . . I suppose it's the difference
between a man and a woman. . . . Even Austin, who was their
father . . . I oughtn't to say it about a man who's dead, but I
always suspected it was *me* that he wanted . . . or not even me!
The one thing that any woman could give him, the *only* thing
that women can give some men and the only thing some men
seem to want. *You're* not like that, are you? Oh, if you *knew* how
I hated talking about these disgusting things!"

As she turned away with scarlet cheeks, I embarked on a
reassuring discourse which I still remember as combining the
maximum of vagueness with the maximum of prudery. Love and
passion, the life-force and the procreative urge that kept the world
populated, the wife-type and the mother-type, the husband-type,
the father-type and the perfect blend of wife-mother and husband-
father: I generalized till the blush of needless shame had faded
from Elizabeth's cheeks and then promised her that she would
never have cause to say of me that I was one of those men who
wanted only one thing.

"I want you as my wife," I told her, "and the mother of our
children, but also as a companion and—that lovely old word!—
helpmeet. Some one to share my life as I hope to share hers, some
one that I can help and protect, which I suppose is the masculine
counterpart of a woman's maternal instinct . . ."

"Do you want children?", she interrupted.

"Never having had any, I find it hard to say. I imagine they
complete things and bind the man and woman together. When
we're old and the age of passion is past . . ."

"I think that side of things is so *horrid*! Until I married
Austin . . ."

I presume she was going to say that she had been brought up
in complete ignorance of the physical aspect of marriage, but at
this point her two boys came into the room and she embarked on
an explanation of my position as their "new daddy" who, after
to-morrow, was going to do all that the "daddy" of the photograph in their nursery would have done if he had "come back".
Listening with one ear, I wondered what part Austin would in

H

fact have played as their father. He would have stopped baby-talk and refused to let a child's nurse be called a "nanny"; it had always been a shibboleth with him that people should "have no nonsense about them" and I could imagine his telling Elizabeth that it was the worst kind of nonsense for a married woman to talk about natural processes as "these disgusting things". It was the first business of every woman to be physically attractive, the second to be a healthy mother and the third to shew herself a good housekeeper. If she fancied that she had a soul above these things, all the professions would become overcrowded and the race would come to an end. All this, he would declare, was mere "feminist nonsense".

Watching and listening to Elizabeth as she talked to her little boys, I wondered how much nonsense the forthright and occasionally harsh Austin had found it necessary to knock out of her. How much had she resented it? And to what extent was she visiting on my head the resentment that she still cherished against Austin? The involved saga of new and old "daddies" seemed to be embracing uncles: we had all been boys together at school, Uncle Philip and Uncle Maurice and Uncle Clayton, that school by Westminster Abbey which would one day be Martin's and Humfrey's school. In a short pause for intellectual digestion, I reminded Elizabeth that, if their children had been girls, Austin and she were committed to Wycombe Abbey. Had she, I asked, been there? Or her sisters?

"I don't know why Austin picked on Wycombe Abbey," she answered. "Phyllis and May were at Heathfield and Kitty at Roedean. When we lived in Saint John's Wood, I went to a day-school for one term, but I had an illness and wasn't sent back. There's nothing wrong with Wycombe Abbey, is there?"

"I believe it's one of the best schools in England. I was only wondering . . . If any of our children are girls . . ."

Elizabeth bit her lip, for all the world as though she thought it indelicate for me to speak of the children that we might naturally expect to have.

"Surely it will be time enough . . .," she began. "Colin, I don't want to turn you out, but Kitty's coming to make the final arrangements about this house and I have a terrible lot of things to do. I *should* like to go to bed early to-night. You don't mind? I'm sure you want to see me looking my best to-morrow! Good-bye, my dear! Say 'Good-bye, daddy', boys."

I returned from Montpelier Square to Grosvenor Road on foot. By this time to-morrow night, I assured myself, Elizabeth and I should be at Bowbury Castle; by ten o'clock to-morrow morning, I continued, we should be in the train, quite old married people, and this ghastly, dull fog of uncertainty would have dispersed. Why, even in jest, had I coined that imbecile phrase about death or sudden illness? If I had said "nothing but the end of the world", I should not be fretting now about Nemesis; but, had any one asked whether I expected sudden illness to attack either of us, I must have answered that I thought nothing less unlikely than that Kitty would telephone to say that Elizabeth had been ordered to bed with a temperature of 104°. She was sick in mind, if not in body; and her sickness was so contagious that I could not attend to my own last preparations till I had unloaded my vague anxieties first on her butler and then on her sister. Would they let me know if there was anything that I could do? Mrs. Gerrold, I thought, had seemed rather tired and overdriven that afternoon.

"Well, you *have* rather rushed things," said Kitty. "A bit unnecessarily, I should have thought."

"When you've made up your minds," I replied, "there's no point in waiting."

"You may be right! I was thinking that, if you had waited, you might make up your minds rather differently. Oh, I don't mean that either of you would call it off: Rella is as grimly set on marrying you as you are on marrying her! With a bit more time, though, you might have agreed what kind of marriage you were trying to bring about. Too late now!"

So long as it was too late now for Elizabeth to draw back, I felt that I could dismiss my fears of an incapacitating illness. What meaning my future sister-in-law intended me to read into her dark utterances I could not imagine and would not enquire. There had never been much love to lose between her and Elizabeth, whom she openly and comprehensively despised; I think it still rankled with her that Austin and I remained friends with Clayton after she had divorced him and I believe her acid comment on our engagement to have been that, if "little Cinderella" could find herself one fairy prince, there was no reason in nature why she should not find herself fifty. Fairy princes, she seemed to hint, must be rather easy to please; and it would be interesting to see how I compared with Austin.

Was a comparison of this kind interesting, perhaps perturbing, Elizabeth at this moment? Had her marriage to Austin left bruises on her spirit and was she wondering whether I should leave more? Impatient and temporarily on edge I knew myself to be; but, if she believed that I should inflict physical or mental cruelty on her, she would surely have broken off the engagement. Kitty's phrase returned to torment me. What kind of marriage did we hope to achieve? Well, what kind of marriage did any average man and woman hope to achieve? I wanted her, however little she liked the word; and I must assume that she did not regard me as physically repellent. Two years of widowhood had taught her, as two months of desolation had taught me, that we were not cut out to live alone. She was devoted to children; and I had little doubt that I should be too, when I had some of my own. In the meantime we craved for companionship and for the loving help that only a man and woman could give each other. I no longer expected romance or rapture; and, despite Kitty's foolish phrase about fairy princes, I doubted whether Elizabeth had ever expected them. When I told her that with the coming of peace we must decide—and decide instantly—whether we intended to make new lives for ourselves, I felt that she asked for nothing better than to reconstruct the life that had been interrupted in 1914.

"Grosvenor Road instead of Montpelier Square," I enumerated, "with me instead of Austin, but anyway a sufficient income for an adequate house and servants, a certain position in the official world of London, a wide and increasing circle of interesting friends. . . . I can't see what Kitty was driving at! If we had *waited* a bit . . ."

For all my self-justification, I felt a stab of conscience when Elizabeth and I stood next morning before the registrar. I certainly had rushed things, perhaps unnecessarily; and she looked utterly exhausted. Throughout the long journey to Devonshire, she only opened her lips to say: "You've stayed with Lord Axminster at Bowbury, haven't you?"; and thereafter, as at one of her dinner-parties in old days, I was left to sustain a monologue on the history and architecture of the castle. I am far from sure that she listened; and that evening, as we were taken round by the house-steward, everything had to be explained a second time.

"They call yours 'The Bishop's Room'," I mentioned, as we

went up to dress before dinner. "The 'Bishop's Man's Room', next door, which has been given me as a dressing-room . . ."

"Is this my private bar?," Elizabeth interrupted, opening the door of the small turret-room in the south-east corner.

The lights had come on as she turned the handle; and I saw a big gate-legged oak table completely filling the room and completely covered with bottles and decanters, syphons and glasses, dishes of olives and jars of caviare.

"It is a foretaste," I answered, "of the hospitality for which Axminster is famous."

"Is this *champagne*?," she asked, fingering the rusty-gold wire of a tappit-hen, as though she needed to touch as well as to see.

"Like most good judges, Axminster would tell you: the bigger the bottle, the better the champagne. I doubt whether he has anything smaller than a magnum in all his cellars. My father belonged to the same school of thought, but he never regarded champagne seriously. As a preventive of sea-sickness or a pick-me-up, with a peach, in the middle of the morning, best of all as an *apéritif*: one glass, while he was dressing for dinner . . . He didn't care about sherry; and cocktail-drinking was a barbarism as inexcusable as smoking over your port. Axminster is more catholic. There's a bowl of ice here: would you like me to mix you a cocktail?"

Elizabeth examined the silver labels round the necks of the decanters, murmuring: "Brandy, rum, whiskey, gin, sherry, madeira," then returned to the tappit-hen.

"Your father said that champagne . . . ,?" she began.

"It's pleasantly stimulating, easily digested and instantly refreshing, without any of the deleterious effects of raw spirits on an empty stomach. Champagne let it be! I'm sorry it's not a pint bottle."

"Well, we needn't finish it all now," said Elizabeth with the first attempt at gaiety that I had seen her make that day. "Your health, Colin! And now, if I'm to be bathed and dressed by half-past eight . . . I wish I wasn't so tired!"

"You'll be better when you have had some dinner," I assured her. "You're *looking* better already for the champagne."

The colour had come back to her cheeks and there was some light in her eyes when we went down to dinner, though she complained of feeling sleepy before the meal was over. I urged her to go up as soon as she liked; when I came to her room, her eyes were closed; and, though she assured me that she was not asleep, I could not have said she was fully awake at any time that night or next morning until the moment when she roused to ask me for a glass of soda-water.

As I turned on the light, I thought that her lips looked parched and, laying my hand on her forehead as she drank, I found it so hot that I tiptoed to my dressing-room and fetched my thermometer. Her temperature was upwards of 103°; and, without saying anything to her, I set about preparing a hot drink.

"What are you doing?," she asked, as I lighted the spirit-lamp which Axminster's forethought had put in the turret-room.

"I suspect you've caught a chill," I answered. "I think a little rum, aspirin, lemon and sugar . . ."

"Oh, my dear, I should be sick! Some more soda-water, if you like."

As I refilled her tumbler, my attention was caught by the champagne bottle that I had opened before dinner. We had drunk, allowing for froth, perhaps two glasses each; and there could hardly have been more than two glasses left now. A tappit-hen held three quarts; and two quarts had disappeared since I went to dress.

It was conceivable, I told myself, that the housemaids had been revelling while we were downstairs; but I could not believe that Lord Axminster's housemaids would revel quite in this way.

XI

"THERE's a tremendous lot of this influenza flying about," Dr. Maxton, the Axminsters' local physician, informed me after his first visit. "And I must warn you that it's highly infectious. Fortunately, most of the servants here have already had it, twelve of them—I may tell you—at the same time and not a nurse to be had for love or money! The excellent Mrs. Becket—Lord Axminster's housekeeper, you know—looked after them all; and, if I may suggest it, I should get her to look after Mrs. Whimboyne. It's only a question of keeping her warm, giving her the medicine I'm sending you and taking her temperature night and morning. I can't tell you how sorry I am that this should have happened while you were on your honeymoon."

"If it's only influenza . . . ," I began.

"You must see to it that it *remains* only influenza. This winter's variety has been complicated by rather a lot of septic throats, leading to bronchitis and even pneumonia. The fact is, Mr. Whimboyne," the grey-haired doctor continued, hoisting himself stiffly to the edge of the table, "we're all paying for more than four years of over-work and under-nourishment: our resistance is weak. I don't suppose you remember it, but we met here once before: when you were Lord Axminster's private secretary and poor Honiton had his coming-of-age. You've changed so much that I hardly recognized you at first; *you* don't look as though you would put up the fight I should like to see, against any stray germs or exceptional strains."

"*I* shall be all right," I assured him, "as soon as I know that *she's* all right. Yes, it's only when the springs uncoil that you realize how tightly you've been wound up. I shouldn't have asked whether it was only influenza with my wife if I hadn't been scared by the time you took to examine her! Nearly an hour! Nerves!"

Dr. Maxton answered with a laugh that, when he was seeing new patients for the first time, he liked to study their background and medical history.

"When I come again," he continued, "I shan't need to stay more than ten minutes. Mrs. Whimboyne is very strong: sound lungs, heart like a bell. As soon as her temperature's normal . . . But you mustn't try to push her," he added, frowning. "Since you've mentioned your own nerves, I can tell you that hers are not in a satisfactory state. I suppose the turmoil of all the wedding-preparations, the excitement of embarking on a new life . . . Who's her man in London, by the way?"

"Vaughan Drake. A schoolfellow of her first husband. Do you want a consultation with him?"

"Not if everything goes on as I hope. She ought to be up and out within the week. And there *my* responsibility ends. I was only thinking . . . If you're not satisfied with her nervous condition when you get back to London, let Drake, who knows more of her history than you and I put together, have a look at her. You're both of you too young to be talking about nerves. Well, I'll come back the day after to-morrow, unless you send for me before. And now, if I may have a word with Mrs. Becket . . ."

What that word was I had no means of knowing; but I suspect

it conveyed forcibly that I was to be kept out of the sick-room until the danger of infection was past. This would have been enough for the silver-haired old autocrat whom I remembered as enjoying the reputation of being almost a match for the autocratic Lord Axminster. I suspected also that Elizabeth had inspired the doctor to keep me away till she sent for me. As I sat down to a solitary luncheon, I was handed a pencilled note of overt apology and hinted reproach.

"My dear, this is a funny sort of honeymoon!," she began. *"I'm sorry to be so feeble, but I'm afraid the last few weeks have been too much for me. I shall be better when I've had a little rest; but I've been sleeping so badly that, now I'm in bed, I feel I don't ever want to get out again! That nice Dr. Maxton is sending me some tablets; and Mrs. Becket is looking after me too wonderfully. So there's no need for you to worry; and I shan't worry unless I find I've given my horrible influenza to you."*

I spent the greater part of the first day of my honeymoon walking to the lighthouse and back.

That evening I received word that Elizabeth's temperature was normal; and two days later Dr. Maxton informed me that I could regard her as convalescent.

"You must expect to find her rather limp," he warned me at parting, "but after a few days' feeding-up . . . I'm old-fashioned enough to recommend my patients the judicious use of alcohol: a glass or two of Lord Axminster's burgundy at luncheon and dinner, a glass of port afterwards. Well, good-bye and good luck!"

As I mounted the perilously overpolished stairs to the Bishop's Room, I wondered whether it was my imagination that the doctor had seemed to stress the words "judicious" and "good luck". Had Elizabeth told him anything about the injudicious use of champagne and, as he gripped my hand with unnecessary warmth, was he hinting that I should need all the good luck I could find if I had married a wife who needed to have the cellar-door locked against her?

I might, unless she was a consummate actress, have spared myself all anxiety. Elizabeth, rather white and very listless, was sipping beef-tea as I sat down by her bedside; and, when I mentioned Dr. Maxton's advice about burgundy, she exclaimed with a grimace that not even to please me, not even as medicine, could she be persuaded to touch it.

"That's one of the things I want to get clear about with you, Colin," she continued. "Now that we're married . . . If we're to make a success of it . . . I'm not a pussyfoot, but I simply loathe the taste of every wine that has ever been offered me. I drank some champagne that first night because you said it was a tonic and I was feeling beat-out. You've seen me taking a sip of sherry with you, out of politeness . . ."

"But in old days," I interrupted, "in Montpelier Square . . ."

"A drop at the bottom of the glass, to please Austin! He said it threw a blight over the party if I insisted on drinking water. The same with smoking: I *hate* it, but just to put the other women at their ease . . . I think it's *cruel* to force people who don't like a thing . . ."

As she broke off with a smothered sob, I assured her that I should never try to impose my tastes on her.

"I shan't even tell you that you don't know what you're missing," I went on. "Indeed, I'm rather surprised that Austin . . . There were so many reputed delicacies that he couldn't himself abide: oysters, olives, artichokes . . ."

"He always said I should *learn* to like wine. And all sorts of other things. Well, I haven't! I suppose it's the way you're made. And it's no good saying that all the rest of the world . . . There must be exceptions to every rule; and apparently I'm one of the exceptions."

Though I could divine the answer before I put the question, I asked Elizabeth whether she had any particular rule in mind. Her whole face flamed, from chin to forehead, as she spat out the word "love-making" at me.

"I hate thinking about it!," she cried; and, as though we had put back the clock a week, I felt that I could see her thinking about it, bolting the door and hurrying to the turret-room with some memory of hearing about people who made themselves too drunk even to think. "I hate talking about it!," she went on; and, as though we had put the clock back a month, I could see her flushing scarlet as we sat after dinner in London and she spurred herself to speak of the "horrid" physical aspect of marriage and the vileness of men who wanted only one thing. I understood Dr. Maxton's rather solemn reference to nerves, his sympathy over the misfortune that had befallen us on our honeymoon and his advice that, when his own responsibility was ended, I should call in the physician who might be presumed to know Elizabeth's history. "All that *side* . . . ," she ended, convulsively covering her face with her hands.

"It's generally regarded as rather an important factor in married life," I observed mildly.

"That's the way Austin used to speak! He was absolutely blasphemous at times, talking about 'immaculate conceptions'!"

"You wanted *children*. . . . Did you say anything to him before you married? I'm afraid *I* never grasped at all . . . *Modesty* I can understand, or *shyness*. . . . To marry, though, either with no intention of consummating the marriage or else with such a horror of the consummation beforehand . . ."

"Well, the marriage has *been* consummated!", Elizabeth answered behind her teeth. "You promised—what was it?—that you would never impose your tastes on me. Oh, I *can't* go on talking about these things, Colin! I suppose I thought you would be different from Austin . . ."

By the calendar on her writing-table I saw that there was still a fortnight of Axminster's hospitality to run; and, as though we had put the clock forward two weeks, I felt that I could see the pair of us on our journey back to London, brooding over our singular honeymoon. For all the time remaining to us here, Elizabeth would continue as limp as Dr. Maxton had warned me to expect. Despite his tablets, she would still be suffering from insomnia; and the presence of any one in her room would prevent her going to sleep. When she hoped to find me different from Austin, I could not be sure whether she had hoped to find me less repellent or less desirous; but I could promise the two of us with equal fervour and good faith that I should never resemble him in asserting any conjugal rights.

"This requires some digesting," I muttered, still staring at the silver-framed calendar.

Nineteen-hundred-and-eighteen. I was a few months over thirty, Elizabeth a couple of years under. Physically, I was as sound as Maxton had declared her to be. There was no obvious reason why we should not both live to be eighty and to celebrate our golden wedding.

"I suppose I've disappointed you," she sighed, much as though she were telling me that she had accepted an invitation to tea before remembering that she was already engaged.

"I was wondering why you bothered to marry me," I answered.

Unless she was a consummate actress, there was no doubting the genuineness of her anger and amazement.

"*That's* a nice thing to say!," she cried. "I married you, Colin, because I loved you. Of *all* Austin's friends . . . I suppose you'll think I was jealous of him. I wasn't, but of all the people who were *so* brilliant, *so* witty, you were the only one who thought me worth talking to. You were the only one who took the faintest interest in Martin and Humfrey, the only one who looked me up when Austin went out, the only one who tried to help me when he was killed. It's a wicked thing to say, but I sometimes thought, even when he was still alive, how different everything would have been if *you* and I . . . When he . . . didn't come back, I swore I would never marry again. I couldn't go through all *that* a second time, but I said I should always have *you*. When I thought you'd dropped out . . ."

As she checked with another dry sob, I reminded her that I had only kept away because she told me that no one at that time could do anything for her.

"I knew about you and Isabel Pryde," she continued, as though she had not heard me. "I loved you so that it nearly broke my heart, because you would never have been happy with her. . . . But I expect you would rather I never mentioned her name!"

"There's no point in digging up what's over and done with," I answered. "It's the future we have to consider. Isabel is as dead to me as Austin is to you."

I fancy I must have winced or faltered over the name, for Elizabeth opened her arms to me as on the night when I collapsed like an hysterical child; but it was not any grieving for Isabel that unnerved me now and no amount of maternal crooning or petting could have soothed me. If indeed I had betrayed any emotion, it was helpless dismay. The more Elizabeth talked about love, the less she seemed to understand the simplest meaning of the word. She liked me as a contrast to Austin's other and more impatient friends; perhaps she idealized me as a contrast to the occasionally rather brutal Austin himself; she was vaguely grateful to me; and no doubt she felt that she could depend on me. This, though, was not my conception of love.

"What do you mean," she asked in honest perplexity, "about the 'future'?"

"I want to arrange something that will preserve us both from murder or suicide! This is not a passing whim? However long we live, you wish us to have separate rooms? So be it! Do you expect me, however long we live, to remain technically faithful? Have you the right to ask that?"

"It would be *adultery* . . . ," Elizabeth began solemnly. "And what you find to laugh at in that . . . !"

"I was laughing at the thought of this conversation at this time, in this place! D'you imagine in all the world's history any other men and women have talked about divorce on their *honeymoon?*"

"*Divorce?* What d'you mean? We've never mentioned the subject! You can't divorce me, I'm your wife, for all we know I'm going to bear you a child! And you're my husband! I couldn't divorce you if I would, I wouldn't if I could! '*Whom God hath joined!*' . . . You're not like Austin, are you, Colin? You don't make mock of sacred things? The way you talk of *murder* and *adultery* . . ."

As she paused, I wondered—idly and unprofitably—whether Austin had in fact ever talked in this way.

"It looks as though we had made rather a mistake in marrying," I said. "No good discussing whose fault it was! Better see what we can save from the ruins! I can't accept a marriage that is no marriage. If you would rather not break it formally and openly, we must break it informally and discreetly. You shall have your freedom, but I must have mine. If the result is adultery, that will be my look-out . . ."

"And you'll say I drove you to it. Men always do!"

So far as my numbed brain allowed me to think, I reflected that I, as a man, had known many other men who had committed adultery, but that none of them had ever said he was driven to it. I found it a little hard to believe that Elizabeth, a woman who regarded sex as "horrid" and would have spoken more delicately of "breaking the seventh commandment", had received enough confessions of adultery to justify her rather bold generalization. At best or worst I could imagine a single dialogue in which one man admitted his unfaithfulness and she exclaimed that this was adultery and he retorted that he had been driven to it.

I could not readily imagine an exchange of this kind between Elizabeth and Austin, as I could not easily believe that he would have tolerated for five minutes a wife, in his favourite phrase, with so much nonsense about her. And yet it was harder to credit that any other man had taken her into his confidence; and of a sudden I recalled my last meeting with Austin, when he expatiated on the wisdom of having a second house to which one could retreat if it ever seemed that husband and wife were seeing too much of each other.

"I shan't say you drove me to being unfaithful," I promised, "unless you find it necessary to tell the world of my unfaithfulness. I'm a man of flesh and blood, though. If I tried to live the life you're suggesting . . . Well, I told you I was considering the best way of avoiding murder or suicide or both."

"You don't seriously mean that you would commit suicide . . . ?," Elizabeth began in horror.

I begged her to make her mind easy on this point. At one season of great unhappiness I had wished myself dead, but always I lacked the courage to take my own life.

"Like that man in Kipling's *Love o' Women*," I added. "I had a perfectly good razor, I could have borrowed my brother's revolver, I had even been giving a sleeping-draught that would have settled my hash in five minutes if I'd drunk the whole bottle. I couldn't! If I'd been serving, I might have persuaded some obliging sniper to put a bullet through my brain, but by 1917 it wasn't so easy for civil servants to get taken into the army as when Austin joined up . . ."

"Colin, are you suggesting that *Austin* . . . ?" She was trying, I suppose, to ask whether I dared to suggest that Austin was so tired of life that he had taken a commission in the hope of meeting an obliging sniper who would do for him what he feared to do for himself. No thought of the kind had ever entered my head; but, as I looked into Elizabeth's tortured eyes, I saw that a thought of this kind was no stranger to her. "Colin!," she repeated peremptorily. "I'm asking you a question! You've already hinted that I drove Austin to adultery! Now you're hinting that I drove him to suicide!"

"I've not said or hinted or thought anything of the kind! I've not mentioned Austin's name except to say that I don't want a *post mortem* on his life with you. It's your life with me, mine with you, that we have to plan. Our marriage, apparently, has come to an end almost before it began. I gather you won't divorce me or let me divorce you. Perhaps you're right: I'm really too dazed to say. Perhaps a *façade* ... For the sake of Martin and Humfrey ... But, if it's all over, we'd better face it frankly and at once."

XII

THOUGH I have more than once stayed in tedious parties that have goaded a desperate fellow-guest to having himself called away by telegram, I have not used this mode of escape for myself nor borrowed it for any character in a play. In general, I am not easily bored; and, though my friends include several aspirants to the title of "Queen Bromide", I am always fascinated by the sound of their unfailing flow as I suppose a lover of billiards is fascinated by the sight of an unending break. Surely, we say, the eye and the hand, the tongue and brain must weary some time. This anchor-cannon, already scoring in thousands, will end before life itself ends; these pretentious platitudes will dry up some day; as the miller wakes when the mill stops, we want to be there when the great silence begins.

My experience, moreover, has been that these inspired telegrams are always too flawless to be wholly convincing. As a civil servant, I could at almost any time have had myself summoned to London by an inconsiderate minister or a harassed under-secretary; but not in the first week of my honeymoon. And my immediate comment, when I received an express-letter calling me to my mother's bedside, was that no one—Elizabeth and Dr. Maxton least of all—would believe that I had not told my brothers to send for me.

Here, indeed, I was entirely wrong. My wife's fear that I, like Austin, might mock at sacred things was varied by a baseless suspicion that I might jest about serious things; but, taste and natural feelings apart, she needed no persuading that I should not invent a fatal illness for my mother as a device for getting away from Bowbury Castle. And that the illness would prove fatal I had little doubt after I had shewn the doctor my brother's letter.

"A few years ago," he told me, "it would probably have been diagnosed as *angina pectoris* or perhaps 'false *angina*'. From the symptoms, I'm inclined to call it thrombosis of the coronary artery. She must be kept absolutely still and quiet, probably for several months. After that, if she avoids all strain, all exertion. . . ."

"There's no cure?," I interrupted.

"Her own man will give her some high-explosive to take if she has another attack, but you must face the possibility of other attacks. And one of them will be the last. It may be the heart, it may be the brain. You may hear that she had been found dead in her bed one morning, which would certainly be an enviable end; or she may have a stroke or succession of strokes, which would be less pleasant. There's nothing *you* can do."

"I must go to her," I said.

"Oh, obviously. And, as I understand the house is yours, no doubt you can arrange a bedroom on the ground-floor for her. Though she's not my patient and it's really no affair of mine, I should *not* advise your taking Mrs. Whimboyne with you. She's well enough, but I think it might alarm your mother if three sons and three daughters-in-law all arrived with anxious faces."

I promised to hand on his opinion to my wife, though I did not say that this was quite certainly what Elizabeth and I were both tacitly hoping that he would recommend. When the remaining fortnight of Axminster's hospitality had run its course, the cleaning and distempering in Grosvenor Road would be finished; before I returned from Ridgeway House, she could dispose the bedrooms for herself and me, for Martin and Humfrey, as she thought best; and, by the time that she brought the boys back from a family Christmas with her parents, I might have roughed out a pattern for the life that we were to lead.

In this, I had divined already, I should receive no help from Elizabeth, who was genuinely convinced that we had no pattern to make. We were married, the marriage had been consummated and, as I must know, there were certain subjects that she could not and would not discuss. For the rest, our design for living had really been settled for us during the few and feverish days of our engagement. It might be said, not unfairly, that I had tossed her my design with one hand (pointing a pistol at her head with the other) and that she had accommodated herself to it without protest.

Was that not the woman's expected part? It was certainly the part that she had played with Austin.

"He was the bread-winner," she recalled, as she gave me back the letter in which I had explained to the Winters that she would

probably arrive in Grosvenor Road before me. "And he had a
career. Well, you have two, Colin! It was my business to look after
the family and the house and to entertain his friends. Used you to
give many parties? I know you have a visiting-list as long as my
arm."

"As a bachelor," I said, "I was more entertained against than
entertaining. I hope I repaid all the cutlets I was offered, but in
general I would always rather dine with one sympathetic person
or alone with a book. . . . Big parties . . ."

"That's what Austin used to *say*, but it never worked out like
that. In all the years we were married, the number of nights when
we dined by ourselves . . ."

I said something banal about his incurable sociability, but I
was thinking of the first time that I had broken bread in Montpelier Square and of Austin's odd and pressing invitation for, I
think, the following night. He had always enjoyed the clash of
mind against mind; in the years that followed this first party I
sometimes wondered how he could afford to entertain so prodi-
gally; and, since Elizabeth had testified that I was the only guest
who troubled to notice her existence, I felt that she had not
extracted much amusement from his so witty and brilliant friends.
Remembering my own conversational agonizings, I wondered a
little uncharitably whether some of Austin's parties had been
expressly contrived to keep him from dining alone with Elizabeth.

"We must see what life in London is going to be like after the
war," I suggested. "If I stay on in the civil service . . . ," I continued in the hope of beginning a general discussion that would
enable us to compare and exchange, perhaps even to blend, what
I have called our patterns.

"But surely all that was *settled*," Elizabeth broke in with a
frown.

And it was at this moment that I saw there was, at least in her
view, no pattern to consider. It had all been settled. The bread-
winner, who had made himself responsible for a wife and a ready-
made family, perhaps—who could say?—for a second family (of
one), would continue in a service that brought him a covenanted
salary and the promise of a pension; he must live in London to be
near his work; and she would therefore uncomplainingly move
herself and the ready-made family into his ready-made home.

I need hardly say that this phrase was not used by her or me;
but I have no kind of doubt that it would have accurately ex-

pressed Elizabeth's mental attitude. Austin was dead; and his best friend, to whose care he had committed her, was now stepping into his shoes.

Meanwhile, my mother's illness and perhaps swiftly approaching death threw all our private petty adjustments into the shade: I must take the first train to Marlborough, Elizabeth would accompany or follow me if her presence would in any way help me; otherwise, in the words of that old song that Austin used to sing before he went out, she would "*keep the home fires burning*" for me.

I did not feel that her presence would help me in any way; and, on reaching Ridgeway House, I quickly found that I should have no time for considering petty adjustments in the life that I was expected to regard as settled. Dr. Maxton's long-distance diagnosis had been accurate enough so far as it went, but my mother's state was already worse than he had led me to expect. She was in bed when I arrived: in the bed that she was to keep till she was found dead in it one brilliant morning in the following early spring. The stroke for which I must be prepared at any time had already incapacitated her right side; and, though her brain seemed clear, she remained till the end so tired that my brothers and I talked to her as we should have talked to a sick child, almost in whispers, almost in baby-language, a dozen simple words at a time.

"It's rough luck on you that this should have happened while you were on your honeymoon," said John the first night, after dinner. "Something had to be arranged, though. I suggest that the three of us should take it in turns to mount guard for a month at a time. If we go by order of age, you'll get a couple of months for settling down in London. I don't know whether you *can* live here and work there, but if Elizabeth takes charge and you come down for week-ends . . ."

"I'm sure something can be arranged," I said. "Perhaps, as I've still a week or two of leave to run, I had better take the first watch."

So in fact it was arranged. By the time John and Blanche arrived to relieve me, Elizabeth had pegged out our spheres in Grosvenor Road and taken her boys for their Christmas gathering; I had sketched an acceptable time-table for my attendance at the Lord Keeper's Department; and, drifting with a notebook and pencil about the dilapidated house and neglected gardens while

I

my mother dozed, I had worked out a crude specification of what needed to be done if Ridgeway House was to be habitable by the standards of 1918.

Who was to inhabit it after my mother I did not trouble myself to ask. It might be a holiday-home for us all, it might be—as in fact it became—the permanent home for Elizabeth and her children when she decided that they needed to live in country air, it might be a week-end retreat in which I joined her, or it might be the permanent home for me when she decided that she needed to live in London near the boys' schools and I decided that I must live in the country to secure peace and quiet for my literary work. Which of all these courses we should adopt as our pattern I should know better when I had spent a few weeks in Grosvenor Road under the pattern favoured by Elizabeth; but the more I brooded over her casual reference to life with Austin the more I felt that I should never step into his shoes, still less into a pair of his shoes altered by her to fit me.

When I was not making simple, bedside conversation to my poor, pathetically tired mother or jotting down ideas for repairs and improvements, I had my hands amply filled with the letters of congratulation and good wishes that followed on the announcement of my marriage. "Masses of friends" had been attributed to me by Elizabeth, who—when I came to think of it—seemed to have no friends of her own; and certainly I was confronted with a flatteringly long list of men and women who insisted on our dining with them the moment we returned to London and who were not to be denied the pleasure of giving a wedding-present by my churlishness in being married privately before a registrar. I forwarded the letters to Elizabeth; and, when I joined her in Grosvenor Road half-way through January, I found that she had completed a businesslike inventory of my effects and compiled a businesslike estimate of the extent to which obvious deficiencies could be made good by the generosity of my solicitous friends.

"Winter tells me he's been on at you for years about a new dessert-service," she informed me. "And Mrs. Winter was talking about little breakfast-sets on trays. I see Clayton says something about a coffee-service, but Winter says we don't need another yet; and Clement Phayre suggests a gramophone. We ought to have a gramophone, Colin."

"I've avoided having one for ten years," I said, "because I can't abide the things."

"It would amuse the boys," Elizabeth replied. "We mustn't think only of ourselves."

"Then let it be kept in the schoolroom," I begged. "Now what about all these people who want us to dine with them?" Without hesitation, Elizabeth answered that I must accept every invitation I had received. If she had to be quite honest, one dinner-party—in her experience—was very like another; but these were my friends and she hoped that in time they would become her friends. She would certainly never be able to forgive herself if any of them ever said that they and I had drifted apart after our marriage.

"I suppose we must go through with it," I said, "but I want you to understand from the beginning that parties, as such, I simply abhor. An *intimate* affair is different: two old friends, like the Oakhirsts, say . . ."

"Violet Oakhirst wants to know whether we should like *books*. I should have thought you had enough books already; but I suppose, as one high-brow to another . . ."

"She's offering me her father's Edinburgh Stevenson," I interrupted. "If she feels in cold blood that she can spare it, I shall accept it gratefully. So would any man in his senses."

I know that I spoke a little impatiently; but I am not sure, even thirty years later, why I felt impatient. Perhaps it was the impatience of the collector with one who condemned all books as dust-traps; perhaps I resented Elizabeth's division of my friends (as of Austin's aforetime) into high-brows and others; perhaps I detected a sneer or a hint of jealousy. Most probably, I think, I did not want to talk about Violet or to picture my first meeting with her after four years. Faithful to my promise, when she wrote from abroad to enquire casually about my rumoured engagement, I had told her before any one else when there was an engagement to announce; she had written to congratulate me in terms which made me feel that my happiness was the one thing that could make her happy; and, since I could never hope to impose on her for two minutes, I suppose I was dreading the scrutiny of those searching brown eyes which would tell her without a word from me that I was not happy.

And yet, if I was not to lose Nigel and Violet, I must meet them some time.

"Let's take them first," I suggested. "The first of the nights they offer . . ."

"Shall I have to sit next to Nigel?," Elizabeth enquired.

"As the bride and guest of honour . . . Don't you like him?"

"I never know what to talk to him about."

I said that I, on the other hand, never knew how to stop Nigel talking. If she needed a subject, I reminded her that he and I had shared this house for a few months before his marriage; she could tell him of the changes that we had made and, after that, he would tell her of the changes that he had made in his Barton Street house until it was time for us all to ask for taxis.

As I spoke, still more as Elizabeth nodded approval of my suggestion, I wondered whether Austin had been consulted in the same way and whether that single question—"Are you working on a new play?" or "Haven't you been out to America since last I saw you?"—had been inspired by him in response to the plaint that she never knew what to discuss with any of her neighbours at a dinner-table. Certainly in the next few weeks I found myself stepping into Austin's shoes to the extent of explaining that A had worked with me at the Ministry of Munitions or B was the man whose novel had lately been banned. I did not always hear Elizabeth's question; but that she had asked it I deduced from the resultant monologue on gun-mountings or the liberty of the press.

It was only for a few weeks, as I was soon recalled to Ridgeway House; and, when I returned to London, I suggested that the inevitable uncertainty of my movements furnished a perfect excuse for avoiding a form of social life that bored us equally.

"We shall have to ask all of them back," Elizabeth sighed. "In common decency . . ."

"In God's good time! If we're still alive, if we're still here . . ."

"What d'you mean: 'if we're still here'?"

"My mother won't be with us for long. When she goes, we must decide what's to be done with Ridgeway House. And we must decide what's to be done with *ourselves*. I won't take you over the ground that we covered at Bowbury Castle; but, if we both insist on our liberty, we must consider how it's to be arranged. When Ridgeway falls vacant, we shall have the chance of a lifetime to put things on a sensible footing. I can stay here and you can live there, meeting amicably at week-ends; or you can stay here . . ."

As I paused, Elizabeth asked angrily why I found it necessary to talk such nonsense.

"How could you possibly live in Wiltshire and work in London?," she demanded.

"I'm perfectly willing to give up working in London."

"And leave me to starve?"

"I hope not! But, as you gave up your own house to come here, I didn't feel it would be fair for me to turn you out if you want to stay here. Once again, though, if you want your liberty, I must have mine. With two houses, it should be quite easy. If you attach importance to appearances, we can quite easily keep them up. Health . . . Exigencies of my work . . . If we're seen living harmoniously together at week-ends, nobody need ever know that we're not living as husband and wife. It's for you to choose which of us lives here."

As I waited for her answer, Elizabeth muttered something that sounded like: "You do hate me, don't you?"

"Not in the least," I said, "but the bottom has dropped out of our marriage and you couldn't put it back if you told me to forget every word you'd spoken at Bowbury. That's all over. I'm as indifferent to you as you are to me, but I'm a normal man and I suspect we shall get very badly on each other's nerves if I try to lead an abnormal life. We can be friends, perhaps . . . In time, perhaps, when the age of passion is over . . . But we mustn't see too much of each other."

"And I shouldn't care if I never saw this house again! It's cold, damp . . . Half the time you *can't* see it for fog! What possessed you to settle in the bed of the Thames . . ."

"If you consider it's unhealthy, you should think twice before sending Martin and Humfrey to Westminster, which is just as much in the river-bed. In spite of that, the school is generally regarded as remarkably healthy. I may be wrong, but I thought the chief attraction of this house was that it lay so near to the school. Martin and Humfrey could live here and go as day-boys . . ."

Since coming to live in Grosvenor Road, Elizabeth informed me, she had thought many more times than twice about sending her boys to a London school. The idea had been Austin's; and she would have abandoned it long ago if I had not backed his choice. Philip was sending Alexander and Hilary to Charterhouse, which stood on a hill; Maurice, in compliment to Lady Jane, had already entered little Angus for Fettes. If they were not so far away, she would have chosen Sedbergh or Rossall or St. Bees'.

"You might do worse than Marlborough," I suggested. "It's within a walk of Ridgeway House. Certainly you should keep this question in mind when you're deciding where and how we're going to live. We can't do anything while my poor mother lingers on; but, as I told you at Bowbury, we must face facts. I'll do my best to help, I'll consider any proposal you care to make, I see no reason why we shouldn't remain friends even if our marriage has not turned out quite as we expected. In many ways I still think that a divorce . . ."

I stopped as Winter came in to say that I was wanted on the telephone. Dropping his mask of reserve, he murmured solicitously that he was afraid it was bad news. My mother, it seemed, had had another stroke; he had ordered a taxi; and the bag that I kept ready-packed was standing in the hall.

I reached Ridgeway House to find her unconscious; and she died early the next morning.

Telephoning to Elizabeth, I said that I should stay in the country till after the funeral. She replied that, though she had never met my mother, she would like to attend it as a mark of respect to her and of sympathy to me.

"I'm *really* sorry, Colin," she added. "I want to help and I want you to help me in helping you. Can't we forget all that we said to each other last night? I still shudder when I remember that your last word before the blow fell was 'divorce'. You must never, never say that again! I'm sorry if I was tiresome, but I really wasn't myself. Colin . . . Can you hear? Colin . . . I'm going to have a baby."

PART TWO

I

DURING the last weeks of my mother's life I had been enquiring among my neighbours for the name of a good local architect; and a day or two after the funeral I arranged with the one of Major Plimsoll's choice, Anstruther Nesbitt of Marlborough, to consider the plans that I had sketched for modernizing the house.

Since my indolent brothers and their supine wives had long since waived all claims of seniority, I felt no obligation to consult them about changes that I should have carried out by now for my mother's benefit, if she had been less ill; but, as her death frustrated the ostensible purpose for which I had bought Ridgeway, I was not sorry to hear their comments if I told them that I had decided to put the place up for sale again. As secretary—since he was invalided out of the army—of the Stonebeach Golf Club, John had been responsible for the refurnishing of the dormy-house; Henry, as agent to Lord Drury, had in the last few years pulled down, rebuilt and sold a not inconsiderable portion of residential Warwickshire. My own experience of builders and decorators was confined to the superficial refurbishing of my London house at the time of my marriage.

"I'm not committed to anything, even mentally," I told my brothers when we were by ourselves after dinner on their last night. "I would have paid a big sum to make our mother a bit more comfortable, but there wasn't time for that. If I like, I have good reason to think that I could get out of the speculation without much loss; and I've always believed that, if I spent several thousands, it would be an extraordinarily good investment. Do I *want* an investment of that kind? Have I time and strength for the labour of revolutionizing the place? Do I want to remodel what is after all our old home for some one else to live in? I don't know yet."

"And obviously Henry and I can't know for you," said John. "Would you get any fun out of making the alterations? Messing about with bricks and mortar has never appealed to me."

I felt that it would have been difficult for the head of the family, impossible for me, to say what did appeal to him. The passage of time, more than worry or work, had powdered his thick black hair, increasing the family-resemblance to our good-looking father, though his flat-cheeked, bony face was still unlined and his brown eyes had not yet acquired our father's melancholy. Had Austin been with us, he would probably have observed that John and Henry, though dead, were not yet decomposing; perhaps he would have charged the squire with compassing their deaths by intriguing them into jobs that required no effort to keep them alive; certainly he would have warned me that I, with my resolve to warm both hands at the fire of life, should not get even good advice from them.

"I'm interested in creating *anything*," I answered, trying not to remember too vividly either Austin's vague hint that this would be an amusing diversion or my own frantic feeling that the responsibilities of Ridgeway might at least help to preserve my sanity against the assaults of Isabel Pryde's ghost.

"You rule out all question of living here yourself?," Henry drawled.

He too, I thought, had become more like our father in the last five years, if only in his addiction to good living; and, though he remained spare and upright, he seemed slower in mind and heavier in body.

"I rule out nothing," I said. "One could work here, but it's a big place for a man's private bolt-hole and it offers no attractions to Elizabeth. Why should it?"

"If she has the eye of faith . . .," Henry began. "Unlike John, bricks and mortar have an endless fascination for me: I can see—after all, it's part of my job—the possibilities of this pláce and I daresay Elizabeth sees them too. She told me to-day that she'd started with rather a prejudice against Ridgeway—chiefly, I think, on account of the expense—but that she now thought you could make something rather good of it without breaking yourself. Who's this fellow Nesbitt, by the way? I don't remember any of his work."

I suggested that we should adjourn for a moment to the library, where Nelson Keys (as I had nicknamed my prospective architect) had left a portfolio of photographs and plans. We could take our wine with us, I added, as I felt sure that the ladies were in no hurry for us to join them: rather to my surprise, Elizabeth seemed to have confided in Blanche and Constance that she was

going to have (what she persisted in calling) a "little" baby and I
suspected that by now the party in the saloon had constituted
itself a jury of matrons. For my part, though I did not tell my
brothers so, I was in no hurry to join the ladies till I had been
given a few moments to think over my wife's change of attitude
to Ridgeway. "My wife", I said to myself, because Elizabeth
seemed—ever since that telephone-conversation after my mother's
death—to be throwing herself heart-and-soul into the part of
present wife, future mother and (to borrow the "lovely old
word" that I had once used) eternal helpmeet. I could not quite
make it all out.

The farther, indeed, that the nightmare of our honeymoon
receded, the less I was able to make Elizabeth out at all. Despite
the delicate euphemisms that we both increasingly employed, she
insisted on her liberty; she did not remind me again that the
marriage, which I called no marriage, had been consummated,
but she hinted unambiguously that she had done her duty and
that only a man with a one-track mind would wish to dwell on
the "horrid" side of marriage now. Who could believe me if I
protested that we had been set apart for ever in the first hours of
our honeymoon?

I paid her the compliment of accepting that she had spoken
the truth about this coming child, but I could no longer feel sure
of her about anything. After her warping experience of one
husband, what had induced her to take a second? In somewhat
less cruel language than her sister Kitty had used about Cinderella
and her fairy princes, I could readily believe that a young woman
who had moved from the shadow of a masterful father and
brothers into that of a yet more masterful husband might feel
unequal to struggling, single-handed and with two small children
at her heels, with the daily problems of life. I could even, with an
effort, force myself to imagine that some phrase during our brief
engagement had misled her into thinking that I was as indifferent
sexually as herself. Was she abnormally stupid? Was she abnormally cunning? Was she a normal woman who was abnormal, to
the point of mania, on a single subject?

"I see our old nursery wing is to be bachelor bedrooms,"
observed Henry, bending over my rough plans.

"A south-east aspect instead of a north-west one," I explained.

"And our mother's old boudoir will be your dressing-room?

You're making bathrooms for Elizabeth and yourself out of our father's old dressing-room?"

"The boudoir will be *a* dressing-room. I don't say it will be mine, because I don't know yet what I'm going to do with the place, but these are the principal *chambres de maître* and nobody in 1919 is going to put up with a Victorian double-bed and a pill-box bathroom between the two. I've been wondering about the billiard-room," I went on to John, who was looking at the ground-floor plan. "The table needs new cushions and a new cloth, but is anybody going to play on it? And a smoking-room when women smoke everywhere . . ."

As I had expected, John declared at once that billiards had been killed by bridge; as I had hoped, Henry asserted that this was untrue of Scotland and the north of England; and, as I had intended, I was able to end the discussion of bedrooms by recalling the advice of Axminster 'that in my travels through England I should always turn south when people began to call a smoking-room a "smoke-room".

"I'm inclined," I added, "to make the billiard-room a book-room."

In fact, this was what I had said to Elizabeth earlier in the day, when she found me inking in my pencilled sketches. If, I added at once, I decided to keep Ridgeway for my own use, but at present I had decided nothing. I had then been told in a fittingly muted tone that on a day like this I could not be expected to decide anything, but that—with John and Henry in the house—I might do worse than take their opinion. As—comparatively—old married men, they might help me.

I had wondered at the time, I wondered again now, what help or advice or opinion my brothers could give if I told them the full and true story of my life since the evening nearly three years ago when I was ushered into Lord Wansborough's drawing-room in Hill Street to find his eldest daughter reading in a circle of lamp-light. I wondered what the full and true story would prove to be when it reached the evening when I asked Elizabeth to marry me. Would they say that we had married on false pretences? Would they tell me that I must go through with it for the sake of my promised child? Would these comparatively old married men talk sagely of a woman's whims, urging me to be patient and reminding me that I must have been in love before I proposed and could not now be as indifferent as I asserted?

"You can make it a good house for entertaining," said Henry, counting the bedrooms on his fingers. "In fact, you *must*. After London, you'll find it pretty quiet here just by yourselves."

"Once again," I replied, "I don't know whether we *shall* live here, whether I may come here to work, whether Elizabeth would like to make this her headquarters, with me coming down for week-ends. As I've told you, until she saw the place, she was prejudiced against it."

And now? Her prejudice now seemed to be against Grosvenor Road, with its imagined damp and rather exaggerated fogs. Strolling on the Downs the afternoon of her arrival, she had filled and emptied and filled her lungs; then, reminding me that it had been my suggestion, she asked me what I thought of Marlborough as a school for Martin and Humfrey, perhaps—in time— for "some one else". On our return to the house, she begged me to explain my proposed alterations; and, after staring rather blankly at the plans, she informed me that she approved in advance anything that I—the bread-winner—thought best for myself and all of them.

"How long," John enquired, "does this fellow Nesbitt think the alterations will take?"

"About two months," I answered.

"Then, from my experience," said Henry, "you should allow four. Even so, if you want Elizabeth to be here when the baby's born . . ."

"That's a thing for her to decide. And a comparatively small thing. On Nesbitt's estimate, I can pay for the alterations out of money that has been lying on deposit simply because I haven't had time to invest it. Until the public tires of me, I can afford a house here and another in London. If and when I write myself out, I've no doubt I could let the one or the other at a profit. And so long as I stay in the Lord Keeper's Department . . . Though I couldn't live here and work there . . ."

I paused as John, apologizing for fraternal bluntness, enquired whether Elizabeth had any money of her own.

"Austin must have left her something," I answered, "but her father literally *enjoys* the reputation of being as mean to his own flesh-and-blood as he's rich. I've no idea! And I sometimes wonder whether she has any idea either."

"She must know whether she was paying her way after Austin died," Henry objected. "And she must surely know whether she can afford to send her boys to Marlborough, which she'll find a deal more expensive than having them as day-boys at Westminster. Of course, if the rich and mean father is making himself responsible for their education . . ."

Knowing nothing, I could say nothing; but I was interested to note how much Elizabeth had apparently said to my brothers and their wives, none of whom she had met before except for an hour or two when we sat waiting, four and a half years earlier, for a reply to the ultimatum of 4 August. Naturally, they took it for granted that we were happily married and that we were considering only the change that my mother's death might make in our plans for a common life. Since she had told them almost as soon as she had told me, they seemed to assume that we both wished her confinement to take place at Ridgeway; and, since she had evidently discussed with them the advantages of Marlborough for Martin and Humfrey, I felt that she and they had decided I must mean to make my home here. Though she might say that she approved in advance whatever I arranged, I suspected that she had arranged in advance what our life was to be and now waited for me to approve it.

"Elizabeth's very keen that you shouldn't give up the civil service," John told me. "I think she's right. I'm only a simple soldier—or *was*, till they invalided me out—, but I don't believe *anybody* knows what the next few years are going to be like."

On this subject too the family seemed to have been taken into her confidence.

"If I stay on," I said, "it will mean that she must either live in London, which doesn't appeal to her as it once did, or forgo the charms of my society for most of the week."

"You can get down, as you've said, for week-ends. And she wouldn't have much chance of enjoying your society if you're working in your department all day and writing masterpieces half the night. However, it's no affair of mine. When you begin your alterations, what will you arrange about your staff? I wouldn't poach any of your servants for the world, but if you're going just to put in a caretaker . . . Good servants are not easy to come by, these days."

"For that reason," I replied, "*if* I undertake these alterations, I think I had better put every one on board wages. I don't want to find myself in three months' time with a new, clean house and nobody to keep it clean."

"You could bring down Elizabeth's lot. Didn't she make them over to her sister with the house and furniture? I thought so! And from something she said I gather they're not altogether happy. With all respect to Kitty, I'm not greatly surprised. She has a temper and she has a tongue!"

I said that I too was not surprised; but, though I did not say so, I was a little surprised that Elizabeth should have discussed with John the staffing of Ridgeway before I had decided whether we were going to live there, still more that she should have talked to him about the excellent Cruikshanks before talking about them to me. In a shadowy corner of memory there lingered the echo of a phrase that I seemed to have heard in Montpelier Square: "I wish *you* would tell Austin that, Colin! He would pay more attention to you." Had she been saying to John: "You're his brother, he would take it from you"?

As we finished our wine and I packed up Anstruther Nesbitt's plans in his portfolio, I wished that I could have added a "Plan For Living" on the lines of Austin's great *Sauve Qui Peut* of my father on the field of Waterloo. Elizabeth seemed to have provided in detail for every emergency. She had successfully enlisted my brothers' support at every stage. There was a line of retreat from every position that might prove untenable; but, if I read her mind aright, she would feel that she had consolidated each position as she won it and that any retreat would be by me.

Did I read her mind aright? Do I now? Some of the sentiments and sentences that we had exchanged between December and April were unforgettable. Her liberty and mine; my indifference to her, which was as complete as her indifference to me; the need for skilful tactics if we were not to get on each other's nerves; murder or suicide if we failed to make a design for life! Even if we had not meant them, we should remember that we had said them, that we had been capable of saying them and that some of them had been said in cold blood. The most mawkish excesses of the First Film Age were still to come, but mawkishness had its addicts in the circulating-libraries and the theatres: I could imagine a strong scene, with all the strength of concentrated saccharine, in which a roving husband was called to heel by the announcement that a "little" baby was expected, but I could not now see Elizabeth in the part. We might, as I had told her, become friends in time; our common interest in this child might make the time shorter, the friendship more cordial; but she knew from my own lips that my interest in her was dead and, so far as I could see, she was planning and contriving that this (however regrettable) should make no difference. There would be no divorce, no scandal, no whisper even of estrangement or coolness; and, turning that word divorce over on my tongue, I seemed to see the two of us in "the Bishop's Room" at Bowbury Castle and to hear Elizabeth shrilly repeating "*Divorce?* But you're my *husband*!" By an appropriate coincidence, my brothers and I reached the saloon in time to hear her saying: "In my opinion it's the duty of every *husband* . . . I mean, with *husband* and *wife* . . ." Then she interrupted herself to ask whether she might have another look at Nesbitt's portfolio.

I said that I would bring it her as soon as we had drunk our coffee; but, remembering the incomprehension that she had displayed in looking at the plans before, I volunteered to arrange a personally-conducted party round the house if anybody wanted to see it and would wait till daylight.

"Including the attics?", Henry enquired.

"If any one cares to see 'Mad Marion's' private apartments," I said.

"Do I know about 'Mad Marion'?," asked Elizabeth.

"Does any one?," John asked in his turn. "She was the third wife of the much-marrying Whimboyne who built this house. We, by the way, are all descended from the second wife, Eleanor, so we owe none of our madness to poor Marion. Well, according to one story, the general dreariness of this place sent her off her head; according to another, she was always so nearly off her head that Hugo brought her to live in the country where she could be kept hidden. At times she became violent; and, as there was no private asylum in those days, the unhappy creature was confined in the attics, where you can still see her handcuffs and leg-irons. If I were you, Colin, I should unload all that on some museum: it's just the least bit gruesome."

I said that, as these dark, unventilated attics were never used even as lumber-rooms, it would be a simple solution to turn a key on them.

"And the 'Ridgeway windows'?," Henry enquired doubtfully. " 'Mad Marion' was always planning ingenious means of suicide," he explained to Elizabeth, "and every window in the house above ground-floor level is barred. It was very well done, too: what you would take for a Georgian small-pane sash-window is really an iron grille encased in wood. The house can be made a complete and perfect prison. In your place, Colin, I shouldn't touch the windows, which are probably unique. And some of them serve a useful purpose: in the nurseries, for instance, when we were children . . ."

As he paused, Elizabeth enquired what had happened to "Mad Marion" at the end.

"I believe she died a natural death," Henry answered. "She was certainly buried with Hugo's first two; and he then married for the fourth time. For what it's worth, she has always had the decency not to haunt the house. I once spent a night in her 'apartments' for a bet."

"Any way, as I don't believe in them," said Elizabeth, "I'm not frightened of ghosts. But do you really mean that all the windows upstairs . . .?"

"The bars were strong enough to contain certain French prisoners in the Napoleonic wars," said John. "I can't say what state they're in now . . ."

"Well, I can," I put in. "I tested them the other day to see whether one *could* break out in case of a fire. They're as strong as they ever were. As Henry says, the house can be made a complete and perfect prison, under a veneer of the most exquisite and delicate Georgian elegance. Examine the doors, look up the chimneys!"

I glanced at Elizabeth as I spoke; but, if she suspected any veiled meaning in these reiterated references to a prison, she was keeping her suspicions to herself. So far as I could hear her murmured conversation with my sister-in-law Blanche, she seemed to be exploring the advisability of putting bars on nursery-windows: they made for safety, of course, but many people thought that they set up that thing with the long name meaning a fear of being shut in.

"Claustrophobia?," Blanche suggested.

"That's the word!"

I did not listen to the rest of the conversation, which seemed to be concerned with the newly fashionable theory of prenatal complexes. A complete and perfect prison Henry had said this house might be made; and John, admitting that he knew little more of "Mad Marion's" husband than of herself, seemed to be suggesting that "old Hugo" with his four (if not five or six) wives must have been the Bluebeard of the otherwise respectable

Whimboyne family. "A complete and perfect prison", I whispered. This, in effect, was what Elizabeth designed to make of Ridgeway House: a prison from which her husband, the father of her next and last child, would never escape. I picked up the telephone-directory with intent to cancel my appointment with Anstruther Nesbitt and tell him that I proposed to sell the place as it stood. At once I saw that this would not help me: the house in Grosvenor Road, any house anywhere, could be made as secure a prison if I were fool enough to walk into it with open eyes and to wait helplessly while the door was slammed and barred behind me.

"I've never understood why our strange father stood out against electric light and yet admitted the telephone," said John, as a bell rang faintly in the library next door.

I went to it and heard, with some difficulty, the voice of Violet Oakhirst, speaking from London. She had not written after my mother's death, she told me, because she did not wish to give me yet another letter to answer, but she would like me to know that she had been with me in spirit at the funeral and hoped very soon to be with me in person. Was I returning to London at once? If not, could I spare her an hour between convenient down and up trains at Marlborough? For reasons that she would explain later, she would rather not come to Ridgeway House: indeed, if a meeting took place, she would rather that no one ever knew anything about it.

"I want your advice, Colin," she continued. "A crisis has occurred. Perhaps I should say, 'another crisis'. I don't know how much you've heard about the earlier ones, but this time I really feel I can't go on. It's not a thing I can discuss by telephone; and letters are no good. If I could see you for just a few minutes . . . Nigel will be in court all day; and as long as I'm back for dinner . . ."

I named a mid-morning train and told Violet that I would give her luncheon. I had heard enough of earlier crises to guess the nature of this latest one. A man could hardly share a house with Nigel in his bachelor days without wondering whether he would change his ways when he married. Though Violet had dropped no hint before, I had sometimes wondered too whether, in turning to me for friendship, she was turning away from a husband who had failed her.

I said that my advice, sympathy and help were hers for the

asking; but, as I went back to my relations in the saloon, I wondered whether in the length and breadth of England any man or woman could have chosen an adviser less competent to advise on a ship-wrecked marriage.

II

As I waited for Violet's train at Marlborough next day, I reflected that, though the Oakhirsts' was the first of many invitations that Elizabeth and I had accepted after the unforgettable honeymoon that we were both so anxious to forget, the party had been postponed at the last moment and I had not been to Barton Street nor they to Grosvenor Road since the outbreak of war in 1914.

As Nigel was in London all the time, I had run into him occasionally on his way from the Temple to the House of Commons or from one to another of the government departments which he successively adorned in these years as parliamentary under-secretary. At these encounters each of us invariably told the other that we must really "fix a night" for dining and talking of old days; but in fact, when we met socially, it was always—by accident or design—in other people's houses.

On reflection, slowly pacing the downside platform, I decided that it must have been by design. An ambitious careerist, who had begun with minor-meteor brilliance at the bar and in parliament, Nigel seemed now to be marking time: I was told that his practice as a silk had not fulfilled his friends' expectations of him as a junior and, though he was still in demand as a platform-speaker, the House tended to empty when he was seen to have caught the Speaker's eye and neither Asquith nor Lloyd George seemed to have felt that the ministry would be strengthened by taking him into the Cabinet. From his punctual exclamations about my "luck" I chose to fancy that he was a little jealous of my moderate successes; and on the day, soon after the "coupon election", when he first talked of Indian provincial governorships I decided he must be feeling that he had shot his bolt in England.

"It's now or never," he told me gloomily.

At three-and-thirty he was too young, he explained, for the High-Court bench; but he had solid claims on his party's gratitude and was anxious to have them recognized while his party

K

controlled at least half of the government's patronage. I remembered asking him, as we came to the parting of our ways on Horse Guards' Parade, how Violet would like a term in Madras or Bombay; his reply was that he had not asked her; and it was the tone of this reply, suggesting that he never considered any one else where his career was concerned, that made me hesitate for once to tell him, however insincerely, that we really must dine together one of these nights. In sudden illumination I saw why Nigel, for all his gifts and mechanical charm, had never made himself liked at Westminster or at Oxford, at the bar, in the House of Commons or any other society where shrewd judges of men reject the counterfeit good-fellow who thinks only of his own advancement. Now that the war was over, even the most charitable of Nigel's critics were saying that, for all the good he had done as a peripatetic under-secretary, he might just as well have put in a bit of fighting.

As an afterthought, he had indeed explained that there was no opportunity for discussing anything with Violet until she had closed her hospital in Normandy; but it occurred to me, now that I had heard her speak of a crisis or a series of crises, that perhaps there was more than one explanation of her protracted absence abroad. If I had wished to describe Nigel in two words from the experience of sharing a house, I should have called him discreetly promiscuous: he would pick up any woman that took his fancy, but no woman was allowed to take his fancy if he suspected that she might bleed him or blackmail him or compromise him in his all-important career. There were rumours before 1914 that he was making Violet rather unhappy; and, when she took her ambulance to France that autumn, I heard whispers that for the Oakhirsts at least the war might be something of a blessing in disguise.

And now the war was over; Violet had returned to England; there was a crisis which made her declare that she could not go on; and she was on her way to seek my advice.

As the train swept in, she was standing by an open window; and, when our eyes met, she gave me one of the smiles that were rare enough for Austin Gerrold to have called her "the aloe that flowers once in a hundred years". The smile put me in such good heart that I was able to forget for a moment her troubles and mine and to remember only the days before either of us married, when we met at "the Master's" house in Russell Square to discuss the technique of playwriting. I was not, indeed, expecting any one so habitually reserved as Violet to appear suddenly old or grief-distraught; but the four years in which we had been separated seemed to have left no mark on her.

"You haven't changed much either, Colin," she told me, as we left the station. "In essence, I mean."

"I should like to think I'm four years wiser," I said.

"So long as you're not forty years sadder . . . ," she began with one of the lightning glances that always seemed to strip me bare. "It's all right!," she added at once, seeing that I had seen what she had seen. Our conversation, progressing by leaps, must usually have been unintelligible to a stranger. "I've come here to talk about *myself*! Where are you taking me to lunch?"

I said that this would depend on the time of the train back to London. I had a car, with a picnic-basket, and, if she could spare me two or three hours, I would drive her up to the Downs or through the Vale of White Horse or wherever else she liked. Otherwise, we could go to an hotel in Marlborough.

"I should like a picnic," she answered, as she settled herself in the car. "Especially if we can dispose of business first and then talk of really interesting things. Colin, my dear, what is Nigel's form as a public man? I mean, will he ever be a law-officer, a judge, a cabinet-minister? The unvarnished truth, please!"

"At the present time and at his present age," I answered, "he might get a good recordership or a police-magistracy, nothing more. In politics he seems to have reached a dead end. The last time I saw him, he was talking about appointments abroad. Well . . . If he's going to be content with the Seychelles or Mauritius . . . I don't believe any one's going to make him governor of Ceylon or Hong Kong. He hasn't the experience and he hasn't the standing."

"In other words, his career isn't a thing we need any of us bother about?"

"I wouldn't quite say that. Perhaps in 'big business' or as a *minor* prancing proconsul . . ."

A short silence followed. Then Violet asked me whether I remembered the fate of the lacrimose Lord Lundy, who sank steadily to becoming Curator of Big Ben and was then ordered by his aged grand sire to "*go out and govern New South Wales*".

"Would it cramp Nigel's style," she enquired casually, "if I divorced him before he went out?"

"I should think it would kill his chance for all time. As the

King's Representative . . . Has it become as bad as that, my dear?"

"It has become so bad that something *drastic* must be done! I've known for years that one woman was not enough for Nigel. I looked the other way so long as he didn't force these creatures on my notice. *And* when they didn't force *themselves* . . . He was too circumspect ever to get entangled with any one in his own world, but his high-heeled, silk-stockinged, cheap-scented secretaries aren't engaged for their shorthand or typing. I continued to look the other way till I thought that one of them was being deliberately insolent to me. The insolence of a servant girl under notice, who has stolen something and challenges you to get it back if you can . . . In what way? To begin with, she wanted to be received by me in Barton Street! The night you and Elizabeth were coming to dine! Some woman had failed at the last moment; and little Miss Blank put Nigel up to suggest that she should fill the empty place. I cancelled the whole party and told Nigel that he must get rid of Miss Blank that day. He blustered, but in the end he admitted that she had become a little too big for her boots. The next thing was a call from Miss Blank. I don't know whether she's a bit mad, but she seemed to be hinting that I should divorce Nigel so that he could marry her! As I rang for her to be shewn out, she informed me that she was going to have a child. Well, Colin, that sort of thing can't go on."

Another and a longer silence fell between us.

"And what advice do you want me to give you?," I then asked. "Apparently you've considered the question of a divorce; and I told you that from *his* point of view . . ."

"Tell me what's best for *myself*, for myself *alone*! This business has made me feel *dirty*; and I shan't feel clean again till Nigel and I are parted. In old days I looked the other way because a scandal would have ruined his career, but you tell me that he has no career to ruin and I shouldn't mind if he had. What I can't and won't endure is having him tied to me. If, as you say, a divorce would kill his chances for ever . . . He'll have to be provided for somehow. . . . I should do better, shouldn't I? to avoid a scandal, help him to the best job that influence or intrigue can buy and then shut the door on him. I've good reason to think he could be governor of the Spice Coast if he liked. Can we strike a bargain, he and I? If he'll go there and not come back, I'll say nothing myself and I'll see that Miss Blank says nothing. Of course he mustn't expect me to accompany him. That's not essential, is it?"

I said that, as the Spice Coast was officially regarded as the unhealthiest of all our colonies, any governor would have a good excuse for not taking his wife with him.

"You'll be his wife still, when he comes back, though," I warned her. "The Colonial Office won't keep him out there more than five years. During that time, too, he'll come on leave . . ."

"I may feel clean enough by then to put up a convincing *façade* while he's in England. When he leaves the Spice Coast for good, he'll be promoted to a better place. If he hasn't died of some tropical disease in the meantime. When he reaches retiring age, which won't be for twenty years or more . . . Oh, anything may have happened! If *I'm* not dead by then . . . Can you suggest anything *better*, Colin?"

"I suggest that we both take a little more time . . . ," I began, but Violet interrupted to say that this was impossible.

If time could be made or bought, she went on, she would not have burst in this way into a house of mourning. For months past Nigel had been industriously pulling every kind of string; and now the colonial secretary had approached him and required an immediate answer. A decision, the one way or the other, had to be reached that night at dinner; and, so far as Violet could see, the choice lay between the Spice Coast with a voluntary separation arranged on her terms and a divorce which would end his career as any kind of public man and leave her to support him.

"He has saved almost nothing," she said, "and he's making very little now. I suppose he could get a county-court judgeship if I didn't divorce him till he'd been appointed?"

"And how will you manage?," I asked.

"Oh, I have some money of my own. My life generally? There are more things that I want to do than I ever have time for . . . What is that attractive-looking house in the belt of beeches?"

I told Violet that I was glad she found the house attractive, as this was Ridgeway. Almost without design, I had driven the car up a farm-road cut deep in the white chalk of the Downs and we were pausing by a shut cattle-gate, at the very spot where

Austin had once pointed an indignant finger at the "mortuary" in which the Whimboynes lay extended on their slabs. Whatever I may have thought overnight, as I sat half-suffocated by the placid pressure of John and his pink-and-white Blanche, of Henry and his dead-gypsy Constance, I did not think that Ridgeway House looked at all like a mortuary in the midday spring sunshine; it was not even the perfect prison that it had seemed the night before with Elizabeth immovably established with her stolid back to the door. No house, I decided, was a prison unless one made it so. Violet, I felt, would retain all her independence of mind in Holloway; and something of her undaunted spirit mingled with the scented breeze blowing over the Downs, with the song of invisible larks and the sweetness of hidden gorse, cleansing and invigorating me. Though I had been asked to advise her, I knew that she had unconsciously been advising me.

"We might stop here for luncheon," I said.

"Perfect setting and perfect timing," she answered, as she picked up the rug and spread it on the grass by the roadside, where we could support our backs against one beech tree and use the stump of another as a table. "I like to dispose of unpleasant things before a meal that I know is going to be pleasant."

"I should just like to say that I'm terribly sorry this should have happened, Violet," I began before the subject was finally dismissed.

"My dear, that's one of the things that go without saying," she broke in, "between *us*. I knew I could always count on your sympathy. And you, my dear . . . I couldn't help meeting people and reading the papers, Colin. *I've* not said how terribly sorry I was that you should have gone through such hell since last I saw you. I'm sure you *know* that. As you said nothing, I felt it would be an impertinence . . ."

As I busied myself with the luncheon-basket, I assured Violet that nothing she could ever say to me would be an impertinence. "Going through hell", I added in an attempt to copy her own lightness of touch, was an over-statement: like other and better men before me, I had burnt my fingers, which was painful at the time, and the best thing was to let them heal without thinking of them. If she cared to hear the whole story, our old and—to me— very precious friendship entitled her to hear it, so far as even now I was able to understand it; if, on the other hand, she felt that an autopsy of this kind would serve no useful purpose, I

wished to say only that nobody was more to blame than anybody
else for the sufferings that I had endured and inflicted.

" '*Man's forgiveness give . . . and take*'," I quoted.

"As though *blaming* ever did any good!," Violet exclaimed. "I
don't blame Nigel for his carryings on: I suppose it's the way he's
made. I *rather* hope, though I don't greatly care, that he doesn't
blame me for refusing to let him carry on like this in my house
and under my nose. I suppose that's the way *I'm* made: an inborn
dislike of being *dirtied* . . . No, Colin, I was only sorry that some
one I've always loved dearly should have burnt even the tip of
one finger. I rejoiced, quite unselfishly, when you wrote to me
about your engagement. You'll never hear me again on this
subject and you wouldn't be hearing me now if I hadn't been
shocked by the look in your eyes when we met at the station.
Burnt fingers? A scorched soul, my dear! When I said 'forty
years sadder' . . . Tell me what you're giving me to eat."

"It's only cold chicken and salad. Well . . . I've had no chance
of proving whether I'm four years *wiser*. You had thought everything out so clearly, with the various choices . . ."

"No, I needed your opinion on the *effect* of a divorce. I nearly
came to you a year ago, when there was a somewhat similar crisis,
but you weren't married then."

"I don't know what difference being married could make to
advice on what is really a matter of fact. Public opinion has
changed a lot since the time of Dilke and Parnell, but divorce is
still a quite insuperable bar to some things. By the way, this is
barsac I'm giving you to drink."

Violet sat for a few moments watching the sunlight glinting
on the molten gold in her glass. Then she set it down, untasted,
and turned to look me in the eyes with an expression that I
remembered in the earliest discussions of "our" plays. "Mental
integrity carried to fanaticism" I had once called it: a scene might
be "good theatre", but neither cajolery nor browbeating, neither
torture nor bribery would persuade her to call a bad scene good.

"Your being married makes a great difference to the advice
I should be willing to follow," she told me. "If you said: 'Divorce
Nigel and make a new start', if you'd said it a year ago . . . Well,
I might not have been quite so detached. If I'd made a new start,
it might have been with you! D'you remember the first time we
met, when I made Nigel so angry by telling Austin that, if I'd
met you before I met him, I should most certainly have chosen

you? Well, you were saved then by the fact that the engagement had been published! You're saved now by the fact that you're married! Heaven knows what might have happened if I'd asked your advice about a divorce twelve months ago! A new start when we were both of us *rather* unhappy . . . D'you remember a day when you came to Barton Street and helped me to arrange darling father's books?"

"When you apologized for the way a respectable young married woman had been declaring herself to a respectable young unmarried man? Violet . . . Violet, why are you talking like this?"

With a shiver she turned away and sat gazing at the mellow red roof of Ridgeway House.

"Because I would do anything to get that look out of your eyes!," she answered between clenched teeth. "I know it's selfish, I'm only an old friend to you, but I happen to love you so dearly that it just breaks my heart to see how you've been suffering. Does it help at *all* to know that I ached and prayed for your happiness, that I shared every torment you went through? . . . I would give the skin of my cheeks to graft on your poor burnt spirit! . . . I'm sorry, Colin! I don't often behave like this, do I? Perhaps my nerves in the last few days . . . This is most delicious wine!"

I told her again that it was a barsac, for which I then and there improvised a theory that it should always be drunk out of doors, in hot sunshine like this. Had I been Axminster, I added, with whom I had first tasted it when he led me at a hand-gallop across the Esterelles from his villa at Valescure, there would have been an attendant car with an ice-bucket.

"My year as travelling secretary to him . . . ," I continued, and then discovered that I could not go on. "Violet . . . When did this trouble with Nigel begin?"

"When did it begin or when did I find out?," she asked. "Not that it matters either way! Before we'd been married a year I knew he was no longer in love with me. Perhaps he never had been. Perhaps he was only in love with himself and his career. I was good value as a hostess, but I daresay he found me over-fastidious. If he hadn't been so much concerned with appearances, Nigel would have been a man for low public-houses and lower conversation and women lowest of all. However, that's all over. Within a week you'll read that he has been appointed

governor of the Spice Coast. And I . . . Will Elizabeth let us go
on being friends, Colin?"

"She can't stop it," I said.

"But will she let you talk to me about what you're writing?
Nigel was only too glad to find any one who would keep me
amused, but I could never be sure that Elizabeth didn't rather
resent some of Austin's literary friends."

I said that this was a matter on which I did not propose to
consult Elizabeth.

"If a man's expected to give up his own friends and interests
when he marries . . . ," I continued. "I daresay *she* will be only
too thankful to you for keeping me amused. If she comes to live
here with her boys, I shall have a good deal of time by myself in
London. No doubt I can get down here for week-ends," I
explained by rote, "and I expect she'll stay in Grosvenor Road
when she comes up for a day's shopping. If I felt that I could
telephone to Barton Street any evening when I was at a loose
end . . ."

Violet interrupted to ask whether this was not another of the
things that, between us, went without saying.

"A pity this place is so far from London," she went on with a
frown. "I can understand, of course, that you wouldn't give it up
for anything. All the same . . . If I may criticize, it doesn't sound
a very *comfortable* arrangement. I quite see that you must be near
your work, but if you're only going to meet at week-ends . . ."

"I, on the other hand, think it's not only the most comfortable arrangement, but also the only possible one. Apparently it
took you a year to find out that Nigel was not in love with you.
Elizabeth and I made that discovery before we'd been married a
week. Unfortunate, but there's nothing any one can do."

Violet tried to speak, but only achieved a choking gasp of
horror.

"Like you," I continued, "I considered the question of a
divorce. Like you, I decided against it. Within four months you
will read that I have been made a proud and happy father."

III

I suppose I have been subjected as often as the next man to such ingenuous questions as: "How do you get your plots?" or "Do you think a play out beforehand or do you just sit down and write?" I should like to believe that my answers, whatever they have been, were occasionally satisfying to the questioners; but I must confess that I have found no convincing answer to my own almost life-long question: "What is the distinctive quality of mind that makes the creative artist?" Devotees of *The Wrong Box* will remember that, whereas a down-hearted drawing-master protested: "*But I can't invent. I never could invent in all my life*", the best solicitor in London proved himself a skilled hand as a narrator of stirring and fictitious incident. Why does a situation, a character, a phrase suggest a dozen stories to one and none to another?

This faculty of constructive imagination is probably inborn; but I fancy it can be cultivated by practice and I at least cannot remember a time when I was not telling myself stories that were inspired by anything or nothing. I used to flatter myself that the most unexpected emergency would never catch me at a loss; and certainly in the days when Violet and I were discussing the *scenario* of a play, any change that she suggested at once reflected itself in a changed scene, changed dialogue, changed characterization and perhaps a changed climax. The new play, imagined with the rapidity of a dream, was in every way as complete and rounded as the old; and, if I could have written as quickly as I thought, my three or four acts would have been finished in three or four minutes.

Could I have spoken as quickly as I was thinking, in the noontide glory of this spring day, I might have sketched the next thirty years of my life in thirty seconds. Nineteen-nineteen to nineteen-forty-nine: I was thirty-one and in nineteen-forty-nine I should be sixty-one. I should have retired from the civil service and perhaps from play-writing, the prime of life would be past, but for thirty years I should have recaptured life.

"I was wrong," I told Violet, "in saying there was nothing any one could do."

"I feel too shattered to say anything," she answered. "I suppose Nigel and I were never really in love, but, when I married, I didn't know what being in love *was*. You *did*, Colin. So, I imagine, did Elizabeth. Surely you must both have known that this wasn't the same thing?"

"There was no passion or romance or glamour about it, but perhaps I thought I'd had enough of that to last me several lifetimes. The war was just over, we were all wondering what we could make of our rather broken lives and I, nearly off my head and lonelier than the last man left alive at the Day of Judgement, felt suddenly that a home, a wife to look after me and for me to look after, children to watch growing up . . . Elizabeth wasn't *exciting*, but she was more than passably attractive. She was devoted to her children, devoted to her house, I thought she'd been devoted to Austin and, if she wasn't yet devoted to me, she gave me something that I needed and prized more than any devotion. What shall I call it? The comforting, healing tenderness of the eternal mother. I quickly discovered that the eternal mother isn't always the eternal wife. Elizabeth wants children, but she doesn't want a husband. We ceased to be husband and wife after the first night of our honeymoon. If I insisted on my conjugal rights, I should send her into an asylum, but the idea of legalized rape is so distasteful that I've no wish ever to see her again. Till I heard about this child, I wanted a divorce, but if I can achieve a practical separation so that we don't spoil each other's lives and kill Life itself . . ."

I have sometimes wondered how often Violet and I used the word LIFE, always in capitals, always flaming with the red of a summer sunrise, during the next hour or so. This was the first spring that the world had been at peace since 1914; and, though Death would always win in the end, Life did seem to have triumphed over Death at the last moment, thrusting him back behind his bars till Youth should have been left behind and we were ready for him at our own proper time. To a very few, laying the odds at a fantastic price, the war had been an opportunity— for escaping from uncongenial grooves, for making money or attaining power—and to one or two it had been an æsthetic or spiritual inspiration; but for most men and women of my age it was a fraud perpetrated on the young and ardent by the incompetent old who could not keep peace or make war, four years of our lives had been stolen from us and we had nearly seen Life itself extinguished. Under cross-examination, I must have admitted that I had experienced no nearer peril than having my windows broken by a Zeppelin bomb and being chased by a submarine on my way back from America; the war, with its demand for light entertainment, had been the making of me financially; and I should still have been an unnoticed item in a rabble of young civil servants if the Ministry of Munitions had not offered me a chance of distinguishing myself. None of this, however, would give me back the Austins and Honitons who had been killed like ants under a giant's heel for more than four years; and, whether or no I was justified in sharing the emotions of the sparse survivors, I had felt since eleven o'clock on Armistice Day that my sole duty to God and to my neighbour and to myself was to secure that Life should not be snatched from me again.

"It did rather look as though I had thrown everything away with both hands," I told Violet. "And this time I couldn't blame the Kaiser or the Little Navyites or Carson."

"I now understand the look I saw in your eyes," she whispered.

"Do you see it now?"

She turned to examine my face, smoothing a wrinkle from my forehead with the tip of one finger.

"You're looking extraordinarily happy, for some reason," she told me.

"For the sufficient reason that I *am* extraordinarily happy."

"Well . . . I'm delighted, of course, but I don't understand."

I pointed down to the house slumbering in the sunshine below us and drew Violet's attention to the dormer windows half-hidden by the balusters of the stone parapet, dummy windows ingeniously painted on the red-brick gable and often—erroneously—explained as having been blocked by a niggardly Whimboyne to evade window-tax. In fact, I told her, the roof had never been pierced; the rooms inside were unfenestrated; they were "Mad Marion's apartments"; and I gave her the history of "Mad Marion" as my brothers and I had given it to Elizabeth the night before.

"Would you understand better," I continued, "if I told you that I saw myself last night and this morning as the modern, male counterpart of Mad Marion, but a thousand times more to be pitied because I wasn't mad yet and knew I should be, knew I should watch myself going mad, knew that I should always retain enough sanity to see how mad I was and to see there was no cure, no escape, that it must go on for ever? . . . This isn't nerves,

Violet, I wasn't dramatizing myself! I was in prison, for life, equally in prison if a Black Maria transferred me to London or Gloucester or Penrith. Perhaps if I had cut and run like Gauguin to the South Seas . . . And then I found you in the next cell to mine! And your solution of the problem was to slip back the bolts and walk out into the sun! I'm more grateful than I can say. *Now* do you understand?"

"I don't understand *how* . . . ," Violet began.

Then it was that I spoke like a man inspired, a man touched by the sun, a man flown with wine or perhaps a man who was something of all these things. That night, I told her, she would make her declaration of independence; and next morning Nigel would begin to buy a tropical outfit for the Spice Coast. That evening, before the light faded, I should take Elizabeth for her promised tour of inspection; and next day Mr. Anstruther Nesbitt would receive his instructions for converting Ridgeway House from a prison into a shrine of liberty, a temple of Æsculapius, where the sick in soul would be healed. I should myself make no declaration of independence, since I had made mine already and Elizabeth had made hers. All that the world expected of a man and a householder, a father and stepfather I would do for Elizabeth and her children, but as a trustee and counsellor, not as a husband or partner in a shared life. I greatly doubted whether Elizabeth would understand anything that I might call a declaration of independence or that she would notice if I put it into effect. She had, in name, a husband for herself and, in fact, a father for our child; she had a permanent supporter at her back and a dependable man of affairs at her beck; she had a home and the means of maintaining it; she had nurses and nurseries for the children; most important of all, perhaps the only important thing of all, she had the children and could devote her whole life to them.

"I honestly believe," I added, "that, *if* I told her *I* was going to the Spice Coast for five years, she would only ask how quickly she could get in touch with me if she needed anything. She would notice when I came on leave, because I should bore her as I bored her by trying to talk intelligently at the old Montpelier-Square parties and as she bores me, but she'll be far happier alone with Martin and Humfrey. And *we*—you and I—shall be standing where we stood before either of us married. On the threshold of Life. Not forty years sadder, not even four years older, but four hundred times *wiser*. I shan't say again, as I said to my tutor at

Oxford, that I was one of Nature's bachelors. You won't say again that you don't know what being in love is!"

"I shall never say that again, Colin," Violet answered. "And that's all I *can* tell you now. It's too much to take in, too much to *bear*! I'm afraid to move, I might wake up! I want to sit here for ever in this golden sunshine, drinking this golden wine."

"There's no need to move, but this is not a dream. If we're too late for the train at Marlborough, I'll drive you over to Swindon or Didcot. I brought a time-table. Which reminds me! Have you ever thought of interior-decoration as a profession? I remember the house in Russell Square, the house in Barton Street, the week-end cottage you had before the war: you have a natural genius for colour-schemes and furnishings. Will you put up a brass plate, advertise in *Country Life* and begin by taking Ridgeway in hand? I shall have to be here quite a lot while the work's going on. If there are any possible trains . . . Yes, I could get to Queen Anne's Gate by half-past ten, with an early start. There's a dining-car in the evening. It won't be too bad for the summer months. I should camp in whatever corner the plumbers and electricians left me; you would have rooms at an hotel in Marlborough. When the place is ready, I can move out and Elizabeth can move in."

As I waited for Violet's answer, I opened the second bottle of wine that I had brought as a precaution against the first's being corked. We should have been light-headed if we had drunk nothing stronger than water, but total immersion in a butt of malmsey would not have clouded our brains.

"You think of everything," she murmured. "I suppose, when you're planning a *scenario* . . . What sort of play had you in mind when you got up this morning?"

"*Hamlet* without Ophelia," I answered. "I should have gone ahead with the house down here, as an escape from Grosvenor Road. If Elizabeth wanted the country, I should have gone back later to London; if she wanted London, I should have settled here to work in peace. There would have been no outward breach, we're perfectly good friends in spite of this unfortunate misunderstanding, but I just couldn't face spending my entire life . . . The play changed when I found that *you* . . ."

"Leave me out for a moment! You and Elizabeth *have* a bond now, or you will have in a few months' time. Are you interested in children?"

"As I told her before we married, I can't say till I've seen one of my own. When I felt that I'd lost Life itself, I thought I could make a sort of substitute by watching a new young life, part of me, taking shape and doing better. Perhaps it was rather sentimental. It may be rather sentimental now to say that I've had a rush of dynastic blood to the head since I bought this place. When I never expected to have it, I never troubled to think about my heir, but we've lived here for the best part of two centuries and I'm by no means the first younger son to inherit. If *my* flesh-and-blood . . . I haven't thought it out at all clearly yet . . ."

As I paused, Violet warned me that I should have to think out my attitude to children generally, and to this child in particular, clearly and immediately. I observed that, perhaps through my speaking of an heir to Ridgeway, we both assumed that the child would be a son.

"It's not *his* fault that his parents are at everlasting logger-heads," she began. "But for him, I would have said: 'Make a clean cut!' I would have made a clean cut myself with Nigel, we could *really* have started afresh."

"*He* will never know there's the faintest discord between his mother and me. Nor will Martin and Humfrey. You must remember that Elizabeth doesn't believe there *is* any. She thinks it's all working out as she planned. Well, I can act a bit. As well as Austin did. To these children I shall be like a commercial traveller who comes home on Saturday after a week on the road. Even if there were no rift, I shouldn't be playing much of an active part while they're still in the nursery."

"You don't think you ought to?"

I replied, now quoting Austin with many others, that for the first six or seven years of a child's life the mother should have an almost unchallenged voice in the mode of its upbringing.

"Of course, if the father thinks there's too much molly-coddling, say . . . ," I continued.

"And you *do*," Violet broke in softly, "or you wouldn't have mentioned it. I've an idea that Elizabeth would choke any cat with cream. It's no business of mine, of course, and except from any duty you may feel to Austin I don't know that it's any business of yours how she brings up her own children. When it's your child as much as hers, it *does* become your business. Mine too. I had a blissfully happy time, Colin, with two parents who adored each other and adored me. I would never see you again if I were going to be the means of depriving any other child of that. In the eyes of the world you must be seen sticking to Elizabeth, in the eyes of all the children it must be a *happy* home. When my mother died, darling father brought his sister and family to live with us so that I shouldn't become a spoilt only child. I think the two-parent idea is terribly important. And, even if you don't yet know whether you're really interested in children, you don't want your son to be spoilt. Your great fresh start is going to bring a great many old duties and responsibilities with it."

"Which will make it all the more precious," I cried, "all the more *necessary*! I can see all the *ROAD UP* signs, all the ropes and red lanterns, all the *NO THOROUGHFARE* boards. We can never marry! You can't be seen about with me perpetually without causing comment! And, except when we're alone, we shall be playing a part for the edification of our servants, our friends, of Elizabeth and Nigel most of all. The more difficulties and drawbacks we find, the more I shall say: 'Isn't it *worth* it?' Think of us early this morning, Violet, cheated of Life and setting our teeth, shrugging our shoulders, telling each other that apparently we had no choice! Think of us now, the first hour we've been together since we found ourselves! We shall be together now every day as long as we live! We shall be together when we're hundreds of miles apart, because each will know that the other's there always! We can stand the other part of our lives if we know all the time that this is the real part. Sitting opposite to Elizabeth at week-ends, taking her to royal garden-parties, visiting the boys for school functions . . . One will go through it all as a sort of sleep-walking, it will be as unreal as a dream. *This* . . ."

"*This* . . . ," Violet echoed. "This is something I shall never forget."

I have no idea how long we sat on. If we said anything, I have forgotten what it was. At some point the broken stable-clock, which never struck the hours, chimed a quarter; and Violet asked me what time it was. I believe I told her that, if she was to catch the train from Marlborough, I must begin to pack the picnic-basket; I believe she insisted, smiling, on helping me as a "symbol".

"Shall we call at my architect's office?," I asked, as we got into the car. "He might know of a house or rooms that would suit you better than an hotel."

"You had better get Elizabeth's approval first," Violet

suggested. "As a formality. She won't *want* to be coming down here every other day and I don't think she's really interested in houses—Austin once told me that he'd planned everything in Montpelier Square—, but it would be a bad beginning if she looked on me as an interloper."

"I'll mention it to-night. Meanwhile, can I tell her—in confidence—about the Spice Coast business? And your idea of house-decoration as a profession?"

Protesting that the idea was wholly mine, Violet broke out with a laugh to say again that she presumed this was how I sketched the *scenario* of a play:

"Preparation . . . Everything thought of and provided for, so that the audience is never taken by surprise unless you set out to surprise it . . . Yes, I think it's an admirable *mise en scéne*, my dear! '*As the curtain rises, Elizabeth and Colin are studying an architect's plan. Elizabeth: "You'll need expert advice about the decoration." Colin: "As a matter of fact . . . You mustn't let this go any farther till you read the official announcement . . ."* ' And, if Elizabeth greets you on your return with the statement that the house is quite unworkable, there'll be another *scenario* all ready. I just couldn't do it! I can criticize something that you've created . . ."

"Or something that has created itself?," I asked. "It's the way one's imagination works. I take no credit for it. Now, when Elizabeth has been alone with me for a few days more, I think it's quite likely that she'll cry out for the lights and sounds of London. Ridgeway was all right for my mother, who was a passionate gardener, and for my father, who had all the interests of the traditional country-gentleman . . . Your train's signalled, but you've plenty of time. Well, we shall be coming back to Grosvenor Road at the end of the week. Before then, I shall have heard the outcome of your talk with Nigel this evening, I hope it won't be distressing, but I feel that after to-day nothing matters, nobody can touch us, other people are shadows and dream-figures."

IV

THE sun was setting as I put Violet into the train. There was but a faint afterglow as I collected myself to leave the station. And, as I drove home, the first lamps were shining with feeble cheerfulness in the cottage windows on either side of the road.

Since my brothers and their wives had left in the morning, Elizabeth and I should be dining alone. Since I must allow some months for Nesbitt and Violet to electrify the house, we should be dining by lamplight. Whether I found the light feebly cheerful after the radiance that had half-blinded me all day would depend in great measure on Elizabeth's reception of my proposal that Violet should undertake the redecoration of Ridgeway.

Though I have just written of driving "home", I remember thinking that it would also depend in great measure on Elizabeth whether Ridgeway became our home or an escape from home. As I had lately told Violet, we were quite good friends despite our one regrettable misunderstanding; we might become better friends within the next few months when a still unpredictable link had been forged between us. And then, before we had been an hour by ourselves, I was wondering whether we could even be friends. For me at least, where there is not perfect trust, there can be no perfect friendship; and the vision of a perfect, if quite impersonal, friendship faded that night as I began to wonder whether I should always have to ask myself whether Elizabeth was meaning what she said or saying what she meant.

Even thirty years afterwards I need to underline that word perfect. After the shock of our honeymoon I had sometimes pondered whether Elizabeth was abnormally stupid, abnormally cunning or a mixture of the two; but, allowing for all the differences in a world where no two people observe precisely the same code or use words in exactly the same sense, I thought that I could in general trust her as well as I could trust my father (who became utterly untrustworthy when his political passions were aroused) or my mother (who was as bad when her prejudice against the Catholic Church came into play) or my brother John (whose laziness amounted to a disease) or my brother Henry (whose greed for easy and good living tended sometimes to blunt his moral sense). Now I was not so sure.

To this day I do not know how much of honest misunderstanding there was, how far each of us argued on certain assumptions that the other found incomprehensible. When we sat down to dinner, Elizabeth mentioned that she had spent most of the day exploring Marlborough College and was enchanted with it.

"If you approve, Colin," she continued, "I should like you to put the boys' names down at once."

"I feel it's entirely a matter for you to decide," I answered.

"As we know, Austin favoured Westminster; but his preference, which may have been due to passing sentiment, isn't binding on you. Personally, I have the highest regard for such Marlburians as I knew at Oxford . . ."

"Can we afford it?," Elizabeth interrupted. "I have the terms here, but I *don't* understand money."

I said that I would gladly advise her to the best of my ability, but that—once again—she must decide how much she could and how much she would spend on her sons' education, whether— for example—she would "spread herself" over their schools and leave them to take their chance at a university or whether she would economize on the school and have a nest-egg for starting them in life later.

"I haven't the faintest idea what your financial position is," I put in parenthetically. "When I suggested a settlement, it didn't appeal to you. I may add that I also haven't the faintest curiosity. I detest talking about money . . ."

"And I don't *understand* it," Elizabeth told me again.

"I presume you know what your income is. If not, I can very soon tell you when my accountants send me my income-tax return. It's the privilege of a husband to pay supertax on the *joint* incomes of his wife and himself, even though he can't recover the tax from her and derives no benefit from her income."

"Well, when you became responsible for me and my ready-made family . . . ," she began with a laugh that died away rather miserably.

If I believed in voices like Joan of Arc's, I should say that this was the moment when a voice whispered to me in deplorably colloquial language: "Have a *show-down*, young man! *Now!*" Through deficiency of school-patriotism I had listened with only one ear to Elizabeth's exaltation of Marlborough above West-minster; I had not made even a mental comment on her question whether "we" could afford this or that for her sons; and I fancy it was her reiterated plaint about her inability to understand money that filled me with quite indefinable suspicion. Why had she refused a settlement? Ostensibly, because in her ignorance and irresponsibility she had not had a marriage-settlement with Austin and therefore could not need one with me; but at the time she had given me a disagreeable impression of wondering whether I was trying to appropriate Austin's money to my own uses. Why did she hide behind solicitors whose very name she refused to divulge? Why, in all discussions of houses in London or the country, of styles of living, of education, of careers for young men in twenty years' time did she never ask me what I could contribute or volunteer what she could contribute herself? I recalled my brother's fraternally blunt question the night before: had Elizabeth money of her own? I recalled my faintly impatient answer, born of a sense that all talk of money was vulgar, that I did not know. Was it imagination that both my brothers had looked rather surprised?

"Until to-day," I said, "everything's been so uncertain that it really seemed rather a waste of time to prepare any kind of budget. We've decided now to keep the house in London; we've decided to go ahead with the alterations here. In due course we must decide what kind of life we're going to lead in both places. Before we can answer that question, we must know the probable income at our disposal and agree who's to pay for what. I can give you my fixed income from salary and investments; my literary income is much bigger, but also much more fluctuating . . ."

"And if I told you I had no income at all?"

I repressed an unworthy impulse to ask: "Was that why you married me?" and repeated instead that, though I felt no curiosity about her affairs, I really did not understand how a woman with no income could have lived and entertained at Montpelier Square, clothed and fed herself and her two small sons, paid the wages of a staff and laid plans for the establishment of her children regardless of cost.

"I had an allowance from father," she explained with the air of one struggling for life in intellectual quicksands, "but I wasn't allowed to call it an allowance. It was a present or something, to avoid income-tax. Oh, I forgot! I have Austin's pension . . ."

"I presume *he* left something?"

"Not to me. Is it called 'in trust'? He left all his money in trust for Martin and Humfrey. I have the control of it till they're twenty-one. I mean to say, there must be *something* to pay for their food and clothes and doctors. I don't know what Austin thought would happen to *me*. . . . Now you know as much as I do, Colin! It's no good going to the solicitors. I've nothing but my share of Austin's army-pension. Therefore, when I said: 'Can we afford it . . .?' I suppose I ought to have said: 'Can *you* . . .?' If we can't afford Marlborough, we can't, but it seems a terrible pity. If we can afford to spend thousands on this place, which you say is *much* too far from London . . . I don't understand it! Perhaps I don't understand you. Certainly I don't understand money. . . . Will you think me very unfriendly if I leave you to finish your dinner by yourself? I'm tired out. Oh, there are the Marlborough terms I told you about."

As I studied the schedule of fees, I decided that I could easily afford to pay for both boys. I did not see so readily why I should. Elizabeth obviously had the spending of some thousands a year, but she had gone to her room without telling me how much in fact she controlled and how much she could contribute, if not to the common purse, at least to the support of her own children.

I finished my solitary dinner with a disagreeable feeling that, where money was concerned, I could not depend on her to tell me the whole truth and nothing but the truth; but I saw no point in mentioning this intuition when I wrote that night to Violet and, whenever we met in the next two or three months, we had pleasanter things to occupy our minds than the people whom I had already dismissed as dream-figures. One of them duly returned to London; another duly embarked for the Spice Coast. Violet took rooms in Marlborough and motored daily to and fro in Anstruther Nesbitt's car. With occasional nights in Grosvenor Road, I made my headquarters at Ridgeway, trekking from bedroom to bedroom as one wing after another was dismantled and abandoned to succeeding waves of sanitary engineers, electricians, painters and paper-hangers. Architect and decorator were pledged to have the last workman out of the house by mid-August; but so much progress had been made by the end of June that I felt justified in suggesting that Violet should dine with me to celebrate the signing of the peace treaty at Versailles. By now the downstairs rooms had at least been wired for electric-light, the chandeliers and sconces converted, the pictures cleaned and the panelling pickled; for many aromatic weeks the french-polishers had been working on the Chippendale tables and chairs; the new carpet chosen by Violet had been laid; and it was a post-card from her, to report that the cream-brocade curtains were now hanging, that inspired me to suggest a preliminary house-warming.

As my mother's old servants, who had only stayed on to oblige me, departed one by one into retirement, the admirable staff which had served Austin and Elizabeth, but was unwilling to serve the tempestuous Kitty Mandeville on any terms what-

soever, had trickled down to replace them; Mrs. Cruikshank in
her new kitchen was cooking—by candle-light—with all the
artistry that I remembered in London and her husband had
polished the silver to a brilliance never surpassed in my father's
most spacious and improvident days.

"It's perfect!," Violet exclaimed, pausing in the doorway.
"Cruikshank's table, I mean. I'm not praising my own handiwork."

"That you can leave to me," I said. "The whole room's
perfect, the whole house. To-night of all nights, when the horrors
of the war-years have been tidied away for ever . . ."

"Do you understand now why I said, that day on the Downs,
that I didn't want to move for fear of waking up? Surely such
perfection, such perfection of happiness, only comes to us in
dreams?"

I relieved Violet of her cloak, and, as I laid it over the back of
a chair, I felt that for the first time in many weeks we were a man
and woman again, no longer a decorator and her client.

"I told you that day," I reminded her, "that *this* was our *real*
life. The dream, the sleep-walking, the *unreal* part is when you're
not here. Why *shouldn't* life be perfect? Why do so many people
spoil it by saying: 'We shall pay for this later'?"

As I paused, Violet pointed to the glowing west and asked
whether I had ever felt that life might be too perfect.

"Like a summer-day when the sun seems to have forgotten to
set?", she continued. "*I* don't. After all, if we're happy now,
Colin, we weren't always so happy. Therefore, I *don't* say 'Touch
wood'!"

"And *I* don't say 'It can't last'. Why shouldn't it? When I look
back on the last few months . . ."

I fell silent as Cruikshank came in with the soup. Looking
back on the last few months, I felt that everything had fallen out a
hundred times better than I had expected. It was to no one's
advantage, I most confidently believed, to change the course that
all our lives were following. Nigel was now established as
governor and commander-in-chief of the Spice Coast, there to
remain for five years, pleasantly excited by the prospect of
greater success than he had achieved at the bar or in the House of
Commons and many thousand miles beyond the reach of the
young lady known as "Miss Blank". He, surely, had no reason
to complain of the hand that Destiny had dealt him. Nor, I

ventured to think, had Elizabeth. With the choice of two spacious houses fresh from the hands of the painters, with a devoted staff in each, with a husband who appeared only for dinner one or two nights a week, with her two boys and unfettered liberty to bring them up as she pleased, the wife of Mr. Colin Whimboyne, C.B., assistant-secretary in the Department of the Lord Keeper, or, if she preferred it, of Colin Whimboyne Esquire, J.P., of Ridgeway House, Wiltshire, or of Whimboyne *tout court*, the now quite well known and still quite successful popular playwright, was no worse off than the wife of the late Austin Gerrold.

And I? Some weeks earlier I had discussed with Violet whether I should abandon the Maugham-and-water kind of comedy that I had written hitherto and, like Maugham himself, try to write something in a class as different as that of the later Maugham's plays. With her perfect honesty of criticism she had told me that by now I must know my powers and my limitations. The "Perfect Painter", she reminded me, was the name given to a flawless craftsman and not to a giant like Raphael or Michael Angelo. The advice, I now felt, might be transferred from art to life: I knew the limitations of the happiness that we had agreed to allow ourselves and within that range I had no fault to find.

"Has Elizabeth had any success about Marlborough?", Violet asked, when I mentioned that I had visited the school on my way from the station. "Then . . . I suppose she'll *live* here, to be near the boys?"

"I think it's more than likely, when the time comes."

Though I did not tell Violet so, Elizabeth had not again raised the question whether "we" or she or the boys' trustees (whoever they might be) could afford this or that. Since our one brief and embarrassing discussion of incomes and expenditure, certain facts had been forced on my notice and certain other facts were being tacitly ignored or taken for granted. Thus, though I paid the wages of the other servants, Elizabeth seemed to be paying those of the nurse and nursery-maid; though all house-keeping bills came to me, the doctor's bills for the children did not; and, though Elizabeth's pension was included in my income-tax return, I was told nothing about her allowance or about the trust-income which had apparently been placed at her disposal until Martin and Humfrey came of age.

I did not mind; if she or her still anonymous solicitors had asked me whether that was a fair apportionment, I should have said that it was; had she failed to keep up any agreed contribution, I should have paid it gladly for her. I did not want any confidences that she felt disinclined to give; and I wanted even less any repetition of a scene in which she could tell me that she had no income and, in the next breath, that she had a pension and an allowance and the use of a trust-fund.

"If Elizabeth's coming here to have her baby . . . ," Violet began, "August, did you tell me? I shall feel that I've earned a holiday by then."

"And I hope you'll spend it here. I suppose I shall have to be within call for the event itself. When she's well enough for visitors . . ."

Violet shook her head slowly, explaining that she had arranged to go abroad with friends.

"I shall never come back here," she continued, "if Elizabeth makes it her home. D'you remember saying that you wouldn't know how you felt about children till you had one of your own? Well, when you have, you may find that you feel quite differently about your son's mother. I can't say, nor can you, but I'm sure Elizabeth believes there'll be a reconciliation, a blending and merging . . . I should never know another moment's happiness, my dear, if I stood in the way of that. So . . . I shan't come back unless you send for me, at all costs we must keep our love unsullied. And, if you send for me, it will be to Grosvenor Road. I haven't *stolen* you from Elizabeth! If she hadn't *abandoned* you when Nigel abandoned *me* . . . But I can't pretend with her that you and I are just literary friends. You wouldn't care to pretend that with Nigel. I know you agree, my darling one! In all these weeks you've never even kissed my hand . . ."

"Because it *would* have spoiled everything if you hadn't wanted it!"

"And I didn't! I don't want to change *anything* until you tell me . . . *Unless* you tell me . . . Oh, how shall I put it? That Elizabeth was wrong, that this child *hasn't* made the difference she expected, that you're still icebergs to each other and that I couldn't steal a love that's not hers . . . And now, my dear, wouldn't it relax the tension if you sent for Mrs. Cruikshank and complimented her on her really admirable dinner?"

"I'll ask them both to drink a glass of wine with us," I said, "Peace-night! That should put them at their ease."

I rang the bell and brought two more chairs up to the table;

but, as Cruikshank gravely thanked me for my invitation, I felt that the last thing he needed was to be put at his ease and, when he returned a few minutes later with his wife, some instinct saved me from saying—as I had intended—that this was not an occasion for speeches. It quickly became evident that he was prepared with a speech and that, when he had done, Mrs. Cruikshank would deliver a speech on her own account. They had obviously been waiting for an opportunity; and the wine was hardly poured before one of them was saying it was a pity that Mrs. Whimboyne could not be present and the other was pointing out that they could perhaps speak more freely in her absence.

"Though you mustn't think, sir," they added in chorus, "nor you either, madam, that there's anything we would say behind her *back* . . ."

I wondered, a little apprehensively, what was coming; and what in fact came would have been embarrassing if it had not been profoundly moving. In alternate sentences, each prompting or explaining the other, they thanked me for giving them this chance of saying how glad they were to be at Ridgeway and in my service. Though I did not know it before, Cruikshank had been a footman, his wife a kitchen-maid, with Austin Gerrold's parents, they had heard of Ridgeway from "Master Austin" in our school-days and they had begun to take an interest in me when they discovered that the young Mr. Whimboyne who came to dine in Montpelier Square was the Mr. Whimboyne who wrote the plays. Since I had assumed the burden of Austin's family responsibilities they seemed to be feeling their way towards a bargain by which they were to take charge of my life at Ridgeway —as my excellent Winters had for so long taken charge of it in London—if I would indicate the lines on which I wished my life to run.

"Master Austin hadn't the *time*, sir . . . ," Cruikshank explained.

"Or the *patience*, poor dear young gentleman . . . ," Mrs. Cruikshank supplemented with a smile and a sigh. "He being the only child, Mrs. Gerrold had done everything for him. And, marrying so young, well, sir, you couldn't expect him to know about a house. Linen and stores and cleaning and the duties of the servants . . . Into my kitchen he *would* not come. 'You tell me that's a "lovely" something-or-other of lamb, Margaret, but to me it's a perfectly horrible lump of dead meat and I thank Heaven I don't have to touch it till it has been cooked!' He always liked his joke, Master Austin did. But, sir, I hope you'll come just *once*, now that Mr. Nesbitt and Mrs. Oakhirst have made everything so nice for me. As soon as the electric light's working . . ."

I said that I would come the moment Mrs. Cruikshank was ready for me and asked whether Mrs. Whimboyne had been favourably impressed when last she came to inspect the progress of the work at Ridgeway. I was told, however, that she had spent all her time in the nurseries and had replied "Whatever you and Mrs. Oakhirst think best . . ." to every question that the architect put to her.

"We calculate, sir," her husband contributed, "that the house is about the same size as Blackdown, Mr. Gerrold's place near Birmingham. Quite *different*, of course! All that black-and-white half-timber that you see so much in Shropshire and Cheshire."

As they talked and sipped their wine, I gathered—for the first time—that Austin's father had been some kind of Midland manufacturer; and, from the reported extent of his entertaining, I judged that he had been a man of wealth. This no doubt accounted for Austin's ability to maintain a style far beyond that of a young civil servant, though it did not explain why he had not given Elizabeth even a conditional life-interest in his estate. Conceivably he considered that she would inherit enough from the Cheshunts; but I felt that it would be unprofitable to enquire into the system which she had more than once described as asking her solicitors whether she could afford this or that and being told that she could or could not.

The light was fading as Mrs. Cruikshank bowed herself out and her husband began to clear the table.

"You're to be congratulated on that couple, my dear," said Violet, when we were alone in the saloon. "They know their job, both of them, from A to Z; and they're as honest as the day."

"So long as Elizabeth doesn't feel that they're taking too much on their own shoulders . . . ," I began.

As though she had not heard me, Violet added that the Cruikshanks were obviously the soul of loyalty.

"They would never criticize the mistress of the house to an outsider or even to her husband," she continued. "Like you, Colin, I never went to Blackdown and I daresay Austin's parents just said to their butler and housekeeper: 'Eighteen for dinner and everything of the best and most expensive'. In these last few months I've certainly felt that Elizabeth was curiously unin- terested in her own house. Too busy exploring the nurseries to bother about the kitchens or the staff wing. I should be *rather* surprised to hear she had visited the kitchen in Montpelier Square more often than Austin. After all, why should she? I was brought up differently and I didn't spend the greater part of my married life bearing and rearing children . . ."

"Do you regret it?", I asked, as she paused.

"Yes and no! I'm a completely normal woman and I've missed the thing for which I was created a woman. We can't have children, you and I; perhaps we can't ever be anything but platonic friends, perhaps . . ." Her voice trembled and then became defiantly cheerful. "Perhaps we can't even be that! You'll know better in the autumn or whenever it is, but nothing can take away what this spring and summer have brought. I shall love you as dearly if we never meet again. If you say we had better not meet, I shall know you're right. That holiday . . . I shall begin it as soon as I've finished here and you've brought Elizabeth down. I'll give you a list of my addresses."

"But, before you go, I shall see you in London. I *must*! There've been times in the last year or two when I thought I should never write again. You've given *that* back to me, my dear, and I want you to see the result. May I dine with you one night in Barton Street? After that . . . Are you committed to being away for any particular time?"

With another shrug, Violet answered that this would depend on me.

"We're starting in the French Pyrennees," she explained, "and going into Provence, if it's not too hot. I suppose I could always be back in a couple of days if you needed me."

This is perhaps the place to record that Violet and her friends were at Saint Jean de Luz when Elizabeth brought Martin and Humfrey to Ridgeway House at the end of July. They had reached Toulouse by the time I telegraphed in August to say a son had been born to me. For the whole of that month I remained in Wiltshire; but, when my leave ran out at the beginning of September, I told Elizabeth that I proposed to spend at least the middle of each week in London. A new play, I mentioned, was going into rehearsal immediately; and in the meantime I was at work on another.

"Then you certainly ought not to wear yourself out with a train-journey night and morning," Elizabeth answered.

"You'll be all right here by yourself?"

"It's hardly 'by myself' with Martin and Humfrey and now Norman!"

"I hope to get down here for most week-ends," I said. "And when the pheasant-shooting begins . . ."

Elizabeth sighed that she had been hoping I could see all I wanted of my friends in London.

"I do find parties so exhausting," she added.

"Well, we can talk about that later. There's nothing you need me for here any longer?"

According to her list of addresses, Violet was at Arles when I telegraphed to say that I was returning to London and hoped to see her immediately about a new play.

"*No news of interest. Stop,*" the telegram ended. "*No change of any kind. Stop. Love always. Stop. Colin.*"

V

THE day chosen by Violet for her return from Provence happened, though I did not know this till later, to be her birthday; the week in which it occurred, though she did not know this till she reached Paris, happened to be, in England, a week chiefly given over to a railway-strike. Leaving her luggage to follow with her friends, she had secured the last place in that day's Handley-Page from le Bourget; and, when I met her at Hounslow, she handed me an empty purse and invited me to admire the exquisite symbolism of her entrance in my new play.

"I spent my last *sou* to telegraph to you," she explained. "If you hadn't come, I should have had to walk from here to Westminster. But I literally flew to you the moment you sent for me. If you like to wish me—or both of us—many happy returns of the day . . . Yes, I'm twenty-eight!"

"And you look about eighteen."

"I don't feel *any* age, though I must seem forty or fifty years younger than my passport-photograph. The man in the office regarded me with the utmost suspicion! So did the customs-people when I couldn't produce even a hand-bag. 'Nothing to declare'. That would make rather a good title for a play, Colin!"

"I should like to think that, if you look younger than your photograph, it's because you've left all your troubles behind. I should also like to think that railway-strikes are not a symbol of the life we're going to mould for ourselves in a world made safe for democracy."

Violet assured me that, if we could circumvent others as easily as she had circumvented this one, we had nothing to fear.

"Can you lend me some money till I get to the bank?", she continued. "I wasn't expected back so soon and Barton Street is still shut up, so I must go to an hotel for a few days."

"I told Mrs. Winter to have a room ready in Grosvenor Road. I understand the hotels are packed like sardine-tins. If you don't mind being alone with me . . . I don't suppose Elizabeth or the children will ever come there," I went on. "For some reason she never liked the place and now she has moved all her belongings down to Ridgeway. In any event the Winters have prepared dinner for us. You can decide later if you'd like me to try for a room at an hotel . . ."

"As though *I* should mind being alone with you now, Colin! If we *are* alone . . ."

"As we never were before! I suppose you've not been seeing the English papers regularly? A few days after you went abroad, the Duchess of Abbotsbury gave birth to twin sons. As Talleyrand observed of Napoleon's death, '*It is no longer an event, it is only a piece of news*'. For some weeks, though . . . or months . . . or *eternities* . . . I was *never* alone, the house was *haunted* by her . . . After you told me that you would never come back to Ridgeway if Elizabeth was there, I said to myself that, if *she* decided to live *there, you* couldn't mind coming *here*. We should be alone . . . and then I wondered whether we *should* be alone, whether it would be *her* turn to haunt the place. . . . I needn't have worried! She never left a mark on Grosvenor Road; and, the day after she'd moved her things down, I could hardly remember that she'd been there even as a visitor. Are you ready to start?"

Violet looked at her watch and asked whether my car could take her first to Barton Street and wait while she packed a case for the night.

"This, of course, is an emergency," she explained, "but we must begin as we mean to go on and, obviously, we can't share a house. Have you planned anything for our new play beyond what you've told me: mid-weeks in London, week-ends and holidays at Ridgeway?"

"It's too early for any of us to plan anything more. After all, it's less than two months since Norman arrived on the scene, less than six weeks since I really began to see Elizabeth in her new frame."

"Meanwhile, to judge from your letters, a number of other people have been busily planning *for* you."

As we got into the car, I said that, if Violet was referring to the Cheshunts, I thought they had all been examining their Cinderella's new frame to see how well it would suit them. The moment Elizabeth was up and about, they had descended on Ridgeway in force: old Alec, whose pointed beard and blue eyes suggested an Elizabethan adventurer more than a stockbroker, and his lady, who like Martha still troubled about many things, the immaculate Philip and the supercilious Lady Mary, Maurice— if anything, more of a barber's block—and the still haughtier Lady Jane, Kitty Mandeville and her future marquis, the Lords Bracton and Scaling with their respective viscountesses. My in-laws, I observed to Violet, had contrived to splash their way over so many pages of *Debrett* that I was afraid Elizabeth and I must have seemed very plebeian; and I owed it entirely to the redecoration of Ridgeway that they had all regarded it so favourably.

"In their different ways they were all impressed," Violet assured me. "There are some things you *can't* buy, as you might buy impoverished Scottish earls' daughters or backwoods Irish peers. A Coverley Court, yes, and the family portraits, which in time you might pass off as your own; but not the things that Austin hated so much and that most English people envy and love quite irrationally."

"The metaphorical certificate from the Land Registry . . ."

"That a place has been in your family since William of Orange or Henry the Eighth or the Conqueror. Your in-laws are a most interesting study! They've made money and bought houses and contracted exalted alliances, but there's still something lacking. Philip and Maurice still drag in too many stories of what their servants said to 'her ladyship'; and their ladyships are still too fond of explaining that the Cheshunt money, for which they sold themselves, is the one good thing in the family. If you can't have too much of a good thing, you can at least see that you have enough! If they can't do anything else, your in-laws can apparently make money. I hope you get on well with them, Colin? You're going to see a great deal of them! It was gratifying to hear that my decoration was as much admired as your alterations! A perfect house for entertaining! If 'Rella' would wake up and take her proper place . . ."

As Violet paused, I mentioned Elizabeth's recent plaint that parties fatigued her and that she hoped I would contrive to gather my friends round me in London.

"*Your* friends, yes; *her* family, no. She'll be as much out of her depth with the county as she was with Austin's high-brows, but she likes hearing your decoration admired and having it taken for granted that it's her own! She likes 'her' food and wine to be praised."

"Always the palm without the dust? I rather suspected from what the Cruikshanks said about old days in Montpelier Square . . ."

"Have you studied this psychoanalysis that every one's talking about?," Violet broke in. "I've long suspected that Elizabeth has suffered all her life from what they call an inferiority-complex. We all want to be admired for something, most of us think we *deserve* it. Elizabeth had good looks and good clothes, but she was always outshone—perhaps snubbed and shouted down—by brothers and sisters with better brains or at least greater personality. Well, she may feel she's coming into her own as a squire's lady, patronizing her own relations. And I think you'll see a lot of her relations because Ridgeway gives them the background they're conscious of lacking. Perhaps it will be easier than if you and she were alone. . . . Here we are in Barton Street. I shan't be more than ten minutes; but I won't ask you to come in, as everything is in curl-papers. If your man would carry my case down for me afterwards?"

I said that I had a purchase to make and would take the car on to the Army and Navy Stores. Until the war, Violet had supplied herself with a five-year diary which enabled her to set down in parallel columns what she had done on the same day in any one of the five years. Since 1914, I remembered her telling me, the practice had lapsed; and, as I wanted to give her a birthday-present, I decided to enquire whether diaries of this kind were again procurable. To my delight, I was shewn an enormous volume with columns for no less than ten years; and, as I drove

back to Barton Street, I recalled a conversation that we had held
in 1914 and wondered whether we should be as wide of the mark
now as then if we looked back on the stirring five years that
had lately closed and assured each other than the next five or ten
could not possibly be as stirring.

What was to be this play that we were to make for ourselves
to live?

"*Act One*," I murmured. "*Scene: a corner house in Grosvenor
Road. Time: a September evening in* 1919 . . . *Colin Whimboyne, an
unremarkable-looking man of thirty-one* . . ."

And, in nineteen-twenty-four I should be thirty-six and
Elizabeth thirty-four, Violet thirty-three, Martin eleven and
Humfrey nine. During my month at Ridgeway I had seen the
two boys at closer quarters than ever before; and I wondered
whether by nineteen-twenty-four or nineteen-twenty-nine parts
would have to be written for them. Even without the Cruikshanks
to say of some gesture or expression that "Master Austin had been
just the same at their age," I felt that I was watching the puppy-
stage of two impetuous, self-assertive creatures who were growing under my eyes into the young Austin that I had known at
school. Though their mother still favoured somewhat longer hair
and more babyish clothes than he—I felt sure—would have
tolerated, they were already as forthright, as certain of themselves,
as fully charged with electricity as he had ever been. And in 1929
Norman, now in his cradle, would be half-way through his time
at a preparatory school.

As I sat in the car outside Violet's slumbering, shuttered
house, I took out the latest of the little note-books in which I
had for the last dozen years been jotting down my impressions of
people and their backgrounds, of situations and problems.
Martin and Humfrey were still too young by many years to be
brought on any stage; but already they possessed dramatic
importance for Elizabeth and me, already there had been some
minor clashes between their mother and their "new daddy",
already I was asking myself whether in one way or another they
would set us even farther apart than we now were.

"*She exercises no control over them,*" I had written, "*and, when they
get out of hand (as all high-spirited, healthy children do sometimes), she
summons me like an ogre from his cave to put the fear of God into them.
If I lift a finger (metaphorically, of course, since no one is allowed literally*

to lift a finger against either of them!) before *being summoned, I am told that children should not be repressed; and, when I have played my assigned ogre-part, she dries their tears and stuffs them with sweets till they're left in no doubt whether Codlin or Short is their friend.*"

I put my note-book away, as the door of Violet's house opened and she beckoned to my chauffeur.

"I'm sorry I was so long," she apologized, "but, as we've waited—what is it, seven years since we first met?—seven years, a few minutes more or less . . ."

"I have been buying you a thoroughly utilitarian birthday-present," I said.

"I don't want any presents if I have you."

"Accept it as another of your symbols," I suggested. "A new diary to cover the new chapter in our lives that opened that day on the Downs."

Violet unpacked the parcel and, seeing the contents, turned to kiss me.

"It's the very thing I wanted!" she exclaimed. "Somehow, after 1914, I didn't care much to compare one year with another when every year seemed rather more hopeless than the one before . . . Bless you, Colin!"

"Unlike your old books," I pointed out, "this runs for ten years. If you like to find a symbol in that . . ."

With her lightning power of divining what I had in mind before I could put it into words, she checked me with a frown that was at once followed by a shrug:

"You mean that in *five* years' time His Excellency will have returned from the Spice Coast? Well, it will make no difference of any kind to the five years after that. *Nothing* will ever make any difference to us *now*! If you'd found me a book to cover twenty years or thirty . . . In five years' time . . . I suppose, if Nigel does well, he'll be given a better governorship. After all, he will still be under forty. So shall we all! And, for you the fifteen years *after* that will be the best years of your life. Nineteen-twenty-four to nineteen-thirty-nine? Thirty-six to fifty-one? They're the best years of a man's prime. After fifty, your *experience* will go on increasing and deepening, your technique will go on improving, but I shan't expect the same furious energy, the same steady output. . . . I always speak quite impersonally, Colin, when I talk to you about your work! Twenty years from now . . ."

M

She paused, as the car stopped at the door of my house. While my chauffeur rang the bell and lifted out the dressing-case, a newspaper-boy approached at a run, hoarsely shouting: "Special Edition! Latest Strike News!" I bought a copy and glanced at the headlines as we went into the house. After nearly half a life-time I cannot remember whether the railway-strike had already ended or was only expected to end within the next few hours. At intervals throughout the evening Winter was coming in with later and yet later editions; I recall that I telephoned once or twice to the Lord Keeper's Department for news; and with a queer anticipation of the General Strike in 1926 I recollect that Violet asked me how soon I thought all private houses would be equipped with wireless installations.

"You were saying that twenty years from now . . .?", I prompted her, as we went into my work-room for a glass of sherry.

"I was wondering what twenty years of science applied to daily life would do for us. D'you suppose that in twenty years' time these films will be a serious rival to the theatre?"

"I believe we may live to see the theatre completely knocked out by them. When the people in charge have outgrown their present childishness, the spectacular effects and your independence of time and space . . ."

"And the actors and actresses . . . ," Violet began, walking slowly round the room to study the signed photographs on the tops of my book-cases.

I said that in twenty years' time (if we were all alive then) I should be little surprised to find myself writing plays exclusively for a camera-*plus*-gramophone. And I saw no reason why they should be worse than what I wrote now. By then, I went on, Gerald du Maurier and Owen Nares, Gladys Cooper and Marie Löhr would—as likely as not—be acting solely in these film-plays. Again, I could see no reason why, with a slightly changed technique, they should not act as well.

Violet looked for a pencil and then seated herself in the winged armchair to the left of the fire-place, her new diary open on her knees.

"I'm going to make an index at the end of this," she told me. "What we were saying five and ten years earlier. Wireless: I asked how soon you thought we should all have it. And film-plays. Oh, you said something at Hounslow about hoping this railway-strike was not a symbol of what life would be in our new peace-time world. I should like to put down what you really think, not only what you hope."

I said that I believed there would be strikes of increasing magnitude and frequency until the people of England learnt the meaning of the word "inflation". The ever-rising cost of living produced strikes for higher wages which in turn increased living-costs and occasioned fresh strikes. The remedy was to produce more and to consume less. I believe Violet made a note of these unoriginal words. I certainly hope that she did so, for everything else that I said before we went up to dress seems in retrospect to have been more fantastically wrong than anything I had said that summer afternoon in 1914, when we agreed that the next five years could hardly be as stirring as the last. Out of hand we dismissed the three spectres that were in fact to haunt the next twenty years, till the generation that (as we said) had at least been spared a European war was enmeshed and mangled in a world-war: "militarism" and "the German peril" would be meaningless phrases to Martin and Humfrey, "unemployment" and "the problem of poverty" could not trouble Norman, who would be an old man before the wastage of the late war had been repaired.

"I'm glad you don't regard the films as an immediate menace," said Violet, as we sat down to dinner.

"I think it's a much greater danger that the theatre-public will demand something that I can't give them," I answered, "and something that other men can. Whatever happens, I shall have had a good run for my money," I added. "And good money for my run. If in five or ten years' time . . ."

Many years have passed since Violet alluded to her record of our prognostications in 1919; and I can remember only the general picture of what we foresaw. We did not expect, I do not think either of us wanted, an easy time: four years of war had cracked and to some extent stripped away the varnish of civilization with which *Homo Sapiens* had been covering his father, the anthropoid ape, for more than four hundred thousand years. Tens of millions had died since 1914, the world's savings had gone up in smoke. Nevertheless, the earth was still fertile on its surface and incalculably rich below its surface; science could make good the deficiencies of our man-power; and who could want a life of ease till the devastation of these war-years had been repaired? We should require, Violet and I told each other, to work harder than ever before, but at least we need work no longer, as in the years before 1914, under the perpetual cloud of potential war. The League of Nations, the Covenant, President Wilson and the war-weary of five continents had put future wars beyond the pale. We were secure abroad; we should be secure at home when economic laws were freed of their war-time pegs.

Though we continued to talk of the new play that we were making and living, I do not remember that we sketched it in any great detail. Once or twice a queer stillness descended on Violet, as though she were saying again that, if she moved, she might wake from a perfect dream; and at some point a long silence fell between us, to be softly broken by a sigh charged with utter happiness.

"May I not share?," I asked.

"You shall share everything." Violet answered. "I was thinking of what you said about Elizabeth: that she had come and gone without leaving the faintest mark on this house. It's true! And that reminded me of something I'd almost forgotten, something—to me—far stranger. Do you *ever* remember that Nigel once occupied this house, that you joined him before he married, that father and I came to dine here regularly while Nigel and I were engaged? For any mark that *he* has left . . ."

"He came . . . And he went. . . . I could see you hardly recognized the place when you walked in. No, *I* find it hard to believe that he ever lived here. As for any *mark* that he left . . . I should like to think that he has left no mark on your life, your memory, your spirit, that he ceases to exist when you don't see him. If I thought about her, I *suppose* I should say that Elizabeth was technically existing at this moment . . ."

"When I'm with you, Colin, *nobody* else exists!"

VI

THE approach of peace in 1918 had stirred to new life certain moribund societies which impulsively invited me to address their members on any theme that I might choose at any time that I might find convenient. In the autumn of 1919, I was required to begin fulfilling my promises.

Sometimes this took the form of a lecture, sometimes I

responded to a toast and sometimes I spoke to a motion which was then debated. In general, this is not a kind of entertainment that I greatly enjoy; but in the last months of the war and the first of the armistice I needed distraction with all the craving of a drug-addict for his poison and, later, as I cast reluctantly about for appropriate subjects, I was somewhat consoled by the discovery that my hosts were feeding and paying me to do something that I must have done in any event as a matter of professional routine. I see that my first discourse was entitled *The Changing Social Scene*; and, though I ranged from a pretentiously styled *Materia Dramatica* for an audience of Cambridge undergraduates to a catchpenny: *When Is A "Problem" Not A Problem?* for an assembly of north-midland artisans stubbornly set on self-improvement, my main line of study was always the same and, when a publisher with more money than authors asked me for a volume of occasional papers, he suggested after a single glance at the typescript that it should be called *The War And The Theatre*.

Probably the least-read book of any that I have produced, it was the pleasantest to write, as I discussed every sentence in it with Violet; and its publication led to a series, not yet ended, of well-paid commissions for newspaper-articles on such subjects as *Career Women And Bachelor Girls* or *The New Poor And The Old Profiteers*. How in fact, we debated from the big chairs on either side of my work-room fire, had the late war disposed for ever of certain old, stock problems, how far was the peace with its economic upheavals and its social revolutions changing the stuff that drawing-room comedies were made on? I remember, after some first-night party, quoting to Violet a lament from Mrs. Patrick Campbell that she could find no plays to suit her; I had asked why she did not revive some of her old successes, such as *The Second Mrs. Tanqueray*; and her reply was that she did not feel drawn at the moment to period pieces. *Mrs. Tanqueray* was "dated"; its morals and manners belonged to a different geological age. Now, if I would write a play, said Stella, and call it *Paula Tanqueray's First Husband*, there might be a fortune in it for both of us. As we drove home, Violet and I amused ourselves for an irreverent half-hour by bringing the morals of the early eighteen-nineties up to-date.

Were they worse, were they better or were they merely different? In 1919, we agreed, if the stiff-jointed Aubrey could have beguiled a vital woman of the half-world like Paula to marry him, his friends at their bachelor dinner would have acclaimed it his social salvation; that colourless daughter of his would have learnt from her step-mother, if not the whole art of sex-appeal, at least the elements of skilful make-up; no one would have been ostracized, no one would have been morally quarantined.

"*A fortiori*, no one," I continued, "would have committed suicide."

"And instead of a play in three or four acts," said Violet, "you would have a slow curtain at the end of the second, with Cayley Drummle explaining that in the present state of morals there was no play to offer an audience and that all money would be returned at the box-office. At least . . . Does any one trouble to explain anything nowadays? Doesn't your *raisonneur* belong to a *Dolly Dialogues* time when button-holed and frock-coated young men of fashion took their gloves and silk hats with them into drawing-rooms?"

"And their closely chaperoned sisters gazed wistfully at the hansom-cabs in which they were forbidden to ride. Picture 'Lady Windermere' driving 'Lord Darlington' home from the play and inviting him in for a drink, as I hope you're going to invite me! With 'Lord Windermere' abroad too!"

As she felt for her latch-key, Violet asked me to picture any dramatist of the nineties planning the act that was to follow our meeting on the Downs above Ridgeway.

"Twelve months elapse," she continued, as we entered the house. "Elizabeth chooses the country for her children's sake, and you only meet her, in a big party, at week-ends. In Nigel's absence, I occupy myself with this decorating business that you persuaded me to take up and, as I've always had a literary circle since the old days in Russell Square, you and I can meet whenever we please. No, there's not the *material* for another act. Your audience would say we should all of us—Nigel included—be very hard to please if we didn't feel that we had all the *conditions* of happiness, or *almost* all . . ."

I asked why she had found it necessary to add that "almost all"; and she answered at once that time alone would shew whether I was artist enough to make art my wife and mistress, whether I should always feel content to be surrounded by the children of my imagination and, as an afterthought, whether she herself would be satisfied with the creatures of some one else's brain.

"I'm more your wife than I ever was Nigel's," she went on, gazing at the fire so steadily that I could see the dancing of the flames reflected in her deep-set grave eyes. "More your wife than Elizabeth ever has been or ever could be. In a rather hackneyed phrase, though, a marriage of minds is all that the world will allow us, in public, and, if we're to be entirely happy, the marriage must be fruitful. You must make me feel that I've helped to create these children of your imagination, that they're *worthy* of us . . ."

"But, dear heart, except when you were abroad, you know that every play I've written . . ."

"Has been—if I may throw myself a bouquet—a little bit licked into shape by me *after* birth. I want *more* than that, Colin! Your work is the biggest thing in your life and you're the biggest thing in mine. I want you to take it more seriously than anything in the world! You're far too ready, my darling one, to say that your vein will be worked out in ten or twenty years' time, but I want to see you planning at least the next *ten* years, mining for a richer vein when life has enriched your experience, sinking new shafts that will make me say: 'This *is* first-rate!' What should we have lost from Galsworthy and Maugham and Arnold Bennett if *they'd* stuck to a single line like you?"

"If I were in the least like any of them . . . ," I began.

I must try my hand, Violet insisted, on novels and short stories. It was Meredith the poet that we now rated higher than Meredith the novelist.

"And Galsworthy the novelist . . . ," she continued reflectively, then abruptly interrupted herself to push a footstool to my chair and clasp my right hand in her own two as though she were willing it to do what I protested it was incapable of doing. "This is only the *beginning*," she whispered. "Twelve months . . . We're still fumbling in this most strange new world, still staring at your changing social scene, still hunting for a pattern. I want you, at the *end*, Colin, to look back on all you've *done*. If you can say, when we're both old, that you've something substantial to shew for your life and that I've helped you by believing in you and keeping you up to the mark . . ."

From memory I was able to quote a list of twelve tentative titles. I had completed a *scenario*, I told Violet, for each of the first five and had made a skeleton outline for each of the remaining seven. The general conditions of the London theatre convinced me that I should never repeat the triumphs of my *annus mirabilis*;

but, if all these seedlings came to flower and I produced only one play in twelve months I could give a good account at least of my industry for somewhat more than ten years.

"Without waiting till we're both old," I added, "I can tell you that in everything I've written since we first argued about technique at Austin's dinner-table, I've felt your hand on mine as it is now. If you took it away . . . When we're old, what I shall say is that the intellectual *companionship* you've always given me . . . No, I'm sorry I *can't* say it!" I apologized, as I found that my voice had suddenly become unsteady. "Let's go back to Stella Campbell! You know, morals and manners change in detail so quickly that I think it would be a mistake to plan *very* far ahead: your play would be dated before it went into rehearsal. Life itself changes so quickly! We assume—and why not?—that your conditions of happiness will continue, but ever since August, 1914, I've rather lost faith in *permanency*. When you look in after years at that diary of yours to see what has happened to our pattern since we first made it . . ."

Though in the next few years we were to talk many times of plans and patterns and the play that we were making of our lives, I do not recall that in fact we often checked our predictions by reference to the diary. History was being made too fast for us to assemble the separate items as they occurred or to see them in perspective until history had become ancient history: hardly had we agreed that the war-to-end-war had in fact ended war in Europe, at least for our time, when we read in swift succession that the Italians were beginning a private war over Trieste, the Turks conducting a war in Asia Minor that threatened the peace of Europe before the ink was dry on the peace-treaties, the French occupying the Ruhr in a desperate effort to discover who had really won the Great War. Hardly had we agreed that to make good the waste and destruction of the war-years we must all of us produce more and consume less before we were witnessing a triple-alliance strike, mass-unemployment, a general strike, a spreading life on the dole and finally a financial collapse with a public default on our debt to America.

"Our great mistake goes back to 1914," Violet told me one night when we had been glancing through my recent contributions to the press. "Most of us honestly believed that a war would bring about a general change of *heart*. We see now that with leopards and Ethiopians . . ."

"Were people of our age either of these things in 1914?," I asked. "We'd been bred and trained to a thousand different ends, from writing poetry to emptying dustbins. None of us, except a hangman's apprentice, was trained to take human life. Between one day and another you tell millions of potential poets and scavengers that their job is to kill the other fellow before they're killed themselves. They're adaptable: you saw them at bayonet-practice on straw-stuffed sacks, but do they adapt themselves *back* again so easily after they've smelt blood, the other fellow's or their own? When we were sketching *The War And The Theatre*, I told you it would be a mistake to plan *very* far ahead: we were still feverish, in a still sick world. Any pattern we might make only twelve months after the cease-fire . . ."

And four years later, the world was somewhat more sick, most of us were somewhat more feverish. This conversation, as I have good reason to remember, belongs to the early weeks of 1924; a second foolhardy publisher was asking for another volume of occasional papers; and Violet had been studying my ephemeral comments on the changing social scene to determine whether any were worth reprinting.

"We agreed then that the pattern other people had made for us was better than any we could have made for ourselves. Do you still think that, Colin?"

"I don't *think*! I *know*! Admittedly, it's not in the least what I expected. If you had told me in 1919 that I should still be a civil servant . . ."

By 1924 the gallery of signed photographs in my work-room was diversified by portraits (generally as unflattering to the subjects as the inscriptions were flattering to me) of the chiefs under whom I had served. The general election of 1922 had brought one new political head to the Lord Keeper's Department; the change of prime minister in 1923 had brought a second; and the general election just ended, with the first Labour government in English history, had brought a third. I had expected nothing of this in 1919, when I looked to see Axminster holding on like the Vicar of Bray until his sinecure was abolished and his staff distributed among other departments.

"It's part of the pattern," Violet laughed, "that you should tell me each year is going to be your last. For five years I've reminded you that, if you retire, you won't have the same excuse for living in London. Perhaps you don't want it. I purposely don't

worry you with questions about Ridgeway and I don't really
know how you expected things to turn out there. . . . May I take
these typescripts home with me? There are one or two small
criticisms . . ."

As I packed them into a parcel for her, I tried to imagine how
I should describe my life in London and Wiltshire if I were now
meeting her for the first time after five years. Throughout that
period I had been going to Ridgeway, according to plan, for
week-ends; and, if I did not spend my annual leaves there, this
was partly because it suited my comfort to go abroad for a few
weeks in the winter and still more because Elizabeth made it clear
that I was in the way when the boys were at home, with their
friends, for the summer holidays. The week-ends, however, were
widely different from anything that I had foreseen. Like Violet,
I had thought that life would be easier if Elizabeth and I did not
face each other for too many silent or platitudinous dinners; but
it soon seemed as if Elizabeth felt that life would be insupport-
able if every room was not filled for every night that I was
there.

"I don't know whether it was the high-brow quality of
Austin's parties that she found so fatiguing . . . ," I began.
"They're not that now."

"I only went to one," said Violet, "when she wanted my
advice about changing two of the carpets. Then it was all family.
Well, for better or worse, Ridgeway is very convenient for
Newbury; and your brothers-in-law knew to a pennyweight what
prestige they got from 'being in the Ridgeway House party'.
There's nothing snobbish about *your* brothers' wives, but John
always follows the line of least resistance and Blanche has never
forgotten that a younger son bought her husband's birthright.
She's going to spoil the Egyptians. Henry? He isn't so lazy as
John, but he's far more greedy; and Constance has been worrying
how to keep him contented ever since his job as Lord Drury's
agent came to an end. At Ridgeway he gets free board and
lodging, two miles of first-rate fishing on the Kennet . . . I'm not
inventing this, my dear! They both know, Constance and
Blanche, that I'm an old friend of yours; they wanted me on their
side, to intercede with you if Elizabeth grew tired of having
them there. And I think it's very much what we might have
expected."

I reminded Violet of a chance prophecy, now five years old,

that Elizabeth would be no more at ease with "the county", as she elected to call it, than with Austin's "intellectuals".

"You spoke of an inferiority-complex," I added.

"She thoroughly enjoys being the bright social light of the neighbourhood. True, she never enters another house and never opens her mouth in her own, but she's a J.P. and a name to conjure with in juvenile courts. If that's *really* her *métier*, if she has found it at last . . . Perhaps you're right, my dear, in still thinking that things have worked out better for us than we could have planned for ourselves."

"But don't *you*?"

"There's nothing *I* would change! I suppose . . . I want to be assured that you too, after five years . . ."

With a sudden feeling of suffocation I interrupted Violet to ask whether all these references to five years meant that she had heard from Nigel.

"We can come to him later," she answered. "It's *you*, Colin . . . There are moments when one can take stock . . . When one *must* . . . Partings of ways . . . To go on or to go back . . . To cut one's losses or double one's stake . . . Things will be changed for us unless we take a hold; and this is your chance, for saying whether you want them changed."

"A chance for both to say whether we're tired of each other?," I asked, but I could not be sure that Violet was listening.

"I always feel that the world of your imagination is your real world, Colin," she continued. "You always needed mental companionship, I think you always needed a woman in your life. Don't *you* feel that the characters you create, the men and women that we—yes, darling heart, I boldly say 'we'—*we* have thought and talked into existence, staring into a fire and speaking in whispers . . . ? And you've known, ever since I first told you that my ruling passion was the theatre, but that I couldn't myself create . . . *My* real life these last five years . . . The people in our plays are a thousand times more vivid than so-called flesh-and-blood people! To watch them taking shape till they stride across your stage . . . To me, it's never Ronald Squire and Yvonne Arnaud playing your 'Sir Guy' and 'Lady Ballance', it's Sir Guy and Lady Ballance giving *them* the chance of coming to life for a few hours. Will you ever know the little Norman you've begotten as you know the Guys and Hilarys and Cynthias that you've invented?"

As she paused, I begged her to explain her dark reference to doubling our stakes.

"There are no losses to cut," I continued.

"You're sure? If I could leave you to enjoy the world of your imagination in peace . . . We've been marvellously favoured by fortune all these years, but we can't expect it to go on. Do we even *want* it to go on? A great deal of water has flown under Westminster Bridge since I asked your advice about divorcing Nigel. Nineteen-nineteen . . . ."

And here we were in nineteen-twenty-four, the end of Nigel's term as governor of the Spice Coast. If he continued in the colonial service, he could hope for promotion; if he retired, he could pick up as many directorships as he fancied. I did not trouble to say how a divorce would affect either career, because I did not believe that Violet could now divorce him. Should she incite him to divorce her, naming me as corespondent? I did not trouble to think how a divorce would affect my position in the Department of the Lord Keeper, because I neither knew nor cared. She would secure her freedom; but she would be unable to use it as we both wished unless I secured mine at the same time. Would Elizabeth divorce me? I was no longer in a position to divorce her.

"You said we could come to Nigel later," I began. "You've heard from him?"

Violet nodded, a little grimly—I thought—and with a pursing of her lips that reminded me of the day when she consulted me about the crisis that had made it impossible for her to continue under the same roof as her husband.

"I didn't know him in his nursery," she sighed, "but I've told you how he always wants to run before he can walk. After five years in which he has never been home on leave, he now considers himself, rightly or wrongly, the greatest living authority on all colonial questions. For all I know he may be: he has good brains and he's a tremendous worker. Well, he feels this is another of the now-or-never moments in his career. Shall he go back into politics, with the hope of being made colonial secretary? Shall he try for a first-class governorship?"

"Where you," I put in, "would—in the eyes of the world— have no very good reason for not accompanying him."

Violet's eyes narrowed; and my memory went back to a night in Grosvenor Road when she turned the pages of her still-new diary and remarked that in five years' time Nigel would be returning to England, but that this would make no difference of any kind to the five years after that.

"Shall he," she continued, "trade his experience for something in Big Business? I shall be interested, Colin, if you can find out what the Colonial Office *really* thinks of him. Are these all day-dreams? Or is he now a man to reckon with? I shall have to reckon with him in another sense," she warned me with a wistful glance round the room where we had spent so many evenings in the last five years. "He's on his way home. I won't read you his letter, but there are one or two phrases which we shall both do well to digest. He's not going out *again* to any white man's grave. He thanks God that our long separation is nearly ended. It has been five years of penal servitude, for him, in solitary confinement. And he thinks that is enough for any man to purge any offence."

VII

In a more robust age, recaptured by older members of the Garrick Club when I was elected, the gallery and pit still expressed disapproval of a play by pelting the actors (and, if they were lucky enough to catch him, the author, too) with decaying or dead vegetable and animal matter. In these softer days, booing and catcalls are generally the worst that the inadequately appreciated playwright has to face; but, though my own fortitude has never been more severely tested than by the occasional failure of an audience to raise even a single cry of "Author!", I am not sure that to sit through one's own "first night" is not the bravest thing that any man can do. My friend Nelson Eversley, who adds a bar to his D.S.O. in every world-war, once assured me that he would not stand—or sit quaking—in my shoes on such an occasion if he were promised a V.C.

Perhaps it was a reflection of my own nervousness that kept Elizabeth from witnessing any play of mine until it had been running a week or two; perhaps she was not deeply interested in the theatre or interested at all in first-night audiences, perhaps she was a little jealous of my success and resentful of the greater interest that her neighbours at the dinner-table took in stageland than in the juvenile courts. It would indeed have seemed odd if she had confessed that she lacked time or inclination for seeing her own husband's productions; but she contrived to combine duty with thrift by asking me for a box, giving a luncheon-party in Grosvenor Road and taking a party of her friends to a *matinée*, after which my bed-of-the-river house knew her no more till next time.

Occasionally, if it were a Saturday, we met at Paddington and travelled together to Marlborough. I still remember—I doubt, indeed, whether I shall ever forget—that this happened on the late-winter evening after she had paid her first and only visit to the Connaught Theatre, where *The Waters of Lethe* was settling down to a run of sixteen months. Of all my plays, this had caused me most searching of heart; of all my first nights this was the most harrowing. Violet, beside me in the shadowy back of the stage-box, might assure me that this was a far, far better thing than I had ever done before; but I could only recall gloomily that with no other production of mine had everything gone so consistently wrong from the beginning. I had hoped to have it directed by Basil Dean, but his hands were already full; I had counted on Marie Tempest to play the lead, but she was on the full flowing tide of a success that threatened to run for ever; I needed an "intimate" theatre and could get nothing smaller than the Connaught, which promised as much "intimacy" as Olympia; and, as an omen for the superstitious, my stage-manager dropped dead in the middle of the first rehearsal.

"None of which," Violet persisted, "affects the quality of the play. It's more *original*, it's better *constructed*. . . . If these people are capable of appreciating good work when they see it . . . And you know, my dear, I haven't *always* said your work was good . . ."

She leant forward to see the first arrival of "these people", as they sauntered to their places. The habitual first-nighters seemed to be there in force; and I heard her murmuring "Sir George Lewis . . . Lady Cunard . . . Eddie Marsh . . . Lady Colefax . . . Gordon Selfridge . . . Lord Lathom." There were actors and actresses not at that moment playing: Seymour Hicks and George Grossmith. Lady Wyndham and old Sir Squire Bancroft. My own friends had rallied gallantly to my support; and Violet's murmur was now of "John Lavery and Hazel . . . Lady Randolph . . . Mrs. Keppel." In sobering contrast to the prevailing white waistcoats, I saw an occasional black tie surmounting a short coat; and I hardly knew whether to be more flattered or intimidated by the eminence of the critics who had thought my play worthy of their attention. "Walkley . . . ," I heard Violet saying. "St. John Ervine . . . James Agate . . ."

Was the company on the other side of the great red curtains as wretched as I? Had I felt less unsure of myself, I should have been "behind" by now with a word of encouragement here, a jest there, a reminder—disguised-as-a-compliment to little Peggy Learoyd who at the dress-rehearsal had so far forgotten to mumble that I could hear every word of every line at the back of the upper circle; I had been told on other occasions that I inspired confidence even if I did not myself feel it and that I achieved at least an air of composure which was soothing to taut nerves strained to snapping-point before that last-trump call of "Be-ginners, please"; but to-night I was more likely to start an epidemic of hysteria. For the first time in a now fairly long experience I seemed to be completely out of accord with my company, my producer and, hardly less, with my collaborator Violet. Not for one moment did I fear that any one would fail me; but the atmosphere was defeatist and I felt that, if a single scene dragged for a single minute, everybody would be saying "Who was right?"

And who, I asked myself as the lights were slowly dimmed and my pulse bounded very much less slowly, *would* prove right? When I completed the first draft in the seclusion of Grosvenor Road, my puppets—at least to me—were so vital that I could see them as children and as old men, long before they made their first entrance and long after they were hidden by the final curtain. When I shewed the script to Gerald du Maurier, he commented that, though he could not spare time to produce it, *The Waters of Lethe* would "play itself". Naturally, when we came to casting, Violet and I did not expect the play of our imagination to be the same as a play interpreted by Dion Boucicault and Irene Van-brugh (if I could get them); but the play that began to take shape at rehearsal (when I had to be content with Nowell Crummock and Jennifer Deane) was something quite different from what Violet and I had imagined and, when Geoffrey Thirsk was engaged to direct the production, it became most unrecognizably different from what I had written.

Violet maintained indignantly that the play was being mur-dered; I, recalling Gerald's criticism, asserted that it was "playing itself" and that in some ways I thought Nowell and Jennifer were making a better play of it. But for the intervention of Geoffrey Thirsk, they might indeed have given me my head or I might have given them theirs, in one way or another achieving artistic integrity; but the nearer we came to our opening night the more I felt that *The Waters of Lethe* had become three plays and that we could not agree whether the acting edition was to be the author's or the producer's or the actors'.

The result was an uneasy compromise, all the less satisfactory to me because I was getting my own way on most points and getting it to please Violet rather than to assert my own convictions. I still thought that Nowell and Jennifer, in studying their parts, had seized on possibilities and significances of which I had hardly been conscious in writing them; their creative contribution, far from murdering my play, had invested a somewhat different play with a gay, breathless spontaneity of their own. In my opinion, I told Violet, this was as it should be: I was not so conceited as to imagine that anything I wrote was incapable of improvement. Violet's reply, after a reference to the Athanasian creed, was that *The Waters of Lethe* suggested to her a play written in English for French actors and produced by a German *impresario*, none of them understanding any language but their own. Who, in three hours' time, would prove to have been right?

In my association with the theatre I have always found a warm-hearted generosity which is sometimes less noticeable in other branches of art. As the house demonstrated that night, the press next day, Violet had been right; and I could tell her so before the first act was half over. Already, however, the door of our box had been quietly opened, my chair quietly pushed forward and the quiet voice of Geoffrey Thirsk was saying: "You needn't hide any longer! This is going to be another of your successes, my boy. I hope I didn't seem very pig-headed in preferring *my* reading: I like yours better." And, after the first curtain, Jennifer Deane danced in, still in her grease-paint, to congratulate me and ask Violet whether she might kiss me. When she had danced away to her dressing-room, I said that I was going to smoke a cigarette; but the anteroom to the box was half-full, compliments were raining down on me and the deep drawl of Bridget Constable had informed me that I was coming to her supper-party in Great Cumberland Place. Would I tell her where she could find a telephone? She would then instruct her butler, who had been trained never to be surprised, to organize one; and her young daughters could get out of their beds and invite people. There would not be more than eighty or a hundred, two hundred at the outside. She had not cared to arrange anything before, as she could not know whether the play was going to be a "flop".

"There are still two more acts," I warned her.

"Oh, you're all right!" she answered.

But was I? Any one who has seen or read *The Waters of Lethe* will remember the sudden twist in the very last lines, which I intended to set the whole play in its proper perspective, as Lewis Carroll sixty years earlier set "Alice's" dream in perspective by making her say: "*You're nothing but a pack of cards!*" and as Arnold Bennett only two years before set *Riceyman Steps* in perspective with the aid of a contents-bill, "*which displayed nothing but 'mysterious Death of a Miser in Clerkenwell'.*" It was novel; if it succeeded, it would be as effective as if the audience had been told to reverse their opera-glasses and view these angry, puzzled, intriguing little people of mine in their true proportions; to my own thinking, I had prepared the way so that no one could complain of being taken unfairly by surprise and I hoped that I had allowed enough time for the reversed opera-glasses to focus themselves on the stage before the curtain fell. Had I, in fact? Would the critics say that I had misled them, the public that I had made fools of them? "*Sir James Barrie*," I made an imaginary writer say, "*who has forgotten more about the theatre than Mr. Colin Whimboyne will ever learn, can play these tricks and play them successfully . . .*" Had I thrown away a winner by trying to be clever? The worst moment in an evening of almost unbearably bad and good moments was introduced by an alarming silence, which shewed that my point had not been taken. I believe that the signal for the curtain was deliberately delayed (as it was delayed in every performance thereafter) for the less nimble-minded to collect their wits. Then began the applause. An enthusiastic voice from the stalls murmured: "I call that a master-stroke!" And for the first time in my experience the audience shouted "Author! Author!" before the actors had taken their calls.

As always, I felt light-headed (and, I am afraid, on the verge of tears) as I made my bow, standing hand-in-hand first with Jennifer and Peggy, then with Nowell and Geoffrey Thirsk, and I heard myself returning thanks. I was still light-headed and very limp when I returned to Violet and piloted her to the stage-door where my car was awaiting us and the doorkeeper asked with a

N

grin whether I was calling a rehearsal at ten for cuts. And I shall
for ever be grateful to Bridget Constable, who met us in the hall
of her house and firmly carried me off to her own room for
cutlets, champagne and a small cigar before I was required to
meet her other guests.

"You were looking done in," she told me. "I don't know
why. This is going to be one of your biggest successes. I suppose,
any first night . . ."

"For some reason," I answered, "this was the most nerve-
racking that I remember."

"Your last curtain was *brilliant*! I won't say it didn't leave
rather a *bitter* taste in the mouth."

And this, in somewhat different language, was Elizabeth's
verdict, on the memorable evening that I have mentioned, when
we travelled down together after she had taken a party of fellow
workers for juvenile welfare to the first Saturday *matinée* of *Lethe*.
I have not mentioned, I think, that we ran into a dense fog before
we reached Slough; and I have sometimes thought that our
journey would not have been memorable at all if the train had not
been an hour and twenty minutes late, if I had not finished my
papers and book with time in hand for conversation, if one of
Elizabeth's friends had not—apparently—been a frustrated
dramatic critic and if Elizabeth's report of her rather crude
literary judgements had not come so soon after Bridget Constable's supper-party at which, though I and my play were the
subject of discussion, I listened to an hour of the best conversation that it has ever been my privilege to hear from "Prof" Ross,
Alfred Sutro, Bridget herself, Arnold Bennett, W. L. Courtney,
Violet and John Drinkwater. Elizabeth's friend, who seemed to
be celebrated enough as "Elspeth" to dispense with a surname,
was tolerant of the device that had been the making of the play,
but she was aesthetically shocked that I had not "prepared" my
audience better. Elizabeth disliked the device itself: it was
"needlessly cynical" and she could not see why a play should not
have a "happy ending".

"So long as happy endings are not yet the rule in *life* . . .," I
began, as the train stopped and I lowered the window to see how
far we had come.

"Oh, Colin, you're letting in all the fog!," Elizabeth exclaimed. "Where are we?"

"Burnham Beeches," I replied, wondering whether in truth

the fog was thicker outside than in. If I remembered rightly, it was Oscar Wilde's "Mrs. Erlynne" who could never make out whether the fog in England produced the serious people or the serious people produced the fogs. It was poor Elizabeth's fate to shroud the austere simplicity of the multiplication-table in mist if any one asked her the answer to "seven times eight." And, unless I withdrew unsociably with the day's crossword-puzzle, I could look forward to another two or three hours of this at our present rate of progress. I refused, as I had now been refusing for more than five years, to admit that I could look forward to another forty years of this if anything came to disturb the happy ending that she and I, Violet and Nigel had contrived for our private dreams; but I could never blind myself to the possibility that circumstances too strong for us might some day compel Elizabeth and me to share a house and make pretence of sharing our lives. "I'm sorry your friend was taken by surprise," I said. "I hoped that by now we had left enough time for my point to sink in, but it's very hard to judge the speed of an audience's reaction. In the play I'm working on at the moment . . ."

"Elspeth wanted to know whether you were writing anything now. I said that you never discussed your work with me."

Perhaps with a feeling that, if I talked without stopping until we reached Marlborough, I might keep Elizabeth from talking, I told her that I would gladly give her an outline of my present comedy if this would interest her and if she would recognize that as yet I had not put pen to paper.

"It's an idea that occurred to me a few days ago," I explained truthfully enough, as I put my feet up and began to fill a pipe. "I can't *promise* you a 'happy ending', as I don't yet know what the ending is going to be. I should like your opinion. Mr. and Mrs. Linden, as I've called them, have been married for ten years and separated for seven of them . . ."

I believe that I afflicted my Mr. Linden with an ungovernable temper at times, but endowed him generally with good sense and good nature so that, since neither he nor his wife wanted to marry again, they had agreed on a private separation—in preference to a divorce—for the sake of their children. My first scene was laid in the office of Mrs. Linden's solicitors, where the senior partner sat knitting his brows over a letter in which—after all these years —she asked his advice about having her marriage dissolved.

After almost a quarter of a century I cannot pretend to

remember the details of a plot which I was inventing piece by piece with a cautious eye on Elizabeth to see how much time she would take before rousing to ask whether I was planning to put our two selves into a play. On reflection, I feel that I need not have troubled. Probably I shall never know whether "divorce", to her, always and exclusively meant divorce-proceedings between us or whether in her eyes any one's divorce constituted the sin for which there was no forgiveness. As I improvised my fantasy, which—incidentally—was far better done by Alan Herbert in *Holy Deadlock*, I could see her placid eyes beginning to kindle, her rather slack mouth hardening; and I felt that we might have been back again at Bowbury Castle in the first week of our honeymoon. It did not matter that my Lindens' marriage was over in all but name, that one or perhaps both now wanted to marry again and that each had been unfaithful to the other. It did not matter that I conveniently got rid of the children who were supposed to be holding them together. In her opposition to divorce Elizabeth went further than the Mosaic code or the Christian doctrine: incompatibility or infidelity, desertion or cruelty provided no excuse, marriages were made in Heaven, marriage-vows were taken in the sight of God, the marriage-tie could be sundered only by death and, if I was really writing a play on this subject, she wished that I had not told her anything about it. Greatly against her will, she had been taken to see Clemence Dane's *Bill of Divorcement*; and it had shocked her to the marrow.

"*Insanity?*", she hissed at me. "When a woman has taken a husband for *better* or *worse*. . . ?"

I was so much interested in this exhibition of impassioned fundamentalism that I thanked Elizabeth with complete sincerity for giving me her point of view so candidly. It was hopeless antagonism of this kind, I said, the irresistible force meeting the immovable body, that provided the stuff of drama. Fortunately for me, I was not a moralist and did not have to take one side or another; but my duty to the public demanded of me that I should stage a fair fight and, if I might regard Elizabeth as the immovable body, I must make Linden or Mrs. Linden—I had not yet decided which—the irresistible force.

"One or other of them," I said, "perhaps both, will fight as hard to break apart as you would fight to keep them together. A new start: it's *vital* to them. If they can't bribe or bully you, they'll try to force your hand somehow . . ."

"They can't. What then?"

"I suppose they'll do what most people do when they can't get what they want: they'll go without it. That doesn't mean they won't make their new start: it only means they'll make it without your help. And that's so easy nowadays that I hardly feel I'm staging a fair fight: you get the honours of war for your point of view, but they win the war without firing a shot. I wonder whether any one has used *The Honours of War* as a title?"

I was not sorry to take out a pencil and pretend to make notes. Elizabeth had given me her answer, though I was unlikely ever to know whether she understood that I had been asking her a question; and I had given her mine. "*Irresistible force and immovable body*". I wrote. "*Mrs. Linden . . . I shall call her Agatha. Agatha Linden. Mutato nomine de te fabula narratur. The other couple! Charles and Hermione Brent. And the force that is going to make it an evenly matched contest . . .*"

I glanced at my evening paper to remind myself of the date. Nigel Oakhirst was not due in England for another week, but I felt that his shadow had been hanging over London ever since he sailed from the Spice Coast. Since the night when Violet told me of his imminent return, his name had not been mentioned between us; but in every plan that we discussed I felt that—in her own phrase—we now had to "reckon with" a third person in our lives. That day I had lain in wait for Sir Matthew Greystoke, of the Colonial Office, invited him to lunch with me and encouraged him to air his everlasting grievance against the inflexibility of the service that he administered.

"No man," he asserted, vigorously peppering his oysters, "should fill an important position at home till he has learnt the difficulties of the man on the spot. And no one should be sent out to become the man on the spot till he has served an apprenticeship at home. If Government House is to understand the Colonial-Office point of view and *vice versa* . . ."

"I suppose," I said, "it's easier to find governorships for promising young men in Downing Street than to find berths in Downing Street for retired governors. Take a man like Nigel Oakhirst, who had no departmental training. He has now finished his term on the Spice Coast, where I understand he has done very well. What's his future? You would now keep him in London? I'm interested in him because we were at school together."

Before answering my question, Greystoke enquired acidly what I meant by "doing very well". Oakhirst had indeed done all that was required of him; but all that was required of any man on the Spice Coast was that he should contend successfully with the climate. There were no problems for him to solve, no opportunities for him to exploit. He must keep on good terms with the trading community; he must be ready to stamp on the ever-smouldering embers of the slave-trade; he must refrain from taking bribes; and he must not drink himself to death from sheer boredom.

"I felt sorry for Oakhirst at first," my companion continued. "So much enthusiasm and so few opportunities. My sympathy rather wilted when he began to pitch in fifty-page memoranda on the coconut-crop and the possibility of growing sisal. I had to read his infernal lucubrations!"

"And now?," I asked.

"If he wants a second term, no one is likely to say him nay. At the moment, there's nothing worth his while that we could offer him elsewhere. And—forgive my saying it of a friend of yours, Whimboyne!—we shouldn't care about having him at the C.O. To begin with, he won't rise any higher: though he's able and hard-working, he doesn't hit it off with people. To go on with, he has too good an opinion of himself. We old stagers don't like being taught our business by a young gentleman who was jobbed into an appointment for political reasons . . ."

Though Greystoke continued to talk in the same strain for a while longer, I felt that I now had an answer for one at least of Violet's questions: the Colonial Office did not think highly of Nigel and *à fortiori* the prime minister would not think highly of him as a future secretary of state for the colonies. The choice before him seemed to be between another five years in a white man's grave, which he had rejected in advance, and an approach to "big business", on which I could express no opinion. When my guest left me, I began a letter to Violet; and, as the train stopped and started and stopped again on its dismal journey through the thickening fog, I tried to bring my letter up to date by giving the heads of my recent conversation with Elizabeth.

"For six years," I began, "I've been asking myself whether I ought not to have walked out and left her to divorce me. I now know that she wouldn't divorce me if I became such a public scandal that I was turned

out of my department and asked to resign from my clubs. That earth is stopped. I see no point in your divorcing Nigel (assuming that you now could) if this set you free while I was still tied. Our position, therefore, is what it was; but what will it become if Nigel remains in England, if he camps on your doorstep in Barton Street, if—as your lawfully wedded husband—he objects to your friendship with me? Nothing is going to make me give that up or change it in any way! If necessary, I would ask you to cut the country with me. To use a phrase that I've just been using with Elizabeth, that is the irresistible force that these immovable bodies must expect to meet . . ."

VIII

IN describing my nervousness on the first night of *The Waters of Lethe*, I said that almost everything seemed to have gone wrong from start to finish; but I can see now that I ought to have said that I had been so much on edge from start to finish that everything would have seemed to be going wrong if an all-wise, all-powerful archangel had been directing the play. In calm retrospect I do not think I had more than my average of troubles, though I magnified each of them into a cross. In more reasonable mood I should have been amply consoled as I watched the play rising in a steady *crescendo* of success; but in fact, until the last curtain fell, I was expecting to see success turning to failure at the eleventh hour; and, when my enthusiastic friends asked if I was not pleased, I preferred to say merely that I was relieved, as the play had been getting on my nerves. It would have been more accurate, I see now, to say that I had lost my nerve.

I had lost it, obviously, on the night when Violet told me that Nigel was on his way back to England. Was this, then, the end? She might declare that his return would make no difference to us; but, if he remained in England, insisting that he had now purged his offence, what then? It was only, I think, as our life together was thus suddenly threatened that I came to see what the last five years had meant to me; I did not really expect the first night of *Lethe* to be much more unnerving than any other, but what if it were to be the last?"

Imagination took the bit between its teeth and bolted with me. By now, rightly or wrongly, I had convinced myself that I should never write another play unless I had Violet by my side; if I gave up writing, I must give up my present style of living, with one house in London and another in Wiltshire, with cars and chauffeurs, with house-parties and dinner-parties for eleven months in every year and with a winter holiday on the Riviera for the twelfth. To cut the country, as I hinted to Violet, would not—on second thoughts—help anybody. Since Elizabeth had set her face as stubbornly against London as against a divorce, I should have to join her at Ridgeway if we were no longer able to maintain separate establishments; and what life at Ridgeway would be like I knew well enough even before our train crawled through the fog to Marlborough and she told me who had been invited for the week-end. They were nearly all my friends, since Elizabeth seemed to have no intimates of her own; they were all intelligent, agreeable and socially well broken; properly matched and mixed, they would have made any party go with a swing; but, unfortunately, in choosing guests, Elizabeth never looked beyond balancing the sexes and, as she made no contribution herself to general conversation after her one pump-priming question, she seemed wholly unaware of the chaos that she habitually created by inviting the wrong people on the wrong occasions, flinging shy welfare-workers at hard-bitten race-goers in a Newbury week and diluting a literary luncheon with worthy, but silent, members of her Women's Institute.

"It's a good thing we've nobody dining to-night," I said, as we stumbled out in search of the car. "We shall be lucky if we're in before eleven."

"We've no one till luncheon to-morrow," said Elizabeth. "Oh, did I tell you that Violet Oakhirst may be coming? I heard from her this morning that she's staying in Marlborough to consult Anstruther Nesbitt about some house she's decorating for him. If they finish their business early . . ."

I answered conventionally that I hoped we should see them both; but I must confess that my heart missed a beat. It was Violet who had written, not young Nesbitt; and, if she felt obliged to invite herself like this to Ridgeway, it could only be to say—as she had said when she invited herself to meet me at Marlborough station all those years ago—that another crisis had arisen.

"It may be the last chance before she goes abroad," Elizabeth continued.

"I didn't even know she was going abroad."

"Well, it's only to Cannes, but she seems to have been given a fairly big job there. Some American millionairess who wants her villa turned upside down. Big enough for it to be worth her while to let the house in Westminster. Didn't she tell you?"

"I've not seen her since the *Lethe* first night. No doubt, to-morrow . . ."

In fact I did not have to wait so long, as I was greeted on my arrival at Ridgeway by an express-letter in which Violet explained that she had not written before because she thought it might save time and argument if she could announce an accomplished fact.

"I've let my house for six months," she went on, *"to a member of parliament, who will take it on month by month after that for as long as it suits me. This does not mean that you will not see me in that time; but for obvious reasons I don't want to be much in London at present. My M.P. moves in as I move out; and Nigel, having no house at his disposal, will have to live at his club. I will tell you all about it when I see you on Sunday."*

As I pocketed the letter until such time as I could burn it, I felt that my lost nerve had been restored to me. Violet was prepared to play her part as an irresistible force; and within the next few weeks I might expect to read that Sir Nigel Oakhirst (he would surely have been made a K.C.M.G. by then) had been reappointed for a further term as governor and commander-in-chief of the Spice Coast. As likely as not, old Matthew Greystoke would telephone to give me the news before it was published; and Mr. Clement Phayre, nosing for scraps among the dustbins of Whitehall, would devote a paragraph or two in his column of gossip to a rehash of Nigel's biography in *Who's Who*, statistics about the Spice Coast from the *Statesman's Year Book* and an account of Violet's pioneer-work as a professional adviser on house-decoration.

"When an irresistible force meets an immovable body . . ."

Like most people (as I had told Elizabeth in the train), if we could not get what we wanted, we resigned ourselves—ostensibly —to going without it. This did not mean, however, that we were going to be baulked of our new start.

"For five years . . . ," I reckoned. "Nigel's term ended in twenty-four. In nineteen-twenty-nine I shall be forty-one. In nineteen thirty-nine . . . But it's no use looking *more* than five years ahead in these uncertain times."

And these in fact were almost the very words that Violet used next day when she and Anstruther Nesbitt arrived for luncheon. I was a little surprised, knowing how it offended her sense of fitness to play the part of a mere friend with literary leanings in a house where Elizabeth and I were playing the part of a happily married couple of young parents, that she had not suggested my meeting her in Marlborough; but, as—at her own request—I took her round the house afterwards to shew how her decoration had stood up to five years of changing fashion and hard wear-and-tear, she explained that, whatever superficial form her future life with Nigel might take, she could not begin to plan the next chapter of her life with me till she had seen with her own eyes the formal (if I liked, the "unreal") other half of the life that I led when I left Grosvenor Road for Wiltshire.

"It would make a good first-act," I said, as I threw open the door of the book-room. "And *Option to Renew* would not be at all a bad title. Two people who have agreed to have a stock-taking every five years, say, and decide whether they want to go on . . . Were things here what you expected? We keep up a tolerable *façade*."

"It was *better* than I expected!" Violet answered. "I suppose conscience makes a coward of me. . . . I told you, years ago, that I should fade out for ever if I stood in the way of a reconciliation between you and Elizabeth. Well . . . There's no more chance of that than of my being reconciled to Nigel. Something has *died* and none of us can bring it to life again."

"So, till our next stock-taking . . . If you really think it's necessary to have one . . ."

"More than ever! I also told you that if I stood in the way of your little Norman . . . I'm not interested in the other boys and you're not responsible for them. For Norman's sake, I wanted to make quite sure that we weren't doing anything or leaving anything undone . . ."

I said that, if Violet had come to tell me that she was returning with Nigel to the Spice Coast next day, I could do no more than I was doing at present.

"As you can see," I continued, "Elizabeth and I bore each other to extinction, though with her copy-book sentimentality she blinks the fact by saying that husbands and wives *oughtn't* to bore each other. She was *horrified* when I told her, years ago, that if we were to avoid murder or suicide . . ."

"Do you believe that was why Austin went to the war?," Violet broke in. "Clayton Mandeville always says *he* was so bored . . ."

"I don't know what to say! Elizabeth *used* to think . . . Or perhaps she was only afraid that other people might think . . . Your perfect bores never understand how boring they are. Even with perpetual house-parties I couldn't stand even the week-ends here if I didn't have you for the rest of the time. If anything brought that to an end, I think I should burn my boats and settle in Hollywood. That's quite the done thing now."

We had been walking from room to room as we talked, and had now reached the one-time day-nursery, where my younger step-son Humfrey was entertaining a party of school-friends from Sudbury House; Martin, who had gone to Marlborough the term before, doubtless felt it beneath his dignity to consort with "prep-school kids" and was engaged in converting one of the night-nurseries into a study for himself. Norman, not yet even of pre-preparatory-school age, was being allowed to "fag" for him. As we turned back from the nursery-wing, Violet assured me that I could dismiss Hollywood from my thoughts for at least another five years.

"Everything will go on as before," she continued. "So far as *I'm* concerned. Five years or *fifty* won't make any difference. I just wanted to make myself a picture of what life was like here. It saddens me that, even living in a crowd, you should find it so boring, but it's only for week-ends. Perhaps it won't be so boring as Norman grows up. He'll need you, if he's not to be spoilt like Martin and Humfrey. I believe you'll find you need him too! Have you ever studied that young son of yours, Colin? He's a most unusual little boy! Remember I've only seen him once before, when he was about two . . ."

"He fell for you at first sight to-day," I said.

"Which was highly flattering, because I don't pretend to understand small children, and even more touching, because he seemed to be so full and running over with affection. Perhaps there's nothing unusual in *that*: if you're healthy and happy and smile at the world in a way that makes the world smile back at you . . . He's not in the least like you or Elizabeth and yet he couldn't conceivably be any one else's child."

I asked Violet in what way she found him unusual; and she asked in her turn whether he shewed any taste for music or drawing.

"I expect I'm talking great nonsense," she went on, "but I shouldn't be the least surprised if he developed into a Beethoven or a Keats. There's something a little bit other-worldly about him: an extraordinary sensitiveness . . . Let me know if you *do* ever catch him writing poetry on the sly."

"So far," I said, "his aesthetic interest is limited to watching me, round-eyed, while I'm writing and then asking to be told a story. Unfortunately, I'm no good at inventing stories for infants and, as he prefers mine to Elizabeth's, I have to eke them out with dramatic effects from my model theatre. Yes, he's a winning child, but I'm prepared to see him growing into a completely commonplace boy. This sensitiveness you think you see . . ."

"I do see it, my dear! So strongly that I should be terribly worried about sending him to school. He might suffer so dreadfully, *or* he might suffer so much *more* dreadfully afterwards if he hadn't had the sensitiveness knocked out of him! I'm glad I shan't have the responsibility of deciding!"

I said that I did not suppose I should have this either. Elizabeth was to have control of him until he went to Sudbury House, after which I should expect to be consulted. I should think many times before deciding that he was too fine a spirit for the rough-and-tumble of a public school; but, if he seemed in danger of being bullied, I would take care that he was taught the scientific use of his fists before he went to Marlborough.

"He's a sturdy young gentleman," I continued. "Physically, quite fearless . . ."

"Which wasn't at all what I meant. He may be as brave as a lion, but, if people even raise their voices, it flays him alive! You'll have to go very carefully with Elizabeth when he's about. He adores you both; if he dreamt that you were on bad terms . . . And he would feel it in the air. I imagine that a man like Marcel Proust, when *he* was a small boy, was hypersensitive in the same way . . ."

As she paused, I invited Violet to tell me candidly whether any one who did not know the facts would imagine for one moment that Elizabeth and I were not on the best of terms.

"Oh, people can't make you out. A really intelligent man so besotted that he doesn't *see* how stupid his wife is! That's your

sister-in-law Kitty, who has never forgiven the simple, despised
Rella for blackmailing her over the Montpelier-Square house.
Elizabeth may not understand about money, but she'll drive a
bargain that would make Shylock blush and it will always be for
her two poor fatherless boys. She's a very odd creature! I used
to think that every one had a main-spring of duty or greed or
vanity or fear, a first principle of some kind; but, if Elizabeth
has one, I can't tell you what it is. Ought we to be going back to
the others?"

"When you've assured me there's nothing the matter. You're
different to-day, Violet, for some reason. You don't regret . . . ?"

Throwing her arms round my neck, she whispered that she
regretted nothing and that there was nothing the matter, though
perhaps she had been foolish to come here.

"Being so near . . . ," she faltered. "Remembering it all so
well . . . Colin, my darling, it seemed such an enormous price to
pay! This big house, your whole *train-de-vie*, the colossal make-
believe: all to give Elizabeth her 'freedom' and to keep your own.
. . . I wanted you to have a chance of asking yourself whether it
was *worth* it. Oh, I knew what you would say! I suppose that letter
of Nigel's upset me. I thought I'd disposed of him! You and I
were so marvellously happy. Oh, you warned me, when I decided
against a divorce, that he would still be my husband in five years'
time! Now I must fly, or I shall lose my train! I shall see you in
London, but I'm not sure it would be wise for you to come out
to Cannes while I'm there."

We returned to the saloon; and a moment later young
Nesbitt brought his car round to the front door. As I shook hands
with Violet, I contrived to whisper that I at least should not
regret this meeting if it had been the means of shewing me the
value of something that I might otherwise have taken for granted.

"I sometimes wonder whether one can take anything for
granted these days," she answered with a shiver, at once adding
in a tone for any one to hear: "Then you'll telephone when you've
seen what your other engagements are? Any time before half-past
eleven, say."

As the car drove away into the darkness, I flirted with the idea
of inventing an excuse for returning to London that night.
Violet, who shared my loathing for telephone-conversations,
must be seriously adrift from her moorings to be asking me to
communicate with her in this unsatisfactory way; there was

nothing she could say from London, more or less inaudibly and with a risk of being overheard, that she could not have said in a safe whisper as we strolled by ourselves through the empty rooms of the house that afternoon. I could only think that she was frightened and knew she would not sleep till I had in some way comforted her. A moment's reflection decided me that I should only arouse gratuitous suspicion if I absented myself from the dinner-party that Elizabeth had arranged; but by careful timing and a good deal of luck I put my call through as Violet's train was due at Paddington and caught her as she entered her house.

"I dressed early," I explained, "so that we shouldn't be interrupted. Can you hear? Every one's upstairs . . ."

"Oh, my dear, there was no need for all these precautions!," Violet answered with a rather joyless laugh. "I just wanted to know when I could see you. I'm leaving on Thursday. Any day or night, lunch or dinner . . . I'm sorry, my dear, but I can't talk, I can't think, I'm not myself when I'm within a mile of a certain person known to both of us. She numbs my brain! I feel like one of those monkeys in the *Jungle Book*, being hypnotized by the boa-constrictor before being devoured!"

"So long as it's nothing worse than that!", I said. "Don't meet her! I was afraid . . . You seemed on edge even when we were by ourselves."

"I suppose I was. I told you the reason. It's the uncertainty. Your lease *may* be renewed in five years' time; but if not . . . You can't even be sure of five years. I can't *promise* that His Excellency will go back for a second term. And, when he comes back in 1929, it *will* be for good. Ten years in a tropical swamp . . . And then we shall have all this to go through again!"

I said that, if we had nothing worse to fear, I should not worry. I should not think of blaming my star, I continued with rather hollow valiance, so long as I felt sure that I was no underling. We had proved that we at least were worthy of the escape that had been offered us when for a moment we had seemed condemned to life-long imprisonment.

"You made your terms quite clear five years ago," I reminded Violet. "Nigel was let off a divorce on condition that he kept out of your life. When he comes back for good . . . He must live at Torquay, for the sake of his health, or in Liverpool, for business reasons. Have you answered that letter of his, about the penal servitude and the solitary confinement and the purging of his offence?"

"Oh, yes! And I've told him I'm only going away to avoid wasting valuable time. I've given him my address in Cannes, to shew that I'm not *afraid* to meet him, but he must see that it will be utterly useless to pursue me out there. I suppose I oughtn't to be worrying. He should know when he's beaten. He can't help knowing that I can be quite useful in making some sort of new career for him if he keeps the right side of me. No, it's the *general* uncertainty! I haven't the same faith in *life* that I had five years ago. If I could trust fate as I trust you, Colin, and you trust me . . . When you look back, though, to that day when we lunched together on the Downs . . . Things haven't worked out quite as we expected."

"They've worked out infinitely better than I ever dared to hope! If the next five years . . ."

Violet broke in to ask whether I thought she was growing old.

"Or perhaps only growing up?" she suggested. "When you're a child, there are all sorts of things that only happen to other people, but year by year you find them happening to *you*. It's *your* friends and relatives who die or contract terrible diseases or else lose all their money or get caught up in frightful scandals. I'm in a thoroughly cheerful mood to-night, as you can see! Heaven knows why! Perhaps I saw to-day what a tiny thread all our happiness hangs by! If Nigel is *kept* in England? He never told me, but I heard lately that he'd had blackwater-fever last year. If he's really a semi-invalid? If anything happened to you that you had to give up writing? If anything happened to the *world* . . . I don't yet see much of that home fit for heroes that we were expecting five years ago, I'm not even sure about that war to end war. But I mustn't go on like this! It's only a rush of realism to the head! May I dine with you to-morrow? Then good-bye till then and forget everything I've said!"

As I hung up the receiver, I heard voices in the hall; and I reached the saloon by one door as Elizabeth entered by another to receive the first of our guests. If I did not forget everything that Violet had said, I did not dwell over-long on what she called her rush of realism and I thought a mood of nervous depression. "If" this! "If" that! By now, as I had told her so often lately, it was idle to look more than a very short time ahead, but I had few misgivings about the next five years.

And by the calendar I was justified: when we came to take stock in 1929, none of her fears had materialized; but she was out in her reckoning by only a very few months. Thus it was not till 1931 that Nigel was sent home after a second and nearly fatal attack of blackwater-fever, not till 1931 that the world-economic crisis ended the spacious days of paper prosperity, not till 1934 that Europe began to prepare for a new war. Of no one year can I say it was then that I gave up writing; but the last of my big successes came at the end of the nineteen-twenties and by the middle of the nineteen-thirties I existed in the theatres of London and New York on increasingly precarious sufferance.

All this notwithstanding, these five years of gathering clouds and increasing friction, of dwindling achievement and advancing age, are amongst the happiest that I have known. Adversity brought Violet and me closer together; and, for both of us, happiness was shewn to have nothing in the world to do with success. Though she had asserted that regular stock-takings were more than ever necessary, I do not remember that we ever had another, though we harked back once or twice to what she called her "Cassandra mood" at Ridgeway.

"I suppose it was what people call nerves," she told me as the second five years drew to their end.

"Or what *you*, in relation to Norman, called hypersensitiveness?," I asked. "If there *is* such a thing as a *Zeitgeist*, I'm the last person to be aware of it, but I find you a wonderfully reliable barometer for the day after to-morrow. In 1919 it was set fair for every one; for me, it was still set fair in 1924, but you seemed to feel in your bones that there was bad weather coming. And you were right! The state of Europe since the Ruhr business, the state of this country since the general strike, the state of the world since this slump in America . . . I don't know what you think the next few years are going to bring . . ."

"A worse time than any we've known or imagined! Don't ask me in what way! I couldn't tell you! I just feel that the whole machine of life is breaking down. Let's hope I'm wrong! We always planned that these next ten years were going to be the best of our lives. Nineteen-twenty-nine to thirty-nine . . ."

"I will remind you of this evening," I said, "when we get to nineteen-thirty-nine."

IX

VIOLET's last words, as I saw her into the Pullman at Victoria, were that I must understand she was going abroad for my sake as much as for her own.

"When I told you my marriage had come to an end," she reminded me, "I said that I should feel *dirtied* if I didn't break away from Nigel. What life I made for myself after that was a matter for my own conscience or taste, but you and I should both have felt dirtied if we'd formed an eternal triangle with him. When you told me your marriage had crashed too, I felt we must never form an eternal triangle with Elizabeth. I didn't want to meet her on false pretences and I didn't want you to meet Nigel on false pretences either. You could hardly have helped meeting him now if I'd remained in London."

"I suspect I'm all the more likely to meet him if you're away," I said. "Men may come and men may go, but the Department of the Lord Keeper continues for ever. During the war it was the first clearing-house for any one who wanted to know who was still alive, who was on leave and so on. I shall be greatly surprised if Nigel *doesn't* look me up."

"Well . . . If he asks you about me, you can tell him that everything's *over*. I should have divorced him if you hadn't warned me it would ruin his chances for any public appointment; and I'm not going to take him back now. It may spare him a journey to Cannes if you can make him understand that in London, but I hope you won't be bothered by him. It was truly to save you the embarrassment of a meeting that I decided to go away."

Whether in fact Nigel would have come to see me in my clearing-house I shall never know. On second thoughts, I feel he might have found it embarrassing, not knowing what I knew, to explain that his wife had not stayed to welcome him home after five years abroad, that their house was let and that he had no idea when she was returning to England. When we met, it was within a stone's-throw of my office; but he would only say that he was on his way to luncheon and then, in the traditional formula, that we must really fix a night for talking about old times.

"How does an English winter feel after the tropics?," I asked.

"I'm told that the first is never so bad as the second: by then

o

your blood has had time to cool down. However, as I shan't be
here to see . . ."

"You're going out again?"

Though his luncheon-party had been vaguely indicated as
lying in the opposite direction, he said that, if I was going to the
Garrick, he would walk a little of the way with me.

"How old would you say I looked, Colin?," he demanded
abruptly, turning his smooth and still boyish face for my inspection.

"I know in fact that you're rising thirty-nine, but you've
changed very little since you were an undergraduate."

"There used to be a ridiculous phrase about men who were
too old at forty. I wonder whether I shall be told that I'm too
young at sixty. I was the 'Baby of the House' when there were a
dozen members younger than me. At the bar, too. And now at the
Colonial Office. D'you know a prize stick-in-the-mud called
Matthew Greystoke?"

"He was lunching with me about a week ago," I said, without
disclosing the purpose or the outcome of our meeting.

Nigel expressed a comprehensive regret that I had not
poured powdered glass into his soup and rat-poison into his
coffee.

"Though I would sooner see him dying as my guest on the
Spice Coast," he added. "I could tell him a whole lot first about
the improving health and falling death-rate of the colony."

"Are you going back there?," I asked.

"I've nowhere else to go! Too young at forty for any of the
plums like Ceylon or Hong Kong. No suitable job at home.
Look here, I must turn back now if I'm not to be late for my
party, but we must meet again. Violet's abroad at present, but
I expect to be in London till my leave's over. Are you still in
our old house in Grosvenor Road?"

"When I'm not in the country. The family . . ."

With an obvious effort, such as I imagined Nigel must always
make in forcing himself to affect an interest in any one else's
affairs, he exclaimed that "of course" I had married poor old
Austin's widow. A bad business about Austin! He had been the
ablest of our generation at Westminster and the House, though
some—including himself—had attracted the lime-light sooner
and others—like me—had probably made more money. It was
an extraordinary thing, if one happened to strike the popular

taste . . . However . . . He seemed to remember that Austin had left a boy or two, but for the life of him he could not remember having heard whether I had any children.

"Violet and I have been spared *that* complication," he continued, without waiting to be told. "And somehow, Colin, I never pictured *you* as the complete *paterfamilias*. How many . . . ? Oh, 'only a little one'. Well, now, when have you a free night?"

"I'll let you know when I've looked at my book," I promised. "At the moment, Grosvenor Road is in the hands of the painters."

And in the hands of the painters, I decided, it should remain until Nigel had returned to the Spice Coast. When he dropped out of Violet's life, he had dropped even more definitely out of mine; and, even if I had not shared her distaste for eternal triangles, I had no wish to exchange memories of school and university days with an egocentric bore who thought of nobody but himself and of nothing but his own advancement, regarding his fellows in general as a gang of conspirators bound together to cheat him of his dues and dividing his more successful intimates into those who had succeeded by cunning and those who owed everything to luck. By now, indeed, his intimates were few; in Greystoke's temperate phrase, he did not get on well with people; and, if he looked on me as a man who would listen untiringly to his grievances for old time's sake, London would very soon prove too small to contain the two of us.

I had in fact arranged for my house to be repainted before I heard that he was on his way home: when I understood I should see very little of Violet for perhaps several months, I decided to distract myself by ordering the first complete (and now long over-due) redecoration of the house inside since the nightmare time when the painters had walked in as I walked out to the Kensington register-office and my honeymoon at Bowbury Castle. I had intended to supervise the work; but I now saw that the presence of the workmen would give me an unchallengeable excuse for being in the country whenever Nigel invited me to fix that night; and, when I wrote to tell Violet of my changed plans, I added that Ridgeway would be my headquarters till she returned from Cannes, even if I heard that Nigel was leaving England next day.

"A chance word of his," I explained, *"has made me feel that I'm not being very much of a* paterfamilias. *For Austin's sake I ought to be interesting myself in his two boys; and, if there's anything in the*

traditional Jesuit boast about the enduring quality of their early influence,
I ought to be keeping a closer eye on Norman in the first seven years of his
life than at any other time. I won't pretend that I relish the prospect, but
it's a duty I shall have to face some day and there won't be much addi-
tional time for being bored if I leave before most good Christians have
breakfasted and don't return till the dining-car train. Inevitably it will
revive bitter-sweet memories of the summer when you were redecorating
Ridgeway and I was camping out there; but I feel that in the last half
dozen years we've learnt to remember only the sweetness of life. Then I was
coming down to see the enchanting house that you were making for me; now,
I shall be sleeping in that house and coming up five days a week to see
whether I'm making anything a hundredth part as enchanting to greet
you the first time you dine with me in Grosvenor Road."

In her reply a week later, Violet expressed approval of my
plans and added that she too, even if she heard that Nigel was
leaving England next day, would have to remain in her present
headquarters for several weeks longer.

"The whole Riviera is booming," she continued, *"and, if I accepted*
half the commissions I'm being offered, I should spend the next ten years
of my life out here. That I do not propose to do, but I must finish my
present job. If you felt inclined to come out here for a week or two, I
believe it might be possible in the not too distant future. And, the sooner
you practise addressing your letters to 'Lady Oakhirst', the better.
Nigel is going to get his K.C.M.G. And any day now you may read that
he has been received in audience by the King and has kissed hands on his
reappointment and so on. I've no idea, though, how soon he will take it up.
For the present, therefore, you must carry on at Ridgeway as you've
arranged. I hope you'll find that most fascinating little Norman of yours a
compensation for the tedium you'll have to endure. Properly approached
(if you were ever capable of dramatizing yourself), you could fill the
whole of one of your little note-books with the experiences of the next few
weeks! You know Ridgeway when the stage is set for your week-end
visits, but what is it like from Monday till Friday? I don't know. I
suppose your faithful Cruikshanks do, but they would be the last people
to tell you."

In fact, I did not take my usually inseparable note-book with
me when I migrated to Wiltshire; and, if I had, I hardly know
what I should have put in it. I hardly knew what to put into the

letters that I wrote almost daily to Violet. To borrow a phrase that I thought Elizabeth overworked, from Monday to Friday— the unknown time-quantity in the life of Ridgeway—the house was organized on a "bread-winner's" basis. Every morning, before her own schoolroom breakfast with the younger children and Norman's governess, she dispensed eggs-and-bacon to me, directed my attention to the waiting car and rang for Cruikshank to help me into my greatcoat. Every evening, after her final visit to the night-nurseries, she came into the book-room with suitable questions about my day's work in London and with a dutiful account of her own activities. These seemed to be concerned chiefly with elementary education, public health and juvenile delinquency, though she found time also for a variety of committee-meetings.

"It's not wildly exciting," I told Violet, *"because she has a queer faculty of taking the interest out of anything she describes, but (even if I can't dramatize myself) I've once or twice wondered whether she was presenting a scene of domestic life as it* ought *to be lived by people like her and me. The bread-winner, the lady of the manor busied with her multifarious duties in his absence, their common life when they meet in the evening to compare notes on the day, the common tie of these boys for whom I've made myself vaguely responsible and of the boy that we combined to create. I came here, as you know, with an idea of taking my responsibility seriously."* I broke off and sat staring at the paper for several minutes, then added lamely: *"But I'll tell you about this later."*

What, though, could I add, then or later, that would interest Violet? I had come to see that these boys were being properly brought up; but at the end of many weeks I could not say whether they were or not. To my masculine eyes, Elizabeth had in earlier days fussed over them ridiculously, stealing up to their doors every night to make sure they were asleep, summoning the doctor for a grazed knee and insisting eternally that they must never be over-tired, over-excited, over-heated. I should have called this mollycoddling; but had it in fact done any harm and was the general spoiling that succeeded it doing any harm now? The independent and outspoken sons of Austin Gerrold had effectively damped her excessive solicitude the moment they went to school by declaring that they would not let their mother or any

one else "make fools of them before the other chaps." Norman
was still of an age, perhaps he would always be of a disposition,
to accept without question whatever came to him from an
obviously loving hand; but I pinned my faith on the corrective
influence of his schools.

"I thought I should get to know the boys better," I wrote to Violet a
week or two later, *"but in fact it's Elizabeth that I'm beginning to get
into focus. I have been helped in this by Clayton, who has been staying
with us, though I doubt whether I shall ever succeed in focusing him anywhere in Elizabeth's entourage. The other day Elizabeth mentioned that
getting up early and giving me my breakfast and seeing me off to work
brought back memories of earliest childhood when the Cheshunts lived in
Saint John's Wood and she was responsible for seeing old Alec off to the
City while her mother 'had her sleep out'. If there'd been time I should
have liked to get at her true feelings about the humble days, when I knew her
brothers in the chrysalis-stage at school, and the gaudy-butterfly phase of
Coverley Court and the utterly different chapter in Montpelier Square
with Austin: which had she liked best and why? If she were planning the
ideal life for herself? At times she thirsts to be a great lady, at times I
think she hankers after her original suburbia. According to Clayton . . ."*

I paused for a moment to consider why, as I had just confessed, I could never quite get Clayton into focus. As one of
Austin's oldest friends, cast in the same mould of mental exuber-
ance and loud argumentativeness, it was understandable that he
should still be invited to Montpelier Square even after he had been
divorced by Elizabeth's sister; but, when Austin was dead and
Elizabeth was remarried to a man who had never gone out of his
way to foster the friendship, I was as much puzzled that she, with
her abhorrence of divorce, should make him welcome at Ridgeway as that he should punctually issue himself invitations to a
house where the hostess bored him. Sometimes, when Elizabeth
spoke of *"poor Clayton"* as "a man more sinned against than
sinning", I fancied that she was administering a retaliatory back-
hander to Kitty for some of her remarks about "poor Rella";
sometimes, when I checked the cellar-book after one of his visits,
I decided that the catering at least must meet with his approval;
but it was only when Elizabeth's efforts to please him became
agonizings to propitiate him that I saw she was afraid of him.
Why?

To my knowledge he had told Violet that Austin had joined the army to get away from his wife; in his cups he had hinted to me that Austin's marriage had been no luckier than his own; and with little encouragement he might have said that, if Austin had not been killed, he would never have come back to Elizabeth. Apparently she hoped to silence him with food and drink; certainly she had succeeded in restricting his confidences, on this occasion which I was describing to Violet, to harmless reminiscences of the Cheshunts before the days of their social greatness. And, accepting his anecdotes as substantially true, I found them far more illuminating than any speculations about Elizabeth and the boys, or even myself, had Austin survived the war.

"If, as I always suspected," I continued to Violet, *"the unhappy Elizabeth never got used even to the modest style of Montpelier Square, what a fish out of water she must have felt at Coverley Court! Old Alec's rise to fortune was so rapid that his eldest child saw the light in a semi-detached villa, with one general servant, and the youngest cut his first tooth on a gold christening-mug presented by the Lord Lieutenant of Hampshire; Clayton, who watched the whole triumphant progress, tells me that all the Cheshunts adapted themselves with successful gusto to their new conditions with the exception of Mrs. Alec, who was too old to learn new tricks, and Elizabeth, who only exchanged her swaddling-clothes for her mother's apron-strings. If true, this explains a lot: the frantic efforts of her brothers and sisters to smarten up poor Rella, poor Rella's stubborn resistance to what she regarded as pretentiousness, the slow wearing-down of opposition and now the paradox of Rella setting out to beat the others at their own game. You once told me how her brothers bragged at Newbury about being in the Ridgeway-House party; and one half of Elizabeth is devoted passionately to being Mrs. Colin Whimboyne, of Ridgeway. She would like to be Lady Whimboyne: when I told her about Nigel's prospective K.C.M.G., she asked how soon I could expect a K.C.B.! The other half of this curiously divided personality hankers after the simpler joys of her childhood; and her rule for the upbringing of the children might be described as ambition tempered by austerity. She would like them to attend a levée but they ought to go by bus. How it will work out I'm not prepared to say yet."*

Nor was I prepared to say several weeks later when within the space of ten days Sir Nigel Oakhirst left London for the Spice Coast, Lady Oakhirst left Cannes for London and Messrs. Higgs and Hill's painters left Grosvenor Road for their next contract. One of my last duties at Ridgeway was to attend a breaking-up party at Sudbury House, where Elizabeth gave away the prizes; and, as Clayton was once again staying with us, I asked him that night after dinner how he, as an impartial outsider, thought that Austin's boys were shaping.

"As you know, they were intended for Westminster," I continued, "but I take full responsibility for agreeing that they should go to Marlborough."

"And in the long run," said Clayton, "it won't make a ha'porth of difference what school they went to or whether they went to none at all. How old are they?"

I said that Martin was rising thirteen and Humfrey eleven. Sudbury House, I added, must be given the credit of having reduced the ego in their cosmos; but, if the alternative to school had been a tutor at home, I thought that they would soon have been unmanageable.

"They'll be that in spite of Sudbury House and Marlborough," Clayton predicted. "As Austin was, in spite of Westminster and the House. Would you have it otherwise, Colin? Those stepsons of yours are high-mettled individualists, like their father, sharp as needles, living—like him—all out as though every moment were going to be their last. Marlborough or any other school can be trusted to kick their backsides if they become *too* uppish, but no school—thank God!—is going to subdue them to the standardized public-school type. Raw material for curates and private secretaries and junior partners in family businesses! Among our contemporaries, is there a single one who has achieved distinction *without* having been a bit unmanageable? You've no cause to worry about those boys."

"I feel that, for better or worse, Austin would have influenced them enormously. He might have repressed them, he might have encouraged them. I'm doing neither. Elizabeth . . ."

"Elizabeth doesn't see that they'll be whatever they're going to be without consulting *her*."

"Do they yet know what *they* want to be?"

Clayton sipped his port in silence and then asked me whether I had carried on my father's practice of initiating the boys into adult manners and conversation on their seventh birthdays.

"You've sometimes told me," he recalled, "that you all grew up under the shadow of dissolution. That was the way the older generation talked in those days, though I don't think it shook *our* faith that everything would go on as before. All that's changed, Colin, since 1914: though they may not put it into words, the younger generation feels that nothing is safe or certain any more. Every one must look after himself nowadays. No, I've not the faintest idea what Martin and Humfrey will do, but subconsciously they and all the boys who were born after our so-called spacious days are out for money, power, *security*. If you have the chance of making yourself snug . . ."

"I should like to know what Austin would have said," I observed. "He was by way of being an idealist."

"With a strong belief in letting people decide for themselves. He would have been disappointed to see his sons becoming pushful, smart little materialists, but he wouldn't have stopped it if he could and he couldn't have stopped it if he would. Martin and Humfrey have his good brain and strong will, but in character they're Cheshunts. The queer family you and I married into, Colin! Pure *Cheshunts*," he repeated, as though this explained everything.

I said I was glad to have an outside opinion.

"I feel a certain responsibility . . . ," I added.

"Which is why you've spent most of this winter here! *I* tumbled to that, if Elizabeth didn't. It's highly to your credit, Colin, if I may say so. I can't think you've really *enjoyed* your time here, as I've never regarded domesticity as your long suit. Well, *you've* done your duty and can go back to London now with a good conscience. There's nothing you or any one can do about those two boys and I don't know that there's anything you should *try* to do. They're going to be very successful. . . . Have you found time to do any work while you were down here? Then the sooner you get back to Grosvenor Road the better!"

"You're very anxious to hunt me out of my own house!," I remarked. "I suppose we ought to be joining Elizabeth. Unless," I added rashly, "you're having more port?"

Observing that he had already drunk enough to float a battleship, Clayton refilled his glass and emptied the rest of the decater over the table.

"*In vino ver'tas*," he muttered a little thickly. "I'm fond of you, old boy, for some reason. You always know when you've had enough. I suppose I do too, but I don't stop, like you. I *admire* you for it. Self-control and all that. I admire you for the way you work. I don't think much of your plays, but you've done devilish well and you've worked devilish hard for it. I admire you for the way you've tackled your life. *Why* you married Elizabeth . . ."

"May we leave your hostess and my wife out of the conversation?," I suggested.

"Always the gentleman," Clayton commented imperturbably. "D'you think Elizabeth will notice anything? I'm just the least little bit drunk, you know. Well, as I was saying . . . I admire you, old boy. I'm fond of you. Not as fond as I was of Austin. I should be sorry to see you going poor old Austin's way. That's why I admire the way you've tackled your life. If old Austin had broken away like you . . . Well, there wouldn't have been that woman whose name I always forget, he wouldn't have taken to the bottle —dreadful thing, old boy, when a man takes to the bottle—and he wouldn't have gone to the war. Now, if you stay here, where a blind man can see you're bored stiff . . ."

"I am in fact returning to London by the bread-winners' train to-morrow," I said. "Therefore, I'm going to bed early to-night. If you like to go up, which I strongly recommend, I'll make your excuses to Elizabeth."

X

HAD Nigel Oakhirst ever been able to regard himself objectively, I think he must have felt that his sojourn in England during the late winter and early spring of 1925 had not been an unqualified success.

When his ship crossed the bar of the Shambree River and steamed slowly between the mangrove-swamps and palm-clad islands on either side, he would enjoy a transient glory by emerging from his cabin in full-dress uniform; his opponents and partners of the last five weeks at deck-quoits and bridge would address him as "Your Excellency"; the guns in the old Portuguese fort would fire a salute, he would inspect the guard of honour drawn up on the jetty, an open carriage would bear him through the dusty glare of Consort Street to Government House; and, when he had taken over the reins of office from the colonial secretary, he would hear the chief justice congratulating him and the colony on the extension of his term for another five years. Then the Governor and Commander-in-Chief of the Spice Coast would shed his helmet and sword, assume his working-dress of white tunic and shorts, send an orderly to summon his A.D.C. and receive from his secretary an outline of the colony's uneventful history since he sailed for home, intending never to return. Every one would felicitate him on his K.C.M.G.; every one would ask for news of England; and every one would wonder why he had come back before his leave had half run its course, why indeed he had come back at all.

The answer, if he had ever seen himself as others saw him, must have been that he had overestimated both his prospects and his powers: he was not wanted for anything better than his present position and he could not make himself wanted. The instant effect of his arrival in London was that every one he most wished to see mysteriously disappeared: this one went abroad, that one retired to the country, the rest were engaged whenever he laid siege to their offices and country-houses.

"Did he in fact try to meet you?," I asked Violet, when she arrived for dinner on the night of her return from Cannes.

"He tried and succeeded," she answered. "While his ship was loading at Marseilles, he jumped into a train and hunted me out. I'd warned him it would do no good. From his point of view it has done definite harm."

"I should have thought he had nothing more to lose."

"*He* didn't think so! Circumstances were against him at the moment, but in undertaking this second term he was doing what no other man had done and the Colonial Office would *have* to recognize his claims. If Sir Matthew Greystoke (who had his knife into him for some reason) retired when he was sixty, those claims would be recognized in much less than five years. And so on. He was bursting with optimism, as he usually is when he's daydreaming. Even if he stayed out there the whole five years, he would be five years older and these old dodderers in the City would no longer be able to say he was too young for their precious boards."

"Why did you say he had done himself harm?," I asked.

With a sudden tightening of her lips, Violet enquired whether I remembered a phrase about Nigel's having purged his offence.

"He hasn't decided yet," she continued, "whether he'll stick to the colonial service or come back here to collect directorships, but, once he's out of his white man's grave, he takes it for granted that he'll have me at his side. Well . . . As I couldn't divorce him now, I suppose it was natural enough: if he settled in London, I couldn't banish him to his own club and, if he got Nigeria or the Gold Coast, I couldn't refuse to accompany him. It's a mistake, Colin my dear, to take things for granted! He never mentioned our bargain, never asked to be released from it, never doubted that all was forgotten and forgiven when it suited Sir Nigel Oakhirst in the interests of his career . . . I let fall in passing that I had a career now. 'Choosing curtain-material for rich Americans who are too ignorant or lazy to choose it for themselves' was his comment. That's one way of looking at it, of course. Do you feel like going into some figures and giving me your advice? It won't take two minutes."

In fact it took two hours; and, though Violet had spoken of seeking my advice, I felt at the end that it would have been more accurate to say that she wanted my approval of a course that she had worked out in minutest detail on the best advice obtainable, a course that she felt obliged to take whether I approved or not, but a course that would affect my life as much as hers and a course, though she accepted all responsibility for it, that she would never have taken if I had not put the idea into her head half-a-dozen years earlier when we sat on the Downs above Ridgeway and I asked why she should not turn her natural genius for interior-decoration to profitable account.

"I told you in one of my letters," she reminded me, as we went in to dinner, "that the whole Riviera was booming. I might have added that I was booming too."

"You said that you would be out there ten years," I answered, "if you accepted all the commissions that you were being offered."

"It was what I had just said to that enterprising financier Sir Colville Shandy. He had a great idea for buying up about five miles of the coast near la Croix and developing it. When I explained that I was a humble adviser on colour schemes, with more work already than I could possibly handle, he decided to develop *me*. Do you *know* that astonishing man, Colin?"

I said that we had occupied adjoining rooms for some eruptive years in the Ministry of Munitions and that I suspected Arnold Bennett of having taken him for the model of his dynamic supermen who would buy an entire hotel between the oysters and the soup if there were no readier means of getting a steak grilled to their liking. Shandy had a diviner's sense of the unseen, subterranean streams of gold that flowed under a derelict watering-place or a bankrupt newspaper, an over-built factory for cheap motor-cars or an under-capitalized department-store. He had made one fortune out of roller-skating rinks and another out of picture-palaces; I was told that he had burnt his fingers over country-clubs, but, if in truth this venture had failed, I was prepared to bet that the far-sighted Sir Colville had got out at the top of the market. Were I a gambler, in the Casino or on the Stock Exchange, I said I should always follow him for fun and luck and the excitement of being swept along by currents and tides of which I understood nothing; and, if I wanted the shrewdest advice of the astutest business-brain in London, I should go to Shandy as indeed I had gone to him in my youthful inexperience for advice about buying Ridgeway.

"He wants to make me a limited company," said Violet. "I may be one already! I don't know how long these things take, but he seemed to be settling it all by telephone from Cannes in one afternoon. That evening he dictated a memorandum which he said I might shew my solicitor. If you would like to look at it after dinner . . ."

I am sorry that I did not ask for a copy of something that was a remarkable document in itself and proved to be the chart by which Violet and I were to steer for many years, if indeed we are not steering by it to this day. Lady Oakhirst, the preamble set out, had been among the first in the comparatively new field where her success was becoming an embarrassment to her. So far, nevertheless, she had worked only one small corner. Obviously she could not undertake more, perhaps she would have to shed part of her present burden, unless she consented to delegate her routine duties and confine herself to tasks worthy of her powers. In brief, Sir Colville wished to buy her name and reputation, her talents and experience and to float her as a company in which she would be the supreme expert-adviser with a team of assistants trained by her and working under her. To his imaginative vision it was not enough for her to evolve schemes and work out estimates: they must have shops to display their fabrics, possibly factories to make them, galleries to exhibit furniture and schools of craftsmen to reproduce it. To organize this would be Lady Oakhirst's province; but, as the public envisaged by Sir Colville would not for ever be satisfied to alter and adorn existing houses, they must build, they must lay out gardens, they must buy land to develop like this tract in the south of France. Architects, surveyors, builders and contractors would follow inevitably, though he did not propose to trouble her with this side of the enterprise at present.

"If you put Cubitt's on top of Hampton's," said Violet, "and a Garden City on top of Cubitt's . . ."

"If the shares are offered to public subscription, I should like to apply for some," I told her.

"They ought to be given you free. It was your idea. So that we should have a chance of meeting at Ridgeway while we were taking hold of Life again . . . When Sir Colville outlined *his* idea, in all seriousness, I saw it as a scheme for *keeping* our hold. I'm accepting his offer. When everything's in train, I shall let Nigel know what *I* mean by a career. An office—Sir Colville is taking an entire house in Old Burlington Street—and a Holy-of-Holies for me at the top, only to be reached when you've produced evidence to my guard of secretaries that you really have an appointment. A bedroom, in case I'm working late . . . or don't want to sleep in Barton Street, for any reason. My own car, to take me about the country, visiting my clients. It can be made to look more impressive than choosing curtain-material for rich Americans. More profitable too: the salary apart from any share of the profits . . . When Nigel comes back . . ."

As she paused, I asked her what advice she thought I could give. Her solicitors would scrutinize any contract before she signed it; and, though Shandy had not attained his present position and wealth without learning how to drive a hard bargain, he would stand by any bargain that he made.

"I'm only afraid he may work you to death," I said. "That was his reputation at the Ministry of Munitions. He doesn't mean to, but he's so tough in himself, his enthusiasm is so infectious . . ."

"I told him I'd only taken this business up as a pastime, I had various other interests that I couldn't sacrifice. He said I could make my work what I pleased by raising my fees like any other fashionable consultant. I want your opinion *generally*, Colin: as a professional psychologist, in our old phrase. I'm afraid I see no opportunity for *drama* . . ."

"And I see very little else! Did you ever read Wells' *Wife of Sir Isaac Harman*? I should call this *The Husband of Lady Oakhirst*; better still, of *Violet Oakhirst Limited*. You began as 'the wife of

Sir Nigel', but this is the part you've cast him for. He won't like it, but he can't help himself. Shall I tell you why you're doing all this? It isn't feminism or desire for money, you haven't been talked into this by Shandy."

"No, *I* talked *him* into it. I was *afraid*, my dear, as you've quite obviously seen. I *won't* let go what we've won! Nigel's calm way of taking it for granted that when he leaves the Spice Coast . . . That *frightened* me! If I could think of something that would keep me in England, if I wanted, take me out of London, if I wanted . . . Well, I'm not his shadow any more. There's only one Chanel, there's going to be only one Violet Oakhirst. Incidentally, the money is not to be sneezed at. If I'm making two or three times more than Nigel can ever hope to earn . . . *I'm* the serious bread-winner. You may say that I've always paid the lion's share of our joint expenses, but I wasn't *making* it then . . . Oh, how I hate talking like this, but you're right, I was *frightened*! I don't want any advice! I want you to say I've done the only wise, right, sensible thing!"

Remembering how the wife of Mr. Nigel Oakhirst had driven him abroad at the pistol's point six years earlier and how Mrs. Oakhirst's husband had been sent abroad again almost without a meeting, I could not understand why she was afraid of him; but, granted that fear, the only wise, right and sensible thing was to grasp it.

"I should like a little time to take it all in," I said. "Most important of all for me: how is this going to affect our life together?"

"It's going to take away the one thing that marred it," Violet answered. "This watching of the clock for five years at a time, this panic whenever any one asks how soon my husband is coming on leave . . . For the rest, you won't know I'm a limited liability company. When I'm in Old Burlington Street, you'll be in your department. When I'm visiting my clients, you'll be spending your week-ends as usual at Ridgeway. If you ever want a change, you can get yourself invited to the houses where I'm working. Quite a lot of my clients are friends of yours. Did you by any chance mention my name to Lord Axminster? I've had an enquiry from him. *Not* about Bowbury Castle! And various other people."

She produced a pencilled list; and we spent a pleasant half-hour choosing the houses within comfortable distance of London where we could meet. My long winter at Ridgeway, I told her, had convinced me that Elizabeth would not hesitate to say: "Yes, of course," if any one asked whether she could spare me for a week-end.

"You said very little in your letters," Violet observed, "about your time in Wiltshire."

"Because," I said, "our sense of fitness has set up a tacit understanding that we shall talk as little about Elizabeth and Nigel as we possibly can. We made our mistake, we repaired it, we don't blame others or pity ourselves. If you let yourself go, you would hate Elizabeth, for not giving me what you would have given me. I sometimes think you almost hate her for taking possession of a place she doesn't appreciate, a place you made a thing of beauty . . ."

"I suppose it's a small price to pay for keeping her away from London. It saddens me, though, to think of that lovely house given over to parties that she hates or a pretence of family-life that drives you distracted. If you could organize your life *vis-à-vis* her as I hope and believe I've organized mine *vis-à-vis* Nigel . . . Perhaps I exaggerate the souring, dwarfing effect of that make-believe existence. I suppose, if it was really as bad as I feared, you would have broken away and joined me at Cannes."

I said that next winter I certainly should, but that—in her own words—I thought I had done the only wise, right and sensible thing in making the redecoration of my London house an excuse for studying Ridgeway House in its workaday dress.

"I *can* now organize my life," I continued, "with an easy conscience. There's nothing I can do for Martin and Humfrey, who will become whatever the sons of Austin Gerrold and Elizabeth Cheshunt might be expected to become when they emerge from the mill of a public school. There's nothing I can do for Norman while he's still in the nursery. I'm not *needed* there and I'm not *wanted*. In an unobtrusive way Elizabeth has organized a life for herself—if you like, a career for herself—and I should upset it grievously if I cast her for the part of Mr. Colin Whimboyne's Wife. As you know, she's not interested in the theatre . . ."

"I should find it hard to say what she *was* interested in," Violet interposed. "Her children, of course, though I really see her as a big child herself, playing with her dolls."

Three or four months earlier I should probably have said the same thing; but during my recent sojourn at Ridgeway I fancied that I had discovered a Monday-to-Friday Elizabeth very

different from the bewildered and inadequate Elizabeth who
presided over unwanted week-end parties and still looked up
from table-plans to say: "I've got Hugh Walpole on my left.
You must tell me what I'm to talk about to him." Within her
chosen range and in the appropriate company I did not doubt
that she could hold her own. The room that in my father's day
had been called "the office" was now the place in which Elizabeth
materialized as a justice of the peace, signing papers and witnessing declarations at a big roll-top desk, giving interviews to
the local constabulary and burying herself under drifts of papers
from the juvenile courts. It was, however, in my mother's old
writing-room that her deepest interests were revealed. One
evening, when she was called to the telephone, I occupied myself
by reading the titles of the books in her well-filled cases; and,
whereas I had sometimes thought that she should never have
married me, I now felt that I ought never to have married her.
*Mothercraft, Sick-room Nursing, Diet and Health, The Religious
Education of Children*: I quote at random the first few books that
caught my attention, but her whole library seemed to be given
over to one subject and, in general, I took no more interest in that
subject than she in Shaw's *Quintessence of Ibsenism* or Walkley's
Playhouse Impressions.

"Anything to do with the upbringing of the young interests
her," I told Violet. "I suppose it ought to interest me; but over
books as over most other things we seem to have decided to go
our own ways. Some lack of mental sympathy . . . I seem to make
every subject boring to her; and she, even on her own chosen
ground . . . I remember, one night, trying to get her on to
Madame Montessori, whom I regard as an inspired revolutionary
among educationists. The *Montessori System* happened to be one
of the few in all her collection that I'd read . . ."

"Had she?"

"I imagine so. Why?"

"Because I gave it her. I saw it that day when I came over with
Anstruther Nesbitt and you took me round the house. She
hadn't even cut the pages! I sometimes wonder whether she's
really interested in anything that requires the faintest effort. But
we said we weren't going to talk about her! If you're right in
thinking that you're neither needed nor wanted at Ridgeway . . ."

I said that I must continue to go there occasionally, to keep
an eye on the place, to see something of my neighbours and to

sit on the bench. After five years of promiscuous entertaining, however, I felt that I owed no hospitality to any one and could indeed begin to accept a few of the invitations that I had hitherto refused on the plea that we had house-parties at Ridgeway for almost every week-end.

"I see no reason under Heaven," I added, "why we shouldn't combine your business with my pleasure. Perhaps with *my* business too. I've been about in England very little since the year when I was dashing to and fro with Axminster. There are all sorts of places I should like to see. And for the purposes of my trade I ought to revise my possibly obsolete ideas of the social scene. If I may have that list of yours again . . ."

And on that word Violet and I planned an itinerary that we had not entirely carried out when circumstances wholly unforeseen on this late-winter evening of 1925 demanded more of her time in London and of mine in Wiltshire.

I had not supposed that Elizabeth would offer any opposition to a change in my routine of life that would substitute my more welcome room for my less welcome presence, but I was not prepared for the enthusiasm with which she greeted my proposal for seeing something of my friends in their own houses. As the bread-winner, it was of course for me to say how much entertaining we should do at Ridgeway; but, without wishing to seem calculating, she had long felt that our hospitality was one-sided and she had sometimes wondered whether we could afford this unceasing stream of parties. "The City" (if she, who would never understand the first thing about money, at least understood the broad hints of her father and brothers) had become pessimistic about the immediate future. Austin's stodgy old solicitors tended more and more to say what she could not afford than what she could; and her father had suspended her "allowance". It really seemed only common sense for us to reduce our expenses. Incidentally, she had been greatly interested to see from the papers that Violet Oakhirst was setting out to earn her living, though— once again to quote her father and brothers—poor Violet had chosen an unfortunate moment to float herself as expert adviser in luxury decoration.

I said that I knew very little at present of Sir Colville Shandy's latest enterprise, but that I expected to see something of Violet's handiwork in the houses that I contemplated visiting. For the rest, though I could not expect my own vogue to last indefinitely,

I had been very little affected as yet by the depression which had become a constant feature of our daily life for several years by 1925.

And, nearly a quarter of a century later, I should be reluctant to say with any confidence when I felt that the tide was definitely running against me. I never again had a success to equal *The Waters of Lethe*, but I never had a failure. Though I did not regain the foothold on Broadway that I lost in the great American slump of 1929, my plays were increasingly in demand in the studios of Hollywood; and I did not feel that my London days were drawing to a close until I observed that, whereas all managers grumbled about the dearth of theatres, they succeeded in presenting Noel Coward and Frederick Lonsdale when they were unable to present me. Whenever this began to happen (and I cannot suggest even an approximate date), I suppose I ought to have said that I was written out. In fact, I did not. In fact, I was thinking of other things. For half-a-dozen years after the flotation of Violet Oakhirst Limited, I was thinking far more of her and of her activities than of myself and mine.

Success, deserved success, the deserved success of a person one loves is the pleasantest of all things to study; and Violet's success was never in doubt from the moment when Sir Colville Shandy gave his house-warming party in Old Burlington Street. As a woman with a career and as a bread-winner, she could meet the Governor and Commander-in-Chief of the Spice Coast on equal terms. I was never again to hear talk about our watching of the clock for five years at a time. Never again did she tell me that she was frightened, until the naturally unnerving day when she received a cable reporting that Nigel was again in hospital with blackwater-fever.

XI

IN the developing and expanding days of Violet Oakhirst Limited there was indeed no occasion for her to use phrases about watching the clock and, when we were compelled to ask the time, I discovered that I too had watched the clock so little that I could not be sure whether it was still going. Nigel's second term should have been from 1924 to 1929; and I believe he was entitled to come home on leave in alternate years. In fact, whenever

I enquired, I heard that he was improving his knowledge of
colonial problems by making expeditions up-country; and 1929
had come and gone before I learnt purely by chance that he was
remaining on the Spice Coast, at his own request, a while
longer. It must have been in June, 1931, that I went up to
Oxford for a gaudy: sitting next to my own medical adviser,
Vaughan Drake, I asked about various contemporaries of ours at
Westminster and the House and he told me that against his own
strong advice Nigel Oakhirst was not coming home yet.

"The man's a fool," Drake added, "and I told him so. He
has had one go of blackwater and, though the Spice Coast isn't
nearly so unhealthy as people make out when they want bigger
salaries for risking their lives in the cause of Empire, Oakhirst
doesn't give himself a fair chance with his busman's holidays. If
he took his leave in Rhodesia or Kenya, it would be another
matter, but to explore equatorial jungles in the hope of finding
rubber . . . I don't know what the Colonial Office think of
private concession-hunting by one of its governors, but even a
directorship of the Spice Coast Development Corporation can be
bought too dearly."

"That's what he hopes for when he retires?," I asked.

"He *says* he has been virtually promised it, but with Oakhirst
the wish is always father to the thought. In his last letter to me he
said that, if we found another Belgian Congo in the hinterland,
we shouldn't need to worry about economic crises."

We talked for a while of the depression that had prostrated
America for two years and was now prostrating Europe. So
far, I told Drake, it did not seem to be affecting the theatre-going
public, which still demanded to be amused; and the business in
which Nigel Oakhirst's wife had interested herself was temporarily
benefiting by the general tightness of money, which was com-
pelling distressed householders with reduced staffs to reorganize
their houses on labour-saving lines.

"It's the rising generation that is feeling the pinch worst," I
continued. "My young stepsons, for instance: Martin's eighteen
and Humfrey's two years younger. They weren't keen on Oxford
in any event, but, whether they could now afford it or not, they
both feel they can't afford the time. Martin's going into his uncles'
office the week after he leaves Marlborough. Anything for a job,
though the Stock Exchange is hardly the job I should choose at
this moment. Humfrey still talks of the bar; but he wants to leave

too, so that he can go into an accountant's office first. Another
string to his bow, I suppose."

"Will they live with you in London," Drake asked.

I said that nothing had been decided yet: Elizabeth was still
prejudiced against London in general and my house there in
particular, but it was out of the question for a couple of schoolboys to fend for themselves and she was torn between her
anxiety to make a home for them and her equal anxiety to keep a
home near Marlborough where she could watch over Norman.
More than this I saw no reason for telling Drake; but for the
first time since we unobtrusively separated, she possessing herself of Ridgeway and leaving Grosvenor Road to me, I felt that
revolutionary changes were confronting us. As ever taking for
her text what "we" could afford, she had lately come nearer to
revealing a rudimentary understanding of money than in all our
married life before. Admittedly, she was speaking from a brief
prepared by old Alcc, but it had been approved by her brothers,
studied without comment by mine and strongly supported by her
own solicitors.

"Now that you spend so little time here," she had written from
Ridgeway on the eve of my departure to Oxford, *"are we really
justified in keeping the place on? In these days of general post, with every
one moving into a smaller house, Anstruther Nesbitt thinks you could
easily let it to some one who's trying to get out of a still bigger barrack,
even if you can't sell it (I don't think you ever told me whether it was
entailed—if that's the right word—on Norman). I have the chance of
getting a tiny pill-box of a place in Marlborough itself, big enough for
Norman and me till he goes away to school and really much handier for
my local duties. It would be an immense saving of money; and everybody
I talk to thinks we ought to cut down. Martin can't expect to make anything for years and I'm told that, if Humfrey goes into an accountant's
office, he actually has to pay for the privilege! He'll have to pay again when
he joins an Inn and when he's called or whatever the word is and when he's
taken as a pupil. Living in London is going to be much more expensive,
too, though we shall pick up something if we have only one house (and, of
course, a cottage here) . . ."*

I had not intended to let Elizabeth's letter mar the rare
pleasure that I always derived from dining in the most beautiful
hall of the most magnificent college in Oxford; but Drake's

question about my stepsons made me wonder whether to him too—as doubtless to Philip and Maurice Cheshunt, to John and Blanche, to Henry and Constance, even to Anstruther Nesbitt— she had said: "I wish *you* would talk to Colin! He might listen to *you*." It was a long letter, even for the number and gravity of the questions that it raised; and yet, when I put it in my pocket as the train came in sight of Oxford, I had reflected that it was not long enough to enlighten me on any of the points that really mattered. Though she seemed to be convinced, without knowing anything of my income, that "we" could not afford to keep Ridgeway in commission, Elizabeth was no more communicative now than she had been at any time in the last twelve years about the trust-funds that the solicitors allowed her to handle until Martin and Humfrey came of age. It had paid for their nurses and governesses, their tutors and doctors, their clothes and schools; doubtless it would pay to admit Martin to the Stock Exchange and Humfrey to the bar; it had—naturally, I thought—never paid the living expenses of what we used to call Elizabeth's ready-made family and she seemed to assume that it would not pay them now. We might indeed save money if we let Ridgeway and all lived instead in Grosvenor Road; but there was a hint towards the end of the letter that, if she and Norman moved into their Marlborough pill-box, it might be better for Martin and Humfrey to go to Philip and Maurice, where one or other of their aunts could look after them. It was, once again, a question of what one could afford for what; the boys would of course have to go as paying-guests, since their uncles could not afford to keep them in these hard times, but she simply had no idea whether "we" could afford to maintain a big London house (when I lived in only a corner of it for only part of the week) and to board Martin and Humfrey out with relations. She ended by hoping that I would discuss the whole subject with some one who understood money better than she did and who had a clearer idea of the way "things" were moving.

"Austin," she recalled, "used to say that you lived in a world of your own at Oxford and I do sometimes feel you're thinking so much about your plays and the people in them that you forget about real people. I don't pretend to understand why everything's got into such a muddle. It seems to me just wicked that farmers should burn their wheat in one place when there's naked starvation in another, but I do know that the real people I meet are really frightened about the future."

Had I rated Elizabeth's literary judgement higher, I might have relished the less her contrast between real people and the people in my plays; but, if indeed I lived so much in a world of my own that I did not understand my neighbours' dismay at the collapse of our international economy, I too was really frightened by one aspect of the future as she seemed to be envisaging it. Ever since she moved herself and her sons from my bed-of-the-river house to the wind-swept Wiltshire Downs, I had come to regard Grosvenor Road and Barton Street as a corner of London sacred to Violet and me. I did not want to make a home there for Martin and Humfrey, who in recent years had sometimes made me feel that even Ridgeway was too small for the three of us; still less did I want to make for seven days a week the utterly artificial life that their mother and I had contrived for week-ends of ever-increasing boredom. If Elizabeth came to Grosvenor Road, Violet would not; and, though we had said twelve years before that I could retire from the civil service and do my work at Ridgeway, I now set greater store by my salary than in the days when the theatre brought me more money than I could spend. We had said twelve years before that, if I settled in Wiltshire, Violet could find herself a cottage in the neighbourhood; but, ever since she became Violet Oakhirst Limited, her headquarters needed to be in London.

"Your practice brings you in touch with all sorts and conditions," I said to Vaughan Drake. "Do *you* find every one very gloomy?"

"I should say that by now most people felt we had the remedy in our own hands or hearts," he answered. "Ever since we gave up barter, our whole existence has been based on *faith*. I must believe in the value of your money before I accept it in place of goods; I must believe in your credit before I accept your promise to pay—in money—at a future date. The moment you begin to *doubt* . . . I fancy it's historically true that the best way of stopping a run on a bank is to tell your customers that you'll stay open all night and pay your depositors to the last farthing: in ten minutes the people who have been drawing out money at one counter will be paying it in at the next. The trouble with the world at present, Colin, is that we've all lost *faith*. If some really big man would point out that we still have all the material and labour that we need . . . Everything else is a matter of adjustment, in which we've temporarily broken down. Once you begin to call in your mortgages and cut your expenses . . . That's defeatism! You're killing faith in a world that lives by faith. I visit my patients in a Rolls-Royce, which does them more good than any prescriptions or pep-talk."

"Do they then order Rolls-Royces for themselves?," I asked. "I'm interested, because my own *entourage* seems to have lost its nerve. Elizabeth would like me to get rid of Ridgeway."

Drake nodded in a way that convinced me this was no news to him; but natural and acquired discretion barred him from saying whether one of his patients had asked him to make another see reason. If she had, I felt that she had not succeeded.

"Where are those brothers-in-law of yours sitting?," he muttered, as he put on his spectacles to study the plan of the tables. "Oh, that's all right: they can't hear. The trouble with them is that they just echo what the Stock Exchange says; and the trouble with Elizabeth is that she just echoes what they say when they want to make her flesh creep. Philip and Maurice are a shade worse than the ordinary run of stockbrokers, because they don't know what will happen to the firm when old Alec is gone. I understand from her that he's not a good life and I've had hints from them that he's been rather heavily dipped in various quarters. All the more need, I maintain, for saying: 'Every day, in every way, things are getting better and better and better'. In your own immediate circle, Colin, it won't help to establish confidence if people go about whispering: 'The Whimboynes have had to shut Ridgeway. The Gerrold boys aren't going to Oxford after all. In fact, the younger one's being taken away from school before the end of his time and shoved into an office. I suppose poor old Colin finds that the theatre has slumped, like everything else'. If you want to stop the rot . . . I should complete the education of these boys even if I had to borrow the money. When I think what my time here meant to me . . ."

"They had decided against it even before the slump," I said. "*I* think it's a pity and I'm trying to infect Norman with my own love of the place. When I shewed him round a few weeks ago, he seemed to feel that he quite belonged here. The freshmen's table, where we dined till we could make up a mess of our own; the guest-table, where I used to entertain his *rather* awe-inspiring grandfather; the training-table, to which I *never* aspired; the Loders' table to which Uncle Philip and Uncle Maurice were duly translated; the B.A.'s table; my old rooms in Peck.; the Junior

Common room; the rooms where Lewis Carroll wrote *Alice*. He was deeply impressed, most of all—I think—by the idea of having rooms of his *own*. I said I could sympathize. Can *you* understand the people who live—for choice—in furnished flats or hotel suites? A house, to me . . ."

As I paused, Vaughan Drake enquired whether I had seen any of the houses that Violet Oakhirst had been transforming in the last few years; and, until the toasts and speeches began, we argued desultorily whether we should either of us feel entirely at home in a house that had been decorated or designed, perhaps even built, by some one else. I have wholly forgotten what conclusion, if any, we reached, as my thoughts were concentrated on Elizabeth's letter and on the reply that I intended to send that night. Drake may have been right in his homily on faith, though I suspected that the rot had by now spread so far and so fast that no optimistic gesture by individuals here and there could arrest it. The budget was unbalanced, we were soon to have a report from the May Committee that would shew we were heading for insolvency; I did not believe that anything I could say or do would accelerate or retard our rake's progress; but, so long as I could keep a roof over my head, I was resolved that it should be the roof under which Violet and I had made a new life for ourselves during the last twelve years. And no one should come to spoil that life!

I had been given a room in college; and, not knowing when the last post would be collected, I excused myself in an interval between speeches and wrote to say that I should be delighted to discuss our financial position with Elizabeth when we met at the week-end, but that I did not feel any need at present for drastic changes in our mode of living. I would get in touch with my accountants, I promised, on my return to London; and, if Elizabeth could obtain the necessary figures from her own solicitors, we should know what we had been spending and venture a guess at what we could afford to spend.

After leaving my letter at the porter's lodge, I sauntered through Tom Quad., where a full moon was effectually paling *"the line of festal light in Christ-Church hall"*. Though I seemed to have the entire quadrangle to myself, I could not feel that I was alone: at one moment I was strolling with my excited small son, at another I was fitting myself into a vast early-morning photograph of a commemoration-ball group and, though I had never met Violet until a year or two after I had gone down, I had a

stronger sense of her proximity than on a thousand occasions
when we were seated on opposite sides of the same fire. In writing
to Elizabeth, I had almost turned to read my letter to Violet.
This was a matter that affected her; she had a right to know what
I was saying; and I had an uncontrolled need to tell her what I had
said. The word "crisis" rang through my head, to be followed by
the word "escape". Assuredly we had talked enough, my neighbours and I up there in Hall, about the economic crisis for an
echo to have pursued me to my rooms at Canterbury Gate; but
it was an apprehension of personal crisis that had sent me hurrying
to write a letter that could surely have waited till the morning. It
would not wait! I was being shut in, as once before I had been shut
into the "perfect and complete prison" of Ridgeway. A tidal
wave of mass-suggestion—from Elizabeth and her brothers,
from my own brothers and their wives—seemed to be sweeping
me from my moorings, sweeping me from freedom and joy, from
love and Life itself, into a perfect and complete prison of frustration and boredom. In the cool calm of the deserted quadrangle
this might be laughed away as an attack of nerves; but I had forced
myself free, as a man forces himself awake from a nightmare, and
I had escaped, as once before I had escaped in an ever-sacred fold
of the Downs above Ridgeway. I wanted Violet to know. This
crisis had brought us nearer together than ever in our lives before.
Though she had gone to Derbyshire on business the day before,
giving me no address, I felt that she was at my side as I walked,
still curiously out of breath, back to Hall. I am not deeply interested in so-called telepathy; but, before mounting the stairs,
I turned to check the time.

"It would be interesting," I murmured to myself, "if she told
me that she too at this moment . . ."

The feeling of proximity was so strong that I stood for
several minutes by the glazed doors of Hall. To-night she must
come no further; but no one could object if she watched the
scene for a while. The High Table alone was lighted up; and the
scarlet gowns of the new doctors who had received honorary
degrees that afternoon blazed in contrast to the prevailing black-
and-white, the rare episcopal purple, the occasional Garter-blue.
A speech was ending; chairs scraped and glasses flashed as the
company rose to honour another toast; I asked, aloud, whether I
really wanted to go back; but by now I was alone and could
return to my place. Vaughan Drake, fanning himself with his

table-plan, asked me whether I had felt faint. I said that I had not been sorry to get a breath of cool air, but that I had gone out to send a letter which—rightly or wrongly—I thought rather important; and my neighbour on the other side presumed jocularly that a cabinet crisis had arisen and that I had been telling the prime minister how to handle it.

"I'm not the power-behind-the-throne that I once was," I answered. "In the golden age, when Axminster was Lord Keeper, I did really know something about what was going on; but, since I ceased to be a private secretary, I seldom hear of a crisis till I find myself being lent to some other department. In Axminster's day . . ."

I paused, as my old "scout's boy", who had been waiting on our table, handed me a letter which he said had been brought by a special messenger.

"And you pretend it isn't a cabinet crisis!," Vaughan Drake exclaimed. "Let's know the worst! Has Ramsay resigned? Has the King sent for Baldwin? And is Baldwin sending for you to tell him how he's to form a government?"

The address on the envelope was typewritten; but the letter inside was in Violet's hand. I answered my neighbours that this too was a personal communication; and, after reading the first lines, I interrupted myself to say that the messenger need not wait as there would be no answer.

"*My dear, I* don't *want you to write, still less to telephone and least of all rush back to London,*" it began. "*I do want you to hear at the earliest possible moment a piece of news that I've just received and to give me your views when you've had time to digest it. The Colonial Office telephoned yesterday—first to Barton Street and then to Old Burlington Street and finally to Derbyshire—to say that Nigel was ill again. The line was so indistinct that I said I would come up at once. And there seems to have been a muddle over the cables, as the C.O. heard that he was 'improving slightly' before any one knew that he was 'holding his own' or even that he was 'seriously ill'. It's blackwater-fever once more; and, if he pulls through, it's the end of the tropics for him.*

"*That's all that anybody can say definitely at present. If all goes well, it will be weeks before he's allowed out of hospital; he must then wait for a boat; there will be the voyage home after that; and then, the C.O. thinks, a long convalescence here. I've heard nothing direct—I expect the poor creature was too ill even to cable—but I've naturally sent my sympathy and good wishes and so on. Now I'm sitting back and trying to get my breath.*

"Colin, my dear, you and I have always known that Nigel, accidents barred, must come back to England some day. At our queer meeting in Cannes—seven years ago is it now?—I expected him back in '29, at the end of his second term; I expected him to remain here, either at the Colonial Office or on his own in the City. As you know, I then and there rearranged my life—shouldn't I say, our lives?—so that I should be completely independent of him. I suppose at the back of my mind I'd always known that he might be struck down by some tropical disease or bitten by a rattlesnake (if they have any on the Spice Coast); I remember now that our doctor, Vaughan Drake, was dead against his going out again after the first attack. As you know, I took the possibly heartless line that after our rupture Nigel had simply ceased to exist for me: I wish no man dead, but a man who's already dead to me must not be allowed to come back and spoil my life a second time.

"What, though, if he isn't alive or dead, the broken pieces of a man and no longer a man? I don't know that he is: he may outlive us both if he stays in the proper climate. The Colonial Office people couldn't help; and obviously, when you may hear at any moment that a man's dead, you can't ask what sort of job he can expect if he doesn't die. Anything's possible, including pretty complete disablement; Nigel as a permanent invalid.

"Do you remember when Norman was on his way into the world, I told you that your first duty was to him? I also told you that I should never know a moment's happiness if I felt that I had got in his way. I'm wondering about Nigel! My first duty is not to him. The account between us is closed. I believe I could make myself blind, deaf and insensitive to what the world might say: 'neglecting her invalid husband for some ridiculous business that she took up to kill time while he was abroad'. The sickness-and-health vow went overboard with his loving-and-cherishing vow. I shouldn't be responsible for him if we'd had a divorce; and I feel no responsibility because we happen still to be technically tied. My conscience is as clear as my head over that! And yet there's something beyond reason that keeps nagging at me! Should I be happy, could you be happy, if we passed by on the other side?

"I don't know! I'm writing to you, my beloved, just because I don't know. I'm frightened! The bottom has dropped out of my world! I put myself in your hands. I'm just a fool of a woman and I don't know, I can't make up my mind, you must make it up for me. Just give me a little time and I'll do whatever you say! It was heaven while it lasted, wasn't it? O my darling heart, this isn't the end, is it?"

As I pocketed the letter, I felt a hand on my wrist and heard Vaughan Drake murmuring:

"Not bad news, I hope?"

"Well, yes, it is," I said. "And a very odd coincidence! We were talking about Nigel Oakhirst at the beginning of dinner: my letter was from his wife to say she'd just heard from the Colonial Office that he'd gone down again with blackwater."

"H'm. That is *not* good. I can't pretend it is. He has a very tough constitution in his favour, or *had* before he began to take liberties with it. And I believe the government hospital out there is extraordinarily good. Everything that *can* be done . . . ."

"It would help," I said, "if you would give me—and Violet— a lecture in words of one syllable about blackwater. She's in London."

Drake studied a small engagement-book and asked whether I could arrange for us both to meet him the following afternoon.

"You would probably get more help from an encyclopaedia," he added. "I can't advise on the strength of the one word 'black-water', applied to a patient of mine that I haven't seen for six years or more. Tell Lady Oakhirst that there's nothing anybody here can *do*: she must be patient, keep a stout heart . . ."

"I think she would like a general talk with you," I said. "In her own words, the bottom has dropped rather suddenly out of her world."

"I can well understand her feeling that. If you can make her see that it's no good worrying, because there's nothing any one can do. . . ."

"I will tell her," I promised, "that everything has already been done that *can* be done. Nigel can be trusted to put up a good fight."

And so, I added to myself, could Violet; so, I hoped, could I. It was only in her imagination that the bottom had fallen out of her world. Everything that could be done had already been done. Her world and mine was not going to be wrecked. By another coincidence, with which I did not see fit to bother Vaughan Drake, that had all been settled while her messenger was still on his way to me, when I wrote a letter—under her eyes—to Eliza-beth and carried it to the porter's lodge, through the moon-lit quadrangle that was empty of all living things except myself and the companion who might so easily have been mistaken for the shadow of my master's gown.

XII

THOUGH Violet—in a rare moment of panic—might say that she was putting herself in my hands, though I—in sublime confidence that I had provided in advance against her fears—might tell her that I asked for nothing better, I feel in looking back on the whole twenty years of superficial peace from 1919 to 1939 that, far from keeping our fates in our own hands or entrusting them to some one else of our own choosing, we slipped by almost imperceptible stages into a fatalistic resignation which began by doubting whether we had any destinies of our own and went swiftly on to deny us any will-power to shape our own destinies if we had any. At the time of the armistice I was blandly telling Elizabeth and any one else who would listen that this was the moment for deciding whether we were going to pick up the old threads or make a new start, whether we could do better for ourselves than our elders had done for us; by the time of the world economic-crisis I was saying that we were impotent victims of wild forces too strong for us to control, perhaps too vast for us even to understand.

By imperceptible stages, I had said; and even in tranquil retrospect I do not feel that there was ever a dividing-line, like the declaration of war in 1939, of which we could say: "Before that, our souls were our own; after that, they were not." With mingled amusement and thankfulness, awe and misgivings, I saw our souls being filched from us many weeks before the Labour government gave place to a National coalition or the country went off the gold-standard or I was hunted across the Atlantic to the Ottawa Conference or Nigel Oakhirst arrived in Barton Street by a motor-ambulance from Tilbury. To be sure, the Lord Keeper's Department, the Garrick Club and Grosvenor Road seemed not only unchanged, but also unruffled, when I returned to them after my one night in Oxford; and it was not until I called to take Violet to our promised lecture by Vaughan Drake in words of one syllable that I became conscious of a different atmosphere.

She was receiving a visit from Sir Colville Shandy when I arrived; and evidently she had been telling him about her interviews at the Colonial Office. When she left us to put on her hat, Shandy subjected me to a fusillade of penetrating, but apparently unconnected, questions about "Whitehall" and "the Treasury view", the Oakhirsts' financial position and Nigel's medical history. He then announced enigmatically that the time had come for him to take a hand; he had too much at stake, indeed, to let things drift; and, as a first step, he proposed to accompany us to Wimpole Street and learn a little about this blackwater-fever for his own purposes. Of a sudden, though no two men seemed to have less in common than this despotic creature and my easygoing, ineffectual brother John, I was reminded of the August day in 1914 when he and Blanche took possession of my house and intimated to us civilians generally, to us civil servants in particular, that we had now better leave things to the soldiers. Shandy's tone was that of a man telling us pigmies that we had better leave things to the giants.

"Lady Oakhirst is worked up over this business," he explained. "She *mustn't* be worked up. See? She's the life of the Old-Burlington-Street concern; and the Old-Burlington-Street concern is the life of a very far-reaching network of other concerns in which I happen to have put a great deal of money. See? It's not for her *beaux yeux*, still less for her husband's. I know nothing about him, but I can't afford to lose her. See? Can't afford to let her become hipped or lose heart or chuck her hand in to play sick-nurse to him. If he dies, he dies. If he lives, he must be provided for. This fellow Drake may tell us what sort of a cracked pitcher he'll be if he pulls through. If he's fit for a home job, if the Colonial Office can find him one . . ."

I interposed, quoting a chance remark of Drake's the night before, that I understood Nigel had been hoping and indeed working to make a career for himself in commerce and finance.

"I don't know," I added cautiously, "that he would care more for Whitehall than Whitehall would care for him."

"So I've heard from my intelligence department," said Shandy. "Well . . . I'm a director of the Spice Coast Development Corporation. *And* of the Bank of Equatorial Africa. *And* of the Green Funnel Line. If he's passably fit . . . Assuming that he can pull his weight . . . That should be some consolation to Lady Oakhirst. And it's for *her* sake . . . Of course, first and foremost for *mine* . . . I've risked a tidy sum on her."

"She won't give up if she can help it. If he came back a complete crock, though . . . These companies of yours all have their headquarters in London, I suppose?"

"None that I should put Oakhirst into," Shandy answered firmly. "Liverpool or Glasgow . . . well, they might not be good for his health. But Southampton, with a house on Southampton Water . . . You doubtless know the Oakhirsts better than I do, Whimboyne, but, though she is an oyster about herself, I've formed a certain impression. There are no children, they've made independent lives for themselves and they've got on so comfortably without each other all these years that perhaps they wouldn't get on so comfortably if they were boxed up together. I don't know! I don't care! It's no affair of mine except in so far as she's too valuable for me to let her chuck herself away on a husband whose existence she hardly mentioned to me until he was taken ill. See? If I can do a little judicious wire-pulling . . ."

He stopped, as Violet came back into the room; but, as we got into his car and heard him instructing his secretary and found that we were both committed to dining with him that night and watched him drafting a cable to Nigel, she threw me a glance which made me feel that she was saying: "Leave it to the supermen!"

There was, indeed, little else that we could do; and, though I value my independence, I would rather surrender it to a man who knows his own mind and gets things done than to pawns and puppets as helpless as myself. And, if I had to describe the mood of that summer in a single word, I should say that it was above all else a mood of helplessness. As a civil servant, I had no politics; but, until the years of puppet-rule that ended with the end of the Chamberlain government, I have never—as a citizen and tax-payer —felt myself to have been quite so much at the mercy of helpless puppets as in the weeks that ended with the end of the second MacDonald government.

It was this that I had in mind a moment since when I wrote of our fatalistic resignation. It was my duty, as assistant under-secretary, to educate the bewildered new Lord Keeper whom the National Government sent as new master of my department; my duty next year to accompany the Treasury delegation to Canada; my duty at every turn to accept uncomplainingly a cut in salary and an increase in work. It was my duty as a patriot that coming winter to keep sterling in the country by taking my leave in England; my duty as an employer not to swell unemployment by reducing my staff; my duty as a consumer to eat and drink and smoke as the Board of Trade in its wisdom might decree. None of this I seriously minded. It was our spirit of "Tell us what to do and we'll do it" that brought us securely to port; but, though I kept my misgivings to myself, I could never—then or later—feel that the leaders whom we followed so unhesitatingly had any clear idea where they were leading us. In our perplexity we asked only—as in effect I had asked of Colville Shandy— that the men from whom we took our orders should at least know their own minds; and I have since thought that those who seemed to know their own minds were as often as not only those with the loudest voices.

This was certainly the feeling that I carried away from the family-council that Elizabeth convened a few weeks later at Ridgeway. The date must have been somewhere in the last days of August or the first of September, as the government had fallen, but the act for the suspension of the gold standard had not yet been passed. The memory of the first and the expectation of the second conditioned our meeting. I suppose I had scarcely imagined that Elizabeth would accept my invitation to a frank stock-taking of our incomes and expenses; when I went to Ridgeway for the week-end after writing to her from Oxford, she informed me that, as I refused even to consider any change in our style of living, she had not wasted her solicitors' time by asking for figures. Thereafter I was kept so busy with the political excitement of attending the reconstitution of the government that I could not leave London; and, when I got away for a week-end, the public and private scene had been so violently changed that we should have only wasted our time by discussing figures that related to another life. It was no longer profitable, old Alec Cheshunt told me, to calculate what our incomes had been in 1930; if we "went off gold", it were even more unprofitable to speculate what our incomes might be in 1932; and he at least felt convinced that Snowden would have to come off gold before September was out. He and his wife, he added, had come to Ridgeway on Elizabeth's pressing invitation; but in the matter of advice I probably knew better than any one in the house whether there was going to be an autumn budget, what new taxes would be imposed and what cuts made in expenditure.

If my father-in-law really believed that I was privy to the government's financial policy and that, if I were, I should be willing to discuss it with him, this was enough to account for his presence; I could only think that Philip and Maurice had been imported by Elizabeth to make me—by dint of hard shouting—

Q

see sense. They certainly shouted hard enough; but I felt that they and Mr. Cheshunt and Elizabeth and my stepsons were all shouting outside an unlocked door. By now, despite Vaughan Drake's homily on the need for faith, I too was scared by the financial outlook; and, though I refused to let any of the servants be discharged, I acquiesced without protest in the programme of petty economies which Mrs. Cheshunt had elaborated and which Elizabeth welcomed with an enthusiasm that made me wonder whether her spiritual home was not really the suburban house, with the one general servant, into which her still humble parents had married. I acquiesced in Martin's decision to enter his grandfather's business and to lodge with his uncle Philip. Tacitly and blindly I acquiesced in whatever terms Elizabeth had made with her brothers for board and bed: in matters of this kind the Cheshunts could very well look after themselves, in the last resort her solicitors could be invoked to say what she could afford and it was really no affair of mine.

It was equally no affair of mine, though my brother-in-law Maurice shouted his loudest at me on this point, if Humfrey was taken away from school at sixteen, though I made it my affair to be sure that his leaving was not a moonlight flitting. Possibly the school, almost certainly his house, was entitled to a term's notice; but a ground-bass of "devil-take-the-hindmost" boomed so harshly through all our faintly hysterical discussions that in the future interests of Norman and the present interest of Ridgeway's good name I called on Mannington-Drax, the boy's housemaster, to satisfy myself that he had not been stampeded out of his dues.

"I would rather pay next term's fees myself," I explained, "than have any misunderstanding."

"I was afraid," Mannington-Drax answered, "you had come to say that Mrs. Whimboyne had changed her mind. That *would* have been awkward, as Humfrey's place has been filled. No, Mr. Whimboyne, it's very good of you, but the question of notice doesn't really arise. In any event, at a time like this . . . You smoke?"

"I think people have rather lost their heads," I said, signalling for permission to fill a pipe. Though I knew the headmaster and was on nodding-terms with several members of the staff, I had never been encouraged by Elizabeth to interest myself in her sons' progress at school; and I welcomed the opportunity of a talk with the man to whose care Norman would be confided in one or two years' time. "I'm sorry Martin isn't going to Oxford, but I'm ten times sorrier that Humfrey's leaving at an age when he might be most useful to the school and the school would be most valuable to him."

Mannington-Drax was silent for a moment or two and then said that he gathered Mrs. Whimboyne shared my view.

"It's the boy's wish," he continued. "And he'll stick at nothing . . ."

"But isn't he happy here?," I asked in some surprise.

"Oh, Mr. Whimboyne, you must know that those two boys would be happy anywhere! With their zest and vitality . . . No, I fancy Master Humfrey decided that he doesn't want to stay on after his brother had left. If there'd been no economic crisis, he would have asked you to send him abroad to learn languages. The eternal desire to be grown-up . . . I felt, long before Mrs. Whimboyne came to see me, that this summer-term would be his last. He would stick at *nothing* . . ."

"That's the second time you've used that phrase," I observed.

Another short silence fell between us; and I saw the shrewd, grizzled housemaster studying my face as though to make sure how freely he could speak. His gaze shifted to a perpetual calendar which still stood at a day in July; and he got up to change it as though he had just remembered that the holidays had begun.

"No harm in saying it now, I suppose . . . ," he murmured. "Mr. Whimboyne, if your stepson hadn't decided to remove himself, I'm not at all sure that we shouldn't have asked you to remove him. If he couldn't leave in any other way . . . Oh, nothing one could take hold of, certainly nothing to his discredit: he just laid himself out, if you'll pardon the phrase, to be a damned nuisance to everybody. I warned him he was heading for trouble. He smiled charmingly and said he *knew* that. Incidentally, he wanted to be sure that, if we expelled him, it wouldn't keep him from going to the bar. I've had a fairly long experience of boys, but that was something new to me."

"Can you explain it?," I asked. "He and Martin will combine against a common enemy—the grown-ups—, but they're not so much attached to each other that they would pine away if they were separated. Under the present scheme they *will* be separated: my two brothers-in-law are dividing the responsibility for them . . ."

"Do they imagine that they'll have a more amusing time in London? Ridgeway is a lovely place, but it may seem a bit quiet for a couple of tempestuous boys. And, being so near Marlborough, they probably feel that they never get away from school even in the holidays."

I said that, though their father in his undergraduate days had spoken disrespectfully of our "mortuary", I had tried to remove that reproach by putting down an *en-tout-cas* court and converting one of the coach-houses for squash. Martin and Humfrey could have whatever friends they liked to stay with them; there was fair shooting, good hunting and first-rate fishing if either of them had ever shewn the least enthusiasm for sport; and, if they felt any thrill in meeting the so-called "great", our week-end parties gave them a wide choice of celebrities.

"Yes, I've heard about them," said Mannington-Drax. "That's the part of their life at Ridgeway that they enjoy most."

"And it's not as though they spend *all* their time there," I persisted. "They've been on some of these cruises, they've been taken winter-sporting . . ."

"By their mother . . ."

I was about to say that my own leave was determined for me by a Treasury scale and that I liked to spend it in places like Cannes and Monte Carlo where I met the kind of people who figured in my plays. If I hesitated, it was to ask myself why Mannington-Drax had said "their mother" and not "Mrs. Whimboyne". Instead, I mentioned that both boys had been given motor-bicycles on the day that they were old enough to have a licence.

"And that's the part of their life they enjoy most of all," he commented. "Dashing about the country . . . May I offer you a glass of sherry? I'm nothing of a judge, but the grateful parent who gave it me seemed to think well of it."

I accepted, less for the sake of the sherry than from a feeling that it was now Mannington-Drax who wished to talk confidentially and, since the other boys had now left, to talk about Norman.

"Do they enjoy it," I asked, "*because* it takes them away from home? I want you to speak quite frankly. My brothers and I didn't have nearly so much done for us when we were their age, but I feel that the charms of the squash-court and so on were quickly exhausted. Have I spoilt them? Is it the general restlessness of the age? They said they *liked* Switzerland, but they never went a second time."

"They might have, if they could have gone with their own friends."

It was not my imagination, then, that to their housemaster at least there was an all-important significance in the fact that they had been taken to St. Moritz and taken by their mother. I remembered now that, when I expatiated—at second-hand—on the delights of winter sports, Elizabeth had spoken only of their dangers, especially the nightmare danger of the Cresta Run. Knowing the two boys, I knew that they would skate or ski, bob or even curl, as it pleased them; knowing Elizabeth, I knew that she would be quelled by a single fierce adjuration not to make fools of them in public by fussing over them. Knowing by now something of Mannington-Drax, I knew the picture that with generous help from Martin and Humfrey he had painted. "Great fun, thank you, sir," they had probably said, when he asked them about their holiday in Switzerland. "It would have been greater fun if our *adoring* mother hadn't spent *all* day and *every* day on her *knees* in her bedroom, *praying* that we should come back alive!"

"Do you think," I asked, "that this passionate desire for London is really a passionate desire to cut the apron-strings?"

"I do. You see it in all boys to some extent. I met Austin Gerrold a few times when we were cramming—I *unsuccessfully!*—for the home civil and I should expect to see it strongly in any sons of his. I'm glad to have had this talk with you, Mr. Whimboyne, because I *do* feel it's been touch-and-go with Humfrey. Do you remember a song in one of the war-time *revues*: *And Her Mother Came Too*? Any one who wanted to bait the Gerrold boys had only to whistle that. Well, they generally gave as good as they received, but it rankled. No doubt, when they've been away from home a year or two and can stand on their own feet . . . I've ventured to talk in this way because I'm fond of Humfrey and should have been sorry to see him cutting off his nose to spite his face. We should really have had no alternative, though."

"And now, thanks to the crisis, he has left without a stain on his character? I'm very grateful to *you* for talking as you have. I hope, when my own boy comes to you . . . After this, you know that you can speak quite openly to me. And I shall have the right to see that anything you say . . . I mustn't bother you with my own affairs, but I've always been in rather a false position over my stepsons. No position at all, I should, say perhaps! The only sons of their mother and she a widow, almost *morbidly* anxious to do the best for them . . . Well, I understand *now* why you said it would have been rather awkward if I'd come to tell you she wanted to change her mind about Humfrey!"

On my return to Ridgeway, I mentioned that I had been calling on the boys' former housemaster and that, all things considered, we were adopting the wisest course in allowing Martin and Humfrey to follow their own inclinations. If my own accountants could help in finding room for a pupil, I would gladly consult them; and, though I knew nothing about the procedure for entering a boy at one of the Inns of Court, I could get all the information required from one of my many barrister friends at the Garrick. Elizabeth told me, rather vaguely, that she believed her brother Maurice was seeing to all this; and thereafter it remained only for the family-council to agree what decisions it had reached.

"*Everything,*" I wrote to Violet, who was at work on a Border castle in Northumberland, "*has been arranged amicably, satisfactorily, in minutest detail and on a tacit understanding that no one should say it would all have to be done again in a week's time. Old Alec did indeed cast a passing doubt on our plans for stopping the clock hands, but it suited us all to accept his conclusion and ignore his premisses. On no account, he said, must I think of selling Ridgeway: land at least did not run away, but, if the Whitehall pundits began monkeying with the pound, everything else would.*

"*This effectually quashed Elizabeth's idea of a pill-box in Marlborough; she will remain where she is and will economize on the lines laid down by her mother (Nobody really needs more than three courses for dinner; and, if you make a napkin 'do' for two meals, you cut one item in your laundry-bill by half). Her boys go to their uncles; and I continue in one corner of a house that is admittedly too big for me. For reasons that I will give you when next we meet, I may find it advisable to spend more time in Wiltshire or to make an excuse for having Norman—without his mother—to spend part of his holidays with me. I've had rather a jolt over Martin and Humfrey; I don't want any jolts of the same kind over Norman.*

"*My dear, I feel that this is really my (rather belated) answer to the letter you sent me in Oxford. Nothing, fundamentally, will ever make any difference to us; but, now that Colville Shandy has tidied up your life for you, I want you to know—chapter and verse—how my in-laws and I have tidied up mine. May I repeat myself: FUNDAMENTALLY,*

NOTHING WILL EVER MAKE ANY DIFFERENCE TO US? But, my dearest dear, what balderdash we've all of us, except old Alec, been talking! I was brought up in a Tory atmosphere, most of my friends have always been Tories and I'm accustomed to seeing them take leave of their senses when a Radical—still worse, a Labour—government is in office. We've all been badly scared (I believe, with very good reason); but, now that we have a National Government, now that Ramsay will take his orders from Baldwin, my simple-minded Tory friends seem to think that the rot has been stopped.

"I wish I could agree! I'm afraid I think things are going to be a lot worse before they begin to be better. And that's why all our solemn contrivings seemed so farcical. If we go off gold? I believe we shall, but I haven't the faintest idea how it will affect our lives generally. It won't affect yours and mine! Nothing is going to sink us! We're two little corks that nothing can sink, but I sometimes think we're only corks, swept along by a vast river in full flood. Six months—no, six weeks!—ago, we were personalities with a certain importance. I don't feel that any one is important now. If Peary landed in Aberdeen after discovering the North Pole, he would hardly be noticed. Disappointing for him, I suppose . . ."

And I suppose it was disappointing to the Governor and Commander-in-Chief of the Spice Coast that, when he landed at Tilbury after coming nearer to death than Peary had ever been in the Arctic Sea, he was only noticed among a couple of hundred disembarking passengers as the one who had to be carried ashore. Though Violet had known for some months that he was out of danger, everything else had become so much worse since I wrote to describe our family council at Ridgeway, we were all so much more like tossing corks than before.

"I want to arrange a meeting between N. and Sir Colville," Violet wrote on the night after she had brought Nigel back to Barton Street. *"Will you help me out? N. has expressed a special desire to see you, as he has a firm belief in your sound common-sense. I'm afraid he thinks we've all got the economic crisis on our brains. Perhaps we have; but, if he'd been through it at close quarters, it might be an obsession with him too. As the home-coming of an empire-builder, to-day's proceedings fell rather flat. And he's very much the empire-builder when he isn't being the spent volcano or the squeezed orange. Which he intends to be ultimately I must leave him to decide; but, as he seemed to be harping dangerously long on the need for a supporting arm, I've brought in a trained*

nurse who has been given my room. As you see from the note-paper, I'm in Old Burlington Street.

"It's too early to make plans at present, I sometimes wonder whether we shall ever again make plans for more than a week ahead! Do you remember those great unwritten masterpieces: The Wife of Sir Nigel Oakhirst *and* Lady Oakhirst's Husband*? The problem-play we have to consider now (as Sir Colville foresaw many months ago) is Wife? or Sick-nurse? As a title, what do you think of No Ministering Angel I?*

"Sir Colville fascinates me! I'm urging him to take up politics, for the single and simple reason that he knows his own mind. I don't feel that about any of our rulers, even after the latest shuffle. Must we go on saying for the rest of our lives: 'Tell us what to do and we'll do it'?"

Half-a-dozen years later, when Violet was helping me to turn out old papers, I came across this letter and, when we had both of us re-read it, I dropped it into the fire without comment. The little corks were still bobbing on a stream still in flood; but for altogether too long we had all done what we had been told to do and by 1938 it seemed that the men who knew their own minds and from whom we cheerfully took our orders were all domiciled in Germany.

PART THREE

I

I⊤ was a privilege of Westminster scholars in my day to attend any service of historic interest in the Abbey and a few in Saint Margaret's. In the exercise of it between 1900 and 1906 I paid my rather uncomprehending last respects to persons as diverse as the Duke of Cambridge and Sir Henry Irving; I was hurried out of school one afternoon to a service of intercession when King Edward the Seventh was struck down with appendicitis on the eve of his coronation; I helped to acclaim him a few weeks later with a dutiful "*Vivat Rex!*" shouted from the triforium; and it was with a queer sense of slipping back into boyhood that I presented my ticket for the memorial service of the late and last Marquis of Axminster on the morrow of the economic crisis which had, in a way, killed him.

Though I had now been an old Westminster for a quarter of a century and was attending in part as a friend of twenty years before and in part as Comptroller to the Department of the Lord Keeper, the feeling that time had played a trick on me was strengthened when I found that my seat in the north transept was between Vaughan Drake, who had been Axminster's last medical adviser (or, since the dead man had never taken any one's advice, I should perhaps say his "consultant extraordinary"), and Clement Phayre, for whom this concourse of fashionable mourners would provide half-a-dozen columns of gossip ready-made. As we waited for the surpliced procession of which we had once formed the undistinguished tail, we exchanged memories of the chapters that we had seen ceremonially ending here from twenty-five to thirty years ago; and, though Drake's professional discretion barred him from saying more of Axminster's death than the one word "heart", Clem Phayre whispered the Fleet-Street version of a climax that he obviously thought I should not accept, though I should have said—with still vivid memories of the dinner that had ended with his asking me to second him in a duel—that it harmonized in every detail with the life and manners, the outlook and language of "Lorenzo the Magnificent", "Billy the Bruiser", "the Flying Dutchman" and "the last of the Whigs".

"He was abroad," Phayre informed me, "when the crisis began. Oh, making his customary royal progress from *palazzo* to *castello*. I suppose nobody had told him that we had gone off gold, though he would as soon have believed that Coutts would return a cheque of his as that any damned foreigner would look twice at a Bank-of-England note. And, by Jove, that's what actually happened! Some luckless restaurant-proprietor ventured to hint that he would like his bill settled in francs, whereupon Billy the Bruiser—who was several years the wrong side of eighty—thrashed him within an inch of his life. Amazing, eh? Since at the same time he was giving his uninhibited opinion of the French, national honour was quickly felt to be involved and some incensed patriot hit the old gentleman over the heart. It didn't kill him, but it was the cause of his death. Of course, the whole thing was hushed up, but that's the true story."

Whether true or false, for me at least it bore the authentic stamp of truth; and, though I doubted whether Axminster believed that he would ever have to die, it seemed likely enough that—once the possibility had been granted for argument's sake— he would have said he had been as happy in the mode as in the moment of his death. The insolent dog of a *restaurateur* would keep his bed for three months, in which time he would learn better than to take liberties with a harmless, peaceful English nobleman. And in very much less than three months, if Axminsters and their like still counted for anything in politics, there would be a new British ambassador in Paris: it was not decent that Lord Tyrrell, however witty and whimsical he might be, should talk—at the Embassy dinner-table—as though there might be something in what this son of a cook had said. If for a single instant Axminster had fancied that he was returning to a different England from the one that he had left six months before, he would as soon die exiled in the Paris flat which he kept fully commissioned (and used perhaps for one night in three years) to spare himself the distress of breaking his journeys at an hotel packed with damned foreigners all jabbering French.

In fact, this was what he did; and a week later, while his coffin was being brought home in his own steam-yacht, Mr. Clement Phayre informed his readers that they would not see the dead man's like again and that, on this account, the world in general and England in particular would be the poorer.

"Not perhaps an *original* sentiment," he admitted, with a death's-head grin, coughing consumptively, "but he *was* the last of that breed."

We were sitting in the severe shadow of Mr. Gladstone's statue; and, though I had not reached Westminster in 1898, Vaughan Drake recalled sceptically that much the same thing had been said then, neither for the first nor for the last time. It was "the end of an era", he continued when Queen Victoria died with the South African war still unfinished; and, if the journalists were to be believed, the world in general, England in particular, had been becoming progressively poorer at every memorial-service that any of us had attended since.

Though I could not wholly accept this dreary view of history, I had for a time thought that the burial of the Unknown Soldier might be taken symbolically to mark the moment of our deepest poverty: in men and money, in statesmanship, in faith, even in hope, the end of a war that had ended our peace-time world without necessarily ending war itself. As I brooded over Clement Phayre's account of Axminster's death, I found myself wondering whether he felt that we had now touched an even lower depth.

It was not my own view; but the vision of my old master's final bout of fisticuffs suggested that any one else who had heard the story might well be asking himself whether we too were battling to preserve something that without our noticing it was already dead. The last of his breed? If indeed "Lorenzo the Magnificent" had fallen in technical defence of the pound sterling, I chose to think that he had really been championing all that the pound represented; and to him, whose ancestors had unmade and made dynasties and fostered revolutions and created new nations, sterling was the symbol of security and power, of certainty and permanence, the guarantee that Bowbury Castle would not melt into thin air. Was that guarantee no longer valid?

"He was a great old character," Vaughan Drake murmured, looking about him in faint surprise as the transept filled, "but I can't feel that his death will make the faintest *difference* to any one."

I was unprepared as yet to give an answer. Ever since that family-council at Ridgeway, when each of us in turn examined

our expectation of continued solvency, I had been trying to
define the change that I could feel as one chapter so obviously
ended and another so much less obviously prepared to open.
"When", I kept beginning, "*I* was the age of Martin or Humfrey
or Norman . . ."; and now, half-closing my eyes, I could see a
fair, chubby Vaughan Drake, an already emaciated Clement
Phayre with smooth black hair and prominent teeth, and myself,
in Eton jackets and black ties or in white ties and scholars'
gowns, when all three of us were all these boys' ages. What were
our youthful successors making of this day? What would they
make of it thirty years hence?

The background of certainty, which, despite that "rascal
Harcourt" and that greater rascal "the Welsh attorney", had
speciously survived the European war, was now gone; and,
herein differing from Drake, I felt that the passing of Axminster
—regarded symbolically—made the difference that henceforth,
in any modern comedy that I might attempt, the stage would be
laid on joists half-consumed with dry rot. For my son and stepsons, for their uncles and grandparents, the boards might hold for
another night or, again, they might not; but there was no longer
any Victorian sense of security in the minds of the players who
strutted over them or of the audience that watched them strutting.

And this, I believe, was the feeling that prevailed in the Abbey
that afternoon. I must have arrived in more than good time, for
the atmosphere of my immediate neighbourhood was long
suggestive more of a conversazione than of the reverent prelude
to a memorial service: strangers obligingly surrendered their
seats to enable obvious friends to sit together, life-histories were
mercilessly exchanged and, when Clem Phayre left me for his
note-book, it seemed almost the natural place and time for Drake
to turn from a newcomer and whisper to me that an old *confrère*
of his and an old confidant of mine was anxious to know whether
I still remembered him. It must have been a dozen years since I
had last seen Dr. Maxton; for a moment I could not recapture his
name; but at the first sound of his deep, deliberate voice I recalled the physician-in-ordinary to Axminster's household, who
had attended Elizabeth on our honeymoon and diagnosed from
a telegram my mother's last illness.

"Bowbury Castle, nineteen-eighteen," I murmured, like a
frightened rider rushing a fence before becoming any more
frightened.

Even twelve years later, I did not care to think of those days.

"I've followed your triumphal career in the papers," Maxton told me, gripping my hand with more of congratulation and less of misgiving than when he bade me good-bye and good luck, on that dark December day which to both of us must have seemed the first in a life-time of dark December days. "I don't get to London often enough to see *all* your plays, unfortunately. You wear well, if I may say so."

"Life has gone well with me," I answered, looking him steadily in the eyes. "I must tell you, though, that I've a son almost of public-school age. I wish my wife could have guessed I was going to meet you: she would have sent all sorts of messages. Like you, though, she lives almost entirely in the country. That house, by the way, where you advised me to rig up a bedroom on the ground-floor for my mother."

"I remember! You, of course, are tied to London?"

"I go to Wiltshire for most week-ends. If," I continued with some idea of shewing how well life had gone with me, "you ever find yourself in that part of the world . . . "

The in-voluntary began; and I stood up with a feeling that in accounting for myself to Dr. Maxton I had accounted for a private sense of satisfaction that in these days of gloom always seemed a little out of harmony with the prevailing pessimism. Life had indeed gone well with me; and, though I might say that the age of certainty was past recall, I did not believe that all the places and people and things that had combined to inspire my boast could all be taken away. Sometimes, I reflected, one built better than one knew. In times of crisis I might feel that, with Nigel Oakhirst permanently in England, I should see less of Violet or that Elizabeth and I, at the spur of poverty, might be driven to see altogether too much of each other; but the guiding spirit of Old Burlington Street was now the dominant partner in Barton Street and, despite old slumps and new cuts, I had saved and invested enough to secure my own happiness and the comfort of all who depended on me. Chapters might close or open; milestones might appear or landmarks disappear; but I seemed to march steadily on.

"Do you mind," Clem Phayre whispered, as he pocketed his note-book, "if I make you say: *Felix opportunitate mortis?*"

"If I don't, some one else will," I whispered back. "I don't *feel* that in the very least."

And I could not imagine that Axminster's incurable buoyancy would long have allowed him to lament that he had better go while the going was still good. Already, by ruthless taxation and rigid economy, the country was beginning to get on its feet again; as yet, while we were still paying for the war and repairing the mistakes of the treaty-makers, no one contemplated the possibility of another war. Peace, we had all been saying since the League of Nations came into being, was one and indivisible; since the world economic-crisis, we were coming to say that prosperity was one and indivisible, demanding an economic League of Nations that should impose an international control of currencies and exchanges, tariffs and quotas, prices and wages. That we should see, that we must see, in the new chapter now dimly opening, if Man was to survive; and, had the social and political Great Saurian to whom we were paying our last tribute lived a few years longer, he would have repeated the new catch-words as vehemently and with as little understanding as the old. At our last meeting, to be sure, he was still unprepared. A world police instead of the British navy? A world unit of value instead of the sterling pound? As well put Esperanto in place of English!

No, on second thoughts, Axminster would never have said that this or that was a good moment for dying. No course could be too long for him.

"I suppose," said Phayre, in an obviously puzzled attempt to assess the news-value of the occasion, "I've known this place as tightly packed for a coronation, but the crowds who've been standing all night in the streets . . . One in a hundred may have seen the old boy driving his coach to Epsom, but not one in a thousand could write you six lines about his life. Is it because he was the Characteristic Englishman, the Englishman they would all like to be, the peer and millionaire statesman—sportsman?"

"Or," I suggested, "because he was always and everywhere a law unto himself? The English like a touch of arrogance, especially when it's directed against foreigners. Palmerston, that 'gay eupeptic son of Belial' . . . Disraeli was a more glittering figure, Salisbury was more solid, but they never gave the man in the street the same truculent sense of *security*. If in fact that has now gone . . ."

For what it may be worth, this was the first time that I thought to associate the sense of insecurity left by the war with the new and growing faith in dictatorships. For ten years now the Italians had submitted to Mussolini's protection; the Germans seemed to think that Hitler would give them a protection that they could not achieve for themselves. Axminster's long list of nicknames did not include "John Bull"; but the thronged Abbey and crowded streets suggested that timorous spirits might be whispering: "John Bull himself is dead."

Looking back on my now distant year as the Lord Keeper's private secretary, I decided that his greatest gift was his power of convincing himself and any one who came in contact with him that, though the skies fell, he and his immediate circle would survive unscathed. I had seen him in a minor shipwreck, a major fire and a medium-sized riot for which the police had to use their truncheons. Though completely fearless, he was intelligent enough to know danger when he saw it; but he seemed sublimely sure that it could never touch him.

"I still retain a little of the charmed-life feeling that I learnt from him," I told Phayre.

"Oh, you were born with a silver spoon in your mouth!," he retorted.

It was not true; but, as the organ crashed into the Dead March, I felt that this was neither the time nor the place for arguing with a soured gossip-writer about luck and destiny. I was beginning to reckon my debt to Axminster and to understand why it had seemed natural to declare a moment since how well life had gone with me. Dead or alive, he remained the man who had carelessly promised to keep an eye on "little Johnnie Whimboyne's youngest boy", the man of whom my pessimistic father had then said that with such a supporter my career was made. Nothing could ever go really wrong with any one who had Lord Axminster at his back. And nothing had.

When the service ended, I escaped into the east cloister and strolled into Little Dean's Yard. Though I had spent half my days within a stone's throw of the school, I had seldom visited it since Elizabeth decided first that her two boys and then that mine should go to Marlborough. Most of the doors were open; and I passed under the Inigo Jones archway and up the steps to see whether my brothers' names and mine had been added to the long Whimboyne list painted on the north wall above the seats of the Monitorial Council. Were evidence needed, my steadily growing pile of note-books would prove that I had all my life been more interested in the people around me than in myself; the drama, if so it could be called, that Elizabeth and Violet, Nigel and I were enacting was one in which I had cast a certain Colin Whimboyne for a part and not one in which "I" was playing. Now, in thinking of what Axminster had done for me, I found myself—as never before—piecing together the scenes that made up my life as scenes that I had helped to make instead of merely watching, with a pencil in my hand. A small new-boy kneeling here for his first Latin prayers, a bigger boy—on a wet half-holiday—asking leave of his housemaster to go with Gerrold to a *matinée*, a boy fully grown and facing the school to read prayers for the last time, a young man returning to the dilapidations of Ridgeway and the calculated hopelessness of his father, an under-graduate on fire to write plays, a made man hastening home to report that the Lord Keeper had appointed him a supernumerary private secretary: until this moment I had never stood aside to review my own progress, in the bitter-sweet months of my association with Isabel Pryde we were interested enough in our-selves, but it hardly occurred to me that any one else could be interested in us and now, when Clem Phayre talked enviously of my silver spoon, when Dr. Maxton revived memories of Bowbury Castle in 1918 and when Nigel Oakhirst stopped me in the cloister to say that Violet really must fix a night for talking over old times, I wondered what drama they would make for me in the improbable event of their being more interested in my life than I was myself.

Our names, I saw, had been duly painted up; and I retraced my steps down School. If, I reflected, I had been born with a silver spoon in my mouth, so had John and Charles and Henry; but in fact the only adventitious help that any of us had received was that mysterious "word" which our father in the last resort could always speak in the "right" quarter. It had wafted me into the anteroom of Lord Axminster, into the Lord Keeper's Depart-ment and—most important of all—into a dignified, leisurely and secure life which enabled me to satisfy my literary inclinations. By any test, I had done better than my indolent brothers; but I chose to think that the happiness I had achieved was due less to luck or favour than to a certain cheerful stoicism, most probably learnt from Axminster, that had kept me from ever taking the world or myself too tragically.

"Even," I mused, "after saying good-bye to Isabel. Even on my honeymoon with Elizabeth."

And, as though to think of Bowbury Castle had taken me back there, I found myself once again face to face with Dr. Maxton. Like me, ostensibly, he had come to see whether his own name was still legible above the doorway leading to Ashburnham House; like me, I felt sure, he had separated himself from the chattering mob by the Abbey doors to effect a private leave-taking and to get his old friend—now muffled in "all the grand investiture of death"—into lasting perspective.

I felt sure, I have just said; but was I in the least sure? If Maxton wanted to be alone, he should not have followed on my heels; and, if he had not noticed me in the cloister, he must have seen me mounting the steps or sauntering up School. He had, I now decided, deliberately followed me. As he acknowledged my presence with no more than a nod, he was clearly not trying to engage me in conversation; but, suddenly remembering the unusual warmth of his handshake in the Abbey, I felt that he was saying: "If you think I can help you in any way, here I am!"

"When we met before," I remarked, "I didn't know that you were an old Westminster."

"Our friend Vaughan Drake would have been the natural person to tell you," he answered. "He has been our only channel of communication. Yes, I've asked him for news of you whenever we've met. A doctor is rather awkwardly placed, Whimboyne: he meets a man as a patient and perhaps would like to meet him as a friend. . . . D'you see what I'm driving at? There were many things I should have liked to discuss with you, but we were meeting professionally . . . One thing you said, though I don't suppose you remember . . ."

"I remember chiefly," I interrupted, "how extraordinarily sympathetic and helpful you were. If you're spending the night in London, I do most sincerely wish you would dine with me."

II

In the last fifteen years or so I have thought many times of my dinner with Dr. Maxton in Grosvenor Road, of my vague expectations when I impulsively invited him to dine and of my still vaguer feelings at the end of our long and very agreeable meeting.

R

I suspect that Axminster's death and the atmosphere of his memorial service had stirred me more than I knew; and I think that for a moment I may have dramatized myself, in the sense that I said: "What is happening to you, my friend, is what you make happen to other people for your most effective curtains." And the critics, a few weeks earlier, were good enough to say that I had beaten my own record for effective curtains in *The Rule of the Road* when "Lord Henry" summed up the second act in the words: "*Mrs. Despard is the only person who can resolve the mystery; and no one knows whether she's been dead these twenty years . . . ,*" to break off as his butler enters to say: "*A lady wishes to speak to you on the telephone, my lord. I said you were engaged, but she would not give me a message. Mrs. Despard, the name is.*" From the first moment of my unexpected encounter with Maxton, I fancy that one part of my brain had been saying "Here is the only man who can explain your own married life to you"; when we met again up School, I felt that he was offering me his help. And, when I had invited him to my house, when he had accepted, when we had talked into the early hours of the morning with hardly a mention of Elizabeth, I wondered—as I have been wondering at intervals ever since— whether in fact he had nothing to tell me, whether in some way I inadvertently froze his apparent communicativeness or whether we both discovered at the outset that we were more interested in the present and future than in the past. I seem to remember that I followed my invitation immediately with an assurance that I should not try to break through his professional reserve. What, another part of my brain was asking, did my married life matter to any one? It was Life, rediscovered by Violet and me, that alone mattered. Life that we refused to allow either Elizabeth or Nigel to mar, Life that I had found a moment since to be still flaming when every one else in that vast, sombre congregation seemed to think that, with Axminster's passing, the sun had lost its heat and light.

For several minutes I could not even be sure that Maxton had heard what I said. Jerking his thumb at the line of Whimboynes, he observed with a frown that he did not know whether to be glad or sorry that since poor Honiton's death in the Great War Axminster had no heir.

"He would have been an impossible man to succeed," he added. "Especially in these times . . . By the way, you mentioned a son of school age. Is he carrying on the family tradition?"

"His mother favours a school in the country," I answered. "As my two stepsons were at Marlborough . . . But perhaps you didn't know there was a first family?"

"I believe Mrs. Whimboyne told me, but it's a good many years ago and my memory, for the circumstances even of my regular patients, is not what it once was."

I pointed to the name of Austin, first and last of the Gerrolds to be commemorated on these walls.

"Missing, believed killed, in the second year of the war," I said. "One of my best friends and, like me, a civil servant. I, all of us who were here or at Oxford with him, always thought he would have gone farther than any of us."

"Perhaps, if we'd had conscription earlier . . . ," Maxton generalized. "I know, in my own profession . . . I rather gathered, though, in the short time I was attending Mrs. Whimboyne, that nothing would have stopped *him*. Which I think was still rankling. Married men oughtn't to have been *allowed* to go while single men were kept at home. Apart from that she said very little about Gerrold, so little that I didn't even know he'd been a friend of yours. I believe I warned you at the time, Whimboyne, that her nerves seemed to be in rather a funny state. The strain of the war, the excitement of the wedding. I encouraged her to tell me anything about herself that she would, but it didn't amount to much. If I heard how many children she'd had . . ."

Then it was that I promised not to embarrass him, if he would dine with me, by talking about Elizabeth unless he gave me a lead to follow.

"Though I'm ready to bet," I could not resist adding, "when you heard she'd been married once, you asked yourself why in the world she had married a second time."

"Well . . . One had met cases enough of women who wanted a home at all costs, with a man to look after them . . ."

"And you found in two minutes or less that under that vague manner she was rather exceptionally well able to look after herself!"

"One had met cases," the doctor continued, "of women who wanted a husband but couldn't be bothered with children. *Too* many, for my taste. One had met women who wanted children, but couldn't be bothered with a husband."

As he paused, I said that from his voice and manner it was evident to me he had not before met a case of two people, no longer adolescents, rushing into marriage without beginning to understand each other's attitude to it.

"It seemed to you quite dreadful," I continued, "that we should have waited till our honeymoon . . ."

"Still . . . As you tell me everything's turned out all right . . . I suppose Gow was headmaster when you were here? I'm so much of an old-timer that I had two years under Scott and the rest under Rutherford."

Though Maxton had seemed to my still young eyes an elderly man when I first met him a dozen years earlier, I calculated from the date of his admission to the school that he must be still in his sixties. If his memory was no longer what it had once been, it was good enough; and yet his deliberate speech and slow movements proclaimed him a man old before his time, possibly a man in failing health and almost certainly a man that I should not see again if I waited another twelve years. It had occurred to me, a few minutes since, that I had never before troubled to piece my life into a dramatic whole; and, though I had less than no wish to inflict the results on him, it occurred to me—as he suddenly discovered that he had not accepted or refused my invitation to dinner—that in some way I could not yet define he could help me as no other man could.

Elizabeth the simple or Elizabeth the cunning? Elizabeth the inhibited, Elizabeth the victim of an inferiority-complex, Elizabeth humble or aspiring in different phases of a split personality, Elizabeth the child of arrested development: how often Violet and I had written an all-explaining new label for her, only to discard it before the ink was dry!

"If it were worth a *post-mortem*," I said, as we came out into the sunshine of Little Dean's Yard, "I could find excuses for both of us, but I mustn't accept sympathy that I don't deserve and, when I say that I don't want to pump you about Elizabeth, my chief reason is that to all intents and purposes we've dropped out of each other's lives. Whether Drake suspects anything . . ."

"Quite the *reverse*! And I'd convinced *myself* that things had somehow worked out better than I'd once expected. After all, if one accepted literally everything that a woman says in a state of high fever . . . It was the so-called 'Spanish influenza', if I remember rightly . . ."

"And long before the temperature was normal, long before that ghastly honeymoon was over, I at least knew that we'd neither of us ever been in love with the other. Very soon I found that, without knowing it, I had been in love for years with another woman. As she was married, we thought we were just friends and should continue to be. Only when I heard that her marriage had crashed as badly as mine . . . When I told you that life had gone well with me . . ."

We had passed through Dean's Yard and the whole length of Great College Street before Maxton spoke. Then, after he had asked where I was taking him and I had explained that I lived in Grosvenor Road, he observed deliberately:

"It *sounds* the best thing that could have happened for everybody. Quite why you told me . . ."

"Haven't you found," I asked, "that people who live alone, as we've lived alone for nearly twelve years now, are apt to get strange ideas about themselves? We *think* it's a world of our own . . ."

"I've never heard a whisper from Drake, if that's what you're driving at," Maxton interposed, "or from Axminster."

"I mean something—to me—more fundamental than that. I suppose it was this service. Whatever Axminster represented was *gone*. And yet I had never felt so certain of myself and my future! The shadows as well as the sunshine. Well, was I all wrong before? When I thought and said that civilization had been surely and steadily collapsing since you and I first met? In the death-chamber of the world, was this a dying man's last illusion: that he was better, that he would recover?"

"*Spes phthisica* we call it," Dr. Maxton murmured. "You feel that life has gone almost *too* well with you?"

I thought that his question would be best answered by himself, when he had seen my house and savoured the atmosphere of peace that it offered, when I had shewn him certain water-colours of Ridgeway and when he had given me his opinion of a charcoal sketch that Sargent had made of Norman on the one occasion when he honoured me with his company.

"Life," I said, "sometimes presents a dream-like quality that makes me wonder whether I am a real person. Shall I, after this meeting, wake up to find myself in the 'Bishop's Man's Room', if that was its name, being called with tea, getting ready to take my daily walk to that dreary lighthouse?"

"If you think my opinion worth having on *any* subject, you're most welcome to it. You'll have to tell me a great deal more than

you've done so far. To the best of my ability, it will be an absolutely true opinion; and you should therefore decide whether
you *really* want the truth."

"You speak as though you suspected I was suffering from an
incurable disease!"

"Isn't *Life* an incurable disease? When you've seen as much
of it as I have . . . However, I'm not going to diagnose before
examination. This is your house? I mustn't stay more than a
moment if I'm to get back to my hotel in time to dress, but I
should like to see your surroundings by daylight. It may surprise
you to hear that you're the first professional writer I've ever met."

In fact we dined without dressing, after a rambling talk that
must have continued for nearly four hours. Deliberately I call it
rambling, for at the time I should have said that Maxton was
examining my playbills and model theatre with an absorbed and
rather ingenuous interest and that I was following him from one
room to another, commenting on the signed photographs,
explaining curiosities in my acting editions and drawing his
attention to odd theatrical trophies that I had been accumulating
for the last twenty years. I should not have said that he had asked
many questions, or that I had volunteered many statements,
about myself or my life, until he observed, almost as though
apologizing for inquisitiveness, that he liked to "get a general
picture" and went on to give a summing-up that I had only
heard equalled by the greatest of judges and parliamentarians.

"Who was the woman," I enquired at the end, "who said that
she never asked questions but none the less seemed to receive a
great many answers?"

"I fancy it was the wife of the *Irish R.M.*," the doctor replied
with a chuckle. "He also mentioned, if I'm quoting him correctly,
'Flurry Knox's' enviable or incommunicable art of 'getting
himself talked to'. I've found in my practice, Whimboyne, that
patients tell me a great deal more about themselves if they don't
feel they're being questioned. God knows I can understand it! I
hate being asked questions! There are so few that, as a medical
man, I can *answer*. Simply, I mean, and without every kind of
qualification. Now, you wanted my opinion whether you were
living in a dream world. If you bang this table, you'll soon find
that your fist and the table are *real* enough. So, by the way, is this
burgundy, though it's the kind of wine one usually meets in a
dream."

"I remember, when you prescribed chambertin for my wife, we agreed that it was the king of wines. That, however, was an episode in a bad-dream world which, with your permission, I would rather not recall. In ten years I don't suppose I've thought of Bowbury Castle for ten minutes . . ."

"Has your wife, so far as you can judge? From your account of her, I should say she has *not*. Her marriage, *prima facie*, has been what she set out to make it. She has her children, she has a husband who makes no demands on her and relieves her of all responsibilities, she has money, position, a fine house. She must feel she has struck a very good bargain with life! So long as you give her no cause for jealousy . . . And you must have practised a commendable discretion if neither she nor any one else has the faintest suspicion. After all, you're a public man. In *that* quarter, I see no reasons why the conditions of the last ten years should ever be disturbed. No fool's paradise *there*! When you tell me, though, that there's a husband, of whom I know nothing . . ."

I thought of Nigel, firmly marooned on the shore of Southampton Water. In that quarter, I expected no disturbance and, even if our discretion broke down, it would make no difference.

"You wonder, then," said Maxton, "why I don't immediately say that you too have struck a good bargain with life? Well, I shouldn't mind changing places with you for five minutes and asking you, as a public servant in the know, to tell an ignorant old medico from the backwoods whether he's living in a fool's *purgatory*. You seemed faintly surprised when I spoke of life as an incurable disease, but I must admit that my study of world-affairs has made a pessimist of me. When you recall the never-again mood of 1914, the new-heaven-and-earth mood of 1918 . . . I say deliberately that you and I and all of us should be living in a fool's paradise if we imagined we weren't worse off in every way than before the war. How would you say *I* ought to feel if I found that my bank had put the shutters up and that my village policeman had downed his truncheon? So far as I understand these things, that is what has happened: international finance has jammed and public order is being left to take care of itself. You see how the Japs are behaving in Manchuria; you see that neither the League of Nations nor any of its members is in the mood to stop it. Our private lives, however prudently we plan them, seem to me to lie at the mercy of world forces that you and

I are powerless to control. If you accept that fundamental limitation . . ."

"I *must*! All my engagements to-morrow are based on the assumption that I *shan't* be run over on my way across Whitehall. Subject to that?"

Dr. Maxton glanced approvingly round my dining-room and complimented me on its atmosphere of perfect peace.

"So may it continue!," he made haste to add. "At the same time . . . I've seen a telephone on every table!"

"But you've *not* seen the switchboard in the pantry, you've not heard my faithful butler protecting me from interruption when I'm working. My name doesn't appear in the directory; only a score of relations and friends know my number; *they* would only telephone at appointed times; and by now Winter knows unerringly whether to say I'm drunk, dining out or merely dead."

"It *sounds* sufficiently armour-plated! I wonder whether you may not have protected yourself *too* well, Whimboyne, or, let me say, given too much thought to protecting yourself. Everything's so snug that you yourself ask me whether I think you're living in a fool's paradise. There's a devastating incompatibility between you and your wife: you so rearrange things that it's now hardly even an evil memory. You thought your stepsons might be rather a responsibility: things arrange themselves so happily that the responsibility falls on their uncles. I won't go on! It's my last wish to ask: 'What's the catch?' or 'Where's the snag'? about every part of the life you've organized, but you might well explore to see whether you're more vulnerable than you supposed. These telephones! I regard them as symbols: they're loop-holes through which the outside world can shoot at you, the flex is a chain tying you to the outside world. As a playwright, you must see that your outside-world is like very many other people's: unless you *keep* it outside, you must expect your average share of troubles. Master Martin telephoning to be bailed out on Boatrace Night, Master Humfrey telling you about a mess he's got into with a girl."

I was about to say that I thought the boys would be more likely to seek help from their uncles than from a stepfather who might betray them to their mother; but Maxton had already turned to my brothers-in-law and their wives, their old father and mother, my own brothers and sisters-in-law.

"You're regarded as the sheet-anchor of the family on both sides," he expounded. "That gathering of the clans you were telling me about, when the economic crisis began."

"In his day," I said, "old Alec Cheshunt spent more money in a week than I could make in two years."

"And apparently that day is over. I thought it a sign of the times that a financier of his calibre should urge you to keep Ridgeway on the ground that land was at least always there. At this moment the moneyed interests just don't know where they are. Do you find me too pessimistic? I promised you my candid opinion of your circumstances and, though I shall probably be dead and buried before you think again of this conversation, I don't want you to write me down too big a fool. We've not mentioned health, for instance: I assume that Drake is satisfied you're a good life, I remember telling you—though it's twelve years ago now—that your wife was sound in wind and limb, but in our average of trouble we must reckon with illness. If either of your brothers became a permanent invalid and had to give up his job . . ."

I said that this thought had been put into my head when I was considering the wisdom of buying Ridgeway. John had a pension, which however would die with him; but, if anything happened to the other one or to either of their wives, they must turn to me. I had therefore, unknown to them, taken out an insurance-policy which seemed to cover every conceivable contingency.

"Then your armour-plating is even thicker than I had supposed," said Maxton. "If, as I hinted, life itself is an incurable disease, you seem to have immunized yourself pretty completely. So it's only the unforeseen that you have to fear; and no one can provide against that. Incidentally, your telephone has not rung a single time since I've been in this house! Perhaps I was wholly at fault in seeing it as a symbol of vulnerability."

"Or perhaps Winter has been accumulating messages for me. There's one, certainly," I added, as a memorandum-block was deposited beside my plate. "If you'll excuse me . . .? No, on second thoughts I'll read it aloud. I may want your professional opinion and I feel this is an odd commentary on what we've just been discussing."

After more than fifteen years I cannot pretend to remember the precise wording of the message nor even to distinguish between what I learnt then and what I heard later that night. The

call was from the metropolitan police—whether Scotland Yard
or a district station I have forgotten—and my number had been
disclosed by the London Telephone Service. A letter signed by
me and addressed to Alexander Cheshunt Esqre had been found
among the papers of a visitor to the Cornwallis Hotel, South
Kensington. Internal evidence made it plain that I was intimate
with, perhaps even related to, Mr. Cheshunt: and the police
asked for my help in establishing whether the visitor, who had
registered in another name, was in fact Mr. Alexander Cheshunt.
It was only right to warn me that the visitor had been found dead
by a chambermaid who had let herself into his room with her
master-key about midday. There was no name on any of the
dead man's clothes and nothing to identify him beyond this letter
of mine and a volume of plays with the inscription: "*Every good
wish for Christmas and the New Year. From Colin Whimboyne.*" The
deceased had apparently died in his sleep: the bedside reading-
lamp was still burning, my book was still open, his tortoiseshell
spectacles—an unusual kind, almost black in colour and with side-
pieces nearly half-an inch broad—were still on his nose.

Winter, it seemed, had promised to deliver the message as
soon as I was available; and on his own responsibility he had
volunteered certain information and asked certain questions. I
was indeed Mr. Cheshunt's son-in-law; Mr. Cheshunt habitually
wore reading-spectacles of the kind described; and Mrs. Winter
remembered packing and posting an inscribed volume of my
plays at Christmas. In return, it was revealed that the deceased
had registered under the name of Arthur Trufitt, engaging the
room for three nights, and that a medicine bottle, three parts
empty, was standing on the bedside table.

"If it's what I think," said Maxton, "the booking for three
nights was an ingenious touch. He wanted to make sure that no
one would burst in with tea or letters before he was ready."

"You believe it was suicide?"

"No! Death by misadventure. Accidental overdose of a
sleeping-draught. That gets him Christian burial and prevents a
scandal, without invalidating his insurances. A very old trick,
Whimboyne, with the burning light and the open book!"

"Assuming it *is* old Alec, why the false name in the register?
It's bound to come out and make some sort of scandal."

Maxton looked at his watch and asked whether I should like
him to accompany me to the Cornwallis Hotel.

"If he'd used his own name, the police would have hunted through the directory for Cheshunts. I suspect he decided to use you as a shock-absorber. Well, this is one of those unforeseen things that nobody can provide against. It's a nuisance for you, but I don't feel it has breached your armour-plating. If you'd like me to come . . ."

I said that I should. Did I feel by intuition that I should not see the doctor again? Certainly he had been long buried before I thought again of this night's conversation and in the meantime that symbolic telephone had been used disturbingly by all the people that he had named and by a number more of whose existence he had been unaware.

III

A JURY of twelve, duly sworn and charged by a coroner with a well-earned reputation for the brisk despatch of business, investigated the circumstances of Mr. Alexander Cheshunt's death and agreed without dissent or even discussion that he had not taken his own life.

Why, as one of the jurors demanded of me on leaving the court, should he have? The medical evidence established that, apart from occasional insomnia, he was in perfect health; his family and friends testified unanimously that he had not complained of depression or worry; his affairs were in order and he would be found to have died a rich man. Some sudden mental derangement, of which there was no sign, would indeed account for anything; but suicide, especially a long-premeditated suicide, required a motive and none was forthcoming.

As I had been delayed on my way to the inquest, I do not know whether anything was said about the false entry in the hotel register; but, as the papers made no reference to it, I think it may have been suppressed as irrelevant. There was no hint of foul play; and, if an elderly gentleman chose to kick up his heels under an assumed name in a dim Kensington hotel, what good was done by revealing the fact?

The anonymous juror who shared my taxi was saying, I found, what almost every one thought. Why should old Alec slink into a corner, like a sick dog evading the light, and over-

dose himself with a sleeping-draught? In his youth, Vaughan
Drake informed me, he certainly had been a plunger, gambling
for gambling's sake; and, if some of his speculations had ended
wrong-side up, perhaps the only escape would have been an
accident with a gun in climbing a stile. With a growing family,
however, and exalted ambitions for it, he had gambled to the
sole end of amassing prestige and wealth for his children and
himself. By name at least every one over twenty could remember
Coverley Court. He could have begun that sort of life again, if it
had amused him, at any time after 1919; or, if it amused him
more, he could have grown old gracefully, with a wise old man's
knowledge of what was worth having. A house in Brighton and
a club in London, a chop and a pint of good claret for his dinner,
a comfortable bed and a book: all these he had enjoyed as his last
indulgences on earth. All these, but for an accident, he might
have enjoyed for another ten years. Why then, asked Vaughan,
should any sane man suppose that he had wanted to cut it short?

"*You will see the verdict in to-morrow's papers,*" I wrote to Dr.
Maxton. "*Are you still of the same opinion? The complete absence of*
motive *has rather shaken me.*"

And of all characteristics common to all Cheshunts I should
have put love of life first.

"*I wonder,*" the doctor wrote in reply, "*whether you'll find a
motive so hard to discover when you're Cheshunt's age. After seventy,
when you've had everything, you may well ask yourself whether life still
offers you enough to pay for the effort of living. The pleasure of having all
that money can buy ended for people like your late father-in-law in 1914.
The more discriminating pleasure of buying what is worth having ended
for him with the economic crisis. His will may be proved for any figure
you like, but would he have enjoyed being rich in the world that he quite
possibly saw stretching ahead of him? Here you have the old pessimist
croaking again! The banks putting up their shutters and the police
downing their truncheons! It would have been interesting to hear a man
like* him *on future prospects! I can well understand his saying: 'The
world as I see it shaping has no attractions for me'.*"

In fact I do not to this day know the amount of old Alec's
unsettled estate. I was not one of his executors; his sons and

daughters never mentioned the subject to me; and, if any particulars were published in the press, I missed them. Is it unduly cynical to suggest that some trouble may have been taken to make me miss them? For several weeks after the funeral I established my headquarters at Ridgeway, ostensibly to help the unhappy, half-stunned Elizabeth in the rather vague task of "deciding what had better be done now"; the papers were always a little late in reaching me, as they were taken first to old Mrs. Cheshunt who had come to recuperate after the shock of her husband's death, and, when *The Times* arrived one morning in a mutilated condition, I wondered whether the missing paragraph was connected in any way with Elizabeth's statement overnight that she did not expect her father to have left her anything.

"He sometimes talked," she continued, "as though he might do something for the boys; but he always said that, if you could afford this place *and* a house in London, I couldn't need any money from him."

This, if Clayton Mandeville was to be believed, had always been old Alec's attitude to marriage-settlements: if his sons-in-law were well-off, they must expect no help from him and, if they were not, they had no business to be his sons-in-law. An allowance, disguised as a present not subject to income-tax, was another matter; but, whenever I troubled to consider the subject, I always felt that it was a toss-up whether ostentation or low cunning would prevail. My father-in-law might stagger his friends by leaving a half-a-million more than any of them expected or he might stagger them in another way by stripping himself till nothing was left to pay out in death-duties.

Had I been really interested, I suppose I could have asked my solicitors to send a clerk to Somerset House and have the will copied; but I have always disliked discussions of money, more especially discussions of other people's money and most especially the discussions that begin with the statement of one vulture that a man "ought to cut up for a tidy sum" or the surmise of another that "there must be a packet coming for each of the children". And both phrases were used to me by Sir Nigel Oakhirst when we met after the funeral.

"We had some good times at that place of his in Hampshire," he recalled, "but I saw very little of him after he sold it. Some one told me he'd changed a lot in recent years: haunted by the rich man's fear of dying in the workhouse."

"I saw no sign of that," I answered. "He became rather a recluse . . ."

"And something of a miser? They say he was working harder and making more money than ever before, but God knows what he did with it. If he's been hoarding it for his fortunate children . . ."

I told Nigel that they would doubtless know all that was to be known within an hour, when the will had been read; I told myself that from my experience of Elizabeth and her brothers all that I should ever know would be that my assessment to surtax had or had not been raised in consequence of my wife's increased income since her father's death. Now, in this brief exchange with Elizabeth, a week or two later, I had learnt that her income was unchanged; and that, I decided, was all that I should ever learn.

"Has anything in fact been left to the boys?," I asked.

"I haven't seen the will," Elizabeth answered; and then, as though even she recognized that she was evading my question, she added hastily: "I should have been none the wiser if I had. You know I don't understand about money. That's why it makes me *desperate* in these hard times to see you throwing it away on these two great barracks, which are always three-quarters empty. Even if you can afford it, Colin, the wicked *waste* . . ."

I pointed out that, while Martin and Humfrey were living at Ridgeway, there was often not a room to spare in the holidays. When the novelty of London had worn off, I continued, they might be more than glad to come here for week-ends. In time, no doubt, they—Norman too—would marry: would she then not be grateful for a place to which they could bring their wives and children? However little, moreover, I might care for a house, I should never call it a barrack if I felt that I owed anything to it; and I thought that we were both under an obligation to a place where we could entertain our friends, almost without limit, whenever they cared to visit us. Since the sale of Coverley Court, I reminded her, Ridgeway was the only house to which our relations on both sides could invite themselves as a matter of course.

"Is that a dig at me for having mother here?," asked Elizabeth.

"It was *my* suggestion that she should come! And I hope she'll stay till she feels steady enough to face the problem of making a new life for herself."

"She never will be. There must always be some one to look after her now. For that reason . . . As Martin and Humfrey have gone . . . One of their rooms for her and the other for her maid . . . Very soon Norman will only be here for his holidays. . . . It would be company for me. . . . And she could have her meals in her room when you had your fashionable friends here."

I said that we might discuss this again when I had been given a little time to think over it. Meanwhile, I hoped that Mrs. Cheshunt would remain as long as she felt that the place was doing her good.

"She has not experienced the Wiltshire Downs in a bad winter," I added.

"She would pay well," said Elizabeth.

"That I *could* not allow! Times may or may not be hard, but we're not yet reduced to taking in boarders."

"But if she's willing? What earthly point is there in turning good money away?"

I replied that as long as I could afford to keep the doors of Ridgeway House open, I should feel dishonoured if I charged my visitors for their board and lodging. It seemed superfluous to underline that I should feel equally dishonoured if my wife made the charge and dishonoured beyond hope of a clean 'scutcheon if I discovered by chance, as in fact I was to discover a month or two later, that she was making the charge to her own ailing mother and pocketing the proceeds.

At the time I thought only that I had killed a proposal which Elizabeth would scarcely have made if she had taken five minutes to consider it. There remained, however, the original suggestion, which I erroneously believed to be a far more delicate and difficult one: did I, did we, did our friends and other relations want to see the old lady established permanently at Ridgeway? To banish her from sight when I had a "fashionable" party was so intolerable an idea that I felt ashamed of Elizabeth for putting it forward; but I thought it might prove irksome for both of us to be saddled with a perpetual visitor who had always been almost a complete stranger to me and who seemed in the last few months to have become a stranger to "little Rella".

"Poor mother has aged a lot," Elizabeth would say when Mrs. Cheshunt had talked for an hour as though she were still at a stage before any of her children was fledged. "All the time now she harks back to the old days in Saint John's Wood before father began to make a splash."

"Perhaps when she looks back," I suggested, "they seem her happiest days. When I said good-bye after my first visit to Coverley Court, I asked her whether this enormous party had tired her out. She assured me there had been nothing for her to do. Possibly she enjoyed life more *without* an army of housekeepers and butlers and secretaries and tutors to take everything out of her hands."

"I don't believe any woman enjoys housekeeping for its own sake; but, if you've had to make yourself a good manager, you hate the sight of *waste*. There was the most *appalling* waste at Coverley Court, mother says there's tremendous waste *here*. She would like to take over the housekeeping."

I said that I was more than satisfied with the results achieved by the Cruikshanks, but that, if any one could keep as good a table at a lower cost, I was not above learning. As I expected, it was my standard in food and wine that Elizabeth and her mother deplored; I recalled that during the family-council at the beginning of the crisis Mrs. Cheshunt had been fertile in suggestions for reducing the staff and simplifying the meals; and I decided that, if in fact the old lady had reverted to her early days of struggle in Saint John's Wood, the less she had to do with the catering at Ridgeway the better.

"If you can afford the best," I propounded in words borrowed from my father, "why put up with the second-best in anything?"

"Does anybody know what he'll be *able* to afford in a few years' time? I should have thought that if you economized and put something by for a rainy day . . ."

"Oh, if we gave up entertaining altogether, we could make a magnificent nest-egg! Personally I would rather do that than lower my standards."

And might this not be the best solution for every one? Elizabeth's sneer at my "fashionable friends" was proof, if proof were needed, that she hated all parties for which I had to prime her with suitable conversation for her intimidating neighbours; her neighbours hated that portion of every party that entailed a sparkling monologue to a completely unresponsive audience; the women, I had been told, habitually met in secret conclave to discover a single subject that they could discuss with their hostess after dinner; and I could sometimes feel my own nerves snapping as I waited for the dull thud of her next platitude. Would it not be better for me to see my friends in London? If Elizabeth wanted society, could she not get it—without any of her more incongruous mixtures—by keeping open house for her friends of the Education Committee and the Women's Institute and the Association of District Nurses? I could never be sure that either she or her mother ever listened to what the other was saying; but their range of infinitely small interests seemed very similar. Why should I not restrict my time at Ridgeway to a few week-ends during Norman's school-holidays? We had drifted along, Elizabeth and I, not too uncomfortably for the last ten or twelve years, but the departure of Martin and Humfrey struck at the foundations of the life that we had contrived together.

And old Alec's death had effected a change of atmosphere whenever two or three of his children were gathered together; at this season they were gathered together at Ridgeway more than usual; and the atmosphere might perhaps be likened to that of a pirate-ship suddenly reft of the captain who had never known a reverse. The Cheshunt sons and daughters had always modelled themselves on their buccaneering father; even Elizabeth tolerated a life of wanton splendour so long as old Alec imposed the standards, not a socially striving brother or an ambitious husband or a pretentious, titled sister-in-law. In all their marauding careers they had never stood on the defensive; and this death by misadventure, which not one of them ascribed to natural causes, seemed to have destroyed their faith in themselves. Elizabeth had scarcely originated that phrase about not knowing what any one would be able to afford in a few years' time: this was the language now current in the family and the words that Nigel had wrongly used of the father might be used rightly, I thought, of all his children for a time at least. They had become miserly, with the rich man's fear of dying in a workhouse.

I said something about spending more time in London one night when Clayton, most faithful of self-invited guests, had been dining. Talking of old Alec, he remarked on the curious and flattering coincidence that my father-in-law was reading a book of mine at the moment of his death and that a letter from me was the sole clue to his identity. Clayton, like Dr. Maxton, evidently believed that, if there was to be any news, I was intended to be made the bearer of it.

"*If* there was to be any news . . .," he continued. "He never

S

talked to you about what would happen after his death? That's characteristic of the man! He *did* to me. And, if he knows anything now, he must know that everything has worked out according to plan. Clever old devil! *Thorough* old devil, never leaving a single thing to chance."

"You knew him longer and better than I did. Obviously you believe he made away with himself. Why?"

"He as good as told me! The intelligence-department in his office could knock spots off Fleet Street and Downing Street combined; and the old boy didn't care much about the prospects that his tipsters painted for him. England, Europe, the World were played out. The war had been too much for us. Here we were, ten, twelve, fourteen years after it was all over, quite unable to tidy up the mess and make a fresh start. Disarmament, reparations, the League of Nations: we were beginning to see them for the pious frauds they were, but we were no nearer than in 1918 to a Europe that had even begun to function. People were becoming disheartened, if they hadn't already become desperate. Nothing was more likely than that the Germans would go the same way as the Russians. As for our own home for heroes! There'd been a first-class capital-and-labour war ever since 1919, but no man or cabinet of men was big enough to do anything about it. A country that drifted, as we'd been drifting ever since the general strike, was finished."

As Clayton paused, I said that I too, if I thought so poorly of what the government and people had done ever since the economic blizzard began, might feel tempted to take the quickest and easiest way out. This was the mood of dark despair that seemed to have numbed the crowds lining the streets for Axminster's memorial-service, the mood that had roused such opposition in me that I felt obliged to ask Maxton whether my fancied well-being was a sick man's last delusion.

"I won't call it also the most cowardly way," I added, "because I'm quite certain *I* haven't the courage to commit suicide."

"Old Alec *had*," my companion assured me, "but he wasn't running away from a corner that had suddenly become too hot for him. His firm rode out this storm; and by some means, you'll find, he died a richer man than he was two years ago. He was as game as they're made, but he was an old man. If another and bigger storm burst in ten years' time, he mightn't be able to ride it out. *Therefore* he wouldn't wait till he was a semi-invalid in a bath-chair."

I objected that no man, in full possession of his powers, had ever thought to cut himself off in his prime for fear of being unable to cope with the daily difficulties of life when he was no longer in his prime.

"Do you remember that operation old Alec had six or eight years ago?," Clayton asked. "It was to remove a malignant growth; and he told me that he could face the knife then, but he might well funk it a few years later. *Is* that bad psychology? Old Alec always seemed to have the rather rare quality of seeing what was under his nose. He had great ambitions for himself and his family before the war; and he dropped them all like a hot coal when he decided—rightly or wrongly—that the world for which he'd been laying his plans had quietly passed away. He could have had his peerage, but it would have been no use to him in the nineteen-twenties and it would probably have been an infernal nuisance to his heirs in the nineteen-thirties and -forties and -fifties. Overboard with it, away with the frills of life, concentrate on what really matters, the daily bread-and-butter. The old boy was a natural patriarch, you know; he wouldn't have died happy if he hadn't arranged everything for all his flesh-and-blood even unto the third and fourth generation. He picked on you to break the news, knowing that Rella would be the first person you'ld tell, knowing that she would rush to her mother's side . . ."

"If," I intervened, "you're suggesting that he picked on me to become responsible for Mrs. Cheshunt, you're a little wide of the mark. It was *my* proposal. And, if the old lady makes her home here, it will be on my invitation."

"But you don't tell me seriously . . .? She would drive *me* off my head in a week!"

For long enough I had fancied that Clayton, the man perhaps more sinned against than sinning, was made welcome by Elizabeth for fear of sinister hints that he might drop about her life with Austin. As he seemed to be considering the problem of Mrs. Cheshunt's presence solely from the standpoint of his own comfort as a fellow-guest, I was stung into saying that, if he found her so tiresome, he had better postpone his next visit till he heard that she had gone for one of her periodical cures at Droitwich.

"I'm not thinking of myself, old boy," he answered imperturbably, "*I* can get on with anybody. I'm thinking of *you*. If you let that old woman dig herself in here, you won't be able to call your soul your own. It will be two to one in everything: Rella will at least have the support she has always lacked in her dealings with you. And very soon it will be about twenty to one, when this becomes the established rallying-point for the entire Cheshunt clan. I *know* them! I was married to one of them! As dear mummie is too old and frail to visit her sons and daughters and grandsons and granddaughters, they'll come to her. Whenever they want a cheap holiday, whenever they're looking for a place to park their young . . . Of course, if you don't *mind* being squeezed out of your own house . . ."

At this point, though I still believe and—for some unaccountable reason—still hope that Clayton did not see it, I lost my temper. Though for a dozen years he had treated Ridgeway as a free hotel, too often leaving me the disagreeable choice of saying that he had now drunk as much of my port as he could carry or that he had better go to bed before any one else noticed that he could not carry what he had drunk, I strained charity to say that his experiences as a war-correspondent had been too much for his nerves; I think it was after our meeting on Armistice Day that I labelled him the Laughing Cavalier who had lost his laugh; and I refused to become censorious over his weaknesses if in fact they were attributable to spiritual shocks that I had been spared. Looking back now over the best part of twenty years, I daresay my recent complacency was shaken by his dogmatic insistence that old Alec was frightened by what these twenty years might bring; but at the time I felt only that I could not stomach the insolent warning that, if I were not more careful about the class of my other patrons, Clayton might have to withdraw his custom.

"I would rather," I said, "see Elizabeth filling the house with her own relations than have it standing empty. In her heart, she doesn't care for the kind of life I've tried to arrange here; I don't think I should care for the kind of life she would arrange if she had a free hand. I have another house where I can entertain as I please. Isn't it really better . . . ?"

"Oh, if you're prepared to abdicate . . . ," said Clayton. "I seem to have got you all wrong! I remember Ridgeway in your father's time, I thought it was the apple of your eye. When you bought your brothers out . . . I thought you were in love with Elizabeth, as Austin had been, as I was in love with Kitty, but I also thought that you had a pretty poor opinion of the Cheshunts.

My God, your queer, sticky old father would turn in his grave if he knew that you were handing the place over to a pack of suburban *arrivistes*. However, it's not *my* affair! I'm only warning you! If that old woman digs herself in . . ."

"You said that before, Clayton," I interrupted. "In some ways the place *is* the apple of my eye . . ."

"In twelve months' time you won't recognize it! I know what I'm talking about. I may be drunk, but I'm *right*. In twelve months' time . . ."

He was certainly drunk. On a long view, I suppose he was also right, though I should not have said so in twelve or twenty-four or thirty-six months' time. Life at Ridgeway in the next few years was somewhat more humdrum when I went there in Norman's holidays; but I had no feeling that I had been squeezed out of any position. It was indeed only when war threatened at the time of Munich that I discovered that I had ceased to count in the life that had been taking shape ever since, as Clayton would have said, I abdicated.

And three times out of four when I went there in the last six or eight years of nominal peace, I found that Clayton was there. He no longer talked of the Cheshunts as suburban *arrivistes* or commented on the strange family into which he and I had married; I was treated to no more hints that Elizabeth had driven Austin to women, wine or war; and she seemed to have outgrown her fear of him. Instead of trying to buy his silence with food and drink, she was letting him earn his keep by being useful to her. Obviously, I cannot say whether she employed with him her old formula: "I wish *you* would say that to Colin! He might listen to *you*"; but throughout the "white war" and the "red" I felt that Clayton had transferred his allegiance from me to Elizabeth.

"*Who wonders? And who cares?*"

In all these years I should have said that nothing Elizabeth or Clayton did together or apart could have the smallest interest or importance for any one but themselves. And on a long view I was disastrously wrong.

IV

IF at any time since I began this scribbling I had been as much interested in Colin Whimboyne as in his playhouse, I suppose I should have enriched my note-books with psychological discoveries about myself. I might have said, for example, that, like most of my fellows, the only criticism that I really resented was the one with a core of truth that I was unwilling to admit. Tell me that I am a dipsomaniac, I might have boasted, and I can shrug my shoulders in good-humoured pity for your silliness; say, as Clayton Mandeville said, that I was a "quitter" and I grow angry. To be sure, he was speaking in his cups; I could have sworn that I never gave his taunts another thought; and yet, when the word "abdication" suddenly sounded on every one's lips, I found that it had been rankling for years. I remember wincing when Violet used the word in Grosvenor Road on the night when we heard that King Edward the Eighth had abdicated.

"Is anything the matter?," she asked, observing my change of expression.

A little shocked that this pinprick had been allowed to fester, I thought to rid my system of its poison by telling her of the conversation that had led to old Mrs. Cheshunt's establishment at Ridgeway nearly five years ago now. As my mother-in-law had been in her grave since 1934, the danger of my being squeezed out of my own house had obviously passed. In fact, I defended myself, I had for various reasons spent more time in Wiltshire during my alleged abdication—usually to end a crisis created by one or other of my stepsons—than when—as Clayton might have said—I was continuing the "excellent squire" or "local tin-god" tradition laid down by my father and, if I no longer entertained there so lavishly as in the nineteen-twenties, the reason was that the paper-prosperity of the years immediately following the war had not survived into the nineteen-thirties. Moreover, though we had weathered the world economic-crisis, we were being buffeted every few months by international crises; and, even if Elizabeth had not made every party a penance for herself and my guests, a good party-spirit was hard to maintain when every one was gloomily asking every one else: "What are these damned Japs up to in Manchuria?" or "What do you make of this fellow Hitler?" or "How has that bombastic ass Mussolini been allowed to get away with his Abyssinian racket?"

"I'm not even conscious," I went on, "that it was ever two to one, as Clayton warned me to expect, during the short time that the old lady was with us. As for a perpetual twenty to one when the Cheshunt hordes are supposed to have entered into possession . . . Do *you* feel that the jungle ever rushed in?"

"It might have shocked your father," Violet suggested, "that no one dressed for dinner when you weren't there. Or that the wireless was brought in as a substitute for conversation at meals. Even that was only schoolboy slackness: I should say that Martin and Humfrey were now greater sticklers than you and your father put together. Why worry, though, about a man who obviously doesn't know the meaning of words?"

I was worrying, I answered, because I suspected that Clayton had flicked me on a raw place of which I was hardly aware.

"I'm wondering now," I went on, as Violet crossed to my chair, "whether I didn't flare up at poor old Clayton over abdication when I ought to have lowered my head at some one quite different, over quite another word. I told you at the time about the visit that old doctor of Axminster's paid me here after the memorial service. He complimented me, I remember, on my armour-plating of life and, as an afterthought, he hinted that perhaps I'd given too much thought to it. When I had to decide what life at Ridgeway was to be with the boys gone, it certainly was the easiest way out to retire gracefully and leave Elizabeth and her mother to keep each other company according to their own ideas. *So* easy as to seem almost like running away. I wish I could have seen more of Maxton: he died suddenly quite a few weeks after our one night here together."

"And before there was time to see whether any of his forebodings . . ."

The telephone was at my elbow; and, pointing to the flex, I told Violet that there had been time for him to see substantiated his warning that this was in truth a chain tying me everywhere and always to the outside world.

"It was the night," I explained, "when the police telephoned to me about old Alec."

"How long ago it seems now! And how utterly unimportant!"

It was, I calculated, only five years; but they had been crowded years, for Violet in Old Burlington Street and for me in my department and in the theatre, even with the protection of armour-plating. For a day or two, as a sign of the times, old

Alec's mysterious death had seemed ominously important; after that, for a year or two, it seemed as unimportant as Violet asserted; for a month or two after that, however, when I recalled Clayton's declaration that the old man had committed suicide because he could not hope to grapple in ten years' time with a world that for him was already finished, I wondered whether his death was so unimportant after all.

"That telephone has certainly been kept busy," I said. And in describing the impenetrability of my armour, I had boasted to Maxton that only a handful of relations and friends even knew my number! They had availed themselves so unsparingly of their knowledge that in moments of impatience I sometimes thought of advertising myself as "*Expert Adviser On Every Subject Under The Sun: Consultations* 8.0 *a.m.*—8.0 *p.m. Sundays included.*" I have forgotten which of the interested parties got in first word, but the earliest storm I was required to compose, about 1933, blew up over Martin's announcement that, as he would be of age in a year's time, he wished to set up for himself in Albany, where he had a week's option on a friend's chambers. While my brother-in-law Philip was charging me to find why the boy was dissatisfied with his present quarters and Elizabeth was reminding me that he would not have a penny of his own till he was one-and-twenty, a second bombardment was opened on my other flank by Humfrey, who informed me that he was joining Martin and would like me to pacify his mother and his inexplicably indignant Uncle Maurice. If, in the event of war, his brother and he were old enough to be taken into the army, they were old enough to look after themselves in a place of their own. Though they were still minors, the money paid to their uncles for board and lodging would amply cover their simple requirements; and—let no one make any mistake about it!—, if their trustees put any difficulties in the way, they would find their own means of raising the wind.

"Your armour-plating didn't help you much then," observed Violet, who as often as not had been present to hear the one-sided conversation.

"The affair wasted a good deal of time," I answered, with a glance at my gradually dwindling number of new playbills, "but I fancy I'd been mentally armour-plated against these two young gentlemen for some years. It was the lips of Martin and Humfrey, but it was the voice of Austin. As I said to Elizabeth and their uncles, why kick against the pricks? They had always done whatever they wanted and they always would."

"You were worried off your head at the time. And I couldn't help! You wouldn't even talk to me about it."

I said that I would talk about it now, if Violet wished, but that any worry had been on account of the part played by Elizabeth and that for many years we had agreed to avoid, as far as possible, even talking about her.

"She always protests that she doesn't understand about money," I continued, "but I can't understand her attitude *to* money. That Albany business brought things to a head. Ever since Austin died, she has had the handling of whatever he left—I should think there was a good bit—to his sons. The same with anything old Alec left them, which again was probably a good bit, to judge by the style in which the boys proposed to live. I've not been told and I haven't asked. Well, she had had her pension, there was an allowance from her father, I naturally paid all the Ridgeway bills. You would have *thought* . . . And yet, when at last I'd convinced her that Martin and Humfrey must be given their heads, she went off at a tangent and said that she would be penniless when they came into their own money. It absolutely defeated me! She *couldn't* have starved *them* to feather her own nest, she has never even splashed money about *for* them. What she has done with their money after paying for their schools and doctors I just can't tell you. The whole subject is most distasteful to me, which is why I wouldn't talk to you about it at the time. This everlasting cry of poverty, this morbid hunt for economies when she has probably had more big sums passing through her hands . . ."

"And now both the boys are engaged, aren't they?," asked Violet with an air of helping me to escape from a subject that we had promised ourselves not to discuss.

I nodded, thumping the telephone with my fist.

"How often I've wanted to tell old Maxton how right he'd been!," I exclaimed. "That bell became such a waking nightmare that my excellent Winter asked whether he mightn't insist on being given a message for me. 'Is that you, Colin? Are you *alone?* I suppose nobody can tap that line of yours?' It was mostly Elizabeth, but Philip and Maurice took a hand, of course Martin and Humfrey tried to get me on their side and the two girls— Barbara and Monica—weren't above pleading their case with a total stranger."

"What could you *do*, for them or for their agitated parents?"

"I suppose I was regarded as the old man of the tribe, perhaps the boys still remembered me as the ogre periodically summoned to enforce discipline on the Ridgeway nursery. As I pointed out to the young people, nobody could stop them calling themselves engaged; as I pointed out to the parents, nobody could stop them getting married on the day they were twenty-one and, from my knowledge of my stepsons, if any one tried to spirit the girls away for a voyage round the world while they recovered their senses, they would almost certainly find themselves faced with a couple of runaway marriages. Elizabeth, of course . . ."

As I checked, Violet asked whether I had any objection to the girls, apart from their youth and inexperience.

"I think those two boys—and all of us—might go a great deal farther and fare a great deal worse," I answered. "Very modern nineteen-year-olds, however pretty, don't—-in any sense of the phrase—say anything to me, but I invited Elizabeth to remember some of the little horrors we'd been spared. As I'd foreseen, Martin and Humfrey found Ridgeway a convenient place for entertaining their friends at week-ends and in their undiscriminating early days they produced some remarkably flashy little gold-diggers. You won't find Barbara and Monica in *Debrett* . . ."

"Perhaps the older generation of Cheshunts have swallowed as many impoverished peers' daughters as the family can assimilate!"

"To me, they're a pair of good-looking, pleasant, totally uninteresting young damsels who will make as good wives as the next pair. If there's to be a double wedding, we must be careful to keep the couples distinct. You did in fact meet both girls at Martin's coming-of-age party, but I shouldn't expect you to remember them."

Ridgeway had been honoured on this occasion by the presence of several press-photographers; and, as I turned the pages of my press-cutting books, Violet and I talked of the dance that Elizabeth had asked me to give two years before. Since my stepsons had no future interest in Ridgeway, my first thought was that the celebrations should take place in London, where most of their friends could be readily assembled; but Elizabeth, arguing that my house was now the only home that Martin and Humfrey could remember, flatly refused my suggestion of an hotel. In a passing lapse from charity, I had wondered whether she was saying that, if I gave the party, she need not contribute to the expense; but for this occasion her habitual parsimony deserted her. Not content with filling the house and having a band from London, she summoned Violet to advise her professionally on the redecoration that we had been putting off from year to year as the slump of the late twenties became the economic crisis of the early thirties. There was no longer any talk of what "we" could afford; and, as though to give the note for what the occasion demanded, Elizabeth told me that she had bought Martin a crocodile fitted dressing-case. I said that I thought a cheque would probably be the most acceptable present from me; and Elizabeth, agreeing, mentioned that the dressing-case had cost upwards of two hundred pounds.

"It was an odd commentary," I observed to Violet, "on her own recent declaration that she would be penniless when the boys came of age. I can only think she has been saving up for this out of her pension. It was always a matter of pride with her how *little* money she spent on clothes."

"She spent a pretty penny on the dress she bought in Martin's honour. And she *hadn't* sold the jewelry that Austin gave her. I know what women's clothes cost, my dear, and I can tell good jewelry when I see it. No, I felt at the time that she'd had to put up with your parties at Ridgeway for untold years and this was going to be hers. She's afraid of the place because it seems too grand for her, but she loves being Mrs. Whimboyne of Ridgeway House, Mrs. Whimboyne, J.P., too: on her own merits and owing nothing to you. When some old gentleman referred to her as 'a brother—or, should I say?—a *sister*-magistrate', you could hear her purring at the other end of the room. Of course, she would justify her extravagance by saying that a boy only came of age once."

"But when you've proclaimed that you're going to be penniless . . . ," I persisted.

By now, Violet and I had by many years passed the stage at which she would say: "Having no children of my own, I can't dogmatize about a mother's feelings . . ."; but a momentary dimming of the brightness in her eyes usually told me when she was thinking that she would never have children of her own and I saw the briefest imaginable shadow of wistfulness passing over her face as she reminded me that she had been present when Martin received his dressing-case.

"It was almost *unbearably* moving!," she exclaimed. "Elizabeth would cut herself into small pieces for her children, but she bores and exasperates them to distraction. Here was a chance of shewing her love and *buying* his! The case was so much handsomer than anything he'd expected that he was speechless! You could fancy his saying to himself, 'The poor old mater really *is* a good soul.' Then he threw his arms round her and lifted her off her feet. I should think it was the happiest moment of her life. And five minutes later he'd forgotten about it all!"

"Evidently you saw a whole lot more than I did," I observed.

"D'you suppose I'm making all this up? I wonder if I am! As you know, Colin darling, Elizabeth is not sympathetic to me, but that night I felt she was transparent. And I was terribly sorry for her. *I* can tell you what she's been doing with the boys' money all these years! Saving every farthing she could, putting it in a stocking, bringing out a great lump of it—oh, like an oxygen-cylinder!—when she felt that their love for her was at its last gasp, *bribing* them back into her heart."

On the same page as the coming-of-age photographs I found a paragraph cut from *The Times* announcement of *Forthcoming Marriages*. Here was a young woman coming to steal Martin from Elizabeth for ever.

"Not if Elizabeth plays her cards properly," said Violet. "About wedding-presents . . . She'll casually ask for suggestions, he'll casually mention an Austin Seven, she'll casually weigh in with a Phantom Rolls. She has been saving up for it . . ."

"Out of *his* money and mine and her mother's and her sister Kitty's!," I put in. "She may not understand anything *about* money . . ."

"And you know your dope-fiend would rob a blind man's plate to get his dope! This craving is a thousand times stronger!"

I must have looked sceptical, for Violet grasped my wrist as though to persuade me by physical force.

"You're thinking: 'And what do *you* know about it'?," she cried. "I know, my darling, because all the love that I might have felt for children has been given to you, all the love I might have had from children has come from you, it's the air I need to live! Once I began to bore or exasperate you, once I saw you turning from me as those boys have turned from their poor, stupid mother, I would steal and kill to buy your love back . . ."

"But it was Elizabeth who fought to have the engagement

published! With any one else you would say she was impatient to get Martin off her hands. It was Barbara's people who played for time. And Monica's: they quite reasonably said that, as Humfrey wasn't even of age yet, as he hadn't yet taken all his examinations . . ."

As I paused, Violet murmured something that sounded like: "And perhaps never would." Then, with an apology for telling me things that she could not explain and did not understand, she mentioned that, possibly unbeknown to me, she—and sometimes Nigel—had seen more of Elizabeth—and much more of her tame counsellor Clayton—in the two years or so since the redecoration of Ridgeway had been put in hand than at any time since Austin Gerrold's death.

"That in fact was their starting-point," she continued, "one day when I was working out a new colour-scheme for the rooms old Mrs. Cheshunt had used. Clayton enquired after Nigel; and Elizabeth reminded me of the days before the war when we were always dining with Austin and her. She said she would like to see him again for old times' sake; and I said that, if I was being invited to Martin's coming-of-age, she had better see whether Nigel could get away from his work at Southampton. Since then, we've met several times—nominally on business—in London and she's been down on Nigel's invitation to shew your young Norman over the *Queen of Sheba*. It was at the beginning of the Abyssinian business. Somebody had given her the idea that we were on the slippery slope of another European war: what did I think, what did Nigel think, what could we any of us do about it?"

"What *does* Nigel think?," I asked.

"It depends how he's feeling. He was in one of his black moods when Elizabeth first talked to him. The way things were going, war was an absolute certainty. Ever since we funked it with Japan over Manchuria. We *might* still save ourselves if we imposed conscription, doubled the navy, quadrupled the air-force, clapped on an income-tax of ten shillings in the pound."

I protested that Nigel had rather gratuitously furnished Elizabeth with ammunition for her campaign against my alleged extravagances.

"She wasn't much interested in that part of his discourse," said Violet. "It was the possibility of another *war*, a thousand times worse than the last, a war largely in the air which we shouldn't be spared by being an island, a war that would hit the civilians as badly as the soldiers, a war that would catch her *sons* . . . Quite literally, she whitened to the lips when Nigel began to talk about conscription. I couldn't help thinking . . ."

"Go on," I encouraged her, as she hesitated.

"Well, we talked about conscription in 1916. You remember the Single-Men-First agitation? And the outcry against the fit young men who were sheltering in government offices? I couldn't help wondering . . . It was so soon afterwards that she swung round over Martin's engagement. Clayton actually said that, if Martin was an old married man by the time the war came, *he* couldn't be taken. Nor Humfrey. There wasn't so much time for Humfrey, if the war came soon, but perhaps he could make himself indispensable beforehand so that he would be exempted. My dear, when I said that Humfrey might possibly *not* take all the bar examinations, it was because Elizabeth was asking Nigel about the shadow-factories and departments that the government was supposed to be setting up in preparation for war. Does this seem to you very far-fetched?"

Before I could answer, my butler had come in to remind me that, if we wished to hear Prince Edward, lately King Edward the Eighth, broadcasting to his former subjects the circumstances of his abdication, the moment had now arrived. It was an historic occasion; and I felt that Violet and I could do no less than listen, but at the end of the speech I switched off the wireless and neither of us commented on this final curtain to a drama that had held the world spellbound for many passionate, self-righteous, sympathetic, censorious and humane months. Its sole importance to us that night was that this discussion had been inspired by my resentful memory of Clayton's charge that I had abdicated from Ridgeway five years earlier.

"Whatever Elizabeth proposes," I said, "it'll be Martin and Humfrey—chips of the old Austin block—that will dispose. Incidentally, what is she suggesting for Norman? He's seventeen. If the war comes any time after a year from now, he'll be fairly caught."

"Unless . . . Colin, has he *ever* expressed any desire to be an empire-builder? It seemed faintly improbable to me, but Clayton was talking to Nigel as though his dearest ambition was to get into the colonial service. I couldn't help wondering . . ."

"Whether she wanted him shipped to the other side of the

world before any unpleasantness breaks out in Europe? To use the most overworked word in the language, that *would* be abdication! But I don't see Norman running away. He has always loved every stick and stone of Ridgeway. Ever since he was old enough to grasp that it would come to him eventually, he has been studying his part. Already I fetch him into the office whenever there's any estate-business of any interest to discuss. No, with him too Elizabeth may propose . . . Perhaps she won't even propose if anything happens to persuade her that another war is *not* really inevitable. So far, she hasn't asked you or Nigel to speak to me?"

"That would advertise her plan of campaign! And she knows you would fight her tooth and nail. This may be all my imagination, Colin, but I do believe the next few years are going to be a battle-royal between you and her for possession of these three boys. And I don't see what you can *do*."

V

I ALSO did not see what I could do, perhaps I doubted whether any one could do anything, in the years of creeping paralysis during which the war that Elizabeth considered a nightmare possibility in 1936 became a nightmare fact in 1939.

After Violet's warning of a battle-royal to come, I was indeed agreeably surprised to find how harmoniously Elizabeth and I worked together in all the trifling family-affairs of this time. In the last days of 1936 Humfrey came of age. To avoid a possible anticlimax and as my brother John had just lost his wife, he himself suggested that, if the occasion was to be celebrated, I should give a dinner in Grosvenor Road and, if we had ever contemplated a dance in his honour, that we should save our money and spend it on carpets and curtains for the flat that he was taking in a converted mews near Shepherd's Market. The dinner, he went on, would provide an opportunity for announcing Martin's and his own engagements; and, if Mr. and Mrs. Whitney or Colonel and Mrs. Brace still thought that Barbara and Monica were too young, they could look out for squalls.

At this point Elizabeth intervened to say that she and I had been on the boys' side from the first and that she was confident of winning over the girls' parents now that there were some concrete facts to offer.

"A career, private means, a house . . . ," she enumerated. "Martin wasn't even a fully-fledged member of the Stock Exchange when he and Barbara became engaged. You hadn't been called to the bar. It's quite different now. Don't you think it's a good idea, Colin, just to have a dinner? Another dance and the *two* weddings . . . It's trying people rather highly in these poverty-stricken days."

We digressed into a general discussion of coming-of-age presents, Christmas presents and wedding presents. I said again, as with Martin, that I thought a cheque would be the most acceptable mark of my regard; Elizabeth announced that she too proposed to give a cheque, though it might seem rather a small one; and Humfrey undertook that Martin and he would "go quietly for a box of cigars apiece" if they might come to Ridgeway for Christmas and bring their future wives with them.

"But of course!," Elizabeth exclaimed. "We haven't done anything about a party, but I asked Violet and Nigel Oakhirst if they could come."

Though this was news to me, I made no comment till the next time I saw Violet, when she confessed a little sadly that she had said nothing because she did not know whether she would do more harm by accepting or by refusing.

"I suppose it's a good thing for Nigel and me to be seen about together occasionally," she sighed, "but you know my views about eternal triangles. I should have declined out of hand if Elizabeth hadn't made a business affair of it. Has she told you her great plans for Ridgeway?"

"Not so far as I know."

"Ah! I expect she was afraid and wanted me to persuade you for her. I was wrong, Colin, about the Phantom Rolls as a wedding-present. She wants me to work out a scheme for doing up the boys' old rooms so that Martin and Humfrey can always count on a place where they can come for week-ends when they're married. She wouldn't put you to any expense after all you paid to tidy the house up for Martin's party, but if she finds she can afford it . . . As a wedding-present to the *girls* . . . It's to be a great surprise; and she doesn't want a word said till she has your permission. I asked her if she had discussed it at all with you, but she said there was really nothing to discuss till I gave her an estimate."

I felt that I now understood why Elizabeth had warned Humfrey that her cheque might seem rather a small one.

"If it will give her any pleasure . . . ," I began. "I can rely on you to see that she doesn't introduce tubular-steel chairs or a cocktail-bar. *Is* there any objection . . . ?"

"It will give them rather a vested interest if they have their own suites, their own furniture, their own garages; but, with a house that size, you can't very well refuse to let Elizabeth have her own sons to stay in their old home. It will give her the most enormous pleasure now, even if it leads to the most enormous disappointment afterwards . . ."

"Why the superlatives?," I asked.

Violet shrugged her shoulders and asked in her turn whether Elizabeth had not still to learn what we already knew:

"You can't mix your generations. I don't suppose she'll ever understand that she drove those two boys away through sheer boredom and will drive them away again if she fusses over them, as she certainly will. It's a convenience to have a country-club where you get the best of everything free of charge, but, unless their wives teach them *not* to be exasperated by their too well-meaning mother, they'll say that convenience can be bought too dearly. In a blind, dumb way Elizabeth knows they've drifted apart, though she pretends that they're only trying their wings and will inevitably come back to the nest she has built for them; but, if her scheme succeeds, it'll be the girls she's buying. In your place, Colin, I should risk the disappointment for the *pleasure* you'll give her. Incidentally, it may save you from having Ridgeway commandeered by the government if you can shew that it's in full occupation."

I said that I did not think any department even in war-time would cast a covetous eye on a house so remote from any camp, aerodrome, factory or port; but Violet, with rather studied vagueness, insisted that, if a war-scare developed, no one could foretell what the government might do.

"It'll be an added kindness to Elizabeth," she continued, "if you give her something else to think about. She has European wars on the brain."

"Is she still convinced that there's going to be another one?"

Instead of giving a direct answer, Violet asked with a wry

T

smile whether I was still convinced that Elizabeth would prove wrong.

"It was a shock to *me*," she continued, "when the Germans reoccupied the Rhineland last March. They *may* only have been taking what belonged to them, we *may* not have carried out all *our* undertakings, but the ugly fact is that Hitler made waste-paper of the Versailles Treaty and nobody dared to do anything but protest. It was another shock in October when Italy and Germany . . . I felt that Mussolini was saying: 'I got away with it in Abyssinia, you've got away with it on the Rhine. There's nothing we can't get away with if we pull together. Just you see.' And now this civil war in Spain is giving them their chance. Like every one else, including the government, I suppose I was too busy in recent months, thinking about the King and Mrs. Simpson, to bother about anything else. And, now that *that's* been tidied up, I suppose we shall be so busy thinking about the coronation. I'm not as much scared as Elizabeth—I haven't three sons!—, but I *do* feel sometimes that we've lost control of the strategic situation, that we've lost the tactical initiative, that we're regularly caught every time any one makes a surprise attack. . . . Heavens, I'm using the very jargon of the *last* war! If I could feel that any one was doing anything about it . . ."

I reminded her that so long ago as March the Prime Minister had appointed Sir Thomas Inskip as Minister for the Co-ordination of Defence.

"Nigel knew him at the bar," she informed me. "I believe he's quite a good lawyer, but to co-ordinate defence . . ."

"He's taking his responsibilities seriously. As you know, I'm always borrowed when there's a crisis in the offing and I was turned on last spring to prepare a report for Tom Inskip, on our *ad hoc* improvisations between '14 and '18; the old Press Bureau and the Ministries of Blockade and Food and Shipping. I couldn't help thinking of the venerable gibe that we *always* prepare for our *last* war."

"When I was abroad almost all the time. Was there any central organization for requisitioning houses?"

"I fancy every minister did that which was right in his own eyes. Why?"

With a second rather unhappy smile, Violet explained that she too had been given a job by Sir Thomas Inskip: to serve on a committee charged to create the machinery for large-scale requisitioning, should this become necessary, and afterwards, if a central department were set up, to place her services at its disposal as general adviser.

"It's a great compliment to Sir Colville Shandy and Old Burlington Street," she continued, "but it did bring back most *unpleasant* memories of the years before 1914 with their almost annual scares. Balkan wars becoming European wars, a civil war in Ireland or a railway-strike here supplying the opportunity for a world-war."

"Even now," I said, "I believe we can stop the rot if we shew we're in earnest. Mussolini and Hitler have been forcing open doors, but if we put ourselves in a position to *defend* them . . . You weren't the only person to be shocked by the Rhineland business, my dear: Martin and Humfrey consulted me about applying for commissions."

With unwonted cynicism, Violet enquired whether the boys had got or ever would get beyond the consulting stage.

"I think," she continued, "you'll find that their engagements and Martin's work in the City and Humfrey's bar examinations and their house-hunting and furniture-buying took up all their time! I am in fact quoting Elizabeth, who happened to call at my office just after my Inskip interview."

Reminding Violet of her prophecy about a fight for possession of Elizabeth's three boys, I said that I believed it would be fought with the ghost of Austin: I at least could not readily picture his sons hanging back.

"They're her sons too," Violet returned, "and all the Cheshunts I know have always looked after themselves first. I don't mean that they'll come out as conscientious objectors! Elizabeth said, like you, that if we shewed we were in earnest . . . Very soon I found that she knew a great deal more about the co-ordination of defence than I did: the mushroom departments that would spring up, the departments that were already springing up as skeletons, with volunteer staffs planning and practising their jobs. Forgive me, Colin, for saying that I hardly recognized *Elizabeth* in this voluble, well-informed enthusiast! Then, of a sudden, she revealed that among those patriotic volunteers who were giving all their leisure were Martin and Humfrey! My dear, where other people's *lives* are involved, I should think many times before telling them what their *duty* was, but it looked to me as though the Rhineland shock had spent itself."

I said that, with me, Elizabeth had always taken the line: "*We* don't want war, therefore *nobody* can want war."

"If we're only to be in earnest up to a point . . . ," I continued. "A *war* job, but not a *fighting* job . . . You spoke, by the way, of creating vested interests: I suppose Elizabeth has considered how her plans may affect Norman? If I walk under a lorry and he succeeds me at Ridgeway, to find his mother and half-brothers permanently established with their families . . ."

"She doesn't think as far ahead as that. The idea of Norman as a grown man! She still sees Martin and Humfrey as little boys, which is what *maddens* them . . ."

"It would madden Norman too if he weren't so frightened of hurting her. You said, while he was still in the nursery, that he was too sensitive to *endure* any air of discord. I've done my best ever since to make him feel that Elizabeth and I are one mind and one spirit."

"And you've succeeded! He adores you both, as Martin and Humfrey never adored their mother or any one else, and he has never had to take sides with one against the other. It can't always have been *easy* for you."

I said that it had perhaps been easier than Violet supposed insomuch as I had given Elizabeth a free hand until Norman left his preparatory school. When he went to Marlborough I took him to my own tailor, but otherwise I had not interfered. He was set on Oxford, without prompting by me, and he had once or twice asked me about the printed-books department of the British Museum, as though this promised to slake his literary thirst.

"You once," I reminded Violet, "begged me never to let him become the rope in a tug-of-war between Elizabeth and me. Well . . ."

I was about to say that the danger had never yet arisen, but I checked to ask myself whether this was true. For his eighteenth birthday Norman had been promoted to the dignity of his first white waistcoat and tail-coat; smoking his first overt cigarette after his first glass of port sipped as of right and no longer swallowed as a dubious treat, he had talked of London as he knew it from my plays and I, recalling that there were several new productions that I ought to have seen, suggested that he should spend his Christmas holidays with me and make a round of the theatres. Before he could answer, Elizabeth was exclaiming enthusiastically that this would be delightful and asking whether she was included in the invitation. I said: "Of course!"; and, glancing down the table to see whether Norman had detected deficient conviction in my tone, I thought that he was looking surprised or even disappointed. Nothing more was said till the day when Humfrey asked whether Martin and he might come to Ridgeway for Christmas. Then Norman reminded me of my invitation, adding at once that he could hardly come for the entire holidays, as I had suggested. If the others were staying over the New Year, he explained, he supposed he ought to stay too; but, after that, he would like to come for a week, if I did not think that life would be a bit flat for his mother all alone at Ridgeway. Neither he nor Elizabeth, I had noticed, again asked whether she was included in the invitation.

"It has occurred to me," I told Violet, "that the more Martin and Humfrey spend their week-ends at Ridgeway, the more Norman will be able to get away without feeling that Elizabeth is being left stranded. I should like him to see all he can of the world before he decides on a career, or before any one decides on it for him. Clayton, who has just remembered that he's Norman's god-father, is coming to us for Christmas and will doubtless monopolize every conversation with plans and suggestions."

My forecast, I was to find, would have been more accurate if I had said that Clayton would come filled with a single, obsessive idea and that others would make bright suggestions on the strength of it. In his checkered odyssey from leader-writer to war-correspondent and from dramatic critic to literary editor, at every change enlisting with a paper of sorrier reputation than the last, he had now taken his final walk down Fleet Street and after a period of unattachment (traditionally gilded by the euphemism of free-lance journalism) was now a ghost-writer of memoirs that his clients were too illiterate or too idle to write for themselves. The friend of a friend had mentioned his name to Axminster's executors; and Clayton seemed to have persuaded them that England and America were clamouring for a full-length biography and that he was the proper person to undertake it. I, it seemed, was to supply the material from my recollections of twelve months spent as "the Flying Dutchman's travelling secretary".

I had little new to tell men like Clayton and Nigel, who remembered Axminster at the peak of his fame; but the younger members of my audience, to whom he was now little more than a

name, were so much diverted by his extravagances and escapades
that it was I who monopolized the conversation at dinner the
first night, carrying them with me on a magic carpet to the
roystering days of the Regency. Since the moods and manners of
Axminster's world were less squeamish than those in which I had
been brought up, I bowdlerized my narrative and was rewarded
at the end by hearing Elizabeth say that it must have been a
wonderful experience for a young man (which, I thought, was
underlining the obvious) and that she wished Martin and
Humfrey could have had my opportunities.

"If you could persuade one of your viceroy friends to do for
Norman what Lord Axminster did for you . . . ," she continued.
"Colin used to have a perfect *collection*," she explained to the
company at large. "Lord Reading, Lord Irwin, Lord Willingdon,
Lord Linlithgow, Lord Tweedsmuir. I can't see any point in
being friends with people like that if they won't do you a
favour occasionally. It would be a marvellous chance for
Norman."

As she seemed to be speaking more than half seriously, I felt
obliged to point out that only the two last-named on her list were
holding office at this moment and that my acquaintance with the
new governor-general of India was limited to a single, twenty-
year-old meeting—most surely forgotten by him—when
Axminster introduced me at some public dinner. Tweedsmuir I
had known—as John Buchan—for half my life; but it was a
literary friendship which did not justify me in asking for my son
to be taken on his staff. In any event he had quite certainly chosen
all the secretaries and A.D.C.'s that he required before going to
Canada.

"If Norman fancies that sort of job," I went on, belatedly
aware that the person chiefly concerned had so far not expressed
an opinion, "we can see what the market's like when he comes
down from Oxford, but you can't pitchfork anybody into that
kind of thing straight from school. Heaven knows, *I* was young
enough; but, as endurance ranked higher with Axminster than
experience, that didn't seem to matter. Even so, I made a number
of pretty bad breaks . . ."

I continued to draw on my recollections for the rest of
dinner; and, though the others egged me on, I noticed that
Violet, seldom talkative in a big party, had been somewhat more
silent than usual. When we adjourned to the saloon, I expressed

the hope that I had not bored her and she answered apologetically that she had not been listening very attentively.

"You've won *that* round," she added enigmatically.

"I didn't know I was fighting any one," I said.

"That business of Linlithgow and Tweedsmuir!"

"But it *would* have been a marvellous thing for Norman. I don't like asking favours, but I would have gone on my knees to John Buchan if he'd been going four or five years later! Twelve months for a boy on the Viceroy's staff at Ottawa! If Norman is as keen as his mother, I'll cheerfully pull every string I can lay hand on with Tweedsmuir's successor, whether I know him or not!"

Violet shook her head slowly and prophesied that I could spare myself the trouble.

"If he went, it wouldn't be for twelve months," she assured me. "He would be away till Elizabeth's war was over. Four or five years from now will be too late for her: she's convinced that her war is coming in two or three."

"I hope she's wrong; but, if it does come, I'll back Norman to do what's expected of him."

"Oh yes! And I'll back her to fight you by every underhand means in her power. As she was so transparently trying to do this evening! However . . . I've come here to advise Elizabeth about the alteration of those rooms for Martin and Humfrey."

VI

WHEN my travels with Lord Axminster brought us from Sicily to Naples, it was little more than two years since the earthquake that had devastated Messina in 1908. As the death-roll was upwards of 77,000, it surprised me to see how the survivors were already building new homes in the rubble-heaps of a town whose recorded history seemed to consist principally of earthquakes. Axminster propounded the comforting theory that, if there had never been two upheavals in a single generation, the average Dago of these parts might fairly expect his roof to stay in place for his own life-time. I argued, against this, that, if these devastations occurred on the average at intervals of—say—

fifty or a hundred years, the second or third generation must feel that to remain on this doomed site beyond a certain date was to invite gratuitously a sudden and awful death. Our Italian interpreter explained that most of these human ants whom we had watched rebuilding their shattered cells had—or thought they had—nowhere else to go; and Axminster, turning over my phrase about inviting death, asserted that most people went on living where they had always lived and doing what they had always done because they did not see what else they could do.

"Those fellers that guide was tellin' us about at that place in Greece or wherever it was," he continued with characteristic contempt for mere corroborative detail. "Combin' their hair before a battle where the odds were thousands to one . . ."

"The Spartans at Thermopylæ?," I suggested.

"Dessay! Dessay! Well, if your number's up, what can you do except carry on in the ordinary way? No *gentleman* would willin'ly go to the block without shavin' first."

I had wholly forgotten this conversation until Clayton, rooting for my personal memories of Axminster, enquired how I supposed he would have reacted to the conditions of 1936. I fancy we had harked back somehow to the abdication, for I remember we were talking at some time in 1937 and by then I was far less interested in Axminster's possible reactions to the past year than in anybody's and everybody's to the one that had begun—as I thought—so badly and had gone on to become so much worse.

" 'When your number's up . . .'," I found myself quoting without at once recognizing the source of the quotation. "I think he would have shrugged his shoulders and carried on. As we're all doing. What else *can* we do! In February you had the rearmament-programme: fifteen hundred millions to be spent in the next five years. 'Pretty hot!,' as Martin remarked, but he and Humfrey went tranquilly ahead with their wedding-arrangements, my brother John made wedding-arrangements on his own account. Till the coronation was over, the man in the street was thinking of nothing else."

"And you? Nothing that you tell me will go beyond these four walls, old son."

Had I cared to be pernickety, I might have replied that for some years now every question of Clayton's seemed to have been inspired by Elizabeth and that every answer of mine, though strictly remaining within the four walls of Ridgeway, found its way to her before the day was out.

"I'm behaving like every one else," I said. "As a private citizen, I happen to believe, rightly or wrongly, that Neville Chamberlain's succession as Prime Minister is going to give a new direction to many things. I may like the prospect or dislike it, as a civil servant I have no views to air; but, if I thought he was driving us over a precipice, it wouldn't affect the plans I've made, as a private citizen, for Norman. What else can I do? He leaves Marlborough in July and goes up to the House in October, I have great hopes that he'll be given my old rooms . . ."

"Have you decided what you're going to do with him afterwards?," asked Clayton; and I felt again that, since his first object now was to stand well with Elizabeth, he had promised to interrogate me on all the subjects that she avoided discussing in my presence.

"If the whole world hadn't changed so much in the last thirty years," I answered, "Norman would like to follow in my footsteps. Moorings in Whitehall, with abundant leisure for literary pursuits and long week-ends as a country gentleman. Unfortunately, those spacious days are over: his housemaster, Mannington-Drax, is very doubtful whether he would get into the civil service; and, if we have conscription, he'll probably go straight from Oxford into the army."

Clayton asked whether compulsory service was one of the new directions that I expected from our new Prime Minister, but I said that I thought Neville Chamberlain would be the last man to meet threats with threats and violence with violence.

"Round-table conferences with no shorthand-writers," I suggested. "Clean sheets, fresh starts. 'If you think you've had a raw deal, say what it was and tell us how we can put it right. You mustn't, of course, mistake reasonableness for weakness: our fighting-spirit is as high as in 1914, *so* high that we don't need a press-gang. *Our* young men are *volunteering* . . .' It remains to be seen," I continued, "whether they *are*, but I meet a growing opinion that we can't afford to be caught again as we were over the Rhineland. The unlikeliest people are putting themselves on a war-footing."

I did not say that the unlikeliest person we could either of us name was Elizabeth; but it was on the first night of Clayton's present visit that she had announced her intention of becoming a

"Vamp". I had not then even heard of the Volunteer Army of Motor Patrols; perhaps it was not then even in existence; but, when I found Elizabeth next day in the seclusion of the back drive, taking lessons from my chauffeur in driving the elderly station-car, I was told that she was a founder-member of a new organization that had taken the proud motto: *"Go anywhere; do anything!"* As local commandant, she did not indeed expect to go anywhere farther than an office in Marlborough; but, when I heard her in the next few months interviewing uniformed young Amazons about first-aid and mobile canteens, their boast that they could and would do anything seemed tolerably well-founded. I had no opportunity of studying the activities of the "Vamps" in other parts of the country; but, when war came, I had good reason to think that any success my own corner of Wiltshire achieved over evacuation or billeting, national registration or rationing was due in great measure to the devotion and tact of these versatile and efficient young women who would fight a fire, set a ditched lorry on the road, apply a tourniquet or serve midnight cocoa to train-loads of refugees with equal confidence and calm.

"If I were Hitler or Mussolini," said Clayton, "I should feel strongly tempted to ask what a round-table conference could give me that I couldn't take for myself."

"At the risk," I asked, "that next time we may say: 'This is really going *too* far!' ?"

"Shall we *ever* say that? I feel these damned fellows have got us on the run! Oh, I suppose, if Mussolini tried to close the Mediterranean or Hitler reoccupied Alsace-Lorraine . . . God knows what their next *coup* will be, but I feel the time's pretty well ripe for another. These dictators work their people hard, but they have to work devilish hard themselves: if they don't bring off miracles at very short intervals, their people say their gods are losing grip. Meanwhile, we carry on as usual!"

In fact, the next *coup*—if such it could be called—did not take place till the following February, when Eden tendered his resignation from the Foreign Office and it was accepted. Though Mussolini had obviously not engineered it, Clayton telephoned from Ridgeway to ask whether I did not think it was as great a personal triumph for him as if he had, inasmuch as the minister who refused to take his word was being replaced by one who would. From information which I was not at liberty to disclose within any four walls, I believed that the full explanation was hardly as simple as this; but we were still wrangling at week-ends about the new policy of so-called appeasement when Clayton's question about round-table conferences was answered by the German occupation of Austria.

Though I did not see him until some weeks later, I felt that his earlier question—about Axminster's reactions to the issues of the day—was being answered at the same time: Axminster would have done nothing because there was nothing that he could do, which was the reason—as I pointed out to Violet when next we dined together—why hardly any one did anything.

"Except talk!," she exclaimed. "Or *pray!*"

"Raymond Asquith," I recalled, "once said: 'I am joining the army because the alternative is to spend the rest of my life in explaining why I did not.' Most of the people I've met lately seem to be spending their time in explaining why it was better to give Hitler a walk-over than to have equipped an army some years ago to resist him. It's only the union of Germans with Germans, they say, so *natural*! It's the sense of *dispersion* that has made Germany the disturbing factor in Europe for so long. Thank Heaven the Austrians didn't provoke *needless* bloodshed by *resisting*. With Hitler reaching out to touch the Brenner, perhaps we shan't hear quite so much of Mussolini in the Mediterranean. And so on! You would say they couldn't be more pleased if they'd suggested it themselves! And in a sense they did! They suggested that they would believe anything, put up with anything, applaud anything so long as they could keep out of vulgar brawling. Isn't that what you've been hearing, my dear?"

"Quite a lot. But I've also heard people praying. Praying that this *is* the end, that we can now settle down in peace. Unless it's my imagination, Colin, this latest crisis has produced a curious confusion of mind: more people than ever are more determined than ever to avoid war at all costs and at the same time they're more *frightened*. What *next?*"

I said that the answer to their question was staring at them from the map of Europe that Hitler had just redrawn. This might indeed be the end; but the rape of Austria had uncovered CzechoSlovakia's flank and in Czecho-Slovakia there were Germans panting to be reunited to their fellow-Germans. Did that seem like the end?

"That's what Nigel was saying," Violet observed. "He

invited himself to lunch with me, which is one reason why I invited myself to dine with you. Not *every one*, mercifully, is talking or praying or whistling to keep his courage up: a few people—scare-mongers and war-mongers, no doubt—are *acting*. Now that I'm an honorary member of the government service, you can tell me if you've heard anything of interest or importance. To *us*, I mean."

I said I had heard nothing that had not appeared in every paper and been discussed at every club. Since completing my report on the improvisations of 1914, I had returned to my routine-work in the Lord Keeper's Department, where in due course I received a letter of thanks from the Minister for Co-ordination of Defence. Whether Inskip or Chamberlain had read my memorandum I was not told; but despite my experience at the Ministry of Munitions I had not so far been seconded for duty in the Great Sciamachy, as some wit had termed our war of shadow-factories, shadow ministries and shadowy ministers. My stepsons, who now spent long week-ends at Ridgeway, did not seem to be learning their way about the embryonic departments which were supposed to be absorbing their patriotic leisure; and, though their mother sometimes alluded darkly to the papers which pursued them into the peace of the country, I suspected that they and their wives might not have honoured our roof so often if so many of their friends, through poverty or depression of spirit or mere uncertainty, had not called a halt to week-end house-parties. I told Violet all that I knew of Elizabeth's activities in her new V.A.M.P. organization and added in confidence that Norman had applied for a commission in the Territorial battalion of the Wessex Regiment, but for fear of upsetting his mother wished nothing to be said until it had been gazetted.

"Who are the scare-mongers and war-mongers that you were mentioning?," I asked.

"Oh, various busybodies who are saying that, if the government won't give them a lead, they can at least have all their own plans cut and dried for any emergency. If there ever is another Ministry of Shipping, Nigel will be in it. Already his people have moved him up from Southampton on a job rather like the one you've been doing, I should imagine: a report on what the Green Funnel Line did in 1914 and what it can do now in the way of arming merchantmen and converting passenger-boats into troop-ships. If there *is* another war, I suppose it would only seem natural for him and me to be under the same roof or in the same cellar. That's all it would be, of course; and nothing *less* than another European war would drive me *that* far. At the moment he's at his club, but I understand his London office is making a bomb-proof shelter in the bowels of the earth where all the important people can work and eat and sleep without ever coming to the surface. And this is nineteen-thirty-eight, in a civilized Christian country! By the way, if Violet Oakhirst Limited doesn't come to an abrupt end, we shall bolt somewhere for safety. I suppose the Requisitioning Committee will give me a steel-lined basement within easy reach of Whitehall."

I said that, if we were involved in another war and if it were at all the kind of war that I expected, I thought her committee's first task would be to requisition every cubic inch in some place like Cheltenham with almost unlimited hotels and boarding-houses for the civil service and with a pump-room where the exiled Houses of Parliament could meet.

"If there *is* a war . . . ," Violet began slowly, "I would sooner have it at our time, Colin, than at Hitler's, though I've wondered ever since Abyssinia whether we're fit to fight a war with any one. . . . But for argument's sake . . . When my peace-at-any-price friends ask me what quarrel we have with any one . . . What *would* involve us, Colin? It's no good pretending at this time of day that any one's going to fight for the Versailles Treaty when we've seen the Germans going back on every part of it that didn't happen to suit their convenience."

"If we felt our own safety threatened . . . ," I suggested without much conviction.

"But hasn't it been threatened at every point for half-a-dozen years? We may pretend that conscription or the Rhineland or Austria doesn't affect us deeply, but if our first line of defence is really on the Rhine . . . Nigel is *scared*; and he has succeeded in scaring me."

I have forgotten what answer I made at the moment, for in looking back on the last eighteen months of peace, so-called, I feel that, though Violet and I now seldom met on more than one night a week, this conversation—begun in mid-March—continued almost without a break, certainly without cues or recapitulations, until mid-September. When we were discussing the storm that had suddenly blown up in Czecho-Slovakia towards the end of May, Violet asked me whether people in England would feel their own safety threatened if the Germans descended on Prague as they had descended on Vienna; I repeated, as though I had said it only five minutes before, that the rape of Austria had exposed the Czechs' flank and that I at least should not feel that the threat to our own safety was over so long as Hitler could point to a single German minority anywhere outside the Reich.

"Have you seen Nigel since this latest development?," I asked.

"Yes, he's rather less gloomy. He met some Czech diplomats at the week-end; and *they* were quite happy in their minds. They would fight to the death, if need be, but they felt sure there would be no war."

"Are they banking on France? I'm told—unofficially, of course—that she won't move a man or a gun to support them. If the French break their plighted word to their own allies, it'll be difficult to persuade people here that it's *their* business to send an army into Central Europe or even to the French coast."

In their turn these were the phrases on which we opened every instalment of our conversation until "Munich". Of the Runciman mission I said again that I did not believe the French would march, but that perhaps the Germans were less eager to march against an enemy who would resist them. If so, Runciman's task would be one of formula-finding and face-saving. And "face-saving" was the first word that we both used on the September night when we learnt that the Prime Minister was flying to Berchtesgaden.

As though to complete the illusion that we had been as near together in body as in mind and that our persons had been as inseparable as our spirits, which seemed still to communicate when we were a hundred miles apart, Violet now adapted to the needs of the moment, with an air of having sat in the armchair opposite mine for eighteen months, the explanation of Raymond Asquith's motive in joining the army which I had quoted to her after the invasion of Austria.

"I'm not sure whether people *would* have fought; the *alternative*, which is what they've chosen, is to spend the rest of their lives explaining why they *didn't*."

"But how *could* we fight without the French?," I demanded.

"You didn't want a repetition of 'sanctions'! It's very impressive to mobilize the fleet, but even the British Navy can't cross mountains. As Runciman failed in his face-saving, Chamberlain's taking a hand. Now that we're on the very brink of war, it's conceivable that Hitler is wondering whether his own people enjoy the prospect any more than the French or ourselves. It may seem a desperate hope, but it's our only one now. An eleventh-hour general return to sanity. Within the next few hours . . . In the meantime, as old Axminster would have said, there's nothing we can *do*."

"Except talk . . . And *pray*."

Recalling the circumstances in which Violet had used the phrase before, I suggested that there were certain changes to remark since we resigned ourselves helplessly to the occupation of Austria. In ever-increasing numbers people were now acting, as witness Nigel with his shipping-board, herself with her requisitioning-committee, Elizabeth with her "Vamps". Since the beginning of this latest crisis, Norman had been sleeping with his kit packed, a car at the door and a telephone by his bedside; until this latest crisis ended, in one way or another, I predicted that Ridgeway would see little of Martin and Humfrey, who were back in London awaiting the word that should give substance to their shadow ministries.

"If I believed in the efficacy of prayer," I concluded, "I should say it could do no *harm* to pray that a mad world may recover its senses."

"So long as it's not *too* one-sided! Pray for the success of Chamberlain's efforts! *Don't* say: 'O God, why don't they give Hitler what he *wants*?!'"

"If you wish me to believe that any one is saying *that* . . ."

My nerves were taut with long strain; and I am afraid I spoke sharply. There was a momentary sharpening in Violet's voice as she answered that she had heard those very words that very day.

"I was taking a short cut home through the Abbey," she explained. "In the cloister there was a woman, huddled in a heap on the ground and weeping so convulsively that I thought she must have injured herself. I went up to see whether there was anything I could do and that's what I heard: 'O God, O God, O God . . .!' Then there was something about 'my boy'. I rather thought of asking this Spartan mother whether she had ever heard anything about coming back from battle *with* your shield or *on* it, but I don't greatly care about reading moral lectures to total strangers. Then I saw that she wasn't a total stranger. Oh, I'm sorry, Colin! I oughtn't to have told you, but it has been haunting me ever since! That wet heap of human misery! The pathos! And the *indignity*! . . . Elizabeth . . . I crept away, only hoping she hadn't seen me!"

VII

THERE were times in the long nightmare between "Berchtes-gaden" and "Munich" when I found myself declaring that, if Violet was still wondering whether Elizabeth had seen her in the Abbey cloister, I was really beginning to wonder whether it was in fact Elizabeth that Violet had seen. Nothing had been said to me about a contemplated visit to London, though I had often and impressively been told of interviews at the War Office ever since the establishment of the V.A.M.P.s; nothing was said, when I was summoned to Ridgeway, if not at the most critical, at least at the most inconvenient, moment of the crisis; and nothing has ever been said to me in the ten years and more that have passed since.

It was in the afternoon following Violet's weekly dinner with me that Cruikshank and his wife, as ever supplementing each other in statement and explanation, created a precedent by telephoning to me at my office and conveying, by strophe and antistrophe, that the situation in one part of East Wiltshire was slipping out of control.

"I must *apologize* for disturbing you, sir . . . ," Cruikshank had begun.

"You must blame *me*, sir," Mrs. Cruikshank interposed. "I told Cruikshank he *ought* to let you know . . ."

After this faintly ominous preamble, the message seemed to me something of an anticlimax. An anonymous young man, I gathered, had called on Elizabeth to survey the house and decide how many refugees could be accommodated if war broke out and London were evacuated. Her first rejoinder seemed to have consisted in hurrying the bewildered young man round the house and putting one room after another out of bounds as being occupied by herself or Norman, Martin or Barbara, Humfrey or Monica. Even when she had confided that both Mrs. Martin and Mrs. Humfrey were expecting "little babies" quite soon, the accommodation appropriated for them and their nurses still left a respectable number of rooms available; but I now learnt—for the first time—that Elizabeth had on some occasion told my two sisters-in-law that, if there ever was another war, they must bring their husbands (who would have been at least as safe in their own houses) to Ridgeway and I gathered that a similar invitation had been extended to her own brothers and their families.

"The oak room for Mr. Philip and Lady Mary, if they come," Cruikshank was saying.

"And the Chinese room for Mr. Maurice and Lady Jane," added his wife.

Possibly suspecting that Elizabeth was not being whole-heartedly co-operative, the persevering youth (who was believed by my butler to be a divinity-student living with the vicar) pressed to be shewn the top storey, which had not been unlocked since the almost forgotten day when I conducted a party round "Mad Marion's apartments". At once Elizabeth declared that she could give no decision about these rooms without consulting me; and, when the amateur billeting-officer asked whether I could be reached by telephone, I was given to understand that she had—"in a rare taking"—resigned the cares of empire to Cruikshank and departed to the office of the V.A.M.P.s. Mrs. Cruikshank, before getting in touch with me, had examined the condition of the attics and now reported that I could bed down a couple of battalions there if the military did not mind the complete lack of windows and fireplaces; but she and her husband had ventured to approach me because they thought that Mrs. Whimboyne was unequal to contending single-handed with the crisis. Her work for the Motor Patrols was sufficient responsibility in itself; but she was worrying herself sick over Mr. Norman and the young gentlemen in London, at one moment giving the gardeners frantic orders to dig shelters in the woods, at another telephoning in all directions for food and yet again at another shepherding the staff to be equipped with gas-masks in Marlborough.

I said that I would come to Ridgeway for the night, but that I must return to London the next day. Whatever should be regarded by others as the most critical moment of the crisis, for me the most critical had occurred about half-an-hour before the Cruikshanks telephoned, when the faithful and faultless secretary who had watched over me ever since I entered the Department of the Lord Keeper came in to announce that she was retiring to

U

hospital next day for a major operation and that, even if she survived it, she would almost certainly be unfit ever to work again.

"I'm sorry this should have happened, Mr. Whimboyne," she ended. "Now, of *all* times."

"I'm very much more than *sorry*, Miss Mainwaring," I said, almost unable to find words. "Leaving on one side the question who's to take your place . . ."

"Well, that's what I wanted to discuss with you. Miss Norbury, my relief when I was on leave this summer . . . I've spoken to her and to the establishment-officer. She's rather junior, but if you wanted to make a similar arrangement with her for doing your literary typing in the evening and at week-ends . . ."

I believe I asked some conventional question about Miss Norbury's experience, but I was too much shocked and dazed to know what I was saying. This reserved and calm model of efficiency, now middle-aged and fingering her own death-warrant, had watched over my literary career since the now distant day when she typed my first script; she knew more about my business-affairs than I did, more about my agreements and rights and royalties than my own agent and, in return, I knew nothing about her except that she quite obviously expected to be dead within a week.

"Which hospital . . .?," I began.

"A private nursing-home," she announced in a tone which suggested that she did not want to be questioned. Was she feeling, I wondered, that beyond giving her tickets for my first nights, I had never taken any personal interest in her and that it was too late to begin now? I preferred to think, as she coloured slightly and thanked me for the "privilege" of working for me, that she had decided a quarter of a century earlier, for lack of husband and child, to adopt me. Twice and thrice she repeated in bitter self-reproach that she could not well have chosen a worse time for leaving me: the least and last that she could do for me was to avoid adding to my burdens.

"As things are shaping," I said, "I don't expect to have much *literary* typing . . ."

"When you do, you'll find Miss Norbury will get into your ways very quickly. She's as clever as a monkey." Miss Mainwaring permitted herself a faint smile. "She *is* rather a monkey, but she's a good-hearted little thing. Well, if you're going to the country, Mr. Whimboyne, perhaps you won't mind if I leave early. There are several things to see to at home . . ."

And on that word she bowed herself out of my room without giving me a chance even to shake hands or wish her good luck. A few minutes later she telephoned down to say that she had reserved me a seat in the dining-car; and a few minutes later again a demure young person with sandy hair and the enquiring green eyes of a month-old kitten came in to pack my papers for me and to explain that Miss Mainwaring had gone home.

This, I supposed, was Miss Norbury, but I hardly noticed her. Throughout my journey to Marlborough it was the greying hair and pale-blue eyes of Miss Mainwaring that I saw; and I am afraid that, when I reached Ridgeway, I could give but per-functory attention to Elizabeth's troubles until I had explained that I myself was suffering from a disabling shock. And, when at last I had pieced together a coherent history of the day's events, I felt that for all the good I could do I might have remained in London: the Motor Patrols had not been mobilized, Norman's Territorial battalion had not been embodied, none of our relations had even hinted at coming to us for shelter and Elizabeth's visitor that morning turned out to be a volunteer, without authority or power, who had been sent round the parish in a laudable attempt by the vicar to have an answer if any official enquiry were addressed to him.

"I've no news of any kind," I told Elizabeth, Norman and Cruikshank in turn. "If you want the gossip of the market-place, there will be no war."

"Because Hitler isn't ready?," asked Norman. "Or because he's afraid we *may* stand firm this time?"

"I should say," I answered, "because the market-place is filled with people so horrified of war that they believe what they want to believe."

"If we don't have it now . . . ," Norman began, to break off politely as his mother—for the first time in my experience openly losing her temper with one of her children—hysterically forbade him to say anything so wantonly wicked as that there must be a war some time or that to strive for peace was only to postpone the evil day. I have no idea whether phrases of this kind had already been used, but Norman's politeness and absence of sur-prise at what surprised me profoundly suggested that this out-burst was not the first of the day. As Elizabeth, choking down a

sob, muttered that she must write at least a dozen letters before
going to bed, he jumped up and put his arm round her shoulders
with a steadying: "If they're important, I'll write them for you;
if they're not, I think bed is a good idea for all of us."

Important or unimportant, he was back again within five
minutes, explaining carelessly that "poor mummy" was "taking
this business rather to heart".

"I'm glad you were able to get down," he added. "If the worst
comes to the worst, I suppose you'll make this your headquarters?"

I fancy I said that my work and place of living would doubtless be decided for me, but we passed immediately to a debate on
what we both meant by the worst coming to the worst and, as we
settled down to talk, filling our pipes and mixing ourselves drinks,
I reflected that this was the first time my own son and I had talked
together as man to man. He used the phrase indeed within a few
minutes of his mother's going upstairs and the Cruikshanks'
retiring for the night; and he might equally well, for his own
purposes, have said: "Now that the lodge is tiled . . ." or "Hand
on heart!" I offered him the collective wisdom of the Lord
Keeper's Department and the Garrick Club, repeating his "Man
to man", but privately giving it a different interpretation. We
had always talked frankly, whether by ourselves or in a mixed
company, perhaps never more frankly than when he stayed with
me in Grosvenor Road for a week of restaurants and theatres or
when I visited him in Oxford to dine alone with him at the guests'
table in Hall. Always, however, we had talked as father and son,
teacher and disciple, man and boy; this evening we talked as men
of the same age, or possibly of no age at all, men faced with
problems that the one could solve as easily as the other and with
responsibilities that they must agree to divide, but problems and
responsibilities that they could not share with women nor delegate
to servants. I suppose I had noticed that a year at the House,
secure from Elizabeth's efforts to keep him the long-haired little
boy of Sargent's drawing, had matured Norman in mind and
manner; for a day or two at least, whenever he returned from
camp, his voice retained the assurance of an officer who had been
commanding men; but it was only as he talked now of Oxford
and Ridgeway, of money and work, of life and death, that I
found him fully and permanently grown-up.

"Like you," he told me, "I feel in my bones that there won't be a war now, but, whether we avoid it by giving Hitler all he wants or force him back, snarling, to *reculer pour mieux sauter*, I feel—*pace* poor mummy—that it's only a question of time unless the Germans themselves chuck him out of the saddle. Even if it blows over for the moment, I don't at all know what chance I shall have of finishing my time at Oxford. If we're all going to arm and train for the next crisis . . . I'm sorry if you were dragged here on a wild-goose chase: I was at the depot all day and mummy was up to her eyes in V.A.M.P. work when this fellow called about billets. *She* became rather rattled and the Cruikshanks became rattled. It was only when she met the vicar in church that she found this was a purely unofficial enquiry."

Until this moment I had not been told that Elizabeth had met the vicar; and, as week-day services were almost unknown in the parish, I assumed that she had gone for private devotion. I remembered Violet's account of her walk through the north cloister of Westminster Abbey the day before; and an incongruous train of thought took me to Norman's old housemaster, Mannington-Drax, and to the talk that I had had with him about my stepsons. I seemed to recall that their mother's eternal "fussing" had not passed wholly unobserved by their schoolfellows; one of us, I believe, had quoted Martin or Humfrey as saying that, when they were out on the Cresta Run, she spent the day on her knees in her bedroom, praying that they would come back with unbroken bones. "Poor mummy" did indeed seem to be "taking this business rather to heart".

"Whatever comes of Chamberlain's mission," I said, "I'm not sorry that your mother should have all this work with her Vamps. If you're too busy to think . . ."

"With some people, when they're worked up," Norman enunciated, "the more they have to do the more they want to do. That was really the trouble with the Cruikshanks to-day. Left to themselves, as they always have been, there's nothing they can't do, but when poor mummy started a panic about our stocks of food . . . If we *are* going to have a war, daddy, I believe you'll find you'll have to take charge here. Mummy and the Cruikshanks are going to get in one another's way *so* appallingly . . ."

I told Norman, as I had lately told Violet, that, if there were a war of the kind that I foresaw, I believed the government and the government service would be forced to leave London.

"So far," I continued, "I've heard nothing official. Nobody

would be a penny the worse if *my* department were moved to the
Outer Hebrides and left there, but I expect I shall be borrowed by
some other ministry."

I was told nothing official when I returned to Queen Anne's
Gate next morning, though I thought that the vague and baseless optimism of the day before had somewhat abated. Thereafter
the temperature rose and fell so abruptly that I wondered whether
Hitler, before abandoning white war for red, was making a last
attempt with his favourite war of nerves. I still received no
instructions and heard no news that was not common property.
Norman was still living with his kit packed and a car at the door;
and so he would continue to live, he told me grimly when I
telephoned from the House of Commons to say that the Prime
Minister had interrupted his speech to announce an invitation,
that moment received, to meet the Führer, this time at Munich.
When I returned to Ridgeway for the week-end, the boy had
indeed changed out of uniform and put his car away, but he
assured me that this was a compromise with his conscience to
which he had submitted from consideration of his mother's
feelings.

"Another day or two would have sent her off her head,"
he continued, frowning. "What she'll be like when war *does*
come . . ."

"You still think it will?"

"I'm not unpacking my kit," he answered. "And I'm taking it
to Oxford with me next month. You won't *tell* her that, *will* you?
This has been a bad dream; and she's still frightened. We must
keep her from brooding over it. Can't you work up some distraction that will knock her off her feet? A holiday in Venice? A
motor-tour among the great cathedrals of France?"

I promised to consider what I could suggest; but, when I
went back to London, I had to tell Norman that I saw no chance
of taking even a week's holiday abroad. The flood-tide of reaction
against the Munich settlement had set in during the week-end,
while I was at Ridgeway, and the country was puzzling over Duff
Cooper's resignation from the Admiralty; a trickle of reaction,
over which I am still puzzling more than ten years later, against
Neville Chamberlain was setting in as I boarded the London train
at Marlborough; and, though my official position barred or
saved me from taking sides in an acrimonious wrangle that even
in more than·ten years has not lost all vitality, this same position

made me an early victim of the Prime Minister's forethought—
according to one school—or—according to another—of his
mental fog. Despite Hitler's signature on the paper promising
peace for our time, the government was taking no unnecessary
risks; those who wished for peace must prepare for war; and
a flattering note from Downing Street invited me to become
chairman of an emergency—and most secret—"Committee of
Planning".

It was so secret that I never mentioned it even to Violet, even
when she asked whether I was too busy to see her, even when she
hinted that another private crisis was threatening her life.

"This time," she wrote, *"it has nothing to do with Nigel, except in
so far as it has to do with us* all; *but I feel that, unless we take a firm hold
on life, we're going to lose control of* Life *and of our lives and freedom and
will and destiny and everything, like the Court at Versailles before the
Revolution or the Russian aristocracy in the last days of the Czar or that
ghastly line of petrified monkeys in the* Jungle Book, *sitting paralysed
till it should suit the pleasure of the boa-constrictor (I'm so tired that I
can't remember names!) to gobble them all. I don't mean that I believe
Hitler is necessarily going to gobble us all up, but ever since Munich I've
felt that, unless you fill me with black coffee and walk me up and down, I
shall sink into a coma."*

Without waiting to finish the letter, I telephoned to ask
whether Violet would dine with me that night; and in accepting
she assured me with a rather mirthless laugh that I should be
thankful to hear she was not going to argue with me about
appeasement.

"You *can't* 'stand up to the dictators'," she continued, "with
phrases like 'collective security'; I believe the well-intentioned
Mr. Chamberlain has *completely* misjudged Hitler and Mussolini;
but, as the French wouldn't fight for the Czechs, we had to accept
pretty well any terms that the Nazis chose to dictate."

"You spoke of 'coma' in your letter," I reminded her.

"And I want you to help me to keep it off by looking *ahead*!
The people I meet, Colin . . . Well, there are the Old Chamberlainites, like Elizabeth, who are now honestly convinced after
seeing war just round the corner for a fortnight that we really *are*
going to have peace for our time. Let's all sit back! The New
Chamberlainites, like me, hope that even the Germans have had a

scare, but I'm not leaving anything to chance in the way of rearming. The Anti-Chamberlainites are certain that war's inevitable and that the appeasers have been giving way vital positions: that's Nigel's class and he is organizing his own show as though he'd been told the date when war would break out."

I said that I thought it was also Norman's class.

"Only time will shew which is right," Violet sighed, "but, if we're not to go under, we—you and I, Colin—must deliberately and firmly take *hold* of Life. Will you please tell Elizabeth that you will be out for luncheon next Sunday? Will you then please find me a suitable train and meet it with a car and a luncheon-basket? Will you see that the luncheon-basket contains cold chicken and salad? I suppose it's too much to hope that you have any of your Liquid Sunshine left after all these years! A barsac, wasn't it? And then will you drive me to the place where we lunched on the most precious and unforgettable day of my life?"

As she paused, I made bold to say that I thought I could improve on her proposal. Elizabeth, I had been told, would be spending the week-end at some rally of her V.A.M.P.s; Norman, I knew, was lunching with friends at Wantage; and, if Violet would come for the week-end, I could promise that she would not meet Elizabeth, that she would meet Norman, that I could offer her a very fair successor to her "Liquid Sunshine" and that I should like to make my invitation a business one.

"As we have to be prepared for all emergencies," I explained, "I must in every sense of the phrase put my house in order. If there's an all-out bombardment from the air, London will be evacuated and a house like Ridgeway will have to take every man, woman and child that it can accommodate. You must advise me what we can do; and I can tell you my own plans for offering shelter to people like yourself and Vaughan Drake and my own colleagues, who have to work in London as long as London is tolerable."

"I may still have my picnic?," Violet asked. "I'm not being sentimental! For a solemn occasion I need an appropriate setting, as I need organ-music and the sun shining through stained glass for a service in a great church. If we're to decide what the future of the world is likely to be, what life we're making for ourselves before our wills are paralysed . . . How long is it since you've written a single line?"

"As a matter of fact, I was beginning a new *scenario* when the crisis began; and I finished it on the night of the Munich announcement. For some reason I always work best when I'm being run off my feet—witness my successes in 1916—and I should have had something to discuss with you if my peerless secretary hadn't been suddenly struck down."

"That nice Miss Mainwaring?"

I said that I was very much afraid she was a dying woman.

"I'm told," I continued, "that the girl who has come to take her place is prepared to do my literary typing, but I haven't tried her yet. At the moment I can't even remember her name and I've become so used to Miss Mainwaring that I have to pull myself together when I ring the bell and a strange young damsel sidles in. Norman, who called the other day to take me out to luncheon, tells me that she is a 'raging beauty', but I'm afraid I shouldn't recognize her if I saw her in the street."

At fifty, Violet warned me, I should be unwise to interest myself in young "raging beauties", who would see me first and foremost as coeval of their own fathers.

"It's different for Norman, though he's still a boy to me. I should like to meet him again."

"The demands of the last few months have matured him, but *I* can't yet see him as a young man with an appraising eye for— I've just remembered her name!—the Miss Norburys of this world. I wonder what they think of him. I wonder what you'll think of him. If I were a Miss Norbury, I think I should fall for him rather quickly and heavily."

VIII

I HAD spoken of Miss Mainwaring as, I feared, a dying woman; and the day after Violet came to Ridgeway I had to report that she was dead.

The news reached me in a letter from Miss Norbury, who had sat with the patient until she finally lost consciousness; the letter was accompanied by several short typescripts; and to the first of these was pinned a slip on which the most conscientious of secretaries had explained to Miss Norbury my idiosyncrasies of spelling and punctuation.

"She would have written exactly the same note," I said, "if she had been going away for her summer holiday without finishing something I'd given her at the last moment. I feel badly about it! I had always taken her so much for granted . . ."

"You shouldn't let that worry you," Violet interrupted. "To begin with, it's not true: no man has ever accepted less as of right what other people do for him. *I* should know, my dear! To go on with, if she had to die, you should only be glad that she died quickly and that she was brave enough to remain quite calm when death called her sooner than she expected. You'll *miss* her, of course . . ."

I gave myself a moment for composure by pretending to study Miss Norbury's notes about the funeral-arrangements.

"It'll be months or years," I then answered, "before I realize how much! In an unobtrusive way she took charge of one department after another: my accounts, the wages and household books. . . . I had only to sign a cheque on the first of each month. And she did it all without ever rubbing people up the wrong way."

"The Cruikshanks?"

I said that Miss Mainwaring had confined her activities to Grosvenor Road. I should have liked her to shoulder a similar responsibility at Ridgeway; but after a single visit of exploration she had begged to be excused.

"I don't know," I continued, "whether with Elizabeth and me and the two Cruikshanks she felt she would be a fifth wheel to the coach. Mrs. Cruikshank, I know, *liked* her. So, I believe, did Elizabeth."

Violet glanced at her watch and stood up as though to warn me that, unless we set out at once, we should become involved in an endless, unprofitable discussion of Elizabeth.

"And, naturally, Miss Mainwaring never gave you her opinion. . . . She never had an opinion to give, a personality to express, till that moment when she said how much she had enjoyed working for you. I can *well* understand, Colin, why she didn't want to be mixed up with this place. You said, laughing, that she must evidently have decided years ago to adopt you; and any woman who made you her chief interest in life would naturally divide all other women into those who worked for your happiness and those who didn't. The first time we met, she studied me most carefully to see which class *I* belonged to. She never had the least

use, by the way, for your stepdaughters-in-law and I should
think that a single week-end here would be enough to shew her
that Elizabeth—how shall I put it?—wasn't conspicuously
working for your happiness. As there was nothing she could do
about it, she preferred to meet you in a different atmosphere."

"And I have achieved such heights or depths of indifference
that Elizabeth can't affect my happiness one way or the other. She
no longer irritates me, she doesn't even bore me! When I think of
her at all, I'm puzzled as after all these centuries we're still
puzzled by la Giaconda's smile, or the Sphinx's secret. Do *you*
find the atmosphere of this place oppressive?"

Violet swept her hand in a half-circle that began with a
beech-ringed round barrow on the skyline to the north and
ended where the white chalk of the estate road joined the black
highway from Marlborough to Hungerford. Though it was an
October morning, the leaves had hardly begun to change colour
and the sun was so hot that the Ridgeway "prison" windows
stood open to their fullest extent. Outside I could see Norman's
car, no longer loaded with his kit, waiting to take him over for
his luncheon-party at Wantage; and, before answering my
question, Violet thanked me for the weather that I always
provided for her.

"It's too early to speak of a 'Saint Luke's summer'," she
murmured, "or even of a 'Saint Martin's'. Shall we call it a 'Saint
Norman's'?"

"He has never *expressed* any desire to be canonized," I
answered.

"If it *is* going to be 'peace for our time' . . . *He* may not feel
it, but you and I know how marvellous it is that he can go back
to Oxford next week as though all this talk of war had been a
bad dream. He has certainly come on, as you told me, but he has
not yet outgrown the *habit* of happiness. Like sleeping well or
having a good appetite, he *expects* to be happy and, thank God, he
is. No, the atmosphere is not oppressive when *he's* here, with his
zest and gaiety and sixth-sense gentleness. Or, perhaps I had
better say frankly, when Elizabeth is *not*. He and you, in this
enchanting house that you both love so dearly, in this heavenly
setting . . . I believe I might throw myself a bouquet and say:
'He and you and I . . .' We've always got on well together,
Norman and I. At dinner last night I couldn't help indulging in
a little childish, useless make-believe. Colin, my dear, if I'd

married you instead of Nigel, if Norman were my son instead of Elizabeth's . . . I should have been a more *sensible* mother for him, a more understanding wife for you, a more appreciative mistress of Ridgeway. Or should I not? If I'd had children, should I have fussed and worried and intrigued for their love as she has done? One simply can't say! If I had sons who were now of military age . . . But that's what I've come to talk to you about! What *do* we believe is going to happen? What does any one believe? How are we going to get back our grip on Life?"

In the few minutes that it took me to drive Violet up to our clump of beeches above the house, I was able to tell her at least what I believed other people believed at this moment.

"And your private opinion?," she asked, when I had done.

"Six of the one and half-a-dozen of the other," I answered. "But, like you, I'm not and never have been content to stand trembling outside the slaughter-house, wondering whether it will be my turn next and bleating that there's nothing I can do. These notes that my poor Miss Mainwaring was typing till the moment she went into hospital . . ."

"May I see them?"

I handed Violet the package that I had thrust, unopened, into a pocket of my rain-coat and left her to examine the contents while I unpacked our luncheon-basket. She was still reading as I came to the end of my preparations; and, when I offered her a glass of sherry, she motioned me to sit down and asked whether we need begin yet.

"Have you any one in your mind for 'Lady Caroline'?," she asked.

" 'Lady Caroline' doesn't yet exist even on paper," I answered. "What you're reading is my usual *scenario* with a few scraps of dialogue that suggested themselves as I went along. I wanted you to see that I *had* been working."

"Your big scene—'Dr. Williamson's Consulting-Room'— mustn't be *touched*! Surely you must have *seen* somebody playing 'Lady Caroline' there? Peggy Ashcroft? Isabel Durban? She must be quite young."

"Honestly, I haven't given a thought to the casting! I've not written the play yet! I don't know that I ever shall! It was an idea that interested me . . ."

Violet read on to the end in silence and then sat in silence, with eyes half-closed, for fully three minutes. When she spoke, it was in half-sentences and the dreamy, remote voice of a woman only half-awake:

"Curious if I've been utterly, utterly wrong . . . *Most* curious . . . All these *years* . . . I was so brutally frank too . . . Cobblers and their lasts . . . I've no idea how old Somerset Maugham was when he changed over . . ."

"The idea seems to interest you too," I observed, as she paused to note the title of what she had been reading and murmured—after several repetitions—that I could do better than with *Flowers By Request*.

"What are the others like?," she asked, flicking the pages of two comedies as yet without names.

"They're a good deal more what the public expects of me," I told her. "I believe something quite creditable might be made of them. Any way, they ought to shew whether my hand has lost all its cunning, whether I've been beaten at my own game by Freddie Lonsdale and Noel Coward. They'll shew too, if ever I write them, whether like ailments call for like medicines. I owed nine-tenths of my success twenty-five years ago to the fact that people wanted to be taken out of themselves. Well, the everlasting *threat* of war is more trying to the nerves than war itself; and if I can make people laugh with well-written fooling . . . I promise you it will be well-written . . ."

"And, if I have any say in the matter, it won't be written at all till you've finished *Flowers By Request*. I don't know whether you *can*! All these years I've praised your wisdom in *recognizing* your limitations. You hadn't it *in* you, I said. Well, if I was wrong . . . But I don't believe I was. Something has happened to you, Colin! You've changed! Do you remember my telling you a thousand years ago that playwriting was like swimming: one day you couldn't and the next you miraculously could? I tell you in all seriousness that yesterday you couldn't fly and to-day you can! I don't know whether it's the rather sobering experience we all had lately: standing on the drop and being suddenly reprieved, seeing the rope being taken from your Norman's neck . . ."

As she stopped, with a shiver, I felt it had been superfluous for Violet to tell me that she was speaking seriously. I doubt whether I had ever heard her or any one else speak with an equal passion of white-hot conviction. Though I might say that this was "only" a *scenario* that she was reading, I had myself worked with something of the same passion. A skeleton of acts and scenes, a frigid outline of entrances and exits, possible "business" and tentative "curtains" were not enough for me: I had written a line or two here, half a page of dialogue there, a full-length scene in a third place. I remembered, I could now confess to her, that I had written them at the top of my voice, ranting and gesticulating, once even seizing a cushion and shaking it as I panted: "You rat! You contemptible little rat!"

This belonged to "Dr. Williamson's Consulting-Room", of which Violet had forbidden me to retouch a word.

And with the steady gaze of her deep-set brown eyes that always seemed to strip my soul bare she had divined a change in me that I had not begun to suspect and was explaining it in a way that I must needs accept. I had flung myself on that play as I might have flung myself on the stones of the Westminster Abbey cloister.

"You think it has possibilities?," I asked.

"Only certainties," she answered. "Take it away now! If I go on as I should like, we shall neither of us get anything to eat!"

I presume, from Mrs. Cruikshank's gratified inspection of the empty luncheon-basket some hours later, that we ate and drank whatever she and her husband had provided. For all that I know, they provided the chicken-breasts, salad and barsac for which Violet had asked. I remember only that we began the meal with a typewritten *scenario* flattened open on her knees and that we ended with a three-act play completed and stored in our heads. It would indeed have to be written out and typed, re-written and re-typed, but this was work that any copyist and proof-reader could finish in a few half-mornings. Somewhat less than six hours sufficed for the completion of a play that either of us could have dictated from memory to any manager in London.

"And you were fifty on your last birthday," Violet observed at the end. "I wonder whether you *are* beginning a second completely different career. How old was Jerome K. Jerome when he wrote *The Passing of the Third-Floor Back*? And what inspired him to write it after things like *Three Men in a Boat*? You say this was just an idea that interested you: have you many more of the same kind?"

"I think I've always had more plays in my head than I've ever had time to put on paper. For some years, too, I've doubted whether it was worth while trying to write anything when the whole world seemed tumbling into ruin."

"But you're not doubting now! Hope for the best and prepare for the worst, but don't sit helplessly watching Life slip
through your fingers! Whatever the future may bring . . . We're
going on . . . Oh, *not* as we were doing before! A thousand times
more marvellously! *Soaring!* In some miraculous way you've
learnt to fly! This play: how long will it take you to finish it?
Three months?"

I said that this would depend largely on my official work;
and she admitted that, if I wanted her criticism, this would be
dependent for her too on the demands of her requisitioning
committee.

"If there *is* a war," she continued, "you should prepare for a
mass-exodus from London. Ridgeway is quite unsuited for a
hospital, but the schoolchildren and their teachers will be the
first to go. I ought to have a look at 'Mad Marion's' attics."

I said that I would take her to them the moment we got back
to the house; but, as I began to pack our luncheon-basket, I was
surprised by the note of a horn followed by a hail from Norman.
As this farm-road was not on his way from Wantage, I feared
that he had come to look for me in answer to some appeal for
help in some new crisis at Ridgeway; but he explained that he
had turned aside to pay a visit and would tell us all about it if we
would promise to keep it a secret.

"I don't want mummie to be worried," he added.

"For heaven's sake don't put me in the position of having
secrets about you from your mother," I begged.

"Oh, she'll hear sooner or later, but I would rather make it
later. I don't want her to come racing back . . ."

"Is anything the matter, Norman?," Violet interrupted.
"You're looking most awfully ill."

I had just time to see his face, which seemed to have become
suddenly green, before he turned with a smothered apology and
vomited over the side of the car. A second apology followed the
first and I thought he was trying to say that this was the very
thing that he wanted to keep from his mother, when he stopped
with a little gasp of pain. A moment later, he was himself again,
lighting a cigarette with a steady hand and begging Violet—
with a flood of returning colour—to forgive him for making
such an exhibition of himself.

"Have you eaten something that has poisoned you?," I
asked.

"No! This happened once before, my second year at Marlborough. Just a passing pain and sickness. Dr. Ribstone called
it a 'grumbling appendix'. If I made a habit of these attacks, he
said, I should have to have the thing out, but he was dead against
—what did he call it?—'cutting into the abdominal wall' unless
it was a matter of life and death. I'm all right now!"

"You'll have to get yourself properly overhauled," I said. "I
don't know how many times makes a habit . . ."

"Ribstone says I may go another six years or sixty without any
more trouble. I've just been to see him. And, if I want to be told
I must have an operation, I must go to another medico. He has a
perfect *horror* of the knife."

I said that I could not readily picture any man setting out in
search of a medical adviser who could be bullied into recommend-
ing, against his better judgement, a major operation; but Norman
assured me sardonically that most doctors, if Ribstone was to be
believed, could tell me of men who had chosen the operating-
theatre in preference to the front line in the last months of the
Great War.

"A job at the base when they came out of hospital," he
continued. "After that, a position on somebody's staff . . .
Remember, *please*, that this is a secret between the three of us
and old Ribstone!"

"You admitted that your mother would have to be told
sooner or later . . ."

"But not by me!," Norman broke in, his cheeks flushing
again. "I can't stop Ribstone, if *he* thinks fit . . . I rather hoped,"
he went on, looking at me and at once lowering his eyes, "that
you might say something. . . . I daresay it *is* the prudent thing to
do: have the damned appendix out while you're in good health,
don't wait till it's within five minutes of bursting. That's what I
wanted when I was at school. You must choose your time,
though: as I told mummie just before Munich, you'll be classed
with that fellow in *The Four Feathers* if you suddenly remember
your old grumbling and rumbling whatnot when you're waiting
to mobilize. . . . Are you going back now? Ribstone says my
temperature's a bit up and he wants me to stay in bed till it's
normal. If you and Lady Oakhirst could bear to have your nuts
and wine in my room . . .?"

"If your father approves," Violet struck in, "I should like to
suggest three dinners on three trays."

Without waiting for my answer, Norman started his car and called back over his shoulder that he would go on ahead and prepare the Cruikshanks for our change of plans.

"I call that a positive brain-wave," he added. "As it happens, there's a lot I want to talk to you both about. These people I was lunching with, the Charlburys: old Charlbury is the head of Charlbury And Anson, the publishers, and my friend Tony Charlbury is very keen on starting a new kind of bookshop. He wants me to come in with him. I told him I couldn't do much till I'd finished at Oxford, but if the offer's still open in two years' time . . . He's twelve months senior to me and he hopes to get under way in the summer or autumn of 1939. I'll tell you more at dinner."

The car started down the road; and Violet watched it in silence till it turned into the stable-yard below us.

"It sounds quite a promising idea," she observed. "The shop will fail and they'll lose a lot of money, but they'll have some fun for it. A Saint Norman's Summer for poor Saint Norman!" she added with a sigh. "Even to talk about it, even if it never gets beyond talk . . ."

"Obviously you believe it won't. *I* shall raise no objection. I can't, of course, speak for old Charlbury."

"O my dear, I'm thinking of the time they've chosen for their *début*! The summer or autumn of next year! We seem to have a crisis every year nowadays! Unless 1939 is going to be an exception . . . What a heavenly evening!"

"To round off a heavenly day!," I said, as I got into the car.

We talked of the weather until we separated to dress for dinner. It was not a profound or stimulating conversation; but perhaps it kept us from thinking and perhaps neither of us wished to think of Elizabeth arguing and pleading with Norman or Dr. Ribstone or both.

"If," I whispered to myself, "she could have him in a nursing-home, preferably under an anæsthetic, when war's declared . . . *If* war's declared . . . ," I corrected myself. "Hope for the best and prepare for the worst."

x

IX

THOUGH Norman touched on this project of a bookshop once or twice during the long and extremely agreeable dinner in his bedroom, he did not get to grips with the subject till some weeks later when he invited me to visit him in Oxford and meet his friend Charlbury, a tow-haired and thin-lipped fanatic with grey eyes that bored like gimlets and a torrential delivery that reminded me of the youthful Austin Gerrold.

A more practical stage was reached when Charlbury and he stayed with me in London and spent two or three mornings in Old Burlington Street, expounding to Violet where they would like their shop to be situated and hearing from her how it should be furnished; but I could not feel that we had progressed beyond a general denunciation of existing bookshops until Norman came for the greater part of his next vacation to Grosvenor Road.

His excuse was that his tutor had advised him to attend certain lectures or consult certain books at the London School of Economics; but I ceased to think it more than a transparent excuse when, making Violet his confidante, he confessed that he could not work at Ridgeway. With the kindest intentions, his mother was always tiptoeing into the room to make up the fire or turn on his reading-lamp; if he did not break off for tea, a tray with a thermos-jug would appear noiselessly and—somehow—reproachfully; and he had given up working at night since the discovery that, however late he might—in her unvarying phrase —"burn the midnight oil", she would not go to bed till the sound of his footsteps by her door convinced her that he really did not want cocoa or hot milk. Though I was cited as having once—rather harshly, I fear—suggested that Norman was really old enough now to tell Cruikshank if he wanted anything, it was intimated that Ridgeway, when I was there, became a different place from Ridgeway when I was in London. To shield his mother, Norman called it "rather on the quiet side"; Violet expressed his feelings for him more bluntly by saying that he was bored beyond endurance. The library of the London School of Economics provided a desperate way of escape that he would certainly not have taken for the mere human pleasure of dining with his friends and going to a theatre.

words: familiar enough to be a parody of something that I had said quite recently and yet inevitably strange because I could not know how my speaking voice sounded to others. Then, as two other voices murmured appreciatively: "Go on, Ginger!" and "Ginger, you are a scream!," I divined what was happening behind the half-open door of Miss Norbury's room. This was the last act of *Flowers By Request*, which I had given her that morning; she was galloping fearlessly through "Dr. Williamson's Consulting-Room", now playing "Lady Caroline", now the cockney drug-addict and now "Dr. Williamson" himself. And she was playing them uncommonly well.

It was an intolerable liberty, I told myself as I went out to luncheon, for the girl to take with a script that had been given to her in confidence; and I should speak sharply to her when I got back. And yet I was far too much interested to feel really angry. If I still believed, after thirty sobering years of disillusionment, in the existence of born actresses, Miss "Ginger" Norbury belonged to that class. The golden voice with which she could do such miracles was wasted in a government-office. I had not, of course, seen her; but, if she had no spark of talent on the stage, she could coo or storm her way to triumph on the air.

"And Violet keeps asking who's to play 'Lady Caroline' ... ," I whispered. "If this girl really has anything more to her than her voice and half-a-dozen elocution-lessons ..."

I hurried through my luncheon and returned to Queen Anne's Gate as Miss Norbury was leaving the memorandum that I had drafted in the morning.

"Have you ever thought about going on the stage?," I asked without preamble.

"The stage?," she repeated, as though she could not have heard me aright.

"Well, you're obviously interested in the theatre," I said. "I inadvertently heard you giving a reading from *Flowers By Request* this afternoon."

"It wasn't a *reading*, Mr. Whimboyne. I took the script home for safety when I went to lunch. I hope I didn't murder it, but I'd only been through it once, in a great hurry."

Even at the time I was conscious that our scene was not developing as I had planned it. I should have been magisterial, irate, formidable, she abashed and tongue-tied; instead, she was completely self-possessed and I agog with curiosity.

"Do you mean to say," I demanded, "that on one admittedly hurried reading . . .?"

"My memory's like that," she answered. "I don't suppose you've noticed, Mr. Whimboyne, but I only take down a word or two when you're dictating. And I don't think I often go wrong."

"You certainly don't. Do you retain it? My first act, for example, which you typed a good many weeks ago now?"

" 'Lady Skipworth' giving the orders to her housekeeper? *'I think that's everything, Mrs. Nairne . . . Sir George will telephone if he can't get down in time for dinner.'* Mrs. Nairne: *'I don't think you said which room Mr. Charles was to have, my lady.'* Yes, I think I remember all that."

I said that most actresses of my acquaintance would give a year of their lives for this power.

"Have you had any training?," I went on.

"In acting? No! I can't *act*, Mr. Whimboyne!"

"What I overheard this afternoon . . . I didn't see you, of course . . . Are you interested in the subject? Would you care to go through a scene or two with me? You know my address: if you're doing nothing to-night, will you dine with me?"

"That's very kind of you!"

"We shall be by ourselves. Later on . . . I believe you may conceivably have a big future on the stage, Miss Norbury. Just those few lines between 'Lady Skipworth' and 'Mrs. Nairne'. They shewed you *could* act. . . . Later on, if I think I'm right, I should like to put you through your paces before a friend of mine. Is half-past eight all right for you?"

Had I discovered a Bernhardt or a Duse blooming unremarked in the typists' room of the Lord Keeper's Department? The "clever little monkey", as Miss Mainwaring had called her, was very much more than the usual clever mimic with a most unusual voice that transformed my demure mouse of a secretary into "Ginger", a public entertainer appreciatively hailed as a "scream"; she was more than a vocal impersonator who had almost succeeded in making me feel that three different people were in her room, playing "Lady Caroline" and the drug-addict and "Dr. Williamson", making me feel that this room which I could not see had been transformed into "Dr. Williamson's Consulting-Room". From a single reading she had apparently memorized every line of a fairly long act; and, without a hint from me of what I had tried to achieve, the hearts and brains of these three characters were dragged into the light for the audience to study.

Her reading of the parts, to be sure, was not quite the same as mine, but that I have never experienced of any actor or producer. It might be better, it might be worse; but it was at least a vital picture, a vital character. "Lady Caroline" had materialized from my manuscript like a genie and taken possession of this girl, as indeed she had taken possession of Violet after one glance at the *scenario*, as—before that—she had taken possession of me.

In my fifty-first year, as I had lately been reminded, and after half a life-time of playwriting, I believe I was more boyishly excited than when my first manager accepted my first play. On reaching Grosvenor Road, I told Winter to light the fire in the one-time studio at the top of the house, always impressively misdescribed by him as "the auditorium-chamber" through incorrigible confusion between an audience-chamber and an audition. I ordered sandwiches to be brought up if the session looked like being a long one. And I said that I did not want to be disturbed by any one on any pretext.

"Mr. Norman telephoned from Oxford, sir," Winter informed me, "to say he was coming up for the night and dining on the way."

"Oh, I don't mind *him*," I answered. "Tell him I've arranged an audition. He can come and hear it, if it would amuse him."

Then, as I dressed for dinner, I tried to get my faintly absurd excitement under control by making notes of the scenes that I would ask Miss Norbury to try. It was one thing, I said, to act a part or several parts before a dozen girls of her own age and kind; but it would be something very different to find herself rehearsing a play with the author, on a stage with windows and doors, with a "*sofa, centre; a writing table with reading-lamp, left-centre, and a revolving bookcase with telephone and small armchair right,*" most of all on a stage whose fourth wall had been equipped with footlights and painted to suggest the vast gloom of an auditorium. That afternoon I had noted with amusement Miss Norbury's perfect self-possession; if she could remain self-possessed in these surroundings, I felt that she would shew yet another quality for which most young actresses would give a year of their lives.

"If *I* think her good," I decided, "I shall try her on Violet. And, if Violet thinks her good, I shall try her on the best producer

I can think of. Violet and I, after all, know something of acting, but we know nothing of the *training* of an actress. I don't suppose any·human being would say: 'There's your "Lady Caroline" ready-made.' Probably she'll have to attend a school of dramatic art. Well, I would most cheerfully pay the fees. Meanwhile, I don't think she even answered my question whether she was interested in the theatre! Never thought about it! All in the day's work! If her 'chief', as she probably calls me, invites her to dine with him, well, it amuses him and doesn't hurt her. Take what the day brings! In her place, I should have been wild with excitement if any one had told me I might possibly have a big career on the stage. She was entirely unmoved ! *'I* can't *act*, Mr. Whimboyne!' If she's really as indifferent as she seemed . . ."

I felt that she had dropped her indifference for a moment when I went downstairs and saw Winter relieving her of a small suitcase. This, she explained, held two or three "changes", as I doubtless remembered that "Lady Caroline" (if indeed I intended to take her through that part) made her first appearance in a coat and skirt, her second in a dance frock and her third in beach-pyjamas. Perhaps, by an odd perversity, her indifference became most noticeable when she herself was the subject of discussion: my "auditorium-chamber" won hardly a glance of interest, but I think she would willingly have spent half the night examining the stage trophies in my workroom.

At dinner, too, she was alert enough when I was talking about the many Lord Keepers under whom I had served, but she lapsed into silence when I tried to find out what chance had brought her to that anachronistic and ever-threatened department. At her background I could make no guess; and, as the word passed through my head, I saw the absurdity of expecting an established background for a chameleon that changed colour with every leaf or twig it met. Miss Norbury, shorthand-typist and secretary-on-probation to the Comptroller of the Office of the Lord Keeper, had nothing in common with the girl called Miss Norbury who was dining with Colin Whimboyne, the dramatist, to talk about his latest play.

And we had reached our coffee before she again relaxed her attitude of personal indifference by asking whether I was prepared to take *Flowers By Request* in full. She had never attended a rehearsal, but once or twice she had visited the dressing-room of a friend who was playing in some musical-comedy of which I had never heard. Miss Norbury confessed that she would never understand the detachment which enabled her friend to knit and write letters while she awaited her next call.

"Even if I'm not on the stage," she exclaimed, "it's my *story*. I shall be no good, Mr. Whimboyne, if you just give me a cue and go through a bit of dialogue with me and then give me another cue. I must have the whole picture. When I'm under the anæsthetic and the doctors are talking about me . . . If you don't take me through that or let me say it to myself, the scene where I leave the nursing-home won't have any meaning for me. I expect this sounds very childish, but it's the only way I can see a play."

"It's the way the audience is intended to see it," I said. "I don't mind if you're prepared for three solid hours of the thing. You'll have to read half-a-dozen different parts. I too. I'm afraid my idea *was* to give you just your cues. If I'm to play in full too, it'll mean dancing in the supper-room scene. I believe I *have* an elderly gramophone somewhere, but I haven't danced for a hundred years."

"Well, you only have to go half-way round the stage before you discover that I'm too drunk to stand. 'Lady Caroline' *was* drunk, wasn't she? It wasn't just excitement? Well, I'm ready as soon as you are."

Even before Miss Norbury withdrew for the third time to the disrobing-room used by models when my "auditorium-chamber" was still a studio, I had made the discovery—with others of greater moment—that the three hours for which I had stipulated might possibly carry us to the end of the second act, no farther. I did not mind, if she did not; and, if she blenched at the prospect of going on even after midnight, we could take the second and third acts on a later occasion. This obviously implied that I thought it worth while for us to take the second and third acts. If at the end she were still too indifferent to ask whether I thought her any good, this was a question that Violet would ask, a question that I had asked myself—without finding the answer—before I thought a second time about inviting Violet to attend the next audition. Would this girl ever be a great actress, a competent actress, an actress of any kind?

" '*I* can't *act*, Mr. Whimboyne'," I repeated, as I shifted the furniture for my supper-room scene and tried a waltz-record on the antiquated gramophone which I believe I had given to Martin and Humfrey when for a few months they were living as small boys in Grosvenor Road.

In any technical, narrow sense, it was true. Never before having trod the stage of even a rehearsal-room, Miss Norbury had no idea of the artificialities which the theatre imposes on the naturalism of the simplest physical movement; despite my line of footlights and my fourth wall painted to represent a crowded and probably critical audience, she played—if I may use the word—as though she and I were alone on the stage—or, perhaps I should say, in the room that I had put on the stage, turning her back on the imaginary audience, dropping her voice to a whisper that even I could sometimes hardly hear, committing every crime that could drive a producer distracted and rejecting every convention by which all playwrights have been bound ever since playwriting began. Half-way through the first act, when we were affecting to eat a stage dinner, Big Ben had struck eleven and I had warned her that we should not at this rate finish by breakfast-time. In an oddly stupid voice, after a long silence, she pointed out that this was a four-course dinner and that she could not be expected to eat it in five minutes. Then, passing her hand over her eyes, she muttered something about having lost the thread and asked me if I would mind going back to her last entrance.

"The cue," she reminded me, as she left the stage, "is: '*I should think that's Lady Caroline now*'."

And it was in giving it that I discovered I should have said "stupefied" to myself, not "stupid"; it was in the moment before she entered that I made my great discovery and then discovered that she had made it for me some hours earlier. "It's my *story*": had that been her phrase? I now understood the dazed look in her green, kitten's eyes, like that of a sleepwalker suddenly awakened, when I broke into her story. In words that I was to use in writing to Violet next day, I whispered to myself:

"She isn't *playing* 'Lady Caroline'. She *is* 'Lady Caroline'. She's in 'Lady Caroline's' bedroom now, changing into one of 'Lady Caroline's' dance frocks. Heavens above, if I can use a genius like that!"

Since the stage-directions laid down that the orchestra should be playing a popular waltz as "Lady Caroline" passed through the revolving door of the restaurant and seated herself at a table for two, I started the gramophone as soon as I heard "Lady Caroline" shutting the door of my model's disrobing-room or of her own bedroom in Grosvenor Square. The next few minutes, I feared, were going to be a bad time for me. I had to join her, double the parts of myself and the waiter to whom I was giving my order for dinner and then suggest that we should dance while we waited for it to be brought. It was true, as she had pointed out, that I should see almost at once that she was hopelessly drunk; but, even before that, she was likely to see that my dancing days belonged to another century.

In fact my powers were never tested. Obviously I shall never know whether in her reading of the part "Lady Caroline" was to find, the moment she was on her feet, that she could not stand, whether she was to cling convulsively to me till I could lead her to a sofa or whether Miss Norbury, who had asked me whether she was supposed to be drunk or only excited, was collapsing from excitement. What happened was that we stood up, as my stage-directions enjoined, that I put my arm round her and, as her head drew near to mine, kissed the lobe of her left ear. She was then to whisper something; we were both to laugh; and then my laughter was to die as she clutched at me and I became aware of her condition. I believe she whispered something that I did not catch; I know we both laughed; and then, before I expected it, she was clinging to me for support and I had all but lost my balance and let her fall.

"Sorry! I'm afraid I muffed that," I said. "I hope I didn't tread on you?"

"No. . . . Do you want it again? If so, you'll have to wind the gramophone. I must go back to the moment when I came in, bowing to the headwaiter as though we didn't both know that I was hopelessly in debt to his restaurant. Haven't you a modern waltz?"

I looked through the pile of records, not sorry for a moment in which to recover my composure. Miss Norbury's "Lady Caroline" was no longer mine. It was drunkenness that had to incapacitate her; but it was not drunkenness that had made her cling to me a moment since.

"Everything here is at least twenty years old," I said. "The middle of the Great War. *If You were the Only Girl in the World* . . . *Widows are Wonderful* . . . *The Broken Doll* . . ."

And not since the middle of the Great War had any girl pressed herself against me with the same abandonment of passion. After more than twenty years, though I had been told

that the only thing I could do for her was to forget her, I found
my hands trembling as I recalled the night of my first meeting
with Lady Isabel Pryde when she invited herself to supper with
me.

"I don't think I know *The Broken Doll*," said Miss Norbury.

"It's not a waltz," I warned her. "I'll put on *Widows are
Wonderful*."

Before I could wind the gramophone, however, the door of
the studio was quietly opened and Norman signalled to know
whether he might come in. I introduced him to Miss Norbury
and explained what we were doing.

"May I stay?," he asked. "Winter gave me your message that
if I thought it would amuse me . . ."

"If it amuses you to see your elderly father making a guy of
himself," I answered. "My worst enemy never called me a
dancing-man . . ."

"But, Mr. Whimboyne, you don't *have* to dance . . .," Miss
Norbury broke in. "Because I *can't* . . . You're all *wrong* . . . Oh,
I'm sorry. That's terribly rude! What I mean is: I don't *agree*.
I've just come on from about five cocktail-parties, full to the
brim. I've pulled myself together for coming in, but I want to
sit down. You ask me to dance. I get up. Everything swims
round me. I drop like a sack of coals. Now, *you* want me to waltz
sedately for two rounds of the stage, whispering and laughing.
It can't be done! I can stand long enough for one kiss, one giggle
and then I pass out. Oh, do let me shew you! Start from: '*I
thought you were out in Cairo with your husband, Caroline*'."

This time the scene went through without a hitch, even if it
was not quite the scene that I had written. I invited myself to sit
at "Lady Caroline's" table, I ordered dinner, I commented on the
music, I suggested that we should dance. As before, I kissed her
ear, we laughed and whispered. This time she steered me towards
the sofa; and I could let her fall without falling myself. As she
had said, I did not have to dance a step. She clung to me conscientiously enough, but there was now nothing to remind me of
a wartime drive through darkened streets twenty-two years and
six months earlier.

"What's this thing you've put on?," Norman asked, jerking
his head towards the gramophone.

"*Widows are Wonderful*," I replied. "I really wanted a waltz."

"It's rather jolly." He turned to Miss Norbury with a smile

that any woman would have found hard to resist. "'*Caroline, I don't believe we've danced together since George Mottram's party for the Leger in 'thirty-five. Shall we?*'"

As they began to dance I looked at my watch and brought in the tray that Winter had left outside the door. It was nearly midnight; and I was tired by all the emotions that I had experienced since I left my room in the Department of the Lord Keeper to carry a memorandum upstairs to be typed before I went out to luncheon. If Miss Norbury was not equally tired, I thought that she had done more than enough for one night. And I thought that Norman too was looking tired when I first saw him framed in the doorway, fair-haired and blue-eyed, eating a sandwich and explaining that he had not after all dined on his way to London.

"I think we might call a halt at the end of this," I suggested, moving towards the gramophone.

Before I could reach it, however, the light footsteps were stilled, I heard a long sigh and turned to see Norman carrying his ashen-faced partner to the sofa.

"Daddy! I believe she's *fainted*!," he exclaimed. "I mean . . . She's not *dead*, is she?"

X

FAR from being dead, Miss Norbury recovered consciousness almost immediately and confessed with admirable candour that she was unaccustomed to drinking wine and that the two glasses of moselle which she had taken from politeness were to her what four cocktail-parties had been to "Lady Caroline".

"Do you want to finish the act?," she asked me.

"Another night," I said. "As soon as I can get Lady Oakhirst."

"And you'll let me know? Then I may as well be going."

I was beginning to ask whether she would like a taxi when Norman volunteered that his car was at the door and that he would be delighted to drive her home.

"I shall only be a few minutes," he told me, when she had given an address in Pimlico. "If you're not going to bed immediately, there's something I should rather like to discuss with you. In fact I've come all the way from Oxford to discuss it."

I said that I had one letter to write; and, as the car started, I tried to give Violet my impressions of Miss Norbury's performance (if such a word were permissible for a completely natural rendering of a part in which she had insinuated herself into the very soul of a character). Violet, I said, must see the girl for herself; and I would arrange another audition when I heard how soon she had a free night. As a spectator, I suggested, she might be able to do what I had found impossible: to decide whether the girl, who kept saying truly enough that she could not act, might be taught to act.

"*If you give her a rudimentary hint or two at the end of a scene,*" I continued, "*we shall see whether she's capable of learning or whether we're simply spoiling a rare (and quite unmarketable) natural talent for impersonation. I can't describe the queer sense she gave me that she was moving and speaking in her sleep. Trilby, singing in the hypnotic sleep induced by Svengali. But unless she can sleep-walk and sleep-talk for a three-dimensional theatre . . .*"

I broke off as the front door slammed and Norman came in to report that he had got Miss Norbury home without a second collapse.

"I hope you're feeling diplomatic," he continued with a faintly sheepish smile. "I can't do it myself without hurting mummy's feelings too dreadfully, but some one really must tell her that second-lieutenants in Territorial battalions are *not* the obvious raw material for a general officer's staff. I expect you know Baird-Cumming? His son Frank is rather a friend of mine and, as Frank was giving the general lunch the same day that mummy was lunching with me, we made a joint affair of the two parties. I'm *sure* it was done with the best intentions," he went on unhappily. "You've very often told me how your father had a regular list of influential people whom he could approach for jobs. I sometimes wonder whether she's trying to take a leaf out of *his* book."

"Did she offer you to the general as an A.D.C.?," I asked.

"She would have in another minute! He's probably hardened by now to wire-pulling mothers who want to give their sons a leg-up, but she doesn't see what it makes *me* look like!"

I remembered Elizabeth's sudden interest in the few governor-generals of my acquaintance who might be cajoled into attaching Norman to their staff; I remembered, before that, her questioning of Nigel Oakhirst about the more remote colonial-service as a career for young men; and, after that, I remembered Norman's own admission that she had tried, in effect, to snatch him from the army on medical grounds.

"*Nobody*," I said emphatically, "is going to doubt the good faith of an officer who, I believe, swore his age up a year or two and took a commission under no sort of compulsion in what it amuses us to call 'peace-time'. I can guess how you feel, though, and I'll see what I can do. How long can you stay for? I was just asking Violet Oakhirst to choose a night for dining here: I want her opinion of Miss Norbury as an *investment*. I should like yours too. If I paid to have her taught the A.B.C. of acting ... Did she make any comment on the evening?"

Before answering, Norman asked what "the evening" was supposed to have been. He had caught sight of Miss Norbury some months earlier in my department and had understood that she was a clerk or something of the kind. Then he had found her an honoured guest in my house. Now she was, apparently, a leading-lady on trial. He could not quite make it all out. Nor, he thought, could she.

I told him of the accident that had revealed a commonplace shorthand-typist as a possible star who would dim the brightness of Mrs. Siddons and Ristori. I was silenced by Norman's disrespectful chuckle:

"I think she rather fancies you've got a crush on her. Is she any good?"

"That's what you and Violet must help me to decide. You've heard of plays written for the study; I've met many, many players for the drawing-room, more or less clever mimics of whom every one says: 'He would make his fortune on the stage.' Would he? Just behind your head there are five volumes of Swinburne's *Tragedies*: not one of them would run three nights! This girl *creates* a living character as Browning created them by the score, on paper, in soliloquies to be *read* ... *My Last Duchess* ... I can *hear* Miss Norbury declaiming that so that you feel you're in the duke's presence, being shewn his treasures, taking his message for '*the count, your master*', listening to the painfully undignified story of the girl who '*had a heart—How shall I say?—too soon made glad*' ... Whether she could do it on any kind of stage ... That we have to see."

As Norman had been granted leave for only one night, I did not really suppose that I should be given the benefit of his opinion; but, when Violet telephoned at breakfast-time to suggest the following Wednesday, he pulled out an engagement-book and, murmuring: "The Ides of March! Well, if *you're* not superstitious . . . ," at once told me that he could easily arrange to come up again. Less shyly than before our "Saint Norman's Summer" began, he recalled the days when he was first allowed to play unattended with my now battered model-theatre. Though he had never aspired to write for the theatre, he had been stage-struck since the night—probably long-forgotten by me— when I took him to see—in his own phrase—"what made the wheels go round", starting at the door-keeper's box as the first arrivals hurried in, visiting the dressing-rooms with the call-boy, watching an act from the wings with the prompter and dodging out of the way as a scene was shifted.

"I was going to ask you some time," he continued, "whether you would let me see a rehearsal."

"If *Flowers By Request* is ever put on," I answered, "I'll try to arrange it, but the last word is with the producer, whoever he may be. Sometimes they are rather sticky about strangers, especially if they think the stranger is of the gilded youth that used to haunt the stage-doors. For my own part . . . I remember perfectly the night you're referring to, Norman, and, if you'll keep it a secret, I'll tell you why it was all arranged. 'Stage-struck' . . . Those Christmas holidays when you stayed here for a round of the theatres: your mother said she hoped you wouldn't become *stage-struck*, meaning that she hoped you wouldn't lose your heart to some diaphanous beauty of a chorus-girl. I said I had a prophylactic against that. Your diaphanous beauty must be simply exuding glamour if she's to stand the test of being seen in the outdoor clothes she has worn to come up by tram from the suburbs, then in her grease-paint, then—worst of all!—as one of a small *army* all exactly alike, all made-up alike, all dressed or undressed alike. . . . I once went to a *revue* that was said to have the nakedest beauty-chorus in London: it may have been beautiful, but it was *too* naked, too reminiscent of Smithfield Market. Well, that's the inner history of the night when I took you behind."

As I talked, deliberately introducing the word "glamour", I was watching Norman's face to see whether my prophylactic had been wasted. Had Miss "Ginger" Norbury, for example, made a glamorous appeal to him? If she had, he did not betray himself; and the only effect of my anecdote was a mumbled wish that his mother would try to see that he was grown-up.

"Stage-struck!," he repeated scornfully; then, before he could say anything undutiful, he asked: "What was the poem you quoted last night? That line about the girl who *'had a heart— How shall I say?—too soon made glad'* has been running in my head ever since. A heart *too soon made glad!*"

"It's *My Last Duchess*. I think, the most nearly perfect short poem that Browning ever wrote, but perhaps I'm not quite sane about Browning."

"Is that why you never put me on to him? Or wasn't I old enough? I remember a great argument about him between you and mummy: she thought it absurd to read a man who needed a Browning Society to explain what he meant."

I refrained from criticizing Elizabeth's literary judgement, which too often—I thought—condemned authors whom she admittedly had not read and disparaged books that had been recommended to her sons by any one but herself.

"I began to read Browning when I was fourteen," I recalled. "If I thought about your age at all on that occasion, it was to wonder whether you weren't too old for me to direct your taste. I wanted you to have preferences of your own."

"Well, this Browning sounds as though he would repay a little attention. Will you lend him to me? And tell me what I ought to read? I don't mind having my taste directed by you, because you never pretend to like a thing if you don't. You told me that you couldn't stand *Tristram Shandy* and that *The Vicar of Wakefield* bored you."

We strolled, talking idly, about my workroom, until it was time for me to set out for Queen Anne's Gate. As I entered my room there, I wondered for a moment whether Miss Norbury's manner would support Norman's idea that she now numbered me among her admirers; and I reflected that, though I account myself fairly observant, she might be faintly chagrined to know that in writing to Violet I had not described her looks because— apart from the hair to which she owed her nickname—I could not remember what they were. As she came in, I tried to take note of them; but she was by now once again so much the demure secretary that I felt reluctant to betray the most frigid personal interest in her.

As we settled down to the morning's dictation, I could not

Y

indeed help asking myself whether this girl, despite her admitted
and demonstrated ignorance of acting, was not a natural actress,
whose nature impelled her to act at every moment of the day. It
was something more fundamental than persistent self-dramatiza-
tion that I had in mind, though I could readily believe that she
saw herself under a spot-light whatever part she was playing:
what I was fumbling to express was that she was always playing a
part.

As she sat now with crossed legs, a yard or two from my
chair, making rare, swift notes in her book, very cool and remote,
very neat and efficient, she was in fact a government office
shorthand-typist; but at this moment she was playing the part of
one who was nothing more. Should I bluntly call it the part of
one who could not be imagined as clinging to a man as she had
clung to me the night before, still less as swooning in the arms of
another man as she had swooned in Norman's a few minutes
later? What part she had played on their short drive together,
what part she would play when she met Violet, I could not guess;
but it would in some way be a part that made it absurd for any
one to think of her as a government-office shorthand-typist from
nine till five.

"Will you feel equal to trying the third act next week?," I
asked, when I had come to the end of my dictating.

"I could have taken it last night, Mr. Whimboyne, if it hadn't
been so late," she answered. "I think it was only a little indiges-
tion, if you're referring to that."

"Lady Oakhirst is free on Wednesday. If that suits you? At
the same time?"

"It's very kind of you. I don't think you said how many
copies you wanted of your memorandum to the Committee of
Imperial Defence."

Whatever the desired number, the Comptroller to the Department of the Lord Keeper now gave it to his secretary; his secretary took a note and left the room; Colin Whimboyne sent a
postcard to his son Norman and telephoned to Violet. My
secretary reappeared at intervals during the day; and Colin
Whimboyne did not see Miss Norbury again until Wednesday
evening when she and Violet entered my house together, Violet
explaining that they had met on the doorstep and introduced
themselves.

If my natural actress had assigned herself a part to play at dinner, I should say it was her former part of a girl, slightly amused and more than slightly puzzled, who knew nothing of acting and was obliging me by assisting at an experiment that she did not wholly understand. Like me, Violet asked her whether she had ever thought of going on the stage; and she replied that the idea had never entered her head. Norman mentioned a friend who was studying at the Central School of Dramatic Art; and she said that she had never heard of it, adding that her "people" had a low opinion of the stage and discouraged her rare visits to the theatre. I suggested that they might change their view if they could be convinced that she had a career ahead of her; and she reminded me that she had played two entire acts without eliciting a word from me to indicate whether I thought she would ever be any good.

"I said nothing," I defended myself, "because I didn't know what to say. I don't know yet. You have an extraordinary power of bringing a character to life, but the stage makes certain orthodox demands. . . . You shall have my opinion when I've given myself a little more time."

"And you're starting to-night with the third act? I shall have to change into my beach-pyjamas. If you'd like me to get ready while you're finishing your coffee . . .? I don't smoke, thanks. It's up the stairs to the very top of the house, isn't it?"

"I'll come and turn on the lights for you," Norman volunteered.

I poured Violet a second cup of coffee and asked her what impression she had formed of my discovery. The evocative power which I had tried to describe in my letter and which was something unique in my experience she would see for herself in a few minutes' time; but was there anything in the feeling, which I had expressed badly enough to myself and was not expressing much better now, that this girl was always playing a part of one kind or another?

"I think you're reading into her more than there really is to see," Violet answered. "She's a pretty, clever little thing, but quite obviously her present surroundings are not what she's used to and she's therefore not at her ease. I don't call it playing a part to be on your best behaviour and to accommodate yourself to your company. If it seems artificial, you must remember that her experience is all derived from the films."

"I meant more than that. When she's taking down my letters,

I feel she's playing the *part* of a stenographer. Completely lost in it for the time being, as she was completely lost in the guest-at-dinner five minutes ago, as she'll be completely lost in whatever part she plays when she gets back to-night to her puritanical 'people'. What she's like when she's *herself*, if she ever is . . ."

"That I *know*, because I've met her kind before. And the others put on quite good gramophone-records and gave quite good imitations of their favourite stars, but they weren't 'completely lost'. If they had been, I should have seen nothing. D'you remember that day on the Downs when I told you about my latest crisis? The girl who wanted me to divorce Nigel or let him divorce me so that she could marry him? She was no more to him than Miss Norbury is to you, but *she* was in love with *him*. Or *thought* she was. And she couldn't help shewing it. Any more than this girl can. Your perfect actress would be able to hide that. I won't insult you, Colin darling, by telling you to be careful, but for her sake—and she seems a nice child—you shouldn't encourage her to daydream at your expense. It might turn a much stronger head than hers to think that the Comptroller of her department, the great Mr. Colin Whimboyne . . . You hadn't noticed anything?"

I said that I had not known till now there was anything to notice. A week ago I certainly had thought that she was emotionally excited: she seemed to have been carried away by the "Lady Caroline" part that she was creating, but, when she fainted in Norman's arms, I had decided that he, if any one, ought to be on his guard.

"I used to think that about Nigel at one time," said Violet. "Though he was young in years and looked younger, he had become very stiff-jointed in mind and I felt that, if they only knew it, these girls would have a much more amusing time with men of their own age and class. I don't think that any more. Apart from your position, if the girl's a scalp-hunter, and your means, if she's a gold-digger, you're much more *interesting* than a dozen Normans, who really have only their youth and high spirits to put in the shop-window. I don't say that *faute de mieux* . . . As you didn't offer to take her up to her dressing-room, she may feel that Norman's better than nothing, but she's conscious all the time that he's still an undergraduate, two or three years younger than she is. For ten minutes' playing with fire while she's changing her dress . . ."

"They've had a good bit more than ten minutes," I answered, as I pushed back my chair.

"You needn't be nervous! Norman is still far too shy, even with a constitutional *allumeuse*, which is what I take this girl to be unless I'm doing her a hideous injustice."

Whether she was or not, we had no means of deciding, as Norman had in fact come downstairs immediately after turning on the lights for her and was standing in the hall reading an evening paper. He did not hear us coming out of the dining-room; he did not seem to see us, though he looked up mechanically at the sound of his own name when I said that we were going to see whether Miss Norbury was ready to begin the performance. This word, I suppose, must have worked its way into his consciousness, since at the end of a long silence he mumbled that he did not know what kind of performance there was likely to be that night.

"You never told me about this little surprise-packet," he continued, frowning and flapping the paper towards me.

"I don't even know what surprise-packet you're referring to," I said.

"Then I should think you're the only person in London . . . Driving here from Oxford, I naturally didn't see a paper. . . . I should think the *Punch* people are feeling a bit foolish."

Violet intervened to say that she had seen no papers since breakfast and had spent the afternoon by herself.

"Then you really don't know . . .? Why, even Neville Chamberlain seems to have come out of his trance! Hitler has issued a snap ultimatum to the Czechs; and his troops began to march on Prague at six o'clock this morning. Chamberlain has been announcing it to the House. Well, it was an even chance since Munich. *I* thought it was an odds-on chance a week ago, when the papers were full of German troop-movements, but that was the moment when our wise leaders decided that the prospects of peace were better than they'd ever been. I must get to the depot and see what's happening. If I'm not wanted, I shall go on to Oxford. Make my apologies to Miss Norbury, will you? I must get under way as soon as I've changed."

As he mounted the stairs three at a time, I rang for Winter to help him with his packing. Since no one had telephoned, I assumed that I was not wanted either in Queen Anne's Gate or Downing Street. Why indeed, I asked Violet, as we went up to

the studio, should I be? The government would issue an indignant protest, but not an ultimatum; we should know better next
time, but, if we would not fight in the week of Munich, we could
not fight now to reverse an accomplished fact. Hitler's next act
of aggression, I prophesied, would be against Poland, which was
the logical inference from Vienna.

"That's what Nigel has been saying ever since the *Anschluss*,"
Violet observed. "I had an open mind. I still believe the German
mass was as glad to be spared war as the French or ourselves."

"But if Hitler can get them the fruits of war without firing a
shot? There'll be no war over Poland if we let them march into
Warsaw unopposed. It's rough luck for poor old Norman!
Whatever happens, this is going to make hay of his remaining
time at Oxford. As for his book-shop! And it will nip in the bud
what you call his 'summer', these very pleasant few months
when the three of us have reached a real understanding and he
seems to have discovered that his allegiance to Elizabeth or me
needn't necessarily rule out the other."

"If we do something *more* than protest this time . . . ,"
Violet began between clenched teeth. "It won't help boys like
Norman, I'm afraid, but I suppose you and I can continue to hope
for the best and prepare for the worst. Anything better than
sitting with both hands folded! In spite of Hitler, we've got back
our grip on life. This play of yours . . . If you go on, *defying* him
to hypnotize or paralyse you . . . Promise me you will!"

I promised readily enough, but I had to excuse myself from
doing anything more that night. I think Miss Norbury, patiently
awaiting us in her beach-pyjamas, was a little surprised, as she
at least knew all about the march on Prague and could not see
that it made any difference to us. I suggested that it would make a
profound difference if the country were declared to be in a state
of emergency, as Americans called it.

"You mean you won't have any time for plays?," she asked.

"I mean—this is in confidence—that I shall probably be
shifted to another job. It means I may ask you to come with me.
It means that there'll be a close time for new plays. I'm afraid it
means that any idea of your training for the stage . . . People
with experience like yours will be told to stay put."

"You mean there'll be conscription for every one? If there's a
war, I should like to join one of the services. I couldn't stand a
government office! Nobody could stop me, surely?"

"I couldn't stop your going, but I might stop you from being accepted anywhere else. Don't let's meet trouble half-way, though! Everything may settle down, but I don't feel like going on with our programme to-night. I hope you're not disappointed? Some other evening . . ."

As she got up from the divan where she had been sitting cross-legged, Miss Norbury once again said that she might as well be going home. When we met in the hall half an hour later, I noticed that this time she had her suitcase with her. She did not say whether she was disappointed, but I felt that whatever dreams she may have entertained about the stage were now ended. As I took Violet back to Barton Street, I felt too that whatever hopes I may have had for this play were now shattered.

She, however, would have none of this.

"You've admitted," she reminded me, "that, even if Miss Norbury's a genius, she'll be useless to you till she has been trained. *Flowers By Request* can't wait one or two years for you to find out whether she'll take training. We stand precisely where we stood when we first talked about casting. This girl may be a gold-mine to you later, but she can't play 'Lady Caroline' at present. She's so curiously uninterested that I don't know whether she'll ever be able to play anything. Frankly, dear Colin, I shouldn't be at all sorry to hear you were quit of her. I think she might prove rather a dangerous young woman. For every one's sake it will be better when you've shaken her off. Assuming you *can* . . ."

XI

NORMAN's reference to *Punch*, which I had not seen that week, eluded me till I took it up to read in bed and discovered that the first cartoon, no doubt settled some days earlier for the Ides of March, depicted John Bull stretching himself in comfortable relief while sinister rumours and scares that had troubled his sleep took wing through the open window. In forecasting Hitler's next move, Mr. Punch had been constrained to guess and he had guessed wrong; but he was wrong in good, or at least numerous, company. Ever since Munich I had felt that peace and war turned on the spin of a coin, but I had not expected that the coin would be spun before the end of the summer.

What did I believe now?

Though in public I had no opinions about Chamberlain or Churchill, Halifax or Eden, I was unshakably convinced that the "Dictators", whether one "stood up to them" or "appeased" them, were gangsters who respected no argument but fraud and force. Europe could have peace if all the other powers were willing to go on being tricked or defied; Europe would have peace if all the other powers combined against Germany and if Germany feared to challenge them. Would they combine? When —in Norman's phrase—the Prime Minister came out of his trance, it was to indulge in a veritable paper-chase of guarantees to the next potential victims of Nazi aggression. Would Germany be frightened? Was Germany even impressed?

This was the staple of all conversations when I went to Ridgeway for a family gathering at Easter. My stepsons, who were there with their wives and their babies, hinted darkly that, if Hitler knew of our preparations, he would think twice before exposing his still frail Third Reich to the fury of another European war; they could not say, however, whether he did know and could only assure me—no longer praying secrecy on their words —that they at least were stripped for action. Martin had not been near the Stock Exchange since "Prague" nor Humfrey the Temple since "Munich". They were working seven days a week in their shadow ministries; and, though they must not reveal what their work was, an important part of it seemed to be a campaign of publicity to convince a sceptical world that we were in earnest this time.

"I believe we are," I answered, when my opinion was asked by Elizabeth who at this time seemed intuitively to divine who was for the moment on her side. "It's unfortunate," I continued, "that we've allowed the Germans such a long start. Being in earnest *now* won't help or hinder any one if we have to wait a couple of years for the men and munitions."

"You think Hitler will have a smack at us before we're ready?," asked Norman.

"He would be a fool not to," I replied, "if he means to strike at all. I think it's a toss-up. If he can't put us out of action in the first weeks, we shall outstay him. And he must know that. We've begun a new armaments-race and we shall outlast him there. That's the big difference between Munich and now: we've begun to *spend* and we're ready to go on. He must either hurry on his war or abandon it. And he must decide now. I don't know modern Germany or Italy at first-hand, but I should have thought that he and Mussolini would be the most popular and powerful men in Europe if they now said, like Louis Napoleon: '*L'Empire c'est paix*' . . ."

That this was not what either of them intended to say became known to us in less than twenty-four hours. Early in the morning of Good Friday, the seventh day of April, Fascist troops began their invasion of Albania. The news, conveyed in a B.B.C. news-bulletin, was brought to me in the book-room by Norman, who glumly "supposed" that he would now have to go through "all the old Munich-Prague racket" again.

"Reporting at the depot," he continued morosely. "Over-hauling my kit. Keeping my car at the front door . . . Do you think my opposite-number Huns and Wops enjoy being kept on their toes like this?"

"The tradition of military service has probably made them better used to it," I said.

"Then I rather wish *I'd* grown up in a conscript country! You could then lay your plans accordingly. I wish you would write a play about people like *us*, daddy! In your day, most men in their second or third year at Oxford knew what they meant to *do*. Some of them, like Martin's father, were engaged to be married before they went down. What's the good, though, *now* of eating your bar dinners when you don't know from one day to another . . .? As for getting engaged! Of course, if a girl doesn't *mind* marrying on a separation-allowance and bringing up a family on her widow's pension . . ."

I said that in my opinion the general prospect for the rising generation was utterly deplorable. My best hope was that, if it seemed equally deplorable to the young men and women of other nations, we might live to see a world-wide uprising against war and rumours of war.

"Simply," I explained, "on the ground that you're going to make what you please of your individual life. The war-lords rap out: 'Mobilize!'; and a great defiant roar goes up, simultaneously, spontaneously: 'We will *not*.' There's certainly the stuff of drama there, though I couldn't handle it, but until then . . ."

"I should have thought for a comedy of manners . . . ," Norman began diffidently; then, flushing and throwing all restraint aside, he continued: "Take me! As soon as I was old enough to understand anything, I had my life all taped: a job, for choice something to do with books, the rest of my time here learning about the place and perhaps being allowed to help you, in God's good time a wife and a jolly little heir for Ridgeway. We-e-ell . . . I couldn't waste my time working for a job that I should have to give up before I'd settled into it: I'm concentrating on a ridiculous bookshop that I can pick up and let fall between scares. I can't take much interest in a place that will still, I hope, be yours thirty years after this world has seen the last of me. As for the wife and children . . . No, thank you! I don't mind having an affair with a girl if any girl is inclined to have an affair with me. Eat, drink and be merry! I don't see why we should lose *all* the fun in life. But if you compare how things have worked out with the way I planned them to work out . . . That's what I meant for the idea of your play," he ended abruptly.

I thought it best to say that this would make an admirable first act: how, though, was the theme to develop? And, filling a pipe, I lay back in my chair and pretended to be awaiting his views. Here, I told myself, was a Norman that I had never seen before, the man begotten of the friendly, grave, sweet-natured child in whom Violet always detected excessive sensitiveness; a Norman that I shrank from seeing again. Still sweet-natured, he would be brave for all his sensitiveness when bravery was needed, but he had ceased to expect that the world would ever be friendly and he was too young by fifty years or all eternity for this philosophy of bitter resignation. Had I even hinted, though, that life was seldom quite so gloomy as I in moments of pessimism had expected it to be, I felt that he might well have replied, like the doomed King of the Beggars in *Hassan*: "*I am a man in the presence of death.*"

"I'm afraid I have no theme to develop," he answered. "It was just the contrast. . . . Oh, if you like, the contrast between the life that mummy had planned for us and the life we shall lead so long as we're leading a life of any kind. Please, daddy, don't think this is self-pity! One occasionally sees things in a flash. '*The one true light . . . one glimpse of it within the tavern caught . . .*' I expect I've been talking the most unmitigated tripe and, once again, I don't want mummy to know that I'm capable of *talking* like this *ever*. *You* can understand it, though, even if it leaves you with an unpleasant taste in the mouth. Eat, drink and be merry . . ."

There was so little merriment in the boy's voice that I felt tempted to bid him eat and drink to his heart's content and beyond if it would make him any happier, but I was checked by the memory of an irrelevant phrase that he had used before repeating this counsel of dreary hedonism. *"One glimpse of it within the tavern caught."* Why had he dragged in that hackneyed line? Was he by any chance faintly uninhibited at this moment? My neighbour and friend Sir James Currie had once silenced an inebriated heckler, who wished to know what good a university education did, by observing that he at least had learnt at Oxford to carry his liquor. Though the tradition was dying out, I had always kept up my father's practice of having port, sherry and a barrel of biscuits brought into the hall in the middle of the morning: if Norman felt the need for Dutch courage, the opportunity was under his hand. If he had seized it, he—like "Jo" Currie—had learnt how to carry his liquor.

Was he taking the too-sensitive man's too-easy way out? When Elizabeth complained that I was putting temptation in young people's way, I had always been able to reply that wine, when it was to be had for the asking, constituted no greater temptation to Martin and Humfrey or Norman than to me. Was it not, she argued, a needless temptation to put in the way of the servants and an unwarrantable extravagance in hard times? I had answered with some heat that I myself was as likely to tipple as Cruikshank; but the heat evaporated rather quickly now when I remembered that the cellar-book disclosed an increased consumption of port into which I had so far been too busy to enquire.

"It would be interesting," I said, "to know how many of your generation have decided that a completely new *approach* is required. Martin and Humfrey, you remember, were among the first to feel that three years at Oxford would be three years wasted. The spacious days were over, there was no going back to 1914. And yet in a rather out-at-elbow way I feel that most of us were trying to make a pale imitation of the social life we'd known or heard about before the Great War. You, quite obviously, feel that the time has come to have a clean cut. I'm interested, Norman, because you're you and because I haven't met this attitude before . . ."

I was talking in the hope of persuading him to talk; but he would only say that, if other people did not share his views, it was because other people did not share his conviction that another European war was inevitable.

"I don't lay claim to much originality," he went on. "If we'd declared war at the time of Munich, the little picture I've painted you would have been exhibited six months earlier. I should have been mobilized. Well, good-bye to Oxford and Modern Greats and a crack at the home civil, good-bye to this place and the handsome piece of plate from the tenants for my coming-of-age, good-bye to the simple country-wedding and the pudding-faced bridesmaids . . ."

"Do you care to say whether you were in fact contemplating . . .? If you think the question's impertinent, consider it unasked."

"It's not impertinent, it's just comic! Marrying and giving in marriage *may* come in again *after* the Flood, but, while the waters are rising, I want to keep my arms and legs free. I sometimes wonder whether Martin and Humfrey would have been in such a hurry . . . After all, if *I* drown, I can sink without dragging any one else down, but if I had a wife who was likely to be bombed or small children who could be poisoned when the water-mains and the sewers unfortunately got tangled up . . . One can't talk to Barbara or Monica about these things, but this attitude of mine, daddy . . . I believe you'll find a great many *girls* who are saying: 'Not good enough.' I don't mean that they're vowing themselves to perpetual spinsterhood! That would only make the world rather more miserable and neurotic than it is at present. I don't mean they're going to lead a crusade *against* marriage. Why should they? It's no business of theirs how other people arrange their lives, it's no business of other people how *they* arrange *their* lives. Mummy would think all this the most frightful depravity. She's still living in an age when mothers told their sons to 'wait till Miss Right comes along'. Does it shock *you*? When all's said and done, you must have been about my age when people were talking about the 'German Peril' and arguing about the Kaiser as they argue now about Hitler."

I said that, speaking for myself, I had not expected the 1914 war until it came.

"You can believe with your head," I explained, "and not with your heart. The warnings were there, but I couldn't persuade myself that anything so monstrous . . . I was wrong, though I always favoured *preparing* for a possible war. I've favoured that in recent years, ever since the League of Nations broke down. Violet Oakhirst and I have a sign and countersign whenever we meet: 'Hope for the best', but 'Prepare for the worst'. All our world-troubles come from our unwillingness to prepare. You're convinced that war is inevitable? Unshakably? I see a *danger* in that. I've said I was wrong, in refusing to see that war was coming in 1914: suppose you're wrong in believing war must come in 1939 or 1940 or 1941? I should say: 'Don't commit yourself irrevocably on your own certainty of war.' It *may* not come."

"And you think . . . ?"

I suppose he was trying to ask whether I thought he was committing himself irrevocably to anything by repeating "Eat, drink and be merry".

"I think, as we said at dinner last night, that it's all a question whether the gangster dictators believe that we're in earnest. I can tell you that the work I've been engaged on ever since Munich has been very much preparing in earnest for all eventualities. Your brothers' shadow-departments are ticking over in earnest. Your mother's work in organizing her 'Vamps', Violet Oakhirst's work in preparing the conversion of this place, her husband's work with his shipping-committee . . . We *are* on our toes this time; but, as I should get cramp if I remained on my toes indefinitely, I'm planning for the time when the present state of emergency is over. That play that you found us rehearsing the other day . . . I'm going ahead with that, hoping for the best, in all the time I can spare from preparing for the worst. I believe you would be wise to do the same, Norman. Don't be caught unaware by peace! You can do a lot in two years: if you're still set on the home civil when you come down . . . You'ld be sorry afterwards to feel that you'd thrown away your chances because it hadn't seemed worth your while to do the necessary collar-work . . ."

I paused as Norman exclaimed that the difference between us was what I had called the difference between believing with the head and with the heart:

"For all I know of astronomy, the sun *might* drop out of the firmament to-morrow, but I don't believe it will. I don't believe we shall have an abiding peace till Hitler's been bumped off. I'm sorry! I just can't help it! Of course, all this is between ourselves: I wouldn't for the world have mummy think that I regarded it as a matter of months or even weeks. . . . I really *will* work this next term; but, if I may, I shall come to you in London for the vacs. I can't keep up pretences all the time! Mummy believes . . . not with the head *or* heart . . . I should say, with her whole nervous-system . . . I shan't be a bit surprised to see her chewing glass when war's declared. She only keeps on her rocker now by toiling day and night for her precious Vamps. It's pure doping."

We digressed for a few minutes—I think, with some relief on both sides—into a discussion of metaphorical drug-taking, "escapism", healthy relaxation and the increased mental concentration attributed by Dr. Johnson to a man very soon to be executed. I mentioned that I worked best at times of emotional crisis, but at once added that I had written *Flowers By Request* as a stimulant when I felt myself being hypnotized by Nazi propaganda.

"And you're going on with that, you said. Will Miss Norbury be any use to you?," Norman asked.

"We've done nothing since that night when we got the news of Prague. I don't know! I thought then, like you, that it was really a waste of time to go on with anything. Later on, I said it was no good standing poised for something that might not happen. . . . You never told us, by the way, how you got on at the depot that night."

"There was nothing to tell. In effect, stand by for orders. It was the same to-day when the news about Albania came through. Nothing *definite*. There never *is* anything definite. You might let me know, when you get back to London, what people are saying there. One's rather cut off from things in Oxford."

I promised to write regularly; and, though there was seldom anything definite enough for his liking, I kept my promise till he came to stay with me for his Easter vacation and again when he went up for what was to be his last summer term. He kept my letters and handed me a bundle of them later with the sardonic comment that in a swiftly changing world I might find it interesting to recall my past opinions from week to week. His own, I was to understand, had never altered.

"*Is there* any *truth*," he enquired in oblique criticism, "*in the story that you can always tell when an earthquake's coming by the way that the birds go to roost even in broad daylight?*"

I was not conscious that I had gone to roost. Indeed, glancing at the letters that I had been writing throughout these spring and summer months, I felt that the whole of my immediate circle had been working calmly and methodically to be ready for whatever the autumn might bring. If we avoided war till after the beginning of October, I told Norman that he could start a new year at Oxford with a new certainty that it would not now be interrupted: the days of white war were over and, if Hitler was risking his Reich on red war, he could not afford to wait. Several times I found myself repeating the advice that he should be prepared for the possibility of peace. Meanwhile I notified him of my own preparations for the possibility of war, I suppose with some idea of shewing that we could—as Violet might have said—still keep our grip without yielding to imbecile optimism or paralysing despair. Acting on official advice to provide against interrupted communications, I told him that Ridgeway was now amply stocked with food; I had installed a capacious petrol-tank and, since I must expect my big car to be commandeered in the event of war, I had bought a second-hand runabout; and I was offering accommodation to various friends and colleagues who would be driven into the country if London were bombarded from the air.

All this, however, was insurance against risks which might never materialize; and I was working at least as hard to convince at least myself that any war of nerves left me unmoved. The complete script of *Flowers By Request*, I reported in May, had now been delivered by Miss Norbury, though I had still failed to arrange for a further audition. He must have asked later how I was getting on, for in June I was telling him that as yet I had no news. Neither on the first nor on the second occasion did I give any reason; but, if I had imagined that I could resolve a mystery by discussing it with him, I might have said that towards the end of May Miss Norbury was absent from the office and at the beginning of June I heard that she was not coming back. Our establishment-officer, presenting her successor, had no explanation to suggest; and the only one that occurred to me was that the girl, without waiting for a declaration of war, had joined one of the women's auxiliary services before any one could stop her. It was a passing vexation to me that I should lose her at a time when I was overworked and she had begun to be useful; but by now I shared Violet's view that Miss Norbury might prove a rather dangerous young person.

Overworked I certainly was; and in my last letter to Norman before he joined me in London for the long vacation I admitted to a feeling of strain and asked whether he would care to come

away somewhere for a fortnight's holiday. In his reply I remember
he said that no single country in the whole of Europe tempted
him at the moment, but that, if we were still at peace in September after he had returned from camp, he would like nothing
better than a motor-tour in Wales or Scotland. Of the time before
his camp, when I would far sooner have gone away, he said
nothing more definite than that he had "fixed up various things
with various people".

Whoever the "people" and whatever the "things", they had
apparently persuaded him to take a less jaundiced view of life
than when we were at Ridgeway together at the time of
Mussolini's invasion of Albania. Though we dined by ourselves
two or three times a week and went for long walks on the
Downs almost every Sunday, I do not recall that he ever returned
to the plight of his generation or to the attitude which it must be
expected to adopt towards careers or marriage. If we now spoke
of war even as a possibility, he seemed indeed more interested in
its effects on me. Would my department be moved out of
London? Should I be seconded for other work? Had Martin and
Humfrey definitely decided to send their wives and children to
Canada? Who were the people that I was inviting to Ridgeway if
London were bombarded?

I said that among those who had conditionally accepted my
offer were Dr. Vaughan Drake and the Oakhirsts, but that I
could accommodate the entire staff of the Lord Keeper's Department if Queen Anne's Gate were evacuated.

"By the way, you never told me that you'd lost your leading-
lady," said Norman.

"I suppose I was waiting till there was something definite to
say," I answered. "How did you hear about it?"

"I met her one night at Ciro's. Where are we now: the
twenty-third of August?"

"The twenty-second, I think. Does it matter?"

"No! I was thinking it must be about two months ago: just
after the end of term."

I said that it must have been about that time that I heard she
was away and, almost immediately afterwards, that she was not
coming back.

"She had to undergo an operation," Norman informed me.

"Nobody at the office seemed to know anything about that.
Was it serious?"

"Well, it hadn't put her out of action for long. To be quite frank, daddy, when young damsels tell me they've had operations and quite clearly don't want to talk about them, I change the subject. She may have been having her tonsils out! I only asked you about her . . ."

Norman broke off through obvious inability to think of a convincing "only" reason why he had asked me about her. The reason that I found convincing was that Miss Norbury had told him to ask. I felt sure he had spoken the truth in saying that they had met at Ciro's; but I did not feel so sure that he had spoken the whole truth in not saying that they had met many times since. I did not want to be sure. If she was responsible for setting my son at peace with himself, that was really all that mattered to me. Like Abraham Lincoln on being told that General Grant drank too much whiskey, I wanted the name of Grant's whiskey-merchant so that I could give it to the other generals so that they might win a few of Grant's victories.

"You don't mind my handing on what you've just said to our establishment-officer?," I asked. "We were a bit worried by the way the girl disappeared without a word."

"She was a bit worried herself," Norman replied. "An uncomfortable feeling that she'd let you down. She's not keen on going back to Queen Anne's Gate, but if you're shifted and still want her as a secretary . . ."

With studied indifference I asked him to let me have her address, if he happened to know it; and he promised to give it in the morning. When the morning came, however, we had other things to occupy our minds. I had been right, the evening before, over the day of the month: it was the twenty-second of August and to-day was the twenty-third. Norman, however, had been right in a matter of graver moment. Ever since Prague, perhaps ever since Munich, he had been saying that war with Germany would come this summer or autumn as certainly as the sun would rise next day. The papers on the morning of Wednesday 23 August, contained the news that a pact of non-aggression had been concluded between Soviet Russia and Nazi Germany.

"I don't think *any one* can have much doubt now . . . ," Norman began and then lapsed into silence. "I'm afraid this will be a jolt for poor mummy," he added soberly. Then with a rather strained smile he asked: "Does Moscow have to join the Rome-Berlin anti-comintern axis?"

XII

WHILE Norman once again went to fetch his car and Winter once again packed for him, I walked by way of Barton Street to Queen Anne's Gate, returning three hours later to Grosvenor Road by way of Downing Street. Though I had known for the best part of a year now that, if war came, I should immediately be borrowed, I had not yet been told when my services would be required nor who was to take my place as Comptroller.

Nor was I told anything definite when I visited the Lord Keeper in his room. With a single exception, none of Axminster's successors had been members of the Cabinet; and, if the Prime Minister even knew the name of Lord Missenden, he probably knew it as that of a completely harmless and completely useless pillar of Home-Counties conservatism whom he had inherited from Baldwin. I hardly expected that Missenden would tell me what Chamberlain or Halifax thought of the Moscow-Berlin pact; but I was to find that he did not even know what would become of his own office if London had to be evacuated.

In Downing Street I was at least begged to remain at call, night and day, until it was seen whether this new crisis would pass; and, when Elizabeth telephoned to ask when I could meet her and various relations "to decide what is to be done", I had to say that for the present all family-councils must be held in Grosvenor Road. She then told me that she had to visit the War Office that afternoon and might have to spend the next night or two in London. I told her that I would have a room ready for her; and Norman surprised me a little by announcing that he could now make Ridgeway his "jumping-off place" instead of an hotel near his depot, as he had intended.

"I don't *like* leaving mummy with no one to support her," he confessed, "but we shall drive each other mad if we go on arguing and arguing whether there's going to be a war and how it might have been prevented. Among all the people you've met this morning, daddy, is there a single one . . .?"

"Every one admits," I said, "that Hitler's in a stronger position than ever before. No danger of a war on two fronts *now*. He can pitch his demands very high. If we stand by our guarantees, though . . . And we shall. If Chamberlain tried to stage another Munich, he would be thrown out. Even Hitler may think twice before plunging into a war to which I at least can see no end. The Maginot Line against the Siegfried Line; and, behind them, the whale and the elephant, each supreme in its own element and both unable to engage the other. You may say it will be a war of air-forces, not of armies and navies, but in Hitler's place I should hesitate to risk everything on a form of fighting that has hardly yet been tried. No, I *don't* regard war as inevitable even now. I've booked rooms in various places for our motor tour and I'm not cancelling my bookings."

"And when you do? *If* you do? I mean, what happened in 1914?"

Reminding him of my recent admission that I had not expected war in 1914 until it came, I now admitted that on this foundation of running sand I had confidently built a skyscraper of expectations which were falsified one after another.

"Then too," I recalled, "we had a family-council and I was required to provide beds for various relations and food for various friends. We sat here waiting to see whether there would be a reply to our ultimatum. I've forgotten who all the people were; but I remember your mother, sitting stunned and then being stunned again when Austin broke the news that he was applying for a commission. I remember your godfather Clayton Mandeville, full of excitement at getting quit of Fleet Street and going out as a war-correspondent. Several ministers had been resigning and withdrawing their resignations. I remember that Nigel Oakhirst was fancying himself for an undersecretaryship. Violet had offered an ambulance to the War Office and was prepared to drive it."

"But didn't all that go according to plan?," Norman asked.

"As regards the others, yes. For myself, I fully expected to be in uniform before August was out. I talked to various people about letting this house. The Winters had been with me a year or two by then; and I remember asking whether they would be prepared to stay on when I went. It never entered my head that I should be forbidden to go or that I should spend half the war helping to organize the Ministry of Munitions and almost the whole of it under this roof. I should say that, if one thing seemed more certain than another, it was that my activities as a play-wright would be suspended *sine die*. Instead of which . . . One reason I talked of letting this house was that I expected to be pretty well broke. Instead of which, I began to coin money till it was literally true that I hadn't time to invest it. If any one had told me on the Fourth of August that I should ever be regarded as a *parti* . . . I thought I was a confirmed bachelor. When we talked of men without ties or responsibilities . . . Instead of which, before the war was over, I had—in the most literal sense of the words—fallen *madly* and quite *hopelessly* in love; and, before the peace-treaties had been signed, I was married to your mother, Norman, and you were on your way into a world that I honestly believed had seen its last big war. I'm telling this to shew you that, if you want me to say what I think the next few months or years will be like, you've come to the worst man in England."

As we went in to luncheon, Norman asked scornfully whether any one else was any better.

"Everybody," he continued, "repeats like a parrot: '*If* there's a war, it'll be hell with the lid off for a few weeks, but, if we can stand that, we shall have won!' I was just wondering how it would affect you personally to have hell let loose over London. I'm not nosing into Cabinet secrets . . ."

I assured Norman that, if he had been, I could not have enlightened him. If war came, I said that I should be seconded for special service; if London proved uninhabitable, I should doubtless be shifted somewhere into the country. Most of the people that I had met that morning seemed to be planning on similar lines: Nigel Oakhirst, for example, had come up from Southampton and would remain here while Violet continued to live in Barton Street. Martin and Humfrey would stay or go as their ministries stayed or went. Whatever happened to Ridgeway, I presumed that Elizabeth would be left a corner from which to direct her V.A.M.P. activities. For the rest, like Norman himself, I must be prepared to go wherever I was sent and to do whatever I was told.

"In fact," I added with a cast back to my telephone-conversation, "I don't really know what your mother wants to discuss with me. We're both in the hands of higher powers. Still, if she wants a family-council . . ."

Norman looked at his watch and announced that he would time himself to start for the depot before the council opened.

"I should think she wants to settle the future of Ridgeway," he observed, with a frown, "and I don't want to be in on that. For years she has been tormenting herself over the expense of the place. You remember her great scheme for taking a cottage in

Marlborough when Martin and Humfrey went to London? It *was* a big place just for her, with me only coming home for the holidays and you turning up for an occasional week-end. She never liked big parties and always thought that people came simply for what they could get to eat and drink. Well, when I'm gone, I fancy she'll press you very hard to get rid of the place."

"And the fact that you love it and that it will come to you when I die?"

"Even if I come through alive, I shall never have the money to keep it in commission. Poor mummy, of course, would never admit the possibility that one of her sons could even be lightly wounded; but, as I happen to believe that the odds against people of my age are rather long, I want to keep out of any dog-fight about the house. You," he continued with sudden tartness, "will go on being terribly careful not to be caught unawares by the possibility of peace; and she will take this war as a heaven-sent opportunity for leading the simple, *inexpensive* life. *Why* she should have this horror of spending money . . ."

I felt tempted to say that it was not her own money that Elizabeth was spending or saving; but from the night when we became engaged her attitude to all financial questions had been so mysterious and unsatisfactory that I did not care to think about them, still less to discuss them with Norman. Whatever the immediate fate of Ridgeway, I told him, I should hold on to it till death relaxed my grasp; and, if a war should take him away for some months or even years, he would find his rooms awaiting him whenever he came on leave and, when the place passed to him, I hoped to leave him enough at least to keep the walls standing and the roof intact.

"At fifty-one," I continued, "I should have ten years of active work ahead of me. I fancy I once told you that I always wrote best under strong nervous or emotional strain. In the 1914 war . . . What I used to call my *annus mirabilis* . . ."

"I hope you'll find it possible in this war. . . . Look here, daddy, I ought to be getting under way and I expect you want to get back to your department. You remember asking me for Miss Norbury's address? I can't put my hand on it, but I have a note of her telephone-number, so you can get in touch with her if you want to. I'll let you know my movements as soon as I know them myself. If things *do* quiet down, you can count on me for that motor-tour. I'm afraid, though . . ."

Leaving the sentence unfinished, he turned on his heel; and, when I set out for Queen Anne's Gate, he was bent over the bonnet of his car with his back ostentatiously turned. He had been gone some hours, I was told, when I came back in the evening; and Winter understood that he was giving a lift home to Miss Norbury, who had called within five minutes of my leaving the house. He added that Mrs. Whimboyne's luggage had arrived an hour ago and that she had sent a message that she would be following it in time for dinner.

Since I could not persuade myself that Elizabeth would regard Miss "Ginger" Norbury as a wholly desirable companion for Norman, I was not sorry that she had come and gone, all the more as she had come to Grosvenor Road when she possibly knew he would be there, at an hour when I was usually lunching at the Garrick. We were likely, I feared, to disagree quite enough over Ridgeway without my giving Elizabeth the idea that our son must not stay with me unchaperoned in London for fear of becoming entangled with a seductive and undeniably warm-blooded young typist.

"Our son," I had called him mentally; and, suddenly mindful of a very old warning by Violet Oakhirst that Elizabeth and I must not engage in a perpetual tug-of-war for possession of Norman, I felt a hopeless heart-ache, as I went upstairs to dress for dinner, at the boy's so obviously divided allegiance. He liked staying with me, if only for a change, but to his mother he must pretend that he was attending lectures at the London School of Economics. Her solicitude tore his nerves to ribbons; but he was so grateful, perhaps so sorry, for her whom he now always called "poor mummy" that he would never—like Martin and Humfrey —callously set up by himself in London to be rid of her. The possibility—for him, the certainty—of immediate war was shocking in its needless, fatuous stupidity; but was it altogether imagination on my part that, when I was describing the last hours of peace in 1914, his eyes had lighted up at the picture of Austin Gerrold girding on his harness? Clayton, in his cups, asserted unwearyingly that Austin had gone to Flanders to get away from Elizabeth; to Norman he would probably say no more than that the war had ended many things that many people could not end for themselves. If a new war came this summer or autumn, it would end for all these young men everywhere the sickening uncertainty of waiting for war; and perhaps for our son it would end a desperate and wretched feeling that his parents had nothing in common but their love of him and that, though in different ways he loved them both equally, he could never give his love to the one without seeming to deny it to the other.

"My God!," I whispered, as I came down to my work-room, "if the unhappy Elizabeth imagined that *he* too in *his* generation was welcoming war as an *escape* . . ."

I had described her to him, on that August afternoon and evening, as sitting stunned; and, when I recalled her pitiful and always unsuccessful efforts to get him into shelter before the storm burst, I could not decide whether I was likely to find her stunned by defeat into resignation or lashed by this latest blow into some wild effort that she knew must be her last. She had failed to smuggle him abroad, failed to secure him a staff appointment, failed to have him declared unfit. We were not indeed as yet at war; perhaps we never should be; but I, remembering her frantic appeal to God in the Westminster Abbey cloister, should hardly have been surprised to find her selling her soul to the Devil if she might secure peace for Norman's time and hers.

There was little, I felt, that I could do. Had she been almost any other woman of my acquaintance, I might have brought her back to sanity, perhaps even to composure, with a word; but for twenty years Elizabeth and I had been strangers, each cultivating a carapace of utter indifference to keep the other from inflaming us to hatred; we lived at different ends of the same house for a moiety of the year, to keep up appearances and to hoodwink our relations. Equally, I imagine, for both of us the most dreadful sentence that any one could pass was that we should live at the same end of the same house. Once for a few weeks I had seemed to be threatened with that fate; and Violet had shewn me the way of escape.

"If it *does* come to war . . . ," I muttered and then fell silent.

How much could Violet and I hope to see of each other? It was very long now since I had bought her that ten-year or twenty-year diary in which we studied our bad guesses in the past and plunged into worse guesses for the future. I could not remember what we expected either of us should be doing in 1939, but I fancied that I was then to be in my physical and creative prime. At our New Year's Eve stocktaking in old days we had concentrated chiefly on the future movements of Sir Nigel Oakhirst, Governor and Commander-in-Chief of the Spice Coast, variously seen as a colonial administrator who must come on leave some day, an empire-builder who must retire some day, a transplanted north European who might be incapacitated any day by a tropical disease. What, we asked, was to happen when Nigel had served his term, or purged his offence, or simply lost his health? Circumstances, firmly directed by Violet, had for many years now left him as conveniently exiled on Southampton Water as in his equatorial swamp, but circumstances had now brought him back to Barton Street.

If he remained there, if Violet had to remain with him, I judged that this would be the most dreadful sentence any one could pass on her; and my hand reached for the telephone. Even if Nigel accompanied her, I must insist on her coming to Ridgeway.

"Which effectually knocks on the head any idea of Elizabeth's that this is the ideal moment for getting rid of the place. Whether I'm there or not . . . Even in war-time we could keep our grip on Life, with a capital, if we met for week-ends, if I went on with my own work, if we felt that we were *creating* a tiny something to put in the scale against the ghastly *destruction* that will be going on everywhere . . ."

Before I could dial her number, the door was thrown open and Elizabeth entered with an apology for her lateness. In her commandant's uniform, with a saluting orderly to take her instructions, she was a world removed from the stunned Elizabeth that I had been expecting, though her officer-corps manner weakened as she asked where Norman was.

"He left here this afternoon," I answered. "He was reporting at the depot and then going on to Ridgeway if he wasn't wanted. Once again, as at the time of Munich, he'll make that his headquarters . . ."

"Does he think . . . he *will* be . . . wanted?," Elizabeth faltered.

"He's sure of it. Much surer than I am. I telephoned to Mrs. Cruikshank, who will see that he has all he wants: I'm under orders to stay here till we see which way the cat's going to jump. You, I suppose . . .?"

"I really don't know. That's what I wanted to talk to you about, Colin. If it really *is* war this time . . ."

She sank into the chair, covering her face with her hands; and across the chasm of twenty-five years, penetrating the disguise of her epauletted tunic and badged cap, I saw the lacrimose and helpless Elizabeth Gerrold who had sunk into a chair and covered her face when Austin, urged to "talk about things", answered brusquely that nobody but a congenital idiot could expect any reply to our ultimatum.

I repeated to her what I had already said to Norman and Violet, to the Lord Keeper and Mrs. Winter. I and my two houses, my movements and life were now in the hands of my superiors.

"What about you?," I asked again. "Has the War Office said anything definite?"

"Well . . . Yes and no," she replied dizzily; and I soon came to feel that "yes and no" would be her answer to every question. "Everything depends on so many things," she continued. "Ridgeway, to begin with."

"Unless and until it's requisitioned, I shall keep it in commission," I said.

"We can't afford it," she pronounced in a tone that I had not heard since our honeymoon.

With all the patience that I could command, I reminded Elizabeth that, ever since my two stepsons had gone to London, I had paid the whole of every bill. Though I refrained from saying that it was not a question—in her irritating phrase—of what "we" could afford, I said that, as figures on her own admission always gave her a headache, she had better leave the business side of our life to me.

"If Norman is away fighting," I added, "it would be hardly the moment for me to sell his birthright."

"But *he'll* never be able to keep the place up, unless ne marries an heiress. When I said we couldn't afford it, I meant that *no one* with any sense of *responsibility* can afford to keep a great barrack four-fifths empty. We ought to cut our expenses to the *bone*! I know I don't understand about business, but I *do* understand about putting first things first. If you think that Martin and Humfrey can live on the pittances they're paid by their skinflint departments . . ."

Before she could say that in marrying her I had married a woman with a ready-made family, I pointed out that, since Martin and Humfrey could not possibly live on what they made on the Stock Exchange and at the bar, I presumed that they must have some private means, inherited from their father or hers or both, but that in the twenty years of our partnership neither she nor her solicitors, neither her brothers nor sons had ever discussed their financial position with me.

"I think it most improbable," I added pacifically, as I felt myself in danger of losing my temper, "that Ridgeway *will* be four-fifths empty for long."

"I hope you don't expect *me* to run it for your friends while you stay here."

"I've no idea whether I *shall* be here. I've no idea whether any of the friends I've invited will accept my invitation or whether I can keep it open indefinitely. If the Lord Keeper's Department, for example, moves out of London . . . If I make the Cruikshanks responsible, there should be no additional work for you."

"That's just as well, because I shall have more work of my own than I can possibly get through. If I could get a bed-sitting-room in our office in Marlborough . . . But we're crowded out as it is. . . . Colin, if your department *doesn't* want Ridgeway, could my Patrols have it? They would pay a good rent."

I was faintly amused, albeit with an acid flavour to my amusement, to observe how little Elizabeth had changed since the night twenty years ago when we sat in this room and I stormed my proposal of marriage at her. Now, as then, she seemed less a single, co-ordinated woman than two halves of two completely dissimilar women: docile and stubborn, trusting and suspicious, simple and cunning. Now, as then, a fog of bovine stupidity was suddenly dispelled by a lightning-flash of shrewdness. Now, as then, after taking a count of nine, she was on her feet and attacking on another, unguarded side. Had she ever been capable of speaking the whole truth and nothing but the truth, I believe she would have said that she had married me to have a man of some kind to look after her and to support her two sons. Ridgeway she had at first neither liked nor disliked, though she hated all parties that made her feel socially and intellectually inferior: she had enjoyed being the great lady of the neighbourhood, enjoyed still more being a magistrate and now commandant of her Mobile Patrols, enjoyed most of all the free run of a house where she met her unsympathetic husband only at week-ends. Of late, however, she had come to hate the house, which she saw devouring money that might have been hoarded for her children. Since I would not part with it, she wished me to understand clearly that she was not going to wear herself out conducting a private hotel for my friends.

Had she told the whole truth, I think she must have said that she had always been jealous of my position in the civil service, always resentful of the flattery poured over a mere writer of plays. Now, if there were a war, she would have her war-work, as important to her as mine to me, perhaps more important to the country; were it paid work, she would be independent of me. Certainly she proposed to make herself entirely independent of Ridgeway and its cares, until she conceived the dazzling notion of making the place her official headquarters (to which I should be admitted, if at all, on sufferance), charging a rent that I should not have dreamt of asking and saving for suitable purposes the money that I was too improvident and "unpractical" to save for myself. Across the gulf of twenty years I could see her telephoning to her sister while I sent Winter to find her a taxi; I could hear Kitty Mandeville, homeless and helpless, commenting, a day or two later, on the house in Montpelier Square: Rella might not understand business, but she understood how to drive a very hard bargain. No, Elizabeth had changed little.

"I'm ready to consider any reasonable offer," I said. "I doubt whether the stabling's adequate for your fleet of cars. In any case, my own department has been given first refusal."

"And what are you doing with *this* house? And the Winters? If there *is* a war," she made haste to add.

I told her again that, unless the entire government migrated to the provinces, my work—which would then have nothing to do with the Lord Keeper—would be in London.

"Or *under* it," I corrected myself. "I've been shewn a cellar that is supposed to be bomb-proof. The Winters are willing to look after me unless the place becomes too hot . . . ."

"But you won't *live* here? If there's a *war*? It won't be *safe*!"

"In war-time . . . ."

"But if anything happened to you? Ridgeway's safer than the very heart of Westminster! Oh, don't you men *ever* think of any one but yourselves?"

No, she had not changed at all, in twenty years or in twenty-five. This was the Elizabeth who had sat in the same corner, drinking a similar half-glass of sherry, on the Fourth of August and girding at Austin for risking his life, shirking his duty and never, never, never thinking of her and the boys. I might have felt flattered by her concern if it had not so obviously been for herself. What indeed would happen to her, to Ridgeway, to her sons and daughters-in-law and grandsons if anything happened to me?

"I could hardly live at Ridgeway and work in London," I said. "In *war-time*. If there *is* a war . . . Have you hurt yourself?"

With one hand Elizabeth was holding a handkerchief to her mouth; and the handkerchief was stained with blood. She was staring at the sherry-glass which she held in the other hand; and the sherry-glass had a small half-moon broken out of the rim.

"I've cut my lip," she answered, whitening as she looked at the handkerchief. "And I'm afraid I've broken one of your best glasses. I'm so sorry, Colin! Do you think it could have been cracked?"

"It must have been! Obviously! I can't imagine how Winter failed to see it!"

My vehemence seemed to reassure her, for after a glance in her mirror she told me that it was only a scratch. Perhaps it reassured me too; and I needed reassurance to make me forget a casual phrase of Norman's that he would not be in the least surprised to see his mother chewing glass if war did come.

"What were we talking about?," I asked.

"I was saying that you couldn't stay here. You *can't* leave me by myself in that great barrack! Norman gone, Martin and Humfrey in the thick of it here! I have my own work! Whatever happens to Ridgeway, I can't look after it! And you can't leave it to the Cruikshanks! No, you must be there! I insist."

It was not, I felt, the moment to ask what she would do if I disregarded her insistence. Certainly I should give her hysterics; perhaps I should send her off her head. This, seen by me for the first time, was the Elizabeth that Violet had found weeping and praying in the cloister at the time of "Munich".

"I can promise nothing till I receive my orders," I said. "Let's come in to dinner! And *do* let's remember that we're not at war yet. Perhaps we never shall be. If it blows over, by the way, I'm taking Norman for a motoring-tour . . ."

I doubt whether Elizabeth paid any attention to what I was saying. I paid little enough myself. For the first time I felt sure that he and I should never take another holiday together, sure that war would be upon us before the autumn, sure that I should be hunted out of Grosvenor Road and that the possibility which had lain in the background of my life for twenty years was now a certainty. Whatever—Elizabeth had just said—might happen to

Ridgeway, she and I were going to be imprisoned there till the war ended or one of us died or both of us were removed to a madhouse.

"About stabling for my 'fleet' of cars," she said, as we moved towards the dining-room. "You could put up temporary buildings on the Downs behind. You know where I mean? There's a farm road and a gate by a clump of beeches . . ."

"I was thinking of that very place at that very moment," I answered. "It has been a favourite spot of mine for picnics, but I don't suppose I shall use it again for picnics."

PART FOUR

I

Writing now some four years after the day chosen to mark the victory of the Allies in Europe, I am inclined to think—in the perspective taught by two world-wars and from the contrasted hopes and fears with which we plunged into these ordeals by fire and emerged the other side—that the six years from 1939 to 1945 were for many, perhaps for most, of us in England a less wretched time than the five years before 1939 or the four years since 1945.

As in some sort a creative artist before anything else, I am the last man to make light of the destroying and defiling which are—to me—among the greatest horrors of war. Rockets and atom-bombs are as dreadful in the spring of 1949 as in the summer of 1945; the torture of the body and the enslavement of the soul, which would have been the price of our defeat, can be no more a matter for flippancy now than then; but I feel that some of us were happier when we were keyed to fight and—quite probably—to die for the survival of civilization than in the earlier years when we did not know whether we should even fight or in these latter years when we are not sure whether civilization has even survived.

Had my house been bombed over my head, I should doubtless feel differently; but, when peace came, I could say in humble thanksgiving that I and the little world about me had escaped lightly by any material standard and I can say four years later that, if I have suffered by any other standards, the war can hardly be held responsible for this. Even when we stood alone after the fall of France, I remember telling those survivors from Dunkirk who asked me what I thought of the war that it was at present, for us in England, not so bad as I had expected.

Was this, I have sometimes asked myself, because from beginning to end it was never in the least what I had expected? In far less than a week from the declaration of war I should have said that we had adapted ourselves grimly to a pattern of life that must continue either until our island was blown out of the

sea by the German air-force or until the German air-force had
been hurled back by our own and we achieved the stalemate
which I had compared a few weeks earlier to the contest of an
elephant and a whale. By the time that I left Grosvenor Road for
my first war-time week-end at Ridgeway, my planning committee was securely underground and I had been formally transferred from the Department of the Lord Keeper. In deference to
Elizabeth's entreaty and in obedience to a general hint from the
government that all who did not have to remain in London should
get themselves into the country, I had arranged to sleep in Wiltshire, to breakfast and dine in the train and to work in London.
The house in Westminster was dismantled except for one room;
and the Winters were under orders to join me at Ridgeway at the
first threat that the *Blitzkrieg* was beginning; a lorry-load of
books and papers was somewhere between London and Marlborough; and I could feel that my quality as a philosopher was
being tested whenever I repeated Violet's words of farewell:
"If we never meet again, nobody can take away these years from
us."

No, from the beginning my expectations were falsified. By
the time that I reached Ridgeway, Norman was under canvas in
Dorsetshire, Elizabeth had disappeared to the regional headquarters of the V.A.M.P.s, Martin and Humfrey had resumed
occupation of their suites until they could send their wives and
children across the Atlantic and the spare rooms were filled with
South-London schoolchildren and their teachers. Since the
Cruikshanks were in highly efficient control of everything, there
was nothing for me to do. The small staff and equipment of the
Lord Keeper's Department, which I had offered to accommodate,
were still in Queen Anne's Gate, where indeed they most unnecessarily remained till the end of the war; the friends whom I
had invited to make Ridgeway their war-time refuge decided to
stay in London as long as it was habitable; and Elizabeth herself
refused the house for her V.A.M.P. organization while it was
occupied by so many of her own relations, with perhaps more to
come. Since the South-London schools were being dispersed as
soon as suitable buildings and billets could be found for them, I
felt after a few weeks that my anticipation of "Hell with the lid
off" had changed to a boring and bored family-gathering.

"I suppose," said Violet at the first of the single luncheons in
each week with which we had to make do now in place of the

dinners that we had exchanged almost without a break for well-nigh twenty years, "Martin and Humfrey are a solace to Elizabeth for the absence of Norman. Perhaps a useful shock-absorber for you?"

"Well, an everlasting *tête-à-tête* would try both of us rather highly," I answered. "And I must do Barbara and Monica the justice of saying that they do behave like well-conducted guests in a house that they were most thankful to have put at their disposal in an emergency. The two boys, I'm afraid, have allowed their mother to get on their nerves so badly that the more she does for them the more they snap at her. You warned me, my dear, of the disappointment that Elizabeth would have after the pleasure of fitting out their married quarters for them. Well, they couldn't stand the emptiness of her conversation before and they can't stand it now. The moment they've decided whether there *is* going to be a lightning-stroke here, which we ought to know as soon as the Germans have finished in Poland, *either* they will send their families away and go back to their dug-outs *or* they'll bring their families back to London. And I shall come too. The Cruikshanks can look after our refugees, Elizabeth is at her office all day and half the night. In addition, my committee needs more elbow-room and I've been asked whether we can use this house for working and keeping our papers. If things become too hot here, we can move bodily to Ridgeway. That would suit me better than this eternal travelling."

It was still September when this conversation took place; and in October I judged that London, at least for the present, was safe. Martin and Humfrey moved back at the same time, though they sent their families to Canada and warned me against too easy optimism: Hitler, they said, was preparing a gigantic peace-offensive and, if it failed, the war from the air would begin at once. We remained, all three of us, in London till the "September *Blitz*" and then returned together to Ridgeway, I shepherding my committee. Thereafter, though we all dodged backwards and forwards several times, I made my headquarters in London and went to Ridgeway only for week-ends or at odd times when Norman was there. Perhaps, for me, the least-expected aspect of the war was this Grosvenor-Road chapter. Ever since that glimpse of my twenty-year-old son bent over the open bonnet of his car, I had thought to see little of him for several years, if indeed I ever saw him alive again; and I never imagined, when we held a stock-

2A

taking in May, 1945, that we should have been more together in the last six years than in all the sixteen before.

"Unless," he observed on the day that the war ended officially in Europe, "I'm sent out to the Far East, I suppose it's all over for us, bar the cheering." He raised his glass to the light and smiled sardonically. "The last time you and I split a bottle of champagne, daddy, was for my coming-of-age. Five years ago now. And the best five years that I can remember. I wouldn't change them for anything! U.W., U.D., B.B.L., . . ."

"I should be more partial to abbreviations," I said, "if I knew what one in fifty stood for. U.W. . . . ?"

"Un-wounded, Un-decorated, But Bloody Lucky. I wonder how many captains, temporary majors, have heard *quite* so few shots fired in anger! I wonder how many 'serving officers' in very nearly six years have done *quite* so much soldiering from a padded chair!"

Even without his obviously sincere admission that he would change nothing in the last five years, I had long believed that Norman was enjoying at least that part of the war which enabled him to devour the books in my work-room at the rate of three volumes a week; and, unless he was cynically hinting that all pleasures had to end some time, I did not understand the unusual bitterness of his tone until, mordantly repeating: "U.W., U.D., B.B.L.," he produced a writing-block and explained that he had been asked to compile his war-record for the headmaster of his preparatory school. Even then I did not understand his mood of self-reproach. After six months' intensive training in various parts of England, he had gone to France in the spring of 1940: as he described it, to be sure, "in comfortable time to be chased out again from Dunkirk". He had then, as soon as he was re-equipped, been sent to the Middle East "in comfortable time to be flown back and popped into hospital". When passed fit for sedentary duty, he was given work at the War Office "in comfortable time to claim a bedroom in Grosvenor Road as soon as the house was put into commission". And there he had passed his heroic days ever since.

"Wasn't there a boy's book," he asked, "called *Deeds That Won the Empire*? I should like to bring it up to date. *My Finest Hour and How I Used It*, by Norman Whimboyne. For all the good I've done, I might just as well have been a conscientious objector."

"About 1915," I recalled, "there was a celebrated recruiting-poster: *What Did You Do In The Great War, Daddy?* In *this* one, with conscription from the start, I feel that the only answer is: 'I did what I was told.' If your superiors see fit to keep you quill-driving in Whitehall . . ."

"I know, I know. And thousands of men must envy me my luck. Do you feel, daddy, that *you've* had a *useful* war? If you do, that may console you for being knocked out of your own work for six solid years. I could let Oxford and any ideas of a career go without a pang if my little efforts had shortened things by five minutes. They didn't. It's no good trying to remake the past, but if I *had* had my damned appendix out at that time . . . What *did* I do in this Great War? Marched valiantly into Belgium and scurried out again like a rabbit! Woke up with a pain in my tummy and wasted a pilot's time bringing me back to England. Sat on my backside, filling up forms and helping illiterate generals with their crosswords. And now it's all over! *Unless*, of course . . ."

"Are you in fact hankering after the Far East?," I asked. "I thought that for many people B.L.A. was interpreted to mean 'Burma looms ahead'."

For answer Norman read me the last line he had written for his record of service.

"'*Demobilized the blank day of blank. Nineteen-forty-blank.*' Thank you, I've no desire to fight the Japs. On the other hand, I've no desire to get into my demob-suit till I see what civilian life can offer a conquering hero. *Not* the civil service, daddy, after these years of passing-to-you-for-necessary-action in the War House! Not that book-shop, if only because my prospective partner has ratted. Didn't I tell you? Tony Charlbury's first love was always teaching; and he's in treaty for a school near Wantage. He would like me to come in with him, but I've no degree yet and I don't see myself going up to Oxford again with a gang of eighteen-year-olds to work for one. Now that it's all over . . . I suppose Barbara and Monica will be bringing their brats home? And Martin will go back to the City. Is Humfrey sticking to the bar? Your most hush-hush committee, I suppose, will die a natural death. The same with mummy's Vamps. . . . D'you mind if I stay on here while I'm looking for a job?"

As he envisaged—piece by piece—the dismantling of the war-machine in its effect on himself and his immediate world, still more as he contrasted an unspectacular career in the army with a most uncertain career in civil life, I felt that Norman, who had extracted at least some excitement from the Dunkirk beaches and some pleasure from his War-Office annexe, was for the first time watching the mist clearing from the landscape of England at peace and that for some reason the prospect dismayed him. When he talked—rather unhappily—about looking for a job, I feared that I might perhaps have frightened him with tales of job-hunting after 1918; but, thinking over his change of tone as he asked whether he might continue to live in Westminster, it occurred to me that he was more dismayed by the prospect of Ridgeway restored to a peace-footing, with his half-brothers and their wives and children creating anew the atmosphere of excessive domesticity that had driven him to divide his Oxford vacations between the London School of Economics and my workroom.

I said that I should be delighted to have him in Grosvenor Road, if he could put up for a while longer with the rough comfort that was the best I had been able to achieve for either of us as a lengthening war intensified the difficulties of service and catering. For the present, I continued, I should have to divide my time between London and the country, as indeed I had been dividing it for half-a-dozen years now, in one peaceful phase living in Grosvenor Road and going to Ridgeway at week-ends to supervise conditions there, in other and more lurid phases living at Ridgeway with my "hush-hush" organization under the same roof and stealing to London at week-ends to see whether my abandoned house was still standing. I might indeed be more in the country, to tidy up after six years of variegated billeting; but I could hold out little hope of tidying up Grosvenor Road at present. When my invaluable Cruikshanks left me to take charge of a hostel and canteen for Violet, I had moved the Winters into their place. The rough comfort that I had mentioned was an improvisation by which Norman and I made our own beds, cooked our own dinners and pinned our hopes for what Violet called "a tolerable standard of dirt and disorder" on the regular arrival of a charwoman.

"In some ways it has been rather fun," said Norman, jumping up with a smiling "*A votre service, m'sieur*," to change our plates. "You never know what you can do till you try, but I didn't think I should live to see you in a hessian apron, scrubbing floors and polishing silver."

"And to most people," I admitted, "it must have seemed misspent labour. I regarded it as a symbol. Over the centuries, Norman, with yawning gaps and glaring anomalies, the English gentry had—in my opinion—reached the highest standard of domestic civilization in the world. The Huns would have battered that out of existence if they'd had their way. When we held 'em, after we'd thrown 'em back, there was still the danger that they might win—through our Fifth-Columnists—by forcing our standards down to theirs. The standards of a gorilla-horde running amok in a native village . . . Once you let your personal fastidiousness go . . . That shocking excuse for slovenliness: 'You seem to forget there's a war on . . .' However, that's only a private obsession of mine."

"I think I share it. And I've *enjoyed* trying my hand at all the things that other people had always done for me. I shall never be any good at sewing, but, honest to God, there are jolly few house-jobs, daddy, that you and I can't do as well as the professionals. Cooking, table-laying, washing-up. I'm not at all sure I shan't offer myself as a single-handed butler. *When* the War House bows me out. And how soon that will be . . . ," he ended with a shrug, his transient gaiety deserting him.

For a few idle minutes, as we set the table for dessert, we exchanged shameful memories of our early adventures in house-craft and agreed that, as grate-cleaning was the domestic duty that we both loved least, we should welcome above all else the advent of a housemaid to undertake this for us.

"Have the Cruikshanks said when they're coming back?," Norman asked, as he sipped the *Château Yquem* that I had opened in honour of our victorious peace.

"They'll be *free* when Violet Oakhirst shuts down her canteen, but how soon that will be . . . Though the war's over in Europe, I believe it will be a long time before we give up communal kitchens, clothing-coupons, even billeting."

"Not to mention food-rationing. Well . . . All things considered, perhaps it will be best if the Cruikshanks stop at their canteen till life generally is more nearly normal. A place like Ridgeway, without a proper staff and with everybody's rations weighed and labelled . . . A sordid, thankless job! I suppose mummy could have done it if she'd had time. Mrs. Cruikshank could have done it if she'd been given a free hand. I did warn you, daddy, after Munich, that you would have to come down and take charge if every one wasn't to get too hopelessly on every one else's nerves . . ."

As he paused, with the old and almost forgotten air of

discomfort that he had shewn before the war in defending his mother to me or justifying me to her, I wondered how much Norman knew or guessed of the friction that had caused the Cruikshanks to give me notice. In six years he had spent little more than six weeks at Ridgeway: one or two on leave before going out to France and, later, to the Near East, one or two after Dunkirk and one or two when he was discharged from hospital after his appendicectomy. For the matter of that, how much had I myself discovered or guessed?

"Did the Cruikshanks make any complaint?," I asked. "The whole business puzzled me. After all, they'd been with your mother since she married the first time; they came on when she married me; and we always got on admirably. *Till* the war. *And* in the early days of *that* they were a tower of strength: when the house was packed and we had all those children and their teachers . . . I should have thought it was good enough war-work for any over-age couple, but they dropped me a hint—oh, before the Battle of France—that they would like something more active. When the schoolchildren left, they became almost insistent. And, when the September *Blitz* began and I moved the Winters down, I really felt that I had no justification for keeping them against their will. They made no complaint to *me*."

"Nor to me. Nor, I would bet any money, to Lady Oak-hirst, but I think she managed to read a bit between the lines."

"She has not confided the result to me."

Norman shrugged his shoulders wearily, as though to pro-claim the futility of any one's ever saying anything to anybody, especially where his own two parents were concerned.

"I should think the trouble began in 1940, when rationing came in," he answered. "If *you'd* been there . . . With all those different people in the house, it was a thing you couldn't possibly leave to a servant and mummy was too busy. If she'd had time, she would have done it to every one's satisfaction. . . . O God, how trivial it all seems! We had more of this, that and the other than we knew what to do with, but because mummy used those blasted 'points' for things we were short of I understand the school-teachers complained she was pinching their rations, to give Martin and Humfrey two meat-meals a day. The Cruikshanks became so sick of the everlasting grumbles that they chucked in their hand. I was away for most of the time, but if they said anything to Lady Oakhirst and if she said anything to you . . ."

I told Norman that, until now, no one had said anything to me. The Cruikshanks had not left till after the last of our refugees: if Elizabeth's handling of other people's ration-books was suspect, they must have feared that, with the children and their teachers gone, she would continue to feed her relatives at the expense of the staff.

"The amount of bad blood this wretched rationing has aroused!," I exclaimed. "But we shan't see the end of it for many a long day yet. Therefore, unless you're prepared to go on roughing it . . ."

" 'Roughing it' be damned! *You* and *I*, daddy . . . I suppose it's because we're *men* . . . The jolly old public-school training . . . Women . . . I suppose no woman really believes that a mere man is capable of looking after himself: otherwise, mummy wouldn't be so keen to come up and take charge here."

"I didn't know she was."

Norman hunted through his tunic-pockets for a crumpled letter and tossed it over to me:

"She suggested it the moment the end of the war came in sight and her Vamps no longer needed her. I believe I was to discuss it with you, as you would be more likely to listen to me. I said it wasn't to be thought of! Good heavens, when I don't know whether my present job will last three weeks or three years! She hates London, anyway! Oh, no! She must stay where she is. If I go to Ridgeway for week-ends, she can see I'm not being starved here. I don't *want* anybody to look after me!," he continued explosively and then apologized for losing his temper. "I know that's damned ungracious, I know mummy has a dull time when she's by herself, I feel a cad for not going down to-night or suggesting that she should come here and join us in our merry-making . . ."

"Won't honour be satisfied," I asked, "if for the present you live here and go to Ridgeway for week-ends?"

"Not in *her* eyes," Norman answered glumly.

II

It was the sole and singular boast of my friend Lord Justice Leighton that he was the best judge of bad brandy in London. While wine-merchants still carried stocks and their customers still kept cellars, Leighton and I used sometimes to meet at Bassetts' or Adamsons' with a row of beakers and a plate of water-biscuits to declare our preferences and to profit by each other's experience. About German wines he had forgotten more than I should ever learn; but, if three brandies were given him to taste, he would say of one:

"This *must* be pretty poor stuff, because I *like* it."

I have sometimes thought that my opinion about the war would have been really valuable if those who discussed it with me had gone away, saying: "Colin Whimboyne is convinced that such-and-such will happen. Therefore it won't." Others, without admitting it, may have been as often wrong; but, thanks to Violet's diary, I have a written and dated record to shew my quality as a prophet from the October day in 1939 when I told Norman that the war would be decided in the air above London or Berlin to the May evening in 1945 when I told him that, as the defeat of Japan would be a task of years, his work at the War Office might continue almost indefinitely.

Of many surprises in these six years the greatest—to every one, I should think—was the discharge of the first atom-bomb; and, for our private lives, I am inclined to think that by hastening the end of the war beyond any one's expectations, it was also the most unsettling. Almost before "V.E. Day" was proclaimed, we civilians at least had adjusted ourselves to the conditions of a new war, but until we had honoured our bond to America it would still be war: Norman might or might not be ordered to the Far East, Martin and Humfrey might or might not continue their activities—in a lately current phrase—as "back-room boys" and Violet's committee on requisitioning might become a committee on "derequisitioning", but our persons and property were still as much at His Majesty's disposal as in the spring of 1940. Elizabeth told me that her V.A.M.P.s would be disbanded as soon as they had been reviewed and thanked by the King, but the organization would still have to be wound up. We were still at war, though a general election threatened us in the very near future.

Counting our domestic blessings, we could indeed say that the black-out was over. A trifling allowance of petrol for pleasure-motoring inspired many of us to plan the first holiday that we had attempted since 1938; but for Norman and me, quartering Cumberland for any hotel that had not been rented by a girls' school or

commandeered by a government department, it was still to be a
war-time holiday, limited to a fortnight, for which we should
equip ourselves with identity-cards, ration-books and our own
towels.

Since the election, however it went, was likely to give me a
new Lord Keeper to train and since Norman apparently judged it
politic to sleep at Ridgeway during the summer months lest his
mother again suggested transferring herself to Grosvenor Road,
it was not till the first week of October that we set out for the
Lakes; and by then the war had ended with the unconditional
surrender of Japan and demobilization was proceeding apace.
As we packed for the journey to Keswick, Norman—sighing
that it had been too good to last—decreed that we must consider
seriously his future activities and added that he had been warned
his present work might have come to an end before he got back.

"It has certainly come sooner than I originally expected," I
said, "but ever since Attlee's announcement of the atomic bomb
in August . . . I'm sorry it didn't come soon enough for both of
us to take as long a holiday as we liked."

"H'm, well . . . I don't know that this is exactly the moment."

He said no more until we were in the train with London and
the London suburbs, the London dormitories and satellite-cities
behind us and were running through the thin belt of timbered
park-land that separated us from the industrial midlands. It was
the first time that I had been as far afield since 1938; and the
imprint of the war lay heavier on the country than on the bombed
towns through which we passed and the scarred tracks that took
us with antiquated rolling-stock and outworn permanent-way
from one to another. Much of the pasture had been ploughed up,
the best trees had been felled and such of the mansions as we
could see were surrounded, three times out of five, by rings of
black huts like inverted fishing-boats. I wondered aloud how soon
these eyesores would be removed; and, for reply, Norman asked
how long I supposed the houses themselves could survive.

"Take Ridgeway!," he challenged me, with a queer explosive-
ness which suggested that he had been bottling this question up
for months or even years. "Even if it lasts your time, daddy, do
you think for one moment that I . . . ? If I didn't love the place,"
he continued, flushing, "I couldn't talk to *you* about . . . Oh, well,
death-duties, but you love it so much too that we *ought* to have a
show-down. I don't want any *figures*! Perhaps I haven't a money-

sense and, if so, I'm *thankful*. The everlasting talk that I hear from Martin and Humfrey and Aunt Kitty and the uncles . . . I don't know whether it's a Cheshunt weakness . . ." Before he could be tempted to complain that his mother was a worse offender than the rest of her family put together, he made haste to say that he was not thinking only of money. "Will places like Ridgeway ever have any servants again?," he asked. "Will people like you ever be able to foot their wage-bill?"

My work at Queen Anne's Gate had kept me in London for most of the summer; but from Norman's accents of exasperation I guessed that, whenever Elizabeth's relations had invited themselves to Wiltshire while he was there, every conversation had tolled the knell of the English country-house. I guessed, too, from the maudlin confidences of Clayton Mandeville when he talked to me for my own good that a fight for the control of Ridgeway was being carried on by everybody with an interest in the house. Never again, he told me, would Elizabeth submit to house-parties of "clever" people to whom she could not talk or of my "fashionable friends", who made her feel inferior; but, as nothing would part me from my "barrack", she hoped to make a tribal home of it for her sons and grandsons. As, however, on the authority of their house-master at Marlborough, it was only the chance of living occasionally on the fringe of "the great world" that had reconciled Martin and Humfrey to spending a single day of their holidays at home, they were insistent that, if I was not going to entertain, I had better sell the place. For Kitty and her brothers, as indeed for Clayton himself, Ridgeway must be the free country-club that they had always made of it when they wanted a week-end or a week or a summer out of London. And Norman—"a peace-at-any-price boy", said his godfather—asked only for the conditions in which he could read and dream and disappear for solitary walks on the Downs and return to congenial society. On some occasion, it seemed, he had told Clayton that his happiest memory of Ridgeway was of a week-end before the war when he had been put to bed with a temperature and Lady Oakhirst and I had sat with him.

Not for the first time I wished that my relations-by-marriage would let me go to the devil or the bankruptcy-court in my own way; but I confined myself to saying that the servant-problem had been exercising my already preoccupied mind ever since our young maids left us in the first year of the war to work in factories;

it had become acute four or five months earlier, when our
"Refugee Brigade" of stopgaps decided that they could now
safely return to London; and, if we failed to solve it, any kind of
country-house life must come to an end. So far, I had to admit,
there had been no time for me to grapple seriously with the
subject or with half-a-dozen others. Whether I was discussing
overdue redecoration with Violet or depleted linen with Mrs.
Winter or glass and china with her husband, I was always brought
up short at the outset by complete inability to say what kind of
life I expected to see any of us living at Ridgeway or anywhere
else.

"Now that Barbara and Monica have brought their boys
back . . . ," I continued, as I began to unpack our luncheon-
basket.

"You won't see much of *them*," Norman prophesied. "I'm
sorry about it, because mummy does so love to have all the family
round her, but Martin and Humfrey have got it into their heads
that she spoils the children. It's true, in a way: she always spoilt
us. . . . And still docs! She has so much love just running to
waste . . ." As though suddenly aware that he had never before
spoken to me of his mother in this vein, he abruptly plunged into
a number of rather crude generalizations about the upbringing of
children and the danger of "mixing one's generations". "Mummy's
ideas about education . . ."

"Fashions change so quickly that it's always a mistake for the
grandparents to interfere. We'll try to avoid that when *your*
time comes, Norman. I suppose it will? The last time we touched
on this subject . . ."

Was it six years or seven since Norman came to me in the
book-room at Ridgeway with the news of yet another international crisis that yet again had made a second European war
inevitable? I could not be sure and I did not think it mattered:
what mattered was that in these six or seven years, when we had
been living together more intimately than ever before, he had
never again discussed himself with me.

"I don't take back anything I said then," he answered reflectively, as he inspected the contents of the luncheon-basket and
opened himself a bottle of beer. "In those days . . . I thought it
was next door to a *crime* for any one in my position to make himself responsible for a wife and children. Now I'm really not sure
that, in the old phrase, it's not worse than a crime: a *blunder*. The

only job I could step into would be Tony Charlbury's prep.-
school at Wantage. It's not the cup of tea I should choose, but it
would please mummy to have me home for week-ends and I
should be earning my keep, even though I could never marry on
an usher's salary. Anything else . . . That new-model book-shop
that we planned so elaborately before the war . . . I came across
Lady Oakhirst's sketches and Tony's estimates the other day. . . .
Well, even if I made a success of it ultimately (which is a big 'if',
when you can't get books for love or money), for years it will be
a bottomless pit of expense. Frankly I can see no justification
under heaven for asking *you* to fill it, daddy."

For a demobilized officer of twenty-six, who had left Oxford
prematurely for the army, to marry on his war-gratuity might
be both a crime and a blunder; but to resign himself to schoolmastering so that his mother might enjoy his society in off hours
seemed an act of insanity.

"You are my only son, Norman," I said. "I too may not have
much of a money-sense, but I've made a certain amount and
I'm only three years off sixty. My precious money won't be much
satisfaction to me if I can't use some of it to give you a start in
life. Whether it's book-selling or holy matrimony or both . . ."
As he was obviously trying to thank me, I spared myself and
perhaps him a moment of hot-cheeked embarrassment by adding
at once: "The one thing I should deplore would be any drifting.
If this book-shop appeals to you seriously, you should make some
enquiries the day after we get back to London . . ."

"I made quite a few the day before I left London. There's
nothing doing in England. Sir Nigel Oakhirst says that if I
started in Johannesburg . . . Lady Oakhirst favours any place in
the south of France with a big English colony: Pau or Menton . . .
I don't know how you would get over the exchange-difficulty . . ."

I felt that Norman need not worry his head with this problem
until it had been faced and solved by the big English colonies
postulated for his book-shop; and, so long as he fluttered con-
versationally from South Africa to the Riviera, occasionally
interrupting himself to say that with the present dearth of paper
it would be somewhat harder to obtain books for export than for
the home market, I suspected that the subject had been introduced
chiefly to shew that he was alive to the need of finding work and
that it had been dismissed to shew that there was at present no
work to be found in this field.

"Perhaps it's just as well," he concluded, with an approving glance at the autumnal landscape that in the midday sunshine seemed to be smiling at him. "I don't *want* to live abroad; and if you think Ridgeway still has a future . . . I sometimes think it's a symbol of the leisured life of a leisured class and that our present rulers are more concerned to smash that than to make any Utopia of their own. They see only the political influence of the country-house world . . ."

"Which was moribund in my father's day," I interposed. " 'The Squirearchy . . .' How many squires could keep the roofs over their heads if they *were* a leisured class? Because my brothers didn't marry heiresses, your grandfather was prepared to let Ridgeway fall down. I was only able to buy it and keep it going all these years by working night and day. Almost literally! My job by day gave me the modest income of a civil servant; my work by night made Grosvenor Road and Ridgeway possible. Any number of men in the same sort of position were doing the same sort of thing: taking directorships in the City or becoming under-writers at Lloyds' so that they could live as country gentlemen at week-ends. It's the only way we can hope to carry on now. If you feel as I do, Norman, that a leisured class is necessary for creating things of beauty and enjoying them and cultivating a spaciousness of outlook for the problems of the day . . ."

"I do! And therefore I must marry money or make it. Which brings me back to my starting-point. As an untrained stopgap in a boys' school . . . Is this Crewe?," he broke off to ask, as he began to repack the luncheon-basket. "If I could ever sleep in a train, I should say: 'Wake me up, please, at Lancaster.' Your Prestons and Warringtons and Wigans . . . How well do you know the Lakes, daddy?"

I said that I had motored wherever it was possible to take a car, but that, as I had walked little and climbed less, I should leave Norman, who had been there on a couple of reading-parties, to decide how we could see most in the time at our disposal. Though he had talked of wanting to discuss his future and to have a "show-down" over the fate of Ridgeway, I felt that he had now said all that he cared to say at present and that I should only spoil a holiday (which he half thought he should not be taking) by warning him a second time against "drifting". As he spread the seat opposite to us with ordnance-maps and planned alternate long and short expeditions for our twelve walking days, he seemed to be saying that, even if this were not the last holiday that we should take together for some years, these were the last weeks of the time that we had spent together, speaking—in an old phrase—as man to man. If he was to lead me "up to Scafell" or "over the Four Passes" or "through Langdale to Bow Fell", as he was industriously plotting in his note-book, I was for a few days longer to guide him as for half-a-dozen years I had guided him round my workroom in Grosvenor Road when he picked out books at random and asked: "This fellow Peacock: ought I to read him?" Long before we reached Penrith, his note-book was as richly filled with names and titles suggested by me as with peaks and tarns that he had decided I must on no account miss.

"I suppose I ought to have been mugging up my Words-worth," he sighed. "It's a pity the old gentleman wrote so much, a greater pity that so much of it is just indifferent prose. At his best . . . I've gone out from Grosvenor Road at all hours of the night to stand on *his* Westminster Bridge. And that thing . . . Is it *The World?*"

" '*A Pagan suckled in a creed outworn'?*," I asked.

"Yes . . . '*Getting and spending, we lay waste our powers*'. Did I tell you that Martin had promised to use his influence if I ever thought of going into Uncle Philip's office? '*Getting and spending*' . . ."

"How did you react?," I asked. "If there's any getting to be done, Philip and Maurice will do it, but I've always understood they were both very good to Martin when he went to them as a very raw schoolboy. As a member of the family in a family business . . ."

As I paused, Norman observed acidly that he feared his admiration and affection for his half-brothers must leave a good deal to be desired.

"I thought their war-service was a poor show," he continued, "but perhaps they're natural cowards and I could no more *blame* a coward than a consumptive. I don't blame them for having both eyes eternally on the main chance: they may have got that from their father." I shook my head at this aspersion on a man whose greatest quality and defect had been that, like some minor Mussolini or Hitler, he had really cared for nothing but the sensation of living dynamically. Norman could hardly have noticed my movement, for he proceeded pensively: "It may be a Cheshunt quality that they've picked up from the uncles. If so, it missed mummy. It's because she's *completely* selfless, asking for *nothing* . . ."

As he stopped abruptly, I began a vague and probably unconvincing defence of a generation that had grown up between the wars to a belief in "Every man for himself". Norman, I suggested, had been too young to mark the crumbling of the new world born, like himself, in 1919 until it crashed in the economic crisis of 1931 which sent Martin and Humfrey from school to seek their fortunes and perhaps persuaded "Old Alec" to let himself out of all his troubles and disappointments while he still retained the strength and courage to unlock the last door of life.

"And now that they've come through alive," said Norman, "it's 'Every man for himself' again. Martin's only comment on his activities for the last six years was that he had made a lot of 'useful contacts'. Humfrey, as you probably know, is going into politics. I don't *mind* it, daddy: if that's the way you're made . . ."

"But you don't want to work with it daily. I never regarded the Stock Exchange as your spiritual home, but for the sake of the money . . ."

"For the sake of *Ridgeway*!," he corrected me. "I was tempted when Martin sounded me after V.E. Day. Perhaps I shall come to it in the end. At the moment I feel that I don't want to be in the same county as any of my relations. Barring you and mummy, of course! And I expressed myself so plainly to many of them that I can't think they'll want me in the same office. You were away that week-end when Barbara and Monica came, for the first time since their return from Canada . . ."

"I'd arranged to be there," I said, "but at the last moment your mother asked me whether I should mind waiting a little for what she called a 'proper celebration'."

Norman asked me whether no one had told me anything about the party.

"It was a *great* affair," he continued ironically. "After all, your cellar hasn't been heavily punished since 1939; and mummy dug out things that she'd been hoarding since Munich. Talk about 'pre-war'! Spanish ham and pickled peaches, champagne to bathe in, chocolates—of all things!—for the children. The *trouble* she'd taken . . . It . . . it . . . it was that," he broke out with a stammer that I had never heard before, "that made me see *red*!"

"You mean that every one took everything for granted?"

His fists clenched and unclenched as he fought to regain his self-control; and I saw his lips moving rhythmically as though he had said to himself: "When you're losing your temper, count twenty before you speak."

"We're running in," he told me, as he jerked round to lift our luggage down from the rack. "Did no one write to complain how *rude* I'd been? I suppose they were all too flabbergasted! It *was* an odd way of speeding the parting guests! I told them how glad I was you hadn't been present. I'd done my best to fill your place. I felt sure you would never want to see any of them inside your house again. I certainly didn't. They made her *cry*, the bloody cads, but I swear I got under their thick hides with some of the things I said. . . . Keswick! I'll lift these out if you'll look for a porter. I'll tell you all about it later, daddy, but, as you haven't heard, I must warn you that I've started a first-class family-row. They'll none of them ever come to Ridgeway again, so you and I shall have to make it up somehow to mummy."

III

HALF-WAY through my holiday in Cumberland, Violet wrote to ask, in general, how Norman and I were getting on and, in particular, whether he had decided what he was going to do with himself when he had been demobilized.

In replying, I described briefly what we had agreed to call my "Lakeland Baptism For Those of Riper Years". It was kept brief from a fear that my enthusiasm would run away with me; but, as Violet had walked the whole district with her father before she married, I could feel sure that she would share reminiscently my mood of intoxication when I tried to recollect in tranquillity my emotion on looking down for the first time, say, on Wasdale from Sty Head or on Ennerdale from the Pillar or on "*all the kingdoms of the world and the glory of them*" as recorded in the devil's third tempting and as shewn me from the summit of Bow Fell.

When I came to write to Norman, I said that I did not think he had yet made up his mind about the future, but that in the last few years he had learnt to keep his own counsel. Of religion and philosophy, of politics and history, of literature and art he would talk with the characteristic gusto of an argumentative freshman and the less characteristic knowledge of a dilettante who had read more widely than most men of his age and had thought somewhat more than he had read; but, where his intimate thoughts and private ethics were concerned, I knew little more of him than in the impulsive days when he motored from Oxford to claim dinner or a bed in Grosvenor Road. We might, for example, debate whether men of his generation would ever know the superficial security that had encouraged me to marry a few weeks after the 1918 armistice had been proclaimed; but he had said no word in the last six days, when we were supposed to be considering his career, or in the six years before that, when I seemed to have won his entire confidence, to indicate whether he was attracted by women or even interested in any woman beyond the few, like his mother and aunts and sisters-in-law, whom he could not help meeting.

In explosive moments I had in fact won his confidence to the extent that he would speak to me as I think he spoke to no one else; but these moments were rare and I could not say with any assurance that he did not always regret them afterwards. On the night of our arrival in Keswick I had been promised the full story of the "first-class family-row" that he had started; but the whole subject seemed to have been forgotten from the moment at bed-time when he tapped the barometer in the hall of our hotel and announced that he would test my powers next day by taking me through the Jaws of Borrowdale to the Honister and home from Buttermere and Crummock Water by Newlands.

And the whole subject seemed to remain forgotten till the beginning of our second week, when we stopped one noon for luncheon in hot October sunshine on the top of Green Gable and he mentioned that he had that morning received a letter which —he most reluctantly supposed—he ought to discuss with me.

"It was from poor mummy," he explained, "about the great Ridgeway bust-up."

"Of which," I reminded him, "I know nothing but the bare fact that there was one."

"It's an unedifying story," Norman sighed, running impatient fingers through his fair, waving hair. "On a long view, the only good the rumpus did was to let *all* of us get certain things off our chests. . . . Of course, a showdown of that kind breaks things that can never be mended. I'm afraid mummy doesn't see that. Even if I felt in the least disposed to apologize . . ."

2B

As he paused, with his under-lip thrust truculently forward, I asked who was thought deserving of an apology.

"Oh, the whole boiling," he answered. "It's Martin and Humfrey that she most wants to placate, for their sakes and their brats', but she can't bear the thought of a breach with her own flesh-and-blood, as she would say, though the uncles—as I told them—only come for what they can get and Aunt Kitty, as I told *her* . . . And now I'm blest if I can remember what I *did* tell her! . . . But, daddy, even without a row, Martin and Humfrey are through with Ridgeway. It isn't that mummy spoils their brats, it's that she spoils *them* and they haven't the gratitude or the grace . . . They've got all that they think worth taking from her and because she never *tries* to be clever . . ." My own charge would have been that Elizabeth never tried even to be intelligent outside her severely limited range of infant-welfare and motor-patrols; I should have expected Norman to be more quickly bored by her mental triviality than his less cultured half-brothers; but, when he now asked with a frown whether I thought that he and I were lacking in intellectual snobbishness, I felt that he had achieved a toleration rather beyond his years. "I *don't* feel superior to the Duke of Wellington," he continued, "because he came to grief over his Latin quantities; his French accent, if he had one, couldn't be worse than mine. If I expected people to be literary, they might expect me to be musical, which would never do. Mummy has never *pretended* to be a high-brow. She's a simple, loving, homely soul. The pomp and circumstance of Ridgeway mean nothing to her, but as a place where she can gather the sneering, ungrateful parasites that she remembers as simple, loving, homely souls before they became rich snobs . . . I'm surprised Aunt Kitty hasn't written to you about me."

"Was the row with her?"

I asked the question with misgiving, for I thought that Kitty of all my sisters-in-law would make the worst enemy. If now too haggard and nerve-racked to be still the handsomest of the Cheshunt sisters, she was still the most vital and occasionally, in conversation, the most brilliant; but as Marchioness of Studland she seemed no happier than as Mrs. Mandeville, her stormy passage through life was scarred with purposeless quarrels and unforgiving feuds, I dreaded her visits to Ridgeway and, if I was careful to avoid a break, I only put up with her for fear of what her reckless tongue might say of Violet and me.

"It was with every one," Norman answered, "but it started with her. Started when she complained that her coffee had been tepid. I told her that there were ten breakfasts to prepare every morning, ten trays to carry up and that mummy had done every blinking thing with her own two hands. Aunt Kitty said it was her own fault for not getting proper servants. I let fly with something that I've completely forgotten, but something that *rowelled* her into whispering across me to Martin: 'Has your brother been at the *bottle*?' I whispered across to Humfrey: 'Has your aunt been at the needle *already*?' "

"Good God!," I ejaculated.

Norman nodded sombrely:

"I know, I know! As I said it, I was thinking what wet tissue-paper our mantle of good breeding is when we're really roused. There was something in me that I just didn't recognize. Daddy, you remember your drug-addict in *Flowers By Request*: was she taken at all from Aunt Kitty? I'd sort of wondered for years, whenever I came up against her raw nerves and vile temper . . ."

"The idea has never entered my head!"

"No? Then I think you must let it enter now. She wouldn't have become such a hell's fury if she hadn't seen I'd found her out. Why doping should be worse than drinking, which was what she'd charged me with . . . Well, after that we all said what we'd all been suppressing all our lives. *Not* edifying, as I told you. And now poor mummy thinks that a suitable expression of regret on my part . . . We're far, *far* beyond that! Aunt Kitty will come back without any apology from me when she wants some one to work off her nerves on. The uncles will forgive and forget when it suits them. But Martin and Humfrey have got what they were looking for. Mummy's a squeezed orange to them! They wanted an excuse for chucking her away. Oh, they'll send her Christmas cards and flowers on her birthday, but *I've* been the means of separating her from two, four, six of the people she loves best in the world. One really ought to control one's temper! I don't know what to say to her letter!"

I asked Norman whether he had brought it with him, but he answered with a second outthrust of his lower lip that he had burnt it after a single reading.

"I now understand," I observed, "your reluctance to join Martin in your uncles' business."

"He'll forgive and forget quickly enough, too, if the firm

really needs another young partner. At the moment that doesn't happen to be what I want. I had another letter from Tony Charlbury the other day . . ."

Guessing only too well what was coming, I strove to affect a sympathetic manner for the moment when Norman should tell me that he was becoming a schoolmaster. It would be a temporary arrangement, he announced at the outset, if indeed anything came of it; and he could not pledge himself elsewhere while he was still on the active list. Charlbury was so desperately short of staff that, as in the parable of the vineyard, he would take in labourers at the eleventh hour and pay them a full term's salary; Norman would not be required to "teach the little beasts football" and it really seemed that, the more he resisted his friend's entreaties, the more monstrous he could make his own terms. Already there was an undertaking that, if he could get the necessary petrol, he might live at Ridgeway and motor daily to Wantage.

"Barring Saturdays," he added. "And, of course, Sundays."

"Does the thing appeal to you at *all*?," I asked him.

"How many people find jobs that really appeal to them?," he fenced. "For its own sake I wouldn't touch schoolmastering with a pole, but if it carries certain special advantages, if I've had the misfortune to smash something that I should like to replace . . ."

As he talked, I found myself reflecting that, in a fairly long experience of the theatre, the saddest sight I could reall was that of a talented actor carrying a play that was unworthy of him. Norman was gallantly doing his best with a part that he felt to be wholly false; I think he suspected that I too felt it to be false; and, when at last he stopped in mid-sentence, his shrug seemed to ask whether either of us thought it was worth while to go on.

"From what you've told me of the Ridgeway row," I said, "you seem to be taking responsibility for certain things that were *not* the consequences of anything you said or did. Martin and Humfrey broke away before and they only went back—to be choked with cream, if you like—because it suited them to have a country-house for their wives at week-ends and a bolt-hole from London in the war. The truth is that they've grown apart . . ."

" '*The good are so harsh to the clever*'," Norman quoted. "Mummy disapproves of Barbara and Monica because they're so 'modern' that they *have* to call a spade a 'bloody shovel'. Or perhaps she kids herself that they've driven a wedge between their husbands and her. She doesn't *always* hide her feelings, either. '*The good are so harsh to the clever. The clever so* rude *to the good'*. They're not as openly rude as Martin and Humfrey, but they don't *ever* hide their feelings. Call it 'growing apart', if you like . . . Uncle Clayton told me that their father had 'grown apart' from mummy till he had to give a dinner-party seven nights a week to avoid being alone with her. The *fact*, however you wrap it up, is that they've walked out. I'm not worrying about Aunt Kitty and the uncles."

As he stopped to point at a black shadow racing up the side of Great End, I wondered how much more Clayton Mandeville had seen fit to tell Norman about Austin Gerrold.

"Are you expecting a storm?," I asked, turning to look at the clouds that had hidden the sun and were throwing this dark carpet on the mountains.

"No, but I always love to watch these shadows on the hillside. It reminds me of the first night I slept out here. Voluntarily, I mean: in my still short experience I'd been caught often enough in a mist and, quite frankly, I disliked it more than most things. On Blencathra, for instance, you run a good chance of breaking your neck if you move and a better chance of getting pneumonia with only a sweat-sodden shirt and shorts to protect you from a northerly gale. I'm still a bit frightened if I'm caught far from a track when the light's going and the clouds are coming down. I wanted to see whether I should be frightened just by spending a night alone, miles from anywhere. I don't quite know *what* you would call the loneliest part of the Lakes: I picked on a place between Pillar and the Haycock."

"And were you in fact frightened?"

"Not in the least! I was *startled* at being called in the morning by an inquisitive sheep, but I don't mind being alone. When night fell, it was just like what you saw a minute ago, only much slower: a tidal wave of darkness gently flooding the valleys. And, when the sun rose, it was like what you're seeing now: the flood-waters or the pall or the carpet being slowly, gently drawn back by a gigantic invisible hand. I never minded being alone in Grosvenor Road during the war. Raids I disliked, because they always gave me a headache. Poor mummy's absolutely terrified of being alone."

I had hoped, as Norman began to talk of the mountains with the shining eyes of a young lover, that he had accepted my estimate of his own limited responsibility for the late unpleas-antness at Ridgeway and of his half-brothers' declaration of independence for which he had no responsibility at all. It had saddened me to hear of his even contemplating work that he detested; and it saddened me more now to find him treating this uncongenial work as the price that he could and perhaps would and certainly should pay to spare Elizabeth the terror of being alone.

"I was just wondering," I said after an uncomfortable silence, "when—if ever—your mother was in fact alone. Before she married, as one of a big family . . . Afterwards with a husband and children and servants . . ."

"It's more than a question of being by yourself in an empty house or even a crowded hotel. I daresay the crowded hotel is worse, if you're made that way. Look here, daddy, this is really *your* job! As a student of psychology . . . I can't express myself properly, because I don't feel that way myself. I think I can *imagine*, though . . . Yes, by Jove, if I landed by parachute in Russia or Tibet, where I couldn't speak a word of the language or read a letter of a street sign, where the people were different in race and features and habits and faith! I *should* feel I was alone! And I think I should be scared the whole time. As mummy," he added almost inaudibly, "has been scared pretty well the whole of her life . . . I suppose she didn't feel quite alone when we were all babies. . . . Unfortunately, babies grow up, grow apart. . . . If you're made that way, daddy, it must be pretty grim to feel yourself aging, to watch other people dying off, to wonder what it will be like if you're left to *die* alone . . ."

It was no longer the good actor exhausting himself to vitalize a bad part. As Norman paused now, his shrug seemed to ask whether it was worth my while to go on when he had posed an unanswerable question.

"How long . . . ?," I began.

"Oh, I've no intention of remaining an usher all my life. If I take this job, I may be able to help mummy through rather a difficult time. We're agreed that, if I'm to keep Ridgeway going, I shall have to make money. I suppose, if I could bring myself to eat humble-pie and go into the City . . . It would mean living in London, wouldn't it?"

A sudden note of eagerness, reminding me of the night when he had declared that he would change nothing in the last six years, suggested that this question should have been put in the form: "*I shall be able to go on living in London, shan't I?*" I heard an answering note of eagerness in my own voice as I assured him that he could not possibly live in Wiltshire and work five days a week in a London stockbroker's office. When he married or—like his half-brothers—set up for himself in bachelor quarters, I must resign myself—like any other father with a grown-up son—to losing him; but, as I was moved to tell him, until this moment I do not think I had at all grasped how much I should miss him.

And, despite the evidence of my own senses, despite Violet's warning that—on his own admission—Elizabeth was "fussing him into an early grave", I had not until this moment at all grasped how much he had always dreaded being alone at Ridgeway with his too solicitous mother nor how much more—even to help her through rather a difficult time—he dreaded being alone with her as she discovered—and did not fail to tell him—that with her other sons and their wives and children gone he was now all that she had left.

"I need hardly say," I told him, "that you will be more than welcome in Grosvenor Road as long as you like to live there. If you continue to spend your week-ends at Ridgeway, nobody can say I'm monopolizing you." As always, I tried to avoid criticizing Elizabeth adversely, even to the extent of saying that her protective love—like that of many mothers—tended to be possessive or that—perhaps like most parents—she could not easily persuade herself that a lately helpless child could ever stand on its own feet; but within the last few minutes we had achieved an intimacy which emboldened me to warn Norman that, if a rivalry ever developed between Ridgeway House and Grosvenor Road, he would be wise to give a wide berth to both.

"You may have to take a leaf out of King Solomon's book . . .," I continued.

"By cutting myself in two . . . ? It's tremendously flattering, of course, to be so much in demand, but I don't feel *that* is a *real* solution. . . . Perhaps if I made the offer . . . If one of you said: 'Half a dead Norman is better than nothing . . .' If the other said: 'I resign my claim! Don't *let* him cut himself in two . . .' That was Solomon's way, wasn't it? of finding the real mother . . ."

As he paused, I said that with a son of twenty-six I had no claim to resign, but that, if he could not please us both, he should harden his heart to pleasing neither.

"When you marry," I went on, "you will leave your father *and* mother and cleave to your *wife*. I know you sometimes talk as though you would never marry. And I don't see how you *can*, if you deliberately take a job that won't support a wife. It all comes back to Ridgeway, doesn't it? If you want to keep that going when I'm dead, if you want your son to succeed you . . ."

"I wonder how mummy would take it if I told her I was engaged."

"If she thought you were going to be happy . . ."

Glancing at the watch on his wrist, Norman jumped to his feet and announced that, if we were going to attack Kirk Fell, we ought to be starting. As he studied his map and pointed the way that we were to go, his voice rose and I had a queer feeling that his conscious mind was shouting down his unconscious.

And, if I was right, his unconscious mind was saying:

"*She*'ll never let you marry! She'll never admit that any one *could* make you happy! If she can't stop it, she'll fawn on your wife as she fawned on Barbara and Monica, but she'll stick at nothing to stop it!"

Meanwhile, the conscious mind was grumbling loudly that we had wasted more daylight than we could afford by taking the best part of two hours over our luncheon.

"Shall I finish what I was beginning to say?," I asked. "If, without waiting to marry or even to become engaged, you think you would be more comfortable by setting up on your own, I shan't blame you . . ."

"Would you blame me if I set up *not* on my own?," he demanded harshly. "Mummy would call it 'living in sin', I suppose."

Had I fancied that it would do any good, I should have said: "*And she would have only herself to thank for driving you to it*," possibly even "*for having already driven you to it*." In fact, perhaps pusillanimously, I replied:

"I don't suppose I should know anything about it. Certainly I'm not such a bigot about marriage that I should *blame* you. It would hardly help to solve the future of Ridgeway, but that's a thing we can discuss some other time."

IV

IF my memory can be trusted, the Imperial Parliament at the end of the First World-War had to pass a short act to define officially when the war had ended. I do not recall that this was found necessary after the Second World-War; but, whatever date had been adopted for legal purposes, the end—for me—did not come with "V.E. Day" and the death-rattle of my planning-committee nor with "V.J. Day" and my Rip-van-Winkle return to Queen Anne's Gate, but with the day when Norman and I made our way back to London after our enchanted fortnight in Cumberland.

For him too it was the end of a war that for six years had dispensed him from grappling with personal questions to which there might be no answer and to which there was certainly no answer that satisfied him; and, as we collected our letters for the last time before going to the station, I felt that many of my correspondents must have said that the war had really ended with my holiday and that, as my holiday had now ended, they must explain at once what their own plans were for a world at peace and enquire about mine. "*Now that it is possible to look ahead . . .*" or some very similar phrase gave the note to four of my letters out of five.

Our journey from Keswick to Penrith reminded me of my journeys back to school more than forty years ago, when my melancholy young friends and I tried to pierce the gloom of a new term to its silver lining by speculating who the house-monitors would be and canvassing our prospects of having been promoted to a study.

As he had expected, Norman's work at the War Office was over; and he could equip himself with his demobilization-suit as soon as he pleased. As he had led me to expect, his friend Charlbury was clamouring for his services even half-way through the school-term; and he had apparently agreed to work at Wantage till the following Easter on condition that he was not asked to remain a day longer.

"It's better than nothing for him," he explained, as we waited at Penrith for the Carlisle train, "and it will suit me while we see how things arrange themselves at Ridgeway. If I'm there during the term, mummy can't grudge me London in the holidays. It goes without saying that I shall come home for Christmas . . ."

"I don't know what kind of party we shall attempt," I said, "with no proper staff . . ."

"I can guess what kind of party you'll achieve! That's my reason for promising to be there. It will be the great test, but I'm prepared to bet it will be only us three."

My letters, as I began to open them, made me less sure. Though I seemed to have heard from most of Elizabeth's relations, only Kitty alluded to the recent eruption at Ridgeway and I feel she had been at pains to shew that she was thinking of every one but herself in venturing to drop me a hint about Norman. While she could protect herself against the rudest of hobbledehoys, it was a pity for boys to become quarrelsome in their cups and a greater pity for them to be filling the wine-cup so early in the morning. For once in her life she agreed with Rella that to have sherry and port standing all day in the hall was to put unnecessary temptation in young people's way. It was, of course, no affair of hers, but others—notably Maurice and Philip —had commented on Norman's failing and had wondered whether I had perhaps not noticed it.

It would have been hard, I thought, to compress more venom into fewer words.

My brothers-in-law magnanimously ignored the insults that had been showered on them and reasoned with me patiently on blind alleys in general and assistant-masterships at small preparatory-schools in particular. They could offer something better if I could persuade my sometimes stubborn son to accept it. Martin and Humfrey pressed the same point from a different side, which I might possibly have overlooked. Did I know anything of Charlbury and his select academy for the backward and difficult sons of freaks? Barbara and Monica had inspected the school with a view to sending their own boys there and had discovered it to be in effect a private home for youthful neurotics who were too "sensitive" for normal establishments.

"*I hear,*" Martin continued, "*that Charlbury means to make a co-ed place of it. He's such a crank that he's quite capable of turning it into a nudist colony. It's an odd job for Major Whimboyne, of Ridgeway, to be taking on! If you feel, as Humfrey and I do, that it's a let-down for the family, it seems only fair to put you wise. By the way, if Norman is deciding definitely against the City, we shall have to look out for an authorized clerk. I simply haven't time to hang about in the House all day.*"

I pocketed the letter with no more comment than that Norman's half-brothers, like his uncles, would come to Ridgeway if and when it suited their convenience; I thought it would suit

the convenience of them all to take in a young partner who would
set them free from buying and selling, to stroll gracefully along
the primrose path of "big business", and I thought it might well
suit Norman's convenience to join them when he had completed his term of self-imposed duty at Ridgeway and had
discovered for himself that his mother would grudge bitterly
every week of holiday that he spent with me in London.

Was he discovering this already? As we steamed out of
Penrith, he threw himself into the seat next to mine and informed
me that on second thoughts he had decided to "give Grosvenor
Road a miss" when he came to London. He could always get a
bed in a friend's flat down Chelsea way and, though he could not
admit that his mother was jealous of me, we agreed that her love
was possessive and he felt sure that it would be more comfortable for all three of us if neither she nor I kept a tally of the days
that he spent with the other. His letters that morning, it seemed,
had included another from her; and I gathered that for Elizabeth,
too, the war was ending this week with the disbanding of her
V.A.M.P.s. What plans were we any of us making? If Norman
intended to be at Ridgeway, she would do her best to look after
him, though the servant-difficulty made it utterly impossible to
recreate the style in which we had all lived before the war; if on
the other hand I could be persuaded to get rid of a house that was
now too big for all of us, she would transfer herself to London.

"You don't really want that, do you?," he asked. "After all
these years? But it's what will happen unless I strike out a line
of my own. Jealousy is an odd thing. . . . Do you suppose that
Aunt Kitty is *jealous* of mummy?"

"Kitty hasn't a great deal to *shew* for her life . . . ," I conceded cautiously.

"And therefore everything that poor mummy has done must
be disparaged! D'you know her second-in-command in the
Vamps, Mrs. Murgatroyd? If she isn't just a cat who can't help
being a cat, she's a damned disloyal friend and neighbour. When
Aunt Kitty had exhausted her own ammunition, she began to
quote Mrs. Murgatroyd. The juvenile court? But every one
knew, Mrs. Murgatroyd (who had sat with her) could *tell* me: a
rare *bustle*, but no *method*, no real *knowledge*, *less* than no willingness to take a decision and the strangest irresponsibility when
something more important came along. She had dropped the
juvenile court like a hot coal when she saw a chance of getting

into uniform and playing at soldiers. Incidentally—as a back-hander for me—that eighteen-hour day at the office, the sandwich-meals and the truckle-bed behind the screen were just dope to keep her from thinking of her gallant boys: the V.A.M.P.s were left to take care of themselves when dear Norman came on leave."

I confessed that I knew little of Elizabeth's qualities as commandant, but I felt sure that, if Kitty had been given the position, the V.A.M.P.s would have mutinied.

"I said something of the kind," Norman answered, "when she began to bite the hand that had just been feeding her. Every one *knew*, Mrs. Murgatroyd could give me a *hundred* instances, that 'poor Rella' knew nothing about running a house and cared less: she had always left the Cruikshanks to arrange everything and engage the other servants. . . . Well, you once told me, daddy, that, when Aunt Kitty took over the lease of mummy's old house, she took over the furniture and staff as well and that every servant had left at the end of a month. I suppose you haven't heard when the Cruikshanks are coming back? We can't go *on* at Ridgeway with about one and a half women coming in by the day and mummy trying to do everything else. Those infernal breakfast-trays, which started all the row! *Ten* of them!"

"I had a letter this morning from Violet Oakhirst," I answered. "She says: '*I feel the war's really over now that my committee work is closing down. The canteen continues, but if you want the Cruik-shanks back and if they want to come . . .*' By the way, Violet wants me to dine with her to-night and discuss some business. You told me you were dining with this friend of yours in Chelsea? If I can send a telegram from Lancaster or Preston . . ."

While Norman studied the time-table, I read the last of my letters and began a reply to Violet. For Nigel Oakhirst too the war had ended that week with the end of his war-time shipping-committee. What the next week would bring or be made to bring he seemed as vague and undecided as any of us; but, since Violet reported that her committee-work—not her committee—was closing down, I thought it likely enough that she had resigned and was returning to her own long-neglected office in Old Burlington Street. Was Nigel going back to his house on South-ampton Water? When it was judged safe for him to emerge from his underground shelter, he had been allowed to sleep in Barton Street and I thought it likely enough that he was asserting a claim to remain there, even that he was urging his directors to have him transferred to London and that the one-time "wife of Sir Nigel Oakhirst" was reminding the present "husband of Violet Oakhirst" that the existence of "Violet Oakhirst Limited" had made her possibly the dominant, certainly an independent, partner in the Oakhirst establishment. I should doubtless hear all about that after dinner; and at dinner itself she would doubtless elucidate her hint about the Cruikshanks.

"They would put their eyes on sticks for you," her letter continued, *"and they would equip Ridgeway with a complete staff from the canteen if they could feel sure that it would be like the old days and that Elizabeth wouldn't interfere as she was doing in the war. I don't know whether you want the old days back when only a millionaire can pay the present wages and you can't get food for entertaining and Elizabeth is grimly resolved to put a spoke in your wheel if you try. Your last letter told me a little about poor Saint Norman and the family-row, but I really believe I can tell you a great deal more. If you feel like writing a pure farce, I can give you all the material from my standpoint as universal confidante for the entire Cheshunt-Gerrold-Whimboyne tangle of families. I've had them all on my doorstep in the last three weeks, all with persuasive little speeches that I'm to make on their behalf to you."*

What followed immediately did not tell me much that I had not suspected already: as I had said a few days earlier to Norman, everything hinged on Ridgeway. Since Elizabeth knew in her heart that she had lost Martin and Humfrey for good, she would cling the more fiercely to the son who remained; and, if their future was not to be a life-long orgy of coddling and being coddled, I must provide diversions to save Norman from a mother who would quickly drive him distracted as well as ruining his chances of making a career for himself or marrying a wife. At all costs she must not be allowed to make servant-problems an excuse for keeping Norman in solitary confinement; he must not be allowed to suffer for the family-row.

"Didn't the Gilbert-and-Sullivan partnership," she continued, *"break down over a carpet? You must not let your three lives be broken up over a breakfast-tray! If there's anything in Humfrey's idea that Norman is in earnest over the damsel that he has been seen about with . . ."*

I pocketed the letter, to finish reading later, as we ran into Lancaster and Norman offered to send off my telegram with one of his own.

"And when I come back," he added, "I shall say: 'Wake me up in time for luncheon, but don't let's lunch till we're out of industrial Lancashire.' I wish we were going the other way, daddy! Lifting up our eyes for the first time to the hills, whence cometh our salvation. Do *you* get that feeling at all . . .?"

"So much so that I felt strongly tempted to reserve the same rooms for next year. I'm a novice, with a novice's perhaps excessive enthusiasm, but I've never met anything like the sense of peace as you walk up and up one of those enchanting valleys, to the sound of running water that becomes fainter and fainter as you approach the source, farther and farther away from the last and remotest farm or bridge or road, beyond the final mountain-ash, into the wind and—most probably—the drenching white cloud at the head of the pass . . ."

"I find that wind and rain so *cleansing* . . .," Norman muttered; then, like a waking dreamer, he asked: "Did you in fact book rooms?"

"I thought you might like different headquarters another year. If you felt like saddling yourself with me again, that is. There's nothing *I* should like better. Perhaps in twelve months' time we shall have enough petrol to bring a car. Incidentally, this is all unknown country to your mother . . ."

As Norman jumped out, calling back over his shoulder that I must not let the train start without him, I felt that he was not sorry to cut short any discussion of what any of us might be doing in a year's time. He too had enjoyed every moment of our holiday, but it was over. Perhaps he resented the reminder that we could not quite ignore Elizabeth in laying plans for twelve months ahead. Perhaps he was saying, as I found myself saying, that by not engaging accommodation I had thrown away an opportunity that would not return.

"An accomplished fact," I murmured, "against a put-up job. Rooms booked by me before he knew anything about it as against rooms booked after I'd hinted that, if we weren't careful, his mother would attach herself to the party. Rather than that, he would forgo the holiday. Rather than make Elizabeth jealous of me, he's reluctantly giving up his room in Grosvenor Road and joining a friend in Chelsea."

And, for all I knew, rather than fight Elizabeth for the right to choose a wife for himself, he was planning a secret life with some girl whose very existence had been a secret to me till this moment. Small wonder that he had looked as though he could hardly bear my praise of the peace that we had left behind.

When he came back to the train, he lingered for some minutes in the corridor and, as I watched him staring moodily north towards the mountains that had brought him healing, I felt he was asking himself whether he would ever see them again and saying, as I was beginning to say and perhaps with the same pang, that he would not see them again with me alone. When at last he threw himself into the seat next mine, his first act—as on our journey up—was to spread out a map of the Lake District; and, when he asked me to give him particulars of hire-service from *The Times*, I guessed that he was brooding over my remark that all this country was unknown to his mother.

"D'you suppose the petrol-position *will* be any better next year?," he asked. "I've been told the trouble is more political than economic. As motoring for pleasure is a luxury of 'the rich', it mustn't be indulged while any necessities are in short supply."

"I was agreeably surprised," I said, "to find the enormous area we could cover from Keswick by motor-bus. Buttermere in one direction, Ambleside and Langdale in another . . ."

"With a hefty walk back sometimes! It was all right for us, but you couldn't take mummy from Dungeon Ghyl, say, over the Stake or Esk Hause . . ."

"Are you working out what can be done by road alone?"

As for me on our journey north, Norman was making a list of sights that his mother must on no account miss.

"She *might* like it," he muttered doubtfully. "Any way it's worth trying. O God, isn't *anything* worth *trying*?"

"You feel she has a dull time when we go away like this?"

"I feel . . . Oh, I suppose I can't get the damned family-row out of my head! Every one pulling in a different direction! I've been thinking . . . For the first time, you may say . . . It *can't* have been easy for you, daddy, . . . Another man's children . . . And a mother with very definite ideas about bringing them up . . . I suppose it was inevitable . . . and *right* . . . that you should go on your own ways. . . . You and she were never really interested in the same things. If I'd been in your place . . . I hope this doesn't sound the most awful cheek! I should have done much the same. Live and let live. If you can't agree, you can agree to differ. The result, though . . . I don't say we're all fighting for our own hands, but we do seem to go our own ways. I wonder whether *that's* right. Surely there are *some* things that you and mummy and I have in common? Things we can share? Let's *try*, at any rate! At Ridgeway, in London, over a holiday up here . . .or somewhere *else*, if she would prefer it. Fair's fair. If we *don't* . . . But surely we can? You're the easiest-going person I've ever met! Half the time I don't think of you as a *father*! Let's *try*!" he repeated. "If we fail . . . Have you ever smoked opium? Nor have I, but I think I shall take to it."

V

SINCE the afternoon—more than a quarter of a century ago now—when Violet flew back from France in answer to the telegram in which I had told her of Norman's birth and of the fact that it made no difference of any kind in my relations with Elizabeth, we had always contrived to meet for dinner on the first night that we both found ourselves in London after our summer holidays. The pleasant ritual was unaffected by the chance that we sometimes spent the holidays together or that one or both of us sometimes went without a holiday. If we could not discuss what we had done together or apart, we could discuss— even in the war-years—what we should have liked to do if we had been able to take even a week's leave; and we could then talk about what we intended to do in the coming twelve months.

In many ways, I used to think, our new year really began at the beginning of October. For long enough I was reporting that Martin had just gone for the first time to a preparatory school, or that Humfrey had joined him for his first term at Marlborough or that within the next week or two Norman would be going into residence at Oxford. More often than not, far more often than not, I came back to Grosvenor Road with the rough idea or even the finished *scenario* of a new play; and, when a so-called autumn season became a regular part of London's social life, the greater number of these twenty-five odd years saw a new comedy of mine going into rehearsal.

Though we always met later for a more traditional stock-taking on New Year's Eve, it was usually in the autumn (when it could not be avoided altogether) that we discussed the latest activities of Nigel or the generally unchanging inactivity of Elizabeth. As a rule we dined at my house, though I had gone to Violet's for some years when I was without servants; sooner or later, one of us would recall our unforgettable drive into London from the Hounslow aerodrome in 1919; and always we ended with a toast to the year that lay ahead of us. Even in 1940 we were able to say from our hearts that, if 1941 were no worse, we should still be counting our blessings in twelve months' time.

"I hope and trust we shall be doing that in 1946," said Violet, when I arrived in Barton Street on my return from Cumberland, "but, like 'Alice', one has to run faster and faster just to remain where one was."

"From the experience of the last fortnight," I replied, "Norman would tell you that for an elderly man of sedentary habits my wind is rather surprisingly good."

"And from the experience of a life-time I want you to tell me everything about Norman."

I promised to do my best; and in the course of dinner I gave Violet almost a word-for-word reproduction of the few and fairly brief conversations that had taken place when some letter from without or some twinge of mental dyspepsia from within came to disturb our holiday trance. At the beginning I warned her to expect nothing subtle, since I regarded Norman as an essentially simple person; summing up at the end, I invited her to regard him—in a phrase which I thought might be useful—as a man with too much *cosmos* in his *ego*.

"Nowadays you won't hear many parents making that complaint about their sons," I concluded. "One sometimes talks of people who look as if they had the cares of all the world on their shoulders; and perhaps, if you substitute 'responsibilities' for 'cares' . . . Because Martin and Humfrey have walked out of their mother's life, Norman feels responsible for making it up to her. Because his friend Charlbury might have helped him in one way and now needs all the help he can get in another . . . Because he'll be *responsible* for Ridgeway when I'm gone, though he *loathes* the idea of the Stock Exchange . . . When he talked about smoking opium, I nearly said that he would at least be following his *own* inclinations for once."

2C

Violet shook her head and bent to blow out the candles before we went up to the drawing-room.

"For that, my dear, you must have a certain hardness or stupidity or certainty of yourself that he doesn't possess. *I* have the hardness and Elizabeth has the stupidity and you have the certainty. Whatever other people may think, *we're* never in two minds about our duty to society and to ourselves."

And where Norman had got his excessive tenderness of heart I could not imagine, but I felt I could never forget his expression as he talked that day on Green Gable of loneliness and fear. "Pretty grim if you're left to *die* alone . . ." He would be so compassionate, I told Violet, both to a murderer and to the murderer's victim that he would confess to a crime he had never committed if that would make things any more comfortable for anybody.

"Well . . . I hope he sticks to what he has said about leaving this school at Easter," she sighed, "but he's going to have a difficult time *till* then, Colin, and you and I must help him."

Looking back on the years that Norman and I had lived by ourselves, I suggested that this might be more easily said than done. He had learnt to keep his own counsel; and he had developed an inflexibility which made it quite impossible for me at least to turn him from his purpose.

"And, Colin, I only want us to *give* him a purpose! If he can be persuaded to feel that Ridgeway and the money to keep it up and a wife and a son to succeed him are his job in life . . . *Not* to comfort his mother or be an intellectual companion to you . . . He said nothing about this girl he's been taking about? Well, it will be something if he can meet her in the holidays, but I'm really thinking of term-time. You'll have to be at Ridgeway more, to give him a respite from Elizabeth."

"You don't think that *will* mean the perpetual tug-of-war you've so often warned me to avoid?"

"Not if the emphasis is on the *place*. The house has been untouched for five years; and it was rather neglected for five years before that, when we were all wondering about another war. As for the garden, since every one was urged to dig for victory . . . Your first duty, now that we're at peace, is to make everything shipshape; and Norman's first duty, as your heir, is to help you. If he makes this his great interest to which everybody and everything else are subordinated . . . I'll gladly undertake the decoration again in return for board and lodging. It may prevent your perpetual tug-of-war to have an outsider there. And, whether I'm useful or not to Norman or you, I can tell you now that you'll be exceedingly useful to me. Don't they speak of a standing counsel at the bar? If I could be your *resident* standing counsel . . ."

It was characteristic of Violet, I thought, that she should hint at the solution of a problem before admitting that there was a problem to solve, yet more deeply characteristic that she should not touch on her own troubles till she had addressed herself to Norman's and mine.

"What has Nigel been up to now?," I asked.

"The lease of this place runs out in March. It's in his name, though of course I've been paying the rent ever since I packed him off to the Spice Coast. He told me casually the other day that he had renewed it for seven—fourteen—twenty-one years."

"What about the house near Southampton?"

"In his state of health he can't fend for himself under present conditions. In all probability, too, his future work would be in London." Perhaps unconsciously, Violet had been imitating Nigel, now innocently off-hand, now studiedly pathetic, now briskly businesslike; as she began to quote his words, her tone changed from wheedling to reasoning and from reasoning to whining: " 'Isn't it time for you to drop the feud after all these years? We've shewn that it's quite possible for us to live under the same roof without fighting. Unless you're modelling yourself on "Irene" in the *Forsyte Saga* . . .' "

As she stopped herself in disgust, I asked whether Nigel fancied that he was modelling himself on "Soames", who at least had been obsessed by his lost piece of human property.

"I expect it's my fault," I continued, "but to me 'Irene' is the one character that needed to be sympathetic and that John completely failed to make sympathetic."

"*I* thought so till Nigel dragged her in," Violet answered. "Then I saw her in a new light. It wasn't the fact that 'the man of property' had treated her as something that you buy and sell, it was that she had never been in love with him, that he bored and antagonized her, that she was in love at different times with two other men and that, if she even pretended to tolerate 'Soames', they would fade out of her life and take all her chance of happiness with them. I know that's not how Galsworthy saw

'Irene', but it's how I see myself." Her eyes rested for a moment on the portrait that McEvoy had painted of her for a wedding-present. "You don't suppose, Colin, that after all these years I harbour a *grudge* against Nigel or his little lights of love? I resent him for himself and for what he might do if I gave him the chance. I wouldn't take him back if you told me *you* were settling at the South Pole for the rest of your life! As I think we both hope that the rest of our lives are going to be very like the last few years . . ."

As she paused, out of breath, I asked where Nigel now was and what she had done.

"I resigned from my committee," she told me, "and reported for regular duty in Old Burlington Street that day. As nearly all the furniture is mine, I *could* have packed it into a pantechnicon and left him alone with his glorious new lease, but that seemed rather petty. Where is he now? At his club. I told him I was starting out on the road at once. *HOW TO KEEP HOUSE WITHOUT A STAFF* is my text. *You're* all right while you have the Winters; you'll be all right if the Cruikshanks come back to you when you move the Winters to London. It's a question of what you can afford to pay, what you think it worth while to pay, what you hope to get in return. Have you thought that out, Colin? I think you should. A new chapter's opening in the lives of us all: long or short, at *our* age it will probably be the last chapter for you and me and Nigel and Elizabeth."

"And for you and me," I said, as I sat beside her and took her hand in mine, "I suppose the first chapter opened in this room, when I came to help you to arrange your father's books. Unless it was at one of those dinners with 'The Master' in Russell Square . . ."

"Or that first dinner with Austin and Elizabeth . . . If you go back far enough, I suppose it would be a dinner before that when Austin found that, though you and Nigel were sharing a house, I'd never met you. He said he thought I should like you . . ."

"I'm wondering," I broke in, "whether it didn't all begin at the moment when I was formally announced to my father as 'a beautiful boy'. If our life together was preordained, my dear . . ."

It had worked out so wonderfully, Violet murmured, as I paused, that she sometimes caught herself believing in destiny.

"It's *more* wonderful," I went on, "than the proverbial

marriage that's been made in Heaven because it was the experience of two marriages made in *Hell* that brought us together. I personally regard all that time as the long prologue to the short act that opened on the Downs above Ridgeway. It still seems short, though it has continued for more than twenty-six years. It'll be too short if it continues another twenty-six years. I shall be an octogenarian if I live that long; but this short act is one that can only be ended by death, only then if we die together. You are as near me as ever when we're apart; you'll be as near me as ever if one of us—shall I say?—goes on a little bit ahead of the other. You ask me what harvest I expect to reap from my last sowing . . ."

I fell silent at a whisper that sounded like:

"Twenty-six *years*?"

"And in that time," I continued, "I've only twice seen you *frightened.*"

"I've been frightened much more often than that, Colin! Whenever I thought I was waking up . . ."

"But you knew I was beside you! When Nigel went down the second time with black water fever . . . You came to tell me—in Oxford—that you were frightened; and I wrote before ever I got your letter telling me why . . . You were frightened when you invited me to dine this evening. You came to tell me in the train to-day; and I telegraphed before you could tell me why. *Need* you be frightened?"

With her disengaged hand Violet drew my head down to her own:

"*Need* I ask you to tell me that you still love me? I know you do, but I'm a woman and women *need* to be told. If I'm a fool, *every* woman is a fool in that. *Twenty-six years* . . . To your Norman, I'm an old woman. What does he imagine you still see in me? Old people, beyond the age of passion . . ."

"And when he's *my* age . . . '*Heaven the vision of fulfilled desire*'," I quoted. "If ever I thought it was, I think so no longer! '*Heaven* the illusion *of fulfilled desire*', if you like . . . or '*Hell the mad pain of* unfulfilled *desire*'. I see passion now as a thing that keeps people unhappy and apart while it's unsatisfied, but a thing of little consequence when they're happy and together. 'One flesh', no! One *spirit*, yes! Age? Looks? The woman I love in spirit has no age, her looks never change! Did you think I should say: 'If Nigel asserts himself, we must accept our fate'? I expect

you at Ridgeway the moment you find it convenient to come.
Did you tell him . . . ?"

"I said I couldn't keep him out of his own house, but, if he
didn't look after himself, I couldn't look after him. I had my own
work, which took me to every part of England. . . . Then I
became tired of pretending and told him frankly that I'd made
this job for myself because I wanted a life of my own."

"If Norman *will* treat Ridgeway as his vocation . . ."

I checked as Violet held up her hand at the distant ringing of a
bell upstairs. Not expecting any one to telephone, she had not
switched back since she went to dress and no one in the kitchen
could hear a bell in her bedroom. With a passing sigh for the
days when a private telephone was hardly more common than a
private tape-machine, she hurried down to the switch-board,
only to hurry back a moment later with the announcement that
the call was for me.

"Is it Norman?," I asked. "He's the only person who knows
I've been dining here."

"It was a woman's voice," said Violet.

"Elizabeth? She knows I'm back in London. If she has tried
unsuccessfully in Grosvenor Road . . ."

"It wasn't Elizabeth. I should have said it was an American.
Or Canadian? I'm not good on transatlantic accents. It might be
Barbara or Monica: they've both come back with a powerful
twang. I'll put it through to you here. If you want me for anything, I shall be in the next room."

I assured her that no one could have anything to say that I
should mind her hearing; but she repeated that she would be in
the next room and, when I brought her back a moment later, her
first words were to ask whether there was anything that she could
do.

"If you're any good at seeing through brick walls . . . ," I
began. "*I* don't know who the woman was. I don't understand
what has happened. . . . *Some one's* doing a healthy lot of lying . . ."

"What did she say?"

As far as I could, I gave the exact words of the message,
which had been delivered in the unmistakable idiom and tone of
Broadway.

" 'Say, is that Mr. Whimboyne? Mr. *Colin* Whimboyne? Oh,
say, listen! I'm speaking on behaff of Mr. Noiman Whimboyne.
Mr. Noiman Whimboyne says: "Please will you *not* sit up for

him if he's late?" There's nothing in the woild to worry about, but something at dinner must have disagreed with him. He says he has often had these attacks before. I'm going right now to the drug-store for a drafft to fix him. Oh! And he says he's gotten his latch-key, so you're not to worry!' "

"In spite of which," Violet observed, "you *are* worrying. Do you know who he was dining with?"

"No, it was somewhere in Chelsea. I assumed that it was with this man, this *friend*, that he talks of sharing a flat with. I've never been told the name and I don't know the address."

"Well . . . If he can't look after himself at this age . . ."

As she paused, I finished her sentence for her in words which she accepted with a slight nod:

"If he can't look after himself, we may be thankful that he has this brisk, business-like New Yorker to look after him. I was a bit startled to find that the unnamed friend in Chelsea was a woman. Assuming she *was* the friend, which I suppose I've no right to do . . . Except that he *has* spoken once or twice . . . As though he were testing my reaction . . . Something I said about setting up by himself, which made him ask what I should think if he set up *not* by himself."

"And you're worrying . . ."

"You too! Otherwise you wouldn't have said you would be in the next room. In case I wanted anything. In case you could help. Before I knew the call had anything to do with Norman. You had a suspicion that something was a bit wrong somewhere."

With a wistful smile, Violet confessed that we knew each other too well by now to keep up even an innocent pretence.

"Something did occur to me as odd," she continued. "I'll tell you when you've explained what you mean by seeing through a brick wall."

"*Well*, my dear! This 'attack' which may keep Norman immobilized till I've gone to bed! You know I don't consider it a hanging offence for a boy to misjudge how many cocktails he can put away with safety. I should think to-night's party has developed into something of an orgy."

I paused to let Violet reveal what had seemed odd to her in her brief exchange with the unknown American.

"I had only half a minute with her," she answered, "but it was mostly hiccoughs on her side. I was *sorry*, for your sake.

Even if there was nothing I could do, I wanted you to feel that you couldn't ask me anything in heaven or earth that I *wouldn't* do. At the moment, we can only leave them to sleep it off. Later on, when I come to Ridgeway, when we're giving poor Norman that great new object in life . . . Assuming that he *does* occasionally try to cheer himself up when everything seems all too difficult . . ."

"I'm wondering what chance we shall have against this woman. Is *she* the girl he's been going about with? If she's really got a grip on him . . ."

"But, Colin darling, for all we know, he'd never met her till to-night! You speak as if she were his old-established mistress, as though the orgy were in her flat, as though he meant her and her flat when he told you that he could always get a bed with a friend in Chelsea. If she's simply a fellow-guest, rather more sober than the others . . ."

"They're not meeting for the first time. She knew something of Norman's 'attacks' in old days. *You* saw one of them. What she didn't know or had forgotten for the moment was that the attacks were due to his appendix and that he had that removed several years ago now. No, I said that some one had done some healthy lying. . . . The sooner you can come to Ridgeway, the better. We're going to have our work cut out for us!"

VI ·

I HAD left for my office before Norman returned to Grosvenor Road; and he had left for Ridgeway before I came back.

A pencilled scrawl on the back of an envelope assured me that he was now all right and thanked me for a perfect holiday. A postscript urged that I should "*say nothing to mummy*"; and I could choose for myself whether he was referring to his indisposition overnight or to the happy fortnight in which Elizabeth had not been included.

When we met at the week-end, I observed a faint uneasiness in his manner, as though he were wondering what I made of his American friend's allusion to an "attack"; but a similar uneasiness manifested itself when I handed him a belated letter that had been forwarded from Keswick and reminded him of a promise to give me a map marked with the dates and distances of all our walks. Obviously, he did not want to talk about our holiday in his mother's presence; and for all his pathetically passionate pleading that there must surely be things we could all three share, I decided that after a week at Ridgeway he had made up his mind that he was not one of the things that could be shared simultaneously by the two of us. I had enjoyed his company for half of October; it was now nearly November and his mother's turn.

To be exact, he had been less than a week at Ridgeway and only three days at the Wantage school; but, when I arrived for the week-end, I found myself being fitted—with him and his mother, with the Winters and the "daily women"—into a routine that seemed as timeless as it was unchanging or at least unchangeable. The day, as I pieced it together, began for Elizabeth at six o'clock, when she got up to cook Norman's breakfast, and for him at half-past six, when she had prepared his bath. As he had not yet secured his supplementary coupons, she filled the tank of his car with petrol amassed by the V.A.M.P.s, cut him sandwiches for luncheon in case the school fare was not to his liking, buttoned him into his great-coat and saw him off for his twenty-odd miles' drive to Wantage. On his working days I gathered that he returned home to find some kind of high tea, followed by bread-and-cheese after he had prepared his lessons for next day. At the week-end he was to have breakfast when he awoke and rang for it; luncheon and dinner were fairly normal repasts, taken at conventional hours, though to spare labour and fuel I found that Elizabeth had arranged for them to be served at a small table in my book-room. This, since Norman had apparently been moved into her boudoir ("to save stairs", as she explained), was now the place where he worked; and, since she no longer had a sitting-room of her own, this was now the obvious place for her to sit while he worked. I am not generally enamoured of dining in a mist of tobacco-smoke nor of talking afterwards in a smell of food, but I forbore to criticize a contrivance which Elizabeth invited me to admire for its convenience and "cosiness". Everything, she pointed out proudly as she stacked a tea-tray and a work-basket on the wireless-cabinet, was in reach of one's hand; but, if I wanted more space or quiet, there was "the office" in which we had formerly attested documents requiring the signature of a magistrate. She might fairly have added that half the tobacco-smoke had come from my own pipe; and, after our first dinner, I felt that, if I had grumbled about talking in a smell of food, Norman might well have enquired whether there had been enough talking before, during or after dinner for any one to notice.

Would there ever be?, I could almost hear him asking as we moved into armchairs round the fire. Was there in fact anything that all three of us could share? I was warned off our own common interests when, in giving me my promised map, he said that he would fill in the dates some time later, but that he did not suppose it would amuse his mother to hear us arguing about places that she did not know. In her turn, Elizabeth was warned off her interest in the Wantage school by the reminder that— Heaven be thanked—Norman had only signed on till Easter. Three days of it, he continued morosely, reminded him of an Oxford friend who, on entering the office of an uncongenial family-business for the first time, observed philosophically that he would have only another forty years of this. I tried to create a common interest by mentioning that I had invited Violet Oakhirst to advise me about decorating the house; and the silence with which my efforts were received, not broken till Norman proposed a stroll in the moonlight before we went to bed, suggested that—as I had told him only a few weeks earlier— everything hinged on Ridgeway and that on this subject the three of us would never all share a single thought.

"Poor mummy suffers from agoraphobia about houses," he observed, when we were out of earshot. "I can't understand it. That place of my grandfather's, Coverley Court . . ."

"You could have put the whole of Ridgeway into one wing," I said. "Perhaps that is the reason. A permanently-lost feeling. She always *has* hankered after a doll's house. When Martin and Humfrey set up in London . . ."

"Well, she has now got the thing she wanted. A place, I mean, where you can touch all four walls without getting up from your chair and where one old-age-pensioner can do all the housework. What have you and Lady Oakhirst in mind?"

I said that I should know better when we had examined the house and that, as he—*in esse* and *in futuro*—was the person chiefly interested, I hoped he would assist at our deliberations.

"According to Mrs. Winter," I went on, "a thorough cleaning is what's wanted first and worst."

"Which mummy hadn't a chance to arrange while she was running her Vamps. She won't have much more chance now if she's going to be a maid-of-all-work. I *did* suggest a thermos of coffee and a breakfast-tray in my room overnight, but she wouldn't hear of it."

"I should have thought that Winter . . . ," I began.

"Mummy thinks his days here are numbered. If you're putting Grosvenor Road into full commission . . . That's their spiritual home. They only came to oblige you when the Cruikshanks left. Incidentally, she thinks it's very doubtful whether *they'll* care about coming back to the kind of life we're all leading nowadays, with butlers helping to make beds and cooks cleaning grates."

From my knowledge of the Cruikshanks I thought that they would cheerfully add car-washing and book-keeping to their duties, if they were asked; but I also thought that Elizabeth, if she had seen them lately, would not have asked them. She might even have hinted that there was now little scope for their services. We were such a small party, I could imagine her saying; she could do anything that had to be done for Captain Whimboyne, as—to his exasperation—she persisted in speaking of Norman after he had broken her of calling him "the major".

It was an incredibly mild night for the end of October; and, though we were walking without overcoats and in thin shoes, neither of us felt drawn back to the house and, when we reached the end of the garden, Norman automatically opened the small gate that led to the Downs.

"How soon is Lady Oakhirst coming here?," he asked.

"As soon as your mother and I can arrange a convenient time," I told him.

"Which may be the day after the Greek Calends. Can you possibly leave it till *after* Easter? I'll tell you why. In her heart, mummy hopes I'm going to stay on at Tony Charlbury's foul seminary. She likes having me here. In fact, she'll be damned lonely when I go. Call it domesticity, call it agoraphobia: she just loves the *snugness* of a small party, living in one room, no frills . . . It'll be a jolt when I convince her that I'm going back to London at Easter, come what may. If at the same time she has to collect a staff and take the house out of its curl-papers . . ."

"I must keep the place in repair," I said, "however we decide

to use it. If it's only a matter of cleaning, there's no hurry for
Violet to come here. Without waiting for her, by the way, there's
one thing that you and I can tackle at once, Norman. The books,
which have multiplied and been duplicated . . ."

For the first time since my arrival Norman roused to interest.

"Funny you should say that!," he exclaimed. "I noticed the
other day that we'd both been getting Hutchinson's *Quarterly
Record of the War* and I meant to suggest that, if one of us was
going for a thing like that, the other should hold his hand.
You've always let me treat your library as my own: if you can
find space for anything I buy on my own . . ."

"Let's make ourselves a selection committee. Ultimately the
whole thing will be yours. An elimination committee, if you like,
too. I've accumulated a vast mass of books of the day, as they're
called, and if you feel that you're never going to read them and
that I shan't ever refer to them again . . . My collection for the
1914–1918 war is as complete as you'll find anywhere outside the
British Museum. . . . If you think there's any market . . ."

"And it's *damned* funny you should say that, daddy. There's a
market for almost any book these days, as the Red Cross can tell
you. Have you tested their incredible organization in Wigmore
Street? They've collected, arranged, indexed, priced every
blessed thing that any one has sent them; you enquire for, oh,
Morley's *Life of Gladstone*; if they've got it, you can have it by
return; if they haven't, *you'll* be indexed and a month later you'll
get a post-card asking whether you still want your *Life of
Gladstone*, as a copy has just come in. It's such thousand *per cent*
efficiency that it oughtn't to be let die. If I could get some of their
trained workers . . . and the overflow of the books here as a
nucleus . . . and a room or two in Grosvenor Road to house them
till I'd seen whether I could make a success of it . . . There
wouldn't be any big capital outlay; I could make a part-time job
of it after office-hours and at week-ends if I *do* go into the City. . . .
And I would, cheerfully, if I had this as a distraction. *Is* there
anything in it?"

Unwittingly I must have hesitated in answering, for Norman
—with a sigh like the air escaping from a pricked balloon—
expressed the caustic hope that I would not ask whether his book-
exchange was intended to be a stick or a crutch.

"My dear boy, nothing was farther from my thoughts!," I
assured him. "I was just considering whether *any one* could point

out *any* snag. . . . *I* can't. It seems to me a wholly admirable idea. I'll start the weeding-out process with you to-morrow morning. And I'll think whether I can suggest any friends who would like *their* libraries hand-weeded. Violet was saying only the other day that she wanted to help the Red Cross, but she just hadn't time to go through her shelves. I'll write to her, for a start."

And, when I wrote, I thought that I could count on her magnanimity to congratulate me on shortheading her in the race to find Norman his great new interest in life. Ridgeway, with its suspected tug-of-war, was forgotten with the "foul seminary" at Wantage; we should have walked to Avebury if I had not heard a remote church-clock striking midnight; and I believe he would have begun work in the book-room then and there if we had not found Elizabeth muffled in the hall and preparing to organize a search-party.

"Where in the *world* have you been?," she demanded indignantly. "I looked for you everywhere in the garden, where you said you were going for a *stroll* . . ."

"It was such a lovely night that we went up to the Downs," said Norman. "And daddy and I have been concocting a *marvellous* scheme!," he continued eagerly and then looked at me out of the corner of one eye in a way that always heralded a quotation in which he feared to find himself less than word-perfect: " '*A scheme of devices, to get at low prices, all goods from cough mixtures to cables, (which* somethinged *the sailors*) . . .' "

" '*(Which tickled the sailors)*'," I prompted him, " '*by treating retailers, as though they were all vegetables* . . .' "

"I haven't the faintest idea what all this nonsense is about," said Elizabeth, directing her rebuke at me, but driving the eagerness from Norman's face more effectually than if she had slapped both his cheeks. "I should have thought there had been time and to *spare* . . ." It was on the tip of her tongue, I felt sure, to say "*when you had him to yourself in Cumberland*," but such a display of naked jealousy daunted her and she substituted "without keeping him out of bed half the night. He was up at cock-crow."

With a complete mastery of whatever his feelings may have been, Norman gaily kissed his mother, gaily told her that, if she did not remember the Lord Chancellor's "nightmare song", he would take her to hear it the next time *Iolanthe* was played in London and somewhat less gaily assured her that we should not have stayed out so late if we had imagined that she was waiting up for us.

"You didn't suppose, did you, that I should go to bed," asked Elizabeth, only half mollified, "not knowing what had happened to you?"

Had it not been common knowledge to us all, she might have said that she never went up till she had made sure there was nothing more that Norman wanted; but he forestalled her by announcing that we had both earned a long drink and that he would carry his to his room and (if she liked) give her an outline of our "marvellous scheme" as he undressed.

"I'll turn out the lights," I said.

Was it only the old playwright's inveterate habit of thinking in dialogue or was there an unspoken line in Norman's heart as he bade me good-night with a joyless smile and began to mount the stairs? Loyalty to his mother would keep him from even hinting that he had even a rhetorical question to ask; but I chose to think that he was wondering whether many lights had been left for me to turn out and I fancied, ten minutes later, that he had his answer when I passed the open door of his bedroom and heard Elizabeth deploring the "dust-traps" that I created by accumulating books that she felt sure I never read a second time. The great new interest, as I wrote to Violet next day, would have to be a hardy plant if it was to survive the blighting chill of Elizabeth's narrow and opinionated criticism.

"In time," I continued, *"Ridgeway may become—for him—all that you and I aspire to make it, but this will require time. At present he is gallantly and most reluctantly making himself the target for what he once called his mother's overflowing love and at the same time trying to make her understand that he cannot and will not give his life to teaching small boys and being treated as a small boy himself. It is his request that you and I should postpone our grand overhaul of the house and garden. I have carried out a preliminary inspection . . ."*

I paused for several minutes and then added that I would tell Violet about it when we met in London. My inspection had answered one question and posed another which at present I could not answer. As the Winters had hinted, the house needed the attention of competent cleaners far more urgently than that of an expert on interior decoration; but what was I to think of the attention that the mistress of the house had given for half-a-dozen years? Elizabeth's attitude since 1939 seemed to have been that, though others ignored the fact, we were at war and that she could spare no more time from her V.A.M.P.s than I from my planning-committee. As our younger servants left, she acquiesced in their replacement by such refugees as the resourceful Cruikshanks could muster; when she fell out with the Cruikshanks over rations, the house was kept functioning by the two Winters with any help that they could obtain anywhere. If one of her sons or brothers came to Ridgeway, Elizabeth would cook and clean in a sketchy manner and for a limited period, but in general she had been living in an ever-narrowing circle. When a window-sash broke, the room was abandoned; when a tap leaked for want of a new washer, a notice in her unformed, round hand was suspended above it, proclaiming that it was *"Out of Order"*. Since Violet and I prepared for mass-evacuation, I had only once been inside "Mad Marion's Apartments"; and I found that they had been converted into a casualty-ward for slightly wounded furniture. The picture with the cracked glass rested against the picture with the broken chain on the sofa with the loose castor and under the screen with the screwless hinge.

Violet's least skilled apprentice would have put everything to rights in a week; and the dexterous Winter would have done the same in a fortnight if he had not been otherwise occupied as boot-boy, scullery-maid, boiler-man and assistant bed-maker.

"I shall not call you in," I concluded my letter to Violet, *"till the Augean stable has been cleaned; and I do not think this squalid make-and-mend programme would offer an alluring introduction to the delights and cares of domestic empire for Norman. At the moment, therefore, I'm concentrating on his book-exchange idea . . ."*

If I remembered rightly, the daughter of my latest Lord Keeper had worked for a time at the Red Cross library that Norman was taking as his model. I had promised him that I would get in touch with her; and a day or two after my return to London, I was invited to call at her father's house in Cadogan Gardens. I went by underground from Saint James' Park to Sloane Square; and on emerging from the station I received a bow from an elegant young woman who made haste to say that she felt sure I did not know her from Eve.

"Give me a moment," I replied, "and I shall remember even your nickname, which I always thought singularly inappropriate. 'Ginger'! Miss 'Ginger' Norbury, unless you've married since last we met, which is a good many years ago now."

"And I've done a good many different things in the interval, but marrying hasn't been one of them. You still have that charming house by the river, where you tried to make an actress of me? 'Lady Caroline'. You haven't produced *Flowers By Request*, have you?"

"Thanks to the late Adolf Hitler, my literary activities have been suspended since that night when our rehearsal was interrupted. Are you still in the government service? I looked out for you when at long last I returned to Queen Anne's Gate."

"I was asked to go back, but I wanted to be on my own. You've heard of jobbing gardeners? Well, I'm a jobbing secretary. I go out one, two, three mornings a week to various people. . . . If you're going down Sloane Street, I must say good-bye: I have to go by the King's Road."

As she stood with hand outstretched, I asked Miss Norbury whether her work as a jobbing secretary included literary typing.

"For years," I explained, "my publishers have talked about bringing out an omnibus volume of my plays. You're familiar with all my peculiarities . . ."

"I couldn't take on anything more, Mr. Whimboyne," she interrupted with decision.

"Don't turn it down out of hand," I begged. "If one of your other clients drops out . . . I'm in no hurry, at least until paper becomes more plentiful. It's work that you could do at home, in your own time. If you'll give me your address . . ."

"I'll think it over," Miss Norbury promised, with a reluctance that she made no attempt to hide. "And *I* can write to *you*, in Grosvenor Road. My 'own time'," she repeated ruefully.

I said again that I was willing to take my place in her queue.

"I'm delighted," I added, "to hear you're so busy. Within reason, too much work is better than too little. Is this your bus? Well, it has been an unlooked-for pleasure to meet you again. I believe I last heard of you from my son, Norman, some time before the war. If you *can* fit me in . . ."

"I'll let you know, but at present I just can't get through the day's work in a day." Gaining the platform of the bus, she turned with an expression of faint defiance to say in a faintly defiant tone: "Your son Norman is a whole-time job."

VII

FOR the two minutes that I stood on the kerb outside Sloane Square station, watching Miss "Ginger" Norbury's bus until it disappeared in the traffic of the King's Road, I told myself dully that I had "known this all along".

For the two years that followed this November afternoon in 1945 I was to tell myself that for any statement made on oath I knew nothing. Nearly two years later again I still do not know for certain whether Miss Norbury was the friend with whom Norman had talked vaguely of sharing a flat in Chelsea; I do not know whether hers was the woman's voice that had spoken to me by telephone with a New York accent; I do not know whether she was the girl with whom Martin and Humfrey had seen their half-brother dining and dancing; and, when Miss Norbury told me that my son was a whole-time job, I do not know whether she was speaking of him as a suitor or an accepted lover or a boon companion or a patient.

Had I asked him, I believe he would have told me; and equally, whether this young woman was his future wife or his present mistress, I feel sure he would have added: "For Heaven's sake don't tell mummy!" Less than a month ago I had heard him on Green Gable, shouting down the unconscious voice that whispered: "*She'll* never let you marry!" and the same voice would whisper now: "It would kill her to know you were living in sin!"

As I walked down Sloane Street, I reflected that it might be better and would certainly be easier for me to know nothing definite at present. Miss Norbury could be trusted to tell Norman of our meeting and of her parting words; he could mention it to me, if he wished, in his own good time; but, whatever their relationship, he would achieve no useful purpose by taking me into his confidence.

"If it's a passing affair," I argued, "he won't want to talk about it. If it's serious . . . If it's serious, he'll fight for her and she'll fight for him." I remembered how Martin and Humfrey had telephoned to inform me of their engagements before acquainting Elizabeth, how the still unknown Barbara and Monica had twittered for me to intercede with their own parents . . . "Unless Norman feels that he'll perhaps get me on his side . . ."

2D

And would he? What should I think if he told me that Miss Norbury and he were engaged? What did I know or suspect of this girl? How should I describe her to Elizabeth and her sisters, to my brothers and their wives, to our neighbours in Wiltshire, to the thousand-and-one friends who would write to me when they read the announcement in *The Times*?

As a natural actress, I felt confident that Miss Norbury would give a flawless performance; but my brothers-in-law and their wives would want to know whether she was "one of the Herefordshire Norburys" and Elizabeth would not fail to ask her how long Norman and she had known each other and where he had met her.

Though by now I had reached my destination, I walked on a few yards towards Knightsbridge to get my thoughts and dates in order.

As my new secretary on probation, he had seen her for a moment—and marked her as a "raging beauty"—in my office; he had danced with her in my private rehearsal-room for a few moments until she fainted in his arms; he had driven her home once or twice, to my knowledge, and omniscient Heaven alone was aware how often they had met since the night when—by his own account—he had "run into her at Ciro's". What must my answer be if I were asked by Philip or Maurice, *Peerage* in hand, whether I approved of her as a daughter-in-law, the future mistress of Ridgeway?

Already late for my appointment, I hurried back to Cadogan Gardens. For the next half-hour I must learn about the Red Cross organization for collecting, classifying and selling second-hand books. Had I not promised Norman that I would telephone that night and tell him what I had found out?

Faithful to my promise, I telephoned; but I am now quite unable to say what I told him and I am doubtful whether I could have said what I was telling him at the time. In a specialized sense of the phrase I feel that I devoted most of the evening—first in a solitary dinner at the Garrick, then in a solitary walk back to Grosvenor Road—to dramatizing myself. Any success that I have had in the theatre may be ascribed, I believe, to a faculty of making my characters speak and act on the stage as they would speak and act in the street outside. My severest critic has never charged me with presenting a "stage" duke or archdeacon or company-promoter. If any High-Court judge of mine hears that his wife has eloped with his chauffeur, I brood over such High-Court judges as I have known and try to imagine how an amalgam of them would speak and act in these circumstances, thus and not otherwise.

Hitherto I had not been required to speculate how an elderly civil servant, with some reputation as a playwright, would comport himself on apprehending that his only son was entangled with a seductive member of the half-world. I had no sketches in any of my note-books either of civil servants or playwrights; and, reversing my usual practice, I now set myself to decide how Colin Whimboyne would act and speak if he found himself cast for this part. If I could keep him from becoming a "stage" father, I might keep myself from behaving like one off the stage. How in fact would a Comptroller to the Office of His Majesty's Lord Keeper behave?

Would he rush for advice to the wisest and best of his friends? This was indeed my first impulse, but Violet was out of London. I must, I said, answer this question by myself; and, as I said it, I felt—as once or twice before—that Violet was beside me, nodding when she agreed and prompting me when I faltered. If we were not talking together, I was thinking aloud so articulately that a strange passer-by checked to ask whether I had addressed him.

"No . . . No . . . ," I answered. "No . . . You see, my dear, the way I regard it is this. Never mind the order! I'm giving you a jumble of ideas, just as they've come into my head. If Norman marries this girl, I back them up through thick and thin. Any one who speaks lightly of her will be answerable to *me*. It's his only chance of happiness! Good God, it's *my* only chance of keeping the least fragment of him! Well, now, this girl . . . The worst thing I suspect about her is that she's oversexed; and that, in itself, means no more to me than if you said she had high blood-pressure. It's the way she's made physically, not a *vice*, though it may land her and other people in trouble if she develops into a man-eating tigress. I don't know that she will. What I *do* know, what frightens me far more is that she and Norman have no background, no tradition, no thought or speech in common. She's a quick, pretty clerk, with great gaiety and zest for life, a good-tempered and good-natured moth. And, I should think, as uncultured, as illiterate almost, as insensitive to any intellectual fineness as the general run of moths. What can she offer Norman

beyond her alluring body? You may ask: What can he offer her
or any girl like her?"

To me, perhaps hearing my own opinions on life and art
echoed with subtle modifications, my son with his clearly
chiselled features and his clearly chiselled mind was an enchanting
companion; Violet might possibly say that the two sides of my
life gave him his two best opportunities for shining, as an
academic among academics. By the death-bed of county society
and in the graveyard of social London he was less at home; and
well-bred toleration was the most that he could give either to the
girl who lived for sport or the one who lived for parties. Always
taking what the day brought, he boasted of his willingness to try
anything once; and usually he admitted afterwards to having
enjoyed his new experience. Once, however, was generally
enough for the popular pleasures of life; and, if I was right in
regarding Miss Ginger Norbury as a "good-timer", I did not
think that Norman would give her a good time for long.

"Dining in modish restaurants," I murmured. "Dancing
afterwards . . . The everlasting film . . . Of course, if she regards
him as a great match . . ."

High rank, vast wealth and autocratic power were still, I
supposed, as much as ever such stuff as day-dreams were made
on, perhaps austerity and egalitarianism had strengthened their
escapist appeal; but in none of these things would Norman ever
cut even a noticeable figure.

"A small country squire," I continued my thinking aloud.
"Any money he has, the money his father made by writing
ephemeral plays . . . If this girl *saw* him in his Ridgeway
frame . . ."

And why should she not? Paula Tanqueray could hardly have
been more devastatingly bored than this girl would be, but I did
not want the luckless Miss Norbury to be invited for the purpose
of being bored. I wanted her to see Norman in a possibly
unimagined setting, I wanted him to see her against his own
background. Before that, I wanted to observe his reactions when
I suggested his inviting her for Christmas, say, to meet his mother
and father.

I would suggest it, I decided, when I telephoned to him that
night; and perhaps the reason that I can remember nothing of
what I said about his book-exchange is that I was thinking chiefly
of what I should say afterwards. His voice, I thought, was sulky

as he snapped: "Ridgeway one-three. Norman Whimboyne? Speaking!"; but it changed at once as he recognized my voice and exclaimed: "Oh, is that you, daddy? This damned telephone . . . All right, mummy, it's for me!" and it changed again, in a way that made me think Elizabeth had left the room, as he continued: "Well, did you find out anything useful for me? I know you *went*, because Yvette Norbury has just rung up to tell me she met you on the way."

"It was only for a moment," I said, "as she was catching a bus. I wish," I continued boldly, "it had been longer. I should have liked, after all these years, to hear a bit more what she had been doing with herself. If you're in touch with her, Norman, bring her to dine one night in Grosvenor Road when I've re-established the Winters there . . ."

I paused at a hardly audible sound of argument; Elizabeth seemed to have come back and asked some question that I did not catch and Norman, with the frozen geniality that he forced to cover his boiling impatience, was saying:

"Heavens, no! There's nothing the *matter*! Daddy promised to get some information for me . . ." Then he must have turned again to the transmitter. "Sorry! Knowing your general hatred of the telephone, mummy was in a flat-spin for fear you'd been taken ill. You were saying?"

"Consider it unsaid!," I resumed. "I've thought of something better: could Miss Norbury be persuaded to come to us for Christmas? You must explain that, if there's a party at all, it will be a family party, but a little outside blood would be rather refreshing." I gave him a moment for consideration: if this young woman was his mistress, he might well pause before asking his mother to receive her. Again, he might swallow his scruples for fear of fostering the idea that she was his mistress. If he aspired to marry her, he might welcome an opportunity of shewing her off. Again, he might excuse himself from shewing her off until they could both choose their own time. In fact, since he said nothing, I continued as though I had not been giving him a chance of saying anything: "I've been thinking about the great family-row, Norman, and Christmas seems an admirable occasion for ending it. I shall make sure of Martin and Humfrey before mentioning it to your mother. Perhaps the Oakhirsts would come to leaven the mass. If Miss Norbury . . . or any one else you can think of . . ."

"I'll suggest it the next time I see her. Could you find out whether the Red Cross affair was carrying on now that the war's over?"

I remember saying that it was not; but I know that I was thinking of one thing and talking of another so that I felt genuinely surprised, at the end of our conversation, when Norman thanked me for the information I had collected and added that it would prove really valuable.

"If it would help your Christmas party," he continued, "for me to eat a little dirt, I don't mind apologizing for my temper."

"I shan't mention the subject," I answered, "and I'm ready to bet that no one else does. They all stand to lose by a break. If you think seriously of going into the City after Easter . . ."

"I loathe the prospect, but anything would be better than my present job. How people can teach small boys for *love* of the thing, like Tony . . . Easter . . . I can hold out till Easter because I've said I would and I can forget about it at week-ends and I've four weeks' holiday to look forward to. Otherwise . . . You'll be coming down on Saturday? I was banking on that. When you're not here . . . I mean, one can't thresh things out properly by telephone. Well, good-night, daddy! Mummy's looking for a chopper to chop off my head if I don't take her candle to light me to bed."

As the line became silent, I paid myself the compliment of thinking that Norman intended to say that life at Ridgeway was quiet, if not dull, when I was not there. His rather ghastly gaiety as he plunged into a nursery rime may have gratified his mother, but it wrung my heart and I made haste to dial Martin's number before I could begin to brood over it. There were times when I felt that Elizabeth's mental development had been arrested when she first opened a nursery in Montpelier Square; it was this that made her two elder sons break away so often and I wondered how long the sensitive, compassionate youngest would bear it.

I wondered, too, how much awe I still inspired in Martin and Humfrey from the now distant days when I was summoned, as a child-eating ogre, to instil discipline. More than a little, I decided, as one brief telephone-conversation succeeded another. Martin had made an engagement for Christmas, but he consented to break it when I told him that he must not disappoint his mother; Humfrey accepted without even this much of appeal to his better feelings. When I went to Ridgeway for the week-end, I was able to tell Elizabeth and Norman that, if they would like a family-gathering, I could arrange it.

"Not that we need confine it to the family," I added, for Norman's benefit.

"Will you be free?," asked Elizabeth. "I'm afraid you were rather squeezed out the last time, but with hardly any regular servants . . ."

"Oh, I shall be here," I answered. "I said I would arrange it. Servants included. I saw Cruikshank this week; and he told me his canteen was closing down for the holiday. He can come, with his wife and all the men and maidens we can possibly need. He can also supply me, at a price, with turkeys. But I needn't bother you with details: I'll arrange it all if the idea appeals to you."

Elizabeth, with something of the dazed helplessness that I remembered from the night when I proposed to her at the pistol-point, said that she would like a little time to think over my proposal. It would, of course, be a joy to have dear Martin and Humfrey; but, if I thought of filling the house from cellar to garret as in old days, this was out of the question.

"The linen, alone . . . ," she continued.

"I had a word with Mrs. Winter about that before dinner," I said. "You needn't worry! I'll arrange it all."

"I think it would be rather fun, daddy," said Norman.

As he reached for a block of paper and began to make notes, I felt he was saying to himself that the battle had been won and that it was the battle, not of a Christmas party, but of Ridgeway and its future, of himself and his life. Was Elizabeth, gazing round the congested book-room in sad silence, telling herself the same thing? I was put in mind of a small child, "playing gipsies" with tent and fire and cauldron, suddenly summoned back to a formal, hated house with stiff servants and a starched frock and needless hand-washing and senseless table-manners. The real world of a summer afternoon faded as she collected her dolls and returned with dragging feet to the make-believe world of grown-ups; Elizabeth's cosy real world of a single living-room, with Norman's great-coat drying before the fire, after his drive home through a flurry of snow, and with his breakfast-tray in readiness on a writing-table, faded as he came down on my side into a make-believe world of servants who fell over one another and of "fashionable" parties and "clever" people who despised her. I had broken down her bridges by saying that I would arrange everything if she would like to gather her family round her; and Norman had burnt her boats by welcoming my suggestion.

"Who besides relations . . . ?," he began.

"I should like to get Violet Oakhirst, if she's free," I said. "I have a rough idea of the redecorating that's needed, but she alone can tell me what it's possible to have done these days."

"*And* what it will cost," Elizabeth murmured. "I *should* have thought, Colin, you would have been wise to wait a year or two. The war's only just over, every one tells me that big country-houses are a thing of the past."

"Until I know the cost," I answered, "I can't say whether I can afford it. I feel, though, that it's a case of all or nothing. If we can't use the house or enjoy the gardens or entertain our friends, we'd better throw up the sponge. I don't want to do that. Nor, I think, does Norman. But we should go the way poor 'Mad Marion' went if we lived in one furtive little corner and never saw any one. If you think the housekeeping will be too much for you, don't give it a thought! I'll arrange all about that."

As Elizabeth sat watching Norman's pencil at work, I suspected she was saying to herself that I seemed to have arranged everything already, without consulting her, making him my accomplice.

"I wonder whether I'm really equal to the fatigue . . . ," she began.

"If you're not, let's call the whole thing off," I said. "I thought, if I *could* get Martin and Humfrey, who are becoming a little 'choosy', as I believe it's called . . ."

"Oh, I should adore to see *them*!"

"And Barbara and Monica and the children?"

Elizabeth nodded, more—I thought—to herself than to me, as though she were admitting that she had been trapped.

"How many at present, Norman?," I asked.

"The three of us, the three Martins, three Humfreys . . . On your side, I suppose Uncle John, Aunt Elsie, Uncle Henry . . . Oh, by the way, daddy, I gave your message to Yvette Norbury, when I was writing to her this week. She says she has not in fact made any plans for Christmas . . ."

"Do I know who Yvette Norbury is?," asked Elizabeth.

Since I had suggested her being invited, I took it upon myself to answer:

"She's a young woman of whom I once had dizzy hopes

of introducing to the world as a new Bernhardt. I was putting her through her paces one night when Norman arrived from Oxford. Well, the war brought my hopes to an end. Norman told me that he'd run into her somewhere, but I lost sight of her completely till a day or two ago in London, when I met her in the street. After all these years I felt I should like to see her again and hear what she'd been doing."

A silence followed, in which I could see Elizabeth's lips moving as though she was repeating: "Yvette Norbury . . . Yvette Norbury?"

"An actress?," she then asked.

"No!," Norman answered. "And never will be! It's a thing she'll never understand about you, daddy: that you should ever have *imagined* . . . In those days she'd only been inside a theatre about twice: her people looked on all actors as rogues and vagabonds."

"And you want to invite her here?"

"I? It was daddy's idea. I don't care one way or the other. If you would rather keep the party undiluted family . . ."

Glancing at her watch, Elizabeth stood up suddenly and announced that she must boil some water for a hot drink if Norman was not to be laid up with a chill after his drive through the snow.

"Arrange it with your father," she added in a tone which conveyed that he and I had already arranged everything else behind her back.

"There's nothing to arrange!," Norman exclaimed with a touch of irritability. "Invite her or not, as you please! It's no favour to *me*. Or to *her* . . ."

"O darling boy, that's not at *all* what I meant! I suppose I was a little bit taken by surprise: I didn't know any one was *thinking* of a big party for Christmas, but apparently it's all cut and dried . . ."

So little, I reminded Elizabeth, was anything cut and dried that the whole idea could be dropped at a word from her.

"Oh, I don't want that," she hastened to assure me. "I love to have you all here. And I should like to meet this friend . . . I'm not clear whether she's your friend, Colin, or Norman's."

"I've known her for a few weeks longer," I said, "but hardly well enough to call her a *friend*."

"I *can*," said Norman. "I saw quite a bit of her when I was in London at odd times before I went out in '40."

"I feel that I know the surname somehow," said Elizabeth, frowning, "but I don't think I knew of her existence, if you understand me, till now. Will you turn out the lights, Colin?"

As they went upstairs together, Norman seemed to be explaining that he must have many other friends of whose existence his mother was unaware. After all, he was twenty-six and had knocked about as much as most.

"I was wondering," he continued with faint uneasiness, I thought, in his voice, "how you had ever come to hear Yvette's name. If you *did*."

But this, it seemed, Elizabeth was unable to tell him.

VIII

DESPITE his hot drink Norman awoke with a slight cold in the head.

As his temperature was subnormal, Elizabeth abandoned her first agitated idea of sending for the doctor and telephoning to the school at Wantage on condition that he remained in bed till luncheon. He in his turn stipulated that she was not to stay away from church on his account; and, though she hurried back without waiting for the sermon, we had upwards of an hour by ourselves for discussing the condition of the house and, when the sun came out at midday, Norman announced that he proposed to get some air and exercise in the afternoon.

"If we're planning the future of this place with Lady Oakhirst," he continued, "we mustn't overlook the gardens. If I were in your shoes, I should let them to a market-gardener and keep only the smallest ring round the house. At the present rate of wages, one man is all that *I* shall be able to afford. Shrubs that can look after themselves, heath to smother the weeds, bulbs that don't require attention once you've put them in, only as much lawn as I can manage with a motor-mower at week-ends."

"Labour-saving is Violet's speciality at the moment," I said. "Cutting down, making do. I felt rather sad at first, Norman, when I remembered what a lovely thing she'd made of the house originally. Money didn't have to be considered in those days; and we were five-and-twenty years younger. Now, all's to be done again, in the most difficult conditions, with our time running out . . ."

"If you're trying to make noises like an old man, daddy . . . ," Norman began.

"I'm never conscious of being any age in particular," I said, "but there comes a time when 'the future' means something we're no longer planning for ourselves. I only said I felt sad at *first*. I should take my grey hairs with great sorrow to the grave, I'm afraid, if I found we couldn't keep Ridgeway or that we had to picnic in a corner of it or that you cared for it no more than your mother . . ."

As I paused, Norman assured me that, if he did not share my love for the place, he would not even think of selling himself into the bondage of a stockbroker's office.

"As I'm willing to do at Easter," he continued resolutely. "Earlier, if Tony will let me off earlier. He sees how I loathe the whole business. I should never have taken it if I hadn't felt that I'd been responsible for splitting the family and it was therefore up to me . . . As you've healed the breach with Martin and Humfrey, I don't feel obliged to stay here, twiddling my thumbs, to keep mummy company. If the uncles still want me when they come here for Christmas . . ."

I said that they were still wanting him when I was talking to them a day or two earlier; and this was the only reference that either of us made to the Christmas party. Miss Yvette Norbury's name was not mentioned; I was indeed asked to say nothing about the Wantage school at present; and, when Elizabeth returned from church, she found us studying a schedule of dilapidations which the Winters had prepared for me to give Violet. Though Norman and I tried in turn to interest her in what we were discussing, she contributed no comment more helpful than that everything (she supposed) wore out sooner or later; and, when he repeated his suggestion for reducing the size of the garden and invited her to come out with us, she would only say that everything seemed to have been settled already and that, if she was not to miss the post, she must devote the afternoon to letter-writing.

"Barbara, Monica . . . ," she enumerated. "You'll let me know this Miss Norbury's address, one of you?"

"You needn't write to Violet," I said. "I shall probably be seeing her this week. She's away in the north at the moment."

And, even if she returned in time for our weekly dinner, I decided that it would do no harm for me to give an outline—so like the *scenario* of one of my own plays!—of what had been happening since the admirable curtain that Miss Norbury had contrived for herself as she boarded her Chelsea bus.

"I stand to be shot at from all sides," I began that night, *"whatever the outcome. Elizabeth will hold me responsible for introducing Norman to this girl and having her invited here. If Miss Norbury finds the party as shatteringly dull as I expect, Norman will blame me for scaring her away. If she sticks it out and they come to me for my blessing, every one will blame me when the marriage crashes. I'm convinced it will crash, if they get that far; but my only hope is to give them a chance of seeing it for themselves before it's too late. You will understand now why your advice and support at the party are absolutely indispensable."*

In her reply, Violet promised me her considered opinion when we next met and, in the meantime, contented herself with the first comments that had occurred to her:

"I don't see how you could let things drift; especially after the young woman had virtually challenged you. From your account of Elizabeth, she would have driven poor Norman off his head if you hadn't seized Ridgeway from her by main force. Once the place is running on its old lines I have good hopes that Norman will make it his big new interest. If he insists on sharing the interest with this girl, there's nothing more that you can do. By the way, I'm thankful that her name is really not 'Ginger', but where have I heard of Yvette Norbury? Was there a case in the papers? If so I've forgotten what it was about."

And, as I had not even heard the name till five or six days ago, there was nothing for me to forget, though it struck a note in Martin's memory when he lunched with me a few days later to report what had been arranged with his uncles and Norman. By now, I was given to understand, "Tony Charlbury's school for freaks" had found a successor to Captain Whimboyne, of Ridgeway, who would be a free man by Christmas. Philip and Maurice were willing to take him into Alexander Cheshunt And Sons if he cared to come; and he could count on a partnership if he put his heart into the business.

"Or, if not his heart," Martin corrected himself, "at least his back. The Stock Exchange is not every one's spiritual home, but he's more likely to make money there than anywhere else I know and he'll need big money if he hopes to carry on with Ridgeway. He's not *limited* to Throgmorton Street, provided he puts it first. There was some chit-chat about a second-hand book-shop. The uncles, whose worst enemies wouldn't call them literary, pulled rather long faces and talked about serving two masters, but as I pointed out, it's no one else's concern how young Norman amuses himself after office-hours. He won't be able to *serve* in his precious shop, but I don't know that we should any of us care to hear him asking whether moddom will *take* the volumes or whether he may have the pleasure of sending them."

"The business he contemplates is not quite of that kind," I said. "An office and a store-room rather than a shop. I've promised him a floor in Grosvenor Road as a beginning, but he says it will take him at least a year to get going and the preliminary organizing will be done by a friend with a good deal more experience of office-management. Have you met her? Miss Yvette Norbury?"

"I've met the *name*. Is she the young lovely I've seen him dining with?"

"That I can't say. She's a pretty girl, though I shouldn't call her lovely; and she's young, though I imagine she's a few years older than he is. You'll meet her at Ridgeway. And, while she lists the books he wants to loot from my library, you can tell him what you've arranged with Philip and Maurice. Frankly, it will be a relief to me if Norman takes kindly to stockbroking: I feel that people of his age have had an unsettling time, with their education interrupted, six years of war, an almost unrecognizable world to come back to . . ."

By talking of Norman, I at least succeeded in keeping Martin from asking me questions about Miss Norbury or trying to remember how he had even heard her name. As likely as not some gossip-writer had recorded in his or her peculiar idiom that: "*Lunching at the Blue Train, I saw pretty Yvette Norbury with Colin Whimboyne's handsome son Norman. I asked him how soon we were to have another play from his father . . .*" I did not want Martin or any of my other guests to approach Miss Norbury with any pre-conceptions that might cause them to change in any way their natural and normal manner in meeting a stranger. This young woman, I felt sure, would give a faultless performance as my leading lady in *The House-Party: A Play In An Undetermined Number of Acts*; but whether the play was a comedy or something more serious, whether it ran to a second act or whether the first and last curtain fell on her reading her own telegram of recall would depend on the rest of the company. If they gave an equally faultless performance, I thought that there would be no more than one act and that her final line would be in a whisper to Norman that, if she spent another hour in this house, she would just simply pass out.

"You remember," I observed to Violet, when we met three weeks later at Paddington, "Austin always called Ridgeway 'The Mausoleum'."

Christmas Day falling this year on a Tuesday, the party was assembling in time for dinner on the Monday; but for various reasons and on various pretexts one or two of the guests were coming on the Saturday. I had suggested to Violet that we should devote the week-end to a survey of the house and its furnishings; Norman, who had been staying with me since the end of his school term to study the accommodation in Grosvenor Road, was bringing Miss Norbury with him to save her having to arrive with a pack of strangers in an over-crowded train on Christmas Eve.

"Family-gatherings are always rather grim," said Violet, "but no one could call the house a mausoleum at other times. If I were this girl, I should be *thrilled* to have the *entrée* to Ridgeway. Watch her to-night, when she's looking through your visitors' book! I don't want to be spiteful, but, if I sized her up rightly at our one meeting, she's a type that—to my cost—I used to know unpleasantly well. Nigel's little friends had always worked out to a farthing what they expected to get out of him and what it was worth their while to put up with to get it."

"Then do you think," I asked, "that I'm simply shewing a cat the way to the dairy?"

"I should like to see her again before saying definitely that she *is* a cat. They've been friends, of one kind or another, for seven years; and she *hasn't* pounced. Seven years is a long time, Colin, for a completely physical affair; he couldn't *afford* to keep her in wanton splendour; and, like you, I can't see any other tie to hold them together. It's puzzling."

The Marlborough train drew in; and we chose our seats,

scattering papers to keep two corners for Norman and Miss Norbury. They arrived before I had time to get out and look for them; and, as we checked our watches by the clock over the main departure-platform, I felt that, if we had shut our eyes, we could wipe out the last seven years and go on from the night when we all met for dinner in Grosvenor Road. Was it the night when we received the news of Hitler's march into Prague? I saw Violet and Miss Norbury coming into my work-room together, after meeting and introducing themselves on the doorstep, I saw Norman arriving by car from Oxford, I could have reproduced Violet's friendly questions and the girl's frank answers at dinner to the moment when she suggested that, as she did not smoke, she should go up to the "auditorium-chamber" and prepare for the beach-pyjamas scene in *Flowers By Request*. Now, as then, she was refusing my offer of a cigarette; and she was thanking me now for my invitation to Ridgeway, as she had thanked me then for my invitation to dinner in Grosvenor Road and, when Violet asked how the war had used her, she picked up the threads of a tiny argument, wholly forgotten by me, about the work that she would be allowed or urged or encouraged to undertake in the event of war.

"I gave you fair warning, Mr. Whimboyne," she reminded me, "that I shouldn't be content to type letters in a government office. One of the services . . . I was with the W.R.E.N.s for most of the time. Pretty hard work, but *interesting*. I expect you know my chief, Admiral Parmint? He wanted me to go back to the Admiralty with him when it was all over, but I couldn't face being just a shorthand-typist in a government office again. As Norman always says, I'd tasted blood: taking responsibility . . ."

"Parmint got a K.C.B., which I maintain should have gone to Yvette," said Norman.

"I believe he recommended me for an M.B.E.," said Miss Norbury, "but I don't know what happened to it and I don't care. What *I* liked, what I would give fifty K.C.B.s for, was his way of saying there was a ticklish job and I must find the best way of doing it. I told you when we met that day, Mr. Whimboyne, that they'd asked me to come back to Queen Anne's Gate, but I did want a job where I could use my own initiative . . ."

"And, from what you told me," I put in, "you're now working for about a dozen people who all present you with ticklish jobs and beg you to find a way out of their difficulties for them."

Miss Norbury assured me, with a smile, that it was only five. Too circumspect even to give their names, she led me to understand that they ranged from a shipping magnate by way of a publisher to one of the opposition-leaders in the House of Lords. Their one common quality seemed to be that, as bachelors, widowers, or husbands of invalid wives, they all needed the services of an active, shrewd and cool-headed young woman to whom nothing had ever to be explained a second time and who could be trusted implicitly when told to use her own discretion.

This, it should go without saying, was not at all the picture that she painted of herself, in her candid and extremely modest answers to Violet's questions. In her own words, used of some more than ordinarily ticklish job, "One just has to do one's best: nobody can do *more* than that"; far from insinuating that she was an omniscient and omnipotent power behind thrones, she confessed frankly how far she often fell short of her own ideals.

"I can't speak a word of any language but my own," she explained. "Therefore, I'm useless to one of my clients or employers or whatever you like to call them when important foreigners come over to see him. I've taught myself a little book-keeping, but I couldn't read a balance-sheet, as one of the others is always begging me to do, to save my life. What I should *like* . . . And I'm sure there's room for it, especially when so many husbands and wives are *both* in public life . . . I don't know Lord McGowan, but, if I worked for him, he ought to feel he could say: 'I'm starting for South America in five minutes. I shall be away six months. Carry on!' "

I looked across at Violet and saw her nodding gently to herself. This, then, she seemed to be saying, was the part that Miss Norbury had chosen: to be herself, naturally and straightforwardly. I had always thought she was a good enough actress to impose herself on any audience that knew nothing of her; but, since Norman and Violet and I all knew something about her, she was not pretending to be anything but what she was. I admired her good sense; so, I thought, did Violet; but from a faintly puzzled frown I felt she was saying that this girl was quite different from anything that she had expected and, later, as our carriage filled and she began to talk in an undertone to Miss Norbury, the friendliness of her manner suggested that she was finding her very much better than she had expected.

At our journey's end, indeed, she said as much:

"More in her than I thought, Colin. Much more."

"If her various jobs are as responsible as she makes out (I've no reason to think they aren't), she couldn't hold them down for a day if she were only a typist in a government office. You seem to have won her confidence."

"Well, we're both career-women. In a way, we've both invented careers for ourselves. Yvette—yes, we're on those terms already!—won't be content with her present work indefinitely. She has ideas. I agree wholeheartedly that there's unlimited scope for able, educated young women of character who will take complete charge of a busy man's private life. Wouldn't you pay the earth, my dear, for some one who took everything off your hands, here and in London, leaving you with proper time and strength for your own work? She was talking to me about starting a school for girls who fancied a life of that kind. I think there's a lot in it."

"Did she say anything about Norman?"

Violet smiled and waited till he and Miss Norbury had packed their luggage and themselves into his car.

"I can't help wondering, my dear," she then said, "whether the whole of this party isn't a work of supererogation! If she marries Norman, it will be because they're in love, not for anything she can get out of him. She's *making* all the money she needs, a great deal more than he is. If she even thinks of marrying him, she won't be put off by any talk about living in a mausoleum. She doesn't care about the 'county', she doesn't want the 'county', it's Norman she wants . . . "

"Ah!"

"Well, a blind man could see they're in love! The odd thing is that they've apparently been in love for about seven years . . . She didn't say it in so many words, but I gathered that Norman had been pressing her hard to marry him and she has always dodged it. I believe that if she found she could marry him without giving up her career, which is a new toy, a new baby to her . . ."

"And she would have to give it up if they married and began to have flesh-and-blood babies . . . Well, here's my car. Elizabeth

2E

couldn't be sure the other day whether Miss Norbury was my friend or Norman's: when he goes ahead like this, she can't be left in much doubt."

As we got into the car, Violet answered a little uncomfortably that no one who saw them together could be left long in doubt that they were in love.

"I'm afraid it may be rather a shock for poor Elizabeth," she added.

"Well, Miss Norbury seems to have left an unexpectedly good impression on you," I said. "If she leaves the same sort of impression on Elizabeth . . ."

"It's unfortunate that Elizabeth should never have heard of her till Yvette is sprung on her after seven years. However, it's too late for us to think about that now."

For Elizabeth, on the other hand, it was not too late. When the family-gathering was first debated, I had told her that I would make all arrangements; and when we arrived, I felt that all my arranging might have been covered by the words: "Put back the clock-hands and start again any moment between 1919 and 1929!" The door was opened for us by Cruikshank; and tea was awaiting us in the saloon, which had been draped in dust-sheets for upwards of six years until now. Though the house wore an air of honourable shabbiness, it was clean and tidy; the housemaids imported by Mrs. Cruikshank from her canteen might have spent their life in our service; and, though I knew that Elizabeth would have preferred to keep Norman to herself in one corner of the house, I thought that she had resigned herself to "going back", as she called it, "to 1939" when the work of managing was taken out of her hands and she could see her family in three generations restored to her. I began to think differently at the end of tea when I asked whether Violet and Miss Norbury would like to see their rooms and Elizabeth found it necessary to ask which rooms they were being given.

"I've been at the depot all day," she explained, "which must be my excuse for being still in uniform. Mrs. Cruikshank told me that you had arranged everything with her, Colin, but she didn't say *what* had been arranged."

"She gave me a list," said Norman pacifically, "which I expect was intended for you. Lady Oakhirst, the oak room; Yvette, the Chinese room."

"Oh, then we're next to each other, Yvette," said Violet. "I thought," she continued to Elizabeth, "that your V.A.M.P.s had been disbanded."

"Not yet. Their work came to an end with the war in Europe, but a great many people have been saying that the organization ought to be retained and turned to civil purposes. We've been having a conference of county commandants." Perhaps belatedly conscious that she had struck a faintly jarring note two or three moments before, Elizabeth explained to me that she had not intended to say anything until there was something definite to say: "When I told you that I might possibly be kept very busy . . . This is a big house to run," she continued to Violet, "when you're working ten or twelve hours a day at an office in Marlborough."

I paid a sincere, if somewhat perfunctory, tribute to the work of the Pioneers in the war; and, as Elizabeth had obviously donned her uniform for the single purpose of demonstrating that she accepted no responsibility for anything that I chose to do at Ridgeway, I rang the bell for Mrs. Cruikshank to shew Violet and Miss Norbury their rooms. Though her methods left something to be desired, I had no complaint to make of Elizabeth's decision. With her loathing for a social life to which she always felt inadequate, the best hope for Ridgeway, for myself, for Norman and for the great new interest that Violet and I hoped to see the house providing for him was that she should have an excuse for being out of it as much as possible.

"Is that Mrs. Cruikshank's list?," she asked, when we were alone and I was studying the paper that Norman had given me.

"Here it is, if you would like to see it," I said. "They all seem to have been given the rooms they usually have. We may expect the rest of the party in time for dinner on Monday."

"I see. Before they arrive, Colin, I should like to know how I stand. Who *is* this Miss Norbury, whom Violet and Norman call 'Yvette'? Are they . . . ? I mean, is she the future Mrs. Norman Whimboyne? Have you invited her to meet the family? I'm completely in the dark! Why have you all made such a mystery about her? If I thought that all this talk of 'arranging' . . . There are some arrangings that I can't allow to be done behind my back. Who *is* she? What stage have she and Norman reached? Why have I been told nothing?"

"I told you pretty well all I knew of her before she was invited," I answered. "It doesn't amount to much. I don't think

I said that she worked for me in Queen Anne's Gate for a few weeks, but I don't feel that really adds anything. As regards her and Norman, you can ask him if you think that would be diplomatic. I can tell you nothing, because I know nothing. Except that this *isn't* a shewing-off party. If I were you, I should wait for Norman to speak. If he ever means to, that is . . ."

IX

THE responsibility—a less contentious word than credit or discredit—for the Christmas party had been taken by me on my own shoulders; it was at my feet that the resultant bouquets fell.

With a single exception, every one in the house complimented me at one time or another on my success; and, as Elizabeth found no audible fault with my arrangements, I might—if I had thought about it—have congratulated myself on winning at least her silent approval. With the exception of a single embarrassing moment at the end, my success was obvious; and, whatever I was expecting or hoping from the experiment of presenting Ridgeway as the background of Norman's life and of inviting Miss Yvette Norbury to say how well or ill she thought she would fit in with it, I had Violet's assurance that in two days I had achieved more to unite the family and safeguard the future, to contrive a pattern of life for Norman and to reconcile Elizabeth to it than she herself could have hoped to see me achieving in two years.

"If I were a cynic," she observed, as we walked back from church on Christmas Day, "I should say that you had studied the weak spot in all these people and gone straight for it. *Every one*, as you often told me, stood to lose by a family feud; for the price of playing old Wardle at Dingley Dell for twenty-four hours you've got Norman a job and Cheshunts a prospective young partner, you've restored their country-club to Martin and Humfrey, who were sick of a servantless life, and you've given them back to their sorrowing mother, thereby liberating Norman. They'll consent to being bored by poor Elizabeth now that they can count on you and the Cruikshanks for a well-run house and as good a table as they'll find anywhere in these difficult times. Elizabeth will be so pleased to have little grandsons crawling over her that she won't mind sitting silent while the 'clever'

people talk. Was it your idea, by the way, that she should breathe
new life into her Vamps?"

"You make me out more Machiavellian than I am," I protested. "They are her refuge and excuse if she finds my parties too
much for her. I've only pointed out to these people which side
their bread is buttered. You'll find that even Kitty will be
prepared to forgive and forget when racing begins again at
Newbury."

"Meanwhile, the important thing is that Norman can make
what he likes of his life."

"He sees it himself. He's in better spirits than at any time since
the war ended. Well, on a long view: Ridgeway, a job that will
enable him to keep it up, this book-exchange as a hobby to
lighten a life of stocks and shares. I haven't had much time to
talk about the various changes that you and I were discussing at
the week-end . . ."

Violet interrupted to say that Norman and she had discussed
little else.

"He's shy of you, my dear," she added, "over plans for
spending your money and still more over plans for the time when
you're dead, but to me, as a specialist . . . I don't need to tell you
that he loves the place, but he *knows* every loose stair-rod, he's
passionately interested in all my suggestions and it's an *intelligent*
interest."

"Did he contribute anything on his own account?"

"Yes. He wanted to know what I thought about dividing the
house into so many separate, self-contained whatever-you-like-
to-call-them. Like Bamborough Castle on a miniature scale. One
flat or wing for you and Elizabeth, one for Martin and his family
at week-ends, one for Humfrey . . ."

As she paused, I asked what he was contemplating for
himself.

"Oh, he had marked out his own corner. Until, as he put it,
the time came for making other arrangements. Meaning, my dear,
what you and I are not afraid to express quite bluntly: when you
die and he succeeds you."

"A corner for himself *alone*?," I asked. "All my long-terms
discussions with him have envisaged a wife, an heir . . ."

"And even to me he doesn't speak freely on that subject. If it
rested with him . . ."

"He would marry Yvette tomorrow! Both my brothers

have asked me when they're to look out for an announcement. And they only met her yesterday!"

And the wives of both Elizabeth's brothers, Violet informed me, had put the same question to her.

"Before I could answer," she continued, "Yvette answered for me by giving her views on women's work. Apparently she had an ailing mother at one time and she told Elizabeth almost brutally that she was more useful helping busy men and making an income for Dr. Dalton to tax than in looking after some one whose value to the community was finished. Somebody, of course, asked whether a woman's natural career was not to marry and bring up a family, but Yvette would only say that—if so—we must reorganize employment in such a way that career-women like her were granted leave of absence so that they could have their babies without giving up their other careers. I fancied that Elizabeth decided from that moment she had nothing to fear."

As Norman passed us with long strides, calling out a reminder that I had promised to meet him in the book-room, I wondered whether he had yet been told of this conversation between his mother and Yvette. If so, what did he make of it? Had they already agreed that, if she married him, he would raise no objection to her going on working? Was Yvette already planning so to reorganize her own employment that she could have her babies without giving up her career? Unless I wholly misread my own son, to marry and produce an heir was a prerequisite to every thought about Ridgeway; if he and Yvette had been friends or more than friends for upwards of seven years, I could not hear him sighing as a lover and obeying as a son if he were told to give her up, I could not picture him with a wife in Wiltshire and a mistress in London and least of all could I imagine him listening to his own or any one else's voice that whispered how affairs of this kind always ended sooner or later, urging him to enjoy himself while he could and to settle down when he must.

Conceivably, if responsibility and initiative were the chief attraction in Yvette's chosen career, they had agreed that she could exercise all the initiative she possessed in setting up her school for personal assistants, all the responsibility she desired in creating the book-exchange. When we reached the house, Norman drew me into the saloon, where a vast Christmas-tree stood waiting to be despoiled after luncheon, and asked whether I knew anything of the service-flats in Pendragon Court, which

Martin had recommended to him. "Poor mummy" might be better reconciled to his leaving her if she knew that there was a staff to cook and clean and air and mend for him; she could, if she liked, telephone nightly, which had hardly been possible when he was sharing a friend's flat; and he could walk in three minutes to Grosvenor Road when Yvette had converted the rooms that I was putting at his disposal.

"All things considered," he said, "it will be best for me to be on my own."

It would be better certainly, I thought, than for him to join me and give Elizabeth the impression that he preferred my society to hers, better than for her to suggest joining both of us, better than for her and me to be left wondering about the establishment in Chelsea.

"We'll ask Violet," I said. "She did the furnishing of Pendragon Court before the war. Will it suit you to make a start with the books to-morrow?"

"We've begun already. And I can tell you that you've laid up treasure, at least on earth, with your first editions of modern works."

To prove his own point, Norman dragged me into the bookroom, where John and his wife were whispering over *The Times* crossword-puzzle, while Henry read out questions from the Christmas general-knowledge paper for Philip and Maurice to answer. Their supercilious ladies seemed to be thawing under the influence of Humfrey's cocktails; and, when Elizabeth—to mark the occasion festive—announced gaily that she would have a sip out of Yvette's glass, I felt that my success had reached its climax.

"I can honestly say," I told Norman, as we went in to luncheon, "that I've never bought a first edition for its own sake. When an author has given me pleasure, I feel that the least I can do is to order his next the moment it's announced. *Jane Our Stranger* or *The Constant Nymph* . . ."

I broke off as Elizabeth, who had a young grandson on either side, coaxed them to say grace; and, while she draped them in bibs, Violet (who had been urged to prepare conversational openings through which the oldest and the shyest could enter without fear) invited Barbara and Monica to say whether Mary Borden and Margaret Kennedy appealed to readers of their generation. When one or other confessed that they were both before her time, somebody—either Philip or Maurice—began to reel off names like Henry Harland or Alfred Mason, with the question: "Does *any one* read him now?" or the statement: "I couldn't possibly say what his *date* was." It was sorry stuff; but it put every one into an amiable mood. When the elders among us had recalled that the Sherlock Holmes *Memoirs* were appearing in the *Strand Magazine* when we first went to our preparatory schools and that Kipling's *Stalky And Co* stories were coming out in the *Windsor* as we left, Yvette Norbury asked me how, in a play not of to-day or yesterday, I could make sure that my characters were speaking the language of the period.

"I suppose," she continued, "if you turned up the old fashion-papers, you could see when hobble-skirts came in, but how do you know when people were using a phrase like 'Sez you'?"

"I turn up the bound volumes of *Punch*," I answered. "Which are also quite invaluable for indicating the collective temper at least of *Punch*-readers. When they thought that 'Spam' was a joke and when they decided that food-rationing had become more than a joke. I admit I'm badly gravelled when I try to date something that's not topical enough for *Punch*, not important enough for the *Annual Register*, and yet the sort of thing that would be in the minds of all my characters."

"Such as?," asked Violet.

I thought for a moment and then told Philip and Maurice that they were not to answer till every one else had guessed.

"Can any one say within five years when the Hatry case was?," I asked. "I can't, though at the time it left an impression far beyond the City of London. In a dinner-party scene my characters might well be talking about it. I can't tell you when the Marconi scandal was: three or four years before the 1914 war, I should say, when the Liberal government was very unpopular and 'Marconi' almost a heaven-set stick to beat it with."

"My trouble," said Philip, "is that, unless it's something that affects *me*, I can never remember what a case was about. There was one that had to do with a 'Slingsby baby': I suppose Humfrey could tell us what great legal principle was involved. That wasn't the same as the Russell case, was it?"

"The Russell divorce-case?," asked Humfrey. "Evidence of non-access and so on?"

At the word divorce, Elizabeth looked anxiously at her small grandsons and reminded us that little pitchers had long ears.

"I thought the carols were better even than usual," she went on. "I told the vicar so. He takes so much trouble . . ."

"As much as you take, mummy, to keep the fun clean!," Martin laughed. "Divorce may be as regrettable as you like, but you won't stop it by refusing to have it mentioned. Lord, what hours Humfrey and I used to spend with the *really* disreputable papers that we borrowed from the servants' hall because your precious *Morning Post* was so sparing of details. A divorce-case *was* a divorce-case in those days. Now, when all the nubbly bits are cut out . . . It's the same with murders . . ."

"Are murders included in the *Annual Register*?," Maurice asked me. "Unlike Philip, I could usually tell you what a *cause célèbre* was about, but I couldn't date it to save my life. The 'Billy Carlton' case: I should *say* it was soon after the 1918 armistice, but that's a pure guess. The *case* . . ."

As he began to outline it, Humfrey turned to ask Yvette whether she had ever attended a murder-trial.

"Thank goodness, no!," the girl answered with a shudder. "I call that *morbid*! The Old Bailey! *You* don't have to practise there, do you?"

"I've never been inside the place. You have? The Commercial Court may be lacking in sensation, but it's comparatively respectable and as I'm exempt from jury-service . . ."

"I've only been summoned once—some action against an insurance-company; and, if I thought I should ever have to sit while a man was being tried for his life, I think I should cut the country!"

Humfrey seized eagerly on the opportunity of explaining the difference between a special and a common jury.

"So the Old Bailey need have no terrors for you," he assured her, "unless you were called as a witness. Who was trying this case you were speaking of? Langborne? He's a good judge still, but appallingly deaf. I suppose you don't remember who was in the case? The counsel, I mean?"

Yvette shook her head:

"They all seemed to be just 'Me learned friend, may it please you, me lord'. There were two—silks, do you call them?—silks, but they always seemed to be in another court, me Lord, and a small army of younger men who did all the work. Are they called juniors? And a mysterious little man with a drooping eyelid, who seemed to be a complete gate-crasher. He was deafer than

the judge! They had a shouting-match for about ten minutes till
the little man got it across that he held—now let me get this
right!—a watching-brief—Would that be it?—for somebody else.
I must say, Mr. Gerrold, I thought the whole business was a
shocking waste of time. When we were all set to begin, it was
time for luncheon; and, when we all came back afterwards, a
fat man with a bottle-nose announced that he and his learned
friend had 'settled', if that's the right word. Why they couldn't
have settled the day before . . ."

"If they had," said Humfrey, "I should have missed the finest
Ruth-Draper performance I've ever heard! Can't you go on, Miss
Norbury? You gave me Langborne, but I can give you the fat
man without being told that he had a bottle-nose, I can give
you the little deaf man with the watching-brief. Go on,
please!"

"But there's nothing to go on with! I don't know these
people's names, but I remember how they looked and spoke.
Ruth Draper, indeed! By the way, what's *her* date? I've never
seen her, but I seem to have heard of her all my life. Let's try
Mr. Whimboyne!"

Several of us indulged in rather wild guesses; Norman
fetched *Who's Who* from the book-room; Philip contrasted the
mimics of an earlier age—Cissie Loftus and Ada Reeve—with
such moderns as Florence Desmond; and Violet again congratulated me on the success of my party.

"I think it's going quite well," I said.

Led by the two small boys, every one was having a second
helping of roast turkey. Another year, Elizabeth was telling one
of them, they must come in time to stir the Christmas puddings;
and Norman was explaining to the other how many "happy
months" they could secure by gobbling all the mince-pies in sight
between now and Twelfth Night.

" 'Another year' . . . ," Violet repeated.

"And we now know the secret for starting general conversation: one's earliest memories of this or that, the difference
between present times and our own young days. I just heard
Elizabeth say that, when *she* was a child, she wasn't allowed to
read *The Wide, Wide World*; her mother—naughty girl—read
Jane Eyre in bed by candle-light."

"Maurice is certainly enjoying himself with his *causes
célèbres*: the Maybrick case, Crippen, the 'brides in the bath' . . ."

She broke off as Philip, on an impulse, looked round him and asked for a pencil and paper.

"A question," he explained, "that you can add to *The Times* general-knowledge paper. 'What were the following? The Tranby Croft Case. The Tichborne Case. The Oscar Slater Case' . . ."

"Philip, *please*!," Elizabeth expostulated with a second agonized glance at her grandsons.

"I said 'Slater', not 'Wilde'," her brother returned, "but I shall have to cut it out, as I'm not absolutely certain what it was. Maurice! The Oscar Slater Case?"

"Wasn't it something to do with cattle-maiming?," asked John.

"*I* associate it," said Henry, "with Conan Doyle. Didn't he do some practical Sherlock-Holmesing to prove that there the been a miscarriage of justice?"

"I believe that *was* it. Well, now," Philip continued, "the Courvoisier Case. The Parnell Case . . ."

"Do you mean the Parnell divorce-case or the Parnell commission?," I asked.

"Oh, you've spoilt it, Colin!," Philip grumbled. "I wanted to see whether these young people had ever heard of Pigott and the forged letters. They all know about Kitty O'Shea. I suppose the Dreyfus Case is *too* easy. And yet it must be the best part of half-a-century old. I remember I was still at school in Hampstead. What was the name, Maurice? Stallard! I was at Stallard's and on my way home I used to pass a paper-shop. I remember pictures of Dreyfus being stripped of his badges of rank, pictures of Devil's Island. . . . The Fell-Maddison Case."

As he wrote down the name, Lady Mary observed that she had never heard of Fell-Maddison.

"He was a doctor who came to grief. Manslaughter, I think the charge was. Any way he was convicted. The interest of the case is that, as he left the dock, he took poison."

"Are you *sure*, Philip?" To my amazement which—I think—was shared by every one, it was Elizabeth speaking, almost for the first time since the beginning of luncheon. "I remember reading about the case. The man who took poison as he left the dock was that fraudulent company-promoter."

"*I* believe mummy's a life-subscriber to the *Police News*," said Martin.

"I read about the case," Elizabeth defended herself, "because I knew something of the woman this doctor killed. No, I mustn't say *that*! The woman for whose death he was responsible."

To the amazement of every one, beginning with me, Yvette Norbury interrupted her conversation with Humfrey to turn, colouring slightly with embarrassment at contradicting her hostess, to insist that Elizabeth was mistaken:

"He didn't kill her. She's alive at this minute. And he didn't commit suicide. He went to prison for two years. You must forgive me for being so positive, but for a few very unpleasant hours *I* was mixed up with the case. You can understand it's not a thing I like to talk about. And you," she continued to Humfrey, "can understand why the very name of the Old Bailey sends a cold shiver down my spine."

With this single exception, my Christmas party—as almost every one sooner or later told me—was a complete success. Those who had wondered for a moment how they knew the name of Yvette Norbury needed to wonder no more.

X

EVER since "Old Alec" Cheshunt's sudden and still mysterious death, I have experienced the utmost difficulty, when talking to any members of his family, in keeping away from the subject of suicide. As it is not one that normally obsesses me, I can only think that my conscious effort to avoid it in some way upsets my unconscious controls, even as a conscious effort to remember how a certain passage of music was fingered may inhibit a pianist from fingering it at all. When my brother-in-law Philip began to compile his list of cases, I felt an innocently perverse, but almost overpowering, temptation to suggest "The Macdonald Case", "The White Case" and "The Kruger Case".

I am convinced that Philip's unfortunate reference to "The Fell-Maddison Case" was occasioned by a similar upset of his unconscious controls. To him, as to Elizabeth and Violet and Martin, the name of Yvette Norbury was vaguely familiar; unlike them, he was able to associate it with the name of Fell-Maddison; and, recalling that the case had been an unsavoury one, he told himself that on no account must he mention or even think of it in Miss Norbury's presence. Banished from his conscious mind, it skulked in his unconscious till it could catch him off his guard. Later that day, when he led me aside to ask whether an apology would only make a bad position worse, he mentioned that the wretched case had invaded his dreams the night before and that he had woken up repeating: "Stamford . . . Portia Stamford."

"Which says no more to me," I observed, "than Fell-Maddison."

"She was one of Kitty's less reputable friends, but a time came when even Kitty had to drop her if she didn't want to be dropped by every one else. It was only drink and man-hunting in the early days; when it became drugs and shop-lifting . . . Surely you've seen her name in the papers?"

"I'm afraid I take very little interest in the vices of people I don't know. Unlike Elizabeth, apparently," I continued with an absence of charity only to be excused by the still rankling knowledge that by their clumsiness at luncheon Philip and Elizabeth had embarrassed one of my guests.

"I fancy Rella too met her with Kitty. Well, of course, if you don't read the papers, you're not likely to have heard of Fell-Maddison. It was the old story! This Stamford girl had got into trouble and went to Fell-Maddison to get her out of it. He must have thought that, as an earl's daughter who had just had a pretty miraculous let-off, she could be trusted to keep her mouth shut. There he didn't reckon with the irresponsible *vanity* of these young fools: anything to shew how clever they are! If Lady Portia didn't brag about what Fell-Maddison had done for her, she bragged about what her 'angel-man' would do for any friend of hers. Talk of that kind gets round: sooner or later, some of it reaches Scotland Yard. One fine day this prosperous middle-aged doctor with the wife and three children finds himself being escorted to Bow Street . . ."

As he paused, I asked how Yvette Norbury had even for a few hours been mixed up with the case.

"I think that was excess of zeal. The man who made the arrest thought there was a regular gang at work and that, as Miss Norbury knew the doctor and Lady Portia, she must be a member of it. In fact, the worst that could be charged against her was that she *may* have introduced them to each other: even that was by no means clear. She was dismissed with an apology from the prosecuting counsel. And, talking of apologies, Colin . . ."

"In your place, I should leave things as they are," I said. "It was a pure accident. And perhaps by now she is feeling rather grateful for it. You say the case was unsavoury. Her name was known to have been mixed up with it. If she's had no chance of clearing herself . . ."

"I thought she shewed great pluck. Well, then, I'll say nothing," he added in an undertone as Norman and Yvette came in to demand my presence in the book-room.

As we set to work, I decided that the subject had been dismissed from both their minds; and I continued to think so that night and next day until the moment, shortly after luncheon, when—the sun breaking suddenly through—I suggested that we should give ourselves half a day's holiday and go for a walk on the Downs. If we did, Norman warned me, we should not finish our work. I proposed a week's adjournment and asked Yvette whether she would come back for the New Year.

"It's terribly sweet of you, Mr. Whimboyne," she answered, "but I'm afraid it's not possible."

"You forget she's a working woman, daddy," Norman added. "If you suggested a party in *London* . . ."

The lines fell so pat as to give me the impression of having been rehearsed: for any one of a dozen reasons I suspected that these two had decided not to repeat the experiment of the last four days and that, if Yvette had asked what she was to say in the event of my telling her to come again soon, Norman had advised her to plead pressure of work. She did not, apparently, object to meeting me; Violet seemed to have won her confidence before they had been talking together in the train for half an hour; and, so far as I could see, she had scored a personal triumph with every member of the party and staff in turn. Had she in fact not enjoyed herself as much as she pretended and was she saying that, now she had passed muster, there was no reason under Heaven why she should come back here to be bored?

"I ought to have remembered that the New Year comes on a working day," I said. "A week-end, though, when there isn't a party and we can really roll up our sleeves . . ."

"That's what we're planning to do in London, if we can finish down here to-day," Yvette explained. "When you spoke to me that day about literary typing, Mr. Whimboyne, I told you I just simply couldn't take on more work. Well, I've gone back on that to the extent of promising Norman to help him till we've seen whether there's a future for this book-business, but it will mean working at week-ends and I shan't be able to do that indefinitely without cracking up."

"That we certainly don't want," I said. "So, if we can finish here to-day, we will. I'm afraid my workroom in London will be a much bigger proposition, as there must be five times as many books there."

"But they're all catalogued," Norman put in. "If you just go through your card-index drawer by drawer . . . Did you ask Lady Oakhirst, by the way, about Pendragon Court?"

I answered that as yet I had not had an opportunity; and Violet, from the top of a step-ladder, called down that, if he wanted any information, he had come to the right person, since she had spent fully half of the previous week looking at bed-sitting-rooms for her husband.

"Did I tell you," she asked me in a tone obviously intended for an audience that might usefully pass her words on, "that the house in Barton Street is being let again? Again to an M.P.? For the next few years I expect to be travelling about the country so much that my flatlet in Old Burlington Street will meet all my requirements on the occasions when I'm in London."

"Nigel put up at his club, didn't he, the time before?"

"Yes, but there's so much competition now that no member may have a bedroom for more than a week on end. If Nigel shifts his headquarters to London, he'll be much more comfortable, as I've told him, in a place of his own." As she paused to let me digest the fact that she had lately surmounted another crisis, I felt that I could hear her telling Nigel the delights of Pendragon Court; and, if he had ventured to say that he would be more comfortable still in Barton Street, I could see her inexorable shake of the head. "All the flats I saw were *good*," she continued to Norman, "but I've no first-hand knowledge of the way they look after you. The person to tell you about that is your godfather: Clayton has lived there for years."

"Lord, *that* rather takes the gilt off the gingerbread . . .," Norman sighed. "If I'm going to run into *him* at all hours . . ."

Violet explained that, as Pendragon Court consisted of four blocks built round a grass quadrangle, it was possible for tenants in different blocks to pass half a lifetime without seeing their neighbours.

"For what it's worth," she added, "I think your mother would feel happier in mind . . ."

"If she thought Clayton was keeping an eye on me? We-ell . . . So long as he keeps it at a distance . . . Are you letting your house for long?," he asked, as though any other subject of conversation would be more welcome than his godfather.

"Three years. By the end of that time we ought to know rather better how things are shaping. I believe my tenant moved in yesterday. I should have liked a little more time, as *I* was contemplating a New-Year's-Eve party . . ."

"Everything points to Grosvenor Road," I said. "That's next Monday, isn't it? Are you all free? Would it amuse you?"

As the idea had really been Norman's, neither he nor Yvette could well think better of it now; but in accepting he asked that the party should be kept small.

"I should like just the four of *us*," he continued. "And I shouldn't be at all sorry if we broke up without *Auld Lang Syne* and the midnight chimes. I have to make my *début* next day as a clear-eyed, clean-complexioned, steady-handed young City clerk."

Perhaps a faint bitterness in his voice, perhaps the loving eagerness with which a moment later he pounced on some unsuspected treasure of mine inspired Violet to come down from her steps and make for the library-catalogue by the fireplace.

"A proposal!," she announced. "Norman, my dear, if you'll explain—I'm really quite intelligent!—what you want done about making these index-cards, your father and I can finish what you and Yvette have been doing. I'm coming back at the week-end on my own job and I should dearly like some fresh air now before the light goes. If I'm to help over your flat, too . . ."

Five minutes later all four of us were on the track leading up to the Downs. I walked with Yvette, setting the pace; and, as the others allowed a generous gap to form behind us, I chose to think that Violet, with the sympathy that Norman could no more withstand than I at his age, both of us knowing it to be born of true understanding and love, was trying to reconcile him to the new work and life that would begin for him in a week's time. For myself, it was the first occasion on which I had been alone with Yvette since we parted in Sloane Square and I fancied that she too must be remembering this when she made me a prim little speech of thanks for my kindness in asking her to Ridgeway.

"I've heard so much of the place from Norman," she continued. "He does so love it. . . . And yet he's so unhappy about it. . . . I *jumped* at your invitation, Mr. Whimboyne, because I felt that, until I'd seen it with my own eyes, I couldn't help him. And I wanted to help. He's terribly pathetic when he's out of love with life. Like a child who can't tell you where the pain is. I'm not all *that* older, but, when things aren't going well—they were going *badly* when he left that horrible school!—he comes to be comforted. I might be his *mother*! I told you he was a whole-time job!"

"And I hope you've enjoyed your short visit well enough to come again," I said.

"It's a lovely house. I *can* understand now why you wouldn't let it go out of the family, why Norman—as he so often says—is *selling* himself to keep it. I used to tell him that was a silly way of talking, because there wasn't anything he wanted to do more, like writing plays or composing music. He adores anything to do with books, but they're a sideshow and he'll have plenty of time for them. . . . Thank goodness the grass is dry! As a complete Londoner, I'm badly off for country shoes."

"Is it as the complete Londoner," I asked, "that you've not yet said whether you've enjoyed this venture in the country? In fairness to the garden, you ought to see it in May."

Yvette assured me that she had enjoyed every moment of her time with us, though she went on at once to say that this was perhaps for other reasons that I supposed:

"If I was to make him . . . oh, at *peace* with himself, I had to see what life here was like. Well . . . May I speak quite frankly, Mr. Whimboyne? Try as he may, he doesn't get on well with his half-brothers. He warned me that I should find them *and* his uncles 'flashy' and 'false', I think he said. I fortunately can take people as they come, but the idea of being boxed up in an office with people whose only thought is to make money and splash it about in what he thinks rather a vulgar way . . . I've told him that he *won't* be boxed up with them *all* the time. He'll have this place at week-ends, he'll have his flat, he'll have Grosvenor Road and you. When all's said and done, most of us have dull, unpleasant patches in whatever our work may be. Surely to goodness, in the *war* . . ."

2F

"I've heard him say that the war spoilt him," I observed. "That's not a charge that many people bring against it . . ."

"And no one could call *him* spoilt! Mrs. Whimboyne may *try*, but Norman just hates having anything done for him. When I tell him he's behaving like a spoilt child, I mean that he's crying for the moon, expecting more of life than life can give, trying to do too much, carrying the whole world on his own shoulders . . ."

"I'm not sure that I quite follow . . .," I began.

As she glanced back over one shoulder, Yvette's green, kitten's eyes and rather characterless mouth seemed to have taken on the faintly defiant expression that I had seen once before as she bade me good-bye in Sloane Square.

"This time I *shan't* ask if I may speak quite frankly," she announced. "Norman tries to do too much by trying to be too many things to too many people. He adores you, he adores his mother. D'you mind my saying that, strange as it may seem, he adores me?"

"It's a self-evident truth. And I think you return the adoration."

"Not in quite the same way, perhaps. I *love* him, I was *in* love with him at one time and maybe I am a bit still. He wanted to marry me, but I told him that was just silly. I'm four years older than he is, I'm not of his world. I don't know how much you care about things like that; Mrs. Whimboyne *does*. Which is one reason why even your flowers in May don't tempt me to come back. She has been very sweet, especially since I told her about my work and said I should never marry, but she would have a blue fit if I said I'd changed my mind. That's neither here nor there, though. If I were four years younger than Norman and a duke's daughter into the bargain, she still wouldn't think I could make him happy. Nobody can but her! We-ell . . . You know all about the row in the summer and the way he blamed himself for it? He wants to be everything you expect him to be, he wants to be everything Mrs. Whimboyne wants—'I'm all she has left'—and, poor soul, he wants to be *himself*. That's what I mean about trying to play three different parts at the same time. It gets on his nerves . . ."

As she paused, I suggested that she might have said: "It *used* to get on his nerves."

"After this week," I explained, "after this party, if you like, he *can* be himself. His mother *won't* be alone, if he comes here at week-ends, he *won't* be all she has left, if Martin and Humfrey park their families here, he'll be everything I should like him to be and everything he wants to be, if he'll join me in running the place, which is what he would like to do. I admit that, until I succeeded in patching things up, he *was* pretty well desperate. That school by day and being the only son of his mother and she a widow at night. I honestly believe that, when we all meet on New Year's Eve, we shall be able to drink with some confidence to the prospect of better times ahead. If you like, you can tell Norman all that I've said, though I should be little surprised if Lady Oakhirst has been saying very much what I've said to you."

What Violet had in fact been saying I could only surmise from the new air of peace which I seemed to feel as they joined us by the first of the round barrows locally known as "The Giants' Graves". I had intended to go up to the summit of the ridge; but, after a glance to get her bearings, she chose a track to the left, saying that it led to her favourite part of the Downs.

"*You* once found us there," she reminded Norman. "That day you were taken ill . . . It's a place," she explained to Yvette, "that I shall remember as, I suppose, Saint Paul remembered to his dying day the place on the road to Damascus where the scales fell from his eyes."

"W-why? I mean, w-what happened?," asked Yvette, awed into a stammer by an intensity of feeling that I myself had only once or twice seen Violet display.

It was a place that I should always remember; but I could not imagine why she was leading these young people to it nor what she could find to say when she got them there.

"I'd been going through a bad time and I came to Mr. Whimboyne for advice. I was feeling like an animal in a trap! Then . . . Didn't Saint Paul on one occasion find that the door of his prison had opened of its own accord? That's what happened to me! As it has happened many times since! As I believe it would happen to most of the people who feel like animals in traps! It's always worth while to see whether the door is in fact locked on you."

Though she was addressing herself to Yvette, it was Norman who—till five minutes before—had seemed a trapped animal; and I divined that, when she nerved herself to expose the most sacred mystery in her life, she was promising herself to complete his cure.

"You mean that most of our prisons are imaginary?," he asked, speaking almost as though he had been drugged.

"A good many. But, even when they're real, there are very few locks you can't break. I used to think some incurable affliction was one; and then I remembered Franklin Roosevelt. This is the place! Unchanged! I had a horrible fear that the trees might have been cut down for the Ministry of Supply."

For our return to the house we changed partners; and this time I left Norman to go ahead.

"I gather you've had to fight another round with Nigel . . . ," I began.

"And you may gather that I won it," Violet interrupted. "That's not what I want to talk to you about. I left you to walk with Yvette: what's your verdict?"

"She isn't going to marry him. *Won't*. Which should be a comfort to Elizabeth. What their relations are I don't know and don't greatly care: she says she *was* in love with him and perhaps still is, but it's much more a maternal feeling. She's an odd young woman," I continued after a pause. "Quick, clever in an uneducated way, shrewd and with a much stronger character than I should have expected. She was a vague, lymphatic little collection of gramophone-records when I first knew her. " 'Yes, Mr. Whimboyne, and one carbon for your own file.' 'But, Mr. Whimboyne, I can't act!' I don't know whether it's the war or this queer job she has made for herself, but she gives me the impression of being extraordinarily sensible. And you?"

I must have waited fully two minutes for Violet's answer, which she prefaced by offering to wager any sum I liked that it would not be what I expected.

"If I wasn't afraid of indiscriminate vitriol-throwing . . . ," she began.

"You're *rather* sorry that she *won't* marry Norman?"

"I'm glad we didn't bet: I should have lost. How did you guess?"

"The thought had already crossed my own mind: he *might* go farther and fare worse. However, as she won't have him, she's safe from having her eyes gouged out by Elizabeth. At the same time, it's not a *satisfactory* position: two young people in love and both knowing that nothing can come of it. As you know, my dear, *I* went through that experience and it pretty nearly sent me off my head."

With the result, I added to myself, that I had married Elizabeth on the rebound; in turn with the result that we had combined to bring Norman into existence.

"It would be a quite hopeless position if nothing came to change it," said Violet. "Something *will*, darling Colin, something *must*! That's why I took them to our Holy of Holies and stripped myself. I don't know what they thought. I don't greatly care. I wouldn't *let* them be prisoners or trapped animals. They won't now."

"How can they help it?"

"He may give her up, for the sake of this place, if the alternative is perpetual celibacy. She may walk out of his life, for *his* sake, if there's no other means. Or she may tell Elizabeth that she has changed her mind about marriage for career-women. There you have *three* ways of breaking the lock. They can't go on as they are. They see it for themselves. It might have been an expensive discovery if they'd been left to *make* it for themselves."

XI

THOUGH Violet still kept her ten-year diary, we had long abandoned the practice of mortifying our spirits by looking back in December to what we had been predicting in January.

For six years after 1939 I do not remember that we wasted much time on predicting anything; and, while we waited by ourselves—after Norman and Yvette had left—to see 1946 in, nothing in the immediate future seemed definite enough to be worth predicting, though I could tell Violet (as I had told Yvette that afternoon on the Downs) that I believed we might now drink confidently to generally better times ahead.

In my opinion, any improvement must come so gradually as to be hardly noticeable; and so, I think, it proved. The whole of 1946, apart from my brother Henry's death half-way through, and indeed the whole of 1947 and the first part of 1948 passed so uneventfully that I should find great difficulty now in picking out any historic or red-letter or even faintly memorable day. My Christmas party produced its first blossom when Martin and Humfrey informed me that they had entered Masters Austin Alexander Colin and Tomlinson Alexander Colin for their old preparatory-school, its first fruits when Barbara and Monica brought the boys to Ridgeway for the beginning of the Easter term. As Elizabeth was to take charge when their mothers returned to London for mid-weeks and as they found it more convenient to accompany their husbands back for long week-ends, Norman could move into Pendragon Court without opposition. Usually he joined me on the Marlborough train on Saturdays for a day and a half of planning and arranging. Yvette came and went at her own times between Chelsea and West-minster while the book-exchange was being organized. I believe that Nigel settled into his new quarters at the same time as Norman; and I am afraid they were both plagued with calls from Clayton while their small stock of whiskey lasted, after which he transferred his attentions to me. A colourable imitation of civilized life was produced in Grosvenor Road when the Winters returned from their long exile at Ridgeway to look after me; and for the first time in six or eight years I felt at leisure to begin work on a new play.

"At leisure and at peace", I told Violet, who throughout these uneventful two years was occupying her flat in Old Burling-ton Street whenever she was not visiting the houses of her clients. "How long the peace will last . . ."

"It's more secure, on the *surface*, than I dared hope for two years ago," she answered. "Norman's earning golden opinions from his uncles; he's as happy as the day is long while he's sorting books here or plotting changes with you at Ridgeway. Until Martin and Humfrey find something that suits them better, Elizabeth can't wail that Norman is all she has left."

"Why did you say 'on the surface'?"

"Because I don't see how things *can* go on as they *are*. When Norman's made a partner, he'll be in a position to marry and start a family. While he couldn't afford it, nobody needed to bother about Yvette's place in his life."

I reminded Violet of the three ways in which she had once said these young people could break the lock that held them in a prison of frustration.

"Well, he hasn't given Yvette up and she hasn't dropped out of his life," Violet assured me. "Only the other day, Nigel asked me who the pretty girl was that he saw dining so often with Norman Whimboyne in the Pendragon restaurant."

"H'm. If Nigel has seen them, Clayton has probably seen them too and it's only a question of time before Elizabeth hears about it. Since the catering at Ridgeway improved, we've been favoured with two or three visits. What did you tell Nigel?"

If, Violet answered, this was the girl she presumed, Norman was considering the possibility of going into partnership with her over some business that I had sponsored when we were all together one Christmas at Ridgeway.

"That shewed," she explained, "that there was nothing furtive about these meetings. But, Colin my dear, when one talks of *partnerships* . . . Are you of the same mind now as then?"

"If they can stick to each other as apparently they've been sticking for a good many years . . . ," I began. "Though that's hardly an argument that I can use with Elizabeth."

"But, if they come for your blessing, you'll back up Yvette through thick and thin? Whoever the girl was, you and Norman would have to fight for her against Elizabeth. *You* don't mind the difference of age, of background?"

"If she's going to make him happy . . . I don't know that Philip and Maurice have got much satisfaction from marrying their ornaments of the peerage. I admit that, if Yvette dropped her aitches or performed that most dangerous and difficult feat of eating peas with a knife . . ."

Though I cannot give the month or even the year of this conversation in the tranquil aftermath of the war, I feel that, if I had known then all that I know now, I should have said that the period which I have called uneventful, the days in which we could look forward to better times ahead, were drawing to their close. Through indifference or design, Norman and Yvette were allowing themselves to be seen together often enough to cause comment; if they chose to disregard it, others would not; and of a sudden I saw myself at little more than Norman's age, confronting my father almost for the last time and being told that my name was being coupled with Isabel Pryde's, that I could not want to get a "gal" talked about or to hear that any "gal" was making a fool of me and that I must either persuade her to marry me or accept my dismissal and bite on the bullet. Even at the time I believe I felt that these uneventful two years or so would end on the day when Philip or Maurice told me that Norman was being taken into partnership or when he and Yvette reported that they had now collected the fifty thousand volumes with which they planned to open their book-exchange. Both these goals, I heard at intervals, might be attained early in 1948; I fancy Norman talked of a dinner to celebrate the double event; and, when Clayton asked me in the course of a week-end visit whether Norman shewed signs of settling down, he made his meaning clear by adding:

"I suppose he can support a wife now. Or will be able to very soon. If not, you'll have to help him, old son. It's this place I'm thinking of."

In fact my cautious period of patient optimism was ended for me some months before Norman had finished his period of probation and some weeks before he was ready to launch his book-exchange; it was ended in the first days of 1948; and I guessed that it was being ended when Violet, who had dined with me the night before, telephoned to ask whether she might dine with me again and discuss a piece of information that she had received in her capacity of universal confidante to all my relations.

"I ran into Martin this afternoon," she explained, when we met. "The first time, as he was careful to remind me, since we were all together that Christmas. That Christmas," she mimicked him, "when young Norman brought Yvette Norbury to Ridgeway. The Christmas, by Jove, yes! when Uncle Philip put all four flat feet into it over the Fell-Maddison case. Martin was so careful to remind me carelessly of so many things that I wondered whether it was pure chance that he should be walking down Old Burlington Street as I came out of my office. Yvette Norbury, by Jove, yes! Had I seen anything of her since? I told Martin that I'd met her several times, with you and Norman, when she came to work on the books here. Martin favoured me with a well-rehearsed whistle and asked me whether I thought you *knew* and, if not, whether you ought to be *told* and, if so, who was the proper person to tell you. I said, rather coldly, that I might be able to answer his questions if I had the least idea what he was talking about. Colin my dear, *he* didn't know and *I* don't know whether there's a word of truth in the story, but you can't want me to beat about the bush as he did?"

I said that, as her tone betrayed that Martin's story was not a pleasant one, the sooner we began it the sooner it would be finished.

"Illegal operations never make a pleasant story," Violet replied, "but I believe Dr. Fell-Maddison was weak rather than

wicked. If a wild-eyed girl threatened to throw herself into the
river unless he 'helped' her . . . It wasn't done for money,
because Yvette had none when *she* went to him. . . . Oh, yes,
that's why she disappeared so suddenly from your department,
though there was fortunately no hint of that in court. Fell-
Maddison was her doctor; Lady Portia Stamford met her with
him; later on, Lady Portia introduced a friend of her own; somebody began to talk; and there was a general round-up of what
was thought to be a gang of abortionists. As Yvette told us,
there was never any question of manslaughter or suicide; I don't
think anything more definite was established against Lady
Portia than that she, like Yvette, had introduced a friend to her
doctor; and this luckless man only came to grief because an
accomplice, a nurse, lost her nerve and gave him away. Well, that
was Martin's story, in outline, but *he* wouldn't vouch for the
truth of it . . ."

"And, if every word of it were true," I broke in, "I don't see
how it affects Yvette now. Assuming that she got into trouble—I
always suspected that was the explanation—and that Fell-
Maddison helped her . . . Well, it's all over, she got away with
it. . . . Unless we say that the only crime is that of being found
out . . . As I can never get into trouble of that kind myself, I
refuse to judge the frightened and desperate girl who does. I
find a certain element of humbug in people who preach and
practice contraception and become stern moralists when contraception fails. Why, though, should Martin bother himself—and
you, my dear!—by asking whether I 'know' and, if not, whether I
ought to be 'told'? It's all finished these many years . . ."

"But *is* it? That's the unpleasant part of an unpleasant story.
If Fell-Maddison 'helped' Lady Portia, if he needed some one to
help him, if Yvette had some knowledge of nursing and volunteered . . ."

"They could make an ugly little scandal and perhaps Scotland
Yard would feel obliged to go for Yvette, though it seems to me
unlikely. But what have this woman and the doctor to gain by
throwing mud? Fell-Maddison has paid his debt to society, Lady
Portia managed to keep out of the Old Bailey racket. Unless you
think they're out for blackmail . . ."

Violet dismissed the suggestion with a quick shake of the
head: so long, she pointed out, as Yvette Norbury's name
remained unsmirched, she might by working six or seven days a

2G

week be earning a gross income of some few hundreds a year. Blackmailers hunted somewhat bigger game.

"Are you afraid of their trying to bleed Norman?," I asked. "If he *married* Yvette, if they threatened him—and me—with a scandal . . ." Litigation had fortunately played so small a part in my life that I could not be sure whether the giants of my boyhood—Sir George Lewis and Sir Charles Russell—were still alive. "I should go to the best solicitors in London," I continued, with a snap, "but it wouldn't be necessary! These people are blown-on. Fell-Maddison knows His Majesty's prisons from the inside. *Blackmail?* Does my worldly-wise stepson *seriously* believe . . .?"

"Does it strike you as at all curious," Violet interrupted, "that he should be so well primed with facts that can only be known as facts to about four people? The doctor, Lady Portia herself, Yvette—if in fact she had any hand in it—: they are the only people who can *testify*. Add all the people to whom they may have told it as a secret! Which of them handed it on to Martin? And *why*?"

"He didn't take you into his confidence over that?"

"He wasn't 'at liberty' to say. I *assumed* it was Kitty. She used to be a friend of Lady Portia's. At one time she had her knife into Norman. If she has heard that he and Yvette are going about together . . . I'm afraid I could believe almost anything of Kitty! And Martin would be the perfect channel for her to choose. He's very conscious of the big position he's making for himself in the City: you remember his agony of mind when Norman—Major Whimboyne of Ridgeway—took that job at a preparatory school. Mix equal parts of Kitty's vindictiveness and Martin's snobbishness . . ."

I asked Violet how long she supposed they had been preparing their brew.

"Martin told me he'd only heard the story that moment," she answered. "He also told me that Barbara and he had at last found the perfect service-flat, with another for Humfrey and Monica in the same block. It looks as though their days at Ridgeway were numbered, but we can talk about that later."

I tried to calculate how soon young Austin and Tomlinson Gerrold would be leaving their preparatory-school and how soon therefore Elizabeth would find herself alone, but I decided that this too could be discussed later.

"If Martin was speaking the truth," I told Violet, "he *hasn't* just heard this story from *Kitty*, who has been abroad for the last year. As the saying goes, we have another guess coming to us, but I don't propose to use it. *I* don't want a *whisper* of scandal, but who stands to gain by making one?"

The question was almost rhetorical: what answer could Violet make but "Nobody"? And yet this was not the answer that she made after a mock-rueful lament for the sheltered life that had left us, on the threshold of old age, so ignorant of crime and criminals.

"I don't know where intimidation ends and blackmail begins," she continued. "Ever since Austin's death you and I have suspected that Clayton was exploiting Elizabeth by playing on her fears. I'm sure he never asked a *price* for keeping his mouth shut about the way Austin was drinking and pursuing other women till the 1914 war gave him his chance of escape. It wouldn't be blackmail if Lady Portia or Fell-Maddison asked an old friend for a temporary loan because they were down and out, but poor Yvette would know they might be awkward people to refuse."

I thought it worth while to say that I had begun to change my opinion of Clayton some years ago: he would die, as he had lived ever since he went to pieces after the 1914 war, a greedy jackal giving his services to the tiger that promised him the best scraps, but never daring to demand them by threats. When he saw his comforts menaced by the arrival of old Mrs. Cheshunt, he would have gladly leagued himself with me to keep her off his hunting-ground; and, when I suggested that he was not obliged to meet her in my house, he had transferred his allegiance and now earned his bed and board by making himself useful to Elizabeth. Had he ever mustered energy to blackmail or intimidate anybody, I should have respected him more.

"Incidentally," I continued, "is Lady Portia on the rocks too?"

"According to Martin," Violet answered, "she would sell her best friend for a supply of whatever her particular drug is. The *fact* may only be known to three or four people, but one of them would shout the whole story from the house-tops if she could get anything by it. Martin . . ."

"By the way, how were things left with Martin?"

With a rare touch of impatience, as though I were deliberately introducing irrelevancies, Violet answered that she had left Martin to convict himself out of his own mouth:

"As he wouldn't say whether he believed his own story, I asked him what in the world there was for him—or, rather, the universal confidante—to hand on to you. If I *have* handed it on, my poor Colin, it's because I hoped that two heads might be better than one. I'm *not* afraid of blackmail or even intimidation, though in any war of nerves I wouldn't count on Yvette *or* Norman to keep theirs, even with the best solicitors in London at their backs. I'm not afraid of anything specific so long as the general position remains unchanged."

"And how do you picture it has been changed? Except in the matter of these perfect service-flats, of which I've just heard for the first time. When Elizabeth finds that the perpetual family-party at Ridgeway is breaking up, she'll take it hard, but she must have known that a change was bound to come when those youngsters went to a public school. Norman can't and won't offer himself up as a sacrifice again, now that he's working in London. And she has no excuse for rushing to look after him when Pendragon Court has looked after him admirably for two years. I'm *sorry* for Elizabeth . . ."

"She'll take it *very* hard if Norman says that now he *is* in a position to marry. . . . If in the meantime a mud-throwing campaign has begun against Yvette . . ."

Again I asked who stood to benefit by raking up a dubious and forgotten scandal about the girl that Norman aspired to marry.

"If she'll have him," I exclaimed, "I'll work myself to the bone to make a success of it."

I checked at a sigh from Violet, followed by a melancholy warning that Elizabeth would work herself to the bone to stop it.

"And if this story of Martin's gets round to *her* . . . ," she continued, "if it has not got round already . . . Colin my dear, I'm saying things just as they come into my head and in the morning they may seem the ravings of delirium. *You* can't suggest it, obviously; *I* can only drop the vaguest of hints. That there *will* be opposition, that you're on their side, that their most venomous ill-wisher can't do anything against an accomplished fact. If they take things into their own hands . . . It's the modern way with young people to cry out against the 'circus' side of marriage. . . . If they marry and tell you afterwards . . . *You* will understand, I shall say. Of *course*, Elizabeth will take it hard, but isn't it better that she should be hurt a little than that they should be hurt a lot? Permanently, mortally, indescribably? If Martin's story is true, Yvette will know what I mean by 'indescribably'! *Is* there anything in the idea, Colin? They'll take things from me that you could never say to them. If I asked them both to dine with me . . ."

"I believe they're in the house at this moment. Norman telephoned to say that Yvette was having an early meal with him at Pendragon Court and coming round for a long session with the books. They always look in on me before leaving, but I can find out whether they came."

I rang the bell; and, as Winter told me that he had not let them in, I sent him to the "vomitorium", as Norman inelegantly termed the suite of rooms in which the spewed outpourings of other people's libraries were being collected and arranged. When he returned with the announcement that the rooms were empty and that certain letters were still waiting for Norman to collect, Violet undertook to telephone to Pendragon Court.

"I suppose it would be more courteous to invite Yvette first," she continued, as she dialled the number, "but she—like you—prefers to keep her name out of the book. Is that . . .? Yes! May I speak to Mr. Whimboyne, please? I have a message from his father. Yes! Lady Oakhirst! Oh, it's you! Listen, my dear! Oh? Oh, I'm sorry. You want to see me? Well, that's very fortunate, because I want to see *both* of you, *urgently*: I was going to ask whether you could spare a night to dine with me. I'm *sorry*. Yes! But of course! If you think my advice or help is going to be any good . . . Yes, I gathered that, reading between the lines. . . . I was sorry. No, I'm not surprised, but I should like a little time for thinking over ways and means. Then you'll let me know what night suits you both? Good-night, my dear! Bless you!"

Putting down the telephone, Violet crossed to my chair and seated herself on the arm, laying one hand on mine.

"I don't know how much of that rather cryptic conversation you took in," she began.

"Norman apparently wants to consult you about something."

"Well, Yvette does! As she was disguising herself behind that New York accent, I didn't recognize her voice at first."

As Violet paused, my memory went back to the now distant night when a woman (whom I had long suspected of being Yvette) telephoned to say that Norman would not be coming to Grosvenor Road that evening; I felt that the pause had been designed to give me time to get my breath.

"He has had another 'attack'?," I asked. "And she's looking after him? That's why you kept on being so 'sorry'. He has been reassuringly free from attacks for the last year or two. *I'm* sorry too . . ."

"You needn't be. It's only a symptom. When everything becomes too much for him . . . Elizabeth's on the war-path. She has told him that he and Yvette are known everywhere as 'the Young Inseparables'. In fairness to the girl, but still more to himself and his family . . . Oh, can't I *hear* her saying it? If Yvette were in any way *suitable* . . . She hasn't said *why* she's unsuitable, but if *she's* the informant whose name Martin wasn't at liberty to disclose . . ."

"What was the advice or help you were offering?"

"She was worried about her 'whole-time job'. After keeping Norman steady all this time . . . She wondered whether it mightn't be best to explode the bomb, get it all over, tell Norman she'll marry him if that's his one hope of salvation from his mother . . . She hasn't discussed it with him. She's wondering how *you* would react . . ."

To this, I told Violet she already knew the answer.

"Will it hold good," she asked, "if the ways and means I mentioned involve a register-office? I *daren't* advise them, Colin, to announce their engagement! If Elizabeth is at the bottom of all this, if she has been building up a case with the help of that awful Lady Portia Stamford . . . I said there wasn't much I wouldn't believe of Kitty, but when Elizabeth's roused, when her back's to the wall . . . I *hate* speaking like this to you . . ."

"I don't think you're telling me anything I didn't know before. Give Norman and Yvette whatever advice you think best and tell him that I'll back them and you to the end. If they or you know of any blanker cheque or *carte* plus *blanche*, bring it to me for my signature."

XII

A LAW of playwriting so obvious and old as scarcely deserving of mention is surely that no character must suddenly behave in a way for which the audience has not been prepared. The spendthrift cannot be suffered to turn miser in the last act to suit his creator's convenience: some hint of excessive parsimony is needed beforehand if he is to achieve psychological integrity. And yet, when the playwright leaves his desk, he seems as ready to expect eleventh-hour conversions as the first twelve men who jostle him in the street.

I had observed this inconsistency in all of my friends when Drama detached itself from the lives of others to take up a position on their own doorsteps; and I observed it in myself when I first tried to direct a play instead of writing one for the players and their producer to inspire with life. Whether or no any last act was opening when I offered Violet my blank cheque, whether or no it would have suited my convenience for certain people to behave in a certain way, I can see now, when the curtain has fallen on everything but a possible, still unwritten, epilogue, that I was expecting almost every member of my closely observed company to do something at variance with the fundamentals of character. I can only think that in creating the men and women of my plays I was compelled to study their mainsprings of action more carefully than those of the men and women whose lives were interwoven with my own.

Perhaps I went astray through misusing that word mainspring. Of my brothers-in-law, Philip and Maurice, of my stepsons Martin and Humfrey, it might be said rather sweepingly that their mainspring was a harsh determination to succeed; but for all I know they had a vision of something beyond social success and financial power, for all I know their harshness was tempered by startling sentimentality and gentleness. For the mainspring of a glittering wrist-watch I should perhaps have used a different metaphor and spoken of the steadying weights in a grandfather clock. It was the checking, rather than the moving, influences in the behaviour of half-a-dozen widely different people that found me most at fault: the decent feeling, to take one example, that survived in strength enough to remind a man whom I in my haste should have dismissed summarily as a hopeless waster that he had once been welcomed by his equals as a scholar and a gentleman.

"Is it all wrong," I asked Violet, "to assume that we all have a dominant feeling—lust for power or fear of poverty, for instance —which is the key to everything else so that if we could discover *that* . . .?"

We were once again dining in Grosvenor Road, this time to

discuss the party that she had given the night before to Norman and Yvette; and she had begun by warning me that she had so far made little use of any blank cheque.

"What would you say was the key-feeling of those two young people?," she enquired in a tone that revealed perplexity, apprehension and a sense of her own complete failure.

"With Norman," I said, "it's an almost morbid fear of hurting any one he's fond of. I don't feel I know Yvette well enough to say yet. To have a good time herself, for which she'll work like a black, and to give a good time to others? That seems almost too vague and superficial to be a guiding principle in life."

"It's true so far as it goes. If it doesn't go very deep, maybe she has no great depth to plumb. She's *really* good-natured; as you've seen, her zest for life took her from job to job till she found an amusing one, but her shrewd little head is screwed on tightly enough to keep her from ever risking security for a whim. She wants to marry Norman, chiefly for his sake, though she sees all the difficulties, but she's not going to give up her career."

I asked whether Violet had made any allusion to her recent conversation with Martin.

"Fortunately, it wasn't necessary," she answered. "Elizabeth's method of persuading Norman that Yvette is an undesirable friend seems to have been to drag up the Fell-Maddison case. Yvette took it more calmly than Norman, presumably refusing to believe that Lady Portia would give herself away for anything she could get by giving any one else away. I don't *think* Elizabeth has said much yet," she continued with a sigh, "but Norman's goaded beyond bearing by her perpetual *hints*. I took your line: that, if he and Yvette had made up their minds, they should go ahead boldly. *You* would back them, I said; and Elizabeth, once the knot was tied . . . She had protested for long enough that Martin and Humfrey were too young to marry; but, when they calmly published their engagements, she doormatted herself to Barbara and Monica. I'm not sure," Violet continued, frowning, "that I was on good ground there."

"It was perfectly true," I said.

"But not a perfect parallel. Martin and Humfrey have never cared how much they hurt their mother, but Norman does. If he has to chose, he'll choose Yvette. They're engaged. He's going to tell you both. But to marry her and tell you afterwards, *no*! It may be *weakness*: Norman shews he has a weak strain by the way he drowns his cares. . . . It may be *strength*. . . . Or *stubbornness*: an idea or code on which he can't compromise . . . I always think he shews superhuman strength in his *patience* with Elizabeth when she's at her most maddening. . . . It may be *blindness*, natural or self-inflicted: if there *is* anything in Martin's story, if Elizabeth gets hold of it . . . They must be running the most frightful risk, just for the sake of doing the right thing. Perhaps they don't see what a risk it is. . . . Or perhaps it isn't a risk at all! What would you consider Elizabeth's dominant feeling?"

I was about to say "mother-love", as indeed I had been saying —with various qualifications—for all the time that I had known her; but by now the qualifications were so many that this key-word seemed incapable of unlocking any doors. Certainly Elizabeth loved her three sons and her two grandsons after her own fashion. She would steal for them, if that were not too crude a description of her record in money matters, though she would not work for them if this entailed the distasteful duty of supervising servants; she would indulge them, but she would leave to others the odium of correcting them for their own ultimate good; she would croon to them in baby-language, but she would not learn to talk intelligently to them when they ceased to be babies. It was a stunted, stupid and selfish love, which sooner or later—I felt—defeated her own ends; and, as the words passed through my head, it seemed to me that mother-love was an end in itself and that, if Elizabeth hoped to be rewarded for it, either this was not my conception of love or love was not her mainspring.

"Norman," I answered, "once talked to me about her over-flowing devotion, but I'm afraid she pours it out because she needs devotion for herself. As men and women give their hearts to a dog or cat. He would say she needs it because she's lonely. And she dreads loneliness because she's *afraid*. . . . If you ask me *what* she fears or *why* . . . She's afraid of being *left* alone; and it's a real fear, because in all her life she has never done anything to attach any one to her or enable her to stand unsupported. Her brothers, her two husbands, two of her three sons: she has allowed or encouraged them to slip away one after another. Now, as Martin and Humfrey are leaving Ridgeway, Norman *is* all she has left; and, as Yvette has said, she would find some insuperable objection to *any* girl he wanted to marry. That's why, my dear, I gave you *carte blanche* in handling them. I'm really rather afraid of what Elizabeth might do if she found herself fighting with her back to the wall, especially if she were armed with a flask of vitriol!"

"And *I'm* afraid," Violet sighed, "that I've not been able to do anything. I don't envy you your week-end at Ridgeway, my poor darling! Norman will have exploded his bomb by then; and as he won't be there to mitigate the shock . . ."

I assured her that anything Elizabeth and I had to say would be said in two minutes.

"She will ask my opinion," I prophesied, "and, when I return the compliment, she will wrinkle her forehead and say she really hasn't had time to think. I shall urge her, for her own sake, to accept the inevitable with a good grace. If she's planning to play rough, she won't tell me beforehand, which is what makes me uncomfortable, but she's so helpless that she couldn't stab a friend in the back unless some one brought her a knife and sharpened it."

I went to Ridgeway for the week-end; and my conversation with Elizabeth the first night followed so closely the lines that I had sketched to Violet that I almost felt we were performing a duologue that I had written. Her one interpolation in my script was the question what I wished her to say when her friends read the announcement. People, she added dolefully, always wanted to know whether the parents were pleased.

"I understand," I told her, "that the engagement *won't* be announced. The modern idea of treating marriage as a private affair . . ."

"They won't get any presents."

"They'll be spared thanking for congratulations and saying what they'd like and being gracious about white elephants and making lists of people to be invited and saving up their rations for a wedding-cake. I rather sympathize! An announcement of the marriage itself in *The Times* . . . Even with that I think they would like to say: 'Please, no letters'."

Almost inaudibly, Elizabeth seemed to be muttering: "As though there were something to *hide* . . ." Aloud she asked in accents of resignation:

"Have you any idea how *soon* . . .?"

I said that I thought this would depend on their success in finding a home bigger than their present bed-sitting-rooms, but I made haste to insist that their home would be in London.

"Where are we now?," I continued. "The fag-end of 1948? I

don't suppose they'll be ready before next spring, but they've said nothing to me and I've really thought it better not to ask them. Nineteen-forty-eight? Norman will be thirty next summer . . ."

"And we shall have been married thirty years this winter. Isn't it called a 'pearl wedding'?."

"I believe it is, but I'm not disposed to advertise the fact. People were embarrassingly generous over our silver wedding."

The conversation, if such it could be called, sank into a languid exchange of inaccurate guesses about the traditional names for wedding-anniversaries; and nothing more was said of Norman and Yvette until bedtime, when Elizabeth, varying her earlier question, asked whether I felt sure that the marriage would not take place till next year.

"One wants a little time to turn round," she added.

"Well, if Norman's coming here next week-end . . ."

"But is he? If so," she went on in a tone of undisguised grievance, "it'll be the first time for a very long while! At the beginning it was this book-exchange, where Yvette could only help him on Sundays. I thought they had finished with all that and were only waiting to find a suitable shop. Now . . ."

It was true that for some months Norman had seldom been at Ridgeway and then only when there was a party or estate-business to discuss with me. I chose to fancy that he was avoiding his mother to escape being questioned or warned by her about Yvette; but I knew from Violet that just before what was called euphemistically his latest "attack" Elizabeth had seen him in the course of a visit to London. I doubted whether it was her only visit.

"We must expect to find him a bit preoccupied," I said. "And I feel," I went on, with greater directness than I had ever employed with Elizabeth before, "that we shall have only ourselves to blame if he drifts away from his old moorings here, like Martin and Humfrey. Marriage always involves a reorientation, but he's devoted to this place and to both of us. If he sees us making Yvette as welcome as we made Barbara and Monica . . ."

"I'm sure I did my best the one time he brought her here. Or *you* . . . I never *did* understand *who* or *why* . . . A total stranger . . . You assured me it *wasn't* to shew her off. *Now* . . ."

"In those days," I interrupted, "nearly three years ago now, I have the best reason for knowing that she wouldn't have Norman.

Now—shall I say?—his constancy is being rewarded. Personally, the more I see of her, the better I like her; but I couldn't separate them if I wished and I may be able to help them and ourselves. It's not a 'great match' in the eyes of your own exalted relations, but if you and I shew that all we care about is their being *happy* together . . . D'you see any reason why Norman should be less happy than Martin and Humfrey? We needed time to get used to Barbara and Monica, with their slang and their patter. I suppose —at my age—the young always do seem so *very* young and empty-headed, their little friends seem even worse than themselves. Do you think that Yvette . . .?"

"I only met her that once. On her own shewing, some of *her* friends . . . However, as Norman wouldn't *listen* to me . . ."

I asked what Elizabeth had tried to tell him, but she would only say with studied vagueness that she had heard some odd names and odd stories. I asked where she had heard them; but she answered impatiently that this was beside the point and that, in my own words, Norman's happiness was all that we had to consider.

"In *your* place . . . ," she began boldly and then broke off as though frightened by her own daring.

"In my place?," I prompted her.

"If I thought that my future daughter-in-law . . . Well, before she had a chance of becoming my daughter-in-law . . . You know I'm a perfect fool about money, Colin, but I've always assumed from the way you threw it about in good times and bad . . . In your place . . . Yes! In your place, for the honour of the family and the happiness of my son, I should ask her what she would take to go out, passage-paid, to Christmas Island and stay there!"

It was, I suppose, the remote and inhospitable Easter Island that Elizabeth meant to choose for Yvette's place of exile as a remittance-woman; but I should not have been surprised if she had said "Devil's Island". My capacity for surprise had indeed been temporarily exhausted by the murderous venom of her tone. Clearly I had been wasting my time in warning her that we should have only ourselves to blame if we lost Norman as the result of his marriage: she seemed not to care whether she lost him or not so long as no one else got him. Perhaps I was wasting my time in wondering whether I had wholly misjudged her in my attempt to find dominant characteristics and key-motives and all-controlling mainsprings of action.

"To get her own way . . .", I reflected, as I went up to bed. "At the time of Munich, she didn't care whether we lost all Europe to Hitler provided she could keep Norman out of a war. She didn't care whether she lost me on our honeymoon, whether she had already lost Austin . . ."

Hitherto I had assumed that for some reason, which perhaps a psychologist might discover, she was abnormal in her approach to what I called the physical, she the "horrid", side of marriage; but this, so far as I could see, had no bearing on her present attitude to Norman and Yvette. Was it for nothing, I asked myself, that she had been nicknamed Cinderella? Was her childhood a bitter and unforgettable history of slights and frustrations, still haunting her with a hardly sane obsession that she would never be allowed to have her own way in anything? I was no longer satisfied with my explanation, suggested by a chance remark of Norman's, that her mainspring was an irrational terror of being left to live and die alone. Looking back on the thirty-odd years that I had known her, the years before that time when I had known of her from the Oakhirsts and Clayton and her own blood-relations, I felt that by some twist of spirit she had contrived to antagonize every man, woman and child who might have lightened the darkness of age and lent her courage for the great last journey that the fearful and the fearless alike had to make alone.

Thirty years, all but a few months, had we been married; and in that time, in the ten or twenty years before that time, she had not only learnt nothing and forgotten nothing, but had even escaped the furrowing and whitening touch of time, the shrinking or spreading of middle age.

Was her mainspring to be found, as I had once thought, in arrested development? She played with babies like a child playing with her dolls; and she was still shocked, like a child, by the facts of procreation. She lied and cheated like a child to whom right and wrong are still imperfectly understood ideas. She displayed a spoilt child's grasping egoism in letting a toy be broken rather than shared. And in eternally overreaching herself she revealed a stupid child's utter inability to associate causes and effects.

In time, I should have thought, the stupidest child learnt from experience; but I sometimes doubted whether Elizabeth, who was now fifty-eight, had learnt anything since she was eight. An incompetent housekeeper, an inadequate hostess, an illiterate companion, she fooled all the people for some of the time by adroitly suggesting that her life's work lay elsewhere; but her pretensions were exposed for ever when her vindictive sister Kitty collected in a single room three witnesses to her record as a magistrate in the Juvenile Court, as Commandant of the V.A.M.P.s and as chairman of the local Care And Health Committee. She did no harm, Kitty summed up the evidence, because she did nothing at all.

Had this been literally true, I should have returned to London less unhappy in mind. Unfortunately, Elizabeth was not always content to do nothing. When roused, she could display a desperate recklessness; and her recent outburst against Yvette shewed her more deeply roused than I ever remembered. If she talked to Norman about the honour of the family or to Yvette about the happiness of my only son, I at least could not forecast what their answer would be. Though she said nothing to me, I heard by telephone a few days later from Clayton that she had been in London; and I thought it unlikely that she had visited him in Pendragon Court without at least trying to see Norman.

I fancy that Clayton was on his way to call on me that same evening when I espied him shambling along Grosvenor Road, but from his lips of all men's I could not bear to be warned that my wife was driving our son to drink. Had I ever smoked opium? No! Nor had Norman; but, if he could not adjust himself better to life, he would really take to it. I turned in my tracks, leaving Winter to say that I was not at home; and, if indeed Clayton caught sight of me, he made no mention of my having cut him when he telephoned again a week or so afterwards to ask whether he might see me on a matter of most serious importance.

"I'm not trying to borrow money," he added, "and you'll be relieved to hear that I'm completely sober."

Perhaps more surprised than relieved, I invited him to dine. He asked to be excused dressing, as his evening clothes were unfit to be seen; but he looked rather unusually presentable in a well-cut suit of grey flannel and I felt that he was trying rather pathetically to wipe out the years of his long decline when his shaking hand invited my attention to a black, pink-striped tie.

"Did these exist in our day?," he asked. "I've never had one before . . ."

"Is that our 'old school tie'?," I enquired. "I believe I was presented with one when they first appeared, but I promptly lost it. Do you ever go to Westminster nowadays? I confess I've avoided it since it was blitzed."

"And I've avoided it for fear of meeting some one like Vaughan Drake or Nigel Oakhirst, who knew me before I became . . . well, what I've become. That's not what I'm here to talk about, though," he continued, sternly waving away my proffered sherry. "Has Elizabeth told you that I dined with her last night?"

I said that I did not know she had been in London; and Clayton, with a sheepish smile, answered that she probably did not wish me to know and would certainly be horrified if I knew how often she had been to Pendragon Court, how frankly she had talked about Norman and how assiduously she was interesting herself in the life of Miss Yvette Norbury. Had she been saying to him: "I wish, Clayton, *you* would talk to Colin. He might take it from you"?

"As you're his godfather," I interposed, "I see no harm in telling you that they're *engaged.*"

"Elizabeth said something about that, but she didn't seem to think it would come to anything."

"The wish is father to the thought," I observed, as we went in to dinner. "They've been friends for the best part of ten years. Norman has been wanting to marry her ever since the war ended. If Elizabeth doesn't want to start a family feud in which *she'll* suffer first and worst . . . These young people are both of age, they're self-supporting; there's nothing Elizabeth can *do*, except make bad blood . . ."

"I'm not so sure. Perhaps if Norman had married this girl and told you afterwards . . ."

I began to say that, though this was a course I myself had favoured at one time, Norman was against it; but I left the sentence unfinished as it became apparent to me that Clayton had something to say and was afraid to say it.

"If he doesn't marry her at once, he never will," he prophesied. "And, if he *does*, I'm not sure that even that would restrain Elizabeth. I suppose I ought to have seen it sooner; but, if I may say so, Colin old man, I'd got used to thinking of her as rather feeble and rather stupid. It never entered my *head* that she was *pumping* me. After all, she has always been so vague that I've had to advise her on a thousand things when she was afraid of exposing her ignorance to you. I never credited her with so much cunning. Her *innocent* questions! I suspected nothing till last night. Or, rather, this morning. I was in no state last night . . . God knows what she gave me to drink! Years ago," he maundered on, "I told you at Ridgeway that I admired you for always knowing when to stop . . ."

"I dislike the consequences of intemperance," I said. "Perhaps, if I could go to bed blind-drunk and wake up feeling none the worse for it . . ."

"I felt considerably the worse for it this morning. Fortunately, my doctor knows how to get me round. At least I call him my doctor, because he writes the prescriptions, though he can't sign 'em. Does Fell-Maddison say anything to you, Colin?"

As the name passed his lips, I remember thinking that I had been expecting this, perhaps ever since Clayton talked of the serious communication he had to make, certainly ever since I heard that Elizabeth had been coming to him regularly for information and advice.

"I know enough," I said, "to spare you any beating about the bush. Has Elizabeth been to him for mud to throw at the unhappy Yvette? Did you make her see that she couldn't throw mud at Yvette without hitting Norman?"

"Fell-Maddison is down and out; but, even so, he would never sell a friend. Nor would I, Colin! I wouldn't willingly give any one away and, if I found that I'd quite innocently made trouble, I should do my best to put it right. After all, you and I, Colin . . . You were joking about the 'old school tie' . . . It's the best part of fifty years now . . . When I came here, I meant to drink only water, but if I'm to make a coherent story . . ."

I fetched a decanter of whiskey from the sideboard and saw his dull eyes become fever-bright as he poured half a tumbler of neat spirit into himself.

"Why did you say that if Norman didn't marry Yvette at once . . .?," I began.

"Because she'll be in gaol. She may find herself there even if she marries him. With Elizabeth in her present mood. Unless she cuts the country. And if you catch Elizabeth reading the article on 'Extradition' in your encyclopaedia . . . Her *cunning* . . . It began years ago, after Yvette Norbury had been to stay with you at Ridgeway. Elizabeth pumped me for anything I could remember about the Fell-Maddison case. Months later she came to me in great trouble because she'd heard stories about the girl:

wasn't it our duty to open poor Norman's eyes? A *scandal*, apart from anything else . . . I didn't know then that she'd been to Lady Portia Stamford. Even if there *was* a case, I said, who was going to stir it up at this time of the day? Unless, I told her, somebody turned common informer and laid an information with the Director of Public Prosecutions. Elizabeth said she had heard of a Common Serjeant, but was there really an official called Common Informer? Last night she returned to the attack. This morning I told Fell-Maddison all I could remember, all I had begun to suspect. There's no sort of doubt, Colin, that this girl has put her head into a noose. She *helped* Fell-Maddison and, though he screened her, Lady Portia can undo all his screening. Can and *will*, if there's anything to be got out of it. Will and *has*, I should think, from some of Elizabeth's innocent questions. As Norman's godfather . . ."

"What did she want *you* to do?," I interrupted.

Clayton replenished his tumbler and surveyed the room with a mournful smile.

"The one thing she *didn't* want me to do," he answered, "is what I'm doing. Telling *you*! May it be accounted to me for righteousness, Colin, when I'm picked up from under a lorry and you come to identify the body! She didn't actually *forbid* it, I certainly gave no *promise*, but she said it would do no good. She had tackled you about paying the girl to live abroad, but you never paid any attention to anything she said. It was Norman's affair, you always told her, not yours. Well, if it was Norman's affair, he ought to be warned. That Yvette Norbury has fallen foul of the criminal law, that the evidence is all there, that a common informer, Scotland Yard, a warrant . . . O my God! It comes back to me! *I* was to persuade *him* that he must persuade *her* to go while the going was still good!"

"And you don't remember what you said to that?"

"I believe I reminded her that it wasn't so easy to get passages anywhere nowadays. Or to take money abroad."

"Doubtless it can be arranged," I said, as I went to the telephone. "Do you mind if I turn you out? I'm asking Norman and Yvette and Violet Oakhirst to come here at once for a council of war. When people begin to talk about warrants, I feel there's no time to waste."

FINALE

THOUGH the crowded days after the council of war quickly lengthened to months, there are still times when I feel that they are a nightmare from which I must surely rouse to find that I have been asleep for no more than a tortured minute or two. It is only in dreams that we act as swiftly, as unexpectedly and with as little sense of incongruity as Elizabeth and I, Violet and Nigel, Norman and Yvette began to act from the moment when I hustled poor Clayton into Grosvenor Road and the first November fog of 1948.

As I shut the door on him, I heard the telephone ringing in my work-room; and, since my number was still known to fewer than a dozen people, I decided with dreamlike certainty that Elizabeth was at the other end of the line. I was right; and, had there been time for me to think what she would say, I might well have guessed that she wanted to talk about the family-gathering that I had rather vaguely suggested for Christmas. Lunching with Monica in the course of a day's shopping, she had heard that Martin and Humfrey were taking their families to Switzerland, which rather knocked the bottom out of my plans; and at present she could get no definite answer from Philip and Maurice, who—Elizabeth hinted—presumably wanted to know who else would be present before committing themselves. The Oakhirsts, of course, had a standing invitation, though Nigel now seldom availed himself of it; and I was more likely than any one else to know whether Violet would care to come this year. Kitty would be back in England, but we could not have her and Clayton at the same time; and, as Norman's godfather, Elizabeth would like him to be included if Norman himself were coming, but she had been unable to get an answer when she telephoned to Pendragon Court.

I said that I would try to find out when next I met him, but that a party comprising two uncles whom he saw five days a week and a godfather whom he saw only when he could not avoid him hardly offered an excess of attractions.

"It might be no bad thing for Norman and for you . . . ," Elizabeth began. "I often say you live in a world of your own,

474

Colin. If you would occasionally pay some attention to the way *ordinary* people think and talk . . ."

With a modicum of encouragement I felt sure she would have said that Martin and Humfrey were taking their wives abroad to escape another meeting with Yvette; Philip and Maurice were waiting to hear whether she had been invited; and it remained to be seen whether Violet, any more than Nigel, would "care to come this year" if Norman or I insisted on including in the party a young woman whom ordinary people considered they should not be asked to meet. Living in this world of my own, I clearly did not see that our relations and neighbours and friends were bidding us choose between them and the object of Norman's infatuation.

I was interested and, so very few minutes after my unnerving conversation with Clayton, enormously relieved. Rightly or wrongly, I decided that Elizabeth would not resort to extremes till she had tried to the utmost the effect of organized hostility and a concerted boycott.

"I always thought it was my *job*," I answered mildly, "to study how ordinary people thought and talked. I admit I've retreated rather into my shell of recent years. Increasing age, the isolations of war . . . Who are the ordinary people you have in mind? What are they saying that I ought to hear?"

"Oh, it's not a thing one can discuss on the telephone! Ask Clayton! Ask any one! I think you know quite well what I'm referring to!"

"I think I do! You remember, though, that, when Martin and Humfrey became engaged before they were even of age, there was nothing we could *do*."

"There was nothing I *wanted* to do, once they were sure they knew their own minds. You didn't have to make *excuses* for Barbara and Monica . . ."

As she paused to see whether I should ask who found it necessary to make excuses for Yvette, I reminded her that Norman must by now be presumed to know his own mind.

"If any one had the *courage* to tell him the truth . . . ," Elizabeth began. "Even *now* . . . It *oughtn't* to be left to *me*!"

"If you could indicate what the 'truth' is . . . So far, you've only spoken of odd stories. If they're really odd and really well-authenticated . . . It won't be an easy or pleasant job—how shall

I put it?—to open Norman's eyes, but I've no wish to shirk the responsibility, even if he said he never wanted to see either of us again. I believe he would, you know, if we upset his apple-cart. And it would be impossible to keep you out of it, if he asked me where I'd got my information."

Elizabeth received my warning in silence so deep and long that a voice from the exchange requested us to replace the receivers if we had finished.

"Don't cut me off!," she then exclaimed. "Are you there, Colin? I've told you this is a thing I can't possibly discuss on the telephone, but there's no need for either of us to be brought in if somebody who knows the facts . . . There's no *doubt* about them! Clayton can give you chapter and verse! And *I* think *he's* the right person! There are some things that parents *oughtn't* to be dragged into!"

"Do you suppose he would consent?," I asked.

"We can but try! Ask him here for Christmas! Explain how *terribly* difficult it would be for me or you! If he would do it, I honestly believe that Norman of his own accord . . . It might take time for him to get over the shock, but there would be no need for us to do anything. *May* I invite him?"

"For Christmas? By all means!," I answered; and to myself I added: "We have till Christmas, then."

It would have been more accurate, I thought, for Elizabeth to say that she would have no need to do anything if she could find a hired assassin to do it for her. Once Clayton or any one else had frightened Yvette out of England or at least frightened Norman into giving her up, there was no need to reveal what part anybody else had played; and, if Norman were not immediately grateful for having his eyes opened, he might be unhappy enough to fling himself for comforting on his mother's bosom.

"We have till Christmas," I repeated, as the telephone-bell rang again and Violet reported that she had that moment received my summons and would come to Grosvenor Road as soon as she could get a taxi. Could I in the meantime give her an idea what problems we had to solve? " '*You have till ten*'." What in the world was the phrase that I was quoting? Something out of *Treasure Island*? The tipping of the black spot by the blind Pew to old Billy Bones?

As I waited for her, the bell rang again and Norman told me that he and Yvette had just come in from a theatre. They were both tired, they both had to be up early in the morning: was it essential that I should see them that night?

"It's not a matter of life and death," I answered, "but you may feel it's somewhat more important even than that. A number of decisions . . . Not a moment to waste . . . We have till Christmas, but no longer."

Some ten minutes later, the council of war opened. Had I ever been required to attend when political prisoners were being interrogated under pressure, I do not suppose I should wish afterwards to dwell minutely on what I had seen and heard. Perhaps I neither saw nor heard very much. In this part of my long nightmare I seem to be everlastingly lying back in my chair and staring fixedly at the ceiling to avoid my companions' eyes; I seem to hear myself speaking rather loudly, to keep any one else from getting a word in. I recall three or four admonitions which I employed again and again: we must keep our heads, we must concentrate on facts and leave moral judgements till later, I knew I could speak for Violet and therefore I must beg Norman and Yvette to believe that she and I would fight for them with the last breath in our bodies.

"There's a way out," I assured them, "if you're prepared to take it. To-morrow morning, Norman, you must apply for a special licence. The moment you're married, you must leave the country. It may be only for a few years, it may be for ever: that depends on other people, who *may* decide to accept the inevitable or *may* pursue you with a relentless vendetta. Wars, big and small, are always easier to start than to stop. I've not yet thought where you ought to go, I've not yet begun to work out how much money I can allow you . . ."

I broke off at the sound of impatient fingers twisting the door-handle; and I suddenly remembered that at an earlier stage of my nightmare, foreseeing something of this kind, I had turned the key and pocketed it. Forcing my gaze down from the ceiling, I saw Norman with his face buried in his hands, Yvette panting by the door and Violet leaning forward in her chair and beseeching me with her eyes either to speak or let her speak for me.

"I wanted to make sure we shouldn't be disturbed . . . ," I told Yvette.

"Well . . . We haven't been," she snapped. "You've said all you wanted to say? I'm off!"

"Where to?"

"As if it mattered! Somewhere, at any rate, where you'll none of you ever be troubled with me again. I can always earn my living! I'm sorry to have been such a nuisance, but if you had all of you left well alone . . . *I* never wanted to gate-crash. . . . If you had never asked me to that ghastly party, never put me through my paces here . . . Too late to think about that now, but the least I can do is to clear up my share of the mess. And the least *you* can do . . ."

As she held out her hand for the key, I said something about our all wanting to do not the least, but the most, the best, for her, for every one.

"Then you can let me go!," she cut in. "And you," she continued to Violet, "you can *really* help . . . or get Sir Nigel to . . . *I* don't know where his ships . . . And don't care either! Some place where English is spoken . . . A shorthand-typist . . . Anywhere but the Sahara . . . The trouble is to *get* anywhere these days: I know from my friends. . . . You can tell Sir Nigel that I'll gladly sign on as a stewardess if there's no other way. . . . Mr. Whimboyne *said*," she ended scornfully, "that you would both fight to your last breath."

Violet nodded and signalled for me to hand over the key.

"And now that you *can* go," she told Yvette, "I hope you'll stay a minute or two longer. You see . . . I don't feel that any of this is going to help Norman much."

"Oh, *he* . . ." Had she continued, I feel sure Yvette would have said: "He's all any of you care about! Well, you've got him and I wish you joy of the hell you've made of everything!"; but, as Violet touched her arm with one hand and pointed with the other to the chair where Norman was still sitting bent and crumpled, with his clenched fists now pressed against his eyes to keep them from seeing, she faltered from the door as though to promise that, if there were indeed anything she could do, she would do it.

"You're the only person who *can* help him," Violet told her; and I felt that, though she was speaking to Yvette, she was projecting all her power of persuasion and strength of will in a mesmeric beam on Norman. "Do you believe, my dear, in the old saying that to understand all is to forgive all? I don't think I do, because I feel I've never understood *all* about *anybody*. If one says, though: '*Until* you understand all, don't rashly declare that there's *anything* you can *never* forgive' . . . I remember once saying to my beloved father—the *wisest* man I ever knew—that somebody was surely a bit mad. He asked me whether I knew any perfectly sane person. They were as rare, he said, as the perfectly healthy people who never had hay-fever or twinges of rheumatism. You alone can teach Norman to allow for the madness in all of us."

"What do you want me to do?"

With her eyes still fixed on Norman, Violet pointed to the chair in which Yvette had been sitting.

"Colin has told you. I've not had much time to think about it, but I'm sure he's right."

"About going . . .? I've said: if Sir Nigel can smuggle me on board any old tramp, you'll none of you see me for dust!"

"I'm sure we shall be able to arrange it. For you *and* Norman: it won't help *him*, my dear, for you to go by yourself. For a time at least you're both of you going to be rather *lonely* young exiles, but if you can face it shoulder to shoulder . . . In time . . . In time you may teach him to understand that love's often cruelly possessive, that you can't help it if you're made that way . . . If he can forgive . . ."

In my nightmare I became conscious of another nightmare that was holding Norman, rocking and groaning, in its grip. How much of what was being said he heard or understood I shall never know; but a word here and there must have penetrated his consciousness to make him spring to his feet now, shouting: "Forgive a common informer?" and then to drop back, as though he had no bones in his body, muttering: "O *Christ*!"

"If he can forgive," Violet repeated, again in that strange mesmeric tone, "he *won't* lose everything. I know it looks rather like that now, I won't try to minimize it, for him or you or any of us. For a time at least I'm going to lose both of you; and I love you both dearly. For a time . . . The trouble with us, Yvette, is that we're *old*, we have very little time *left*. Colin will soon be retiring: he was looking forward to a peaceful evening at Ridgeway, getting the place ready to hand over. I don't need to tell you what it means for *him* to lose you and Norman, even for a time. I believe with all my heart and soul that it's *only* for a time. This *madness*—and it's nothing else!—*must* pass! The maddest of us, when we see that we've thrown everything away, that we're alone in the wilderness we've created . . . But it won't pass all in a moment, you'll be in danger till it does, in *great* danger if you and Norman refuse to be argued apart, in *mortal* danger if you do what Colin and I are urging you to do and if you're found out. There's no reason you should be . . ."

"We're being watched already!"

"I can have you in my flat till the boat sails! If need be, I'll lie and say you've lost your nerve and bolted. Once Norman has got you to Johannesburg, your worst enemy won't try to get you back: they'll know they're beaten and they'll try to make terms . . ."

Yvette crossed to Norman's chair and whispered something that, for me, was drowned by the crash of Big Ben striking midnight. As we waited for the last reverberation to die away, a ghostly figure, which I recognized as myself then, seemed to be reminding another ghostly figure, which I recognized myself as now, that some thirty years ago in this room a distracted man had stormed at a distraught woman, both of them temporarily mad, demanding to know whether she would marry him, pausing to let Big Ben strike eleven and then, when she begged for time, barking that she had been given time enough.

"When I lived in Barton Street," Violet told me, "I never even noticed that. Now, I suppose, it will wake me up once an hour for the first night or two."

For a moment I thought she was talking to me so that Yvette and Norman could talk without being overheard; but, when I asked dully whether her tenant was giving up the house, she answered that she would have it back at Christmas.

"And no doubt," she added with a twisted smile, "I can have Nigel back at the same time. It will make no difference to *us*, my dear, except that I shall dine with you more often, if you want me, instead of asking you to dine with me. It will make no difference to him or me, except that he'll be more comfortable than in a service-flat."

"Then *why*, after all these years . . .?," I began.

"It's the one thing I can offer in return for all he's going to do for us. And he's going to do a great deal! We haven't been such friends these last thirty years, he and I, that I can ask favours. I shall have to tell him the whole story, too, if he's to help. I believe there are always one or two cabins in reserve for Very Important People, but it's a tall order to disappoint some diamond magnate for a honeymoon couple. No, I must tell him *why* it's so important. Don't look up!," she added in a whisper, at the sound of moving chairs and shuffling feet.

The door opened, shut and opened again. Norman, it seemed, was telephoning for a taxi; and Yvette had come back to explain that she was taking him home.

"You can imagine that he didn't want to say any 'good-nights'," she added. "I think he'll be all right now, but I shall stay with him. And the spies can make what they like of that! You say I'm safe till Christmas, Mr. Whimboyne? I hope you're right; but I give you fair warning that, if any one puts a hand on my shoulder and tells me to come quietly, I shall stage a Hermann-Göring act. I've got the stuff!"

"And I hope," said Violet, "that by this time to-morrow you will have dropped it down the nearest drain! I want you to lunch with me in Old Burlington Street. You too, Colin. I shall have seen Nigel by then about sailings. And perhaps he'll be able to tell me something about the book-trade in South Africa. If only as a stop-gap occupation . . . You remember that was *his* idea, years ago, when Norman talked about starting a library on the Riviera. With luck, my dear, you'll have something definite to discuss by the evening."

"And with luck," I continued, "I shall have found out the procedure about special licences. It's thirty years since I got one for myself."

Outside, I could hear an engine throbbing. Yvette called out that she was coming. Violet asked whether half-past one would suit us both for luncheon. All three of us moved towards the open door, which Yvette softly closed before turning to face me.

"Are you sure this is really what you want?", she asked. "I don't know what the Right Reverend and Honourable the Most Noble Lady Portia Stamford has said, but it's probably all true. I *did* help Tommy Fell-Maddison . . . And *her*! And I would do it again, though not for *her*, thank you, if I wasn't scared! I knew it was illegal and I didn't care a brass farthing if it was immoral! When a girl's frightened, as *I* had been only a very few years before . . . Oh, to *Hell* with being moral when you're frightened! Well, that's the sort of person I am! I thought you ought to know. Have you nothing to say?"

"I was trying to remember some lines that Norman used to be very fond of quoting. *The Ebb-Tide*, I think it was. Yes! ' "*What*

am I? A coward!" "the description hardly strikes one as exhaustive"'
Well, now . . ."

"God, poor Norman's going to miss it when he hasn't you
to talk books with! I'm not literary, I'm afraid. I won't offer you a
lift, Lady Oakhirst, because I honestly believe I'm the only living
creature that boy can stand in his present mood."

I fancy I answered that I would get Violet a taxi. I presume
that I failed or that she suggested we should walk in search of
one, for the next thing I remember is that we were trudging
through Parliament Square, with her saying that we might hope
to sleep if we had some air and exercise first.

"I think Yvette's truthful," she observed, "but I'm sure
that's the truest word she ever spoke."

"About being the only living creature . . .? I hope she doesn't
talk to *him* about putting on a Hermann-Göring act: he's quite
equal to stealing what she calls the stuff for himself."

"Instead of which, she'll give him the strongest dope that her
'Tommy' Fell-Maddison can prescribe. Norman may or may not
come to in time to go to the City. I purposely didn't suggest that
he should lunch with us: he won't be in any state to help and
we've no time to let anybody hinder. When the moment arrives,
I should think Yvette had better have a diplomatic illness: you
and I can tidy up after them in her flat and Pendragon Court, but
she won't like walking out on all the people she's been working
for."

"I believe he or she must apply in person for the licence," I
said. "And they must choose a register-office in the district where
one of them has been living for a certain time. I can find it all out
from *Whitaker*, but I wish I'd asked Yvette what she meant about
being 'watched'. After Clayton's account of Elizabeth's 'cunning',
I wouldn't put it past her to picket the registrars of Westminster
and Chelsea. Whether even she would still strike when she *knew*
it was too late . . . But it's idle to talk about what people 'know'
when they're seeing red on any subject! I assume, from our talk
on the telephone, that she'll do nothing till Clayton has tried his
hand at Christmas."

And, until then, I felt that I could rely on Clayton to keep me
informed of any new brain-storms that might sweep Elizabeth
from her moorings. Wholly mistrusting my own powers of
dissimulation, I borrowed Violet's suggestion of a diplomatic
illness and invented an attack of influenza to keep me from

Ridgeway for a week-end or two. By the time I felt fit to be interrogated about Norman, I hoped that our plans would be completed; and the headlong speed of my nightmare whirled me too swiftly along to allow time for wondering what Elizabeth made of Norman's inability to leave London for these same week-ends. The licence was obtained; a double cabin for Mr. and Mrs. N. Whimboyne reserved on the Green Funnel liner *Capetown*; Yvette, for greater security, moved to Old Burlington Street; and her various clients were informed that in consequence of a regretted indisposition she was obliged to hand over her responsi-bilities to a deputy. By the time that I went at last to Ridgeway, whether Norman and Yvette spent Christmas there or on the high seas depended on a word, a hint, a single gesture or expression from Elizabeth.

Was there one to report? We seemed to spend most of our time together in discussing the arrangements for our Christmas party. Clayton was coming; also Philip and Maurice, with their wives; and, as I was shewn the present that Elizabeth had bought for Norman, I assumed that he was expected, though I gathered that he had not written or telephoned for some days or even weeks. Martin and Humfrey, as I had been warned, were taking their families to Switzerland, for which Elizabeth held Barbara and Monica responsible.

Perhaps I ought to have seen that she was describing a lost battle: from the day when their engagements were announced, she had tried to keep her sons attached to her through their wives, and now, when she talked of the wedge that Barbara and Monica had driven into all our lives, I might have guessed that Martin and Humfrey were ending the latest Ridgeway chapter a good deal more definitely and emphatically than I had been told. With their talent for making the best of all worlds, they were leaving their country clothes in the suites that they had occupied ever since the house was divided after the war; but their mother opined gloomily that she hardly expected to see much of them.

"Those young women have outgrown the need of anything I can do," she repeated.

"Isn't it in the course of nature . . .?", I began, meaning to add the threadbare commonplace that the young in every genera-tion wanted homes and lives of their own.

"For men's wives to be jealous of their mothers?," Elizabeth interrupted bitterly. "I *hope* not. I hardly knew your mother,

Colin, but I never *resented* the way you devoted yourself to her when she was ill. There was room enough, *surely*, for us both. I shall always remember . . . She died just as I came to know that I was going to have Norman. . . . I thought of you and your two brothers, hurrying to the old lady's bedside. . . . In those days I was still quite young. . . . Death-beds and death itself, in spite of the war . . . Death was still a *surprise*. . . . Not like *illness*: I'd seen plenty of that. It was your mother's *illness*, ever since her heart went wrong, that I thought of, much more than of her *death*. I wondered . . . In my bones I knew he would be a boy, I think I knew we should call him 'Norman'. I wondered . . . If *I* were ill . . . Would Martin and Humfrey be like your brothers? Would Norman be like you?."

I reminded Elizabeth that, when her own mother began to fail, she had made her home with us at Ridgeway. It was an irrelevant observation; but, whether it was Barrie's "Mary Rose" or her present disciple, I always felt embarrassed by the sight and sound of a young woman looking ahead to the days when her infant or even unborn son should play the nurse to her decrepitude.

"There's no *need* for jealousy," I continued, "if people can reconcile two precepts that are not necessarily irreconcilable: about *honouring* your father and your mother and about *leaving* your father and your mother and cleaving to your wife. Of course, if either side is too possessive or insists on always knowing what's best for the other . . ."

Looking back on this solitary week-end with Elizabeth, the only one that I spent in all the long nightmare of those autumn days, I believe that this brief plunge into a generalized discussion was our sole relief to a forty-eight-hour debate on meals and rooms and presents for the servants and Christmas-boxes for the tradesmen. Perhaps, on that account, I should have paid more attention to it. As at the time of Norman's "first-class family-row" more than three years earlier, she was convinced that she had lost her two elder sons, with their wives and children, for ever; the youngest was now all that she had left; and him too she would lose if and when his wife, whoever she might be, took her inevitable turn in wedge-driving. Probably I was wasting my breath in sermonizing about possessiveness; and I should have wasted more if I had told her that her only chance of keeping Norman lay in her not knowing best whether he would be well advised to marry Yvette Norbury.

Should I have done any good by mentioning her name? Could I have safely told Elizabeth: "Those two are now married. There is nothing that you can do even if you knew their whereabouts"? She might have made a show of surrendering in the hope of snatching something out of her defeat, but I could not trust her. When I returned to London on the Sunday night, I had been told again that Clayton was coming to us for Christmas, but nothing was said of the talk that he was to have with Norman; I had been told again that Elizabeth never got a reply when she telephoned to Pendragon Court, but—on the authority of his uncles—they were shorthanded at the office and he had been working unusually long hours. On the subject of Yvette we both maintained an unavowed conspiracy of silence.

Perhaps my readiness to join the conspiracy aroused her suspicions; perhaps the watching to which Yvette had alluded, though it was never proved satisfactorily, had in fact been steadily pursued; perhaps Elizabeth had nothing but her suspicions, perhaps I really had nothing to fear, perhaps—in the words that I had used and used again in the first phase of my nightmare—we still "had till Christmas". I shall never know for certain, as the one man who might have told me is no longer available for me to ask. When I arrived in Grosvenor Road, Winter was awaiting me on the doorstep; and, as I got out of the taxi, he told the driver to wait and then explained apologetically to me that I should probably need it.

"Bad news, sir, I'm afraid," he continued. "Mr. Mandeville. They've just telephoned from Pendragon Court. An accident . . ."

"Jump in with me, Winter," I said. "You can tell me as we go along. I conclude he's still alive?"

"He was when they telephoned, sir. And conscious. Asking for you, sir. And something that I didn't rightly understand, but the message said that you would. He was picked up from under a lorry. Only a few yards from his own flat, so he wasn't taken to hospital. And *so*, sir, you wouldn't need to identify the body. It sounded like some joke, sir, between you and him, though I'm afraid it'll be about his last joke in this world, poor gentleman. The doctor or whoever it was that sent the message seemed to think he was going fast. Bit wandering already, I shouldn't be surprised: there was something about sending you in his account for righteousness."

"I think I understand," I said.

I was not surprised: nothing, in a nightmare of this kind, could really surprise me. I had known, as one knows only in a dream, that this would happen and I also knew that Clayton would still be alive when I reached him. He would tell me that he had kept himself alive till I came. He would be very weak, in scarcely tolerable pain. I should have to put my ear down to his lips. He would whisper something; and the whisper would die away before he had finished. A dim figure would advance from a shadowy background; a dim head would nod to me; dim fingers would close the staring eyes. Within five minutes I should be in the street again.

"You had better wait," I told Winter, "If anything's wanted . . . ," I added, though I knew that nothing would be wanted.

And it was all over, almost in every detail as I had foreseen, in slightly less than five minutes. He was muttering deliriously: " 'count it me, old boy, righteousness" when I entered the room; and he recognized me at once and achieved a ghastly smile as he thanked me for coming.

"Just time, old boy," he whispered. "Can you hear me? Tell those two hurry! God, she's cunning, but I was cunninger. Is there such word? You're lit'ry man! Ought know! Tell 'em skip!" The effort of saying this last word above a whisper was too much for him. The whisper, as I had foreseen, died away before he had finished; as I had not foreseen, he roused to add: "Warrant out. Must believe. Know it fact."

Then, after a short silence, the doctor gave me the nod that I was expecting.

Though I have reason to remember—for what it may be worth—that this was a Sunday night, I could not, if my liberty or life depended on it, give a day of the week or even an hour of the day or night for anything that happened after I had sent Winter back to Grosvenor Road with my luggage and had taken another taxi to Old Burlington Street. It proved easier, I found, to cope with the crisis than to wait for it: now that war had been declared, we all rose to the occasion as in 1914 and again in 1939, avoiding regrets and recriminations, going swiftly and quietly about our tasks, speaking gently and to the point, resisting all temptation to argue and pre-eminently agreeing not to look more than one stage ahead. I had not quoted Clayton's last words about a warrant, but I repeated his warning that "those two" had no time to lose.

They lost none; and, again as in 1914 and 1939, when I had played a small part in assembling the machine that we should set working if war came, I had the satisfaction of seeing the wheels noiselessly revolving as my fingers touched the switch. Every one knew his station and went to it. Ever since leaving the register-office, Yvette had been hidden in Violet's flat; Nigel had driven, every night, alone to the door, left his car and, later, driven away with Violet's secretary. He would continue to drive here alone and to drive away with a single passenger until the night when he drove Yvette to Southampton and escorted her aboard the *Capetown*. Norman would join her there independently, travelling by train after working till the last possible moment in the City: if Elizabeth had spies planted in her brothers' office, they could only report that Norman was coming and going as usual, making appointments that would keep him tied to London till Christmas Eve.

The parting, when it came, was to take place in London; Nigel was to give the signal; and, when Norman's secretary telephoned to the Lord Keeper's Department to announce with the utmost possible publicity that he was at a loose end that evening and would dine with me if I were disengaged, I knew that he would be leaving for Southampton next day. With the utmost possible publicity, I invited him to dine with me at the Garrick. We were joined, before we had finished our soup, by Vaughan Drake, who wanted to hear about Clayton's death; and in bandying reminiscences of the days when we had been at Westminster together I was denied or spared an opportunity of talking to Norman alone till we left the club.

" *We took no tearful leaving*," he quoted, as we came out into Garrick Street. " *We bade no long good-byes . . .'* "

" *Men talked of crime and thieving*," I continued. " *Men wrote of fraud and lies*. You had better not try to communicate with me till I tell you it's safe."

"I won't. When will it be safe to publish this?"

He handed me the announcement of his marriage, in London, to Emma Jane ("Yvette"), only daughter of two deceased Norburys whose Christian names I have forgotten.

"We shall do no harm by publishing it now," I said. "It's too late to do any *good*. Only time and the logic of facts . . . I'll take it round to *The Times* now, though I don't suppose it will appear to-morrow. Yes . . . I hope it's only for a short time, Norman, but I would rather say good-bye to you in a crowded street than by ourselves. *If* anybody's following us . . . We'll shake hands, you can thank me for your dinner, I'll say 'good-night, my dear boy! God bless you!'. I shall mean it, Norman."

"And I . . . Well, good-night, daddy! See you again soon! And many thanks for a most admirable dinner!"

With a wave of the hand, he strode away in the direction of Westminster. I turned east, towards Printing House Square. I suppose I handed my announcement in, but I do not remember clearly what happened to me for the rest of this night. Walking interminably, I was guided by some unconscious will which took me to Pendragon Court and back to Old Burlington Street. I stood vaguely staring at dark windows. I talked to policemen about heaven-knows-what. I was accosted by a belated prostitute. I had coffee somewhere in a cabmen's shelter. And suddenly the sky began to lighten; and I turned my dragging steps towards Grosvenor Road.

Though I knew that I should not sleep, I went to bed for fear of sowing suspicion in Winter's mind; and I gave a convincing pretence of being asleep when he called me with my letters. After collecting my clothes, he went to the door and stopped with a faintly sheepish smile to ask whether he might take the liberty of congratulating me.

"Thank you very much, Winter," I answered, reaching for *The Times*. "It's in, then?"

"Yes, sir. The names caught my eye as I came up. Here, sir, if you'll pardon me, you not having your spectacles . . . Shall I read it? 'PEARL WEDDING. Whimboyne—Gerrold. *On December* 2, 1918, *at the Register-Office, Kensington,* Colin Whimboyne *to* Elizabeth Gerrold. *Present Address: Ridgeway House, Marlborough, Wilts'*."

THE END